MW00885657

Christian D. Larson

Collection (7 Books)

Your forces and how to use them

The ideal made real

Mastery of fate

How the mind works

Thinking for results

Brains, and how to get them

Concentration

CONTENTS

BOOK ONE

YOUR FORCES AND HOW TO USE THEM

How We Can Change For The Better And Secure What We Persistently Desire

ABOUT THIS BOOK

In this masterpiece, Larson not only states but demonstrates that human beings are full of dormant potentials. If wisely developed and used, we can change any circumstance for the better, and secure anything that we persistently desire. After all, in this life, he can who thinks he can.

As Larson writes: "Man can do far more with himself and his life than he has been doing in the past; he can call into action, and successfully apply, far more ability, energy and worth than his forefathers ever dreamed of. So much has been proven during this brief introductory period of the new-age. Then, what greater things may we not reasonably expect when we have had fifty or a hundred years more in which to develop and apply those larger possibilities which we now know to be inherent in us all.

It is the purpose of the following pages, not only to discuss these greater powers and possibilities in man, but also to present practical methods through which they may be applied. We have been aware of the fact for centuries that there is more in man than what appears on the surface, but it is only in recent years that a systematic effort has been made to understand the nature and practical use of this "more," as well as to work out better methods for the thorough and effective application of those things on the surface which we have always employed."

FOREWORD

"There are a million energies in man. What may we not become when we learn to use them all." This is the declaration of the poet; and though poetry is usually inspired by transcendental visions, and therefore more or less impressed with apparent exaggerations, nevertheless there is in this poetic expression far more actual, practical truth than we may at first believe.

How many energies there are in man, no one knows; but there are so many that even the keenest observers of human activity have found it impossible to count them all. And as most of these energies are remarkable, to say the least, and some of them so remarkable as to appear both limitless in power and numberless in possibilities, we may well wonder what man will become when he learns to use them all.

When we look upon human nature in general we may fail to see much improvement in power and worth as compared with what we believe the race has been in the past; and therefore we conclude that humanity will continue to remain about the same upon this planet until the end of time. But when we investigate the lives of such individuals as have recently tried to apply more intelligently the greater powers within them, we come to a different conclusion. We then discover that there is evidence in thousands of human lives of a new and superior race of people -- a race that will apply a much larger measure of the wonders and possibilities that exist within them.

It is only a few years, not more than a quarter of a century, since modern psychology began to proclaim the new science of human thought and action, so that we have had but a short time to demonstrate what a more intelligent application of our energies and forces can accomplish. But already the evidence is coming in from all sources, revealing results that frequently border upon the extraordinary. Man can do far more with himself and his life than he has been doing in the past; he can call into action, and successfully apply, far more ability, energy and worth than his forefathers ever dreamed of. So much has been proven during this brief introductory period of the new-age. Then, what greater things may we not reasonably expect when we have had fifty or a hundred years more in which to develop and apply those larger possibilities which we now know to be inherent in us all.

It is the purpose of the following pages, not only to discuss these greater powers and possibilities in man, but also to present practical methods through which they may be applied. We have been aware of the fact for centuries that there is more in man than what appears on the surface, but it is only in recent years that a systematic effort has been made to understand the nature and practical use of this "more," as well as to work out better methods for the thorough and effective application of those things on the surface which we have always employed.

In dealing with a subject that is so large and so new, however, it is necessary to make many statements that may, at first sight, appear to be unfounded, or at least exaggerations. But if the reader will thoroughly investigate the basis of such statements as he goes along, he will not only find that there are no unfounded statements or exaggerations in the book, but will wish that every strong statement made, had been made many times as strong.

When we go beneath the surface of human life and learn what greater things are hidden beneath the ordinary layers of mental substance and vital energy, we find man to be so wonderfully made that language is wholly inadequate to describe even a fraction of his larger and richer life. We may try to give expression to our thoughts, at such times, by employing the strongest statements and the most forceful adjectives that we can think of; but even these prove little better than nothing; so therefore we may conclude that no statement that attempts to describe the "more" in man can possibly be too strong. Even the strongest fails to say one thousandth of what we would say should we speak the whole truth. We shall all admit this, and accordingly shall find it advisable not to pass judgement upon strong statements but to learn to understand and apply those greater powers within ourselves that are infinitely stronger than the strongest statement that could possibly be made.

Those minds who may believe that the human race is to continue weak and imperfect as usual, should consider what remarkable steps in advance have recently been taken in nearly all fields of human activity. And then they should remember that the greater powers in man, as well as a scientific study of the use of his lesser powers, have been almost wholly neglected. The question then that will naturally arise is, what man might make of himself if he would apply the same painstaking science to his own development and advancement as he now applies in other fields. If he did, would we not, in another generation or two, witness unmistakable evidence of the coming of a new and superior race, and would not strong men and women become far more numerous than ever before in the history of the world?

Each individual will want to answer these questions according to his own point of view, but whatever his answer may be, we all must agree that man can be, become and achieve far more than even the most sanguine indications of the present may predict. And it is the purpose of the following pages to encourage as many people as possible to study and apply these greater powers within them so that they may not only become greater and richer and more worthy as individuals, but may also become the forerunners of that higher and more wonderful race of which we all have so fondly dreamed.

1. THE RULING PRINCIPLE OF MAN

PROMISE YOURSELF

To be so strong that nothing can disturb your peace of mind. To talk health, happiness and prosperity to every person you meet. To make all your friends feel that there is something in them. To look at the sunny side of everything and make your optimism come true. To think only of the best, to work only for the best, and to expect only the best. To be just as enthusiastic about the success of others as you are about your own. To forget the mistakes of the past and press on to the greater achievements of the future. To wear a cheerful countenance at all timed and give every living creature you meet a smile. To give so much time to the improvement of yourself that you have no time to criticize others. To be too large for worry, too noble for anger, too strong for fear; and too happy to permit the presence of trouble. To think well of yourself and to proclaim this fact to the world, not in loud words but in great deeds. To live in the faith that the whole world is on your side so long as you are true to the best that is in you.

The purpose of the following pages will be to work out the subject chosen in the most thorough and practical manner; in brief, to analyze the whole nature of man, find all the forces in his possession, whether they be apparent or hidden, active or dormant, and to present methods through which all those forces can be applied in making the life of each individual richer, greater and better.

To make every phase of this work as useful as possible to the greatest number possible, not a single statement will be made that all cannot understand, and not a single idea will be presented that anyone cannot apply to everyday life. We all want to know what we actually possess both in the physical, the mental and the spiritual, and we want to know how the elements and forces within us can be applied in the most successful manner. It is results in practical life that we want, and we are not true to ourselves or the race until we learn to use the powers within us so effectively, that the greatest results possible within the possibilities of human nature are secured.

When we proceed with a scientific study of the subject, we find that the problem before us is to know what is in us and how to use what is in us.

After much study of the powers in man, both conscious and subconscious, we have come to the conclusion that if we only knew how to use these powers, we could accomplish practically anything that we may have in view, and not only realize our wants to the fullest degree, but also reach even our highest goal. Though this may seem to be a strong statement, nevertheless when we examine the whole nature of man, we are compelled to admit that it is true even in its fullest sense, and that therefore, not a single individual can fail to realize his wants and reach his goal, after he has learned how to use the powers that are in him.

This is not mere speculation, nor is it simply a beautiful dream. The more we study the lives of people who have achieved, and the more we study our own experience every day, the more convinced we become that there is no reason whatever why any individual should not realize all his ambitions and much more.

The basis of this study will naturally be found in the understanding of the whole nature of man, as we must know what we are, before we can know and use what we in inherently possess. In analyzing human nature a number of methods have been employed, but there are only three in particular that are of actual value for our present purpose. The first of these declares that man is composed of ego, consciousness and form, and though this analysis is the most complete, yet it is also the most abstract, and is therefore not easily understood. The second analysis, which is simpler, and which is employed almost exclusively by the majority, declares that man is body, mind and soul; but as much as this idea is thought of and spoken of there are very few who actually understand it. In fact, the usual conception of man as body, mind and soul will have to be completely reversed in order to become absolutely true. The third analysis, which is the simplest and the most serviceable, declares that man is composed of individuality and personality, and it is this conception of human nature that will constitute the phases of our study in this work.

Before we pass to the more practical side of the subject, we shall find it profitable to examine briefly these various ideas concerning the nature of man; in fact, every part of our human analysis that refers to the ego, simply must be understood if we are to learn how to use the forces we possess, and the reason for this is found in the fact that the ego is the "I Am," the ruling principle in man, the centre and source of individuality, the originator of everything that takes place in man, and that primary something to which all other things in human nature are secondary.

When the average person employs the term "ego," he thinks that he is dealing with something that is hidden so deeply in the abstract that it can make but little difference whether we understand it or not. This, however, does not happen to be true, because it is the ego that must act before any action can take place anywhere in the human system, and it is the ego that must originate the new before any step in advance can be taken. And in addition, it is extremely important to realize that the power of will to control the forces we possess, depends directly upon how fully conscious we are of the ego as the ruling principle within us.

We understand therefore, that it is absolutely necessary to associate all thought, all, feeling and all actions of mind or personality with the ego, or what we shall hereafter speak of as the " I Am." The first step to be taken in this connection, is to recognize the "I Am" in everything you do, and to think always of the "I Am," as being you -- the supreme you. Whenever you think, realize that it is the "I Am" that originated the thought. Whenever you act, realize that it is the " I Am" that gives initiative to that action, and whenever you think of yourself or try to be conscious of yourself, realize that the "I Am" occupies the throne of your entire field of consciousness.

Another important essential is to affirm silently in your own mind that you are the "I AM," and as you affirm this statement or as you simply declare positively, "I Am" think of the "I Am" as being the ruling principle in your whole world, as being distinct and above and superior to all else in your being, and as being you, yourself, in the highest, largest, and most comprehensive sense. You thus lift yourself up, so to speak, to the mountain top of masterful individuality; you enthrone yourself; you become true to yourself; you place yourself where you belong. Through this practice you not only discover yourself to be the master of your whole life, but you elevate all your conscious actions to that lofty state in your consciousness that we may describe as the throne of your being, or as that centre of action within which the ruling "I Am " lives and moves and has its being.

If you wish to control and direct the forces you possess, you must act from the throne of your being, so to speak or in other words, from that conscious point in your mental world wherein all power of control, direction and initiative proceeds; and this point of action is the centre of the " I Am." You must act, not as a body, not as a personality, not as a, mind, but as the "I Am," and the more fully you recognize the lofty position of the "I Am," the greater becomes your power to control and direct all other things that you may possess. In brief, whenever you think or act, you should feel that you stand with the "I Am," at the apex of mentality on the very heights of your existence, and you should at the same time, realize that this "I Am" is you -- the supreme you. The more you practice these methods, the more you lift yourself up above the limitations of mind and body, into the realization of your own true position as a masterful individuality; in fact, you place yourself where you belong, over and above everything in your organized existence.

When we examine the mind of the average person, we find that they usually identify themselves with mind or body. They either think that they are body or that they are mind, and therefore they can control neither mind nor body. The "I Am" in their nature is submerged in a bundle of ideas, some of which are true and some of which are not, and their thought is usually controlled by those ideas without receiving any direction whatever from that principle within them that alone was intended to give direction. Such a one lives in the lower story of human existence but as we can control life only when we give directions from the upper story, we discover just why the average person neither understands their forces nor has the power to use them.

They must first elevate themselves to the upper story of the human structure, and the first and most important step to be taken in this direction is to recognize the "I AM" as the ruling principle and that the "I Am" is you. Another method that will be found highly important in this connection is to take a few moments every day and try to feel that you -- the "I Am" -- are not only above mind and body, but in a certain sense, distinct from mind and body; in fact, try to isolate the "I Am" for a few moments every day from the rest of your organized being. This practice will give you what may be termed a perfect consciousness of your own individual "I Am," and as you gain that consciousness you will always think of the supreme "I Am" whenever you think of yourself. Accordingly, all your mental actions will, from that time on, come directly from the "I Am"; and if you will continue to stand above all such actions at all times, you will be able to control them and direct them completely.

To examine consciousness and form in this connection is hardly necessary, except to define briefly their general nature, so that we may have a clear idea of what we are dealing with in the conscious field as well as in the field of expression. The "I Am" is fundamentally conscious: that is, the "I Am" knows what exists in the human field or in the human sphere and what is taking place in the human sphere; and that constitutes consciousness. In brief, you are conscious when you know that you exist and have some definite idea as to what is taking place in your sphere of existence.

What we speak of as form, is everything in the organized personality that has shape and that serves in any manner to give expression to the forces within us. In the exercise of consciousness, we find that the "I Am" employs three fundamental actions. When the "I Am" looks out upon life we have simple consciousness. When the "I Am" looks upon its own position in life we have self-consciousness, and when the "I Am" looks up into the vastness of real life we have cosmic consciousness

. In simple consciousness, you are only aware of those things that exist externally to yourself, but when you begin to become conscious of yourself as a distinct entity, you begin to develop self-consciousness. When you begin to turn your attention to the great within and begin to look up into the real source of all things, you become conscious of that world that seemingly exists within all worlds, and when you enter upon this experience, you are on the borderland of cosmic consciousness, the most fascinating subject that has ever been known.

When we come to define body, mind and soul, we must, as previously stated, reverse the usual definition. In the past, we have constantly used the expression, "I have a soul," which naturally implies the belief that "I am a body"; and so deeply has this idea become fixed in the average mind that nearly everybody thinks of the body whenever the term "me" or "myself " is employed. But in this attitude of mind the individual is not above the physical states of thought and feeling; in fact, he is more or less submerged in what may be called a bundle of physical facts and ideas, of which he has very little control. You cannot control anything in your life, however, until you are above it. You cannot control what is in your body until you realize that you are above your body. You cannot control what is in your mind until you realize that you are above your mind, and therefore no one can use the forces within them to any extent so long as they think of themselves as being the body, or as being localized exclusively in the body.

When we examine the whole nature of man, we find that the soul is the man himself, and that the ego is the central principle of the soul; or to use another expression, the soul, including the "I Am," constitutes the individuality, and that visible something through which individuality finds expression, constitutes the personality. If you wish to understand your forces, and gain that masterful attitude necessary to the control of your forces, train yourself to think that you are a soul, but do not think of the soul as something vague or mysterious. Think of the soul as being the individual you and all that that expression can possibly imply. Train yourself to think that you are master of mind and body, because you are above mind and body, and possess the power to use everything that is in mind and body.

2. HOW WE GOVERN THE FORCES WE POSSESS

Man is ever in search of strength. It is the strong man that wins. It is the man with power that scales the heights. To be strong is to be great; and it is the privilege of greatness to satisfy every desire, every aspiration, every need. But strength is not for the few alone; it is for all, and the way to strength is simple. Proceed this very moment to the mountain tops of the strength you now possess, and whatever may happen do not come down. Do not weaken under adversity. Resolve to remain as strong, as determined and as highly enthused during the darkest night of adversity as you are during the sunniest day of prosperity. Do not feel disappointed when things seem disappointing. Keep the eye single upon the same brilliant future regardless of circumstances, conditions or events. Do not lose heart when things go wrong. Continue undisturbed in your original resolve to make all things go right. To be overcome by adversity and threatening failure is to lose strength; to always remain in the same lofty, determined mood is to constantly grow in strength. The man who never weakens when things are against him will grow stronger and stronger until all things will delight to be for him. He will finally have all the strength he may desire or need. Be always strong and you will always be stronger.

Whenever you think or whenever you feel, whenever you speak, whenever you act, or whatever may be taking place in your life, your supreme idea should be that you are above it all, superior to it all, and have control of it all. You simply must take this higher ground in all action, thought and consciousness before you can control yourself and direct, for practical purposes, the forces you possess. Therefore, what has been said in connection with the "I Am," the soul and the individuality as being one, and as standing at the apex of human existence, is just as important as anything that may be said hereafter in connection with the application of the forces in man to practical action. And though this phase of the subject may appear to be somewhat abstract, we shall find no difficulty in understanding it more fully as we apply the ideas evolved. In fact, when we learn to realize that we, by nature, occupy a position that is above mind and body, this part of the subject will be found more interesting than anything else, and its application more profitable.

We can define individuality more fully by stating that it is the invisible man and that everything in man that is invisible belongs to his individuality. It is the individuality that initiates, that controls or directs. Therefore to control and use a force in your own system, you must understand and develop individuality. Your individuality must be made distinct, determined and positive. You must constantly know what you are and what you want, and you must constantly be determined to secure what you want. It is individuality that makes you different from all other organized entities, and it is a highly developed individuality that gives you the power to stand out distinct above the mass, and it is the degree of individuality that you possess that determines largely what position you are to occupy in the world.

Whenever you see a man or woman who is different, who seems to stand out distinct, and who has something vital about them that no one else seems to possess, you have someone whose individuality is highly developed, and you also have someone who is going to make their mark in the world. Take two people of equal power, ability and

8

efficiency, but with this difference. In the one individuality is highly developed, while in the other it is not. You know at once which one of these two is going to reach the highest places in the world of achievement; and the reason is that the one who possesses individuality lives above mind and body, thereby being able to control and direct the forces and powers of mind and body. The man or woman, however, whose individuality is weak, lives more or less down in mind and body, and instead of controlling mind and body, is constantly being influenced by everything from the outside that may enter their consciousness.

Whenever you find a man or a woman who is doing something worthwhile, who is creating an impression upon the race, who is moving forward towards greater and better things, you find the individuality strong, positive and highly developed. It is therefore absolutely necessary that you give your best attention to the development of a strong, positive individuality if you wish to succeed in the world and make the best use of the forces in your possession. A negative or weak individuality drifts with the stream of environment, and usually receives only what others choose to give, but a firm, strong, positive, well-developed individuality, actually controls the ship of their life and destiny, and sooner or later will gain possession of what they originally set out to secure. A positive individuality has the power to take hold of things and turn them to good account. This is one reason why such an individuality always succeeds. Another reason is that the more fully your individuality is developed, the more you are admired by everybody with whom you may come in contact. The human race loves power, and counts it a privilege to give lofty positions to those who have power, and every man or woman whose individuality is highly developed, does possess power -- usually exceptional power.

To develop individuality, the first essential is to give the "I Am" its true and lofty position in your mind. The "I Am" is the very centre of individuality, and the more fully conscious you become of the "I Am" the more of the power that is in the "I Am" you arouse, and it is the arousing of this power that makes individuality positive and strong. Another essential is to practice the idea of feeling or conceiving yourself as occupying the masterful attitude. Whenever you think of yourself, think of yourself as being and living and acting in the masterful attitude. Then in addition, make every desire positive, make every feeling positive, make every thought positive, and make every action of mind positive. To make your wants distinct and positive, that is, to actually and fully know what you want and then proceed to want what you want with all the power that is in you, will also tend to give strength and positiveness to your individuality; and the reason is that such actions of mind will tend to place in positive, constructive action every force that is in your system.

A most valuable method is to picture in your mind your own best idea of what a strong, well-developed individuality would necessarily be, and then think of yourself as becoming more and more like that picture. In this connection it is well to remember that we gradually grow into the likeness of that which we think of the most. Therefore, if you have a very clear idea of a highly developed individuality, and think a great deal of that individuality with a strong, positive desire to develop such an individuality, you will gradually and surely move towards that lofty ideal. Another valuable method is to give conscious recognition to what may be called the bigger man on the inside. Few people think of this greater man that is within them, but we cannot afford to neglect this interior entity for a moment. This greater or larger man is not something that is separate and distinct from ourselves. It is simply the sum-total of the greater powers and possibilities that are within us. We should recognize these, think of them a great deal, and desire with all the power of heart and mind and soul to arouse and express more and more of these inner powers.

Thus we shall find that the interior man, our real individuality, will become stronger and more active, and our power to apply our greater possibilities will increase accordingly. The value of individuality is so great that it cannot possibly be overestimated. Every known method that will develop individuality, therefore, should be applied faithfully, thoroughly and constantly. In fact, no one other thing we can do will bring greater returns.

The personality is the visible man. Everything that is visible in the human entity belongs to the personality, but it is more than the body. To say that someone has a fine personality may and may not mean that that personality is beautiful, in the ordinary sense of the term. There might be no physical beauty and yet the personality might be highly developed. There might be nothing striking about such a personality, and yet there would be something extremely attractive, something to greatly admire. On the other hand, when the personality is not well developed, there is nothing in the visible man that you can see, besides ordinary human clay. Everything existing in such a personality is crude and even gross; but there is no excuse for any personality being crude, unrefined or undeveloped. There is not a single personality that cannot be so refined and perfected as to become strikingly attractive, and there are scores of reasons why such development should be sought.

The most important reason is that all the forces of man act through the personality, and the finer the personality, the more easily can we direct and express the forces we possess. When the personality is crude, we find it difficult to apply in practical life the finer elements that are within us, and here we find one reason why talent or ability so frequently fails to be its best. In such cases the personality has been neglected, and is not a fit instrument through which finer things and greater things can find expression.

The personality is related to the individual as the piano is to the musician. If the piano is out of tune the musician will fail no matter how much of a musician they may be; and likewise, if the piano or instrument is crude in construction, the finest music cannot be expressed through it as a channel. To develop the personality, the principal essential is to learn how to transmute all the creative energies that are generated in the human system, a subject that will be given thorough attention in another chapter.

When we proceed to apply the forces within us, we find three fields of action. The first is the conscious field, the field in which the mind acts when we are awake. The second field is the subconscious, that field in which the mind acts when it goes beneath consciousness. It is also the field in which we act when asleep. The term, "falling asleep," is therefore literally true, as when we go to sleep, the ego goes down, so to speak, into another world -- a world so vast, that only portions of it have thus far been explored. The third field is the super-conscious, the field in which the mind acts when it touches the upper realm, and it is when acting in this field that we gain real power and real inspiration; in fact, when we touch the super-conscious, we frequently feel as if we have become more than mere man.

To know how to act in the super-conscious field, is therefore highly important, even though the idea may at first sight seem to be vague and somewhat mystical. We are constantly in touch, however, with the super-conscious whether we know it or not. We frequently enter the super-conscious when we listen to inspiring music, when we read some book that touches the finer intellect, when we listen to someone who speaks from what may be termed the inner throne of authority, when we witness some soul-stirring scene in nature. We also touch the superconscious when we are carried away with some tremendous ambition, and herein we find practical value in a great measure.

When men of tremendous ambition are carried away, so to speak, with the power of that ambition, they almost invariably reach the higher and finer state of mind -- a state where they not only feel more power and determination than they ever felt before, but a state in which the mind becomes so extremely active that it almost invariably gains the necessary brilliancy to work out those plans or ideas that are required in order that the ambition may be realized. It can readily be demonstrated that we get our best ideas from this lofty realm, and it is a well-known fact that no one ever accomplishes great or wonderful things in the world, without touching frequently this sublime inspiring state.

When we train the mind to touch the super-conscious at frequent intervals, we always find the ideas we want. We always succeed in providing the ways and means required. No matter what the difficulties may be, we invariably discover something by which we may overcome and conquer completely. Whenever you find yourself in what may be termed a difficult position, proceed at once to work your mind up into higher and higher attitudes, until you touch the super-conscious, and when you touch that lofty state you will soon receive the ideas or the methods that you need.

But this is not the only value connected with the super-conscious. The highest forces in man are the most powerful, but we cannot use those higher forces without acting through the super-conscious field. Therefore, if you want to understand and apply all the forces you possess, you must train the mind to act through the super-conscious as well as the conscious and the subconscious. However, we must not permit ourselves to live exclusively in this lofty state; though it is the source of the higher forces in man, those forces that are indispensable to the doing of great and important things; nevertheless, those forces cannot be applied unless they are brought down to earth, so to speak, and united with practical action.

He who lives exclusively in the super-conscious, will dream wonderful dreams, but if he does not unite the forces of the super-conscious with practical action, he will do nothing else but dream dreams, and those dreams will not come true. It is when we combine mental action in the conscious, subconscious and super-conscious, that we get the results we desire. In brief, it is the full use of all the forces in mind through all the channels of expression that leads to the highest attainment and the greatest achievements.

When we proceed with the practical application of any particular force, we shall not find it necessary to cause that force to act through what may be termed the psychological field, and the reason is that the psychological field in man is the real field of action. It is the field through which the undercurrents flow, and we all understand that it is these undercurrents that determine, not only the direction of action, but the results that follow action. This idea is well illustrated in the following lines:

"Straws upon the surface flow; He who would seek for pearls must dive below."

The term "below" as applied to the life and consciousness of man, is synonymous with the psychological field, or the field of the undercurrents. Ordinary minds skim over the surface. Great minds invariably sound these deeper depths, and act in and through the psychological field. Their minds dive below into the rich vastness of what may be termed the gold mines of the mind, and the diamond fields of the soul.

When we enter the psychological field of any force, which simply means the inner and finer field of action of that force, we act through the undercurrents, and thereby proceed to control those currents. It is in the field of the undercurrents that we find both the origin and the action of cause, whether physical or mental. It is these currents, when acted upon intelligently, that remove what we do not want and produce those changes that we do want. They invariably produce effects, both physical and mental, according to the action that we give to them, and all those things that pertain to the personality will respond only to the actions of those currents; that is, you cannot produce any effect in any part of the mind or body unless you first direct the undercurrents of the system to produce those effects.

To act through the undercurrents therefore is absolutely necessary, no matter what we may wish to do, or what forces we may wish to control, direct or apply; and we act upon those undercurrents only when we enter the psychological field. In like manner, we can turn to good account all things in practical everyday life only when we understand the psychology of those things. The reason is, that when we understand the psychology of anything, we understand the power that is back of that particular thing, and that controls it and gives it definite action. In consequence, when we understand the psychology of anything in our own field of action or in our own environment, we will know how to deal with it so as to secure whatever results that particular thing has the power to produce.

But this law is especially important in dealing with forces whether those forces act through the mind or through any one of the faculties, through the personality or through the conscious, subconscious or superconscious fields. In brief, whatever we do in trying to control and direct the powers we possess, we must enter the deeper life of those powers, so that we can get full control of the undercurrents. It is the way those undercurrents flow that determines results, and as we can direct those currents in any way that we desire, we naturally conclude that we can secure whatever results we desire.

3. THE USE OF MIND IN PRACTICAL, ACTION

Man lives to move forward, To move forward is to live more. To live more is to be more and do more; and it is being and doing that constitutes the path to happiness. The more you are the more you do, the richer your life, the greater your joy. But being and doing must always live together as one. To try to be much and not try to do much is to find life a barren waste. To try to do much and not try to be much is to find life a burden too heavy and wearisome to bear. The being of much gives the necessary inspiration and the necessary power to the doing of much. The doing of much gives the necessary expression to the being of much. And it is the bringing forth of being through the act of doing that produces happiness that is happiness. Being much gives capacity for doing much. Doing much gives expression to the richest and the best that is within us. And the more we increase the richness of that which is within us, the more we increase our happiness, provided we increase, in the same proportion, the expression of that greater richness. The first essential is provided for by the being of much; the second, by the doing of much; and the secret of both may be found by him who lives to move forward.

In the present age, it is the power of mind that rules the world, and therefore it is evident that he who has acquired the best use of the power of mind, will realize the greatest success, and reach the highest places that attainment and achievement hold in store. The man who wins is the man who can apply in practical life every part of his mental ability, and who can make every action of his mind tell.

We sometimes wonder why there are so many capable men and admirable women who do not reach those places in life that they seem to deserve, but the answer is simple. They do not apply the power of mind as they should. Their abilities and qualities are either misdirected or applied only in part. These people, however, should not permit themselves to become dissatisfied with fate, but should remember that every individuality who learns to make full use of the power of their mind will reach their goal; they will realize their desire and will positively win.

There are several reasons why, though the principle reason is found in the fact that when the power of the mind is used correctly in working out what we wish to accomplish, the other forces we possess are readily applied for the same purpose, and this fact becomes evident when we realize that the power of mind is not only the ruling power in the world, but is also the ruling power in man himself. All other faculties in man are ruled by the power of his mind. It is the action of his mind that determines the action of all the other forces in his possession. Therefore, to secure the results desired, he must give his first thought to the scientific and constructive application of mental action.

In a preceding chapter, it was stated that the "I Am" is the ruling principle in man, and from that statement the conclusion may be drawn that the "I Am" is the ruling power as well, but this is not strictly correct. There is a difference between principle and power, though for practical purposes it is not necessary to consider the abstract phase of this difference. All that is necessary is to realize that the "I Am" directs the mind, and that the power of the mind directs and controls everything else in the human system. It is the mind that occupies the throne but the "I Am" is the power behind the throne. This being true, it becomes highly important to understand how the power of the mind should be used, but before we can understand the use of this power, we must learn what this power actually is.

Generally speaking, we may say that the power of mind is the sum-total of all the forces of the mental world, including those forces that are employed in the process of thinking. The power of mind includes the power of the will, the power of desire, the power of feeling, and the power of thought. It includes conscious action in all its phases and subconscious action in all its phases; in fact, it includes anything and everything that is placed in action through the mind, by the mind or in the mind.

To use the power of the mind, the first essential is to direct every mental action toward the goal in view, and this direction must not be occasional, but constant. Most minds, however, do not apply this law. They think about a certain thing one moment, and about something else the next moment. At a certain hour their mental actions work along a certain line, and at the next hour those actions work along a different line. Sometimes the goal in view is one thing, and sometimes another, so the actions of the mind do not move constantly toward a certain definite goal, but are mostly scattered. We know, however, that every individual who is actually working themselves steadily and surely toward the goal they have in view, invariably directs all the power of their thought upon that goal. In their mind not a single mental action is thrown away, not a single mental force wasted. All the power that is in them is being directed to work for what they wish to accomplish, and the reason that every power responds in this way is because they are not thinking of one thing now and something else the next moment. They are thinking all the time of what they wish to attain and achieve. The full power of mind is turned upon that object, and as mind is the ruling power, the full power of all their other forces will tend to work for the same object.

In using the power of mind as well as all the other forces we possess, the first question to answer is what we really want, or what we really want to accomplish; and when this question is answered, the one thing that is wanted should be fixed so clearly in thought that it can be seen by the mind's eye every minute. But the majority do not know what they really want. They may have some vague desire, but they have not determined clearly, definitely and positively what they really want, and this is one of the principal causes of failure. So long as we do not know definitely what we want, our forces will be scattered, and so long as our forces are scattered, we will accomplish but little, or fail entirely.

When we know what we want, however, and proceed to work for it with all the power and ability that is in us, we may rest assured that we will get it. When we direct the power of thinking, the power of will, the power of mental action, the power of desire, the power of ambition, in fact, all the power we possess on the one thing we want, on the one goal we desire to reach, it is not difficult to understand why success in a greater and greater measure must be realized.

To illustrate this subject further, we will suppose that you have a certain ambition and continue to concentrate your thought and the power of your mind upon that ambition every minute for an indefinite period, with no cessation whatever. The result will be that you will gradually and surely train all the forces within you to work for the realization of that ambition, and in the course of time, the full capacity of your entire mental system will be applied in working for that particular thing.

On the other hand, suppose you do as most people do under average circumstances. Suppose, after you have given your ambition a certain amount of thought, you come to the conclusion that possibly you might succeed better along another line. Then you begin to direct the power of your mind along that other line. Later on, you come to the conclusion that there is still another channel through which you might succeed, and you proceed accordingly to direct your mind upon this third ambition. Then what will happen? Simply this: You will make three good beginnings, but in every case you will stop before you have accomplished anything.

There are thousands of capable men and women, however, who make this mistake every year of their lives. The full force of their mental system is directed upon a certain ambition only for a short time; then it is directed elsewhere. They never continue long enough along any particular line to secure results from their efforts, and therefore results are never secured. Then there are other minds who give most of their attention to a certain ambition and succeed fairly well, but give the rest of their attention to a number of minor ambitions that have no particular importance. Thus they are using only a fraction of their power in a way that will tell. The rest of it is thrown away along a number of lines through which nothing is gained.

But in this age efficiency is demanded everywhere in world's work, and anyone who wants to occupy a place that will satisfy their ambition and desire, cannot afford to waste even a small part of the power they may possess. They need it all along the line of their leading ambition, and therefore should not permit counter attractions to occupy their mind for a moment.

If you have a certain ambition or a certain desire, think about that ambition at all times. Keep that ambition before your mind constantly, and do not hesitate to make your ambition as high as possible. The higher you aim, the greater will be your achievements, though that does not necessarily mean that you will realize your highest aims as fully as you have pictured them in your mind; but the fact is that those who have low aims, usually realize what is even below their aims, while those who have high aims usually realize very nearly, if not fully, what their original ambition calls for.

The principle is to direct the power of mind upon the very highest, the very largest and the very greatest mental conception of that which we intend to achieve. The first essential therefore, is to direct the full power of mind and thought upon the goal in view, and to continue to direct the mind in that manner every minute, regardless of circumstances or conditions. The second essential is to make every mental action positive. When we desire certain things or when we think of certain things we wish to attain or achieve, the question should be if our mental attitudes at the time are positive or negative. To answer this we only have to remember that every positive action always goes toward that which receives its attention, while a negative action always retreats. A positive action is an action that you feel when you realize that every force in your entire system is pushed forward, so to speak, and that it is passing through what may be termed an expanding and enlarging state of feeling or consciousness.

The positive attitude of mind is also indicated by the feeling of a firm, determined fullness throughout the nervous system. When every nerve feels full, strong and determined, you are in the positive attitude, and whatever you may do at the time will produce results along the line of your desire or your ambition. When you are in a positive state of mind you are never nervous or disturbed, you are never agitated or strenuous; in fact, the more positive you are the deeper your calmness and the better your control over your entire system. The positive man is not one who rushes helter-skelter here and there regardless of judgement or constructive action, but one who is absolutely calm and controlled under every circumstance, and yet so thoroughly full of energy that every atom in his being is ready, under every circumstance, to accomplish and achieve.

This energy is not permitted to act, however, until the proper time arrives, and then its action goes directly to the goal in view. The positive mind is always in harmony with itself, while the negative mind is always out of harmony, and thereby loses the greater part of its power. Positiveness always means strength stored up, power held in the system under perfect control, until the time of action; and during the time of action directed constructively under the same perfect control. In the positive mind, all the actions of the mental system are working in harmony and are being fully directed toward the object in view, while in the negative mind, those same actions are scattered, restless, nervous, disturbed, moving here and there, sometimes under direction, but most of the time not.

That the one should invariably succeed is therefore just as evident as that the other should invariably fail. Scattered energy cannot do otherwise but fail, while positively directed energy simply must succeed. A positive mind is like a powerful stream of water that is gathering volume and force from hundreds of tributaries all along its course. The further on it goes the greater its power, until when it reaches its goal, that power is simply immense. A negative mind, however, would be something like a stream, that the further it flows the more divisions it makes, until, when it reaches its goal, instead of being one powerful stream, it has become a hundred small, weak, shallow streams.

To develop positiveness it is necessary to cultivate those qualities that constitute positiveness. Make it a point to give your whole attention to what you want to accomplish, and give that attention firmness, calmness and determination. Try to give depth to every desire until you feel as if all the powers of your system were acting, not on the surface, but from the greater world within. As this attitude is cultivated, positiveness will become more and more distinct, until you can actually feel yourself gaining power and prestige. And the effect will not only be noticed in your own ability to better direct and apply your talents, but others will discover the change. Accordingly, those who are looking for people of power, people who can do things, will look to you as the one to occupy the position that has to be filled.

Positiveness therefore, not only gives you the ability to make a far better use of the forces you possess, but it also gives you personality, that much admired something that will most surely cause you to be selected where people of power are needed. The world does not care for negative personalities. Such personalities look weak and empty, and are usually ignored, but everybody is attracted to a positive personality; and it is the positive personality that is always given the preference. Nor is this otherwise but right, because the positive personality has better use of their power, and therefore is able to act with greater efficiency wherever they are called upon to act.

The third essential in the right use of the mind is to make every mental action constructive, and a constructive mental action is one that is based upon a deep seated desire to develop, to increase, to achieve, to attain -- in brief, to become larger and greater, and to do something of far greater worth than has been done before. If you will cause every mental action you entertain to have that feeling, constructiveness will soon became second nature to your entire mental system; that is, all the forces of your mind will begin to become building forces, and will continue to build you up along any line through which you may desire to act.

Inspire your mind constantly with a building desire, and make this desire so strong that very part of your system will constantly feel that it wants to become greater, more capable and more efficient. An excellent practice in this connection is to try to enlarge upon all your ideas of things whenever you have spare moments for real thought. This practice will tend to produce a growing tendency in every process of your thinking. Another good practice is to inspire every mental action with more ambition. We cannot have too much ambition. We may have too much aimless ambition, but we cannot have too much real constructive ambition. If your ambition is very strong, and is directed toward something definite, every action of your mind, every action of your personality, and every action of your faculties will become constructive; that is, all those actions will be inspired by the tremendous force of your ambition to work for the realization of that ambition.

Never permit restless ambition. Whenever you feel the force of ambition, direct your mind at once in a calm, determined manner upon that which you really want to accomplish in life. Make this a daily practice, and you will steadily train all your faculties and powers not only to work for the realization of that ambition, but become more and more efficient in that direction. Before long your forces and faculties will be sufficiently competent to accomplish what you want.

In the proper use of the mind therefore, these three essentials should be applied constantly and thoroughly. First, direct all the powers of mind, all the powers of thought, and all your thinking upon the goal you have in view. Second, train every mental action to be deeply and calmly positive. Third, train every mental action to be constructive, to be filled with a building spirit, to be inspired with a ceaseless desire to develop the greater, to achieve the greater, to attain the greater. When you have acquired these three, you will begin to use your forces in such a way that results must follow. You will begin to move forward steadily and surely, and you will be constantly gaining ground. Your mind will have become like the stream mentioned above. It will gather volume and force as it moves on and on, until finally that volume will be great enough to remove any obstacle in its way, and that force powerful enough to do anything you may have in view.

In order to apply these three essentials in the most effective manner, there are several misuses of the mind that must be avoided. Avoid the forceful, the aggressive, and the domineering attitudes, and do not permit your mind to become intense, unless it is under perfect control. Never attempt to control or influence others in any way whatever. You will seldom succeed in that manner, and when you do, the success will be temporary; besides, such a practice always weakens your mind.

Do not turn the power of your mind upon others, but turn it upon yourself in such a way that it will make you stronger, more positive, more capable, and more efficient, and as you develop in this manner, success must come of itself. There is only one way by which you can influence others legitimately and that is through the giving of instruction, but in that case, there is no desire to influence. You desire simply to impart knowledge and information, and you exercise a most desirable influence without desiring to do so.

A great many men and women, after discovering the immense power of mind, have come to the conclusion that they might change circumstances by exercising mental power upon those circumstances in some mysterious manner, but such a practice means nothing but a waste of energy. The way to control circumstances is to control the forces within yourself to make a greater human being of yourself, and as you become greater and more competent, you will naturally gravitate into better circumstances. In this connection, we should remember that like attracts like. If you want that which is better, make yourself better. If you want to realize the ideal, make yourself more ideal. If you want better friends, make yourself a better friend. If you want to associate with people of worth, make yourself more worthy. If you want to meet that which is agreeable, make yourself more agreeable. If you want to enter conditions and circumstances that are more pleasing, make yourself more pleasing. In brief, whatever you want, produce that something in yourself, and you will positively gravitate towards the corresponding conditions in the external world.

But to improve yourself along those lines, it is necessary to apply for that purpose, all the power you possess. You cannot afford to waste any of it, and every misuse of the mind will waste power. Avoid all destructive attitudes of the mind, such an anger, hatred, malice, envy, jealousy, revenge, depression, discouragement, disappointment, worry, fear, and so on. Never antagonize, never resist what is wrong, and never try to get even. Make the best use of your own talent and the best that is in store for you will positively come your way. When others seem to take advantage of you, do not retaliate by trying to take advantage of them. Use your power in improving yourself, so that you can do better and better work. That is how you are going to win in the race.

Later on, those who tried to take advantage of you will be left in the rear. Remember, those who are dealing unjustly with you or with anybody are misusing their mind. They are therefore losing their power, and will, in the course of time, begin to lose ground; but if you, in the meantime, are turning the full power of your mind to good account, you will not only gain more power, but you will soon begin to gain ground. You will gain and continue to gain in the long run, while others who have been misusing their minds will lose mostly everything in the long run. That is how you are going to win, and win splendidly regardless of ill treatment or opposition.

A great many people imagine that they can promote their own success by trying to prevent the success of other, but it is one of the greatest delusions in the world. If you want to promote your own success as thoroughly as your capacity will permit, take an active interest in the success of everybody, because this will not only keep your mind in the success attitude and cause you to think success all along the line, but it will enlarge your mind so as to give you a greater and better grasp upon the fields of success. If you are trying to prevent the success of others, you are acting in the destructive attitude, which sooner or later will react on others, but if you are taking an active interest in the success of everybody, you are entertaining only constructive attitudes, and these will sooner or later accumulate in your own mind to add volume and power to the forces of success that you are building up in yourself.

In this connection, we may well ask why those succeed who do succeed, why so many succeed only in part, and why so many fail utterly. These are questions that occupy the minds of most people, and hundreds of answers have been given, but there is only one answer that goes to rock bottom. Those people who fail, and who continue to fail all along the line, fail because the power of their minds is either in a habitual negative state, or is always misdirected. If the power of mind is not working positively and constructively for a certain goal, you are not going to succeed. If your mind is not positive, it is negative, and negative minds float with the stream.

We must remember that we are in the midst of all kinds of circumstances, some of which are for us and some of which are against us, and we will either have to make our own way or drift, and if we drift we go wherever the stream goes. But most of the streams of human life are found to float in the world of the ordinary and the inferior. Therefore, if you drift, you will drift with the inferior, and your goal will be failure .

When we analyze the minds of people who have failed, we invariably find that they are either negative, non-constructive or aimless. Their forces are scattered, and what is in them is seldom applied constructively. There is an emptiness about their personality that indicates negativeness. There is an uncertainty in their facial expression that indicates the absence of definite ambition. There is nothing of a positive, determined nature going on in their mental world. They have not taken definite action along any line. They are dependent upon fate and circumstances. They are drifting with some stream, and that they should accomplish little if anything is inevitable. This does not mean, however, that their mental world is necessarily unproductive; in fact, those very minds are in many instances immensely rich with possibilities. The trouble is, those possibilities continue to be dormant, and what is in them is not being brought forth and trained for definite action or actual results.

What these people should do, is to proceed at once to comply with the three essentials mentioned above, and before many months there will be a turn in the lane. They will soon cease to drift, and will then begin to make their own life, their own circumstances, and their own future. In this connection, it is well to remember that negative people and non-constructive minds never attract that which is helpful in their circumstances. The more you drift, the more people you meet who also drift, while on the other hand, when you begin to make your own life and become positive, you begin to meet more positive people and more constructive circumstances.

This explains why "God helps them that help themselves." When you begin to help yourself, which means to make the best of what is in yourself, you begin to attract to yourself more and more of those helpful things that may exist all about you. In other words, constructive forces attract constructive forces; positive forces attract positive forces. A growing mind attracts elements and forces that help to promote growth, and people who are determined to make more and more of themselves, are drawn more and more into circumstances through which they will find the opportunity to make more of themselves. And this law works not only in connection with the external world, but also the internal world.

When you begin to make a positive determined use of those powers in yourself that are already in Positive action, you draw forth into action powers within you that have been dormant, and as this process continues, you will find that you will accumulate volume, capacity and power in your mental world, until you finally become a mental giant. As you begin to grow and become more capable, you will find that you will meet better and better opportunities, not only opportunities for promoting external success, but opportunities for further building yourself up along the lines of ability, capacity and talent. You thus demonstrate the law that "Nothing succeeds like success," and "To him that hath shall be given." And here it is well to remember that it is not necessary to possess external things in the beginning to be counted among them "that hath.." It is only necessary in the beginning to possess the interior riches; that is, to take control of what is in you, and proceed to use it positively with a definite goal in view.

He who has control of his own mind has already great riches. He has sufficient wealth to be placed among those who have. He is already successful, and if he continues as he has begun, his success will soon appear in the external world. Thus the wealth that existed at first in the internal only will take shape and form in the external. This is a law that is unfailing, and there is not a man or woman on the face of the earth that cannot apply it with the most satisfying results.

The reason why so many fail is thus found in the fact that they do not fully and constructively apply the forces and powers they possess, and the reason why so many succeed only to a slight degree is found in the fact that only a small fraction of their power is applied properly. But anyone can learn the full and proper use of all that is in them by applying faithfully the three essentials mentioned above. The reason why those succeed who do succeed is found in the fact that a large measure of their forces and powers is applied according to those three essentials, and as those essentials can be applied by anyone, even to the most perfect degree, there is no reason why all should not succeed.

Sometimes we meet people who have only ordinary ability, but who are very successful. Then we meet others who have great ability but who are not successful, or who succeed only to a slight degree. At first we see no explanation, but when we understand the cause of success as well as the cause of failure, the desired explanation is easily found. The man or woman with ordinary ability, if they comply with the three essentials necessary to the right use of mind, will naturally succeed, though if they had greater ability, their success would of course become greater in proportion. But the individual who has great ability, yet does not apply the three essentials necessary to the right use of mind, cannot succeed.

The positive and constructive use of the power of mind, with a definite goal in view will invariably result in advancement, attainment and achievement, but if we wish to use that power in its full capacity, the action of the mind must be deep. In addition to the right use of the mind, we must also learn the full use of mind, and as the full use implies the use of the whole mind, the deeper mental fields and forces, as well as the usual mental fields and forces, it is necessary to understand the subconscious as well as the conscious.

4. THE FORCES OF THE SUBCONSCIOUS

When you think of yourself do not think of that part of yourself that appears on the surface. That part is the smaller part and the lesser should not be pictured in mind. Think of your larger self, the immense subconscious self that is limitless both in power and in possibility. Believe in yourself but not simply in a part of yourself. Give constant recognition to all that is in you, and, in that all have full faith and confidence. Give the bigger being on the inside full right of way. Believe thoroughly in your greater interior self. Know that you have something within you that is greater than any obstacle, circumstance or difficulty that you can possibly meet. Then in the full faith in this greater something, proceed with your work.

In using the power of the mind, the deeper the action of thought, will and desire, the greater the result. Accordingly, all mental action to be strong and effective, must be subconscious; that is, it must act in the field of the mental undercurrent as it is in this field that things are actually done. Those forces that play upon the surface of mind may be changed and turned from their course by almost any outside influence, and their purpose thus averted. But this is never true of the undercurrents. Anything that gets into the mental undercurrents will be seen through to a finish, regardless of external circumstances or conditions; and it is with difficulty that the course of these currents is changed when once they have been placed in full positive action.

It is highly important therefore that we permit nothing to take action in these undercurrents that we do not wish to encourage and promote; and for the same reason, it is equally important that we cause everything to take action in these currents that we do wish to encourage and promote. These undercurrents, however, act only through the subconscious, and are controlled by the subconscious. In consequence, it is the subconscious which we must understand and act upon if we want the power of mind to work with full capacity and produce the greatest measure possible of the results desired.

In defining the subconscious mind, it is first necessary to state that it is not a separate mind. There are not two minds. There is only one mind in man, but it has two phases -- the conscious and the subconscious. We may define the conscious as the upper side of the mentality, and the subconscious as the underside. The subconscious may also be defined as a vast mental field permeating the entire objective personality, thereby filling every atom of the personality through and through.

We shall come nearer the truth, however, if we think of the subconscious as a finer mental force, having distinct powers, functions and possibilities, or as a great mental sea of life, energy and power, the force and capacity of which has never been measured. The conscious mind is on the surface, and therefore we act through the conscious mind whenever mental action moves through the surface of thought, will or desire, but whenever we enter into deeper mental action and sound the vast depths of this underlying mental life, we touch the subconscious, though we must remember that we do not become oblivious to the conscious every time we touch the subconscious, as the two are inseparably united.

That the two phases of the mind are related can be well illustrated by comparing the conscious mind with a sponge, and the subconscious with the water permeating the sponge. We know that every fibre of the sponge is in touch with the water, and in the same manner, every part of the conscious mind, as well as every atom in the personality, is in touch with the subconscious, and completely filled, through and through, with the life and the force of the subconscious.

It has frequently been stated that the subconscious mind occupies the Fourth. Dimension of space, and though this is a matter that cannot be exactly demonstrated, nevertheless, the more we study the nature of the subconscious, as well as the Fourth Dimension, the more convinced we become that the former occupies the field of the latter. This, however, is simply a matter that holds interest in philosophical investigation. Whether the subconscious occupies the Fourth Dimension or some other dimension of space will make no difference as to its practical value.

In order to understand the subconscious, it is well at the outset to familiarize ourselves with its natural functions, as this will convince ourselves of the fact that we are not dealing with something that is beyond normal mental action.

The subconscious mind controls all the natural functions of the body, such as the circulation, respiration, digestion, assimilation, physical repair, etc. It also controls all the involuntary actions of the body, and all those actions of mind and body that continue their natural movements without direction from the will. The subconscious perpetuates characteristics, traits, and qualities that are peculiar to individuals, species and races. What is called heredity therefore is altogether a subconscious process. The same is true of what is called second nature. Whenever anything has been repeated a sufficient number of times to have become habitual, it becomes second nature, or rather a subconscious action. It frequently happens, however, that a conscious action may become a subconscious action without repetition, and thus becomes second nature almost at once.

When we examine the nature of the subconscious, we find that it responds to almost anything the conscious mind may desire or direct, though it is usually necessary for the conscious mind to express its desire upon the subconscious for some time before the desired response is secured. The subconscious is a most willing servant, and is so competent that thus far we have failed to find a single thing along mental lines that it will not or cannot do. It submits readily to almost any kind of training, and will do practically anything that it is directed to do, whether the thing is to our advantage or not.

In this connection, it is interesting to learn that there are a number of things in the human system usually looked upon as natural, and inevitable, that are simply the results of misdirected subconscious training in the past. We frequently speak of human weaknesses as natural, but weakness is never natural. Although it may appear, it is invariably the result of imperfect subconscious training. It is never natural to go wrong, but it is natural to go right, and the reason why is simple. Every right action is in harmony with natural law, while every wrong action is a violation of natural law. It has also been stated that the aging process is natural, but modern science has demonstrated that it is not natural for a person to age at sixty, seventy, or eighty years. The fact that the average person does manifest nearly all the conditions of old age at those periods of time, or earlier, simply proves that the subconscious mind has been trained through many generations to produce old age at sixty, seventy, eighty or ninety, as the case may be, and the subconscious always does what it has been trained to do.

It can just as readily be trained, however, to produce greater physical strength and greater mental capacity at ninety than we possess at thirty or forty. It can also be trained to possess the same virile youth at one hundred as the healthiest man or woman of twenty may possess. In fact, practically every condition that appears in the mind, the character and the personality of the human race, is the result of what the subconscious mind has been directed to do during past generations. It is therefore evident that as the subconscious is directed to produce different conditions in mind, character, and personality -- conditions that are in perfect harmony with the natural law of human development, such conditions will invariably appear in the race. Thus we understand how a new race or a superior race may appear upon this planet.

There are a great many people who are disturbed over the fact that they have inherited certain characteristics or ailments from their parents, but what they have inherited is simply subconscious tendencies in that direction, and those tendencies can be changed absolutely. What we inherit from our parents can be eliminated so completely that no one would ever know it had been there. In like manner, we can improve so decidedly upon the good qualities that we have inherited from our parents that any similarity between parent and child in those respects would disappear completely.

The subconscious mind is always ready, willing and competent to make any change for the better in our physical or mental make-up that we may desire, though it does not work in some miraculous manner, nor does it usually produce results instantaneously. In most instances its actions are gradual, but they invariably produce the results intended if the proper training continues. The subconscious mind will respond to the directions of the conscious mind so long as those directions do not interfere with the absolute laws of nature. The subconscious never moves against natural law, but it has the power to so use natural law that improvement along any line can be secured. It will reproduce in mind and body any condition that is thoroughly impressed and deeply felt by the conscious mind. It will bring forth undesirable conditions when directed to produce such conditions, and it will bring forth health, strength, youth and added power when so directed.

If you continue to desire a strong physical body, and fully expect the subconscious to build for you a stronger body, you will find that this will gradually or finally be done. You will steadily grow in physical strength. If you continue to desire greater ability along a certain line and expect the subconscious to produce greater mental power along that line, your ability will increase as expected, but it is necessary in this connection to be persistent and persevering. To become enthusiastic about these things for a few days is not sufficient. It is when we apply these laws persistently for weeks, months and years that we find the results to be, not only what we expected, but frequently far greater.

Everything has a tendency to grow in the subconscious. Whenever an impression or desire is placed in the subconscious, it has a tendency to become larger and therefore the bad becomes worse when it enters the subconscious, while the good becomes better. We have the power, however, to exclude the bad from the subconscious and cause only the good to enter that immense field.

Whenever you say that you are tired and permit that feeling to sink into the subconscious, you will almost at once feel more tired. Whenever you feel sick and permit that feeling to enter the subconscious, you always feel worse. The same is true when you are weak, sad, disappointed or depressed. If you let those feelings sink into your subconscious, they will become worse. On the other hand, when we feel happy, strong, persistent and determined, and permit those feelings to enter the subconscious, we always feel better. It is therefore highly important that we positively refuse to give in to any undesirable feeling. Whenever we give in to any feeling, it becomes subconscious, and if that feeling is bad, it becomes worse; but so long as we keep undesirable feelings on the outside, so to speak, we will hold them at bay, until nature can readjust itself or gather reserve force and thus put them out of the way altogether.

We should never give in to sickness, though that does not mean that we should continue to work as hard as usual when not feeling well, or cause mind and body to continue in their usual activities. When we find it necessary, we should give ourselves a complete rest, but we should never give in to the feeling of sickness. The rest that may be taken will help the body to recuperate, and when it does the threatening ailment will disappear. When you feel tired or depressed, do not admit it, but turn your attention at once upon something that is extremely interesting -- something that will completely turn your mind towards the pleasing, the more desirable or the ideal. Persist in feeling the way you want to feel, and permit only wholesome feelings to enter the subconscious. Thus wholesome feelings will live and grow, and after awhile your power to feel good at all times will have become so strong that you can put out of the way any adverse feeling that may threaten at any time.

In this connection, we may mention something that holds more than usual interest. It has been stated by those who are in a position to know, that no one dies until they give up; that is, gives in to those adverse conditions that are at work in their system, tending to produce physical death. So long as he or she refuses to give in to those conditions, they continue to live. How long a person could refuse to give in even under the most adverse circumstances is a question, but one thing is certain, that thousands and thousands of deaths could be prevented every year if the patient in each case refused to give in. In many instances, the forces of life and death are almost equally balanced. Which one is going to win depends upon the mental attitude of the patient. If he or she gives over the mind and will to the side of the forces of life, those forces are most likely to win, but if they permit the mind to act with death, the forces of death are most certain to win.

So long as one continues to persist in living, refusing absolutely to give into death, they are throwing the full power of mind, thought and will on the side of life. They thereby increase the power of life, and may increase that power sufficiently to overcome death. Again we say that it is a question how many times a person could overcome death by this method, but the fact remains that this method alone can save life repeatedly in the majority of cases; and all will admit after further thought on this subject that the majority will be very large.

This is a method, therefore, that deserves the best of attention in every sickroom. No person should be permitted to die until all available methods for prolonging life have been exhausted, and this last mentioned method is one that will accomplish far more than most of us may expect; and its secret is found in the fact that whenever we give in to any condition or action, it becomes stronger, due to the tendency of the subconscious to enlarge, increase and magnify whatever it receives. Give in to the forces of death, and the subconscious mind will increase the powers of that force. Give in to the forces of life, and the subconscious mind will increase the power of your life and you will continue to live.

Concerning the general possibilities of the subconscious, we should remember that every faculty has a subconscious side, and that it becomes larger and more competent as this subconscious side is developed. This being true, it is evident that ability and genius might be developed in any mind even to a remarkable degree, as no limit has been found to the subconscious in any of its forces. In like manner, every cell in the body has a subconscious side, and therefore, if the subconscious side of the personality were developed, we can realize what improvement would become possible in that field.

There is a subconscious side to all the faculties in human nature, and if these were developed, we understand how man could become ideal, even far beyond our present dreams of a new race. It is not well however to give the major portion of our attention to future possibilities. It is what is possible now that we should aim to develop and apply, and present possibilities indicate that improvement along any line, whether it be in working capacity, ability, health, happiness and character can be secured without fail if the subconscious is properly directed. To direct the subconscious along any line, it is only necessary to desire what you want and to make those desires so deep and so persistent that they become positive forces in the subconscious field. When you feel that you want a certain thing, give in to that feeling and also make that feeling positive. Give in to your ambitions in the same manner, and also to every desire that you wish to realize. Let your thought of all those things that you wish to increase in any line get into your system, because whatever gets into your system, the subconscious will proceed to develop, work out and express.

In using the subconscious, we should remember that we are not using something that is separated from normal life. The difference between the individual who makes scientific use of the subconscious and the one who does not, is simply this; the latter employs only a small part of their mind, while the former employs the whole of their mind. And this explains why those who employ the subconscious intelligently have greater working capacity, greater ability and greater endurance. In consequence they sometimes do the work of two or three people, and do excellent work in addition. To train the subconscious for practical action is therefore a matter of common sense. It is a matter of refusing to cultivate only a small corner of your mental field when you can cultivate the entire field.

5. TRAINING THE SUBCONSCIOUS FOR PRACTICAL RESULTS

When you have made up your mind what you want to do, say to yourself a thousand times a day that you will do it. The best way will soon open. You will have the opportunity you desire. If you would be greater in the future than you are now, be all that you can be now. He who is his best develops the power to be better. He who lives his ideals is creating a life that actually is ideal. There is nothing in your life that you cannot modify, change or improve when you learn to regulate your thought. Our destiny is not mapped out for us by some exterior power; we map it out for ourselves. What we think and do in the present determines what shall happen to us in the future.

When we proceed to train the subconscious along any line, or for special results, we must always comply with the following law: The subconscious responds to the impressions, the suggestions, the desires, the expectations and the directions of the conscious mind, provided that the conscious touches the subconscious at the time. The secret therefore is found in the two phases of the mind touching each other as directions are being made; and to cause the conscious to touch the subconscious, it is necessary to feel conscious action penetrating your entire interior system; that is, you should feel at the time that you are living not simply on the surface, but through and through. At such times, the mind should be calm and in perfect poise, and should be conscious of that finer, greater something within you that has greater depth than mere surface existence.

When you wish to direct the subconscious to produce physical health, first picture in your mind a clear idea of perfect health. Try to see this idea with the mind's eye, and then try to feel the meaning of this idea with consciousness, and while you are in the attitude of that feeling, permit your thought and your attention to pass into that deep quiet, serene state of being wherein you can feel the mental idea of wholeness and health entering into the very life of every atom in your system. In brief, try to feel perfectly healthy in your mind and then let that feeling sink into your entire physical system. Whenever you feel illness coming on, you can nip it in the bud by this simple method, because if the subconscious is directed to produce more health, added forces of health will soon begin to come forth from within, and put out of the way, so to speak, any disorder or ailment that may be on the verge of getting a foothold in the body.

Always remember that whatever is impressed on the subconscious will after a while be expressed from the subconscious into the personality; and where the physical conditions that you wish to remove are only slight, enough subconscious power can be aroused to restore immediate order, harmony and wholeness. When the condition you wish to remove has continued for some time, however, repeated efforts may be required to cause the subconscious to act in the matter. But one thing is certain, that if you continue to direct the subconscious to remove that condition, it positively will be removed.

The subconscious does not simply possess the power to remove undesirable conditions from the physical or mental state. It can also produce those better conditions that we may want, and develop further those desirable conditions that we already possess. To apply the law for this purpose, deeply desire those conditions that you do want, and have a very clear idea in your mind as to what you want those conditions to be. In giving the subconscious directions for anything desired in our physical or mental makeup, we should always have improvement in mind, as the subconscious always does the best work when we are thoroughly filled with the desire to do better. If we want health, we should direct the subconscious to produce more and more health. If we want power, we should direct the subconscious not simply to give us a great deal or a certain amount of power, but to give us more and more power. In this manner, we shall secure results from the very beginning.

If we try to train the subconscious to produce a certain amount, it might be some time before that amount can be developed. In the meantime, we should meet disappointment and delay, but if our desire is for steady increase along all lines from where we stand now, we shall be able to secure, first, a slight improvement and then added improvement to be followed with still greater improvement until we finally reach the highest goal we have in view. No effort should be made to destroy those qualities that we may not desire. Whatever we think about deeply or intensely, the subconscious will take up and develop further. Therefore, if we think about our failings, shortcomings or bad habits, the subconscious will take them up and give them more life and activity than they ever had before. If there is anything in our nature therefore that we wish to change, we should simply proceed to build up what we want and forget completely what we wish to eliminate. When the good develops, the bad disappears. When the greater is built up, the lesser will either be removed or completely transformed and combined with the greater.

That the subconscious can increase your ability and your capacity is a fact that is readily demonstrated. Whenever the subconscious mind is aroused, mental power and working capacity are invariably increased sometimes to such an extent that the individual seems to be possessed with a super human power. We all know of instances where great things were accomplished simply through the fact that the individual was carried on and on by an immense power within them that seemed to be distinct from themselves and greater than themselves; but it was simply the greater powers of the subconscious that were aroused and placed in positive, determined action. These instances, however, need not be exceptions. Any individual, under any circumstances, can so increase the power of their mind, their thought and their will as to be actually carried away with the same tremendous force; that is, the power within them becomes so strong that they are actually pushed through to the goal they have in view regardless of circumstances, conditions or obstacles.

This being true, we should arouse the subconscious no matter what it is we have to do. No day is complete unless we begin that day by making alive everything that we possess in our whole mind, conscious and subconscious. Whenever you have work to do at some future time, direct the subconscious to increase your ability and capacity at the time specified, and fully expect the desired increase to be secured. If you want new ideas on certain studies or new plans in your work, direct the subconscious to produce them and you will get them without fail. The moment the direction is given, the subconscious will go to work along that line; and in this connection, we should remember that though we may fail to get the idea desired through the conscious mind alone, it is quite natural that we should get it when we also enlist the subconscious, because the whole mind is much greater, far more capable and far more resourceful than just a small part of the mind.

When demands are urgent, the subconscious responds more readily, especially when feelings at the time are also very deep. When you need certain results, say that you must have them, and put your whole energy into the "must." Whatever you make up your mind that you must do, you will in some manner get the power to do. There are a number of instances on record where people were carried through certain events by what seemed to be a miraculous power, but the cause of it all was simply this -- that they had to do it, and whatever you have to do, the subconscious mind will invariably give you the power to do. The reason for this is found in the fact that when you feel that you must do a thing and that you have to do it, your desires are so strong and so deep that they go into the very depths of the subconscious and thus call to action the full power of that vast interior realm.

If you have some great ambition that you wish to realize, direct the subconscious several times each day and each night before you go to sleep, to work out the necessary ways and means; and if you are determined, those ways and means will be forthcoming. But here it is necessary to remember that we must concentrate on the one thing wanted. If your mind scatters, sometimes giving attention to one ambition and sometimes to another, you will confuse the subconscious and the ways and means desired will not be secured. Make your ambition a vital part of your life, and try to feel the force of that ambition every single moment of your existence. If you do this, your ambition will certainly be realized. It may take a year, it may take five years, it may take ten years or more, but your ambition will be realized. This being true, no one need feel disturbed about the future, because if they actually know what they want to accomplish, and train the subconscious to produce the idea, the methods, the necessary ability and the required capacity, all these things will be secured.

If there is any condition from which you desire to secure emancipation, direct the subconscious to give you that information through which you may find a way out. The subconscious can. We all remember the saying, "Where there is a will there is a way," and it is true, because when you actually will to do a certain thing, the power of the mind becomes so deep and so strong along that line, that the entire subconscious mind is put to work on the case, so to speak; and under such circumstances, the way will always be found. When you put your whole mind, conscious and subconscious, to work on any problem, you will find the solution.

If there is any talent that you wish to develop further, direct the subconscious every day, and as frequently as possible, to enlarge the inner life of that talent and to increase its brilliancy and power. When you are about to undertake anything new, do not proceed until you have submitted the proposition to the subconscious, and here we find the real value of "sleeping over" new plans before we finally decide. When we go to sleep, we go more completely into the subconscious, and those ideas that we take with us when we go to sleep, especially those that engage our serious attention at the time, are completely turned over, so to speak, during the period of sleep, and examined from all points of view. Sometimes it is necessary to take those ideas into the subconscious a number of times when we go to sleep, as well as to submit the matter to the subconscious many times in the day during the waking state, but if we persevere, the right answer will finally be secured.

The whole mind, conscious and subconscious, does possess the power to solve any problem that may come up, or provide the necessary ways and means through which we can carry out or finish anything we have undertaken. Here, as elsewhere, practice makes perfect. The more you train the subconscious to work with you, the easier it becomes to get the subconscious to respond to your directions, and therefore the subconscious mind should be called into action, no matter what comes up; in other words make it a practice to use your whole mind, conscious and subconscious, at all times, not only in large matters, but in all matters. Begin by recognizing the subconscious in all thought and in all action. Think that it can do what you have been told it can do, and eliminate doubt absolutely. Take several moments every day and suggest to the subconscious what you want to have done. Be thoroughly sincere in this matter; be determined; have unbounded faith, and you can expect results; but do not permit the mind to become wrought up when giving directions. Always be calm and deeply poised when thinking out or suggesting to the subconscious, and it is especially important that you be deeply calm before you go to sleep.

Do not permit any idea, suggestion or expectation to enter the subconscious unless it is something that you actually want developed or worked out, and here we should remember that every idea, desire or state of mind that is deeply felt will enter the subconscious. When there are no results, do not lose faith. You know that the cause of the failure was the failure of the conscious to properly touch the subconscious at the time the directions were given, so therefore try again, giving your thought a deeper life and a more persistent desire. Always be prepared to give these methods sufficient time. Some have remarkable results at once, while others secure no results for months; but whether you secure results as soon as you wish or not, continue to give your directions every day, fully expecting results. Be determined in every effort you may make in this direction, but do not be over-anxious.

Make it a point to give special directions to the subconscious every day for the steady improvement of mind, character and personality along all lines. You cannot give the subconscious too much to do because its power is immense, and as far as we know, its capacity limitless. Every effort you may make to direct or train the subconscious, will bring its natural results in due time, provided you are always calm, well balanced, persistent, deeply poised and harmonious in all your thoughts and actions.

6. THE POWER OF SUBJECTIVE THOUGHT

THE PATH TO GREATER THINGS

Dream constantly of the ideal; work ceaselessly to perfect the real. Believe in yourself; believe in everybody; believe in all that has existence. Give the body added strength; give the mind added brilliancy; give the soul added inspiration. Do your best under every circumstance, and believe that every circumstance will give its best to you. Live for the realization of more life and for the more efficient use of everything that proceeds from life. Desire eternally what you want; and act always as if every expectation were coming true.

The first important factor to consider in connection with the study of thought is that every thought does not possess power. In modern times, when thinking has been studied so closely, a great many have come to the conclusion that every thought is itself a force and that it invariably produces certain definite results ; but this is not true, and it is well, for if every thought had power we could not last very long as the larger part of ordinary human thinking is chaotic and destructive.

When we proceed to determine what kinds of thought have power and what kinds have not, we find two distinct forms. The one we call objective, the other subjective. Objective thought is the result of general thinking, such as reasoning, intellectual research, analysis, study, the process of recollection, mind-picturing where there is no feeling, and the usual activities of the intellect. In brief, any mental process that calls forth only the activities of the intellect is objective, and such thinking does not affect the conditions of mind and body to any extent; that is, it does not produce direct results corresponding to its own nature upon the system. It does not immediately affect your health, your happiness, your physical condition nor your mental condition. It may, however, affect these things in the long run, and for that reason must not be ignored.

Subjective thinking is any form of thinking or mind-picturing that has depth of feeling, that goes beneath the surface in its action, that moves through the undercurrents, that acts in and through the psychological field. Subjective thought is synonymous with the thought of the heart, and it is subjective thought that is referred to in the statement, "As a man thinketh in his heart so is he."

Subjective thought proceeds from the very heart of mental existence; that is, it is always in contact with everything that is vital in life. It is always alive with feeling, and originates, so to speak, in the heart of the mind. The term "heart" in this connection has nothing to do with the physical organ by that name. The term "heart" is here used in its metaphysical sense. We speak of the heart of a great city, meaning thereby, the principal part of the city, or that part of the city where its most vital activities are taking place; likewise, the heart of the mind is the most vital realm of the mind, or the centre of the mind, or the deeper activities of the mind as distinguished from the surface of the mind.

Subjective thinking being in the heart of the mind is therefore necessarily the product of the deepest mental life, and for this reason every subjective thought is a force. It will either work for you or against you, and has the power to produce direct effects upon mind or body, corresponding exactly with its own nature. But all thinking is liable to become subjective at times. All thoughts may sink into the deeper or vital realms of mind and thus become direct forces for good or ill. Therefore, all thinking should be scientific; that is, designed or produced with a definite object in view. All thought should be produced according to the laws of right thinking or constructive thinking. Though objective thinking usually produces no results whatever, nevertheless there are many objective thoughts that become subjective and it is the objective mind that invariably determines the nature of subjective thinking.

Every thought therefore should have the right tendency, so that it may produce desirable results in case it becomes subjective, or may act in harmony with the objective mind whenever it is being employed in giving directions to the subjective. In this connection, it is well to remember that subjective thinking invariably takes place in the subconscious mind, as the terms subjective and subconscious mean practically the same; though in speaking of thought, the term subjective is more appropriate in defining that form of thought that is deep, vital and alive, or that acts through the mental undercurrents.

To define scientific thinking, it may be stated that your thinking is scientific when your thought has a direct tendency to produce what you want, or when all the forces of your mind are working together for the purpose you desire to fulfill. Your thinking is unscientific when your thought has a tendency to produce what is detrimental, or when your mental forces are working against you. To think scientifically, the first essential is to think only such thoughts and permit only such mental attitudes as you know to be in your favor; and the second essential is to make only such thoughts subjective. In other words, every thought should be right and every thought should be a force. When every thought is scientific, it will be right, and when every thought is subjective it will be a force.

Positively refuse to think of what you do not wish to retain or experience. Think only of what you desire, and expect only what you desire, even when the very contrary seems to be coming into your life. Make it a point to have definite results in mind at all times. Permit no thinking to be aimless. Every aimless thought is time and energy wasted, while every thought that is inspired with a definite aim will help to realize that aim, and if all your thoughts are inspired with a definite aim, the whole power of your mind will be for you and will work with you in realizing what you have in view. That you should succeed is therefore assured, because there is enough power in your mind to realize your ambitions, provided all of that power is used in working for your ambitions. And in scientific thinking all the power of mind and thought is being caused to work directly and constantly for what you wish to attain and achieve.

To explain further the nature of scientific thinking, as well as unscientific thinking, it is well to take several well-known illustrations from real life. When things go wrong, people usually say, "That's always the way"; and though this may seem to be a harmless expression, nevertheless, the more you use that expression the more deeply you convince your mind that things naturally go wrong most of the time. When you train your mind to think that it is usual for things to go wrong, the forces of your mind will follow that trend of thinking, and will also go wrong; and for that reason it is perfectly natural that things in your life should go wrong more and more, because as the forces of your mind are going wrong, you will go wrong, and when you go wrong, those things that pertain to your life cannot possibly go right.

A great many people are constantly looking for the worst. They usually expect the worst to happen; though they may be cheerful on the surface, deep down in their heart they are constantly looking for trouble. The result is that their deeper mental currents will tend to produce trouble. If you are always looking for the worst, the forces of your mind will be turned in that direction, and therefore will become destructive. Those forces will tend to produce the very thing that you expect. At first they will simply confuse your mind and produce troubled conditions in your mental world; but this will in turn confuse your faculties, your reason and your judgment, so that you will make many mistakes; and he who is constantly making mistakes will certainly find the worst on many or all occasions.

When things go wrong, do not expect the wrong to appear again. Look upon it as an exception. Call it past and forget it. To be scientific under these circumstances, always look for the best. By constantly expecting the best, you will turn the different forces of your mind and thought to work for the best. Every power that is in you will have a higher and finer ideal upon which to turn its attention, and accordingly, results will be better, which is perfectly natural when your whole system is moving towards the better.

A number of people have a habit of saying, "Something is always wrong"; but why should we not say instead, "Something is always right"? We would thereby express more of the truth and give our minds a more wholesome tendency. It is not true that something is always wrong. When we compare the wrong with the right, the wrong is always in the minority. However, it is the effect of such thinking upon the mind that we wish to avoid, whether the wrong be in our midst or not. When you think that there is always something wrong, your mind is more or less concentrated on the wrong, and will therefore create the wrong in your own mentality; but when you train yourself to think there is always something right, your mind will concentrate upon the right, and accordingly will create the right. And when the mind is trained to create the right it will not only produce right conditions within itself, but all thinking will tend to become right; and right thinking invariably leads to health, happiness, power and plenty.

The average person is in the habit of saying, "The older I get"; and they thereby call the attention of the mind to the idea that they are getting older. In brief, they compel their mind to believe that they are getting older and older, and thereby direct the mind to produce more and more age. The true expression in this connection is, "The longer I live." This expression calls the mind's attention to the length of life, which will, in turn, tend to increase the power of that process in you that can prolong life. When people reach the age of sixty or seventy, they usually speak of "the rest of my days," thus implying the idea that there are only a few more days remaining. The mind is thereby directed to finish life in a short period of time, and accordingly, all the forces of the mind will proceed to work for the speedy termination of personal existence. The correct expression is "from now on," as that leads thought into the future indefinitely without impressing the mind with any end whatever.

We frequently hear the expression, "I can never do anything right," and it is quite simple to understand that such a mode of thought would train the mind to act below its true ability and capacity. If you are fully convinced that you can never do anything right, it will become practically impossible for you to do anything right at any time, but on the other hand, if you continue to think, "I am going to do everything better and better," it is quite natural that your entire mental system should be inspired and trained to do things better and better.

Hundreds of similar expressions could be mentioned, but we are all familiar with them, and from the comments made above, anyone will realize that such expressions are obstacles in our way, no matter what we may do. In right thinking the purpose should be never to use any expression that conveys to your mind what you do not want, or what is detrimental or unwholesome in any manner whatever. Think only what you wish to produce or realize. If trouble is brewing, think about the greater success that you have in mind. If anything adverse is about to take place, do not think of what that adversity may bring, but think of the greater good that you are determined to realize in your life.

When trouble is brewing, the average person usually thinks of nothing else. Their mind is filled with fear, and not a single faculty in their possession can do justice to itself. And as trouble is usually brewing in most places, more or less, people have what may be called a chronic expectation for trouble; and as they usually get more or less of what they expect, they imagine they are fully justified in entertaining such expectations. But here it is absolutely necessary to change the mind completely. Whatever our present circumstances may be, we should refuse absolutely to expect anything but the best that we can think of. The whole mind, with all its powers and faculties, should be thrown, so to speak, into line with the optimistic tendency, and whatever comes or not, we should think only of the greater things that we expect to realize. In brief, we should concentrate the mind absolutely upon whatever goal we may have in view, and I should look neither to the left nor to the right.

When we concentrate absolutely upon the greater things we expect to attain or achieve, we gradually train all the forces of the mind and all the powers of thought to work for those greater things. We shall thereby begin in earnest to build for ourselves a greater destiny; and sooner or later we shall find ourselves gaining ground in many directions. Later on, if we proceed, we shall begin to move more rapidly, and if we pay no attention to the various troubles that may be brewing in our environment, those troubles will never affect us nor disturb us in the least.

The mental law involved in the process of scientific thinking may be stated as follows: The more you think of what is right, the more you tend to make every action in your mind right. The more you think of the goal you have in view, the more life and power you will call into action in working for that goal. The more you think of your ambition, the more power you will give to those faculties that can make your ambitions come true. The more you think of harmony, of health, of success, of happiness, of things that are desirable, of things that are beautiful, of things that have true worth, the more the mind will tend to build all those things in yourself, provided, of course, that all such thinking is subjective.

To think scientifically, therefore, is to train your every thought and your every mental action to focus the whole of attention upon that which you wish to realize, to gain, to achieve or attain in your life. In training the mind along the lines of scientific thinking begin by trying to hold the mind upon the right, regardless of the presence of the wrong, and here we should remember that the term "right" does not simply refer to moral actions, but to all actions. When the wrong is coming your way, persist in thinking of the right; persist in expecting only the right. And there is a scientific reason for this attitude, besides what has been mentioned above. We know that the most important of all is to keep the mind right or moving along right lines, and if we persistently expect the right, regardless of circumstances, the mind will be kept in the lines of right action. But there is another result that frequently comes from this same practice. It sometimes happens that the wrong which is brewing in your environment, has such a weak foundation that only a slight increase in the force of the right would be necessary to overthrow that wrong completely; in fact, we shall find that most wrongs that threaten can be overcome in a very short time, if we continue to work for the right in a positive, constructive, determined manner.

It is when the individual goes all to pieces, so to speak, that adversity gets the best of them; but no individual will go to pieces unless their thinking is chaotic, destructive, scattered, confused and detrimental. Continue to possess your whole mind and you will master the situation, no matter what it may be, and it is scientific thinking that will enable you to perform this great feat. To make thinking scientific, there are three leading essentials to be observed. The first is to cultivate constructive mental attitudes, and all mental attitudes are constructive when mind, thought, feeling, desire and will constantly face the greater and the better.

A positive and determined optimism has the same effect, and the same is true of the practice of keeping the mental eye single on the highest goal in view. To make every mental attitude constructive the mind must never look down, and mental depression must be avoided completely. Every thought and every feeling must have an upward look, and every desire must desire to inspire the same rising tendency in every action of mind.

The second essential is constructive mental imagery. Use the imagination to picture only what is good, what is beautiful, what is beneficial, what is ideal, and what you wish to realize. Mentally see yourself receiving what you deeply desire to receive. What you imagine, you will think, and what you think, you will become. Therefore, if you imagine only those things that are in harmony with what you wish to obtain or achieve, all your thinking will soon tend to produce what you want to attain or achieve.

The third essential is constructive mental action. Every action of the mind should have something desirable in view and should have a definite, positive aim. Train yourself to face the sunshine of life regardless of circumstances. When you face the sunshine, everything looks right, and when everything looks right, you will think right. It matters not whether there is any sunshine in life just now or not. We must think of sunshine just the same. If we do not see any silver lining, we must create one in our own mental vision. However dark the dark side may seem to be, we cannot afford to see anything but the bright side, and no matter how small or insignificant the bright side may be, we must continue to focus attention on that side alone.

Be optimistic, not in the usual sense of that term, but in the real sense of that term. The true optimist not only expects the best to happen, but goes to work to make the best happen. The true optimist not only looks upon the bright side, but trains every force that is in them to produce more and more brightness in their life, and therefore complies with the three essentials just mentioned. Their mental attitudes are constructive because they are always facing greater things. Their imagination is constructive because it is always picturing the better and the ideal, and their mental actions are constructive because they are training the whole of their life to produce those greater and better things that their optimism has inspired them to desire and expect.

In this connection, we must remember that there is a group of mental forces at work in every mental attitude, and therefore if that attitude is downcast, those forces will become detrimental; that is, they will work for the lesser and the inferior. On the other hand, if every mental attitude is lifted up or directed towards the heights of the great and the true and the ideal, those forces will become constructive, and will work for the greater things in view.

In the perusal of this study, we shall find it profitable to examine our mental attitudes closely, so as to determine what our minds are actually facing the greater part of the time. If we find that we are mentally facing things and conditions that are beneath our expectations, or find that our imaginations are concerned too much about possible failure, possible mistakes, possible trouble, possible adversity, etc., our thinking is unscientific, and no time should be lost in making amends. When you are looking into the future, do not worry about troubles that might come to pass. Do not mentally see yourself as having a hard time of it. Do not imagine yourself in this hostile condition or that adverse circumstance. Do not wonder what you would do if you should lose everything, or if this or that calamity should befall. Such thinking is decidedly unscientific and most detrimental. If you entertain such thoughts you are causing the ship of your life to move directly towards the worst precipice that may exist in your vicinity. Besides, you are so weakening this ship through wrong treatment, that it will someday spring a leak and go down.

Think of the future whenever it is unnecessary for you to give your attention to the present, but let your thought of the future be wholesome, constructive, optimistic and ideal. Mentally see yourself gaining the best that life has to give, and you will meet more and more of the best. Think of yourself as gaining ground along all lines, as finding better and better circumstances, as increasing in power and ability, and as becoming more healthful in body, more vigorous and brilliant in mind, more perfect in character, and more powerful in soul. In brief, associate your future with the best that you can think of along all lines. Fear nothing for the days that are to be, but expect everything that is good, desirable, enjoyable and ideal. This practice will not only make your present happier, but it will tend to strengthen your mind and your life along wholesome constructive lines to such a degree that you will actually gain the power to realize, in a large measure, those beautiful and greater things that you have constantly expected in your optimistic dreams.

In living and building for a larger future, we should remember that our mind and thoughts invariably follow the leadership of the most prominent mental picture. The man or woman who clearly and distinctly pictures for themselves a brilliant future will inspire the powers of their entire mental world to work for such a future; in fact, all the forces of thought, mind, life, personality, character and soul will move in that direction. They may not realize as brilliant a future as they have pictured, but their future is certainly going to be brilliant, and it is quite possible, as is frequently the case, that it may become even more brilliant than they dreamed of in the beginning.

When the average mind thinks of the future, they usually picture a variety of conflicting events and conditions. They have nothing definite in mind. There is no actual leadership therefore in their mind, and nothing of great worth can be accomplished.

When we look into the lives of men and women who have reached high places, we always find that they were inspired with some great idea. That idea was pictured again and again in their mental vision, and they refused to let it go. They clung tenaciously to that idea, and thereby actually compelled every force and element within them to enlist in the working out of that idea. It is therefore simple enough that they should realize every aim and reach the highest places that achievement has in store. Such men and women possibly did not understand the science or the process, but they were nevertheless thinking scientifically to a most perfect degree. Their ambition pictured only that lofty goal which they wanted to reach. All their mental attitudes were constantly facing that lofty goal, and thereby became constructive; and all the actions of mind were directed toward the same goal. Accordingly, everything within them was framed to work for the realization of their dream, and that is what we mean by scientific thinking; that is what we mean by thinking for results. And anyone who will train themselves to think for results in this manner, will positively secure results; though in this connection it is well to remember that persistence and determination are indispensable every step of the way.

When we do not secure results at once, we sometimes become discouraged, and conclude that it is no use to try. At such times, friends will usually tell us that we are simply dreaming, and they will advise us to go to work at something practical, something that we really can accomplish; but if we ignore the advice of our friends, and continue to be true to the great idea that we have resolved to work out, we shall finally reach our goal, and when we do, those very same friends will tell us that we took the proper course. So long as the man with ambition is a failure, the world will tell him to let go of his ideal; but when his ambition is realized, the world will praise him for the persistence and the determination that he manifested during his dark hours, and everybody will point to his life as an example for coming generations. This is invariably the rule. Therefore pay no attention to what the world says when you are down. Be determined to get up, to reach the highest goal you have in view, and you will.

There are a great many ambitious men and women, who imagine that they will succeed provided their determination is strong and their persistence continuous, regardless of the fact that their thinking may be unscientific; but the sooner we dispel this illusion, the better. Unscientific thinking, even in minor matters, weakens the will. It turns valuable thought power astray, and we need the full power of thought, positively directed along the line of our work if we are going to achieve, and achieve greatly. The majority of the mental forces in the average person are working against them, because they are constantly entertaining depressed mental states or detrimental habits of thought; and even though they may be ambitious, that ambition has not sufficient power to work itself out, because most of the forces of their mind are thrown away.

We therefore see the necessity of becoming scientific in all thinking, and in making every mental habit wholesome and beneficial in the largest sense of those terms. But scientific thinking not only tends to turn the power of thought in the right direction; it also tends to increase mental power, to promote efficiency and to build up every faculty that we may employ. To illustrate the effect of right thinking upon the faculties, we will suppose that you have musical talent, and are trying to perfect that talent. Then, we will suppose that you are constantly expressing dissatisfaction with the power of that talent. What will be the result? Your mental action upon that faculty will tend to lower its efficiency, because you are depressing its action instead of inspiring those actions.

On the other hand, if you encourage this talent, you will tend to expand its life, and thereby increase its capacity for results.

In this respect, talents are similar to people. Take two people of equal ability and place them in circumstances that are direct opposites. We will suppose that the one is mistreated every day by those with whom he is associated. He is constantly being criticized and constantly being told that he will never amount to anything; he is blamed for everything that is wrong, and is in every manner discouraged and kept down. What would happen to the ability and efficiency of that man if he continued under such treatment year after year? He simply could not advance unless he should happen to be a mental giant, and even then, his advancement would be very slow; but if he was not a mental giant, just an average man, he would steadily lose ambition, self-confidence, initiative, judgment, reasoning power, and in fact, everything that goes to make up ability and capacity.

We will suppose the other man is encouraged continually. He is praised for every thing, he is given every possible opportunity to show and apply what ability he may possess; he is surrounded by an optimistic atmosphere, and is expected by everybody to advance and improve continually. What will happen to this man? The best will be brought out in his power and ability. He will be pushed to the fore constantly and he will climb steadily and surely until he reaches the top.

Treat your talents in the same way, and you have the same results in every case. To state it briefly, make it a point to encourage your talents, your faculties and your powers. Give every element and force within you encouragement and inspiration. Expect them all to do their best, and train yourself to think and feel that they positively will. Train yourself to think of your whole system as all right. Deal with your mental faculties in this manner, under all circumstances, and deal with your physical organs in the same way.

Most people among those who do not have perfect health, have a habit of speaking of their stomachs as bad, their livers as always out of order, their eyes as weak, their nerves as all upset, and the different parts of their systems as generally wrong. But what are they doing to their physical organs through this practice? The very same as was done to the unfortunate man just mentioned, and we shall find, in this connection, one reason why so many people continue to be sick. They are keeping their physical organs down, so to speak, by depressing the entire system with unwholesome thinking; but if they

37

would change their tactics and begin to encourage their physical organs, praise them and expect them to do better, and to treat them right from the mental as well as a physical standpoint, they would soon be restored to perfect health.

In training the mind in scientific thinking, the larger part of attention should be given to that of controlling our feelings. It is not difficult to think scientifically along intellectual lines, but to make our feelings move along wholesome, constructive, optimistic lines requires persistent training. Intellectual thought can be changed almost at any time with little effort, but feeling usually becomes stronger and stronger the longer it moves along a certain line, and thus becomes more difficult to change.

When we feel discouraged, it is so easy to feel more discouraged; when we feel dissatisfied, it is only a step to that condition that is practically intolerable. It is therefore necessary to stop all detrimental feeling in the beginning. Do not permit a single adverse feeling to continue for a second. Change the mind at once by turning your attention upon something that will make you feel better. Resolve to feel the way you want to feel under all circumstances, and you will gradually develop the power to do so. Depressed mental feelings are burdens, and we waste a great deal of energy by carrying them around on our mental shoulders. Besides, such feelings tend to direct the power of thought towards the lower and the inferior.

Whenever you permit yourself to feel bad, you will cause the power of mind and thought to go wrong. Therefore, persist in feeling right and good. Persist in feeling joyous. Persist in feeling cheerful, hopeful, optimistic and strong. Place yourself on the bright side and the strong side of everything that transpires in your life, and you will constantly gain power, power that will invariably be in your favor.

7. HOW MAN BECOMES WHAT HE THINKS

Life is growth and the object of right thinking is to promote that growth. Give less time trying to change the opinions of others, and more time trying to improve your own life. Life becomes the way it is lived; and man may live the way he wants to live when he learns to think what he wants to think. Create your own thought and you become what you want to become because your thought creates you. We all know that man is as he thinks. Then we must think only such thoughts as tend to make us what we wish to be. The secret of right thinking is found in always keeping the mind's eye stayed upon the greater and the better in all things.

Scientific research in the metaphysical field has demonstrated the fact that man is as he thinks, that he becomes what he thinks, and that what he thinks in the present, determines what he is to become in the future; and also that since he can change his thought for the better along any line, he can therefore completely change himself along any line. But the majority who try to apply this law do not succeed to a great degree, the reason being that instead of working entirely upon the principle that man is as he thinks, they proceed in the belief that man is what he thinks he is.

At first sight there may seem to be no difference between the principle that man is as he thinks and the belief that man is as he thinks he is, but close study will reveal the fact that the latter is absolutely untrue. Man is not what he thinks he is, because personality, mentality and character are not determined by personal opinions. It is the thought of the heart, that is, the mental expression from the subconscious that makes the personal man what he is; but the subconscious is effected only by what man actually thinks in the real field of creative thought, and not by what he may think of himself in the field of mere personal opinion.

It is subjective thought that makes you what you are; but to think that you are thus or so, will not necessarily make you thus or so. To create subjective thought you must act directly upon the subconscious, but it is not possible to impress the subconscious while you are forming opinions about your personal self. A mere statement about yourself will not affect or change the subconscious, and so long as the subconscious remains unchanged, you will remain unchanged. While you are thinking simply about your external or personal self you are acting upon the objective, but to change yourself you must act upon the subjective.

Man may think that he is great, but so long as he continues to think small thoughts, he will continue to be small. No matter how high an opinion he may have of himself, while he is living in the superficial, his thoughts will be empty, and empty thoughts are not conducive to high attainments and great achievements. Man becomes great when he thinks great thoughts, and to think great thoughts he must transcend the limitations and circumscribed conditions of the person, and mentally enter into the world of the great and the superior. He must seek to gain a larger and a larger consciousness of the world of real quality, real worth and real superiority, and must dwell upon the loftiest mountain peaks of mind that he can possibly reach. He must live in the life of greatness, breathe the spirit of greatness, and feel the very soul of greatness. Then, and only then, will he think great thoughts; and the mind that continues to think great thoughts will continue to grow in greatness.

It is not what you state in your thought but what you give to your thought that determines results. The thought that is merely stated may be empty, but it is the thought with something in it that alone can exercise real power in personal life. And what is to be in your thought will depend upon what you think into your thought. What you give to your thought, your thought will give to you, and you will be and become accordingly, no matter what you may think that you are. The cause that you originate in the within will produce its effect in the without, regardless of what your opinions may be. Your personal life will consequently be the result of what you think, but it will not necessarily be what you think it is.

Having discovered the fact that the physical body is completely renewed every eight or ten months, you will naturally think that you are young, but to simply think you are young will not cause the body to look as young as it really is. To retain your youth you must remove those subconscious tendencies and conditions that produce old age, and you must eliminate worry. So long as you worry you will cause your personality to grow older and older in appearance, no matter how persistently you may think that you are young. To simply think that you are young will not avail. You must think thoughts that produce, retain and perpetuate youth. If you wish to look young, your mind must feel young, but you will not feel young until the whole of your mind produces the feeling of youth. To develop the feeling of youth in the whole mind, you must become fully conscious of the fact that youth is naturally produced in your entire system every minute, and you must train the mind to take cognizance only of the eternal now.

So long as we feel that we are passing with time, we will imagine that we feel the weight of more and more years, and this feeling will invariably cause the body to show the mark of years, growing older and older in appearance as more years are added to the imaginary burden of age. You will look young when you feel young, but to simply feel that you are young will not always cause you to feel young. The real feeling of youth comes when we actually think in the consciousness of youth and give the realization of the now to every thought.

You may think that you are well, but you will not secure health until you think thoughts that produce health. You may persistently affirm that you are well, but so long as you live in discord, confusion, worry, fear and other wrong states of mind, you will be sick; that is, you will be as you think and not what you think you are. You may state health in your thought, but if you give worry, fear and discord to that thought, your thinking will produce discord.

It is not what we state in our thoughts, but what we give to our thoughts that determine results. To produce health, thought itself must be healthful and wholesome. It must contain the quality of health, and the very life of health. This, however, is not possible unless the mind is conscious of health at the time when such thought is being produced. Therefore, to think thoughts that can produce health, the mind must enter into the realization of the being of health, and not simply dwell in the objective belief about health. Again, to produce health, all the laws of life must be observed; that is, the mind must be in that understanding of law, and in that harmony with law where the guiding thought will naturally observe law. To simply think that you are well will not teach the mind to understand the laws of life and health, nor will that thinking place you in harmony with those laws. That thinking that does understand the laws of life will not come from the mere belief that you are well, but from the effort to enter into the understanding of all law, the spirit of all law, the very life of health, and into the very soul of all truth.

You may think that your mind is brilliant and may undertake most difficult tasks in the belief that you are equal to the occasion, but the question is if your conception of brilliancy is great or small. If your conception of brilliancy is small, you may be right to that degree in thinking you are brilliant; that is, you may be brilliant as far as your understanding of brilliancy goes. Whether that is sufficient or not to carry out the task that is before you is another question. Your opinion of your mental capacity may be great, but if your idea of intelligence is crude, your intelligence- producing thought will also be crude, and can produce only crude intelligence. It is therefore evident that to simply think that you are brilliant will not produce brilliancy, unless your understanding of brilliancy is made larger, higher and finer.

What you understand and mentally feel concerning intelligence, mental capacity and brilliancy, is what you actually think on those subjects, and it is this understanding or feeling or realization that will determine how much intelligence you will give to your thought. Your thought will be as brilliant as the brilliancy you think into your thought, and how much brilliancy you will think into your thought will depend upon how high your realization of brilliancy happens to be at the time. When your thinking is brilliant, you will be brilliant, but if your thinking is not brilliant you will not be brilliant, no matter how brilliant you may think you are. To make your thinking more brilliant, try to enter into the consciousness of finer intelligence, larger mental capacity, and the highest order of mental brilliancy that you can possibly realize. Do not call yourself brilliant at any time, or do not think of yourself as lacking in brilliancy. Simply fix the mental eye upon absolute brilliancy, and desire with all the power of mind and soul to go on and on into higher steps of that brilliancy.

When all the elements and forces of your system are working in such a way that beauty will naturally be produced, you will be beautiful, whether you think you are beautiful or not, and it is the actions of the subconscious that determine how the elements and forces of the system are to work. Therefore, the beautiful person is beautiful because her real interior thinking is conducive to the creation of the beautiful. That person, however, who is not beautiful, does not necessarily think ugly thoughts, but her interior mental actions have not been brought together in such a way as to produce the expression of beauty; that is the subconscious actions have not been arranged according to the most perfect pattern. But these actions can be arranged in that manner, not by thinking that one is beautiful. but by thinking thoughts that are beautiful. When you think that you are beautiful, you are liable to think that you are more beautiful than others, and such a thought is not a beautiful thought. To recognize or criticize ugliness and inferiority in others is to create the inferior and the ugly in yourself, and what you create in yourself will sooner or later be expressed through your mind and personality.

So long as you worry, hate or fear, your thought will make you disagreeable in mind and character, and later on in the person as well; and no amount of affirming or thinking that you are beautiful will overcome those ugly states of mind that you have created. You will thus be as you think -- worried, hateful and ugly, and not beautiful as you may try to think you are.

The personal man is the result, not of beliefs or opinions, but of the quality of all the mental actions that are at work throughout the whole mind. Man is as he thinks in every thought, and not what he thinks he is in one or more isolated parts of his personal self. You may think that you are good, but your idea of goodness may be wrong. Your thought therefore will not be conducive to goodness. On the contrary, the more you praise yourself for being good, the less goodness you will express in your nature. In addition, to think of yourself as good will have a tendency to produce a feeling of self-righteousness. This feeling will cause the mind to look down upon the less fortunate, and a mind that looks down will soon begin to go down, and you will be no better than those whom you criticized before.

You are only as good as the sum total of all your good thoughts, and these can be increased in number indefinitely by training the mind to perpetually grow in the consciousness of absolute goodness. To grow in the consciousness of goodness, keep the mental eye upon the highest conception of absolute goodness. Try to enlarge, elevate and define this conception or understanding of goodness perpetually. Pattern your whole life, all your thoughts and all your actions after the likeness of this highest understanding. Then never look back nor try to measure the goodness that you may think you now possess. Press on eternally to the higher and larger realization of absolute goodness, and leave results to the law. More and more real goodness will naturally appear in all your thoughts and actions. You will therefore become good, not by thinking that you are good, but by thinking thoughts that are created in the image and likeness of that which is good.

From the foregoing it is evident that man is as he thinks, and not necessarily what he thinks he is. But there is still more evidence. That your personal self is the result of your thought has been demonstrated, but what thought? To make yourself thus or so, the necessary thought must first be created but to think that you are thus or so, will not create the thought that can make you thus or so. The reason is because it is subconscious thought alone that can produce effects in your nature, physical or mental, and you cannot enter the subconscious while you are thinking exclusively of your personal self. What you think about yourself is always objective thought, and mere objective thought is powerless to effect or change anything in your nature.

To think thoughts that can give you more life, you must enter into the consciousness of absolute life, but you cannot enter the absolute while you are defining or measuring the personal. If you wish to possess more quality, you must give your thoughts more quality and worth, you must forget the lesser worth of the personal and enter into the consciousness of the greater worth of absolute worth itself. So long as you think that you are thus or so in the personal sense, your thought will be on the surface. You will mentally live among effects. You will not create new causes, therefore will not produce any changes in yourself. You will continue to be as you are thinking deep down in the subconscious where hereditary tendencies, habits, race thoughts and other mental forces continue their usual work, regardless of your personal opinion or empty thoughts on the surface.

To change yourself you must go to that depth of mind where the causes of your personal condition exist. But your mind will not enter the depth of the within so long as your thought is on the surface and your thought will be on the surface so long as you are thinking exclusively about your personal self. The secret therefore is not to form opinions about yourself or to think about yourself as being thus or so, but to form larger conceptions of principles and qualities. Enter the richness of real life and you will think richer thoughts. Forget the limitations, the weaknesses and the shortcomings of your personal self as well as your superficial opinions of your personal self, and enter mentally into the greatness, the grandeur, the sublimity and the splendor of all things. Seek to gain a larger and a larger understanding of the majesty and marvelousness of all life, and aspire to think the thoughts of the Infinite. This is the secret of thinking great thoughts, and he will positively become great whose thoughts are always great.

In like manner, he who thinks wholesome thoughts, and wholesome thoughts only, will become healthful and wholesome. Such thoughts will have the power to produce health, and thoughts never fail to do what they have the power to do. Place in action the necessary subconscious thought and the expected results will invariably follow. Man therefore is not what he thinks he is because such thinking is personal, and consequently superficial and powerless. The thought that determines his personality, his character, his mentality and his destiny is his subjective thought, the thought that is produced in the subconscious during those moments when he forgets his personal opinions about himself and permits his mind to act with deep feeling and subjective conviction. But those thoughts that enter the subconscious are not always good thoughts.

Man's subjective thinking is not always conducive to the true, the wholesome and the best, as his thinking is not always right. For this reason, man himself is not always good, nor his life as beautiful as he might wish to be. His thinking is in his own hands, however. He can learn to think what he wants to think, and as he is and becomes as he thinks, we naturally conclude that he may, in the course of time, become what he wants to become.

8. THE ART OF CHANGING FOR THE BETTER

The greatest remedy in the world is change; and change implies the passing from the old to the new. It is also the only path that leads from the lesser to the greater, from the dream to the reality, from the wish to the heart's desire fulfilled. It is change that brings us everything we want. It is the opposite of change that holds us back from that which we want. But change is not always external. Real change, or rather the cause of all change, is always internal. It is the change in the within that first produces the change in the without. To go from place to place is not a change unless it produces a change of mind a renewal of mind. It is the change of mind that is the change desired. It is the renewal of mind that produces better health, more happiness, greater power, the increase of life, and the consequent increase of all that is good in life. And the constant renewal of mind -- the daily change of mind -- is possible regardless of times, circumstances or places. He who can change his mind every day and think the new about everything every day, will always be well; he will always have happiness; he will always be free; his life will always be interesting; he will constantly move forward into the larger, the richer and the better; and whatever is needed for his welfare today, of that he shall surely have abundance.

Personal man gradually but surely grows into the likeness of that which he thinks of the most, and man thinks the most of what he loves the best. This is the law through which man has become what he is, and it is through the intelligent use of this law that man may change for the better and improve in any way desired. The thought you think not only effects your character, your mind and your body, but also produces the original cause of every characteristic, every habit, every tendency, every desire, every mental quality and every physical condition that appears in your system.

Thought is the one original cause of the conditions, characteristics and peculiarities of the human personality, and everything that appears in the personality is the direct or indirect effect of the various actions of thought. It is therefore evident that man naturally grows into the likeness of the thought he thinks, and it is also evident that the nature of his thought would be determined by that which he thinks of the most. The understanding of this fact will reveal to all minds the basic law of change, and though it is basic, its intelligent use may become simplicity itself. Through the indiscriminate use of this law, man has constantly been changing, sometimes for the better, sometimes not, but by the conscious, intelligent, use of this law he may change only for the better and as rapidly as the sum total of his present ability will permit.

The fact that mental conditions and dispositions may be changed through the power of thought, will readily be accepted by every mind, but that mental qualities, abilities, personal appearances and physical conditions may be changed in the same way all minds may not be ready to accept. Nevertheless, that thought can change anything in the human system, even to a remarkable degree, is now a demonstrated fact. We have all seen faces change for the worse under the influence of grief, worry and misfortune, and we have observed that all people grow old who expect to do so, regardless of the fact that the body of the octogenarian is not a day older than the body of a little child.

We have unlimited evidence to prove that ability will improve or deteriorate according to the use that is made of the mind. A man's face reveals his thought, and we

44

can invariably detect the predominating states of the mind that lives in a groove. When a person changes their mental states at frequent intervals, no one state has the opportunity to produce an individual, clear-cut expression, and therefore cannot be so readily detected, but where one predominating state is continued in action for weeks or months or years, anyone can say what that state is, by looking at the face of the one who has it. Thus we can detect different kinds of disposition, different grades of mind, different degrees of character and different modes of living, and convince ourselves at the same time, that man in general, looks, acts and lives the way he thinks.

The fact that every mental state will express its nature in body, mind and character, proves that we can, through the intelligent use of mental action, cause the body to become more beautiful, the mind more brilliant, character more powerful and the soul life more ideal. To accomplish these things, however, it is necessary to apply the law continuously in that direction where we desire to secure results.

When a person thinks of the ordinary for a few weeks, they invariably begin to look ordinary. Then when something impels them to think for a while of the ideal, the true and the beautiful, they begin to look like a new creature; but if reverses threaten, they will feel worried, dejected and afraid, and everybody observes that they look bad. Then if the tide turns in their favor, they will begin to look content, and if something should suggest to their mind the thought of the wholesome, the sound and the harmonious, they will begin to look remarkably well. In this manner they are daily using the law of change, but never intelligently. They do not take the law into their own hands, but use the law only as suggestions from their environment may direct. They advance one day and fall back the next. One week their physical mansion is painted with colors of health and beauty; the next week only the conditions of age and disease are in evidence. They plant a flower seed today, and tomorrow they hoe it up to plant a weed in its place.

Thus the average person continues to live, and every change comes from the unconscious, indiscriminate use of the power of their thought. This power, however, can be employed more wisely, and when the many begin to do so, the progress of the race will be remarkable indeed.

The basic law of change must be taken into our own hands, and must be employed directly for producing the change we have in view; and to accomplish this the love nature must be so trained that we shall love only what we want to love, only what is greater and better than that which we have realized up to the present time. In this respect strong, highly developed souls will have no difficulty, because they have the power to see the great, the beautiful and the ideal in all things, but those who have not as yet acquired that power, must train their feelings with care, lest love frequently turns thought upon the low, the common or the ordinary.

What you admire in others will develop in yourself. Therefore, to love the ordinary in anyone is to become ordinary, while to love the noble and the lofty in all minds is to grow into the likeness of that which is noble and lofty. When we love the person of someone who is in the earth earthy, we tend to keep ourselves down in the same place. We may give our kindness and our sympathies to all, but we must not love anything in anyone that is not ideal. It is a misdirection of love to love exclusively the visible person. It is the ideal, the true and the beautiful in every person that should be loved, and as all persons have these qualities, we can love everybody with a whole heart in this more sublime manner.

In this connection a great problem presents itself to many men and women who aspire to a life of great quality. These people feel that they cannot give their personal love to husbands, wives, relatives or friends that persist in living in the mere animal world; but the problem is easily solved. We must not love what is ordinary in anyone; in fact, the ordinary must not be recognized, but we can love the real life in everyone, and if we will employ our finer perceptions we will find that this real life is ideal in every living creature in the world. We need not love the perversions of a person, but we can love the greater possibilities and the superior qualities that are inherent in the individual.

It is not the imperfections or appearances that should be loved, but the greatness that is within; and what we love in others we not only awaken in others, but we develop those very things more or less in ourselves. To promote the best welfare of individuals under all sorts of circumstances, personal loves should be exchanged only by persons who live in the same world. When the woman has found the superior world, the man must not expect her personal love unless he also goes up to live in the same world. It is simply fair that he should do so. The woman who lives in a small world must not expect the love of a man who lives in a great world. He would lose much of his greatness if he should give his personal love to such a woman.

The tendency of all life is onward and upward. Therefore, to ask anything to come down is to violate the very purpose of existence. If we wish to be with the higher, the greater and the superior, we must change ourselves and become higher, greater and superior; and this we all can do.

In the application of the basic law of change, no factor is more important than that of pleasure. We are controlled to a great extent by the pleasures we enjoy, ofttimes so much so that they may even determine our destiny. The reason why is found in the fact that we deeply love what we thoroughly enjoy, and since we think the most of what we love the best, we naturally become like the pleasures we thoroughly enjoy, because man gradually grows into the likeness of his predominating thought. It is therefore unwise to permit ourselves to enjoy anything that is beneath our most perfect conception of the ideal, and it is likewise unwise to associate personally with people who care only for the ordinary and the common. What we enjoy becomes a part of ourselves, and for the good of everybody, we cannot afford to go down; but when we love only those pleasures that are as high as our own ideal of joy, then we are truly on the great ascending path.

To overlook the wrongs, the defects and the perversions of life, and to look only for that beautiful something in every soul that we simply want to love, even without trying, is one of the greatest things that we can do; but we must not permit our conception of the beautiful within to become a mere, cold abstraction. It is most important that we be as emotional as we possibly can without permitting ourselves to be controlled by our emotions. The heart should be most tender and warm, and every feeling constantly on fire; but if all such feelings are turned into the secret realms of soul life, we shall find that the forces of love are drawn insistently towards the highest, the truest, and most noble and the most beautiful that our inspired moments have revealed. When this is done we can readily love with the whole heart any noble quality, or high art, or great work upon which we may direct our attention, and what we can love at will, that we can think of as deeply and as long as we may desire.

When we have formulated in our minds what changes we wish to make, the course to pursue is to love the ideal that corresponds to those changes. This love must be deep and strong, and must be continued until the desired change has actually taken place. Know what better qualities you want; then love those qualities with all your mind and heart and soul. To love the higher and the greater qualities of life is to cause the creative qualities of mind to produce those same qualities in our own nature; and in consequence, we steadily grow into the likeness of that which we constantly love. This is the great law -- the law that governs all change for the better. But to use this law intelligently the power of love must cease to respond to every whim or notion that the suggestibility of environment may present to the mind.

The power of love is the greatest power in the world, but it can cause persons or nations to fall to the lowest state, as well as rise to the highest state. Every fall in the history of the race has been caused largely by the misdirection of love, while every step in advance has been prompted largely by the power of love turned upon better things. To misdirect love is to love that which is beneath our present stage in advancement; it is turning the forces of life backward, and retrogression must inevitably follow. In the average person, love is directed almost exclusively upon the personal side of life. In consequence, the love nature becomes so personal, so limited and so superficial, that materialism follows. In many other minds, it is mere appearances that attract the power of admiration, and the finer things in mind, soul and character, are wholly ignored. The result is that the finer qualities of such people gradually disappear, and grossness, both in thought and in appearance naturally follow.

But we must not conclude in this connection that it is wrong to admire the beautiful wherever it may be seen in the external world. We should love the beautiful everywhere, no matter where it may be found; we should admire the richness of life, both in the external and in the internal; and by living a complete life, we shall enjoy more and more of the richness and the beautiful in life, in the within as well as in the without. But the power of love must direct the greater part of its attention upon that which is rich and beautiful in mind and soul. It is that which is finer than the finest of external things that must be loved if man is to grow into the likeness of the great, the superior and the ideal, because man is as he thinks, and he thinks the most of what he loves the best.

When any individual begins to love the finer qualities in life, and gives all the power of mind and soul to that love, they have taken the first step in the changing of their destiny. They are laying the foundation for a great and a better future, and if they continue as they have begun, they will positively reach the loftiest goal that they may have in view.

There are many laws to apply in the beginning of a great life, but the law that lies at the foundation of them all is the law of love. It is love that determines what we are to think, what we are to work for, where we are to go, and what we are to accomplish. Therefore, among all great essentials, the principal one is to know how to love. To apply this essential for all practical purposes, the secret is to love the great, the beautiful, and the ideal in everybody and in everything; and to love with such a strong, passionate love that its ascending power becomes irresistible. The whole of life will thus change and go up with the power of love into the great, the superior and the ideal; everything, both in the being of man and in his environment will advance and change accordingly, and the dreams of the soul will come true. The ideal will become real, the desires of the heart will be granted, and what man has hoped to make his own will be absent no more.

9. HE CAN WHO THINKS HE CAN

When failure comes be more determined than ever to succeed. The more feeling there is in your thought the greater its power. You steadily and surely become in the real what you constantly and clearly think that you are in the ideal. The more you believe in yourself the more of your latent powers and possibilities you place in action. And the more you believe in your purpose the more of your power you apply in promoting that purpose. To him who thinks he can, everything is an opportunity. Depend only upon yourself but work in harmony with all things. Thus you call forth the best that is in yourself and secure the best that external sources have to give.

The discovery of the fact that man is as he thinks, has originated a number of strange ideas concerning the power of thought. One of the principal of these is the belief that thought is a domineering force to be used in controlling things and in compelling fate to come our way. But that this belief is unscientific in every sense of the term has been demonstrated any number of times. Those who have accepted this belief, and who have tried to use thought as a compelling force, have seemingly succeeded in the beginning, but later on have utterly failed, and the reason is that the very moment we proceed to apply thought in this manner, we place ourselves out of harmony with everything, both within ourselves and in our environment. The seeming success that such people have had in the beginning, or for a season, is due to the fact that a strong compelling force can cause the various elements of life to respond for a while, but the force that compels, weakens itself through the very act of compelling, and finally loses its power completely; and then, whatever has been gathered begins to slip away.

This explains why thousands of ardent students of metaphysics have failed to secure the results desired, or have succeeded only in spurts. They have taken the wrong view of the power of thought, and therefore have caused their power to work against them during the greater part of the time. The power of thought is not a compelling force. It is a building force, and it is only when used in the latter sense that desirable results can be produced. The building capacity of thought, however, is practically unlimited. Therefore there is actually no end to what might be accomplished, so long as this power is employed intelligently.

To apply the full building power of thought, we should proceed upon the principle that he can who thinks he can, and we should act in the full conviction that whatever man thinks he can do, he can do, because there is no limit to the power that such thinking can bring forth. The majority among intelligent minds admit that there is some truth in the statement that he can who thinks he can, but they do not, as a rule, believe it to be a very large truth. They admit that we gain more confidence in ourselves when we think that we can do what we have undertaken to do, and also that we become more determined, but aside from that, they see no further value in that particular attitude of mind. They do not realize that he who thinks he can, develops the power that can; but this is the truth, and it is one of the most important of all truths in the vast metaphysical domain.

The law that governs this idea, and its process while in action, is absolutely unlimited in its possibilities, and therefore is in a position to promise almost anything to one who is faithful. When a person begins to think that they can do certain things that they desire to do, their mind will naturally proceed to act on those faculties that are required in the working out of their purpose; and so long as the mind acts upon a certain faculty, more and more life, nourishment and energy will accumulate in that faculty. In consequence, that faculty will steadily develop. It will become larger, stronger and more efficient, until it finally is competent to do what we originally wanted done. Thus we understand how he who thinks he can develops the power that can.

When someone begins to think that they can apply the power of invention, their mind will begin to act upon the faculty of invention. The latent powers of this faculty will be aroused. These powers will accordingly be exercised more and more, and development will be promoted. This, however, is not all. Whenever the mind concentrates its attention upon a certain faculty, additional energy will be drawn into that faculty; thus power will be added to power, much will gather more, and as this may continue indefinitely there need be no end to the capacity and the ability that can be developed in that faculty. In the course of time, be it in a few months or in a few years, that person will actually have developed the power of invention to such a degree that they can invent successfully; and through the application of the same law, can further develop this same faculty, year after year, until they may finally become an inventive genius.

When an individual has some inventive power in the beginning, they will secure, through the application of this law, more remarkable results and in less time than if there were originally no indications of that faculty; but even if there were no original indications of individual power, that power can be developed to a high degree through the faithful application of the great law -- he can who thinks he can, or to state it differently -- one who thinks they can develops the power that can.

There is no faculty that we all do not possess, either in the active or in the latent state. Every faculty that naturally belongs to the human mind is latent in every mind, and it can be awakened and developed, provided the proper laws are faithfully applied. It should be our object, however, to accomplish as much as possible in the present. It is therefore advisable to proceed in the beginning to work through, and develop, those faculties that already indicate considerable power. The mind that has some talent for invention should proceed to think that they can invent. Thus they will accumulate more and more inventive ability or genius. The mind that has some talent for music, should proceed to think that they can master the art of music. They will thereby cause the creative energies of their mentality to accumulate more and more in the faculty of music, until that faculty will be developed to a greater and greater degree. The mind that has some talent for art should apply the same law upon that talent. The mind that has literary ability should proceed to think that they can write what they want to write, and they will finally secure that literary ability or genius with which they can write what they want to write. The mind that has ability in any line of business should proceed to think that they can conduct that business in the most successful manner. Should they enter that business and continue to think that they can, combining such thought with good work, enterprise and the full use of their personal ability, their success will continue to grow indefinitely.

Whatever man or woman may think that they can do, let them proceed to carry out that undertaking, constantly thinking that they can. They will succeed from the beginning, and their advancement will be continuous. However, no mind need be confined to a single purpose. If we have talent for something better than we are doing now, or if we wish to awaken some talent that we long to possess, we may proceed now to think that we can do what we long to do. We shall thus give more and more power to that faculty until it becomes sufficiently strong to be applied in actual practice. In the meantime, we should continue to think that we can do better and better what we are doing now. We shall thereby advance steadily in our present work, and at the same time, prepare ourselves for a greater work in the coming days.

When we think that we can, we must enter into the very soul of that thought and be thoroughly in earnest. It is in this manner that we awaken the finer creative energies of mind, those forces that build talent, ability and genius -- those forces that make man great. We must be determined to do what we think we can do, This determination must be invincible, and must be animated with that depth of feeling that arouses all the powers of being into positive and united action. The power that can do what we think we can do will thus be placed at our command, and accordingly we may proceed successfully to do what we thought we could do.

10. HOW WE SECURE WHAT WE PERSISTENTLY DESIRE

The fact that you have failed to get the lesser proves conclusively that you deserve the greater. So therefore, dry those tears and go in search of the worthier prize. Count nothing lost; even the day that sees "no worthy action done" may be a day of preparation and accumulation that will add greatly to the achievements of tomorrow. Many a day was made famous because nothing was done the day before. Know what you want and continue to want it. You will get it if you combine desire with faith. The power of desire when combined with faith becomes invincible. Some of the principal reasons why so many fail to get what they want is because they do not definitely know what they want or because they change their wants almost every day.

The purpose of desire is to inform man what he needs at every particular moment to supply the demands of change and growth in his life; and in promoting that purpose, desire gives expression to its two leading functions. The first of these is to give the forces of the human system something definite to do, and the second is to arouse those forces or faculties that have the natural power to do what is to be done. In exercising its first function, desire not only promotes concentration of action among the forces in man, but also causes those forces to work for the thing that is wanted. Therefore, it is readily understood why the wish, if strong, positive, determined and continuous, will tend to produce the thing wished for.

If you can cause all the elements and powers in your being to work for the one thing that you want you are almost certain to get it. In fact, you will get it unless it is so large that it is beyond you, or beyond the power of your present capacity to produce; though in that case you have exercised poor judgment; you have permitted yourself to desire what lies outside of your sphere; and what you could neither appreciate nor use were you to get it. What you can appreciate, enjoy and use in your present sphere of existence, you have the power, in your present state of development, to produce; that is, you can produce it if all your power is applied in your effort to produce it; and when you desire any particular thing with the full force and capacity of your desire you cause all your power to be applied in producing that particular thing.

In exercising its second function, desire proceeds directly into that faculty or group of forces that can, if fully applied, produce the very thing that is desired. In its first function it tends to bring all the forces of the system together, and inspires them with the desire to work for what is wanted. It acts upon the system in general and gives everything in the system something definite to do, that something definite in each case being the one thing desired. In its second function it acts upon certain parts of the system in particular; always upon those parts that can do what is wanted done; and it tends to arouse all the life and power that those particular parts may contain.

How desire proceeds, and how it secures results in this respect is easily illustrated. We will take, for example, a man who is not earning as much as he feels that he needs. Naturally, he will begin to desire more money; and we will suppose that this desire becomes stronger and stronger until it actually stirs every atom of his being. Now what happens? He is not only arousing a great deal of latent and unused energy, but all of his active energy is becoming more and more alive. But what becomes of all this energy? It goes directly into his moneymaking faculties, and tends to increase decidedly the life, the power, the capacity and the efficiency of those faculties. There is in every mind a certain group of faculties that is made by nature for financial purposes. In some minds these faculties are small and sluggish, while in other minds they are large and active. And that the latter kind should be able to make more money and accumulate things in a greater measure is quite natural.

But is it possible to take those faculties that are small and sluggish and make them large and active? If so, those who now have limited means may in the course of time have abundance. To answer this question, we will ask what it is that can arouse any faculty to become larger and more active, and we find that it is more energy, and energy that is more alive. No matter how sluggish a faculty may be, if it is thoroughly charged, so to speak, with highly active energy, it simply must become more active. And no matter how small it may be, if it continues to receive a steady stream of added life, energy and power, day after day, month after month, year after year, it simply must increase in size and capacity. And whenever any faculty becomes greater in capacity and more alive in action it will do better work; that is, it will gradually gain in ability and power until it has sufficient ability and power to produce what you wished for.

Returning to the man in our illustration, we will see how the principle works. His money-making faculties are too small and too sluggish to produce as much money as he needs. He begins to desire for more. This desire becomes strong enough to arouse every element and force in his money-making faculties; for here be it remembered that the force of any desire goes directly into that faculty that can, by nature, produce the thing desired. This is one of the laws of mind. In addition, the action of his desire tends to arouse all the other forces of his system, and tends to concentrate those forces upon the idea of making more money. In the beginning, no important change in his financial ability may be noticed, except that he feels more and more confidence in his power to secure the greater amount desired. In a short time, however, possibly within a few months, he begins to get new ideas about the advancement of his work. His mind is beginning to work more actively upon the idea of increased gain. Accordingly, suggestions as to how he might increase the earning capacity of his business are constantly coming up in his mind, and ways and means and plans are taking shape and form more and more completely. The actions of his money-making faculties are also beginning to change; that is, they are becoming finer, more penetrating, and more keen so that his insight into financial matters is steadily improving. He is therefore securing the necessary essentials to greater financial gain, and as he applies them all things will naturally begin to take a turn.

To state it briefly, his strong, persistent desire for more money has aroused his money-making faculties. They have become stronger, more active, more wide-awake and more efficient. And as a strong, wide-awake faculty can do many times as good work as one that is only partly alive, we understand how his desire for more money has given him the ability to make more money. As he continues this desire, making it stronger and more persistent, his financial ability will increase accordingly, and his financial gains continue to increase in proportion.

Many may doubt the efficiency of the plan just presented, because as is well known, most people desire more money but do not always get it. But do they always wish hard enough? It is not occasional desire, or half-hearted desire that gets the thing desired. It is persistent desire; and persistent desire not only desires continually, but with all the power of life and mind and soul. The force of a half alive desire, when acting upon a certain faculty, cannot cause that faculty to become fully alive. Nor can such a desire marshal all the unused forces of the system and concentrate them all upon the attainment of the one thing wanted. And it is true that the desires of most people are neither continuous nor very deep. They are shallow, occasional wishes without enough power to stir to action a single atom.

Then we must also remember that results do not necessarily follow the use of a single force. Sometimes the force of persistent desire alone may do wonders, but usually it is necessary to apply in combined action all the forces of the human system. The force of desire, however, is one of the greatest of these, and when fully expressed in connection with the best talents we may possess, the thing desired will certainly be secured.

We may take several other illustrations. Suppose you have a strong desire for more and better friends. The action of that desire, if deep, whole-hearted and persistent will tend to impress the qualities of friendship upon every element of your character. In consequence, you will in time become the very incarnation of friendship; that is, you will become a better and a better friend, and he who becomes a better friend will constantly receive more and better friends. In other words, you become like the thing you desire, and when the similarity has become complete you will get what you want through the law of like attracting like.

You may desire to succeed in a certain line of work; we will say, in the literary field. If your desire for success in that field is full and persistent, the power of that desire will constantly increase the life, the activity and the capacity of your literary faculties, and you will naturally do better work in that field. The same is true with regard to any other line of work, because your desire for greater success in your work will arouse to fuller action those faculties that you employ in that work. But, in every case, the desire must be deep, whole-souled, persistent and strong. It is therefore evident that results in all lines of endeavor depend very largely upon the power of desire, and that no one can afford to let their desires lag for a moment.

The law should be: Know what you want, and then want it with all the life and power that is in you. Get your mind and your life fully aroused. Persistent desire will do this. And that it is most important to do this is proven by the fact that in thousands of instances, a partly alive mind is the only reason why the goal in view has not been reached. It is necessary, however, that your desires continue uninterruptedly along the lines you have chosen. You may desire a score or more of different things, but continue each desire without change, unless you should find that certain changes are necessary to secure the greater results you have in mind.

To desire one thing today and another tomorrow means failure. To work for one thing this year and another thing next year is the way to empty handedness at the end of every year. Before you begin to apply the power of desire, know with a certainty what you want because when you get what you have desired, you may have to take it. If you do not know definitely what you really do want, desire a better judgment, a clearer understanding and a more balanced life. Desire to know what is best for you, and the force of that desire will tend to produce normal action in every part of your system. Then you will feel distinctly what the highest welfare of your nature actually demands. In deciding upon what you want, however, do not be timid, and do not measure the possible with the yard-stick of general appearances. Let your aspirations be high, only be sure that you are acting within the sphere of your own inherent capacity; though in this connection it is well to remember that your inherent capacity is many times as great as it has been supposed to be; and also that it can be continuously enlarged.

In choosing what you are to desire, act within reason, but go after the best. If the full power of desire is applied upon all the elements of your mind and character, what is latent within you will be aroused, developed and expressed; you will become much more than you are and thereby will not only desire the best, but be able to be of service to the best. And this latter fact is important. When we desire the great and the wonderful we must ask what we have to give the great and the wonderful in return. It is not only necessary to get the best -- to realize our ideal, but it is also necessary to be so good and so great that we can give to the best as much as we are receiving from the best.

Before we begin to wish for an ideal, we must ask what that ideal is going to get when it comes. Coupled with our desire for the ideal, therefore, we must have an equally strong desire for the remaking of ourselves so that we may become equal to that ideal in every respect. If we want an ideal companion, we must not only wish for such a companion, but we must also desire the development of those qualities in ourselves that we know would make us agreeable to that companion. If we want a different environment we should wish for such an environment with all the life and soul we possess, and should at the same time wish for the increase of those powers in our own talents that can earn such an environment. If we want a better position we should desire such a position every minute and also desire that we may become more competent to fill it when it comes.

The power of desire not only tends to arouse added life and power in these faculties upon which it may act, but it also tends to make the mind as a whole more alert and wide-awake along those lines. This is well illustrated by the fact that when we have a strong, continuous desire for information on a certain subject, we always find someone or something that can give us that information. And the reason is that all the faculties of the mind are prompted by the force of this desire to be constantly on the look-out for that information . That the same law will apply in the desire or search for wisdom, new ideas, better plans, better opportunities, more agreeable environments and more ideal companions, is clearly understood. And when we couple this fact with the fact that the power of desire tends to increase the life, the ability, the working capacity and the efficiency of these faculties or forces that can produce what we desire, we must certainly admit that those who have found the secret of using desire have made a great find indeed.

But, as stated before, and it cannot be repeated too often, the desire must be persistent and strong, as strong as all the life and soul we possess. In other words, we must wish hard enough, and we wish hard enough when our desires are sufficiently full and deep and strong to thoroughly arouse those faculties that have the natural ability to fulfill those desires. Many desires are only strong enough to arouse their corresponding faculties to a slight degree -- not enough to increase the activity or working capacity of these faculties, while most desires are too weak to arouse any force or faculty in the least. The act of wishing hard enough, however, does not imply hard mental work. If you make hard work of your wishing, you will use up your energy instead of turning it into those channels where it can be applied to good account. It is depth of desire and fullness of desire combined in an action that is directed continuously upon the one thing desired that constitutes true desire. To wish hard enough is simply to wish for all that you want with all that is in you. But we cannot wish with all that is in us unless our wish is subconscious as well as conscious because the subconscious is a part of us -- the larger part of us.

To make every desire subconscious, the subconscious mind should always be included in the process of desire; that is, whenever we express a desire we should think of the subconscious, and combine the thought of that desire with our thought of the subconscious mind. Every desire should be deeply felt as all deeply felt mental actions become subconscious actions. It is an excellent practice to let every desire sink into the deeper mental life, so to speak; and also to act in and through that deeper mental life, whenever we give expression to desire; or, in other words, when we turn on the full force and power of that desire. To become proficient in these methods requires some practice, though all that is necessary to become proficient is to continue to try. No special rule is required. Begin by feeling your desires through and through. Make them as strong and as deep as you can, and always combine the living action of your desire with your thought of those faculties through which you know that desire is to work.

To illustrate: If you desire greater success in your work, think of those faculties that you are using in your work whenever you give full expression to your desire. If you are a business man, think of your business faculties whenever you desire greater business success. If you are a musician, think of your musical faculties whenever you desire greater proficiency in your music. Though in case your desires should be such that you do not know through what kinds of faculties it will naturally be expressed, never mind. Continue to desire what you want; the power of that desire, if persistent and strong, will find a way to make your wish come true.

When we understand how desire works, and know that it works only when it is persistent, we realize that we have found, not only a great secret, but also a simple explanation for many of the failures in life as well as many of its greatest achievements. And from the facts in the case we conclude that no matter what an individual's condition or position may be today, if they will decide upon that something better that they want, they may get it, provided their wish for it is as strong as their own life and as large as their own soul.

11. CONCENTRATION AND THE POWER BACK OF SUGGESTION

The optimist lives under a clear sky; the pessimist lives in a fog. The pessimist hesitates, and loses both time and opportunity; the optimist makes the best use of everything now, and builds themselves up, steadily and surely, until all adversity is overcome and the object in view realized. The pessimist curbs their energies and concentrates their whole attention upon failure; the optimist gives all their thought and power to the attainment of success, and arouses their faculties and forces to the highest point of efficiency. The pessimist waits for better times, and expects to keep on waiting; the optimist goes to work with the best that is at hand now, and proceeds to create better times. The pessimist pours cold water on the fires of their own ability; the optimist adds fuel to those fires. The pessimist links their mind to everything that is losing ground; the optimist lives, thinks and works with everything that is determined to press on. The pessimist places a damper on everything; the optimist gives life, fire and go to everything. The optimist is a building force; the pessimist is always an obstacle in the way of progress. The pessimist lives in a dark, soggy unproductive world, the optimist lives in that mental sunshine that makes all things grow.

The purpose of concentration is to apply all the active forces of mind and personality upon that one thing which is being done now, and it may therefore be called the master key to all attainments and achievement. In its last analysis, the cause of all failure can be traced to the scattering of forces, and the cause of all achievement to the concentration of forces. This does not imply however, that concentration is the only essential, but it does imply that concentration must be perfect, or failure is inevitable no matter how many good methods one may employ. The ruling thought of concentration is, " This one thing I do," and it can be stated as an absolute truth that whenever the mind works completely in the attitude of that thought, concentration is perfect.

The value of concentration is very easily illustrated by taking, for example, a wheel of twenty spokes with every spoke a pipe, and all those pipes connected with another conveying steam. The steam will thereby pass out through twenty channels. Then connect an engine with one of the pipes. That engine will accordingly receive only one twentieth of the steam conveyed through the wheel, while nineteen twentieths will pass out in waste. But suppose the other nineteen pipes were plugged so that all the steam would pass out through the one pipe connected with the engine. The engine would then have twenty times as much power as before. The average mind is quite similar to such a wheel. An enormous amount of energy is generated at the hub, so to speak, or at the vital centre of mental life; but as a rule, that power passes out through a score of channels, so that the channel of action receives only a fraction of the power generated in the human system. But here we must remember that you can apply your power effectively only in one direction at a time; therefore, if all your power is to be applied in that one direction, all other channels must be closed up for the time being; or in other words, all the power of mind and thought must be concentrated where you are acting at the time.

In learning how to concentrate, it is necessary in the beginning to remember that the usual methods are of no value. You cannot develop concentration by fixing thought or attention upon some external object. Real concentration is subjective, and subjective thought is deep; that is, it acts through the deeper or interior realms of mind. When you fix your attention, however, upon some external object, like a spot on the wall, as has been suggested by some would-be instructors in this field, your thought goes out towards the surface, so that you are actually getting away from the true field of concentration. Any method, or any line of thinking that tends to draw the mind out towards the surface, will produce a superficial attitude, and when the mind is in such an attitude, deep mental action is not possible; but deep mental action is absolutely necessary in all concentration.

There is no use trying to concentrate unless the action of the mind is deep. That is the first essential. In other words, the mind must go into the psychological field; the mind must act, not on the surface of things, but through the deeper life of its thought process. To develop concentration, all that is necessary is to apply consciously those two factors that are invariably found in natural concentration. In the conscious application of these two factors, the following two methods will be found sufficient; in fact, nothing further will be required in the attainment of concentration to any degree desired. The first method is to train the mind to act in the subjective or psychological field; in other words, cause all thinking, all feeling and all actions of thought, will and desire to become deeper and finer; in fact, deepen as far as possible all mental action. Whenever you concentrate or turn your attention upon any subject or object, try to feel deeply, try to think deeply and try to turn thought into deeper realms of feeling. The moment your mental action begins to deepen, you will find your attention directed upon the object in mind with perfect ease and with full force.

Whenever you are thinking about anything, try to feel your thought getting into the vital life of that something, and wherever you turn your attention, try to feel that the force of that attention acts through your whole mind instead of simply on the surface of your mind. To state it briefly, whenever you concentrate, deepen your thought, and the deeper your thought becomes, the more perfectly will the full force of your mind and thought focus upon the point of concentration. Whatever you have to do, deepen your thought while giving that work your attention, You will find that you will thereby give all your energy to that work and this is your purpose.

The second method is to become interested in that upon which you desire to concentrate. If you are not interested in that subject or object, begin at once to look for the most interesting point of view. You will be surprised to find that no matter how uninteresting a subject may seem, the very moment you begin to look for the most interesting viewpoints of that subject, you will almost immediately become interested in that subject itself. And it is a well-known fact that whenever we are thoroughly interested in a subject we concentrate thoroughly and naturally upon that subject. To make concentration perfect, so that you can turn all the power of mind and thought upon any subject or object desired, these two methods should be combined.

Always look for the most interesting points of view, and while you are looking for those viewpoints, deepen the action of your mind by trying to feel the real vital life of those actions. You thereby become interested in the subject on the one hand, and you make every action of the mind subjective on the other hand; and when perfect interest is combined with subjective mental action, you have perfect concentration. The constant practice of these two methods will develop the power of concentration to such an extent that you can concentrate completely at any time and for any length of time, by simply deciding to do so; and that such an attainment is of enormous value is evident when we understand how much power there is in man, and how concentration can turn all of that power upon the one thing that is being done now.

All modern psychologists agree that there is enough power in any human being to accomplish what they have in view, provided it is all constructively applied in that one direction. And when man can concentrate perfectly, he can use all of his power wherever he may choose to act. Then, if we combine scientific thinking and constructive mental action with concentration, nothing can prevent us from realizing our very highest ambition. Another important essential in the use of the forces of mind and thought, is that of understanding suggestion and the power back of suggestion; and this becomes especially true when we realize that there is no factor or condition that we may come in contact with anywhere or under any circumstances, that does not suggest something. To define suggestion, it may be stated that anything is a suggestion that brings into mind some thought, idea or feeling that tends to undermine some similar idea, thought or feeling that happens to be in the mind at the time.

When you have certain ideas or feelings, and you meet circumstances that tend to remove those ideas or feelings, the power of suggestion is working in your mind. If your mind is in a wholesome state and an unwholesome picture removes that wholesome state by replacing something that is degrading, your mind is in the power of suggestion. If you feel joyous and some idea given to you makes your mind depressed, you are in the hands of suggestion; in fact, when anything enters your mind in such a manner as to remove certain similar or opposite states already in your mind, it exercises the power of suggestion. It is therefore necessary to understand how this power works, so that we can take advantage of good suggestions and avoid those that are not good.

The great majority are receiving all sorts of suggestions every hour, and they respond to a very large number of them; in fact, we can truthfully say that most people are controlled, most of the time, by suggestions that come to them from their environment. Those minds, however, who understand the power of thought, and who know the difference between detrimental and beneficial suggestions, can close their minds to the former and open them fully to the latter. And the method to apply is this, that whenever you are in the presence of an adverse suggestion, concentrate your attention upon some idea or mental state which you know will act as a counter suggestion; in other words, when adverse suggestion is trying to produce in your mind what you do not want, persist in suggesting to yourself what you do want. This practice, if employed frequently, will soon make you so strong in this direction that you will unconsciously, so to speak, be on your guard; in fact, the very moment that an adverse suggestion is given, your mind will spring up of its own accord with a wholesome suggestion to meet the requirements.

To avoid becoming a victim to adverse suggestions -- and we have such suggestions about us almost constantly -- fill your mind so full of good, wholesome thoughts and suggestions that there is no room for anything else. Feel right at all times, and nothing from without can tempt you to think wrong. Make every good thought subconscious, and no adverse thought from without can possibly get into your subconscious mind at any time.

A great many suggestions do not produce results, a fact which should be perfectly understood, because every thought that we think does contain some suggestion. When we are trying to impress good thoughts upon our minds, we want the good suggestions conveyed by those thoughts to take effect, but frequently they do not, and the reason is that a suggestion takes effect only when we exercise the power that is back of suggestion. The outward suggestion itself is simply the vehicle through which another power is acting, and that other power is nothing more nor less than the real life of that idea which the suggestion intends to convey.

To simplify this matter, we will suppose that you are suggesting to yourself that you are well. The suggestion itself is simply a vehicle conveying the idea of health, but if your mind is not in touch with the interior or living force of that idea of health at the time you are giving the suggestion, you have not exercised the power back of suggestion, and the idea of health will not be conveyed to your subconscious mind. On the other hand, if you can actually feel the power of this interior idea of health when you are giving the suggestion, you are in mental touch with the power back of that suggestion, and whenever you touch the power back of suggestion you use that power. Results, therefore, will be forthcoming.

To explain further, we might say that you use the power back of suggestion whenever you mentally feel that vital idea which the suggestion aims to convey. When you feel that idea, you respond to the suggestion, but when you do not feel it, you do not respond. This explains why the power of suggestion so frequently fails, not only in everyday life, but also in mental healing. When you think health, you will produce health in your system if you feel the real or interior life of health at the time. When you think harmony you will produce harmony in your system, if your mind actually goes into the soul of harmony at the time. When you place yourself in the mental world of happiness whenever you are thinking happiness, you will actually produce happiness in your mind, because you are applying the power that is back of the thought that suggests happiness.

Two men may present the same proposition under the same circumstances, and you will accept the proposition from the one, while ignoring the arguments of the other completely. The reason will be that while the one is talking about his proposition, the other is talking through his proposition. The mind of the one goes on the outside of his arguments and his suggestions, while the mind of the other goes through the real inner life of those arguments and suggestions. Therefore, the one is only using suggestion, while the other is also using the power back of suggestion; and it is the power back of suggestion that produces results, whenever results are secured. The same idea is illustrated when a person is speaking on a certain subject. If their description deals simply with the shell of that subject, they do not attract attention, but the moment they touch the vital or inner factors of that subject, everybody is interested. The reason is, they have touched the power back of their theme. But we all have ideas or suggestions to present at frequent intervals. Therefore, if we can use the power back of our suggestion at such times we may receive a hearing, but if we cannot, we attract little or no attention.

Thus we understand the value of knowing how to use the power back of suggestion, and we can learn to use this power by training ourselves to get into the real life of every idea and every thought that we may try to think or convey. When we try to live our ideas and thoughts, we will begin to express that interior power, and we shall succeed in living our ideas when we try to feel consciously and constantly the real life and the real truth that is contained in those ideas.

To secure the best results from the power of thought in its various modes of application, we must understand that there is something back of everything that takes form or action in life, and that it is through this something that the actions of mind should move whenever we use thought or suggestion in any manner whatever. When we are conscious only of the body of our ideas, those ideas convey no power. It is when we become conscious of the soul of those ideas that we have aroused that something within that alone produces results in the mental world. Any thought or suggestion that conveys simply the external form, invariably falls flat. There is nothing to it. It is entirely empty, and produces no impression whatever. But our ideas and suggestions become alive with the fullness of life and power when we also convey the real life or the real soul that is contained within the body of those thoughts. We have, at such times, entered the depths of mental life. We are beginning to act through undercurrents, and we are beginning to draw upon the immensity of that power that exists in the vast interior realms of our own mental world.

12. THE DEVELOPMENT OF THE WILL

Say to yourself a hundred times every day, and mean it with all your heart: I will become more than I am. I will achieve more and more every day because I know that I can. I will recognize only that which is good in myself, only that which is good in others; only that in all things and places that I know should live and grow. When adversity threatens I will be more determined than ever in my life to prove that I can turn all things to good account. And when those whom I have trusted seem to fail me, I will have a thousand times more faith in the honor and nobleness of man. I will think only of that which has virtue and worth. I will wish only for that which can give freedom and truth. 1 will expect only that which can add to the welfare of the race. I will live to live more. I will speak to give encouragement, inspiration and joy. I will work to be of service to an ever-increasing number. And in every thought, word and action my ruling desire shall be, to enrich, ennoble and beautify existence for all who come my way.

No force in the human system can be properly used unless it is properly directed, and as the will is the only factor in man that has the power to direct or control, a thorough development of the will, as well as a clear understanding of its application under every circumstance, becomes absolutely necessary if we are to use all the forces within us to the very best advantage.

To define the will with absolute exactness is hardly possible, though a clear knowledge as to its general nature and special functions must be secured. In a previous chapter, it was stated that the "I Am" is the ruling principle in man, and it may be added here that when the "I Am" exercises this function of rulership anywhere in the human system, will power is the result; or, it may be stated that the will is that attribute of the "I Am" which is employed whenever there is a definite intention followed by actual action, with a view of initiating, controlling or directing. To state it briefly therefore, will power is the result of the "I Am" either taking initiative action or controlling and directing any action after it has been taken.

Among the many functions of the will, the principal ones are as follows: The will to initiate; the will to direct; the will to control ; the will to think; the will to imagine; the will to desire; the will to act; the will to originate ideas; the will to give expression to those ideas; the will to will into action any purpose, the will to carry through that purpose; the will to employ the highest and most perfect action of any force or faculty in mind; and the will to push up, so to speak, any talent in the mind to its highest point of efficiency. This last mentioned function has been ignored, but it is by far the most important in the practical life of attainment and achievement.

To illustrate this idea, we will suppose that you have a group of faculties, all of which are well developed, and contain a great deal of ability and power. But how can those faculties be caused to act? The fact is they will not act in the least until the will wills them into action. The will therefore must first be applied, but the act of initiating action among those faculties is not its only function. To illustrate again, we will suppose that your will is very weak. It therefore stands to reason that the original impulse given those faculties will also be weak. Then when we understand that it is necessary for the will to continue to prompt or impel the continued action of any faculty we realize how weak, half-hearted and limited such an action will necessarily be when the will is weak. On the other hand, if your will is very strong, the original impulse given to the faculty will be strong and the continued action of that faculty will be much stronger, larger and more efficient.

In brief, when a faculty is backed up, so to speak, with a powerful will, it easily doubles its capacity and efficiency; in other words, it is pushed up to a higher state of action. We understand therefore the great importance of having a strong will, though such a will is not only an advantage in promoting a fuller and larger expression of any faculty we may possess, but also in promoting a larger and more perfect expression of any force that may be applied, either in the personality, in character or in mind. A powerful will, however, is never domineering or forceful. In fact, a domineering will is weak. It may be seemingly strong on the spur of the moment, but it cannot be applied steadily for any length of time. A strong will, however, is deep, continuous, and persistent. It calls into action your entire individuality, and as you exercise such a will you feel as if a tremendous power from within yourself had been calmly, though persistently aroused.

When we analyze the human mind, in the majority we find the will to be weak, and in fact, almost absent in a great many. Such people do not have the power to take a single original step. They have no initiative, and accordingly drift with the stream. Among others, who are a little higher in the mental scale, we find a will somewhat stronger, but not sufficiently strong to exercise with any degree of efficiency a single one of its functions. Among what can be called "the better class," we invariably find the will to be fairly well developed, and among the great leaders in all the different phases of human life and action, we find the will to be very strong in fact, there is not a single mental or spiritual giant in history, who did not have a tremendous will, and this was one their great secrets.

To illustrate further with regard to the last mentioned of the special functions, we will suppose that you have some talent for music. If you should will to exercise that talent to a slight degree only, it is evident that your efficiency along that line would not be marked. On the other hand, if your will was so strong that you could push up, so to speak, your musical faculty to its very highest point of efficiency, you would soon find yourself on the verge of musical genius; in fact, musical genius is absolutely impossible unless you have a strong will, no matter how much musical talent you may possess.

Though it must be remembered in this connection that it is not sufficient simply to have a strong will. The majority do not possess a strong will, and most of those who do have a strong will, have not learned how to apply it so as to secure greater efficiency in anything they may do; and here it is important to state that anyone who will increase the power of their will, and properly train it for the purpose just indicated, may expect to increase their efficiency anywhere from twenty-five to two hundred per cent. The majority have many times as much ability and working capacity as they are using at the present time; in fact, they apply only a small fraction of what is in them, and the principal reason why they do not apply all that is in them, is that they do not have sufficient power of will to act on this larger scale.

In this connection, we find another condition which is very important, and especially with regard to overcoming circumstances. A great many people have good intentions, and they have sufficient will power to originate those intentions, but they have not sufficient will power to carry them out; in other words, they have the will to think, but not the will to act. And here we can use our own imagination in picturing that state of human affairs that would inevitably come into being if all good intentions became actions. Thousands of people start out right, but they have not the power of will to continue, so that where ten thousand make a good beginning, less than a score finish the race. We find this condition in all walks of life and in all undertakings, and it illustrates most eloquently the necessity of a strong will in every mind.

Realizing the importance of a strong will, and knowing that the will is weak in the minds of the great majority, we may well ask what might be the cause of this weakness; and the answer is that there are several marked causes, all of which we shall proceed to consider. The first among these causes is alcohol. The use of alcohol weakens the will, not only in the individual who partakes of it, but in their children and grandchildren, and many generations following. It has been estimated by those who have studied this subject carefully, that the use of alcohol from generation to generation through the centuries is one of the principal causes for this weakness in the human will that we find to be almost universal. And when we study the psychology of the subject we soon discover the reason why. Nearly every nation, as far back in history as we can go, has been using alcohol in some form or other, and as its weakening effect upon the will is transmissible from one generation to another, we realize that practically every member of the race has been burdened, more or less, with this adverse inheritance. But in this connection, we must remember that it is not necessary to be disturbed by this dark picture, because no matter what we have inherited, we can overcome it absolutely. However, we do not wish to do anything that will be in our own way, or in the way of generations that are to follow.

It is therefore necessary that we consider this subject thoroughly, and act upon it accordingly. The fact that the human race has transmitted a weak will from generation to generation explains why the human family does not have enough power to produce more than an occasional mental giant. Here and there we find in history, men and women who tower above the rest. Their minds are strong, their wills powerful, and their souls invincible; but how different is the condition among the majority. Most of them constitute mere driftwood, and follow blindly the leadership of these mental giants the race has produced. This, however, is not the intention of nature. Nature intends all men and women to be mental and spiritual giants, and does not intend that anyone should follow the will of another. But the human race has, in this respect, ignored the intentions of nature.

The reason why the use of alcohol weakens the will, is very easily explained. When you take anything into the system that tends to take control over your desires, feelings or intentions, you permit yourself to be controlled by an outside agency, and accordingly the will for the time being is laid aside; and the law is, that whenever the will is laid aside by anything whatever it is weakened; that is, you undermine, so to speak, that element of the will which gives it the power to direct and control. When this practice is continued and repeated a number of times, we can readily understand how the power of the will is gradually decreased more and more, until its very foundation has been practically removed.

When you permit an outside agency to control your feelings and emotions at frequent intervals for a prolonged period, your system will soon get into the habit of submitting to the control of this outside agency, and will not respond any longer to any effort that the will may make to regain its original power of control. This being true, we find an explanation for a number of perplexing questions. We learn why great men and women are not more numerous. We learn why the majority are so easily influenced by temptations. We learn why powerful characters are found only here and there, and we also learn why every great nation of past history has fallen.

When we study history, we find that every great nation, after coming to a certain point of supremacy, began to decline, and there are several reasons for this strange termination of national power. But there is only one reason that stands out as the most vital of them all, and as possibly the cause of them all. We refer to the fact that a decrease of great men and women invariably precedes the decline of a nation. To keep any great nation up to a high standard of civilization there must be enough superior characters to hold the balance of power, but the very moment the balance of power gets into the hands of second grade men and women, a decline of that nation is inevitable. Therefore, if any great nation in the present age is to continue to grow in real greatness and real power, we must make a special effort to increase the number of great men and women in every generation. The greater a nation becomes, the more great men and women are required to govern and direct the forces of progress and growth that are at work in that nation. We therefore understand what is required of us in this generation if we want present civilization to advance and rise in the scale.

Another cause of this weakness in the will is found in what may be called psychical excess. And it is unfortunate that so many people have permitted themselves to be placed under psychical influences during the last fifty or seventy-five years; though it is a fact that a great many people have permitted their minds to be controlled or influenced by the psychical or the occult in every age. Another tendency therefore towards weakness in the will has been transmitted from generation to generation down through the ages, and we all have the effect of this misuse of mind also to overcome at the present time; but again let us remember that we have the power to overcome anything that we might have inherited.

Whenever you give up your individuality, or any part of your mind or thought, to some unknown force or influence that you know little or nothing about you are permitting an outside agency to usurp the function of the will. You lay the will aside, you undermine its power to some extent, and thereby weaken those elements in its nature that constitute self-mastery and self-control. That psychical excess has this tendency to a most pronounced degree is well illustrated by the fact that every individual, who is fascinated with psychical experience, invariably lacks in self-control. Such people are usually so sensitive that they are swayed in every direction by every suggestion or influence or environment with which they may come in contact.

But here we may well ask what we are living for -- if we are living to give up to the influence of environment, visible or invisible, or if we are living to attain such full control over the powers and talents that are within us, that we cannot only control, modify, and perfect environment, but also so perfectly control ourselves that we can become all that nature intends that we should become. If we are to rise in the scale, we must attain greater degrees of self-mastery, but we cannot learn to master ourselves so long as we are constantly permitting ourselves to be mastered by something else; and those who indulge in psychical experiences to any degree whatever, are permitting themselves to be mastered by something else. They are therefore losing ground every day. Their characters are becoming weaker, their standards of morality and rightness becoming more and more lax, as we all have discovered, and their power to apply those faculties and forces in their natures through which they may accomplish more and achieve more, are constantly decreasing both in working capacity and in efficiency.

If man wants to live his own life as it should be lived; if he wants to master circumstances and determine his own destiny, he must have the power to say under all sorts of conditions what he is going to think and what he is going to do; but he cannot exercise this power unless his own will is permitted to have absolute control over every thought, effort and desire in his life.

Emotional excess is another cause that weakens the will, and by emotional excess we mean the act of giving way to uncontrolled feelings of any kind. To give way to anger, hatred, passion, excitability, intensity, sensitiveness, grief, discouragement, despair, or any other uncontrolled feeling, is to weaken the will. The reason is that you cannot control yourself through your will when you permit yourself to be controlled by your feelings; and any act that rules out the will, weakens the will. Whenever you permit yourself to become angry, you weaken the will. Whenever you permit yourself to become offended or hurt you weaken your will. Whenever you permit yourself to become despondent or discouraged, you weaken your will. Whenever you give way to grief, mental intensity or excitability, you weaken your will. You permit some artificial mental state to take possession of your mind, and your will at the time is put aside. We therefore should avoid absolutely all emotional excess. We must not permit any feeling whatever to take possession of us, or permit ourselves to be influenced in any form or manner by anything that may enter the mind uncontrolled through the emotions; but this does not mean that we should ignore emotion. Emotion is one of the most valuable factors in human life, and should be used and enjoyed under every normal circumstance, but should never become a ruling factor in mind, thought or feeling.

You may look at a beautiful picture, and lose yourself, so to speak, in its charms. You may listen to exceptional music, and be carried away, or be thrilled through and through by the joy of its harmony; or you may witness some scene in nature that causes your soul to take wings and soar to empyrean heights. You may permit yourself to enjoy any or all of these ecstasies at any time, provided you have conscious control over every movement of your emotions at the time. Whenever you feel the touch of some sublime emotion, try to direct the force of that emotion into a finer and a higher state of expression; thus you will not be controlled by it, but will exercise control over it, and accordingly will enjoy the pleasure of that emotion many times as much.

It is a well-known fact that whenever we control any feeling, whether it be physical or mental or spiritual, and try to turn it into a larger sphere of expression, we enjoy far more the pleasure that naturally comes through the exercise of that feeling. To control our emotions therefore is to lose nothing and gain much.

Another cause of weakness in the will is what might be called mental dependence. To depend upon anybody or anything outside of yourself, is to weaken the will, for the simple reason that you let the will of someone else rule your actions, while your own will remains dormant. Nothing, however, that remains dormant can grow or develop. On the other hand, it will continue to become weaker and weaker, like an unused muscle, until it has no strength whatever. We therefore understand why those multitudes of people, who have followed blindly the will and leadership of others, not only in religion but in all other things, have practically no will power at all. And here we wish to state that it is positively wrong for any individual or any group of individuals to follow any one man or any one woman or any group of men or women under any circumstances whatever.

We are here in this life to become something. We are here to make the best use of what we possess in mind, character and personality, but we cannot cause any element, faculty or power within us to express itself to any extent so long as we are mere dependent weaklings. In everything, depend upon yourself, but work in harmony with all things. Do not depend even upon the Infinite, but learn to work and live in harmony with the Infinite. The highest teachings of the Christ reveal most clearly the principle that no soul was created to be a mere helpless instrument in the hands of Supreme Power, but that every soul should act and live in perfect oneness with that Power. And the promise is that we all are not only to do the things that Christ did, but even greater things.

Man is no credit to Supreme Creative Power if he remains in the puppet stage, but he is a credit to that Power if he becomes a giant in character, mind and soul. In our religious worship we have given unbounded praise to God for His wonderful power in creating man, and the very next moment we have announced the hymn, "Oh To Be Nothing." The absurdity of it all is too evident to need comment, but when we understand that character and manhood, as well as practical efficiency in life, are the products of strength and not of weakness, we must come to the conclusion that every system of thought in the present age, be it religious, moral, ethical, or philosophical, needs complete reconstruction.

We are here to become great men and women, and with that purpose in view, we must eliminate everything in our religion and philosophy that tends to make the human mind a dependent weakling. If you would serve God and be truly religious, do not kneel before God, but learn to walk with God, and do something tangible every day to increase the happiness of mankind. This is religion that is worthwhile, and it is such religion alone that can please the Infinite.

Another cause which is too large and diversified to outline in detail, is that of intemperance; that is immoderation in anything in life. To indulge excessively any desire or appetite, be it physical or mental, is to weaken the will. Partake only of that which is necessary and good, and observe moderation. Control yourself under all circumstances, and resolve never to go too far in anything, because too much of the good may be more of an evil than not enough of it. The effects of weakness in the will are numerous, but there are two in particular that should receive marked attention. The first is that when the will is weak, the human system becomes incapable of resisting temptations, and therefore moral weakness or a complete moral downfall is inevitable. Character in the largest sense of the term is impossible without a strong will, and it is impossible to accomplish anything that is of permanent value without character.

The second is that weakness in the will inevitably implies weak mental actions; that is, no matter how much ability you may possess, if your will is weak, you will apply only a fraction of that ability; and there are thousands of able men and women who are failures in life simply because they have not the will to apply all their ability. If they would simply increase the power of their will, and properly train that will, they would immediately pass from failure to success, and in many instances, remarkable success. It is the power of the strong will alone that can give full expression to every talent or faculty you may possess, and it is only such a power that can push up the actions of every faculty to a point of high efficiency.

In learning to develop the will and to use the will, realize what the will is for. Understand clearly what its functions actually are, and then use it in all of those functions. Avoid anything and everything that tends to weaken the will, and practice every method known that can strengthen the will. Do not give in to any feeling or desire until you succeed in directing that feeling or desire as you like. Feel only the way you want to feel, and then feel with all the feeling that is in you. Whatever comes up in your system, take hold of it with your will and direct it so as to produce even greater results than were at first indicated. Use the will consciously as frequently as possible in pushing up your faculties to the highest point of efficiency; that is, when you are applying those faculties that you employ in your work, try to will them into stronger and larger actions. This is a most valuable practice, and if applied every day will, in the course of a reasonable time, not only increase the capacity and ability of those faculties, but will also increase decidedly the power of the will.

Whenever you will to do anything, will it with all there is in you. If no other practice than this were taken, the power of the will would be doubled in a month. Depend upon the power that is in you for everything, and determine to secure the results you desire through the larger expression of that power. Never give in to anything that you do not want. When a certain desire comes up that you do not care to entertain, turn your attention at once upon some favorable desire, and give all the power of your will to that new desire. This is very important, as the average person wastes more than half of their energy entertaining desires that are of no value, and that they do not intend to carry out. Whenever any feeling comes up in the system ask yourself if you want it. If you do not, turn your attention in another direction; but if you do want it, take hold of it with your will and direct it towards the highest states of mind that you can form at the time.

In brief, every action that enters the system, whether it comes through thought, feeling, desire or imagination, should be redirected, by the power of the will and turned into higher and greater actions. Whenever you think, make it a practice to think with your whole mind. Make your thinking whole-hearted instead of half-hearted. Whenever you act, act with all there is in you. Make every action firm, strong, positive and determined; in other words, put your whole soul into everything that you feel, think or do. In this way, you turn on, so to speak, the full current of the will, and whenever the will is used to its full capacity, it will grow and develop.

Try to deepen every action of mind and thought; that is, do not think simply on the surface, but also think subconsciously. Think and act with your deeper mental life. You thereby give the power of the will a deeper field of action, and it is established in the larger life of your individuality instead of in the surface thought of your objective mind.

The difference between a superficial will and a deeply established will is readily found in everyday experience. When you will to do anything and your intentions are easily thwarted by the suggestion of someone else, your will is on the surface. But when your intentions are so deeply rooted in the subconsciousness of your mind that nothing can thwart those intentions, your will has gained that great depth which you desire. The more easily you are disturbed, the weaker your will, while the stronger the will, the more difficult it is for anything to disturb your mind. When the will is strong, you live and exercise self-control in a deeper or interior mental world, and you look out upon the confusions of the outer world without being affected in the least by what takes place in the external.

Whenever you exercise the will, try to place the action of that will as deeply in the world of your interior mental feeling as you possibly can; that is, do not originate will-action on the surface, but in the depth of your own supreme individuality. Try to feel that it is the "I Am" that is exercising the power of the will, and then remember that the "I Am" lives constantly upon the supreme heights of absolute self-mastery. With this inspiring thought constantly in mind, you will carry the throne of the will, so to speak, farther and farther back into the interior realms of your greater mental world, higher and higher up into the ruling power of the supreme principle in mind. The result will be that you will steadily increase the power of your will, and appropriate more and more the conscious control of that principle in your greater nature through which all the forces in your possession may be governed and directed.

13. THE BUILDING OF A GREAT MIND

He who would become great must live a great life. Happiness adds life, power, and worth to all your talents and powers. It is most important, therefore, that every moment should be full of joy. However much you may do, always remember you have the ability to do more. No one has as yet applied all the ability in their possession. But all of us should learn to apply a greater measure every year. While you are waiting for an opportunity to improve your time, improve yourself. The man or woman who never weakens when things are against them, will grow stronger and stronger until they will have the power to cause all things to be for them.

A great mind does not come from ancestors, but from the life, the thought and the actions of the individual; and such a mind can be constructed by anyone who understands the art of mind building, and who faithfully applies this art. You may have a small mind today, and your ancestors for many generations back may have been insignificant in mental power; nevertheless, you may become even exceptional in mental capacity and brilliancy if you proceed to build your mind according to the principles of exact science; and those principles anyone can apply.

There are two obstacles, however, that must be removed before this building process can begin, and the first one of these is the current belief in heredity. That we inherit things is true, but the belief that we cannot become any larger or any better than our inheritance is not true. As long as a person believes that greatness is not possible to them because there were no great minds among their ancestors, they are holding themselves down, and cannot become any more than they sub- consciously think they can; while on the other hand, the person who expects to become much because they had remarkable grandfathers is liable to be disappointed because they depend too much upon their illustrious forefathers and not enough upon themselves.

Blood will tell when combined with ambition, energy and enterprise, but the very best of blood will prove worthless in the life of one who expects ancestral greatness to carry them through. When we have received good things we must turn them to good account or nothing is gained. Our success will not come from the acts of our forefathers, but can come alone from what we are doing now. Those who have inherited rich blood can use that richness in building greatness in themselves, but those who have not the privilege of such inheritance need not be discouraged. They can create their own rich blood and make it as rich as they like.

Whether your forefathers were great or small matters not. Do not think of that subject, but live in the conviction that you may become what you wish to become by using well the good you have received, and by creating those essentials that you did not receive. If you have inherited undesirable traits, remember that evil is but valuable power misdirected. Learn to properly direct all your forces and your undesirable traits will be transformed into elements of growth, progress and advancement.

We all have met men and women with remarkable talents who persisted in thinking that they would never amount to anything because there was no genius among their ancestors. But if there had been a genius in the family some time during past generations, the question would be where that genius actually received their genius. If we all have to get greatness from ancestors, where did the first great ancestor get their greatness? There must be a beginning somewhere to every individual attainment, and that beginning might just as well be made by us now. What others could originate in their time, we can originate in our time. The belief that we must inherit greatness from someone in order to attain greatness is without any scientific foundation whatever, and yet there are thousands of most promising minds that remain small simply because they entertain this belief.

To believe that heredity is against you and that you therefore will not accomplish anything worthwhile, is to make your work a wearing process instead of a building process. In consequence, you will not advance, and you will constantly remain in the rear; but the moment you realize that it is in your power to become as much as you may desire, your work and study will begin to promote your own growth and advancement. When you live, think and act in the belief that you can become much, whatever you do will cause you to become more.

Thus all your actions will develop power and ability, and living itself will become a building process.

That man may become great regardless of the fact that there were no great minds among his ancestors many thinkers will admit, provided there are indications of exceptional ability in the man himself, but they entertain no hope if they see nothing in the man himself. And here we have the second obstacle to the building of a great mind. This obstacle, however must be removed in every mind that aims to rise above the ordinary, because the belief that the average person has nothing in them is the cause of fully three-fourths of the mental inferiority we find in the world. But the new psychology has conclusively demonstrated the fact that the man or woman who has nothing in them does not exist. All minds have the same possibilities, though most of those possibilities may be dormant in the minds of the majority.

The difference between a great mind and a small mind is simply this, that in the former the greater possibilities have come forth into objective action, while in the latter those possibilities are still in subjective inaction. When we say that a man has nothing in them we are contradicting the very principle of existence, because to be a man, a man must have just as much in him as any other man. What is in him may not be in action, and his mentality may appear to be small, but the possibilities of greatness are there. There is a genius somewhere in his mind, because there is a genius in every mind, though in most minds that genius may as yet be asleep.

When every child is taught the great truth that it has unlimited possibilities within its own subconscious mind, and that it can, through the scientific development of those possibilities, become practically what it may desire to become, we shall have laid the foundation for the greatest race of people that the ages have known. But we need not wait for future generations to demonstrate the possibilities of this truth. Every mind that begins to apply the principle of this truth now may begin to enlarge their mind now, and they may continue this process of enlargement indefinitely.

When we have removed the two obstacles mentioned and have established ourselves in the conviction that we have unlimited possibilities within us, more than sufficient to become whatever we may desire, we are ready to proceed with the building of a great mind. To promote the building of a great mind, the two prime essentials, scope and brilliancy, must be constantly kept in the foreground of consciousness. The mind that is not brilliant is of little value even though its scope may be very large. Likewise, the mind that is narrow or circumscribed is extremely limited, however brilliant it may be. A great mind is great both in capacity and ability. It can see practically everything and see through practically everything. To see everything is to have remarkable scope. To see through everything is to have exceptional brilliancy.

To give scope to the mind, every action of mind must be trained to move toward that which is greater than all persons or things. Those feelings or desires that cause the mind to become absorbed in some one thing or group of things, will limit the mental scope. Therefore in love, sympathy, and purpose the sphere of action must be universal. When we live only with that love that centres attention upon a limited number of persons, one of the greatest actions of mind will work in a limited world. When our sympathies go only to a chosen few, the same thing occurs, and when our purpose in life has a personified goal, we keep the mind within the limitations of that personification. To give universality to our feelings and actions, may require considerable training of the mental tendencies, but it is absolutely necessary if we will develop a great mind.

It is only those mental forces that move towards the verge of the limitless in every direction that can cause the mind to transcend limitations; therefore, all the forces of the mind should be given this transcending tendency. To develop mental scope, consciousness must move in every direction, and it must move along right lines, so that no obstacle may be met during that continuous expansive process. Such obstacles, however, are always produced by limitations of thought. Therefore, they may be avoided when all the actions of mind are placed upon a universal scale.

In the mental actions of love, we find many forces, all of which are true in their own places, but all of these forces must be exercised universally; that is, they must act upon a scale that is without bounds in the field of your own consciousness. The mind must go in every direction as far as it possibly can go in that direction, and must act in the conviction that wherever it may go it can go farther still. The understanding must know that there is no obstacle where the mind may seem to cease in its onward action, and that the mind is forever growing, thereby going as far each day as that day's development requires. When this idea is applied to a personal love between man and woman, the feeling of love must be based upon the principle that those two souls have the power to love each other more and more indefinitely; that the larger the love becomes the more lovable will the objects of that love become, and that the consciousness of perfect unity in pure affection increases constantly as the two souls become more and more individualized in their own sublime nature.

It is possible to make conjugal love universal and continuous between one man and one woman when the love of each is directed toward the sublime nature of the other. Through this law, each individual develops through the consciousness of the largeness of the real nature of the other, and the more the two love each other in this universal sense, the more they will see in each other to love. In addition, the minds of both will constantly enlarge in scope, because when love acts upon this larger scale, the whole mind will act upon this larger scale, as there is no stronger power in mind than love.

The love between parent and child can, in like manner, be made universal. In this attitude, the parent will love all of the child, not only the visible person, but the undreamed-of wonders that are waiting in that child-mind for expression. The child already loves the parent in this larger sense, and this is one reason why the child-mind lives so much nearer to the limitless, the universal, the ideal and the beautiful. And when the parent will do likewise, there will arise between the two a love that sees more and more to love the more love loves in this larger, sublime sense.

The idea is not only to love the tangible, but also that other something that transcends the tangible -- that something that appears to the soul in visions, and predicts wonders yet to be. That such a love will expand and enlarge the mind anyone can understand, because practically all the elements of the mind will tend to follow the actions of the love nature, when that nature is exceptionally strong. But we must not imagine that we shall, through this method, love the person less. The fact is, we shall love the person infinitely more, because we shall discern more and more clearly that the person is the visible side of that something in human life that we can only describe as the soul beautiful -- that something that alone can satisfy the secret longings of the heart.

The love of everything can, through the same law, become universal. Even friendship, which is always supposed to be confined to a small world, may become universal and limitless in the same way; and when it does, you will see more to admire in your friend every day. You will both have entered the boundless in your admiration for each other, and having entered the boundless, you will daily manifest new things from the boundless, and thus become delightfully surprised at each other constantly. The same may be employed in making sympathy universal; that is, never sympathize with the lesser, but always sympathize with the greater. The lesser is combined in the greater, and by sympathizing with the greater, the mind becomes greater.

In the fields of motives, objects, aims and purposes, we find that nearly every mental action is occupying a limited scope, and is acting in such a manner that its own limitations are being perpetuated. This tendency, however, must be removed if a greater mind is to be constructed, because every action of the mind must aim to change itself into a larger action. To cause every aim or purpose to become universal in its action, the mind must transcend shape, form, space and distance in its consciousness of everything that it may undertake to do. When we confine our thought to so far or so much, we place the mind in a state of limitations, but when we promote every object with a desire to go as far as the largest conception of the present may require, and proceed to attain as much as present capacity can possibly appropriate, we are turning all purposes and aims out upon the boundless sea of attainment. And we shall not only accomplish all that is possible in our present state of development, but we will at the same time constantly enlarge the scope of the mind.

It is absolutely necessary to have a fixed goal whatever our purpose in life may be, but we must never give special shape or size to that goal. We must think of our goal as being too large to be measured, even in the imagination. When we have a goal in mind that is only so and so large, all the creative energies of the mind will limit themselves accordingly. They will create only so and so much, regardless of the fact that they may be able to create many times as much. But when we think of our goal as being too large to be measured, the creative energies will expand to full capacity, and will proceed to work for the largest attainment possible. They will act constantly on the verge of the limitless, and will cause the mind to outdo itself every day.

In the field of desire, the same law should be applied, and applied constantly, as there are no actions in the mind that exercise a greater influence over the destiny of man than that of desire. When desire is low or perverted, everything goes down or goes wrong, but when desire changes for the better, practically everything else in the human system changes to correspond. To train desire to become universal in action, every individual desire should be changed so as to set only for the promotion of growth. Those desires which when fulfilled, do not make for the enlargement of life, are detrimental. The power of all such desires therefore must be changed in their course.

Your object is to become more and achieve more, and to constantly promote that object, development and growth must be perpetual throughout your system. For this reason, every action must have growth, for its purpose, and as every action is the result of some desire, no desire must be permitted that is not conducive to growth. It is not necessary, however, to remove a single desire from the human system to bring about this change, because every desire can be trained to promote the building of a greater life. When every desire is caused to move towards the larger and the greater through the mind's irresistible desire for the larger and the greater, all the creative forces of the mind will move towards the same goal, and will constantly build a greater mind.

The principle is this, that when all the actions of mind are trained to move towards the larger, they will perpetually enlarge. The first essential to the building of a great mind will thereby be promoted. To promote the second essential, mental brilliancy, the actions of mind must be made as high and as fine as possible; that is, the vibrations of the mental life must be in the highest scale attainable. To see through everything the mind will require the very finest rays of mental light, and as this mental light is produced by the vibrations of the actions of mind, these actions should be as high in the scale as we can possibly reach at every stage of our mental ability.

The light of intelligence is created by the mind itself, and the more brilliant this light becomes, the greater will become the powers of intelligence, discernment, insight, understanding, ability, talent and genius. And the power of mind to create a more brilliant mind increases as the mind places itself more and more in the consciousness of the absolute light of universal intelligence. To cause the mind to become more brilliant, all the tendencies of mind should fix their attention upon the highest mental conception of mental brilliancy. Every expression of the mind should be animated with a refining tendency. Every force of the mind should rise towards the absoluteness of mental light. Those states of mind that tend to magnify the inferior must be eliminated, and this is accomplished by thinking only of the superior that is possible in all things. All mental actions that are critical, depressing or depreciative must be replaced by their constructive opposites, as every action of the mind must concentrate its attention upon the largest and the best in all fields of consciousness. The mind must be kept high in every respect, because the higher in the mental scale the mind functions, the more brilliant will become the mental light.

74

To increase the rapidity of the vibrations in these higher mental states, creative energy must be supplied in abundance, and to comply with this requirement, all that is necessary is to retain in the human system all the energy that is already created. The human system creates and generates an enormous amount of creative energy every day. Therefore, when all this energy is retained and transmuted into finer mental elements, the mind will be abundantly supplied with those finer energies that can increase both the power and the brilliancy of thought and mind. The mind that is animated with a strong desire to constantly refine itself, and that is thoroughly charged with creative energy, will always be brilliant, and will become more and more brilliant as the laws given above are faithfully and thoroughly applied.

14. HOW CHARACTER DETERMINES CONSTRUCTIVE ACTION

Remove the sting; remove the whine; remove the sigh. They are your enemies. They are never conducive to happiness; and we all live to gain happiness, to give happiness. From every word remove the sting. Speak kindly. To speak kindly and gently to everybody is the mark of a great soul. And it is your privilege to be a great soul. From the tone of your voice remove the whine. Speak with joy. Never complain. The more you complain, the smaller you become, and the fewer will be your friends and opportunities. Speak tenderly, speak sweetly, speak with love. From all the outpourings of your heart, remove the sigh. Be happy and contented always. Let your spirit sing, let your heart dance, let your soul declare the glory of existence, for truly life is beautiful. Every sigh is a burden, a self-inflicted burden. Every whine is a maker of trouble, a forerunner of failure. Every sting is a destroyer of happiness, a dispenser of bitterness. To live in the world of sighs is to be blind to everything that is rich and beautiful. The more we sigh, the less we live, for every sigh leads to weakness, defeat, and death. Remove the sting, remove the whine, remove the sigh. They are not your friends. There is better company waiting for you.

All the elements of life are good in themselves; and should produce good results when in action; that is, when the action is properly directed; but when any action is misdirected, evil follows, and this is the only cause of the ills of human existence. Everything that is wrong in the world has been produced by the perversion and the misuse of the good. Therefore, to eliminate wrong, man must learn to make the proper use of those things that exist in his sphere of action.

The misuse of things comes either from ignorance or lack of character, or both. That person who does not understand the elements and the forces of the world in which they live will make many mistakes, and will make the wrong use of nearly everything unless they are guided by instructions of those who understand. The leadership of greater minds is therefore necessary to the welfare of the race, but this leadership is not sufficient. Guidance from great minds will help to a limited degree so long as the actions of the individual are simple, but when greater development is sought, with its more complex actions, the individual must learn to master the laws of life for themselves. They can no longer depend upon others. Therefore, though the leadership of greater minds be necessary to the welfare of the race, it is also necessary for that leadership to be used, not for keeping the multitude in a state of simplemindedness and dependence, but for promoting the intelligence of each individual until external guidance is needed no more.

The true purpose of the strong is to promote greater strength in the weak, and not to keep the weak in that state where they are at the mercy of the strong. Our united purpose should be to develop more great men and women, and to do everything possible to lead the many from dependence to independence. Every state of individual attainment is preceded by a childhood period, but this period should not be unnecessarily prolonged, nor will it be, when every strong mind seeks to develop strength in the weak instead of using the weakness of the weak for their own gain.

Those who understand the laws of life may inform the ignorant what to do and what not to do, and may thereby prevent most of the mistakes that the ignorant would otherwise make. But this guidance will not prevent all the mistakes, as experiences demonstrate, because it requires a certain amount of understanding to even properly apply the advice of another. Those who do not have the understanding will therefore misuse the elements of life at every turn, no matter how well they are guided by wiser persons, while those who do have this understanding will invariably begin to do things without consulting their so-called superiors. It is therefore evident that more understanding for everybody is the remedy, as far as this side of the subject is concerned, but there is also another side.

A great many people go wrong because they do not know any better. To them, a better understanding of life is the path to emancipation. They will be made free when they know the truth, but the majority of those who go wrong do know better. Then why do they go wrong? The cause is lack of character. When you fail to do what you want to do, your character is weak. The same is true when you preach one thing and practice another. When you fail to be as perfect, as good or as ideal as you wish to be, or fail to accomplish what you think that you can accomplish, your character is at fault. It is the character that directs the action of the mind. It is the lack of character, or a weak character that produces misdirections; and when you fail to accomplish what you feel you can accomplish, something is being misdirected.

What you feel that you can do that you have the power to do. Therefore, when you fail to do it, some of the powers of your being are being misdirected. To be influenced to do what you would not do if you were normal, means that your character is weak, and to be affected by surroundings, events, circumstances and conditions against your will indicates the same deficiency. A strong character is never influenced against their will. They are never disturbed by anything, never become upset, offended or depressed. No one can insult them because they are above small states of mind, and stronger than those things that may tend to produce small states of mind.

All mental tendencies that are antagonistic, critical or resisting indicate a deficiency in character. The desire to criticize becomes less and less as the character is developed. It is the mark of a fine character never to be critical and to mention but rarely the faults of others. A strong character does not resist evil, but uses their strength in building the good. They know that when the light is made strong, the darkness will disappear of itself. A strong character has no fear, never worries and never becomes discouraged. If you are in the hands of worry, your character needs development. The same is true if you have a tendency to submit to fate, give in to adversity, give up in the midst of difficulties, or surrender to failure or wrong.

It may be stated, without any exceptions or modifications whatever, that the more temper, the less character. Anger is always misdirection of energy, but it is the function of character to properly direct all energies. Therefore, there can be no anger when the character is thoroughly developed. The mind that changes easily, that is readily carried away by every new attraction that may appear, and that does not retain a well-balanced attitude on any subject lacks character. A strong character changes gradually, orderly, and only as each step is thoroughly analyzed and found to be a real step forward. The more individuality, the more character, and the more one is oneself, the stronger the character.

Practice being yourself, your very best self, and your very largest self, and your character will be developed. The more one is conscious of flaws and defects, the weaker the character, and the reason is because nearly everything is being misdirected when the character is weak. The strong character is conscious only of the right because such a character is right, and is causing everything in its sphere of action to do right.

To the average person, character is not important as far as this life is concerned; and as most theological systems have declared that it was repentance and not character that would insure human welfare in the world to come, the development of character has naturally been neglected. But when we realize that it is character that determines whether our actions in daily life are to go right or wrong and that every mistake is due to a lack of character, we shall feel that the subject requires attention.

It is the power of character that directs everything that is done in the human system or by the human system. Character is the channel through which all expressions must pass. It is character that gives human life its tone, its color and its quality, and it is character that determines whether our talents and faculties are to be their best or not. The man or woman who has a well-developed character is not simply good. They are good for something, because they have the power to turn all their energies to good account. A strong character not only turns all the elements and energies of life to good account, but has the power to hold the mind in the right attitude during the most trying moments of life, so that they will not make mistakes nor fall a victim to insidious temptation. A strong character will keep all the faculties and forces of life moving in the right direction, no matter what obstacles we may meet in the way. We shall turn neither to the right nor to the left, but will continue to move directly towards the goal we have in view, and will reach that goal without fail.

Thousands of people resolve every year to press on to higher attainments and greater achievements. They begin very well, but before long they are turned off the track. They are misled or switched off by counter attractions. They have not the character to keep right on until they have accomplished what they originally set out to do. True, it is sometimes wisdom to change one's plans, but it is only lack of character to change one's plans without reason, simply because there is a change of circumstance. To change with every circumstance is to drift with the stream of circumstance and those who drift can only live the life of a log. They will be victim of every external change that they may meet. They will control little or nothing, and will accomplish little or nothing.

We all can develop the power to control circumstances or rather to cause all circumstances to work with us and for us in the promotion of the purpose we have in view; and this power is character. Never permit circumstances to change your plans, but give so much character to your plans that they will change circumstances. Give so much character to the current of your work that all things will be drawn into that current, and that which at first was but a tiny rivulet, will thus be swelled into a mighty, majestic stream.

When the various forces of the system are properly directed and properly employed, the development of the entire mentality will be promoted; and this means greatness. The power that directs the forces of the system is character, and it is character that causes the mind to use those forces in the best and most instructive manner. There must be character before there can be true greatness, because any deficiency in character causes energy to be wasted and misdirected. It is therefore evident that the almost universal neglect in the development of character is one of the chief reasons why great men and women are not as numerous as we should wish them to be.

Many may argue, however, that great minds do not always have good characters, and also that some of our best characters fail to manifest exceptional ability. But we must remember that there is a vast difference between that phase of character that simply tries to follow the moral law, and real character -- the character that actually is justice, virtue and truth. Then we must also remember that character does not mean simply obedience to a certain group of laws, but the power to use properly all the laws of life. That person who uses mental laws properly, but fails to comply with moral laws does not possess a complete character. Nevertheless, the character of this person is just as good as that of the person who follows moral laws while constantly violating mental laws.

In the study of character, it is very important to know that the violation of mental laws is just as detrimental as the violation of moral laws, though we have been in the habit of condemning the latter and excusing the former. That person who uses properly the mental laws, will to a degree promote the development of the mind even though they may neglect the moral laws; and this accounts for the fact that a number of minds have attained a fair degree of greatness in spite of their moral weakness. But it is a fact of extreme importance, that those minds who attain greatness in spite of their moral weakness could become two or three times as great if they had also developed moral strength. That person who complies with the mental laws but who violates the moral laws, wastes fully one-half of the energies of their mind, and sometimes more. Their attainment and achievement will, therefore, be less than one-half of what they might be if they had moral character as well as mental character. The same is true, however, of that person who complies with the moral laws, but who violates the mental laws; fully one-half of their energy is wasted and misdirected. This explains why the so-called good characters are not any more brilliant than the rest, for though they may be morally good, they are not always mentally good; that is, they do not use their minds according to the laws of mind, and therefore cannot rise above the level of the ordinary.

The true character tries to turn all the energies of the system into the best and most constructive channels, and it is the mark of a real character when all the various parts of the being of man are working together harmoniously for the building of greatness in mind and soul. When the character is weak, there is more or less conflict among the mental actions. Certain actions have a tendency to work for one thing, while other actions are tending to produce the very opposite. The same is true of the desires. A character that lacks development will desire one thing today, and something else tomorrow. Plans will change constantly, and little or nothing will be accomplished. In the strong character, however, all actions work in harmony and all actions are constructive. And this is natural because it is the one supreme function of character to make all actions in the human system constructive -- to make every force in the human life a building force.

15. THE ART OF BUILDING CHARACTER

Be good and kind to everybody and the world will be kind to you. There may be occasional exceptions to this rule, but when they come pass them by and they will not come again. Ideals need the best of care. Weeds can grow without attention, but not so with the roses. Not all minds are pure that think they are. Many of them are simply dwarfed. It does not pay to lose faith in anybody. It is better to have faith in everybody and be deceived occasionally than to mistrust everybody and be deceived almost constantly. When you meet a person who does not look well, call their attention to the sunny side of things, and aim to say something that will give them new interest and new life. You will thereby nip in the bud many a threatening evil, and carry healing with you wherever you go.

Character is developed by training all the forces and elements of life to act constructively in those spheres for which they were created, and to express themselves in those actions only that promote the original purpose of the being of man. Every part of the human system has a purpose of its own -- a purpose that it was created to fulfill. When those elements that belong to each part express themselves in such a way that the purpose of that part is constantly promoted, all actions are right; and it is character that causes those actions to be right. Character is therefore indispensable, no matter what one's object in life may be. Character is the proper direction of all things, and the proper use of all things in the human system. And the proper use of anything is that use that promotes the purpose for which that particular thing was created.

To develop character it is therefore necessary to know what life is for, to know what actions promote the purpose of that life, and to know what actions retard that purpose. When the secret of right action is discovered, and every part of man is steadily trained in the expression of right action, character may be developed. But whatever is done, character must be applied in its fullest capacity. It is only through this full use, right use and constant use that anything may be perpetuated or developed. Character develops through a constant effort to cause every action in the human system to be a right action; that is, a constructive action, or an action that promotes the purpose of that part of the system in which the action takes place. This is natural because since character is the power of right action, every effort to extend the scope of right action will increase the power of character.

To have character is to have the power to promote what you know to be the purpose of life, and to be able to do the right when you know the right. To have character is to know the right, and to be so well established in the doing of the right that nothing in the world can turn you into the wrong. The first essential is therefore to know the right; to be able to select the right; to have that understanding that can instinctively choose the proper course of action, and that knows how each force and element of life is to be directed so that the original purpose of human life will be fulfilled.

The understanding of the laws of life will give this first essential in an intellectual sense, and this is necessary in the beginning; but when character develops, one inwardly knows what is right without stopping to reason about it. The development of character enables one to feel what is right and what course to pursue regardless of exterior conditions or intellectual evidence. The intellect discerns that the right is that which promotes growth and development; character inwardly feels that the right leads to greater things and to better things, and that the wrong leads invariably to the inferior and the lesser.

The presence of character produces a consciousness of growth throughout the system; and the stronger the character, the more keenly one can feel that everything is being reconstructed, refined, perfected and developed into something superior, This is but natural because when the character is strong, everything in the system is expressed in right action, and the right action of anything causes the steady development of that particular thing. To distinguish between the right and the wrong becomes simplicity itself when one knows that the right promotes growth, while the wrong retards growth. Continuous advancement is the purpose of life; therefore, to live the right life is to live that life that promotes progress and growth, development and advancement in everything that pertains to life. For this reason, that action that promotes growth is in harmony with life itself, and must consequently be right. But that action that retards growth is at variance with life; therefore it is wrong; and wrong for that reason alone.

Everything that promotes human advancement is right. Everything that interferes with human advancement is wrong.

Here we have the basis of a system of ethics that is thoroughly complete, and so simple to live that nobody need err in the least. An intellectual understanding of the laws of life will enable anyone to know what action promotes growth and what action retards growth, but as character develops, one can feel the difference between right and wrong action in one's own system, because the consciousness of right becomes so keen that anything that is not right is discerned at once. It is therefore evident that the power to distinguish the right from the wrong in every instance will come only through the development of character. No matter how brilliant one may be intellectually, they cannot truly know the right until they have a strong character. The external understanding of the right can be misled, but the consciousness of the right is never mistaken; and this consciousness develops only as character develops.

The second essential is to create a subconscious desire for the right -- a desire so deep and so strong that nothing can tempt the mind to enter into the wrong. When this desire is developed, one feels a natural preference for the right; to prefer the right, under all circumstances becomes second nature, while every desire for the wrong will disappear completely. When every atom in one's being begins to desire the right, the entire system will establish itself in the right attitude, and right action will become the normal action in every force, function and faculty. In addition, this same desire will produce mental tendencies that contain the power of right action, which always means constructive action.

It is a well-known fact that all the forces and energies of the system, and all the movements of mind follow mental tendencies; therefore, when the mental tendencies are right actions, everything that takes place in the system will produce right action; and everything will be properly directed. The desire for the right may be developed by constantly thinking about the right with deep feeling. Every thought that has depth, therefore, will impress itself upon the subconscious, and when that thought is inspired with a strong desire for the right, the conscious impression will convey the right to the subconscious. Every impression that enters the subconscious will cause the subconscious to bring forth a harvest of that which the impression conveyed; therefore, when the right is constantly held in mind with deep feeling, the right thought will soon become the strongest in the mind; and our desires are the results of our strongest thoughts. You always desire that which is indicated in your strongest thought. You can therefore change those desires completely by thinking with deep feeling about that which you want to desire. No desire should be destroyed. All desires should be transmuted into the desire for the right, and when you subconsciously desire the right, every action in your being will be a right action.

The two fundamental essentials, therefore, to the development of character are to know the right and to desire the right, but the term "right" as employed here must not be confounded with that conception of right which includes only a few of the moral laws. To be right according to the viewpoint of completeness, is to be in harmony with all the principles of life, and all the laws of the present sphere of human existence. To know the right, it is necessary not simply to memorize rules that other minds have formulated, but to inwardly discern what life is for, and what mode of thought and action is conducive to the realization of that which is in life. To desire the right, according to this view of the right, the mind must actually feel the very soul of right action, and must be in such perfect touch with the universal movement of right action, that all lesser and imperfect desires are completely swallowed up in the one desire -- the desire that desires all that is in life, and all that is in perfect harmony with that which is in life.

It is the truth, that when we come into perfect touch with the greater, we cease to desire the lesser, and the closer we get to the one real desire, the less we care for our mistaken desires. Therefore, to remove an undesirable desire, the course is not to resist that desire, but to cultivate a greater and a better desire, along the same line. In this connection, we must remember that the adoption of a greater desire does not compel us to sacrifice those things that we gain from the lesser desires. He who adopts the greater loses nothing, but is on the way to the gaining of everything.

To know the right and to desire the right, according to the complete significance of the right we must interiorly discern the very right itself.

We cannot depend upon another's definition of the right, but must know fully the spirit of the right with our own faculties. That faculty that knows and feels the right, and that naturally knows and desires the right is character. Therefore, it is through the development of character that each individual will know for themselves how to live, think and act in perfect harmony with the laws of all life. When the consciousness of right action has been attained, a clear mental picture should be deeply impressed upon mind and every desire should be focused upon that picture. This concentration should be made as strong as possible, so that all the energies of the system are not only aroused, but caused to move towards the ideal of right action. And by right action, we mean that action that is thoroughly constructive, that builds for greater things and greater things only. Everything is right that builds for greater things. If it were not right, it could not produce the greater.

To clearly picture upon the mind the image of right action, and to concentrate with strong desire the whole attention upon that mental image, will cause all the tendencies of mind to move in the same direction. There will therefore be perfect harmony of mental action, and that action will be right action, because everything that moves towards the right must be right. This mental picture of right action should always be complete; that is, one's mental conception of the right should not be confined to certain parts of the system only, but should include every action conceivable in the being of man. That person who pictures themselves as virtuous, but forgets to picture themselves above anger, fear and worry, is not forming a complete picture or ideal of the right. They are not giving the creative energies of the system a perfect pattern; the character that those energies are to build will therefore be one-sided and weak.

First ask yourself what you would have all the energies, powers, functions and faculties in your system do. Answer that question in the best manner possible, and upon that answer, base your picture of right action. Whenever a new line of action is undertaken, the mind should continue in that original line of action until the object in view has been reached. To do this in all things, even in trivial matters, will not only cause every action to produce the intended results, but real character will steadily be made stronger thereby. The habit of giving up when the present task is half finished and try something else is one of the chief causes of failure. The development of a strong character, however, will remove this habit completely.

To constantly think of the highest and the greatest results that could possibly follow the promotion of any undertaking or line of action will aid remarkably in causing the mind to keep on. To expect much from what we are doing now is to create a strong desire to press on towards the goal in view. To press on towards the goal in view is to reach the goal, and to reach the goal is to get what we expected.

An essential of great importance in the building of character is the proper conception of the ideal. No mind can rise higher than its ideals, but every mind can realize its ideals no matter how high they may be. Our ideals therefore cannot be too high. The ideal should not only be a little better than the present real, but should be perfection itself. Have nothing but absolute perfection in all things as the standard and the goal, and never think of your goal as anything less. Do not simply aim to improve yourself in just one more degree. Aim to reach absolute perfection in all your attainments and all your achievements, and make that desire so strong that every atom in your being thrills with its power. To form all one's ideals in accordance with one's mental conception of absolute perfection, will cause the mind to live above the world of the ordinary, and this is extremely important in the building of character. A great character cannot be developed so long as the mind continues to dwell on the ordinary, the trivial or the superficial. Neither can true quality and true worth find expression so long as thought continues on the common plane; and the life that does not continue to grow into higher quality and greater worth has not begun to live.

When character is highly developed, both the personality and the mentality will feel the stamp of quality and worth. High mental color will be given to every characteristic, and the nature of man will cease to be simply human. It will actually be more. In building character, special attention must be given to hereditary tendencies or those traits of character that are born in us. But as all such traits are subconscious, they can be changed or removed by directing the subconscious to produce the opposite characteristics or tendencies. It matters not in the least what we may have inherited from our ancestors. If we want to change those things, we can do so. The subconscious will not only respond to any direction that we may make, but is fully capable of doing anything in the world of mind or character that we may desire to have done.

Examine the tendencies of your mind and character, and fix clearly in consciousness which ones you wish to remove and which ones you wish to retain. Those that you wish to retain should be made strong by daily directing the subconscious to give those tendencies more life, more power and more stability. To remove those tendencies that you do not wish to retain, forget them. Do not resist them nor try to force them out of the mind. Simply forget them and direct the subconscious to create and establish new tendencies that are directly opposite to the nature of the ones that you wish to remove. Build up those qualities that constitute real character, and every bad trait that you have inherited from your ancestors will disappear.

To build up those qualities, picture in your mind the highest conceptions of those qualities that you can possibly form; then impress those conceptions and ideas upon tile subconscious. Such impressions should be formed daily and especially before going to sleep as the building process in the subconscious is more perfect during sleep. By impressing the idea of spotless virtue upon the subconscious every day for a few months, your moral tendencies will become so strong that nothing can tempt you to do what you know to be wrong. Not that physical desire will disappear; we do not want any natural desire to disappear, but your control of those desires will be so complete that you can follow them or refuse to follow them just as you choose. And your desire to remain absolutely free from all wrong will become so strong that nothing can induce you to do what your finer nature does not wish to have done.

There are millions of people who are morally weak in spite of the fact that they do not wish to be, but if these people would employ this simple method, their weakness would soon disappear, because by impressing the idea of spotless virtue upon the subconscious, the subconscious will produce and express in the personality the power of virtue; and if this process is continued for some time, the power of virtue in the person will become so strong that it can overcome and annihilate instantly every temptation that may appear.

Impress upon the subconscious the idea of absolute justice, and your consciousness of justice will steadily develop until you can discriminate perfectly between the right and the wrong in every imaginable transaction. Whatever quality you wish to develop in your character, you can increase its worth and its power steadily by applying this subconscious law; that is, what is impressed upon the subconscious will be expressed through the personality, and since the seed can bring forth ten, thirty, sixty and a hundred fold, one tiny impression, therefore, may have the power to bring forth a great and powerful expression. Everything multiplies in the subconscious, whether it be good or otherwise. Therefore, by taking advantage of this law and giving to the subconscious only those ideas and desires that have quality and worth, we place ourselves in the path of perpetual increase of everything good that the heart may desire.

The two predominating factors in character are justice and virtue. The former gives each element in life its proper place. The latter turns each element to proper use. The

84

consciousness of justice is developed through the realization of the fact that nothing can use what is not its own. To try to use what is not one's own will result in misuse. When the consciousness of justice is thoroughly developed, everything in the human system will be properly placed. That very power of the mind that feels justice -- the true placing of things -- will cause all things within man to be properly placed. And when justice rules among all things in the interior life of man, that man will naturally be just to all things in the exterior life. It is not possible for any person to deal justly with people and matters in the external world until they have attained the consciousness of justice within themselves. They may think they are just, or may try to be just, but their dealings will not be absolutely just until they can feel justice in their own life. To feel justice within oneself is to keep the entire system in a state of equilibrium. The mentality will be balanced and no force or element will be misplaced. It is therefore something for which we may work with great profit.

To be virtuous in the complete sense of the term, is to use all things properly, and the proper use of things is that use that works for greater things. Virtue is therefore applicable to every force, function and faculty in the being of man, but in its application there must be no desire or effort to suppress or destroy. Virtue means use -- right use -- never suppression. When things cannot be used in their usual channels, the energies in action within those things should be turned in their courses and used elsewhere. When creative energy cannot be properly applied physically, it should be employed metaphysically; and all energy can be drawn into mind for the purpose of building up states, faculties, talents or powers. (Practical methods through which this may be accomplished will be given in the next chapter.)

When a certain desire cannot be expressed with good results in its present purpose, the power of that desire should be changed and caused to desire something else -- something of value that can be carried out now. The power of that desire therefore is not lost, neither is enjoyment sacrificed, because all constructive forces, give joy to the mind. "And the greatest of joys shall be the joy of going on."

The desire for complete virtue is developed through the realization of the fact that the greatest good comes only when each part fulfills, physically and metaphysically, what nature intended. In the application of virtue, the purpose of nature may be fulfilled metaphysically when the physical channel does not permit of true expression at the time; though when physical expression may be secured, the metaphysical action should always be in evidence, because the greatest results always follow when physical and metaphysical actions are perfectly combined.

In the building of character, the two principal objects in view should be the strong and the beautiful. The character that is strong but not beautiful may have force, but cannot use that force in the building of the superior. The character that is beautiful but not strong will not have sufficient power to carry out its lofty ideals. It is the strong and the beautiful combined that builds mind and character, and that brings into being the superior man.

16. THE CREATIVE FORCES IN MAN

When the creative energies are daily transmuted, and turned into muscle, brain and mind, a virtuous life can be lived without inconvenience. Besides, the body will be healthier, the personality stronger and the mind more brilliant. Hold yourself constantly in a positive, masterful attitude, and fill that attitude with kindness. The result will be that remarkable something that people call personal magnetism. Creative energy when retained in the system will give vigor to the body, sparkle to the eye, and genius to the brain. There is enough power in any man to enable him to realize all his desires and reach the highest good he has in view. It is only necessary that all of this power be constructively applied.

The human system may well be termed a living dynamo, as the amount of energy, especially creative energy, generated in the mind and personality of man is simply enormous. If we should try to measure the amount produced in the average healthy person, we should become overwhelmed with surprise; though we should naturally become even more surprised after learning how much power nature gives to man, and then finding that he applies only a fraction of it. We shall soon see the reason for this, however, and learn exactly why all of this vast amount of energy is not turned to practical use.

What is called creative energy in its broadest, largest sense, is that power in man that creates, forms or reproduces anywhere in the human system, and it divides itself into a number of groups, each one having its special function. One group creates thought, another brain cells, another nerve tissues, another muscular tissues, another manufactures the various juices of the system, another produces ideas, another creates talent and ability, another reproduces the species, and a number of other groups produce the various chemical formations in the system. We therefore have all kinds of creative processes going on in the human system, and corresponding energies with which these processes are continued.

One of the most interesting facts in connection with this study is that Nature generates more energy for each group than is required for normal functioning through its particular channel. In consequence, we find a great deal of surplus energy throughout the system. Each function supplies a certain percentage, and as it is not used by the function itself, the larger part of it naturally goes to waste. And here is where our subject becomes decidedly important. All kinds of creative energy are so closely related that they can be transformed and transmuted into each other. What is wasted in one function can therefore be turned to actual use in another function. An extra supply can thereby be secured for the creation of thoughts and ideas if such should be necessary, or an extra supply can be secured for the manufacture of the different juices of the system, or for the increase of muscular activity or functional activity in any one of the vital organs. Each group will readily change and combine with any other group, thus producing additional power in any part of the system at any time.

More than half of the energy generated in the human system is surplus energy, and is not needed for normal functioning, either in mind or body, though there are many personalities that generate so much energy that fully three-fourths of the amount generated is surplus. The question is therefore what shall be done with this surplus energy, and how any amount of it can be applied through any special function or faculty desired? If a person can accomplish a great deal, sometimes remarkable things by only using a fraction of his energy, it is evident that he could accomplish a great deal more if some means could be found through which he might apply all of his energy. In fact, if such means were found, his working capacity, as well as his ability, might be doubled or trebled, and his achievements increased in proportion.

If a certain amount of energy produces a certain degree of working capacity, twice as much energy would naturally double that working capacity, and this has been demonstrated a number of times. A great many people, who have tried to transmute their creative energies, and direct those energies into some special faculty, have found that the working capacity of that faculty has been increased for the time being to a remarkable degree, but this is not the only result secured. The same process will also increase the brilliancy of the mind, and here let us remember that genius, in most instances, is accounted for by the fact that practically all of the surplus energy of the personality flows naturally into that faculty where genius is in evidence.

To illustrate the idea further, take two men of equal personal power. Let one of them permit his surplus energy to flow into the different functions as usual, giving over a part to normal requirements, and the other to mere waste. We shall not find this man doing anything extraordinary. But let the other man give over to normal functions only what is actually required, and then turn the remainder into his mind, or those parts of his mind that are being applied in his work. We shall find in this second case that ability will rapidly increase, and that in the course of time actual genius be developed. That genius could be developed by this process in every case, has not been demonstrated, though it is quite probable that it could be demonstrated without a single exception. However, no individual can turn surplus energy into any faculty without becoming more able, more efficient and more competent in that faculty.

To learn how this process can be carried out successfully under any circumstances is therefore thoroughly worthwhile. To proceed, we must first learn how these different groups of creative energy naturally act; and we find that each group goes, either naturally or through some habit, into its own part of mind or body; in other words, we find in the human system, a number of streams of energy flowing in different directions, performing certain functions on their way, using up a fraction of their power in that manner, the rest flowing off into waste. Knowing this, the problem before us is to learn how to redirect those streams of energy so as to turn them to practical use where they can be used now, and thus not only prevent waste, but increase the result of our efforts in proportion.

In brief, we want to know how we can take up all surplus energy, that is, all energy that remains after normal functioning has been provided for, and use that surplus in promoting more successfully the work in which we are engaged. And to learn how to do this, we must study the art of transmutation. What we call transmutation is not some mysterious something that only a few have the power to understand and apply, but one of the simplest things in Nature, as well as one of the most constant of her processes. Nature is continually transmuting her energies, and it is in this manner that extraordinary results are found anywhere in the realms of Nature, or anywhere in human nature where unconscious actions along greater lines have been the cause.

Whenever any individual has accomplished more than usual, it is the law of transmutation through which the unusual has been secured. The use of the law may have been unconscious, though everything that is applied in past and unconsciously, can be applied fully and thoroughly through conscious action. When anyone is using his mind continually along a certain line, and is so thoroughly absorbed in that line of action that it takes up his whole attention, we invariably find that the mind while in that condition, draws an extra amount of energy from the body. Sometimes it draws too much, so that every desire of the body is, for the time being, suspended and the vitality of the different physical organs decreased below normal.

A man while in this condition frequently loses desire for food, and we all know of inventors who have been so absorbed in their experiments that they have neither taken nor desired food for days. We have also found the same condition in many others, especially among authors, composers and artists, where the mind was given over completely to the subject at hand. And what is the cause but transmutation? When the mind takes up for its own use a great deal of the energy naturally employed in the body, the power of normal functioning will have so decreased that the desire for normal functioning will have practically disappeared for the time being.

Another illustration with which we are all familiar, is where every natural desire of the body disappears completely, for a time, when the mind is completely absorbed in some entirely different desire; and here we find the law that underlies the cure of all habits. If you would turn your mind upon some desire that was directly opposite to the desire that feeds your habit, and if you would give over your whole attention to that opposite desire, you would soon draw all the energy away from that desire which perpetuates the habit. The habit in question therefore would soon die of starvation. In the same way, people who are inclined to be materialistic could overcome that tendency entirely by concentrating attention constantly and thoroughly upon the idealistic side of life. In this case, those forces of the system that are perpetuating materialistic conditions would be transmuted into finer energies, and would thereby proceed to build up idealistic or more refined conditions of body, mind and personality.

Both Nature and human experience are full of illustrations of transmutation, so that we are not dealing in this study with something that lies outside of usual human activity. We are dealing with something that is taking place in our systems every minute, and we want to learn how to take better control of this something, so that we can apply the underlying law to the best advantage.

In learning to apply the law of transmutation, our first purpose should be to employ all surplus energy either in promoting our work or in developing faculties and talents. This process alone would practically double the working capacity of any mind, and would steadily increase ability and talent; and also to turn energy to good account that cannot be used in its own channel now. To illustrate, suppose you have a desire for a certain physical or mental action, and you know that it would not be possible to carry out that desire at the time. Instead of permitting the energy that is active in that desire to go to waste, you would turn that energy into some other channel where it could be used to advantage now.

Our second purpose should be to direct all surplus energy into the brain and the mind in case we had more energy in our body than we could use, or that was required for physical functioning, and thereby become stronger and more efficient in all mental activities.

Our third purpose should be to transmute all reproductive energy into talent and genius when there was no need of that energy in its own particular sphere. And in this connection, it is well to mention the fact that a man who is morally clean, other things being equal, has in every instance, greater agility, greater capacity, and greater endurance by far than the man who is not. While the latter is wasting his creative energies in useless pleasures, as well as in disease producing habits, the former is turning all of his creative energy into ability and genius, and the result is evident.

In carrying out these three purposes we can prevent all waste of mental and personal power. We can control our desires completely; we can eliminate impurity, and we can turn life and power into channels that will invariably result in greater mental power and brilliancy, if not marked ability and rare genius. To experiment, turn your whole attention upon your mind for a few minutes, and desire gently to draw all your surplus energy into the field of mental action. Then permit yourself to think along those lines where the mind is inclined to be most active. In a few moments you will discover the coming of new ideas and in many instances, you will for several hours receive ideas that are brighter and more valuable than what you have received for some time. Repeat the process later, and again and again for many days in succession, and it will be strange indeed, if you do not finally secure a group of ideas that will be worth a great deal in your special line of thought or work.

Whenever you feel a great deal of energy in your system, and try to direct it into the mind, you will have the same result. Ideas will come quick and rapidly, and among them all you will surely find a few that have exceptional merit.

In learning the art of transmutation, the first essential is to train your mind to think that all surplus energy is being turned into the channel you have decided upon; that is, if you are a business man, you naturally will want all your surplus energy to accumulate in your business faculties. To secure this result, think constantly of your surplus energy as flowing into those faculties. This mode of thinking will soon give your energies the habit of doing what you desire to have done. It is a well-known law, that if we continue to think deeply and persistently along a certain line, Nature will gradually take up that thought and carry it out. Another law of importance in this connection is that if we concentrate attention upon a certain faculty or upon a certain part of the system, we create a tendency among our energies to flow towards that faculty or part. We understand therefore the value of constantly hearing in mind the idea that we wish to realize. What we constantly impress upon the mind through our thoughts and desires, finally becomes a subconscious habit, and when any line of action becomes a subconscious habit, it acts automatically; that is it works of itself.

Before taking up this practice, however, it is necessary to determine positively what you actually desire your surplus energy to do. You must know what you want. Then continue to want what you want with all the power of desire that you can arouse. Most minds fail in this respect. They do not know with a certainty what they wish to accomplish or perfect. Their energies therefore are drawn into one channel today and another tomorrow, and nothing is finished. If you are an inventor, train your mind to think that all your surplus energy is constantly flowing into your faculties of invention. If you are a writer, train your mind to think that all your surplus energy is flowing into your literary talents; or whatever it is that you may be doing or want to do, direct your energy accordingly. You will soon find that you will increase in power, ability, and capacity along the lines of your choice, and if you continue this process all through life, your ability will continue to increase, no matter how long you may live.

The second essential is to desire deeply and persistently that all your surplus energy shall flow into those functions or faculties that you have selected for greater work. Wherever your desire is directed, there the force of your system will also tend to go, and herein we find another reason why persistent desire has such extreme value. The use of desire in this connection, however, must always be deep and calm, and never excited or over wrought.

The third essential is to place your mind in what may be termed the psychological field, and while acting in that field, to concentrate upon that part or faculty where you want your surplus energy to accumulate. This essential or process constitutes the real art of transmutation, though it is by no means the easiest to acquire. To master this method a great deal of practice will be required, but whenever you can place your mind in the psychological field and concentrate subjectively upon any part of your system where you want surplus energy to accumulate, all your surplus energy positively will accumulate in that part within a few moments' time.

Through the same process, you can annihilate any desire instantaneously, and change all the energy of that desire into some other force. You can also, in the same way, reach your latent or dormant energies, and draw all of those energies into any channel where high order of activity is desired; in fact, through this method, you can practically take full possession of all the power, active or latent, in your system, and use it in any way that you may wish. That you should, after you learn to apply this method successfully, become highly efficient in your work, is therefore evident, though this is not all. Extraordinary capacity, mental brilliancy and genius can positively be developed through the constant use of this method, provided, however, that nothing is done, either in thought, life or conduct, to interfere with the underlying law of the process.

To place your mind in the psychological field, try to turn your conscious actions into what may be termed the finer depths of the personality; that is, try to become conscious of your deeper life; try to feel the undercurrents of mind and thought and consciousness, and try to act in perfect mental contact with those deep, underlying forces of personality and mentality that lie at the foundation of your conscious activity.

An illustration in this connection will be found valuable. When you listen to music that seems to touch your soul, so that you can feel the vibrations of its harmony thrill every atom of your being, you are in the psychological field. You are alive in another and a finer mental world, a mental world that permeates your entire personal existence. You are also in the psychological field when you are stirred by some emotion to the very depth of your innermost life. A deepening of thought, feeling, life and desire will take the mind, more or less, into the psychological field; and whenever the mind begins to act in that field, you should concentrate your attention upon that faculty or part of your system where you wish extra energy to accumulate.

Make your concentration alive, so to speak, with interest, and make every action of that concentration as deep as possible, and all your surplus energy will positively flow towards the point of concentration. The power of this process can be demonstrated in a very simple manner. Place your mind in the psychological field, and then concentrate subjectively upon your hand, arousing at the time a deep desire for the increase of circulation in your hand. In a few moments, the veins on the back of your hand will be filled to capacity, and your hand, even though it might have been cold in the beginning, will become comfortably warm. Another experiment that is not only interesting in this connection, but may prove very valuable, is to concentrate in this same manner upon your digestive organs, in case the digestive process is retarded. You will soon feel more energy accumulating throughout the abdominal region, and any unpleasant sensation that you might have felt on account of indigestion will disappear entirely; in fact, even chronic indigestion can be cured in this way if the method is applied for a few minutes immediately before and after each meal.

The idea is simply this, that when you give extra energy to an organ, it will be able to perform its function properly, and whenever any function is performed properly, any ailment that might have existed in the organ of that function, will disappear. A number of similar experiments may be tried, all of which will prove equally interesting, and besides, will train the mind to apply this great law of transmutation.

The following effects may be secured through transmutation: Working capacity in any part of the personality or mentality may be constantly increased; all the energy generated in the system may be employed practically and successfully; the mind may be made more brilliant, as it is an extraordinary amount of creative energy going into the mind that invariably causes mental brilliancy. Any faculty selected can be given so much of this surplus energy of the system, that it will almost from the beginning, manifest an increase in ability, and will, in the course of time, manifest rare talent and even genius.

Moral purity may become second nature, as all that energy that was previously squandered in impure thought, impure desire or impure action can be transmuted readily, and applied in the building of a more vigorous personality and a more brilliant mind. A better control of all the forces of the personality may be obtained, and that mysterious something called personal magnetism may be acquired to a remarkable degree. The attainment or accumulation of personal magnetism is something that we all desire, and the reason why is evident. What is called personal magnetism is the result of an extra amount of creative energy stored up in the personality and caused to circulate harmoniously throughout the personality. And the effect of this power is very marked. People who possess it are invariably more attractive, regardless of shape and form, and they are invariably more successful, no matter what their work may be.

Hundreds of illustrations could be mentioned proving conclusively the extreme value of personal magnetism, though we are all so familiar with the fact that we do not require proof in the matter. What we want to know is what this power really is, how it may be produced, and why those who possess it have such a great advantage over those who do not possess it. To illustrate, we may take two women who look alike in every respect; who have the same character and the same mentality, and who are equals in every respect but one, and that is that the one has personal magnetism while the other has not. But we need not be told of the fact. The woman who does not possess this power cannot be compared in any way with the woman who does possess it. The woman who does possess this power is far more attractive, far more brilliant, and seems to possess qualities of far greater worth; and the reason is that personal magnetism tends to heighten the effect of everything that you are, or that you may do.

If we should compare two business men of equal ability and power, the one having personal magnetism and the other one not, we should find similar results. The one having this power would be far more successful, regardless of the fact that his ability and power in other respects were the same as his associate. Even men of ordinary ability succeed remarkably when they have personal magnetism; and we all know of women who are as plain as nature could make them, and yet being in possession of personal magnetism, are counted among the most attractive to be found anywhere.

The most ordinary human form becomes a thing of beauty if made alive with this mysterious power, and a personality that had no attraction whatever, will fascinate everybody to a marked degree if charged with this power. We all know this to be true; we are therefore deeply interested to know how this power might be secured. In the first place, we must remember that personal magnetism does not exercise its power by controlling or influencing other minds as many have supposed. The fact is if you try to influence others, you will lose this power, and lose it completely no matter how strong it may be at the present time.

The secret of personal magnetism simply lies in the fact that it tends to bring out into expression the best that is in you, and tends to heighten the effect of every expression; or, in other words, it causes every expression to act to the best advantage; though we find this power exercising its peculiar effect not only in the personality and in the mentality of the individual, but also in his work.

When a musician has this power, his music charms to a far greater degree than if he does not possess it. There is something not only in the singing voice, but also in the speaking voice that indicates the absence or presence of this power. What it is no one can exactly describe, but we know it is there, and it adds immeasurably to the quality of what is expressed through the voice.

In the field of literature we find the action of this power to be very marked. A writer who does not possess this mysterious force may write well, but there is something lacking in what he has written. On the other hand, if he has this power, he gives not only added charm to what he has written, but his ideas invariably appear to be more brilliant. In fact, there seems to be a power in everything he writes that is not ordinarily found on the printed page.

On the stage this power is one of the principal factors, and we frequently find that the only difference between the good actor and a poor one, is the possession of a high degree of personal magnetism. No matter how well an actor may act, if he lacks in this power, he cannot succeed on the stage. When we go into the social world, we find the same fact. Those who possess this power are invariably the favorites, even though they may be lacking in many other qualities. In the business world we find in every case that a man who is lacking in personal magnetism is at a disadvantage, while the one who has an abundance of this power will have no difficulty, other things being equal, in working himself to the fore.

In a deeper study of this force, we find that it affects every movement of the body, every action of the mind, and every feeling or expression that mind and personality may produce; that is, it seems to give something additional to every action or movement, and makes everything about the individual more attractive. We might say that this force sets off everything about the person to a greater advantage. This power therefore does not act directly upon others, but acts directly upon the one who has it, and thereby makes the individual more striking, as well as more attractive, both in appearance and in conduct.

What is good in you is made better if charged with this force, and every desirable effort that you may make produces a better effect in proportion. Added charm, added attractiveness and added efficiency -- these invariably follow where the individual is in possession of a marked degree of this power. That which is beautiful is many times as beautiful where personal magnetism is in action, and that which is brilliant, becomes far more brilliant when combined with this mysterious force.

Many people are born with it and apply it unconsciously, though the majority who have it, have acquired it through various forms of training. Any system of, exercise that tends to harmonize the movements of the body, will tend to increase to some extent the power of this force; though when such exercises are combined with the transmutation of creative energy, the results will be far greater. The reason for this is found in the fact that what is called personal magnetism is the result of a great deal of creative energy held in the system, or transmuted into harmonious muscular or mental activity.

The development of this power depends upon the proper training of the body in rhythmic movements, and the training of the surplus energy in the system to act harmoniously along the lines of constructive action in mind and body. A very important essential is to cultivate poise, which means peace and power combined. Try to feel deeply calm throughout your entire system, and at the same time, try to give full and positive action to every power in your system. Try to hold in your system all the energy generated, and the mere desire to do this will tend to bring about what may be called accumulation of energy.

To experiment, try for several minutes to hold all your energy in your personality, and at the same time, try to give all of that energy harmonious action within your personality. In a few moments, you will actually feel alive with power, and if you have succeeded very well with your experiment, you will really feel like a storage battery for the time being. You will have so much energy that you will feel as if you could do almost anything. Experiment in this way at frequent intervals until you get your system into the habit of carrying out this process unconsciously. You will thereby cause your surplus energy to accumulate more and more in your system, and you will produce what may be called a highly charged condition of your personality, a condition that invariably means the attainment of personal magnetism.

To secure this result, however, it is necessary to keep the mind in an undisturbed attitude, to avoid all bad habits, physical or mental, to be in harmony with everything and everybody, and to exercise full self-control under every circumstance. In cultivating this power realize that it is the result of surplus energy held in the system, and caused to circulate harmoniously through every part of the system; remember that it is a power that does not act intentionally upon persons or circumstances; that its aim is not to control or influence anybody, but simply to act within the individual self, and heighten the effect of everything that he may be or do.

17. THE BUILDING POWER OF CONSTRUCTIVE SPEECH

Never think or speak of that which you do not wish to happen.

The whine, the sting, and the sigh -- these three must never appear in a single thought or a single word.

You can win ten times as many friends by talking happiness as you can by talking trouble. And the more real friends you have the less trouble you will have.

Speak well of everything good you find and mean it. When you find what you do not like keep quiet. The less you think or speak of what you do not like the more you have of what you do like.

Magnify the good; emphasize that which has worth; and talk only of those things that should live and grow.

When you have something good to say, say it. When you have something ill to say, say something else.

There is a science of speech, and whoever wishes to promote his welfare and advancement must understand this science thoroughly and regulate his speech accordingly. Every word that is spoken exercises a power in personal life, and that power will work either for or against the person, depending upon the nature of the word. You can talk yourself into trouble, poverty or disease, and you can talk yourself into harmony, health and prosperity. In brief, you can talk yourself into almost any condition, desirable or undesirable.

Every word is an expression and every expression produces a tendency in some part of the system. This tendency may appear in the mind, in the body, in the chemical life of the body, in the world of desire, in character, among the various faculties, or anywhere in the personality, and will work itself out wherever it appears. Our expressions determine largely where we are to go, what we are to accomplish, and how we are to meet those conditions through which we may pass.

When our expressions produce tendencies towards sickness and failure, we will begin to move towards those conditions, and if the tendency is very strong, all the creative energies in the system will move in the same direction, focusing their efforts upon sickness and failure, or taking those conditions as their models, and thereby producing such conditions in the system. On the other hand, when our expressions produce tendencies towards health, happiness, power and success, we will begin to move towards those things, and in like manner create them in a measure. Every word has an inner life force, sometimes called the hidden power of words, and it is the nature of this power that determines whether the expression is to be favorable or not. This power may be constructive or destructive. It may move towards the superior or the inferior. It may promote your purpose in life or it may retard that purpose, and it is the strongest when it is deeply felt. Therefore the words which we inwardly feel are the words that act as turning points in life. When you feel that trouble is coming, and express that feeling in your speech, you are actually turning in your path and are beginning to move towards that trouble. In addition you are creating troubled conditions in your system. We all know that the more trouble we feel in the midst of trouble, the more troublesome that trouble will become. And we also know that that that

95

person who retains poise and self-control in the midst of trouble, will pass through it all without being seriously affected; and when it is over, is much wiser and stronger for the experience.

When you feel that better days are coming, and express that feeling in your speech, you turn all the power of your being towards the ideal of better days, and those powers will begin to create the better in your life. Whenever you talk about success, advancement, or any desirable condition, try to express the feeling of those things in your words. This inner feeling determines the tendencies of your creative powers; therefore, when you feel success in your speech, you cause the creative powers to create qualities in yourself that can produce success, while if you express the feeling of doubt, failure or loss in your words, those creative powers will produce inferiority, disturbance, discord, and a tendency to mistakes. It is in this way that the thing we fear comes upon us. Fear is a feeling that feels the coming of ills or other things we do not want; and as we always express through our words the feelings that we fear, we form tendencies toward those things, and the creative powers within us will produce them.

Whether the inner life force of a word will be constructive or destructive depends upon several factors, the most important of which are the tone, the motive and the idea. The tone of every word should be harmonious, wholesome, pleasing, and should convey a deep and serene expression. Words that express whines, discontent, sarcasm, aggressiveness and the like are destructive; so much so, that no one can afford to employ them under any circumstance whatever. Nothing is ever gained by complaints that are complaining, nor by criticisms that criticize. When things are not right, state so in a tone of voice that is firm and strong, but kind. A wronged customer who employs sweetness of tone as well as firmness of expression is one who will receive the first attention and the best attention, and nothing will be left unturned until the matter is set right. The words that wound others do far more injury to the person who gives them expression. No one therefore can afford to give expression to a single word that may tend to wound. Words of constructive power are always deeply felt. They are never loud or confusing, but always quiet and serene, filled with the very spirit of conviction. Never give expression to what you do not wish to encourage. The more you talk about a thing the more you help it along. The "walls have ears " and the world is full of minds that will act upon your suggestion. Never mention the dark side of anything. It will interfere with your welfare. To tell your troubles may give you temporary relief, but it is scattering sited broadcast that will produce another crop of more trouble. If you have troubles, turn your back upon them and proceed to talk about harmony, freedom, attainment and success, and feel deeply the spirit of these new and better conditions. Thus you will begin to create for yourself a new life, new opportunities, new environment and a new world. Never speak unless you have something to say that gives cheer, encouragement, information or wholesome entertainment. To talk for the mere sake of talking is to throw precious energy away, and no human chatterbox will ever acquire greatness.

The motive back of every word should be constructive, and the life expressed in every word should convey the larger, the better, and the superior. Such words have building power, and are additions to life of extreme value. Every word should express, as far as possible, the absolute truth, and should never convey ideas that are simply indicated by appearances. What is meant by speaking the absolute truth, however, is a matter that the majority do not understand, and as it is a very large subject, it would require pages to give even a brief scientific definition. But for practical purposes, the subject can be made sufficiently clear through the use of a few illustrations taken from the world's daily speech. People who think they have to say something and have nothing in particular to say, always take refuge in a brief description of the weather. In their descriptions they usually employ such expressions as "It is terribly hot," " it is an awful day," " This is terrible weather," "This is a miserably cold day," and so on. But such expressions do not change the weather, and there is no use of talking if your words are not to be of value in some way. You may say all sorts of disagreeable things about the weather without changing the weather in the least, but will such expressions leave you unchanged? Positively not ! Whenever you declare that something is horrible, you cause horrible thoughts to send their actions all through your nervous system. These actions may be weak, but many drops, no matter how small, will finally wear away a rock.

When people talk about themselves, they seldom fail to give expression to a score of detrimental statements. Here are a few: "I can't stand this," "I feel so tired," "I cannot bear to think of it," " I am thoroughly disgusted," " I am so susceptible to climatic changes," "I am so sensitive and so easily disturbed," "I am getting weak and nervous," "My memory is failing," "I am getting old," " I cannot work the way I used to," " My strength is gradually leaving me," "There is no chance for me anymore," "Everything in life is uphill work," "I have passed a miserable night," " This has been a hard day," "I have nothing but trouble and bad luck," "You know I am human and so very weak," " There is always something wrong no matter how hard you try," "You know I have to be so very careful about what I eat as nearly everything disagrees with me."

A thousand other statements, all of them destructive, might be mentioned, but anyone who understands the power of thought will realize at once that such statements can never be otherwise but injurious and should therefore be avoided absolutely. But these statements are not only injurious -- they are also untrue -- absolutely untrue in every sense of the term.

The fact is you can stand almost anything if you forget your human weakness and array yourself in spiritual strength. You do not have to get tired. Work does not make anyone tired so long as he gets eight hours of sleep every night. It is wrong thinking that makes people tired. These are scientific facts. That person who permits himself to become disgusted at anything whatever is talking himself down to the plane of inferiority. When you feel disgusted you think disgusting thoughts, and such thoughts clog the mind. You cannot afford to think disgusting thoughts simply because something else is disgusting, because we daily become like the thoughts we think. We cannot improve disagreeable things by making ourselves disagreeable. Two wrongs never made a right. The proper course is to forgive the wrong-doer, forget the wrong and then do something substantial to right the whole matter. When we think kindly of the weather, place ourselves in harmony with Nature, think properly and dress properly, we shall not be susceptible to changes in the atmosphere; but so long as we say that we are affected by changing atmospheres, we not only make ourselves negative and susceptible, but we also produce detrimental effects in our systems through our own unwholesome beliefs.

The man who constantly thinks he is easily disturbed disturbs himself. When we are in harmony with everything including ourselves and refuse to be otherwise, nothing will ever disturb us. That person who is nervous can make the matter worse by saying that he is nervous, because such a statement is a nervous statement and is full of discord. When we begin to feel nervous, we can remedy the matter absolutely by resolving to remain calm, and by employing only quiet, wholesome and constructive speech. Your words will cause you to move in the direction indicated by the nature of those words, and it is just as easy to use words that bring calmness and poise, as those that bring inharmony and confusion.

Modern science has demonstrated conclusively that there is nothing about a person that gets old. Therefore, to say that you are getting old is to persist in speaking the untruth, and it is but natural that you should reap as you sow. We must remember that a false appearance comes from the practice of judging from appearances. To state that your strength is failing is likewise to speak the untruth. There is but one strength in the universe -- the strength of the Supreme -- and that strength can never fail. You may have as much of that strength as you desire. All that is necessary for you to do is to live in perfect touch with the Supreme, and never think, do or say anything that will interfere with that sublime oneness. The strength of the Supreme is just as able to fill your system with life and power now as it was at any time in the past. Therefore, there is no real reason whatever why your power should diminish. Be true to the truth and your power will perpetually increase.

The belief that there are no opportunities for you is caused by the fact that you have hidden yourself in a cave of inferiority. Go out into the life of worth, ability and competence, and you will find more opportunities than you can use. The world is ever in search of competent minds, and modern knowledge has made it possible for man to develop his ability. No one therefore has any legitimate reason for speaking of hard luck or hard times unless he prefers to live in want. The more you complain about hard times, the harder times will become for you, while if you resolve to forget that there is such a thing as failure and proceed to make your own life as you wish it to be, the turn in the lane will surely come.

The idea that the pathway of life is all uphill work is also a false one, and if we give that idea expression we are simply placing obstacles in our way. Nothing is uphill work when we approach it properly, and there is nothing that helps more to place us in true relationship with things than true expression.

If the night has been unpleasant, never mention the fact for a moment. To talk about it will only produce more unpleasantness in your system. There is nothing wrong about the night. The unpleasantness was most likely produced by your own perverse appetite, or by some reckless inexcusable act. Forgive yourself and declare that you will never abuse nature any more. Such powerful words if repeated often, will turn the tendency of your habits, and your life will become natural and wholesome. No day would be hard if we met all things with the conviction that we are equal to every occasion. Live properly, think properly, work properly and talk properly, and trouble and ill-luck will not trouble you seriously anymore. That person who declares that there is always something wrong is always doing something to make things wrong. When we have wrong on the brain we will make many mistakes, so there will always be something wrong brewing for us. When wrong things come, set them right and look upon the experience as an opportunity for you to develop greater mastership.

When you agree with yourself, all wholesome and properly prepared food will agree with you. But you cannot expect food to agree with you so long as you are disagreeable; and to declare that this or that always disagrees with you, is to fill your system with disagreeable thoughts, disturbed actions and conditions of discord. That nature can digest food under such circumstances no one can justly expect. There is nothing that injures digestion more than the habit of finding fault with the food. If you do not think that you can eat this or that, leave it alone, but leave it alone mentally as well as physically. it is not enough to drop a disagreeable thing from your hands; you must also drop it from your mind.

Remember, you are mentally living with everything that you talk about, and there is nothing that affects us more than that which we take into our mental life. It is therefore not only necessary to speak the truth about all things, but also to avoid speaking about those things that are unwholesome. To speak about that which is wrong or inferior is never wholesome, no matter how closely we think we stand by the facts. Seeming facts, or what is called relative truth, should never receive expression unless they deal with that which is conducive to higher worth; and when circumstances compel us to make exceptions to this rule, we should avoid giving any feeling to what we say.

The greatest essential, however, is to make all speech constructive. Search for the real truth that is at the foundation of all life, and then give expression to such words as convey the full significance to that truth. The results, to say the least, will be extraordinary.

In daily conversation, the law of constructive speech should be most conscientiously applied. What we say to others will determine to a considerable degree what they are to think, and what tendencies their mental actions are to follow; and since man is the product of his thought, conversation becomes a most important factor in man.

We steadily grow into the likeness bf that which we think of the most, and what we are to think about depends largely upon the mode, the nature and the subject matter of our conversation. When conversation originates or intensifies the tendency to think about the wrong, the ordinary or the inferior, it becomes destructive, and likewise it tends to keep before mind the faults and defects that may exist in human nature. To be constructive, conversation should tend to turn attention upon the better side, the stronger side, the superior side of all things, and should give the ideal the most prominent place in thought, speech or expression. All conversation should be so formed that it may tend to move the mind towards the higher domains of thought, and should make everybody more keenly conscious of the greater possibilities that exist within them. No word should ever be spoken that will, in any way, bring the person's faults or short-comings before his mind, nor should any form of speech be permitted that may cause sadness, offence, depression or pain. Every word should convey hope, encouragement and sunshine.

To constantly remind a person of his faults is to cause him to become more keenly conscious of those faults. He will think more and more about his faults, and will thereby cause his faults to become more prominent and more troublesome than they ever were before. The more we think about our weakness, the weaker we become; and the more we talk about weakness, the more we think about weakness. Conversation therefore should never touch upon those things that we do not wish to retain or develop. The only way to remove weakness is to develop strength, and to develop strength we must keep attention constantly upon the quality of strength. We develop what we think about provided all thinking has depth, quality and continuity.

Conversation has exceptional value in the training of young minds, and in many instances may completely change the destinies of these minds. To properly train a child, his attention should be directed as much as possible upon those qualities that have worth and that are desired in his development; and the way he is spoken to will largely determine where he is to give the greater part of his attention. To scold a child is to remind him of his faults. Every time he is reminded of his faults he gives more attention, more thought, and more strength to those faults. His good qualities are thereby made weaker while his bad qualities are made worse. It is not possible to improve the mind and the character of the child by constantly telling him not to do " this " or " that." As a rule, it will increase his desire to do this other thing, and he will cease only through fear, or after having wasted a great deal of time in experiences that have become both disgusting and bitter.

It is the tendency of every mind to desire to do what it is told not to do, the reason being that negative commands are nearly always associated with fear; and when mind is in the attitude of fear, or dread or curiosity, it is very easily impressed by whatever it may be thinking about.

When we are warned we either enter a state of fear or one of curiosity, and while in those states, our minds are so deeply and so easily impressed by that from which we are warned, that we give it our whole attention. The result is we think so much about it that we become almost completely absorbed in it; and we are carried away, so to speak, not away from the danger, but into it. When anyone is going wrong, it is a mistake to warn him not to go further. It is also a mistake to leave him alone. The proper course is to call his attention to something better, and frame our conversation in such a way that he becomes wholly absorbed in the better. He will then forget his old mistakes, his old faults and his old desires, and will give all his life and power to the building of that better which has engaged his new interest.

The same law may be employed to prevent sickness and failure. When the mind becomes so completely absorbed in perfect health that all sickness is forgotten, all the powers of mind will proceed to create health, and every trace of sickness will soon disappear. When the mind becomes so completely absorbed in higher attainments and in greater achievements that all thought of failure is forgotten, all the forces of mind will begin to work for the promotion of those attainments and achievements. The person will be gaining ground every day, and greater success will positively follow.

To cause the mind to forget the wrong, the lesser and the inferior, constructive conversation may be employed with unfailing results; in fact, such conversation must be employed if the mind is to advance and develop. Our conversation must be in perfect accord with our ambitions, our desires, and our ideals, and all our expressions must aim to promote the real purpose we have in view.

It is the tendency of nearly every mind to try to make his friends perfect according to his own idea of perfection, and he usually proceeds by constantly talking to his friends about their faults, and what they should not do in order to become as perfect as his ideal. Parents, as a rule, do the same with their children, not knowing that through this method many are made worse; and it is only those who are very strong in mind and character that are not adversely affected by this method.

To help our friends or our children to become ideal, we should never mention their faults. Our conversation should deal with the strong points of character and the greater possibilities of mind. We should so frame our conversation that we tend to make everybody feel there is something in them. Our conversation should have an optimistic tendency and an ascending tone. It should deal with those things in life that are worthwhile, and it should always give the ideal the greatest prominence. Weaknesses of human nature should be recognized as little as possible, and should seldom, if ever, be mentioned.

When people engage in destructive conversation in our midst we should try to change the subject, by calling their attention to the better side. There always is another and a better side; and when examined closely will be found to be far greater and infinitely more important than the ordinary side. Admirable qualities exist everywhere, and it will prove profitable to give these our undivided attention.

18. IMAGINATION AND THE MASTER MIND

The first mark of a master mind is that he is able to promote his own perpetual improvement. The second is that he is able to be strong, joyous and serene under every circumstance.

The imagining faculty is the creative faculty of the mind, the faculty that creates plans, methods and ideas. Our imagination therefore must always be clear, lofty, wholesome, and constructive if we would create superior ideas and build for greater things.

Before you can have greater success you must become a greater man. Before you can become a greater man you must reach out toward the new and the greater along all lines; and this is possible only through the constructive use of imagination.

You get your best ideas when your mind acts in the upper story. And in all fields of action it is the best ideas that win.

The forces of the human system must have something definite to work for; that is, they must have an ideal upon which to concentrate their attention, or some model or pattern to follow as they proceed with their constructive actions.

To form this model, it is the power of imagination that must be employed, and that power must, in each case, be applied constructively. What we imagine becomes a pattern for the creative energies of mind and personality, and as the creations of these energies determine what we are to become and attain, we realize that the imaging faculty is one of the most important of all our faculties. We therefore cannot afford to lose a moment in learning how to apply it according to the laws of mental construction and growth.

To proceed, imagine yourself becoming and attaining what you wish to become and attain. This will give your energies a model, both of your greater future self and your greater future achievements. When you think of your future, always imagine success and greater things, and have no fear as to results. If you fear, you give your creative energies a model of failure, and they will accordingly proceed to create failure. Then we must also remember if we wish to succeed, our faculties must work successfully, but no faculty can work successfully when filled with fear. It is only when constantly inspired by the idea of success that any faculty or power in the human system can do its best.

To inspire our faculties with this idea, we should always imagine ourselves obtaining success. The picture of success should be placed upon all the walls of the mind, so that the powers within us will see success, and success only as their goal. Hang up pictures in your mind that will inspire you to do your best; hang up pictures in your mind that will cause you to think constantly of that which you desire to accomplish, and this you may do by imagining yourself being that greater something that you want to be and doing that greater something that you want to do.

An excellent practice is to use your spare moments in creating such pictures in your imagination and placing them in the most conspicuous position of your mind, so that all your faculties and powers can see them at all times. We are always imagining something. It is practically impossible to be awake without imagining something. Then why not imagine something at all times that will inspire the powers within us to do greater and greater things?

To aid the imagination in picturing the greater, the higher and better, we should "hitch our wagon to a star." The star may be something quite out of reach as far as present circumstances indicate, but if we hitch our wagon to something in such a lofty position, our mind will begin to take wings. It will no longer be like a worm crawling in the dust. We shall begin to rise and continue to rise.

The only thing that can cause the mind to rise is imagination. The only thing that can make the mind larger than it is, is imagination. The only thing that can make the mind act along new lines is imagination. This being true, it is unwise to use the imagination for any other purpose than for the best that we can think or do.

In this connection, there are a few suggestions that will be found of special value. First, make up your mind as to what you really want in every respect. Determine what surroundings or environment you want. Decide upon the kind of friends you want and what kind of work you would prefer. Make all those ideals so good and so perfect that you will have no occasion to change them. Then fix those ideals so clearly in mind that you can see them at all times, and proceed to desire their realization with all the power of mind and soul. Make that your first step.

Your second step should be to imagine yourself living in those surroundings that you have selected as your ideal; then make it a point to live in that imagination every moment of every day. Instead of imagining a number of useless things during spare moments, as people usually do, imagine yourself living in those surroundings and those ideals. Imagine yourself in the presence of friends that are exactly what you wish your ideal friends to be, and permit your fancy to run as far as it may wish along all of those idealistic lines. If you have not found your work, proceed to imagine yourself doing what you wish to do. If you have already found your work, imagine yourself doing that work as well as you would wish, and imagine the coming of results as large as your greatest desires could expect. Devote every moment of your spare time to the placing of those ideals before your attention, and you will give your power and forces something strong and definite to work for.

Every mental force is an artist, and it paints according to the model. What you imagine is the model, and there is not a single mental action that is not inspired or called forth into action by some picture or model which the imagination has produced.

The imagination can call forth the ordinary or the extraordinary. It can give the powers of your being an inferior model or an extraordinary model, and if the imagination is not directed to produce the extraordinary and the superior, it is quite likely to produce the ordinary and the inferior. Your second step, therefore, should be to imagine yourself actually living in those surroundings that you have selected as your ideal, and in actually becoming and doing what you are determined to become and do.

This practice would, in the first place, give you a great deal of pleasure, because if you have definite ideals and imagine yourself attaining those ideals, you will certainly enjoy yourself to a marked degree for the time being. But in addition to that enjoyment, you will gradually and steadily be training your mind to work for those greater things. The mind will work for that which is upper most in thought and imagination. Therefore, we should invariably place our highest ideals uppermost, so that the whole of our attention may be concentrated upon those ideals, and all the powers of our mind and personality directed to work for those ideals.

Your third step should be to proceed to apply the power of desire, the power of will, the power of scientific thought, and in brief, all your powers, in trying to realize those beautiful ideals that you continue to imagine as your own. Do as the ancient Hebrews did. First make your prediction. Then go to work and make it come true. What you imagine concerning your greater future is your prediction, and you can cause that prediction to come true if you apply all the power in your possession in working for its realization every day

The constructive use of imagination therefore will enable you to place a definite model or pattern before the forces of your system, so that those forces may have something better and greater to work for. In brief, instead of permitting most of your energies to go to waste and the remainder to follow any pattern or idea that may be suggested by your environment, or your own helter-skelter thinking, you will cause all your energy to work for the greatest and the best that you may desire.

This is the first use of imagination, and it easily places this remarkable faculty among the greatest in the human mind. Another use of the imagination is found in its power to give the mind something definite to think about at all times, so that the mind may be trained to always think of that which you really want to think; that is, through this use of the imagination, you can select your own thought and think your own thought at all times; and he who can do this is gradually becoming a master mind.

The master mind is the mind that thinks what it wants to think, regardless of what circumstances, environment or associations may suggest. The mind that masters itself creates its own ideas, thoughts and desires through the original use of imagination, or its own imaging faculty. The mind that does not master itself forms its thoughts and desires after the likeness of the impressions received through the senses, and is therefore controlled by those conditions from which, such impressions come; because as we think, so we act and live. The average mind usually desires what the world desires without any definite thought as to his own highest welfare or greatest need, the reason being that a strong tendency to do likewise is always produced in the mind when the desires are formed in the likeness of such impressions as are suggested by external conditions. It is therefore evident that the person who permits himself to be affected by suggestions will invariably form artificial desires; and to follow such desires is to be misled.

The master mind desires only that which is conducive to real life and in the selection of its desires is never influenced in the least by the desires of the world. Desire is one of the greatest powers in human life. It is therefore highly important that every desire be normal and created for the welfare of the individual himself. But no desire can be wholly normal that is formed through the influence of suggestion. Such desires are always abnormal to some degree, and easily cause the individual to be misplaced. A great many people are misplaced. They do not occupy those places wherein they may be their best and accomplish the most. They are working at a disadvantage, and are living a life that is far inferior to what they are intended to live. The cause is frequently found in abnormal or artificial desires. They have imitated the desires of others without consulting their present needs. They have formed the desire to do what others are doing by permitting their minds to be influenced by suggestions and impressions from the world, forgetting what their present state of development makes them capable of doing now. By imitating the lives, habits, actions and desires of others, they are led into a life not their own; that is, they are misplaced.

The master mind is never misplaced because he does not live to do what others are doing, but what he himself wants to do now. He wants to do only that which is conducive to real life, a life worthwhile, a life that steadily works up to the very highest goal in view.

The average mind requires a change of environment before he can change his thought. He has to go somewhere or bring into his presence something that will suggest a new line of thinking and feeling. The master mind, however, can change his thought whenever he so desires. A change of scene is not necessary, because such a mind is not controlled from without. A change of scene will not produce a change of thought in the master mind unless he so elects. The master mind changes his thoughts, ideals or desires by imaging upon the mind the exact likeness of the new ideas, the new thoughts, and the new desires that have been selected.

The secret of the master mind is found wholly in the intelligent use of imagination. Man is as he thinks, and his thoughts are patterned after the predominating mental images, whether those images are impressions suggested from without, or impressions formed by the ego acting from within. When man permits his thoughts and desires to be formed in the likeness of impressions received from without, he will be more or less controlled by environment and he will be in the hands of fate, but when he transforms every impression received from without into an original idea and incorporates that idea into a new mental image, he uses environment as a servant, thereby placing fate in his own hands.

Every object that is seen will produce an impression upon the mind according to the degree of susceptibility. This impression will contain the nature of the object of which it is a representation. The nature of this object will be reproduced in the mind, and what has entered the mind will be expressed more or less throughout the entire system. Therefore, the mind that is susceptible to suggestions will reproduce in his own mind and system conditions that are similar in nature to almost everything that he may see, hear or feel. He will consequently be a reflection of the world in which he lives. He will think, speak and act as that world may suggest; he will float with the stream of that world wherever that stream may flow; he will not be an original character, but an automaton.

Every person that permits himself to be affected by suggestion is more or less an automaton, and is more or less in the hands of fate. To place fate in his own hands, he must use suggestions intelligently instead of blindly following those desires and thoughts that his surroundings may suggest. We are surrounded constantly by suggestions of all kinds, because everything has the power to suggest something to that mind that is susceptible, and we are all more or less susceptible in this respect. But there is a vast difference between permitting oneself to be susceptible to suggestion and training oneself to intelligently use those impressions that suggestions may convey.

The average writer on suggestion not only ignores this difference, but encourages susceptibility to suggestion by impressing the reader with the remark that suggestion does control the world. If it is true that suggestion controls the world, more or less, we want to learn how to so use suggestion that its control of the human mind will decrease steadily; and this we can accomplish, not by teaching people how to use suggestion for the influencing of other minds, but in using those impressions conveyed by suggestion in the reconstruction of their own minds. Suggestion is a part of life, because everything has the power to suggest, and all minds are open to impressions. Nothing therefore can be said against suggestion by itself. Suggestion is a factor in our midst; it is a necessary factor. The problem is to train ourselves to make intelligent use of the impressions received, instead of blindly following the desires produced by those impressions as the majority do.

To proceed in the solution of this problem, never permit objects discerned by the senses to reproduce themselves in your mind against your will. Form your own ideas about what you see, hear or feel, and try to make those ideas superior to what was suggested by the objects discerned. When you see evil do not form ideas that are in the likeness of that evil; do not think of the evil as bad, but try to understand the forces that are back of that evil -- forces that are good in themselves, though misdirected in their present state. By trying to understand the nature of the power that is back of evil or adversity, you will not form bad ideas, and therefore will feel no bad effects from experiences that may seem undesirable. At the same time, you will think your own thought about the experiences, thereby developing the power of the master mind.

Surround yourself as far as possible with those things that suggest the superior, but do not permit such suggestions to determine your thought about the superior. Those superior impressions that are suggested by superior environment should be used in forming still more superior thoughts. If you wish to be a master mind, your thought must always be higher than the thought your environment may suggest, no matter how ideal that environment may be. Every impression that enters the mind through the senses should be worked out and should be made to serve the mind in its fullest capacity. In this way the original impression will not reproduce itself in the mind, but will become instrumental in giving the mind a number of new and superior ideas. To work out an impression, try to see through its whole nature. Look at it from every conceivable point of view, and try to discern its actions, tendencies, possibilities and probable defects. Use your imagination in determining what you want to think or do, what you are to desire and what your tendencies are to be. Know what you want, and then image those things upon the mind constantly. This will develop the power to think what you want to think, and he who can think what he wants to think is on the way to becoming what he wants to become.

The principal reason why the average person does not realize his ideals is because he has not learned to think what he wants to think. He is too much affected by the suggestions that are about him. He imitates the world too much, following desires that are not his own. He is therefore misled and misplaced. Whenever you permit yourself to think what persons, things, conditions or circumstances may suggest, you are not following what you yourself want to think. You are not following your own desires but borrowed desires. You will therefore drift into strange thinking, and thinking that is entirely different from what you originally planned. To obey the call of every suggestion and permit your mind to be carried away by this, that or the other, will develop the tendency to drift until your mind will wander. Concentration will be almost absent and you will become wholly incapable of actually thinking what you want to think. One line of constructive thinking will scarcely be begun when another line will be suggested, and you will leave the unfinished task to begin something else, which in turn will be left incomplete. Nothing, therefore, will be accomplished. To become a master mind, think what you want to think, no matter what your surroundings may suggest; and continue to think what you want to think until that particular line of thought or action has been completed. Desire what you want to desire and impress that desire so deeply upon consciousness that it cannot possibly be disturbed by those foreign desires that environment may suggest; and continue to express that desire with all the life and power that is in you until you get what you want. When you know that you are in the right desire, do not permit anything to influence your mind to change. Take such suggestions and convert them into the desire you have already decided upon, thereby giving that desire additional life and power. Never close your mind to impressions from without. Keep the mind open to the actions of all those worlds that may exist in your sphere and try to gain valuable impressions from every source, but do not blindly follow those impressions. Use them constructively in building up your own system of original thought. Think what you want to think, and so use every impression you receive that you gain greater power to think what you want to think. Thus you will gradually become a master mind.

19. THE HIGHER FORCES IN MAN

Follow the vision of the soul. Be true to your ideals no matter what may happen now. Then things will take a turn and the very things you wanted to happen will happen.

The ideal has a positive drawing power towards the higher, the greater, and the superior. Whoever gives his attention constantly to the ideal, therefore, will steadily rise in the scale.

Take things as they are today and proceed at once to make them better.

Expect every change to lead you to something better and it will. As your faith is so shall it be.

To be human as not to be weak. To be human is to be all that there is in man, and the greatness that as contained in the whole of man is marvelous indeed.

It is the most powerful among the forces of the human system that we least understand, and though this may seem unfortunate, it is not unnatural. All advancement is in the ascending scale. We learn the simplest things first and the least valuable in the beginning. Later on, we learn that which is more important. We find therefore the greatest forces among those that are almost entirely hidden, and for that reason they are sometimes called the hidden forces, the finer forces, or the higher forces.

As it is in man, so it is also in nature. We find the most powerful among natural forces to be practically beyond comprehension. Electricity is an illustration. There is no greater force known in nature, and yet no one has thus far been able to determine what this force actually is. The same is true with regard to other natural forces; the greater they are and the more powerful they are, the more difficult it is to understand them. In the human system, there are a number of forces of exceptional value that we know nothing about; that is, we do not understand their real nature, but we can learn enough about the action, the purpose and the possibilities of those forces to apply them to practical life; and it is practical application with which we are most concerned.

The field of the finer forces in mind may be termed the unconscious mental field, and the vastness of this field, as well as the possibilities of its functions, is realized when we learn that the greater part of our mental world is unconscious. Only a fraction of the mental world of man is on the surface or up in consciousness; the larger part is submerged in the depths of what might be called a mental sea of subconsciousness. All modern psychologists have come to this conclusion, and it is a fact that anyone can demonstrate in his own experience if he will take the time.

In the conscious field of the human mind, we find those actions of which we are aware during what may be called our wide-awake state; and they are seemingly insignificant in comparison with the actions of the vast unconscious world, though our conscious actions are found to be highly important when we learn that it is the conscious actions that originate unconscious actions. And here let us remember that it is our unconscious actions that determine our own natures, our own capabilities, as well as our own destiny. In our awakened state we continue to think and act in a small mental field, but all of those actions are constantly having their effect upon this vast unconscious field that is found beneath the mental surface.

To realize the existence of this unconscious mental world, and to realize our power to determine the actions of that world, is to awaken within us a feeling that we are many times as great and as capable as we thought we were, and the more we think of this important fact, the larger becomes our conscious view of life and its possibilities.

To illustrate the importance of the unconscious field and your finer forces, we will take the force of love. No one understands the nature of this force, nor has anyone been able to discover its real origin or its actual possibilities; nevertheless, it is a force that is tremendously important in human life. Its actions are practically hidden, and we do not know what constitutes the inner nature of those actions, but we do know how to control those actions in a measure for our own good; and we have discovered that when we do control and properly direct the actions of love, its value to everybody concerned is multiplied many times. It is the same with a number of other forces with which we are familiar. They act along higher or finer lines of human consciousness, and they are so far beyond ordinary comprehension that we cannot positively know what they are, but we do know enough about them to control them and direct them for our best and greatest good.

In like manner, the unconscious mental field, though beyond scientific analysis, is sufficiently understood as to its modes of action, so that we can control and direct those actions as we may choose. When we analyze what comes forth from the unconscious field at any time, we find that it is invariably the result of something that we caused to be placed in that field during some past time. This leads up to the discovery of unconscious mental processes, and it is not difficult to prove the existence of such processes.

Many a time ideas, desires, feelings or aspirations come to the surface of thought that we are not aware of having created at any time. We come to the conclusion, therefore, that they were produced by some unconscious process, but when we examine those ideas or desires carefully, we find that they are simply effects corresponding exactly with certain causes that we previously placed in action in our conscious world. When we experiment along this line we find that we can produce a conscious process at any time, and through deep feeling cause it to enter the unconscious mental world. In that deeper world, it goes to work and produces according to its nature, the results coming back to the surface of our conscious mentality days, weeks or months later.

The correspondence between conscious and unconscious mental processes may be illustrated by a simple movement in physical action. If a physical movement began at a certain point, and was caused to act with a circular tendency, it would finally come back to its starting point. It is the same with every conscious action that is deeply felt. It goes out into the vastness of the unconscious mental field, and having a circular tendency, as all mental actions have, it finally comes back to the point where it began; and in coming back, brings with it the result of every unconscious experience through which it passed on its circular journey.

To go into this subject deeply, and analyze every phase of it would be extremely interesting; in fact, it would be more interesting than fiction. It would require, however, a large book to do it justice. For this reason, we can simply touch upon the practical side of it, but will aim to make this brief outline sufficiently clear to enable anyone to direct his unconscious process in such a way as to secure the best results.

Every mental process, or every mental action, that takes place in our wide-awake consciousness will, if it has depth of feeling or intensity, enter the unconscious field, and after it has developed itself according to the line of its original nature, will return to the conscious side of the mind. Here we find the secret of character building, and also the secret of building faculties and talents. Everything that is done in the conscious field to improve the mind, character, conduct or thought will, if it has sincerity and depth of feeling, enter the unconscious field; and later will come back with fully developed qualities, which when in expression, constitutes character.

Many a man, however, after trying for some time to improve himself and seeing no results, becomes discouraged. He forgets that some time always intervenes between the period of sowing and the period of reaping. What he does in the conscious field to improve himself, constitutes the sowing, when those actions enter the conscious field to be developed: and when they come back, it may be weeks or months later, the reaping time has arrived. Many a time, after an individual has given up self-improvement, he discovers, after a considerable period, that good qualities are beginning to come to the surface in his nature, thereby proving conclusively that what he did months ago along that line was not in vain. The results of past efforts are beginning to appear. We have all had similar experiences, and if we would carefully analyze such experiences, we would find that not a single conscious process that is sufficiently deep or intense to become an unconscious process will fail to come back finally with its natural results.

Many a time ideas come into our minds that we wanted weeks ago, and could not get them at that time; but we did place in action certain deep, strong desires for those ideas, at that particular time, and though our minds were not prepared to develop those ideas at once, they finally were developed and came to the surface. The fact that this process never fails indicates the value of giving the mind something to work out for future need. If we have something that we want to do months ahead, we should give the mind definite instruction now and make those instructions so deep, that they will become unconscious processes.

Those unconscious processes will, according to directions, work out the ideas and plans that we want for that future work, and in the course of time, will bring results to the surface. To go into detail along the line of this part of our study would also be more interesting than fiction, but again, a large book would be required to do it justice. However, if we make it a practice to place in action our best thoughts, our best ideas and our best desires now and every moment of the eternal now, we will be giving the unconscious mental field something good to work for at all times; and as soon as each product is finished, or ready to be delivered from the unconscious world, it will come to the surface, and will enter the conscious mind ready for use.

Some of the best books that have been written have been worked out during months of unconscious mental processes; the same is true with regard to inventions, dramas, musical compositions, business plans, and in fact, anything and everything of importance that could be mentioned. Every idea, every thought, every feeling, every desire, every mental action, may, under certain circumstances, produce an unconscious process corresponding with itself, and this process will in every instance bring back to consciousness the result of its work. When we realize this, and realize the vast possibilities of the unconscious field, we will see the advantage of placing in action as many good unconscious processes as possible. Give your unconscious mental world something important to do every hour. Place a new seed in that field every minute. It may take weeks or months before that seed brings forth its fruit, but it will bring forth, after its kind, in due time without fail.

We understand therefore, how we can build character by sowing seeds of character in this field, and how we can, in the same way, build desirable conduct, a different disposition, different mental tendencies, stronger and greater mental faculties, and more perfect talents along any line. To direct these unconscious processes, it is necessary to apply the finer forces of the system, as it is those forces that invariably determine how those processes are to act. Those forces, however, are very easily applied, as all that is necessary in the beginning is to give attention to the way we feel. The way we feel determines largely what our finer forces are to be and how they are to act, and there is not an hour when we do not feel certain energies at work in our system. All the finer forces are controlled by feeling. Try to feel what you want done either in the conscious or the unconscious mental fields, and you will place in action forces that correspond to what you want done. Those forces will enter the unconscious mental world and produce processes through which the desired results will be created.

Whenever you want to redirect any force that is highly refined, you must feel the way you want that force to act. To illustrate, we will suppose you have certain emotions in your mental world that are not agreeable. To give the energies of those emotions a new and more desirable force of action, change your emotions by giving your whole attention in trying to feel such emotions as you may desire. And here let us remember that every emotion that comes up in the system is teeming with energy; but as most emotions continue to act without any definite control, we realize how much energy is wasted through uncurbed emotions. We know from experience, that whenever we give way to our feelings, we become weak. The reason is that uncontrolled feeling wastes energy . A great many people who are very intense in their feelings, actually become sick whenever they give way to strong or deep emotions. On the other hand, emotions that are controlled and properly directed, not only prevent waste, but will actually increase the strength of mind and body.

Here is a good practice. Whenever you feel the way you do not wish to feel, begin to think deeply and in the most interesting manner possible, of those things that you wish to accomplish. If you can throw your whole soul, so to speak, into those new directions, you will soon find your undesired feelings disappearing completely. Every individual should train himself to feel the way he wants to feel, and this is possible if he will always direct his attention to something desirable whenever undesired feelings come up. Through this practice he will soon get such full control over his feelings that he can always feel the way he wants to feel, no matter what the circumstances may be. He will thus gain the power not only of controlling his emotions and using constructively all those energies that invariably appear in his emotions, but he will also have found the secret of continued happiness. Whenever mental energy moves in a certain direction, it tends to build up power for good along that line. We realize therefore the value of directing all our attention upon those things in mind, character and life that we wish to build and develop.

In building character we find the results to be accumulative; that is, we make an effort to improve our life or conduct, and thereby produce an unconscious process, which will later on, give us more strength of character to be and live the way we wish to be and live. This in turn will enable us to produce more and stronger unconscious processes along the line of character building, which will finally return with a greater number of good qualities. The result of this action will be to give us more power to build for a still greater character, and so this process may be continued indefinitely.

The same is true with regard to building the mind. The more you build the mind, the greater becomes your mental power to build a still greater mind: but in each case, it is the unconscious process that must be produced in order that the greater character or greater mind may be developed from within. In this connection, it is well to remember that the principal reason why so many people fail to improve along any line is because their desires or efforts for improvement are not sufficiently deep and strong to become unconscious processes. To illustrate, it is like placing seed on stony ground. If the seed is not placed in good, deep soil it will not grow. You may desire self-improvement for days, but if those desires are weak or superficial, they will not enter the unconscious field; and any action, however good it may be, if it fails to enter the unconscious field, will also fail to produce results along the line of self -improvement. With regard to the building of character, we must also remember that character determines in a large measure the line of action of all the other forces in the human system. If your character is strong and well developed, every force that you place in action will be constructive; while if your character is weak, practically all your forces will go astray. This is not true in the moral field alone, but also in the field of mental achievement. If the character is weak, your ability will be mostly misdirected no matter how hard you may work, or how sincere you may be in your effort to do your best. This explains why a great many people do not realize their ideals. They have paid no attention to character building, and therefore, nearly every effort that they may have made in trying to work up towards their ideals, has been misdirected and sent astray. Whatever our ideals may be therefore, or how great our desires may be to realize those ideals, we must first have character; and even though we may be able to place in action the most powerful forces in the human system, we will not get results until we have character. It is character alone that can give the powers of man constructive direction, and it is a well-known fact that those people who have a strong, firm, well-developed character easily move from the good to the better, no matter what the circumstances.

What may be called the higher forces in man act invariably through our most sublime states of consciousness, and as it is these higher forces that enable man to become or accomplish more than the average, it is highly important that we attain the power to enter sublime consciousness at frequent intervals. No man or woman of any worth was ever known, who did not have experience in these sublime states; in fact, it is impossible to rise above the ordinary in life or achievement without drawing, more or less, upon the higher realms of consciousness.

People are sometimes criticized for not being on the earth all the time, but it is necessary to get above the earth occasionally in order to find something worthwhile to live for and work for while upon earth. The most powerful forces in human life can be drawn down to earth for practical use, but to get them we must go to the heights frequently. No one can write music unless his consciousness touches the sublime. No one can write real poetry unless he has the same experience. No one can evolve ideas worthwhile unless his mind transcends the so-called practical sphere of action, and no individual can rise in the world of attainment and achievement unless his mind dwells almost constantly on the verge of the sublime.

Examine the minds of people of real worth, people who have something in them, people who are beyond the average, people who are rising in the scale, people whom we truly admire, people that we look up to, people who occupy high positions -- positions that they have actually won through merit -- and we find in every instance, that their minds touch frequently the sublime state of consciousness. When we touch that state, our minds are drawn up above the ordinary, and mental actions are developed and worked out that are superior to ordinary or average mental actions. It is therefore simply understood that experience in sublime consciousness if properly employed, will invariably make man greater and better.

When we look upon a man that we can truthfully say is a real man, we find that something unusual has been or is being expressed in his personality; and that something unusual is hidden in every personality. It is a hidden power, a hidden force, which, when placed in action, gives man superior worth, both as to character, ability and life. Real men and real women, people who are real in the true sense of the term, are always born from the sublime state of consciousness; that is, they have, through coming in contact with higher regions of thought, evolved greater worth in their own minds and personalities; and as this possibility is within reach of every man or woman, we see the importance of dealing thoroughly with these higher powers in human nature.

Whenever we touch those finer states in the upper regions of the mind, we invariably feel that we have gained something superior, something that we did not possess before; and the gaining of that something invariably makes life stronger as well as finer. The ordinary has been, in a measure, overcome, and that which is beyond the ordinary is being gradually evolved. If we would rise in the scale in the fullest and best sense of the term, we must pay close attention to those higher forces and make it a practice to enter frequently into close touch with higher states of consciousness; in fact, we simply must do it, because if we do not we will continue to move along a very ordinary level. Then we must also bear in mind that it is our purpose to use all the forces we possess, not simply those that we can discern on the outside or that we are aware of in external consciousness, but also those finer and more powerful forces which we can control and direct only when we ascend to the heights.

In dealing with these greater powers in man, it will be worth our while to reconsider briefly the psychological field. As long as the mind acts on the surface of consciousness, we have very little control of those finer elements in human life, but when the mind goes into the depths of feeling, into the depths of realization, or into what is called the psychological field, then it is that it touches everything that has real worth or that has the power to evolve, produce or develop still greater worth. It is the active forces of the psychological field that determine everything that is to take place in the life of man, both within himself and in his external destiny. We must therefore learn to act through the psychological field if we would master ourselves and create our own future.

The psychological field can be defined as that field of subconscious action that permeates the entire personality, or that fills, so to speak, every atom of the physical man on a finer plane. The psychological field is a finer field, permeating the ordinary tangible physical elements of life, and we enter this field whenever our feelings are deep and sincere. The fact that the psychological field determines real worth, as well as the attainment of greater worth, is easily demonstrated in everyday experience. When a man has anything in him, his nature is always deep. The same is true of people of refinement or culture: there is depth to their natures, and the man of character invariably lives in that greater world of life and power that is back of, or beneath, the surface of consciousness. If there is something in you, you both live and act through the deeper realms of your life, and those realms constitute the psychological field.

Among the many important forces coming directly through emotion or feeling, one of the most valuable is that of enthusiasm. In the average mind, enthusiasm runs wild, but we have found that when this force is properly directed it becomes a great constructive power. When you are enthusiastic about something, it is always about something new or something better -- something that holds possibilities that you did not realize before. Your enthusiasm, if properly directed, will naturally cause your mind to move towards those possibilities, and enthusiasm is readily directed when you concentrate attention exclusively upon that something new that inspires enthusiasm. By turning your attention upon the thing that produces enthusiasm, the mind will move forward toward those greater possibilities that are discerned. This forward movement of the mind will tend to renew and enlarge the mind so that it will gain a still greater conception of those possibilities. This will increase your enthusiasm, which will in turn impel your mind to move forward still further in the same direction. Thus a still larger conception of those possibilities will be secured, which in turn will increase your enthusiasm and the power of your mind to take a third step in advance.

We thus realize that if enthusiasm is directed upon the possibilities that originally inspired that enthusiasm, we will not only continue to be enthused, but we will in that very manner, cause the mind to move forward steadily and develop steadily, so that in time it will gain sufficient power to actually work out those possibilities upon which attention has been directed. In this connection, we must also remember that we can grow and advance only as we pass into the new. It is new life, new thought, new states of consciousness that are demanded if we are to take any steps at all in advance, and as enthusiasm tends directly to inspire the mind to move towards the new, we see how important it is to continue, not only to live in the spirit of enthusiasm, but to direct that spirit upon the goal in view. It is invariably the enthusiastic mind that moves forward, that does things, and that secures results. Two other forces of great value, belonging to this group, are appreciation and gratitude. Whenever you appreciate a certain thing you become conscious of its real quality, and whenever you become conscious of the quality of anything, you begin to develop that quality in yourself. When we appreciate the worth of a person, we tend to impress the idea of that worth in our own minds, and thereby cause the same effect to be produced, in a measure, in ourselves. The same is true if we appreciate our own worth, in a sensible and constructive manner. If we appreciate what we already are, and are ambitious to become still more, we focus our minds upon the greater, and employ what we already possess as stepping-stones towards the greater attainment; but when we do not appreciate ourselves, there are no stepping stones that we can use in attaining greater things. We thus realize why people that do not appreciate themselves never accomplish much, and why they finally go downgrade in nearly every instance. When we appreciate the beautiful in anything, we awaken our minds to a higher and better understanding of the beautiful. Our minds thus become, in a measure, more beautiful. The same is true with regard to any quality. Whatever we appreciate, we tend to develop in ourselves, and here we find a remarkable aid to the power of concentration, because we always concentrate attention perfectly, naturally and thoroughly upon those things that we fully appreciate. Thus we understand why it is that we tend to develop in ourselves the things that we admire in others.

Whenever you feel grateful for anything, you always feel nearer to the real quality of that particular thing. A person who is ungrateful, however, always feels that there is a wall between himself and the good things in life. Usually there is such a wall, though he has produced it himself through his ingratitude. But the man who is grateful for everything, places himself in that attitude where he may come in closer contact with the best thing; everywhere; and we know very well that the most grateful people always receive the best attention everywhere. We all may meet disappointment at some time and not get exactly what we wanted, but we shall find that the more grateful we are, the less numerous will those disappointments become. It has been well said that no one feels inclined to give his best attention to the man who is always "knocking," and it is literally true. On the other hand, if you are really grateful and mean it, it is very seldom that you do not receive the best attention from everybody wherever you may go. The most important side of this law, however, is found in the fact that the more grateful you are for everything good that comes into your life, the more closely you place your mind in contact with that power in life that can produce greater good.

Another among the finer forces is that of aspiration. No person should fail to aspire constantly and aspire to the very highest that he can possibly awaken in his life. Aspiration always tends to elevate the mind and tends to lift the mind into larger and greater fields of action. And when the mind finds itself in this larger field of action, it will naturally gain power to do greater things. We all realize that so long as we live down in the lower story, we cannot accomplish very much; it is when we lift our minds to the higher stories of the human structure that we begin to gain possession of ideas and powers through which greater things may be achieved.

The same is true of ambition. Ambition not only tends to draw the mind up into higher and larger fields, but also tends to build up those faculties through which we are to work. If you are tremendously ambitious to do a certain thing, the force of that ambition will tend to increase the power and ability of that faculty through which your ambition may be realized. To illustrate, if you are ambitious to succeed in the business world, the force of that ambition if very strong, will constantly make your business faculties stronger and more able, so that finally your business ability will have become sufficiently great to carry your ambition through. You cannot be too ambitious, provided you are ambitious for something definite and continue to give your whole life and soul to that which you expect or desire to accomplish through that ambition.

When we know the power of ambition, and know that anybody can be ambitious, we realize that anyone can move forward. No matter what his position may be, or where he may be, he can, through the power of ambition begin to gain ground, and continue to gain ground indefinitely. The average mind, however, has very little ambition, and makes no effort to arouse this tremendous force; but we may depend upon the fact that when this force is fully aroused in any mind, a change for the better must positively come before long.

The force of an ideal is another among the finer forces that should receive constant and thorough attention. When you have an ideal and live for it every second of your existence, you place yourself in the hands of a drawing power that is immense, and that power will tend to draw out into action every force, power and faculty that you may possess, especially those forces and qualities that will have to be developed in order that you may realize that ideal.

Have an ideal, and the highest that you can picture. Then worship it every hour with your whole soul. Never come down, and do not neglect it for a moment. We all know very well that it is the people who actually worship their high ideals with mind and heart and soul that finally realize those ideals. It is such people who reach the high places and the reason why is easily explained. Give your attention, or rather, your whole life to some lofty ideal, and you will tend to draw into action all the finer and higher forces of your system -- those forces that can create greater ability, greater talent, greater genius -- those forces that can increase your capacity, bring into action all your finer elements and give you superior power and superior worth in every sense of the term -- those forces which, when aroused, cannot positively fail to do the work you wish to have done.

A fact well known in this connection is that when the mind is turned persistently upon a certain ideal, every power that is in you begins to flow in that direction, and this is the very thing you want. When we can get all that is in us to work for our ideals and to work towards our ideals, then we shall positively reach whatever goal we have in view.

Closely connected with our ideals, we find our visions and dreams. The man without a vision will never be anything but an ordinary man, and the people who never dream of greater things, will never get beyond ordinary things. It is our visions and dreams that lift our minds to lofty realms, that make us feel that there is something greater and better to work for; and when we become inspired with a desire to work for greater and better things, we will not only proceed to carry out those desires, but will finally secure sufficient power to fulfill those desires. "The nation that has no vision shall perish." This is a great truth that we have heard a thousand times, and we know the reason why; but the same truth is applicable to man. If he has no vision, he will go down; but if he has visions, the highest and most perfect visions he can possibly imagine, and lives constantly for their realization, he will positively ascend in the scale. He will become a greater and a greater man, and those things that were at one time simply dreams, will, in the course of time, become actual realities.

The power of love is another force in this higher group that is extremely valuable, and the reason is that it is the tendency of love to turn attention upon the ideal, the beautiful and the more perfect. When you love somebody, you do not look for their faults; in fact, you do not see their faults. Your whole attention is turned upon their good qualities, and here, let us remember that whatever we continue to see in others, we develop in ourselves. The power of real love always tends to draw out into expression the finer elements of mind, character and life. For that reason, we should always love, love much, and love the most ideal and the most perfect that we can discover in everybody and in everything that we may meet in life.

We have all discovered that when a man really loves an ideal woman, or the woman that constitutes his ideal, he invariably becomes stronger in character, more powerful in personality, and more able in mind. When a woman loves an ideal man, or her ideal, she invariably becomes more attractive. The beautiful in her nature comes forth into full expression and many times the change is so great that we can hardly believe that she is the same woman. The power of love, if genuine, constant and strong, tends to improve everything in human life; and as this power is one of the higher forces in human nature, we readily understand the reason why. We can therefore without further comment, draw our own conclusions as to how we will use this power in the future.

The last of these finer forces that we shall mention, and possibly the strongest, is that of faith; but we must remember if we wish to use this force, that faith does not constitute a belief or any system of beliefs ; it is a mental action -- an action that goes into the very spirit of those things which we may think of or apply at the time we exercise faith. When you have faith in yourself you place in action a force that goes into the very depth of your being and tends to arouse all the greater powers and finer elements that you may possess. The same is true when you have faith in a certain faculty or in a certain line of action. The power of faith goes into the spirit of things and makes alive, so to speak, the all that is in you. The power of faith also produces perfect concentration. Whenever you have faith along a certain line, you concentrate perfectly along that line, and you cause all the power that is in your mind or system to work for the one thing you are trying to do. It has been discovered that the amount of energy latent in the human system is nothing less than enormous, and as faith tends to arouse all this energy, we realize how important and how powerful is faith.

The effect of faith upon yourself therefore is beneficial in the highest and largest sense, but this is not its only effect. The more faith you have in yourself, the more faith people will have in you. If you have no confidence in yourself you will never inspire confidence in anybody; but if you thoroughly believe in yourself, people will believe in you and in your work. And when people believe in you, you can accomplish ten times as much as when they have no confidence in you whatever.

When a man has tremendous faith in himself, he becomes a live wire, so to speak. It is such a man that becomes a real and vital power wherever he may live or go. It is such a man who leads the race on and on. It is such a man who really does things, and it is people of such a type that we love the best. They invariably inspire others to love the nobler life and to attempt greater things in life, and for this reason their presence is of exceptional value to the progress of the race. To go into details, however, is not necessary. We all know and appreciate the value of faith. We all know that it is one of the highest and one of the greatest forces that man can exercise; we therefore realize how important it becomes to train ourselves to have unbounded faith in everything and in everybody at all times, and under all circumstances.

20. THE GREATEST POWER IN MAN

With All Thy Faults I Love Thee Still

Thus sings the poet, and we call him sentimental; that is, at first thought we do. But upon second thought we change our minds. We then find that faults and defects are always in the minority, and that the larger part of human nature is so wonderful and so beautiful that it needs must inspire admiration and love in everybody. With all their defects there is nothing more interesting than human beings; and the reason is that for every shortcoming in man there are a thousand admirable qualities. The poet, being inspired by the sublime vision of truth, can see this; therefore, what can he do but love? Whenever his eyes are lifted and whenever his thoughts take wings, his soul declares with greater eloquence than ever before, " What a piece of work is man!" Thus every moment renews his admiration, and every thought rekindles the fire of his love.

It is the conclusion of modern psychology that the powers and the possibilities inherent in man are practically unbounded. And this conclusion is based upon two great facts. First, that no limit has been found to anything in human nature; and second, that everything in human nature contains a latent capacity for perpetual development. The discovery of these two facts -- and no discovery of greater importance has appeared in any age -- gives man a new conception of himself, a conception, which, when applied, will naturally revolutionize the entire field of human activity. To be able to discern the real significance of this new conception becomes, therefore, the greatest power in man, and should, in consequence, be given the first thought in all efforts that have advancement attainment or achievement in view.

The purpose of each individual should be, not simply to cultivate and apply those possibilities that are now in evidence, but also to develop the power to discern and fathom what really exists within him. This power is the greatest power, because it prepares the way for the attainment and expression of all other powers. It is the power that unlocks the door to all power, and must be understood and applied before anything of greater value can be accomplished through human thought or action. The principal reason why the average person remains weak and incompetent is found in the fact that he makes no effort to fathom and understand the depths of his real being. He may try to use what is in action on the surface, but he is almost entirely unconscious of the fact that enormous powers are in existence in the greater depths of his life. These powers are dormant simply because they have not been called into action, and they will continue to lie dormant until man develops his greatest power -- the power to discern what really exists within him.

The fundamental cause of failure is found in the belief that what exists on the surface is all there is of man, and the reason why greatness is a rare exception instead of a universal rule can be traced to the same cause. When the mind discovers that its powers are inexhaustible and that its faculties and talents can be developed to any degree imaginable, the fear of failure will entirely disappear. In its stead will come the conviction that man may attain anything or achieve anything. Whatever circumstances may be today, such a mind will know that all can be changed, that the limitations of the person can be made to pass away, and that the greater desires of the heart can be realized. That mind that can discern what exists in the depths of the real life of man does

119

not simply change its views as to what man may attain and achieve, but actually begins to draw, in a measure, upon those inexhaustible powers within; and begins accordingly to develop and apply those greater possibilities that this deeper discernment has revealed.

When man can see through and understand what exists beneath the surface of his life, the expression of his deeper life will begin, because whatever we become conscious of, that we tend to bring forth into tangible expressions, and since the deeper life contains innumerable possibilities as well as enormous power, it is evident that when this deeper life is clearly discerned and completely taken possession of in the consciousness, practically anything may be attained or achieved.

The idea that there is more of man than what appears on the surface should be so constantly and so deeply impressed upon the mind that it becomes a positive conviction, and no thoughts should be placed in action unless it is based upon this conviction. To live, think and act in the realization that " there is more of me " should be the constant aim of every individual, and this more will constantly develop, coming forth in greater and greater measure, giving added power and capacity in life to everything that is in action in the human system.

When the average individual fails, he either blames circumstances or comes to the conclusion that he was not equal to the occasion. He therefore easily gives up and tries to be content with the lesser. But if he knew that there was more in him than what he had applied in his undertaking he would not give up. He would know by developing and applying this more, he positively would succeed where he had previously failed. It is therefore evident that when man gives attention to his greater power -- the power to discern the more that is in him -- he will never give up until he does succeed, and in consequence he invariably will succeed.

That individual who knows his power does not judge according to appearances. He never permits himself to believe that this or that cannot be done. He knows that those things can be done, because he has discovered what really exists within him. He works in the conviction that he must, can and will succeed, because he has the power ; and it is the truth -- he does have the power -- we all have the power.

To live, think and work in the conviction that there is more of you within the real depths of your being, and to know that this more is so immense that no limit to its power can be found, will cause the mind to come into closer and closer touch with this greater power within, and you will consequently get possession of more and more of this power. The mind that lives in this attitude opens the door of consciousness, so to speak, to everything in human life that has real quality and worth. It places itself in that position where it can respond to the best that exists within itself, and modern psychology has discovered that this best is extraordinary in quality, limitless in power, and contains possibilities that cannot be numbered.

It is the truth that man is a marvelous being -- nothing less than marvelous; and the greatest power in man is the power to discern the marvelousness that really does exist within him. It is the law that we steadily develop and bring forth whatever we think of the most. It is therefore profitable to think constantly of our deeper nature and to try to fathom the limitlessness and the inexhaustibleness of these great and marvelous depths.

In practical life this mode of thinking will have the same effect upon the personal mind as that which is secured in a wire that is not charged when it touches a wire that is charged. The great within is a live wire; when the mind touches the great within, it becomes charged more and more with those same immense powers; and the mind will constantly be in touch with the great within when it lives, thinks and works in the firm conviction that "there is more of me," -- so much more that it cannot be measured.

We can receive from this deeper life only that which we constantly recognize and constantly realize, because consciousness is the door between the outer life and the great within, and we open the door to those things only of which we become conscious.

The principal reason therefore why the average person does not possess greater powers and talents, is because he is not conscious of more; and he is not conscious of more because he has not vitally recognized the great depths of his real life, and has not tried to consciously fathom the possibilities that are latent within him. The average person lives on the surface. He thinks that the surface is all there is of him, and consequently does not place himself in touch with the live wire of his interior and inexhaustible nature. He does not exercise his greatest power -- the power to discern what his whole nature actually contains; therefore, he does not unlock the door to any of his other powers.

This being true, we can readily understand why mortals are weak -- they are weak simply because they have chosen weakness; but when they begin to choose power and greatness, they will positively become what they have chosen to become.

We all must admit that there is more in man than what is usually expressed in the average person. We may differ as to how much more, but we must agree that the more should be developed, expressed and applied in everybody. It is wrong, both to the individual and to the race, for anyone to remain in the lesser when it is possible to attain the greater. It is right that we all should ascend to the higher, the greater and the better now. And we all can.

THE END

BOOK TWO

THE IDEAL MADE REAL

Change your fate and obtain health, happiness and prosperity

FOREWORD

The purpose of this work is to present practical methods through which anyone, the beginner in particular, may realize his ideals, cause his cherished dreams to come true, and cause the visions of the soul to become tangible realities in every-day life.

The best minds now believe that the ideal can be made real; that every lofty idea can be applied in practical living, and that all that is beautiful on the heights of existence can be made permanent expressions in personal existence. And so popular is this belief becoming that it is rapidly permeating the entire thought of the world. Accordingly, the demand for instructive knowledge on this subject, that is simple as well as scientific, is becoming almost universal.

This book has been written to supply that demand. However, it does not claim to be complete; nor could any work on "The Ideal Made Real" possibly be complete, because the ideal world is limitless and the process of making real the ideal is endless. To know how to begin is the principal secret, and he who has learned this secret may go on further and further, forever and forever, until he reaches the most sublime heights that endless existence has in store.

No attempt has been made to formulate the ideas, methods and principles presented, into a definite system. In fact, the tendency to form a new system of thinking or a new philosophy of life, has been purposely avoided. Closely defined systems invariably become obstacles to advancement, and we are not concerned with new philosophies of life. Our purpose is the living of a greater and a greater life, and in such a life all philosophies must constantly change.

In preparing the following pages, the object has been to take the beginner out of the limitations of the old into the boundlessness of the new; to emphasize the fact that the possibilities that are latent in the human mind are nothing less than marvelous, and that the way to turn those possibilities to practical use is sufficiently simple for anyone to understand. But no method has been presented that will not tend to suggest new and better methods as required for further advancement.

The best ideas are those that inspire new ideas, better ideas, greater ideas. The most perfect science of life is that science that gives each individual the power to create and recreate his own science as he ascends in the scale of life.

Great souls are developed only where minds are left free to employ the best known methods according to their own understanding and insight. And it is only as the soul grows greater and greater that the ideal can be made real. It is individuality and originality that give each person the power to make his own life as he may wish it to be; but those two important factors do not flourish in definite systems. There is no progress where the soul is placed in the hands of methods; true and continuous progress can be promoted only where all ideas, all methods and all principles are placed in the hands of the soul.

We have selected the best ideas and the best methods known for making the ideal real, and through this work, will place them in your hands. "We do not ask you to follow these methods; we simply ask you to use them. You will then find them all to be practical; you will find that every one will work and produce the results you desire. You will then, not only make real the ideal in your present sphere of life, but you will also develop within yourself that Greater Life, the power of which has no limit, the joy of which has no end.

1. THE IDEAL MADE REAL.

To have ideals is not only simple but natural. It is just as natural for the mind to enter the ideal as it is to live. In fact, the ideal is an inseparable part of life; but to make the ideal real in every part of life is a problem, the solution of which appears to be anything but simple. To dream of the fair, the high, the beautiful, the perfect, the sublime, that everyone can do; but everyone has not learned how to make his dreams come true, nor realize in the practical world what he has discerned in the transcendental world. The greatest philosophers and thinkers in history, with but few exceptions, have failed to apply their lofty ideas in practical living, not because they did not wish to but because they had not discovered the scientific relationship existing between the ideal world and the real world. The greatest thinker of the past century confessed that he did not know how to use in every day life the remarkable laws and principles that he had discovered in the ideal. He knew, however, that those laws and principles could be applied; that the ideal could be made real, and he stated that he positively knew that others would discover the law of realization, and that methods would be found in the near future through which any ideal could be made real in practical life; and his prophecy has come true.

To understand the scientific relationship that exists between the real and the ideal, the mind must have both the power of interior insight and the power of scientific analysis, as well as the power of practical application; but we do not find, as a rule, the prophet and the scientist in the same mind. The man who has visions and the man who can do things do not usually dwell in the same personality; nevertheless, this is necessary. And every person can develop both the prophet and the scientist in himself. He can develop the power to see the ideal and also the power to make the ideal real. The large mind, the broad mind, the deep mind, the lofty mind, the properly developed mind can see both the outer and the inner side of things. Such a mind can see the ideal on high, and at the same time understand how to make real, tangible and practical what he has seen.

The seeming gulf between the ideal and the real, between the soul's vision and the power of practical action is being bridged in thousands of minds today, and it is these minds who are gaining the power to make themselves and their own world as beautiful as the visions of the prophet; but the ideal life and the world beautiful are not for the few only. Everybody should learn how to find that path that leads from the imperfections of present conditions to the world of ideal conditions—the world of which we have all so frequently dreamed.

The problem is what beginners are to do with the beautiful thoughts and the tempting promises that are being scattered so widely at the present time. The average mind feels that the idealism of modern metaphysics has a substantial basis. He feels intuitively that it is true, and he discerns through the perceptions of his own soul that all these things that are claimed for applied metaphysics are possible. He inwardly knows that whatever the idealist declares can be done will be done, but the problem is how. The demand for simple methods is one of the greatest demands at the present time—methods that everyone can learn and that will enable any aspiring soul to begin at once to realize his ideals. Such methods, however, are easily formulated, and will be found in abundance on the following pages. These methods are based upon eternal laws; they are as simple as the multiplication table and will produce results with the same unerring precision. Any person with a reasonable amount of intelligence can apply them, and those who have an abundance of perseverance can, through these methods, make real practically all the ideals that they may have at the present time. Those who are more highly developed will find in these methods the secret through which their attainments and achievements will constantly verge on the borderland of the marvelous. In fact, when the simple law that unites the ideal and the real is understood and applied, it matters not how lofty our minds and our visions maybe we can make them all come true.

To proceed, the principal obstacle must first be removed, and this obstacle is the tendency to lose faith whenever we fail to make real the ideal the very moment we expect to do so. This tendency is present to some degree in nearly every mind that is working for greater things, and it postpones the day of realization whenever it is permitted to exercise its power of retrogression. Many a person has fallen into chronic despondency after having had a glimpse of the ideal, because it was so very beautiful, so very desirable, in fact, the only one thing that could satisfy, and yet seemingly so far away and so impossible to reach. But here is a place where we must exercise extraordinary faith. We must never recognize the gulf that seems to exist between our present state and the state we desire to reach. On the other hand, we must continue in the conviction that the gulf is only seeming and that we positively shall reach the ideal that appears in the splendors of what seems to be a distant future, although what actually is very near at hand.

Those who have more faith and more determination do not, as a rule, fall down when they meet this seeming gulf; they inwardly know that every ideal will sometime be realized. It could not be otherwise, because what we see in the distance is invariably something that lies in the pathway of our own eternal progress, and if we continue to move forward we must inevitably reach it. But even to these the ideal does at times appear to be very far away, and the time of waiting seems very long. They are frequently on the verge of giving up and fears arise at intervals that many unpleasant experiences may, after all, be met before the great day of realization is gained; however, we cannot afford to entertain such fears for a moment nor to think that anything unpleasant can transpire during the period of transition; that is, the passing from the imperfections of present conditions to the joys and delights of an ideal life. We must remember that fear and despondency invariably retard our progress, no matter what our object in view may be, and that discouragement is very liable to cause a break in the engine that is to take our train to the fair city we so long have desired to reach.

The time of waiting may seem long during such moments as come when the mind is down, but so long as the mind is on the heights the waiting time disappears, and the pleasure of pursuit comes to take its place. In this connection we should remember that the more frequently we permit the mind to fall down into fears and doubts the longer we shall have to wait for the realization of the ideal; and the more we live in the upper story of life the sooner we shall reach the goal in view. There are many who give up temporarily all efforts toward reaching their ideals, thinking it is impossible and that nothing is gained by trying, but such minds should realize that they are simply making their future progress more difficult by retarding their present progress. Such minds should realize the great fact that every ideal can be made real, because nothing is impossible.

To reach any desired goal the doing of certain things is necessary, but if those things are not done now they will have to be done later; besides, when we give up in the present we always make the obstacles in our way much greater than they were before. Those things that are necessary to promote our progress become more difficult to do the longer we remain in what may be termed the "giving up" attitude, and the reason why is found in the fact that the mind that gives up becomes smaller and smaller; it loses ability, capacity and power and becomes less and less competent to cope with the problems at hand. Whenever we give up we invariably fall down into a smaller mental state. When we cease to move forwards we begin to move backwards. We retard progression only when we cease to promote progression. On the other hand, so long as we continue to pursue the ideal we ascend into larger and larger mental states, and thus increase our power to make real the ideals that are before us. The belief that it is impossible to make real the ideal has no foundation whatever in truth. It is simply an illusion produced by fear and has no place in the exact science of life. When you discern an ideal you discover something that lies in your own onward path. Move forward and you simply cannot fail to reach it; but when you are to reach the coveted goal depends upon how rapidly you are moving now. Knowing this, and knowing that fear, doubt, discouragement and indifference invariably retard this forward movement, we shall find it most profitable to remove those mental states absolutely.

The true attitude is the attitude of positive conviction; that is, to live in the strong conviction that whatever we see before us in the ideal will positively be realized, sooner or later, if we only move forward, and we can make it sooner if we will move forward steadily, surely and rapidly during every moment of the great eternal now. To move forward steadily during the great eternal now is to realize now as much of the ideal as we care to appropriate now; no waiting therefore is necessary. To begin to move forward is to begin to make real the ideal, and we will realize in the now as much of the ideal as is necessary to make the now full and complete. To move forward steadily during the great eternal now is to eternally become more than you are; and to become more than you are is to make yourself more and more like your ideal; and here is the great secret, because the principle is that you will realize your ideal when you become exactly like your ideal, and that you will realize as much of your ideal now as you develop in yourself now. The majority, however, feel that they can never become as perfect as their ideal; others, however, think that they can, and that they will sometime, but that it will require ages, and they dwell constantly upon the unpleasant belief that they may in the meantime have to pass through years and years of ordinary and undesirable experience; but they are mistaken, and besides, are retarding their own progress every moment by entertaining such thoughts.

If all the time and all the energy that is wasted in longing and longing, yearning and yearning were employed in scientific, practical self-development, the average person would in a short time become as perfect as his ideal. He would thus realize his ideal, because we attract from the without what corresponds exactly to what is active in our own within. When we attain the ideal and the beautiful in our own natures, we shall meet the ideal and the beautiful wherever we may go in the world, and we will find the same things in the real that we dreamed of in the ideal. When we see an ideal we usually begin to long for it and hope that something remarkable may happen so as to bring it into our possession, and we thus continue to long and yearn and wait with periods of despondency intervening. We simply use up time and energy to no avail. When we see an ideal the proper course to pursue is to begin at once to develop that ideal in our own nature. We should never stop to wait and see whether it is coming true or not, and we should never stop to figure how much time it may require to reach our goal. The secret is, begin now to be like your ideals, and at the proper time that ideal will be made real.

The very moment you begin to rebuild yourself in the exact likeness of your ideal you will begin to realize your ideal, because we invariably gain possession of that of which we become conscious; and to begin to develop the ideal in ourselves is to begin to become conscious of the ideal. To give thought to time is to stop and measure time in consciousness, and every stop in consciousness means retarded progress. Real progress is eternal; it is a forward movement that is continuous now, and in the realization of such a progress no thought is ever given to time. To live in the life of eternal progress is to gain ground every moment. It means the perpetual increase of everything that has value, greatness and worth, and the mind that lives in such a life cannot possibly be discouraged or dissatisfied. Such a mind will not only live in the perpetual increase of everything that heart can wish for, but will also realize perpetually the greatest joy of all joys, the joy of going on. The discouraged mind is the mind that lives in the emptiness of life, but there can be no emptiness in that life that lives in the perpetual increase of all that is good and beautiful and ideal.

The only time that seems long is the time that is not well employed in continuous attainment, and the only waiting time, that seems the hardest time of all, is the time that is not fully consecrated to the highest purpose you have in view. When we understand that we all may have different ideals we will find that we have an undeveloped correspondent in ourselves to every ideal that we may discern, and if we proceed to develop these corresponding parts there will be some ideals realized every day. Today we may succeed in making real an ideal that we first discovered a year ago. Tomorrow we may reach a goal towards which we have been moving for years, and in a few days we may realize ideals that we have had in view during periods of time varying from a few weeks to several years; and if we are applying the principles that underlie the process of making real the ideal, we may at any time realize ideals of which we have dreamed for a life time. Consequently, when we approach this subject properly we shall daily come into the possession of something that is our own. All the beautiful things of which we have dreamed will be coming into our world and there will be new arrivals every day.

This is the life of the real idealist, and we cannot picture a life that is more complete and more satisfying; but it is not only complete in the present. It is constantly growing larger and more desirable, thus giving us daily a higher degree of satisfaction and joy. When we discern an ideal that ideal has come within the circle of our own capacity for development, and the power to develop that ideal in ourselves is therefore at hand. The mind never discerns those ideals that are beyond the possibility of present development. Thus we realize that when an ideal is discerned it is proof positive that we have the power to make it real now.

Those who have not found their ideals in any shape or form whatever have simply neglected to make their own ideal nature strong, positive and pronounced. To live in negative idealism is to continue to dream on without seeing a single dream come true; but when the ideals we discern in our own natures become strong, positive working-forces our dreams will soon come true; our ideals will be realized one after the other until life becomes what it is intended to be, a perpetual ascension into all that is rich, beautiful and sublime.

Whether we speak of environments, attainments, achievements, possessions, circumstances, opportunities, friends, companions or the scores of things that belong in our world, the law is the same. We receive an ideal only when we become just like that ideal. If we seek better friends, we shall surely find them and retain them, if we develop higher and higher degrees of friendship. If we wish to associate with refined people, we must become more refined in action, thought and speech. If we wish to reach our ideals in the world of achievement, we must develop greater ability, capacity and power. If we desire better environments, we must not only learn to appreciate the beautiful, but must also develop the power to produce those things that have true quality, high worth and real superiority. The great secret is to become more useful in the world; that is, useful in the largest and highest sense of that term. He who gives his best to the world will receive the best in return.

The world needs able men and women; people who can do things that are thoroughly worthwhile; people who can think great thoughts and transform such thoughts into great deeds; and to secure such men and women the world will give anything that it may hold in its possession. To make real the ideal, proceed to develop greatness, superiority and high worth in yourself. Train the mind to dwell constantly upon the borderland of the highest ideals that you can possibly picture; but do not simply yearn for what you can see, and do not covet what has not yet become your own. Proceed to remake yourself into the likeness of that ideal and it will become your own. To proceed with this great development, the whole of life must be changed to conform with the exact science of life; that is, that science that is based upon the physical and the metaphysical united as the one expression of all that is great and sublime in the soul. The new way of thinking about things, viewing things and doing things must be adopted in full, and this new way is based upon the principle that the ideal actually is real, and therefore should be approached not as a future possibility, but as a present actuality. Think of the ideal as if it were real and you will find it to be real. Meet all things as if they contained the ideal, and you will find that all things will present their ideals to you, not simply as mere pictures, but as realities. View the whole of life from the heights of existence; then you will see things as they are and deal with things accordingly; you will see that side of the whole of existence that may be termed the better side, and in consequence, you will grow into the likeness of that better side. When you grow into the likeness of the better side of all things, you will attract the better side of all things, and the ideal in everything in the world will be made real in your world.

2. HOW TO BEGIN: THE PRIME ESSENTIALS.

To formulate rules in detail that will apply to each individual case is neither possible nor necessary. All have not the same present needs nor the same previous training; but there are certain general principles that apply to all, and these, if followed according to the individual view-point, will produce the results desired. If the proper beginning is made, the subsequent results will not only be greater and be realized in less time, but much useless experience and delay will be avoided. These principles, or prime essentials, are as follows:

1. Learn to be still. When you undertake to live an ideal life and seek to promote your advancement in every direction, you will find that much cannot be gained until your entire being is placed in a proper condition for growth; the reason being that the ideal is ever advancing toward higher ideals, and you must improve yourself before you can better your life. It has been found that all laws of growth require order, harmony and stillness for proper action; therefore, to live peacefully, think peacefully, act peacefully and speak peacefully are important essentials. This will not only put the entire being into proper condition for growth, but will also conserve energy, and when you begin to live the larger life you will want to use properly all your forces; neither misusing or wasting anything. To acquire stillness never "try hard," but simply exercise general self-control in everything you do. Never be anxious about results, and they will come with less effort, and in less time. "Whenever you have a moment to spare relax the whole person, mind and body; just let everything fall into the easiest position possible. Make no effort to relax, simply let go. So long as you try to relax you will not succeed. While in this relaxed condition be quiet; do not move a muscle; breathe deeply but gently, and think only of peace and stillness. Before you go to sleep at night relax your entire system, and fall asleep with peace in your mind; bathe your mind and body, so to speak, in the crystal sea of the beautiful calm. These methods alone will work wonders in a few weeks. While you are at work hold yourself from anxious hurry or disturbed action; work in the attitude of poise and you will accomplish much more in the same given time and you will be a far better workman. Train yourself to come into the realization of perfect peace by gently holding a deep strong desire for peace and by ordering all your actions to harmonize with the peaceful goal in view. The result will be "the peace that passeth understanding," and for this alone your gratitude will be both boundless and endless.

2. Rejoice and be glad. Cheerfulness is not only a good medicine, but it is food for mind and body. The cheerful life will fill every atom with new life, and it is to the faculties of the mind what sunshine is to the flowers and trees. To be happy always is one of the greatest things that man can do, and there are few things that are more profitable in every sense of that term. No matter what comes, be glad; and live in the conviction that all things are working together for good to you. As your conviction is so is your faith; and as your faith is so it shall be unto you.

"When you live in the conviction that all things are working together for good you will *cause* all things to work together for good, and you will understand the reason why when you begin to apply the real science of ideal living. No matter how dark the cloud, look for the silver lining; it is there, and when you always look at the bright side of things you develop brightness in yourself. This brightness will strengthen all your faculties so that you can easily overcome what obstacles may be in your way, and thus gain the victory desired. Direct your attention constantly to the bright side of things; refuse absolutely to consider any other side. At first this may not be possible in the absolute sense, but perseverance never fails to win. However, do not try hard; gently direct your attention to the bright side and know that you can. Ere long it will be second nature for you to live on the sunny side. The value of this attainment is very great; first, because joyousness will increase life, power, energy and force; this we all know from personal experience, and we wish to have all the life and power that we can possibly secure; second, because the happiest soul never worries, which is great gain. Worry has crippled thousands of fine minds and brought millions to an early grave. We simply cannot afford to worry and must never do so under any condition whatever. If we have that habit we can remove it at once by the proper antidote, which is joyousness. After you have trained yourself to look only for the bright and the best, the bright and the best will come to you, because you will be using your powers to bring those very things to pass; therefore, rejoice and be glad every moment. Let your heart and your soul sing at all times. When you do not feel the joyous music within, produce it with your own imagination, and ere long it will come of itself with greater and greater abundance; your soul will *want* to sing because it *feels* music, and there are few joys that equal the joy that comes when music is felt in the soul. There are so many things that are sweet and beautiful in life that when we once find the key to harmony we shall always rejoice. In the meantime, be happy for the good you have found, and through that very attitude you will develop the power to attract better things than you ever had before. This personal existence is brimful of good things and happy souls will find them all.

3. Love everybody and be kind. If you wish your path to be strewn with roses, just be kind. Give your best to the world, and the best will come to you without fail; if it does not come today, never mind; just go on being kind and refuse to consider disappointments. Never hold in mind those things that you do not wish to retain; you thus cause those things to pass away. This "shall also pass away" is true of everything that is not pleasant; but unpleasant things will not pass away so long as we hold them in thought. That which you let go from your mind will pass away from you entirely. Train yourself to be kindness in a permanent state of mind, because you cannot afford to criticize, condemn or be angry at any time. We know that anger not only disturbs the mind, but also destroys the cells of the body, and no one can be angry without losing a great deal of life and energy. To find fault never pays; it simply brings enmity, discord and criticisms; besides, the faults we constantly see in others will develop in ourselves. The critical mind is destructive and the critical attitude is weakening to the entire system; therefore, no one can be his best who permits himself to think or talk about the flaws of life. Be good and kind to everybody; it is one of the royal paths to happiness and peace. When anyone does wrong, do not condemn; help him out; help him find the better way. "Cast your bread upon the waters;" it will surely return; sometimes more quickly than you expect it. Therefore, give abundantly of all that is best in your life, and nothing is better than kindness and love. When you begin to live an ideal life you will desire more and more to live the largest life possible, and to accomplish this you must learn to be much to everybody. Your purpose must be to be useful in the largest and

truest sense of that term; and nothing can promote this purpose so thoroughly and so extensively as universal kindness. This does not imply, however, that you are to permit yourself to be imposed upon or unjustly used by the unscrupulous. It is our duty, as well as our privilege to demand the right at all times, and to demand justice for everybody and from everybody, but this should be done in kindness, with the antagonistic attitude eliminated. The love that loves everybody is not the love that seeks to gain personal possession of some object of affection. We refer to that larger kindness that excludes no one from our whole souled good wishes. This form of love is the greatest power in the world, and the one who loves the most in this larger, truer sense will accomplish the most. The reason why is found in the fact that a great love invariably brings out all that is large, great and extraordinary in human nature. To state that the one who takes the greatest interest in the welfare of the world does the most to promote his own interests may seem to be a contradiction of terms; but it is true, and it proves conclusively that the one who gives his best to the world will invariably receive the best in return. Never permit yourself to say that you cannot love every creature that lives; say that you do love everything that lives, and mean it. What you say you are doing that you will find yourself doing.

This greater love illumines the mind, gives new life to every fibre in your being, removes almost every burden and eases the whole path of existence. Love removes entirely all anger, hatred, revenge, ill-will, and similar states, a matter of great importance, for no one can live an ideal life while such states of mind remain. To have a sweet temper and loving disposition and a kind heart is worth more than tons of gold. We are all finding this to be true, and we realize fully that the person who loves everybody with that larger loving kindness has taken a long step upward into that life that is real life. This is not mere sentiment, but the expression of an exact scientific fact. A strong, continuous love will bring all good to anyone who lives and acts as he inwardly feels.

4. Have faith in abundance. Have faith in God; have faith in man; have faith in yourself; have faith in faith. Believe in everything, and you relate yourself to the best that is in everything. We all know the value of self-confidence, but faith is infinitely deeper, larger and higher. Self-confidence helps us to believe in ourselves, as we are at present, and thus helps us to make a better use of the talents we now possess; but faith elevates the mind into the consciousness of our larger and superior possibilities, and thus increases perpetually the power, the capacity and the efficiency of the talents we now possess. Faith brings out the best that is within us and puts that best to work now. He who follows faith may frequently go out upon the seeming void, but he always finds the solid rock. The reason is that faith has superior vision and goes instinctively to the very thing we desire to find. Faith does not expect things to come of themselves. Faith never stands and waits; it does things; but while at work *believes* that the goal will be reached and the undertaking accomplished. The person who works in the attitude of faith can never fail; because through faith he draws upon the inexhaustible. The person who works in the attitude of doubt can never be at his best. Through the feeling of doubt he lowers his own ability; he holds back his best power and employs but a portion of his capacity; but the one who works in faith will press on to the very limit of his present capacity and then go on further still, because the more faith he has the more fully he

realizes that there is no limit to his capacity, that the seeming void that lies before is positively solid rock all the way and he may safely proceed. Whatever you do *believe* that you can succeed in; do not for a moment permit yourself to doubt; know that the Infinite is your source, that you live in the universal and have the boundless upon which to draw for supply. If people or things do not come up to your ideal never mind; give them time; continue to have faith in their better selves; they will also scale the heights. Expect them all to do their best, and most of them will do so now; the others will soon follow, if you live in the faith that they will. The unbounded faith of one soul can elevate the lives of thousands. This is a statement that is just as true as it is great, and we should constantly give it the highest place in mind. The man who has faith in the whole race is an inspiration to everybody. Many a person has risen rapidly in the scale because someone had faith in him. Faith is the greatest elevating power that we know in the world. Faith can convert any failure into success and can promote the advancement of everybody, no matter what the circumstances may be. Have faith in yourself and you will advance as you never advanced before. Have faith in others and they will inevitably follow. Have faith in the Infinite and the Supreme Power will always be with you. This power will see you through, whatever your goal may be. Therefore, if you would enter the new life, the better life, the ideal life, and inspire others to do the same, have faith in abundance.

5. Pray without ceasing. The true prayer is the whole-souled desire for the larger, the higher and the better while the mind is stayed upon the Most High; and to pray without ceasing is to constantly live in that lofty desire. The forces of mind and body always follow our desires; therefore, if we would use our powers in building up a larger life we must have high desires and true desires. Turn your desires upward and keep them there; desire the greater things only; never desire anything less. Those powers within you will cause you to become as true, as great and as perfect as your heart has prayed that you might become. To cause our desires, thoughts and states of consciousness to rise to the very highest states of being, we should employ the silence daily; that is, we should enter into the absolute stillness of the secret life of the soul. Through the silence we shall find the secret of secrets, the path to that inner world from which everything proceeds. To begin, be alone and comfortably seated. Or, you may enter the silence in association with someone that is in perfect harmony with yourself. Relax mind and body; close your eyes and be perfectly quiet; turn your attention upon the inner life of the soul and gently hold your mind upon the thoughts of stillness and peace. Affirm with deep, quiet feeling, "Peace is mine." "I am resting in the stillness of the spirit." "I have entered the beautiful calm." "I am one with the Infinite." "I am in the kingdom of the great within." "I am in the secret places of the Most High," and similar states. While you make these statements *feel* that you are peaceful and still and that you are now in that inner world where all is quiet and serene. When you feel this deep, sublime stillness you can use other affirmations according to your present needs. You may affirm that you are well and strong and happy and harmonious, and that you have full possession of all those qualities that you know have existence in real life. To feel the perfect peace of the soul, however, is the first essential. After that is attained your consciousness will deepen and you will enter the great within to a greater and greater degree. While the mind is in this interior state of being every thought you think

133

will be a power, and every desire you express will modify or change everything in your life according to the nature of that desire and in proportion to its depth and unity with the Supreme. For this reason you should train yourself to think only right thoughts and create only the truest desires while you are in the silent state. That which you think or do while in the silence will have a greater effect upon your life than that which you may attempt while on the surface of outer consciousness. Therefore, everything that is important should be taken into the silence and through the silence to the Infinite. This corresponds perfectly with the statement "Take it to the Lord in prayer." The real purpose of the silence is to enable the mind to enter the inner life and not only re-create all thought according to the higher truth, but to enter into a more perfect touch with the divine source of things. The silence should be entered every day for ten, twenty or thirty minutes. This is a daily practice of extreme value. Though you may not have any real results at first, simply continue; you will reach your goal. "When you begin to become conscious of your interior life and begin to live more or less in touch with the world beautiful that is within you, you will find that you can live in this high, peaceful state the greater part of the time and thus be in the silence almost constantly. This is not only a most desirable attainment, but it is *the one great* attainment toward which every soul should work. When a person can live in these higher realms always and constantly, and desire the realization of the highest and the best that he knows, the prayer without ceasing, the true spiritual prayer is being fulfilled. Such a prayer will be answered eternally. Every day will bring us something that we truly wished for, and every moment will be supplied with all that is necessary to make the present full and complete.

6. Think the truth. When we learn to think the truth we have actually come to the "parting of the ways." Here we find where the old leaves off and the new begins. In this state the wrong disappears and the right is discerned and realized in an ever increasing manner. The foundation of all truth is expressed in the basic statement—MAN IS A SPIRITUAL BEING CREATED IN THE IMAGE AND LIKENESS OF GOD. Being created in the image of God man is now divine and in possession of all the divine attributes. Each individual is now in possession of infinite wisdom, infinite power, infinite love, eternal life, perfect peace, everlasting joy, universal truth, universal freedom, universal good, divine wholeness, spotless virtue, boundless supply. True, these attributes exist principally in the potential state, that is, they are possibilities waiting in the within for unfoldment, development and expression; nevertheless, they do exist in every soul and to a degree that is limitless. Therefore, every soul does actually possess those attributes, and to speak the truth we must recognize their existence and even now claim their possession. To think the truth you must think that you are divine in your true being, and that you possess these attributes, because this is the truth. You *are* divine in your true being, because you are created in the image of God, and you *do* possess the divine attributes just mentioned because that which is divine must necessarily possess the attributes of the divine. To think contrary to this would be wrong thought, and from wrong thought comes all the wrong in the world. The average person does think contrary to this thought; therefore, he is almost constantly in bondage to sin, sickness or trouble of some kind. Divine wholeness, that is, perfect health of body and mind is yours now, always was and always will be; therefore it would

134

be wrong for you to say, "I am sick. "Your real being is never sick, never will be, because it is divine and you are the real being; you are not the body; you possess a body, and that body may be indisposed, if you create wrong thought, but that body is not you. You are a spiritual being created in the image of God, therefore you are always well. When sickness appears on the surface, that is, in the body, know that it is on the surface only; that sickness is not in you; you are real being, and in real being perfect health reigns absolutely and eternally. The sickness that sometimes appears in the body is the result of a recognition of untruth, either expressed in wrong thinking or wrong living. Right thought, that is, that thought that invariably follows the recognition of absolute truth, would not produce sickness; and no person could become sick that is always filled and protected with the power of right thought. When the light reigns supremely, darkness cannot enter. Wrong thought comes from a false conception of yourself, and false conceptions will continue to form in mind so long as you are ignorant of the truth. When you know the truth, that you are the image of God, perfect in your own true being, you will think this truth and all your thought will be right; consequently, only right conditions can exist in your life, and all will henceforth be well with you. When you see yourself as you are in your true being, that you are even now strong and well, in full possession of peace, love, power, wisdom, freedom and all the good that is in God you will think of yourself accordingly, and such thought is right thought. The result will be right conditions in mind and body. From center to circumference your entire being will be well and perfect, as it always was and ever will be in the truth. To think the absolute truth at first seems a contradiction of known facts, because we are so used to judging from appearances, but when we find that appearances are simply the result of thought, that right thought produces good appearances, and wrong thought produces adverse appearances, and learn that true being is the image of God, we shall no longer see contradiction in thinking absolute truth. When we think the truth about ourselves we shall always think the truth about others; we shall, therefore, not think of them as they appear on the surface but as they are in the perfection of real spiritual being. We shall overlook, forgive and forget the wrong appearance, knowing that it is but a temporary effect of wrong thought, and we shall proceed to inspire everyone to change that appearance by thinking right thought, the thought of truth.

7. Live in the spirit. To express this statement in its simplest terms, we would say that to live in the spirit is to live in the upper story of mind and thought, or to live on the good side, the bright side and the true side of everything. To the beginner this is sufficient, because this simple change in living must come before the higher spiritual consciousness can be realized; but the change though simple at first will completely revolutionize life. Ere long, however, the consciousness of the true side and the better side will become so clear that to live in the spirit will mean infinitely more than to simply dwell in the upper story of mind, and when this larger experience comes we shall know from our own illumined understanding what it means to live in the spirit. When we begin to think the truth all kinds of illusions and false beliefs will gradually vanish, and we shall not only understand that we are spiritual beings, but we shall feel that we are all that divine life can be. We shall positively know that we are eternal souls living in a spiritual world now, expressing ourselves in a physical world, and we shall realize that we are actually created in the image and likeness of the Infinite, united with the

135

Infinite and living in the life of Infinite being. Through the fuller realization of truth we will learn that the spiritual is not some vague, far away something that saints alone can know, but that spirit is the essence of all things, the very life of all things visible and invisible, and that spirit is in itself absolutely good and perfect. We will realize that there is but one substance from which all things proceed and that substance is the expression of spirit; we will see that there is but one life, the spiritual life, and that there is but one law, the eternal coming forth in a greater and greater measure of life. We will find that spirit is the basis of all things, the *soul* of all things, and that therefore all things are in reality very good and very beautiful. We will find through the spirit that evil is but a temporary condition produced by man's misunderstanding of the goodness and the completeness of real being and that to so live that we realize the absolute goodness and the perfect harmony of the whole universe is to live in the spirit. When we realize this we are on the true side of all things and we feel that we are. When we are in harmony with all things we are in harmony with the Infinite and can feel His presence always; and we also find that to "dwell in the secret places of the Most High" is to realize that we are in that great sea of life, the great spiritual sea, the universal state of being, the world of divine existence. While we are in this upper state, that is, in the spirits, we are away from the false, and actually in the true. We are in the spirit, and from the light of the spirit we can see clearly the truth concerning everything. From this place we may ascend to other and greater heights and enter into the ever increasing realms of life where existence becomes fairer and higher, too beautiful for tongue to ever describe. What is held in store for the soul that lives in the spirit, eternity alone can reveal, but that the life that is lived in the spirit is the only true life thousands have learned, both in this age and in ages gone by. To the beginner, however, the first essential is to get away from material life, that is, the common, the gross, the superficial, the ordinary, the perverted and the wrong; then to go up higher, to enter the world of light and live in the more beautiful realms of sublime existence. To live in the spirit, live in the highest and most perfect state now, and do not for a moment come down. At first this state will simply be a life that is finer, larger and more harmonious, where things move more smoothly and where the value of life seems to constantly increase; but ere long living in the spirit will mean far more than merely a pleasing state of existence, and the further we advance the more this wonderful life will be, until we begin to understand the great soul who declared: "Eye hath not seen nor ear heard, neither hath it entered into the heart of man what God has prepared for them that love Him." In this connection we must bear in mind that it is not necessary to reach the supreme heights in spiritual life before we can live in the spirit. We can live in the spirit no matter where me may be in the scale of life, because the spiritual life has just as many degrees as there are human souls. Live in the realization that this universe has *soul,* that this soul is divine, and that you live and move and have your being in that great soul. Realize this as fully as your present state of development will permit, and you have begun to live in the spirit. The realization of the divinity of the soul-side of all things will reveal to your mind the great truth that all things are perfect in their real state of being, and that the real of everything lives in a universe of spirit, a universe that is everywhere within us all and about us all. However, before we begin we must be convinced of the great truth that the spiritual life is not mere sentiment nor a mere feeling of mind and soul. The spiritual life is the real life, the foundation of all life, the essence of all life, the soul of all life, and every true statement concerning the spiritual life is an exact scientific fact readily demonstrated by anyone who will apply the principle. And happy is the soul that does apply this principle, for such a soul will find life in the spirit, not only to be real, but to be infinitely more perfect, more wonderful and more beautiful than anyone has ever dreamed.

3. THE FIRST STEPS IN IDEAL LIVING.

Give your best to the world no matter how insignificant that best may be, and the world will invariably give its best to you. There was nothing great or remarkable about the widow's mite, but it did produce remarkable results, and the reason was she gave her very best. When we give our best we not only receive the best in return from the outer world, but we also receive the best from the inner world.

"When you give your best you bring forth your best, and it is the bringing forth of your best that causes you to become better and better. When you become better you will meet better people and enter into better environments, and everything in your life will change for the better, because like does attract like. To give much is to become much, provided we give our best and give with the heart. The giving that comes simply from the hand does not count, no matter how large it may be. It brings nothing back to us nor does it bring permanent good to anybody else. When you give your best you do not give from your over-supply or from that which you cannot use. If you have something that you cannot use, it does not belong to you, and you cannot give, in the true sense of the term, what is not your own. To give does not mean simply to give money, unless that is the best you have; but rather to give your own service, your own talents, your ability, your own true worth and your own real self. The man who lives a real life at all times and under all circumstances is giving his best and the very best possible that can be given. A real life truly lived in the world is a power, and the person who lives such a life is a power for good wherever he may be. The presence of such a person is an inspiration and a light, as we all know. The man who loves the whole world with heart and soul, and loves without ceasing is doing far more for the race than he who endows universities, and will receive a far greater reward. "We must remember, however, that such a love is not mere sentiment. Real love is a power and will cause the person who has it to do his very best for everybody under every possible circumstance. That person whose heart is with the race will never be satisfied with inferior work. He will never shirk nor leave the problems of life to somebody else; he will go in and push wherever something good is being done, and he will constantly endeavor to render better and better service wherever his field of action may be. Such a person will give his best to the world, whether he gives through the channels of art or mechanics, music or literature, physical labor or intellectual labor, ideas or real living. What he does will be the best, and what he receives in return will be the best that the world is able to give. Give the best that you are through every thought, word and deed; that is the principle; and your life will be constantly enriched both from without and from within. Through the daily application of this principle you will develop superiority in mind, soul, character and life, and the world will be better off because you are here.

Expect the best from everybody and everybody will do their best for you. There may be occasional exceptions to this rule, but through close examination we shall find that these exceptions are due solely to our own negligence in applying the law to every occasion. The man who expects the best from everybody and has faith in everybody will certainly receive more love, more kindness, better friendship, better service and more agreeable associates by far than the one who has little or no faith in anyone. But our faith in people must be alive, and our expectations must have *soul*. To live constantly in the fear that people will do this or that, and that such and such mistakes may be made, is to live in a confused mental world, and where there is much confusion there will be many mistakes. Mental states are contagious; how that can be is not a matter for present discussion, but the fact that they are is extremely important, and we all know that they are; therefore, if we live in fear and confusion we will be a disturbing element among all those with whom we associate, and if our associates are not mentally strong and positive, they will be more or less confused by our presence, and they are very liable to produce the very mistakes we feared. On the other hand, when we have faith in people we help them to have faith in themselves, and the more faith a person has in himself the fewer his mistakes and the better his work. When we have faith in everybody and are constantly expecting the best from everybody we create wholesome conditions in our own minds, conditions that will tend to develop the best in ourselves; that person, however, who has no faith in others will soon lose faith in himself, and when he does there will be a turn for the worse in his life. True, he may continue to possess a mechanical self-confidence or an exaggerated state of egotism, but such a state will soon produce a reaction, and failure will follow. The self-confidence that brings out the best that is within us is always founded upon a living faith in the inherent greatness of man; therefore, no one can have real faith in himself unless he also has faith in the greater possibilities of the race, and no one can expect the best from himself and give soul to that expectation unless he also expects the best from others. This is a scientific fact that anyone can prove in his own daily experience. To expect the best from everybody will cause everybody to do their best for you.

Look for the best everywhere and you will find the best wherever you go. Why this is so is a matter upon which many delight to speculate, but the why does not concern us just now. It is the fact that this law works that concerns us, and concerns us very much. Not everybody can fully understand why the best is always found by him who never looks for anything but the best, but everybody can look for the best everywhere and thereby find the best; and it is the finding of the best that attracts our attention. It is real results that we are looking for, and the simpler the method the better. The man who will constantly apply this law will not remain in undesirable environments very long, nor will he occupy an inferior position very long; better things will positively come his way and he will not have to wait an age for the change. The man who looks for the best is constantly thinking about the best and constantly impressing his mind with the best thought about everything; and since man is as he thinks we can readily understand why such a man will become better and better; therefore, by looking for the best everywhere he will not only find the best in the external world, but he will create the best in his mental world; this will give him a greater mind, which in turn will produce higher attainments and greater achievements. That man, however, who is always looking for the worst will constantly think about the worst and will fill his mind with inferior thoughts; that he, himself, will become inferior by such a process is a foregone conclusion. We shall positively find, sooner or later, what we constantly look for; it is, therefore, profitable to look for the best everywhere and at all times; we become like those things that we constantly and deeply think about; it is, therefore, profitable to think only of the best whatever may come or not. The average person may not find the best the very first day this principle is applied. Most of us have strayed so far away from this mode of thinking and living that it may take some time to get back to the path that leads to the best; but one thing is certain, whoever will look for the best everywhere, and continue to do so for a reasonable length of time, will find that path; besides, he will have more delightful experiences while he is training himself to apply this principle than he has had for any similar period before. This, however, will be only the beginning; the future has far greater things in store, if he will continue to look for the best and never look for anything else.

When things are not to your liking, like them as they are. In other words, while you are working for greater things make friends with the lesser things, and they will help you to reach your goal. The person who is dissatisfied with things as they are and discontented because things are not to his liking is standing in his own way. We cannot get away from present conditions so long as we antagonize those conditions, because we are held in bondage to that which we resist. If you want present conditions to become stepping-stones to better things, you must get on the better side of present conditions, and you do that by liking things as they are while they remain with you. We must be in harmony with the present if we wish to advance, because in order to advance we must use the present, but we cannot use that with which we are not in harmony. This is a fact that deserves the most thorough attention and will, when understood, explain fully why the average person seems powerless to rise above his surroundings. We must be on friendly terms with everything that exists in our present world if we wish to gain possession of all the building material that our present world can give, and we cannot secure too much material if we desire to build a larger life and a greater future. That which we dislike becomes detrimental to us, no matter how good it may be; nevertheless, it will always be with us because it is impossible to eliminate permanently that which we antagonize; when we run away from it in one place we shall meet it elsewhere in some other form; but that which we love will constantly serve us and help us on to greater things; when it can serve us no longer it will disappear. To like those things, however, that are not to our liking may seem difficult, but the question is why they are not to our liking; when we know that everything in our present world is a stepping-stone to something still better it will be natural for us to like everything. Those things may not come up to our ideals, but that is not their real purpose; it is not the mission of present things to serve as ideals, their mission is to help us to reach our ideals, and they positively can do this if we will take them into friendly co-operation. When you take a drive to an ideal country place you do not dislike the horse because he is not that country place; if you are humane, you will love that horse because he is willing and able to take you where you wish to go. If you should dislike and mistreat that horse or should fail to hitch him to the vehicle, you would not reach your destination. This, however, is the very thing that the average person does with the things of his present world; these things are the horses and the vehicles that can take us to the ideal places we desire to reach; but we must hitch them up; we must treat them right and use them. To cause all things that are about us now to work together with us, we must be in perfect harmony with them; we must like them as they are, and that becomes comparatively easy when we know that it is necessary for them to be what they are in order that they may serve as our stepping-stones; if they were different there would be no stepping-stones, and we would have to remain where we are. When we realize that everything that exists in our present world has the power to promote our advancement, if we properly use that power, and when we realize that it is necessary to be in harmony with all things to use the power that is within those things, we shall no longer dislike anything; we shall even make friends with adversity, because the power that is in adversity can be tamed by kindness and love; and when that power is tamed it becomes our own. These are great facts and easily demonstrated by anyone, and whoever will apply these principles will find that by liking everything that he finds he will secure the co-operation of everything, and anyone can move forward rapidly when all things are working with him; consequently, by liking what he finds he will find what he likes.

When you do not get what you want take what you can get and call it good. It is better to have something than nothing; besides, we must use what we can get before we can become so strong and so able that we can get whatever we may want. When a person fails to realize his ideals, there is a reason; usually the cause is this: He simply longs for the ideal but does not work himself up to the ideal. And to work himself up to the ideal he needs everything that he can get and use now; by taking what he can get he secures something to work with in promoting his present progress, and by looking upon this something as good he will turn it to good account. It is a well-known fact that we get the best out of everything when we meet everything in the conviction that it is *good for something*, because this attitude invariably brings the mind into conscious touch with the real value of that which is met. "What we constantly look for we are sure to find, therefore, by calling everything good that we get and by constantly looking for the real worth of that which we get, the good in everything that we get will be found; the result is that everything we receive or come in contact with will be good for something to us and will have something of value to give us. Gradually, the good will so accumulate that we shall have all that we want; life will be filled with that which has quality and worth, which means that the development towards greater worth will constantly take place, and development towards greater worth means the constant ascension into the realization of our ideals. By accepting and using the good that we can now secure we add so much to the worth of our own life that we become worthy of the greater good we may desire; in consequence, we shall positively receive it. This process may not satisfy those who expect to reach the top at once or expect to receive the better without making themselves better, but it will satisfy those who would rather move forward gradually and surely than stand empty handed waiting and waiting for ages hoping that some miraculous secret may be found through which everything can be accomplished at once. The idea, however, is not that we should meekly submit to things as they are and be satisfied with what little fate may seem willing to give us; that is the other extreme and is just as detrimental to human welfare. Take everything that legitimately comes your way; do not refuse it because it seems too small; take it and call it good, because it is good for something; then make the best possible use of it with a view of getting greater good through that use; expect everything to multiply in your hands; have that faith; accept little things, as well as large things in that conviction, and every good that you do accept will be instrumental in bringing greater good to you. To live in the attitude of turning everything to good account has a most wholesome effect upon mind and character, because that mental attitude will tend to turn everything within yourself to good account; the result will be the constant development of a finer character and a more capable mind. By combining all the results from this mode of living and by noting the greater results that will invariably come from these combined results we must conclude that the total gain will be great, and that he who turns to good account everything that comes into his life, will positively receive everything that he may require to live an ideal life.

Live in the cheerful world, even if you have to create such a world in your own imagination. Resolve to be happy regardless of what comes; you cannot afford to be otherwise. Count everything joy; meet everything in the spirit of joy, and expect everything to give you joy. By creating a cheerful world in your own imagination you develop the tendency to a sunny disposition, and by meeting everything in the attitude of joy you will soon meet only those things that naturally produce joy. Like does attract like. Much sunshine will gather more sunshine, and the happiest mind meets the most delightful experiences. When exceptions occur pass them by as of no consequence, because they are of no consequence to you; you are interested only in happy events; it is only such events that you desire to meet; therefore, there is no reason whatever why you should pay any attention to the other kind. It is a fact that the less attention we pay to unpleasant conditions the less unpleasantness we meet in life. That person who looks for the disagreeable everywhere and expects to find it everywhere will certainly find what he is looking for in most places, if not in all places. On the other hand, the person who expects only the pleasant will seldom find anything else. We attract what we think of the most. There is no better medicine than cheerfulness, especially for the circulation and the digestive functions. Keep your mind full of living joy and your circulation will be strong in every part of your being, and a strong full circulation is one of the secrets to perfect health. Another great secret to health is a good digestion, and it is well to remember that so long as you are thoroughly bright and happy you can digest almost anything. The greatest value of cheerfulness, however, is found in its effect upon the mind; that is, in its power to make faculties and talents grow, just as sunshine makes flowers grow. It is a well-known fact that the most cheerful mind is the most brilliant mind, other things being equal, and that the brightest ideas always come when you are in the brightest frame of mind. This makes cheerfulness indispensable to those who wish to improve themselves and develop superior mental power. The depressed mind is always dull and never sees anything clearly; while the cheerful mind learns more readily, remembers more easily and understands more perfectly; but we must not conclude that cheerfulness is all that is necessary to the development of a fine intelligence; there must be mental power and mental quality as well; but the power and the quality of the mind, however great, cannot be fully expressed without an abundance of mental sunshine.

Though the warmest sunshine may fail to make a gravel-knoll productive, still the most fertile soil will remain barren so long as the sunshine is absent. There are thousands of fertile minds in the world that are almost wholly unproductive, because they lack mental sunshine. If these would cultivate real genuine mental brightness every part of the world would sparkle with brilliant ideas. What the acorn is to the oak bright ideas are to a great and successful life, and we all can produce bright ideas through the development of mental ability and the cultivation of mental sunshine. Cheerfulness keeps the body in the best condition and brings out the best that there is in the mind. To attain the cheerful state we must remember that it is a product of the inner life and does not come from circumstances or conditions; therefore, the first essential is to create a cheerful world in the imagination; picture in mind the brightest states of existence that you can think of and impress joy upon mind at all times; feel joy, think joy, and make every action of mind and body thrill with joy; ere long you will have created within yourself the subconscious cause of joy, and when this is done cheerfulness and brightness will become permanent elements in yourself.

Live in the present only, and seek to make the great eternal now as full and complete as possible. It is what we do for the present that counts; the past is gone, and the future is not ready to be acted upon. Give your time, your talent and your power to that which is now at hand and you will do things worthwhile; you will not waste thought upon what you expect to do, but you will turn all your energies upon that which you now can do; results will positively follow. The man who does things worthwhile in the present will not have to worry about the future; for such a man the future has rich rewards in abundance. The greater the present cause the greater the future effect. Nine-tenths of the worries in the average life are simply about the future; all of these will be eliminated when we learn to live in the present only. Instead of giving anxious thought to the bridge we may have to cross we should give scientific thought to the increase of present ability and power; thus we make ourselves fully competent to master every occasion that may be met. To judge the present by the past is not sound doctrine, because if we are advancing, the present is not only larger than the past, but quite different in many if not all respects. To follow the past is to limit one's self to the lesser accomplishments of the past and thus prevent the very best from being attained in the present. The present moment should be dealt with according to the needs of the present moment regardless of what was done under similar conditions in the past. There is sufficient wisdom at hand now to solve all the problems of the present moment, if we will make full, practical application of that wisdom. He who lives for the present only will live a larger life, a happier life, a far more useful life; this is perfectly natural, because he will not scatter his forces over past ages and future ages, but will concentrate his whole life, all his power, all his ability upon that which he is trying to do now; he will be his best today, because he will give all of his best to the life of today, and he who is his best today will be still better tomorrow.

Never complain, criticize or condemn, but meet all things in a constructive attitude of mind. The critical mind is destructive to itself, and will in time become wholly incompetent to even produce logical criticism. To complain about everything is to constantly think about the inferior side of everything, thus impressing inferiority upon the mind; this will cause the entire process of thinking to become inferior; in consequence, the retrogression of the man himself will inevitably follow. Refuse to complain about anything; complaints never righted a wrong and never will. When you seek to gain justice through complaint you temporarily gain something in one place and permanently lose something in another; besides, you have harmed your own mind. The fact is that the more you complain the worse things will become; and the more you criticize what you meet today the more adverse and inferior will be the things you are to meet tomorrow. The reason why is simple; the complaining mind attracts the cheap and the common, and the critical spirit goes directly down into weakness and inferiority. However, we must remember in this connection that there is a marked difference between the critical attitude and the discriminating attitude. When things are not right we should say so, but while saying so we should not enter into a "rip and tear" frame of mind; the facts should be stated firmly but gently and without the slightest trace of ill feeling or condemnation; simply discriminate between the white and the black and state the facts, but let no hurt whatever appear in your voice. What we say is important, but the way things are said is far more important; even truth itself, can be expressed in such a way that it hurts, harms and destroys; this, however, is not true expression. It is truth misdirected, and always produces undesirable effects. To state your wants in a friendly manner is not complaint, but when there are hurts and whines in your voice you are making complaints and you are harming yourself; besides, you are producing unfavorable impressions upon those with whom you come in contact. It is far better to have faith in people than to criticize and complain, even though everything seems to go wrong, because when we have faith in people we shall finally attract those who are after our own hearts, and who are competent to do things the way we wish to have them done. Instead of complaining, or stating that there is always something wrong, we should live constantly in the strong faith that everything is eternally coming right; we thus place ourselves in harmony with those laws that can and will make things right. This is no idle dream, nor shall we have to wait a long time to secure results. The very day we establish faith in the place of complaints, criticisms and distrust, the tide will turn; things will change for the better in our world, and continue to improve perpetually.

Make the best use of every occasion, and nothing but opportunities will come your way. He who makes the best of everything will attract the best of everything, and it is always an opportunity to meet the best. There are occasions that seem worthless, and the average person thinks he is wasting time while he is passing through such states, but no matter how worthless the occasion may seem to be the one who makes the best use of it while he is in it will get something of real value out of it; in addition, the experience will have exceptional worth, because whenever we try to turn an occasion to good account we turn everything in ourselves to good account. The person who makes the best use of every occasion is developing his mind and strengthening his own character every day; to such a person every occasion will become an opportunity and will consequently place him in touch with the greater world of opportunities. Much gathers more and many small opportunities will soon attract a number of larger ones; then comes promotion, advancement and perpetual increase. "To him that hath shall be given." Every event has the power to add to your life, and will add to your life, if you make the best use of what it has to give; this will constantly increase the power of your life, which will bring you into greater occasions and better opportunities than you ever knew before. Make the best use of everything that comes your way; greater things will positively follow; that is the law, and he who daily applies this law has a brilliant future before him.

Never antagonize anything, neither in thought, word nor deed, but live in that attitude that is non-resisting to evil while positively and continuously inclined towards the good. You give your energy to that which you resist; you thereby give life to the very thing you seek to destroy. To resist evil is to increase the power of evil, and at the same time take life and power away from that good which you wish to develop or promote. The antagonistic mind develops bitterness in itself and thereby becomes just as disagreeable as the thing disliked; frequently more so, and we cannot expect to be drawn into the more delightful elements of the ideal while we ourselves are becoming less and less ideal. To live in the antagonistic attitude is to perpetuate a destructive process throughout mind and body, and at the same time suffer a constant loss of energy. We therefore cannot afford to be antagonistic at any time, nor even righteously indignant, no matter how perfectly in the right we may be; though in this connection it is well to remember that indignation never can be righteous. There are a number of minds that have the habit of feeling an inner bitterness towards those beliefs or systems of thought which they cannot accept. Frequently there can be no logical grounds for such a feeling. In many instances it is simply hereditary, or the result of foundationless prejudice; nevertheless, it is there and is actually sapping life and power out of the mind that has it. This habit is therefore responsible for much mental weakness, inability and consequent failure; and as everything that tends to decrease the life and the power of the individual tends to shorten his life, as well as decrease the value and usefulness of his life, it is evident that we cannot afford to feel bitter toward any religion, any belief, any doctrine, any party or any person whatever; we harm ourselves by so doing and do not add to the welfare or happiness of anybody. Be on friendly terms with the entire universe and feel kindly towards every creature in existence; leave the ills of perverted life to die; let the "dead bury their dead." It is our privilege to press on and promote the greatest good that we know; and when we give our whole time and attention to the highest attainment of the greatest good, evil will die of itself. This is what it means to overcome evil with good, and it is the one perfect path to complete emancipation, both for the individual and for the race. If you wish to serve the race do not antagonize systems, doctrines, methods or beliefs; be an inspiration to the race by actually *living* the very best you know now.

4. THE FIRST THOUGHT IN IDEAL THINKING.

But seek ye first his kingdom, and his righteousness; and all these things shall be added unto you.—Mat. 6: 33.

The kingdom of God is a spiritual kingdom within man and manifests through man as the spiritual life. His righteousness is the right use of all that is contained in the elements of the spiritual life. The spiritual life being the complete life, the full expression of life in body, mind and soul, it is evident that the right use of the spiritual life will produce and bring everything that man may need or desire. The source of everything has the power to produce everything, provided the power within that source is used according to exact spiritual law. The spiritual life being the source of all that is necessary to a full and perfect life, and the kingdom within being the source of the spiritual life, we can readily understand why the kingdom should be sought first; and also why everything that we may require will be added when the first thought is given to spiritual living, ideal thinking and righteous action. Righteous action, however, does not simply imply moral action, but the right use of the elements of life in all action.

The kingdom of God is the spiritual side of all things. This spiritual side is within the manifested or visible side; that is, everything is filled with an inner, finer something that is perfect and complete. Every part of the outer world is filled and permeated with an inner world, and everything that appears in the outer world is a partial manifestation or expression of what exists in a perfect and complete state in the inner world. This inner world is the kingdom referred to, and as it is inexhaustible in every sense of that term, there is nothing we cannot receive when we learn to draw upon the riches of this vast inner realm. In the life of man we have the outer and the inner worlds; the personal life in the without and the great spiritual life in the within. What appears in the outer world of man, that is, in his personal existence, is the result of what he has sought and brought forth from his inner world. According to one of the greatest of metaphysical laws we express whatever we become conscious of. We, therefore, understand clearly why the personal man, or his outer world, is the direct result of what he has become conscious of in his interior world. Man is what he is in the without, because he has sought the corresponding elements in the within, and he may change the without in any manner desired by seeking first in the within those qualities and attributes that he may desire.

To seek and find the within is to become conscious of the within, and what is thus sought and found will express itself in personal life; but its real value will depend upon whether it is properly used or not. To seek the richer kingdom within is the first essential, but to promote the righteous use of these greater riches is the second essential, and is just as important as the first. To give the first thought at all times to the great spiritual kingdom within, it is not necessary to withdraw attention from the outer world nor to deny one's self the good things that may exist in the outer world. To seek the kingdom first is to give one's strongest thought to the spiritual life, and to make spiritual thought the predominating thought in everything that one may do in life; in other words, live so closely to the spiritual kingdom within that you are fully conscious of that kingdom every moment, and depend absolutely upon supreme power to carry you through whatever you may undertake to do. To seek the kingdom first the heart must be in the spirit; that is, to live in the full realization of the inner spiritual life at all times must be the one predominating desire. However, the mental conception of the spiritual life must not be narrow, but must contain the perfection of everything that can possibly appear in life.

To think of the spiritual life as being distinct from mind and body, is to prevent the elements of the great interior life from being expressed in mind and body, and what is not expressed cannot be lived. The spiritual life in this larger sense must be thoroughly lived in mind and body. The power of the spiritual must be made the soul of all power, and the law of spiritual action must be made the rule and the guide in all action. "When the spiritual is lived in all life the richness and the quality and the worth of the spiritual will be expressed in all life, and spiritual worth means the sum-total of all worth.

There are any number of minds in the world who now realize this greater worth and who have found the spiritual riches within to an extraordinary degree, but they have not in every instance sought righteousness; therefore, these spiritual riches have been of no use; frequently they have become obstacles in the living of a life of personal welfare and growth.

Real righteousness means right living and exact scientific thinking; that is, the correct expression of everything of which we are now conscious. To be righteous does not simply mean to be moral and truthful and just, but to live in harmony with all laws, physical, mental, moral and spiritual. To be in harmony with physical law, is to adapt one's self orderly to everything in the external world; to resist no exterior force, but to constructively use every exterior force in such a manner that perpetual physical development may take place. To be in harmony with mental laws is to promote scientific thinking; that is, to think the truth about everything and to see everything from the universal view-point. Scientific thinking is that mode of thinking that causes all the forces of mind and thought to constantly work for greater things. To be in harmony with moral laws is to live a life of complete purity; and purity in the true sense of the term is the doing of all things at the right time, in the right place and with the right motive; in other words, every action is a pure action that leads to higher and better things. All other actions are not pure, therefore not moral. To be in harmony with spiritual laws is to live in constant conscious touch with the inner or higher side of everything. To apply the spiritual law is to seek the spiritual first, no matter what the goal in view may be; to seek first the spiritual counterpart that is within everything, to make the spiritual thought the predominating thought and to dwell constantly in the spiritual attitude. "We enter the spiritual attitude when we enter the upper story of the mind and mentally face that supreme side of life that is created in the likeness of the Supreme. Briefly stated, to be righteous is to be in harmony with the outer side of life, to think the truth, to live in real purity, to dwell on the spiritual heights and to give full and complete expression to the highest and the best of which we are now conscious. When this is done we shall rightly manifest whatever we may find in the kingdom within. Righteousness, however, is not a definite goal but a perpetual process of attainment that involves the entire being of man. The righteous man is right and perfect as far as he has ascended in the scale of life at present, though not simply in a moral sense, but in every sense, including body, mind and soul.

The righteous man is never weak, never sick, and is never in a state of discord or disorder. This is a great truth that we should not fail to remember. Sickness, weakness, discord and all other adverse conditions come from the violation of law somewhere in human life, but the righteous man violates no law. He is true to life as far as he has ascended in the scale of life. To be righteous in the absolute sense of the term is to use everything in our present world as God uses everything in His world, which means in harmony with its own nature, in harmony with its sphere of action, and in harmony with that law that leads upward and onward forever. Righteous action is that action that is always harmonious and that always works for better things, greater things, higher things. The great majority of those minds that are awakened to the reality of the spiritual side of things have already found an abundance of good things in the vast interior life that is ready for manifestation in personal life, but as most of these have neglected the law of real righteousness this abundance remains inactive in the potential state and all other things as promised are not added. That all other things will be added when His kingdom and His righteousness are sought first may not seem clear to everybody, because the kingdom of God has been looked upon as a far away place that we are to enter when we leave the body, and righteousness has been looked upon as simply a moral, just and honest mode of living. But when we realize that the kingdom is the great spiritual world within us, and that from this world comes all wisdom, all power, all talent, all life; in brief, everything that we now possess in body, mind and soul, and that everything we are to receive in the future must come from the same source, we understand clearly why the kingdom must be sought first.

We cannot secure anything unless we go to the source, and the spiritual kingdom within us is the one only source of everything that is manifested in human life. When we desire more wisdom and a greater understanding it is evident that we can obtain these things only by entering real mental light, and that light is within us in the spirit. By entering into the consciousness of the illumined world within we naturally receive more light. We, ourselves, become illumined to a degree, frequently to a great degree, and we thus gain the power to understand perfectly what we could neither desire nor comprehend before. When we seek more life and power we can find the greater life only in the eternal life, and the eternal life is the life of the spirit in the kingdom within.

"They that wait upon the Lord shall renew their strength." To wait upon the Lord is to enter into the spiritual presence of the Infinite, and whenever we enter into the presence of the Infinite we enter into the life of the Infinite and we are thus filled through and through with the supreme power of that life. When we enter into the spiritual kingdom within we enter into the Christ consciousness and in that consciousness we receive the life more abundant, because to be in the Christ consciousness is to be in the very spirit of the limitless life of the Christ. When we seek health we can find it in the kingdom, because in the spirit all is always well. There is a realm within man where perfect health reigns supremely and eternally. In that realm everything is always perfectly whole and to enter into that realm is to enter into absolute health and wholeness. No one who lives constantly in the spirit can possibly be sick, because sickness can no more enter the spiritual state than darkness can enter where there is absolute light. To enter the kingdom within is to enter health, happiness and harmony in the highest, largest degree; therefore, by seeking the kingdom, health will be added, happiness will be added, harmony will be added. It is impossible, however, to gain health, happiness and harmony, in the true sense, from any other source. But to seek these qualities in the kingdom is not sufficient. We must also seek righteousness or the right expressions of those things. If we misuse any organ, faculty, function or power anywhere in body, mind or soul, we cannot remain in health, no matter how spiritual we may try to be.

To enter the kingdom within is to enter the perpetual increase of power, because there is no limit to the power of the spirit, and the more power we enter into or become conscious of the more power we shall give to mind and body; in consequence, the more spiritual we become the stronger we become, the more able we become, the more competent we become and the more we can accomplish whatever our work may be; and he who can do good work in the world invariably receives the good things of the world. To his life will be added all those things that can make personal existence rich and beautiful. To enter the kingdom within is to enter the life of freedom. There is no bondage in the spirit, and as we grow in the spirit we grow out of every form of bondage. One adverse condition after another disappears until absolute freedom is gained. Therefore, when we seek first His kingdom and His righteousness we shall find the life of complete emancipation. Perfect freedom in all things and at all times will positively be added.

There are thousands of aspiring souls in this age that are trying to develop their powers and talents so that they might be of greater use in the world, but if these would seek the kingdom first, they would find within themselves the real source of every talent; and as the only way to permanently increase anything is to increase the expressions of its source we understand perfectly why greatness can come only when we begin to live in the great within. We must always bear in mind that what we become conscious of we bring forth into personal expression, but we cannot become conscious of the larger source of any quality or talent unless we enter into the spirit of that quality and talent, and as the spirit of all things has its source of real existence in the kingdom within, we must enter this interior world if we wish to become conscious of a larger and a larger measure of those things that we wish to express.

That any person can improve his environment or overcome poverty by seeking the kingdom first may not seem possible, but the truth is that adverse conditions will positively disappear after one begins to actually live the full spiritual life. Poverty has two causes; lack of ability and the misplacing of ability. To improve ability to any degree the within must be awakened. We must learn to draw upon the inexhaustible sources of the inner life and become conscious of the greater capacity that lies latent within us. This is accomplished by seeking the kingdom first. By giving your first thought, your predominating thought to the great and mighty world within, your mind will gradually enter more deeply into the life of this inner world. You thus become conscious of the larger powers within, because consciousness always follows the predominating thought. What you think of the most develops in yourself. "When you think the most of the spiritual, consciousness will follow your spiritual thought and thus enter more deeply into the spirit. The result is you become conscious of a larger spiritual domain every day, you become conscious of a greater capacity within yourself every day, and since you always express what you become conscious of you will cause greater ability and capacity to be developed and expressed in yourself every day; you thereby remove the first cause of poverty and place yourself in a position where you will be in greater demand, and the greater the demand for your service the greater will be your recompense.

There are a number of people who have misplaced their talents that may have considerable ability, but they are not in the work for which they are adapted, and therefore do not succeed. They may have been forced into their present positions by necessity, or they may have chosen their present places through inferior judgment, but both of these causes may be changed by seeking the kingdom first. When we enter the spiritual everything clears up. We not only see our mistakes, but also how to correct them; therefore, if you are in the wrong place, enter the spiritual light of the kingdom within, and you will see clearly where you belong. If you do not know whether you are in the proper sphere or not, enter the spirit. Constantly live in the spirit and you will soon know; you will also know when and how to change. By entering this state where the outlook is infinitely greater you will see opportunities, open doors, possibilities, and pastures green that you never saw before, and you will also see clearly which one you have the power and the capacity to take advantage of now. If you have been forced into the wrong place by necessity, the larger mental life that will come when you seek the kingdom will give you the power to command something better, and the superior wisdom that comes through the light of the spirit will guide you in your choice. Instead of adversity and constant need you will have peace, harmony and abundance. You will pass from the world of poverty and limitations to a world that can offer a future as brilliant as the sun.

The man who fights adversity and complains of his lot will continue in poverty and need. He will remain in mental darkness; he will be daily misled, and will always be doing the wrong thing at the wrong time. Such a life breeds ill luck and misfortune and perpetuates the poverty that already exists. However, let this person enter into harmony with his present fate, count everything joy, and realize that he can make his present misfortune a stepping-stone to better things; then let him give his first thought to the kingdom, to the greater life and power and capacity within, to the superior creative powers of his own mind, those powers that are able even now to create for him a better fate, if he will but place before them a better pattern; the results will be peace of mind first, then hope of the better, then the vision of great changes near at hand, then the faith that the new life, the new time and the better days are now being created for his world. And when a person begins to inwardly feel that things are taking a turn, that better days are coming and that the good is beginning to accumulate in his life, the victory is nearly won. A little more faith and perseverance and the crowning day is at hand. From that moment all things will begin to work together for good things and for still greater things, providing the mind is held in constant conscious touch with the spiritual kingdom within, and all the laws of life are employed according to the highest ideal of righteousness.

Many a person, however, has failed while on the very verge of his victory, because he neglected the kingdom when he began to see the change coming. By giving his first thought to the material benefits that he expected to secure, his consciousness is taken away from the spirit and becomes confused in those things that had not as yet been placed in the true order of perpetual increase. The result is a scattering of forces and his loss upon the hold of the good things that were beginning to gravitate towards his world. While ascending this upward path we must at every step keep the eye single upon the kingdom, upon the spiritual, upon the larger and the higher life within. When the other things are being added we must not forget the kingdom and give our first thoughts to the other things. We shall enjoy these other things so much the more, if we continue to give the first thought to the spirit. This is evident, because while giving the first thought to the spirit everything that comes into our world will be spiritualized, refined and perfected, and will thus be given added power and worth. When we continue to give the first thought to the spiritual kingdom those other things that are added will enter our world at their best and we shall thus receive the best that those things may have to give.

We are always at our best when we are on the heights, and we gain the power to create, produce and attract those things from every part of life that correspond to the life on the heights.

Therefore, by living on the heights in the spiritual kingdom we gain everything that we may require; we gain the best of everything that we may require, and we are in that condition where we can make the best use of what comes, and enjoy what comes to the highest and most perfect degree. We can thus readily understand that when we seek the kingdom of God constantly, giving our first thought to the spiritual and seeking to live righteously according to this larger view of righteousness, all problems of life will be solved. All the crooked paths of life will be made straight; obstacles will disappear; our circumstances will change to correspond with our ideas, and we will daily enter into a better life and a greater state of existence than we ever knew before. The problems of the world can be solved in the same way. Therefore, the greatest thing that we can do for the human race is to make clear this law, that is, the law through which His kingdom and His righteousness may be sought first by any individual, no matter what the degree of that individual's understanding may be. To promote a real spiritual movement on the largest possible scale is to cause the ills of humanity to gradually, but surely, pass away. This planet will then become, not a vale of tears, but what it is intended to be, the kingdom of heaven realized upon earth.

The human race, however, is the product of human thought; therefore, the prime essential is to inspire the human mind with the power to give His kingdom and His righteousness the first thought. To make the ideal real upon earth, all thinking must be ideal; and to cause all things to become ideal the foundation of all things must be based upon pure spiritual thought; that is, every thought that is created in the mind must be animated with this great first thought, the thought of the kingdom within and the full righteous expression of that kingdom.

When we seek first the kingdom and his righteousness all other things are added, not in some mysterious manner, nor do they come of themselves regardless of conscious effort to work in harmony with the law of life. "We receive from the kingdom only what we are prepared to use in the living of a great life and in the doing of great and worthy things in the world. We receive only in proportion to what we give, and it is only as we work well that we produce great results; but by entering the spiritual life we receive everything that we may require in order to give as much as we may desire, to do as much as we may desire. We gain the power and the talent to do everything that is necessary to give worth and superiority to our entire state of existence. When we enter the spiritual life we gain every quality that is necessary in making life full and complete now, and we gain the power to produce and create in the external world whatever we may need or desire. In other words, we receive everything we want from within and we gain the power to produce everything we want in the without. We, therefore, need never take anxious thought about these other things. By seeking first His kingdom and His righteousness we shall positively receive these other things. The way will be open to all that is rich, beautiful and superior in life, and we shall be abundantly supplied with the best that life can give.

5. THE IDEAL AND THE REAL MADE ONE.

When the elements of the ideal are blended harmoniously with the elements of the real the two become one; the ideal becomes real and the real gives expression to the qualities of the ideal. To be in harmony with everything at all times and under all circumstances is therefore one of the great essentials in the living of that life that is constantly making real a larger and larger measure of the ideal; and so extremely important is continuous harmony that nothing should be permitted to produce confusion or discord for the slightest moment. Discord wastes energy, while harmony accumulates energy. If we wish to be strong in mind and body and do the best possible work, harmony is absolutely necessary and we must be in the best possible condition to make real the ideal. The person who lives in perpetual harmony with everything will accomplish from ten to one hundred per cent more than the average during any given period of time; a fact that gives the elements of harmony a most important place in life. When harmony is absent there is always a great deal of mental confusion, and a confused mind can never think clearly, therefore makes mistakes constantly. To establish complete and continuous mental harmony will reduce mistakes to a minimum in any mind; another fact that makes the attainment of harmony one of the great attainments.

The mind that is living in continuous harmony is realizing a great measure of heaven upon earth regardless of his personal attainments or external possessions. He has made real that ideal something that makes existence thoroughly worthwhile, and he is rich indeed. To live in harmony is to gain the joy everlasting, the contentment that is based upon the real value of life, and that satisfaction that grows larger and better for every day that passes by. On the other hand, to live in discord is to live in perpetual torment, even though our personal attainments may be great and our personal possessions as large as any mind could wish.

To live the good life, the ideal life, the beautiful life, we must be at peace with all things, including ourselves, and every thought, word and deed must be harmonious. Whatever we wish to do or be it is wisdom to make any sacrifice necessary for the sake of harmony, although that which we sacrifice for the sake of harmony is not a sacrifice. When we enter into harmony we will regain everything that we were willing to lose in order that we might possess harmony. When we establish ourselves in perfect harmony we shall be reunited with everything that we hold near and dear and the new unity will be far sweeter, far more beautiful than the one we had before. "My own shall come to me" is a favorite expression among all those who believe that every ideal can be made real, and many of these are waiting and watching for their own to come, wondering in the meantime what can be done to hasten that coming. There are many things to be done, however, but one of the most important is the attainment of harmony. No person who lives in perpetual harmony will be deprived very long of his own whatever that own may be. Whatever you deserve, whatever you are entitled to, whatever belongs to you will soon appear in your world, if you are living in perfect harmony.

To enter harmony is to enter a new world where everything is better, where opportunities are greater and more numerous, and where persons, conditions and things are more agreeable. You will not only enter a better world, however, but the attitude of harmony will relate your life so perfectly to the good things in all worlds that may exist about you, that the best from every source will naturally gravitate towards your sphere of existence. But harmony will not only cause the good things of life to gravitate towards you; it will also cause you to radiate the good qualities in your own being and thus become a perpetual benediction to everybody. To be in the presence of a person who dwells serenely in the beautiful calm is, indeed, a privilege, especially to those who can appreciate the finer elements of a truly harmonious life. Whenever we are in touch with real harmony, whether it comes from the music of human life, the music of nature or the music of the spheres, we are one step nearer the Beautiful. We can therefore realize the great value of being able to actually live in perfect harmony at all times. The life of harmony is the foundation of happiness and health and is one of the greatest essentials to achievement and real success. When we look into the past we can always find that our failures originated in confusion; likewise our troubles and ills. On the other hand, all the good things that have happened to us in the past, or that are happening in the present, had their origin and their growth in the elements of continuous harmony; the ideal and the real were made one, and we consequently reached the goals we had in view.

The mind that works in perpetual harmony does more work and far better work than is possible in any other condition; besides, harmonious work is invariably conducive to higher development and growth. To work in harmony is to promote increase and development in all the qualities and powers of the personality; while to work in confusion is to weaken the entire system and thus originate causes that will terminate in failure.

The majority state that they have no time for self-development, but to live in harmony and work in harmony is to promote self-development every moment, and this development will not be confined simply to those muscles or faculties that we use directly, but will express itself throughout the entire system; and the mind especially will, under such conditions, steadily gain both in power and in worth. In the presence of these facts we can realize readily that no person can afford to permit discord, disturbance or confusion at any time. The many declare, however, that they cannot help it, but we must help it and we can. There is no reason why our minds should be excited or our nerves upset at any time. "We can prevent this just as easily as we can refuse to eat what we do not want.

To proceed, we must apply exact reason to this great subject. We should learn to understand that no wrong will be righted because we permit ourselves to "fly to pieces;" also that the act of becoming nervous over a trouble will never drive that trouble away. To live in a constant strain will not promote our purpose nor arrange matters the way we want them. This is a fact that we should impress deeply upon our minds, and then impress our minds to take another and a better course. The average person feels that it is a religious duty to be as excited as possible, and to string up all his nerves as high as possible, whenever he is passing through some exceptional event; in consequence, he spoils all or practically all of that which might have been gained; besides, he places his system in a condition where all sorts of ills may gain a foothold. There are many reasons why such a large number of undertakings fail, but one of the principal reasons is found in the fact that few people have learned to retain perfect harmony under all kinds of circumstances. Discord and confusion are usually present to a great degree, and in consequence, something almost invariably goes wrong. But when a person is in perfect harmony and does his very best, he will succeed at least in a measure every time, and he will thus prepare himself for the greater opportunities that are sure to follow. To believe that intelligent, well educated people almost daily break down over mere trifles is not mere simplicity, but the fact that it is the truth leads us to question why. Intelligence and education should give those who possess it the power to know better. Modern education, however, does not teach us how to use ourselves. We have learned how to mix material substances so as to satisfy every imaginable taste, and we have learned how to use the tangible forces of nature so as to construct almost anything we like in the physical world, but we have not learned how to combine the elements of mind so as to produce health, happiness, strength, brilliancy and harmony whenever we may so desire. A few, however, have made the attempt, but the elements of the mind will not combine for greater efficiency and higher states of expression unless the mind is in perfect harmony.

We have all learned to remember, but few have learned to think. To repeat verbatim what others have thought and said is counted knowledge and with such borrowed knowledge the majority imagine they are satisfied, the reason being they have not discovered the art of thinking thoughts of their own. This is an art that every person must learn; the sooner the better, if the ideal is to be made real. Original thinking is the secret of all greatness, all high attainments, all extraordinary achievements and all superior states of being; but no mind can create original thought until a high state of mental harmony is attained. To produce mental harmony we must first bear in mind the great fact that it is not what happens that disturbs us, but the way we think about that which happens; and our thought about anything depends upon our point of view. The way we look at things will determine whether the experience will produce discord or harmony, and it is in our power to look at things in any way that we may desire. When we are face to face with those things that usually upset the mind we should immediately turn our attention upon the life and the power that is back of the disturbing element, having the desire to find the better side of that life and power constantly in view. Everything has its better side, its ideal side, its calm and undisturbed side, and a mere desire to gain a glimpse of that better side will turn the mind away from confusion and cause attention to be centered upon that calm state that is being sought. This will decrease discord at once, and if applied the very moment we are aware of confusion we will entirely prevent any mental disturbance whatever. To meet all circumstances and events in this way is to develop in ourselves a harmonious attitude towards all things, and when we are established in this harmonious attitude nothing whatever disturbs us; no matter what may happen we will continue to remain in harmony, and will consequently be able to deal properly with whatever may happen.

The mind that is upset by confused circumstances will lose ground and fail, but the mind that continues calmly in harmony with everything, no matter what the circumstances may be, will master every occasion and steadily rise in the scale. He will continue to make real the ideal, because he is living in that harmonious state of being where the ideal and the real are harmoniously blended into one. To promote the highest and most perfect state of continuous harmony we must learn to meet those persons, things and events, with which we come in daily contact, in the right mental attitude. The result of such an attitude is determined directly by the nature of our own attitude of mind, and as we can express ourselves through any attitude we desire, it is in our power either to spoil the most promising prospects, or convert the most unpromising conditions into the greatest success. We should train ourselves to meet everything in that attitude of mind that expects all things to work out right. When we deeply and continually expect all things to work out right we relate ourselves more perfectly with that with which we come in contact; we take things, so to speak, the way they ought to be taken, and we thereby promote harmony and co-operation among all things concerned.

Though this be extremely important, it is insignificant, however, in comparison with another great fact in this connection; that is, the way things respond to the leading desires of the ruling mind; whether it is the exercise of the mysteries of mental force or the application of a mental law not generally understood, does not concern us just now; but it is a fact that things will do, as a rule what we persistently expect them to do. To understand why this is so may require some study of the great laws of mind and body, and everybody should seek to understand these laws perfectly; but in the meantime anyone can demonstrate the fact that things will work out right if we constantly expect them to do so. No matter what may happen we should continue in the faith that all things will come right, and as our faith is so it shall be. To place ourselves in perfect harmony with all things, the domineering attitude of mind must be eliminated completely.

The mind that tries to domineer over things will not only lose control of things, but will lose control of its own faculties and forces. At first it may seem that the domineering mind gains ground, but the gain is only temporary. When the reaction comes, as it will, the loss will be far greater than the temporary gain. When you try to domineer over persons and things you gain possession and control of those things only that are too weak to control themselves. That is, you gain a temporary control over negatives, and negatives have no permanent value in your life; in fact, they soon prove themselves to be wholly detrimental. Occasionally a domineering mind may attract the attention of better things, but as soon as his domineering qualities are discovered those better things will part company with him at once. The law of attraction is at the foundation of all natural constructive processes; therefore, to promote construction, growth, advancement and real success we must work in harmony with that law. If we wish to attain the superior, we must become superior, because it is only like that attracts like. If we wish to gain the ideal, we must become ideal. If we wish to make real the ideal, we must live the ideal in the real.

When you want good things, make yourself better, and better things will naturally be attracted to you; but good things do not submit to force. Therefore, to try to secure better things through forceful methods, or through the domineering attitude can only result in failure; such methods gain only the inferior, those things that can add neither to the welfare nor the happiness of any one. This fact holds good, not only among individuals, but also among nations and institutions.

The more domineering an institution is the more inferior are its members, and the more autocratic the nation the weaker its subjects. On the other hand, we find the best minds where the individual is left free to govern himself and where he is expected to act wisely, to be true to the best that is within him. In order that the individual may advance he must steadily grow in the mastery of himself, and must so relate himself to the best things in life that he will naturally attract the best things; but these two essentials are wholly interfered with by the domineering attitude. Such an attitude repels everything and everybody that has any worth. It spoils the forces of mind, thus weakening all the mental faculties, and it steadily undermines whatever self-control a person might possess. Never try to control anything or domineer over anything, but aim to live in perpetual harmony with the highest, the truest and the best that is in everything.

Whatever happens we should approach that event in that attitude that believes it is all right. We should never permit the attitude that condemns, not even when the things concerned have proved themselves to be wrong. The attitude that condemns is detrimental to our own minds, because it invariably produces discord. When you meet all things in the expectation of finding them right, you always find something about them that is right. This something you may appropriate and thus gain good from everything that happens. That person, however, who expects to find most things wrong will fail to see the good that may exist among the things that come his way; therefore, he gains far less from life than his wiser neighbor. But what is equally important, the man who expects to find everything right wherever he may go, will gradually gravitate towards those people and circumstances that are right. The man who expects to find everything wrong usually finds what he expects. The effect of these two attitudes upon mind and character is even more important, because the man is as his mind and character, and as the man is so is his destiny. The man who expects to find most things wrong and meets the world in that attitude is constantly impressing the wrong upon his mind, and as we gradually grow into the likeness of that which we think of the most, he is building upon sinking sand. The mind that is constantly looking for the wrong cannot be wholesome. Such a mind is not in harmony with the law of growth, power, and ability; therefore, can never do its best. Unwholesome thoughts will steadily undermine the finest character and mind, and the world is full of illustrations. There is always something wrong in the life of that person who constantly expects to find things wrong, and the reason why is simple. His own expectations are reacting upon himself; by thinking about the wrong he is creating the wrong and thus bringing forth the wrong in every part of his life.

The man, however, who expects to find everything right and meets the world in that attitude is daily nourishing his mind with right thoughts, wholesome thoughts and constructive thoughts; he thinks the most of that which is right, and is therefore steadily growing more and more into the likeness of that which is right, perfect, worthy and good; he is daily changing for the better, and through this constant change he steadily rises in the scale and thereby meets the better and the better at every turn. By expecting to find everything right he finds more and more of that which is right, and as he is becoming stronger in mind, character and soul he is affected less and less by those few things that may not be as they should be. "When you meet a disappointment meet it in

157

the conviction that it is all right, because through this attitude you enter into harmony with the power that is back of the event at hand, and you thus convert the disappointment into a channel through which greater good may be secured. Those who doubt this should try it; they will find that it is based upon exact scientific fact. Transcend disappointment, and all the powers of adversity will begin to rise with you and will begin to work with you and help you reach the goal you have in view. You will thus find that it is all for the best, because through the right mental attitude you made everything work out in such a way that the best transpired as a final result.

To live in what may be termed the "all right" attitude, that is, in that attitude that expects to find everything all right and that constantly affirms that everything is all right, is to press on to the realization and the possession of those things that are as you wish them to be. Disappointments and failures, when met in this attitude, simply become open doors to new worlds where you find better opportunities and greater possibilities than you ever knew before. When the average person meets disappointment he usually declares, "Just my luck;" in other words, he enters that mental attitude that faces ill luck; he thus fails to see anything else but misfortune in that which has happened; and so long as that person consciously or unconsciously expects misfortune, into more and more misfortune he will go. He who believes that he is fated to have bad luck will have bad luck in abundance. The reason is he lives in that mental attitude that places his mind in constant contact with those confused elements in the world that never create anything else but bad luck. That person, however, who thoroughly believes that everything that happens is simply a step to greater good, higher attainments and greater achievements, will steadily rise into those greater things that he expects to realize; the reason being that he is living in that mental attitude that places his mind in contact with the building power of life. Those powers will always build for greater things to those with whom they are in harmony, and we all can place ourselves in harmony with those powers; therefore, we can all move upward and onward forever, eternally making real more and more of that which is ideal.

What we expect comes if our expectation is filled with all the power of life and soul, and what we believe our fate to be, that is the kind of a fate we will create for ourselves. To meet ill luck in the belief that it is your luck, your particular kind of luck, and that it is natural for you to have that kind of luck is to stamp your own mind as an unlucky mind. This will produce chaotic thinking, which will cause you to do everything at the wrong time, and all your energies will be more or less misdirected; in consequence, bad luck and misfortune must necessarily follow. Bad luck comes from doing the wrong thing, or from being your worst; while good luck comes from being your best and from doing the right thing at the right time. It is therefore mere simplicity to create good luck at any time and in the measure that we may desire. The person that fears misfortune or expects misfortune and faces life in that attitude is concentrating attention upon misfortune; he thereby creates a world of misfortune in his own mind; and he who lives in mental misfortune will produce misfortune in his external life. Like causes produce like effects; and this explains why the things we fear always come upon us. We create mental causes for those things, and corresponding tangible effects always follow. Train the mind to expect the right and the best, regardless of present circumstances, conditions or events. Call everything good that is met. Declare that everything that

158

happens, happens for the best. Meet everything in that frame of mind, and no matter how wrong or adverse conditions seem to be, you cause them all to work out right.

"When the mind expects the best, has the faith that the right will prevail, and constantly faces the superior, the true mental attitude has been gained. Through that attitude all the forces of mind and all the powers of will become constructive, and will build for man the very thing that he expects or desires while his mind is fixed upon the ideal. He relates himself harmoniously to the best that is in all things and thus unites the ideal with the real in all things; and when the ideal becomes one with the real, the ideal desired becomes an actual fact in the real; and this is the goal every true idealist has in view. He takes those elements that have been revealed to him through the vision of the soul and blends them harmoniously with the actions of daily life. He thus brings the ideal down to earth and causes the real of everyday life to express the ideal in everything that he may undertake to do. His life, his thought, his action, his attainments, his achievements, all contain that happy state where the ideal and the real are made one. His dreams have become true. The visions of the soul are actually realized, and the tangible is animated with that ideal something that makes personal existence all that anyone could wish it to be.

6. THE FIRST STEP TOWARDS COMPLETE EMANCIPATION.

To forgive everybody for everything at all times, regardless of circumstances, is the first step towards complete emancipation. Heretofore, we have looked upon forgiveness as a virtue; now we know it to be a necessity. To those who possessed the spirit of forgiveness we have given our highest praise, and have thought of such people as being self-sacrificing in the truest sense of that term. We did not know that the act of forgiving is the simplest way to lighten one's own burdens. According to our former conception of this subject, the man who forgives denies himself a privilege, the privilege of indignation and revenge; for this reason we have looked upon him as a hero or as a saint, thinking that it could not be otherwise than heroic and saintly to give up the supposed pleasure of meting out revenge to those who seemed to deserve it. According to the new view, however, the man who forgives is no more saintly than the one who insists upon keeping clean, because in reality the act of forgiving simply constitutes a complete mental bath. When you forgive everybody for everything you cleanse your mind completely of every wrong thought or adverse mental attitude that may exist in your consciousness. This explains why forgiveness is a necessity and why the man who forgives everything emancipates himself from all kinds of burdens. It is therefore profitable, most highly profitable, to forgive everybody, no matter what they have done, and this includes also ourselves. It is just as necessary to forgive ourselves as to forgive others, and the principal reason why forgiveness has seemed to be so difficult is because we have neglected to forgive ourselves.

We cannot let go of that which is not desired until we have acquired the mental art of letting go, and to acquire this art we must practice upon our own minds. That is, we must learn to let go from our own minds all those things that we do not wish to retain. When you forgive yourself completely you wash your mentality perfectly clean. You let go of everything in your mental system that is not good. You emancipate yourself completely. Whatever you held against yourself or others you now drop entirely out of your mind; in consequence, you are freed from your mental burdens, and when mental burdens disappear all other burdens will disappear also. The ills that we hold in mind are the only things that can actually burden our lives. Therefore, when we forgive everybody for every ill we ever knew we no longer hold a single ill in our own minds; we thus throw off every burden and are perfectly free. This also includes disease, because disease is nothing but a temporary effect of a wrong that we mentally hold in the system. Forgive everybody, including yourself, for everything, and all disease will vanish from your system. This may at first sight appear to be a startling statement, but it is the truth, and anyone can prove it to be the truth. "Asa man thinketh in his heart so is he." Therefore, when every wrong is eliminated from the heart of man there can be no wrong in the man himself, and every wrong is eliminated from that heart that forgives everything in everyone. Many persons, however, will state that they hold no ill against anyone yet suffer just the same. So they may think, nevertheless they are mistaken and will see their mistakes when they learn the truth about mental laws. You may not hold direct ill against any person just now, but your mind has not always been absolutely pure and absolutely free from every wrong thought. You have had many wrong desires in your heart, and have had many mistaken ideas. To hold a mistaken idea is to hold a wrong in your heart. To have wrong desires is to hold ills against yourself, as well as others. To blame yourself, criticize yourself, feel provoked at yourself or condemn yourself for your shortcomings is to hold ills against yourself, and there are very few who are not doing this every day to some degree.

When we forgive all and still suffer we may not believe that forgiveness produces emancipation; but the fact is that suffering is impossible when forgiveness is absolute. When we forgive completely we shall also eliminate completely every trouble or ill that may exist in our world. When you have trouble forgive those who have caused the trouble; forgive yourself for permitting yourself to be troubled, and your troubles will pass away. When you have made a mistake do not condemn yourself or feel upset; simply forgive yourself, and resolve that you will never make the mistake again. As you make that resolution, desire more wisdom, and have the faith that you will secure the wisdom you require. "According to your faith so shall it be."

There are many who will think that the practice of forgiving everybody for everything will produce mental indifference and thus weaken character, but it is the very opposite that will take place. To forgive is to eliminate the useless, everything that is not good; and to free the mind from obstacles and adverse conditions is to enable that mind to be its best, to express itself fully and completely. This will not only strengthen the character and enlarge the mind, but will cause the greatness of the soul to come forth. There is many a character that appears to be strong on account of its open hostility to wrongs, but such a character is not always strong. Too often it is composed of a few borrowed ideas about morality backed up by mere animal force.

The true character does not express hostility and does not resist or antagonize, but overcomes evil by giving all its power to the building of the good. A strong character meets evil with a silent indifference; that is, indifference in appearance only. The true character does not pass evil by because he does not care, but because he does care. He cares so much that he will not waste one single moment in prolonging the life of the wrong; therefore gives his whole time and attention to the making of good so strong that evil becomes absolutely powerless in the presence of that good. No intelligent person would antagonize darkness. By giving his time to the production of light he causes the darkness to disappear of itself.

When we apply the same principle to the elimination of evil a marvelous change for the better will come over the world. No person can forgive everybody for everything until he desires the best from every person and from every source. In other words, we cannot forgive the wrong until we desire the right.

Therefore, the letting go of the inferior and the appropriation of the superior constitutes one and the same single mental process. "We cannot eliminate darkness until we proceed to produce light, and it requires only the one act for removing the one and bringing forth the other. From these facts it is evident that when we let go of the wrong we gain more of that power that is right, and we thus increase the strength of character. To eliminate diseased conditions from the body will increase the strength of the body and will place the body in a position for further development, if we desire to promote such development. Likewise, to eliminate all ill feelings, all hatred, all wrong thoughts and all false beliefs from the mind will increase the power of the mind and place every mental faculty in proper condition for higher development. The same effect will be produced in the character, and all awakened minds know that the greatness of the soul can begin to come forth only when we have completely forgiven everybody for everything.

The man who finds it easier to forgive than to condemn is on the verge of superior wisdom and higher spiritual power. He has entered the path to real greatness and may rapidly rise in the scale by applying the laws of true human development. Instead of producing weakness and indifference the act of absolute forgiveness will produce a more powerful character, a more brilliant mind and a greater soul. Try this method for a year. Forgive everybody for everything, no matter what happens, and do not forget to forgive yourself. You will then conclude that forgiveness, absolute forgiveness, is not only the path to complete emancipation, but is also the "gates ajar" to a better life, a larger life, a richer life, a more beautiful life than you ever knew before. You will find that you can instantaneously remove disease from the body, perversion and wrong from the mind by complete and unrestricted forgiveness; and you can in the same way steadily recreate yourself into a new and better being. Forgive the imperfect, and with heart and soul desire constantly the realization of the perfect; the imperfect will thus pass away and the more perfect will be realized in a greater and greater abundance.

Whatever our place in life may be, we must eliminate every burden of mind or body, if we wish to rise in the scale, and the first step in this direction is to forgive everybody for everything. When you begin to practice forgiveness on this extensive scale you will find obstacles disappearing one after the other. Those things that held you down will vanish and that which was constantly in your way will trouble you no more; your pathway will be cleared. You will have nothing more to contend with, and everything in your life will move smoothly and harmoniously towards greater and greater things. This is perfectly natural, because by forgiving everybody and everything you have let every form of evil go. You have invited all the good, and have therefore populated your own world with persons and things after your own heart. Through perpetual and complete forgiveness your mind will be kept perfectly clean. Not a, single weed will ever appear in the beautiful garden of your mind, and so long as the mind is clean neither sickness nor adversity can exist in human life. This may be a strong statement, but those who will try the principle and continue to live it will find it to be the truth.

Since forgiveness is a necessity to all who wish to eliminate the lesser and retain the greater, or in other words make real the ideal, it will be highly important to present the simplest methods through which anyone may learn to practice this great art. It has been said that to know all is to forgive all; but it is not possible for anyone to know all. Therefore, if we wish to forgive absolutely, we must proceed along a different line. When we ask ourselves why people live, think and act as they do we meet the great law of cause and effect. In our study of this law we find that every cause is an effect of a previous cause, and that that previous cause is also an effect of a cause still more remote. We may continue to trace these causes and effects far back along the chain of events until we are lost in the dimness of the past; but what do we learn by such a process of analysis? Nothing whatever. We fail to find anything definite about anybody, and consequently cannot fix the blame for anything; but it is not possible to justly blame anybody when we cannot fix the blame for anything. Therefore, we have only one alternative, and that is to forgive. We can never find the real cause of a single thing. We may first blame the individual, but when we discover the influence of environment, heredity and early training we cannot wholly blame the individual. If we blame the parents, we must find the reason why those parents were not different, also why previous generations were not different. If we accept the theory that the individual has lived before and that he came into his present environments because he was what he was in a previous state of existence, we must explain why he did not live a different life in that other existence; why did he act in such a manner in the past that he should merit adversity and weakness in the present. If he knew no better in the past, what is the reason that he did not know any better? If we accept the belief that we have all inherited our perverted tendencies from Adam and Eve, we must explain why those two souls were not strong enough to rise above temptation. If they were tempted, we must explain why; we must explain why the original man who was created in the image and likeness of God did not express his divine nature in the midst of temptation. But there is no way in which we can explain these things; therefore, to fix the blame for anything is absolutely impossible.

The more we try to find the original cause of anything the more convinced we become that to look for sin or the cause of sin is nothing but a waste of time. Every individual is himself a cause, and his life comes constantly in touch with a number of other causes; therefore, it is never possible to say which one of these causes or combination of these causes produced the original action. Back of every action we find other actions that lead us to the one that we may now consider, but we do not know how those other actions were produced. To trace them back to their original source simply leads us into what appears to be a beginningless beginning. For this reason it is the height of wisdom to let the "dead bury its dead," to let the past go, to forgive every sinner and forget every sin, and to use our time, talent and power for the building of more lofty mansions in the great eternal now. To look for the blame is to find that we are all more or less to blame, and also to find that there is no real fixed blame anywhere. We may then ask what we are to do with this great subject; are we to talk, theorize, speculate, condemn and punish? We know too well that all of that is but a waste of time. The sensible course to pursue is to forgive everybody for everything, to drop ills, mistakes, wrongs, disagreeable memories and proceed to use those laws of life that we understand now in making life better for everybody now.

The man who is habitually doing wrong is mentally or morally sick. Punishment is a waste of time; besides, it is absolutely wrong, and one wrong cannot remove another. Such a person should be taken where he can be healed and kept there until he is well. We should not hate him or condemn him anymore than those who are physically sick. Sickness is sickness whether it appears in the body, the mind or the character, and he who is sick does not need a prison; he needs a physician. To absolutely remove this hatred for the wrong-doers in the world we must cultivate a higher order of love, that love that loves every living creature with the true love of the soul, and such a love is readily attained when we train ourselves to look for the ideal soul of life that exists in everything everywhere in the world.

This idea may cause many to come to the conclusion that the act of forgiving the wrong-doer will have an undesirable effect upon society, because we may be liable to let people in general do as they please; but in this they are wholly mistaken. Reason declares that you cannot justly blame anyone, and love does not wish to blame anyone; forgiveness must therefore inevitably follow when reason and love are truly combined; but reason and love will never permit man in general to do as he pleases. When we love people we are not indifferent about their future. We do not wish them to go down grade. We want them to improve, to do the right and the best and we will do everything in our power to emancipate and elevate the entire race. Reason understands how the laws of life can be applied in producing those results we may have in view; therefore, the desires of love can be carried out through the understanding of reason, and thus every high purpose may be promoted by the right spirit and the proper methods. Others may declare that these methods are in advance of our time and cannot be carried out at present; therefore, it is useless to even talk about it. However, be that as it may, the fact remains that forgiveness is a necessity to the true life, the emancipated life, the superior life, the ideal life. For that reason every person who desires to make real the ideal in his world must begin to practice absolute forgiveness at once. If we can forgive everybody for everything now, we should do so, whether the world in general can do so or not. The man who wishes to move forward must not wait for the race. It is his privilege to go in advance of the race; thus he prepares the way for millions.

When he has demonstrated by example that there are better ways of living, the race will follow. What the few can do today the many will do tomorrow, but if the few should wait until tomorrow, the many would have to wait until the day following, or possibly longer still. Be what you can be now. Do what you can do now, no matter how far in advance of this age such actions may be. If you are capable of greater things today, you owe it to the race to demonstrate those greater things now. You sprung from the race. You are composed of the finer elements that exist in the race, and should consider it a privilege to cause those elements to shine as brilliantly as possible; and one of the greatest of all demonstrations in this age is that of absolute forgiveness, to demonstrate the power of forgiving everybody for everything at all times and under every possible circumstance. We therefore conclude that complete emancipation from everything that is not desired in life can be realized only when we forgive absolutely in this great universal sense; and when we have forgiven everybody for everything, then we can say with the great Master Mind, "My yoke is easy and my burden is light."

7. PATHS TO PERPETUAL INCREASE.

The universe is overflowing with all manner of good things and there is enough to supply every wish of every heart with abundance still remaining. How every heart is to proceed, however, that its every wish may be supplied, has been the problem, but the solution is simple. In consequence, everybody may rejoice. This world is not a "vale of tears," but is in truth a most delightful place, and is endowed with everything that is needful to make the life of man an endless song. "We now know that we do not live to be miserable, but to rejoice. The bitterness that sometimes appears in life is not a real part of life. The greatness of existence alone is intended for man. To know the bitter from the sweet and to appropriate the latter and always reject the former is a matter, however, that is not clearly understood. There may by thousands who know the bitter when they see it, but they do not always know how to reject it. To throw off the ills of life is an art that few have mastered. But those who can eliminate the wrong are not always able to distinguish the right from the wrong, the reason being that we have not looked at things from the view-point of that power that produces things. The philosophers, the theologians and the scientists, as a rule, make life very complex and difficult to live. Their profound expressions confuse the multitudes, while ills and troubles continue as before; but to live is simple. Even a child can be happy; it therefore should not be difficult for anyone else.

When we realize happiness in its highest, broadest sense, we find that it comes in its fullness only when we have everything that the heart desires; and since the desires of the heart increase in size and number with the enlargement of life, the joy of living will increase in proportion providing all the desires of the heart are supplied. This fact, however, may at first sight seem to make happiness very difficult to secure. If we cannot enjoy the allness of joy until we have everything that heart can wish for, then happiness is far away; so it may seem, but things are not always what they seem. All things are possible, and the most difficult things become comparatively easy when we know how; therefore, the way of wisdom is not to look for those difficulties that ignorance has connected with things, but look for that simplicity that is the soul of all knowledge. When we learn to do things as they should be done, all difficulties disappear, and even the largest life becomes simple.

The doing of things is the universal theme in this age. Those who simply tell us what to do are no longer acceptable. We want practical instructions that tell us how. The greatest man of this age and of the future will not be the one who can move as he wishes the emotions of multitudes by the magic art of eloquence and bring whole nations to his feet by the artistic juggling of eloquent phrases. The great man will henceforth be the man who can tell us how, and who can express himself so clearly that anyone can understand. This, however, we are now beginning to do, and ere long the many will come back to the truth itself and understand the real truth in all its original simplicity. The path of truth and life is perfectly straight and is illumined all the way. It is therefore simplicity itself to follow this path when we find it, but the many have strayed into the jungles of illusions and misconceptions. These must all come back to the simple path, and when they do the difficulty of living will wholly disappear.

To teach the race how to find the simple things, the true things and the real things is now the purpose of every original thinker, and whoever can add to the world's wisdom in this respect becomes a light to the race, indeed. One of the first principles in this new understanding of things is that which deals with man's power to place himself in perfect touch with the source of limitless supply; in other words to enter the path of perpetual increase. As previously stated, the world is overflowing with good things, because life is in touch with the limitless source of all good things, and there is so much of everything that the wish of every heart can be gratified. We do not have to take from another to have abundance, because there is more than sufficient for all. The fact that someone has abundance does not prove that he has taken some or all of his wealth from others, although this is what a great many believe to be the truth. Whenever we see someone in luxury we wonder where and how he got it, and we usually add that many are in poverty because this one is in wealth. Such doctrine, however, is not true. It is thoroughly false from beginning to end. The world is not so poverty stricken that the few cannot have plenty without stealing from the many. The universe is not so bare and so limited that multitudes are reduced to want whenever a few persons undertake to surround themselves with those things that have beauty and worth. True, there is injustice in the world. There are people who have secured their wealth, not upon merit, but through the art of reducing others to want; but the remedy is not to be found in the doctrine that thousands must necessarily become poor when one becomes very rich. This doctrine is an illusion, and illusions cannot serve as foundations for a better order. There is enough in life to give every living person all the wealth and all the luxury that he can possibly appropriate.

God is rich; the universe is overflowing with abundance. If we have not everything that we want, there is a reason; there is some definite cause somewhere, either in ourselves or in our relations to the world, but this cause can be found and corrected; then we may proceed to take possession of our own. Among the many causes of poverty and the lack of a full supply there is one that has been entirely overlooked. To overcome this cause is to find one of the most important paths to perpetual increase, and the remedy lies within easy reach of everyone who has awakened to a degree the finer elements in his life.

There may be exceptions to the rule, but there are thousands who are living on the husks of existence because they were not grateful when the kernels were received. Multitudes continue in poverty from no other cause than a lack of gratitude, and other thousands who have almost everything that the heart may wish for do not reach the coveted goal of full supply because their gratitude is not complete.

We are now beginning to realize more and more that the greatest thing in the world is to live so closely to the Infinite that we constantly feel the power and the peace of His presence. In fact, this mode of living is the very secret of secrets revealing everything that the mind may wish to know or understand in order to make life what it is intended to be. We also realize that the more closely we live to the Infinite the more we shall receive of all good things, because all good things have their source in the Supreme; but how to enter into this life of supreme oneness with the Most High is a problem. There are many things to be done in order to solve this problem, but there is no one thing that is more important in producing the required solution than deep, whole-souled gratitude. The soul that is always grateful lives nearer the true, the good, the beautiful and the perfect than anyone else in existence, and the more closely we live to the good and the beautiful the more we shall receive of all those things. The mind that dwells constantly in the presence of true worth is daily adding to his own worth. He is gradually and steadily appropriating that worth with which he is in constant contact; but we cannot enter into the real presence of true worth unless we fully appreciate the real worth of true worth; and all appreciation is based upon gratitude.

The more grateful we are for the good things that come to us now the more good things we shall receive in the future.

This is a great metaphysical law, and we shall find it most profitable to comply exactly with this law, no matter what the circumstances may be. Be grateful for everything and you will constantly receive more of everything; thus the simple act of being grateful becomes a path to perpetual increase. The reason why is found in the fact that whenever you enter into the mental attitude of real gratitude your mind is drawn into much closer contact with that power that produces the good things received. In other words, to be grateful for what we have received is to draw more closely to the source of that which we receive. The good things that come to us come because we have properly employed certain laws, and when we are grateful for the results gained we enter into more perfect harmony with those laws and thus become able to employ those laws to still greater advantage in the immediate future. This anyone can understand, and those who do not know that gratitude produces this effect should try it and watch results.

The attitude of gratitude brings the whole mind into more perfect and more harmonious relations with all the laws and powers of life. The grateful mind gains a firmer hold, so to speak, upon those things in life that can produce increase. This is simply illustrated in personal experience where we find that we always feel nearer to that person to whom we express real gratitude. When you thank a person and truly mean it with heart and soul you feel nearer to that person than you ever did before. Likewise, when we express whole-souled thanksgiving to everything and everybody for everything that comes into life we draw closer and closer to all the elements and powers of life.

In other words, we draw closer to the real source from which all good things in life proceed.

When we consider this principle from another point of view we find that the act of being grateful is an absolute necessity, if we wish to accomplish as much as we have the power to accomplish. To be grateful in this large, universal sense is to enter into harmony and contact with the greatest, the highest and the best in life. We thus gain possession of the superior elements of mind and soul and, in consequence, gain the power to become more and achieve more, no matter what our object or work may be. Everything that will place us in a more perfect relation with life, and thus enable us to appropriate the greater richness of life, should be employed with the greatest of earnestness, and deep whole-souled gratitude does possess a marvelous power in this respect. Its great value, however, is not confined to the laws just mentioned. Its power is exceptional in another and equally important field.

To be grateful is to think of the best, therefore the grateful mind keeps the eye constantly upon the best; and, according to another metaphysical law, we grow into the likeness of that which we think of the most. The mind that is always dissatisfied fixes attention upon the common, the ordinary and the inferior, and thus grows into the likeness of those things. The creative forces within us are constantly making us just like those things upon which we habitually concentrate attention. Therefore, to mentally dwell upon the inferior is to become inferior, while to keep the eye single upon the best is to daily become better. The grateful mind is constantly looking for the best, thus holding attention upon the best and daily growing into the likeness of the best. The grateful mind expects only good things, and will always secure good things out of everything that comes. What we constantly expect we receive, and when we constantly expect to get good out of everything we cause everything to produce good. Therefore, to the grateful mind all things will at all times work together for good, and this means perpetual increase in everything that can add to the happiness and the welfare of man.

This being true, and anyone can prove it to be true, the proper course to pursue is to cultivate the habit of being grateful for everything that comes. Give thanks eternally to the Most High for everything and feel deeply grateful every moment to every living creature. All things are so situated that they can be of some service to us, and all things have somewhere at some time been instrumental in adding to our welfare. "We must therefore, to be just and true, express perpetual gratitude to everything that has existence. Be thankful to yourself. Be thankful to every soul in the world, and most of all be thankful to the Creator of all that is. Live in perpetual thanksgiving to all the world, and express the deepest, sincerest, most whole-souled gratitude you can feel within whenever something of value comes into your life.

When other things come, pass them by; never mind them in the least. You know that the good in greater and greater abundance is eternally coming into your life, and for this give thanks with rejoicing; you know that every wish of the heart is being supplied; be thankful that this is true, and you will draw nearer and nearer to that place in life where that can be realized that you know is on the way to realization. Live according to this principle for a brief period of time, and the result will be that your life will change for the better to such a degree that you will feel infinitely more grateful than you ever felt before. You will then find that thanksgiving is a necessary part of real living, and you will also find that the more grateful you are for every ideal that has been made real, the more power you gain to press on to those greater heights where you will find every ideal to be real. And when this realization begins you are on the path to perpetual increase, because the more you receive the more grateful you feel, and the more grateful you feel for that which has been received the more closely you will live to that Source that can give you more.

8. CONSIDER THE LILIES.

Consider the lilies of the field, how they grow; they toil not, neither do they spin; yet I say unto you, that even Solomon in all his glory was not arrayed like one of these—Mat. 6; 28, 29.

The greatest service that anyone can render to the race is to properly fill the place he occupies now, to be himself today; but it is not only others that will benefit by such individual actions. The individual himself will receive greater good from life through this method than through all other methods combined. The great secret of secrets is to live your own life in your own world as well as you possibly can now. In this age thousands are seeking the path of spiritual growth and high intellectual attainments, while millions are dreaming of the life beautiful; accordingly, systems almost without number are springing up everywhere, claiming to reveal the hidden path to these greater goals; but it is the truth that when everything has been said, the one statement that rises above them all is this: *Be all that you are today and you shall be even more tomorrow.* If you are in search of higher spiritual and intellectual attainments enter into every form of wisdom that surrounds you today and fill your life with as much spirit as you can possibly realize. If you wish to live an ideal life, then aim to make real the most beautiful life that you can think of today. If you are longing for greater accomplishments and a larger sphere of usefulness, then be your very best in the place that you occupy now.

The mighty oak grows great because it grows in the present; it does not think of the past or the future; it is what it is now; it does not wish to become mighty; it simply grows on silently and continually. The lily of the field is beautiful because it is perfectly satisfied to be a lily, but it is not satisfied to be less than all a lily can be. It does not strive or work hard to become beautiful; it simply goes on being what it is, and the result is it has been made immortal by the greatest mind that ever lived. When we follow the example of the lily we find the real secret of life, so simply and clearly stated that anyone can understand. Be what you are today. *Do not be satisfied to be less than you can today and do not strive to be more.* Progress, growth, advancement, attainment—these do not come through overreaching. The mind that overreaches will have a reaction; he will fall to the bottom and will have to begin all over again. Real attainment comes by being your best where you are just for today, by filling the present moment with all the life you are conscious of; no more. If you try to express more life than you can comfortably feel in consciousness, you are overreaching and you will have a fall. The great mistake of the age is to strive, to go about our work as if it were extremely difficult. The man who works the hardest usually accomplishes the least; while the truly great man is the man who has trained his life and his power to work through him.

The lilies of the field are not engaged in hard labor, and yet their usefulness cannot be measured; they are fulfilling their true purpose; they are making real the ideal in their own world and they are living inspirations to every soul in existence. They live to be beautiful and they become beautiful, not by being ambitious for beauty, but by permitting all the beauty they possess to come forth. What is within us is constantly pressing for expression. We do not have to call it forth nor labor so much to bring it into action. All we are required to do is to permit ourselves to be what we are, to permit what is within to express itself fully and completely. We do not have to work so hard to become great. We are all naturally great, and our potential greatness is ever ready to manifest, if we would only cease our striving and let life live. The lily is beautiful because it does not hinder its own inherent beauty from coming forth to be seen; but if the lily should take up the strenuous life it would in one generation become a despised weed. The human race today resembles in too many instances the useless weed. Millions in every generation come and go without accomplishing anything whatever. They do not even live a life that gives contentment.

The reason is they strive too much, and in their striving destroy the very powers that can produce greatness. We have worked hard for results, not knowing that the only cause of results was within us, ready to produce the very results we desired, just for the asking. We have in many instances destroyed our brains trying to invent methods for producing health, happiness, power and success, not knowing that these things already existed within us in abundant supply, and that by wholesome thinking they would appear in full external expression.

The secret of secrets is to let the best within us have full right of way; this, however, most of us have failed to do. In consequence, the majority are undeveloped weaklings of little use to themselves or to the world. The lily permits that which *is* to have right of way. It does not interfere, but man does interfere. He usually refuses to accept the gifts which nature wishes to bestow upon him, and he hardly ever accepts assistance from a higher power. He sets out for himself and works himself into old age and death trying to gain what was actually given to him in the beginning. He leaves the real riches of life and enters the world of personal ambition expecting to find something better and create something superior through his own efforts, but he fails because man alone can do nothing. The average person does not realize that to create something from nothing is impossible, nor has he learned that the necessary something can come only from the life that is within. He may try to accomplish much and become much through personal ambition and hard work, but no one can build without material, and the material that is needed in building greatness can be secured only by giving right of way to the life and the power of the inner world. The man who expects to build greatness upon personal limitations will pass away in the effort, leaving his unfinished work to be taken up by someone else who will possibly build upon the same useless foundation. Thus one generation after another comes and goes, each expecting to succeed where predecessors failed; in the meantime very little is accomplished by man, and he fails to receive what infinite life is ever waiting to give.

This is the truth about man in general. The multitudes have come and gone during countless ages and have accomplished but little. There have been a few great exceptions in every age, but these were exceptions because they refused to follow the ways of the world. They learned the lesson that the lilies have taught, and they chose to let life live, to let the greatness from within come forth, to let power work, and to let that which *is* in the real of man have full right of way. When a person discovers what he is and permits that which he is to have full expression, his days of weariness, trouble and failure are gone. Henceforth he will live as the flower. His life will be full. He will fulfill his purpose and eternally become more and more of that which already is in the great within. When a flower, which has so little of soul within itself, can become so much by permitting itself to be itself, how much more might man become if he would permit himself to be himself. Man is created in the image of God, therefore marvels are hidden within his wonderful soul. When these marvels are given full expression then man begins to become that which the Infinite intended that he should be. In the soul of the lily is hidden the spirit of beauty; nothing more. But the lily does not hinder this spirit from appearing in visible form; therefore, it becomes an inspiration of joy to all the world. In the soul of man even the Infinite is hidden; we can therefore imagine what man will become when he permits the spirit of divinity to express itself in his personal form. This is a great truth, indeed, and deserves constant attention from every mind that has learned to think.

We may believe that every step forward that we have taken has been produced through personal efforts and hard work, but in this we are mistaken. In the first place, those achievements that have followed hard work are always insignificant and never of any permanent value, but those steps forward that have permanent value and that are truly great we find were taken during those moments when we permitted real life to live. "We therefore find that striving accomplishes nothing, while we may through *living*, accomplish anything. There are times when many of us cease our strenuous labor for a few moments and unconsciously open our souls to that higher something that we feel so much the need of when wearied with misdirected labors, and the influx of real life that comes at such times is the cause of those real steps upward and onward that we have taken. At such times we chose to be like the lily; we permitted the good that was to come forth; we gave up, so to speak, to higher power and did not interfere with its highest, fullest expression. What we gain at such moments is always with us and never fails to give us strength, power and inspiration even when we decide for the time being to adopt the ways of the world once more. But since every step in advance comes when we refuse to go the way of the world, we should now understand that the way of the world is a mistake. We should therefore free ourselves from that mode of life, thought and action absolutely.

The world seeks to gain greater things through personal ambition and hard work. The true way to attain greater things is to permit the greatness that is within to have full expression; likewise when we seek health, happiness and harmony or a beautiful life, the true course is to permit those things to come forth and act through us; they are ready to appear. We do not have to work for them or strive so hard to secure them. They are now at hand and will express themselves through us the very moment we grant them permission. We have all discovered that whenever we become perfectly still and permit supreme life to live in us we can feel power accumulating in our system until we feel as if we could move mountains. We have also felt that while turning attention to the everlasting joy within and opening the mind fully to this joy that there came into being a state of happiness, comfort and contentment that seemed infinitely more perfect than the imagination has ever pictured the joys of heaven to be. Likewise when we failed to find health in the without or through external means we invariably found the precious gift coming from within, the moment we gave up, so to speak, to its wholesome life and power.

In this age personal ambition is one of the ruling factors, and nearly everybody is trying to outdo someone else. The result is we build up and tear down in the outer world, but as a race we improve but little. The great within is ignored, held back or prevented from free expression, while there are few things in the great without that are really worthwhile. There never was a time when we should consider the lilies of the field more than now. The human race is breaking itself down striving to gain hold upon phantoms, while the great prize that has already been given is lost sight of in the dust and confusion. But to inspire the present generation with a desire to return to nature and her beautiful ways cannot be done to any extent, however, except through living examples. It is the living of life that will change the life of the world. The world at large does not listen to reason, nor can those who are in the mad rush stop to think; besides, such minds are not sufficiently clear to understand the principles upon which the living of life is based. Seeing is believing, as far as the world is concerned, and therefore they require living examples of those who have proven the superiority of the better way; accordingly, those who know how to live as the lilies live should consider it a privilege to place their light wherever it can be seen. When you can prove through your own life and experience that personal ambition and hard work are not necessary to greater things, but are actual hindrances, and that greater things come of themselves to those who will permit themselves to *be* themselves, you have caused a great light to spring up, and few there are who will not see it.

Those who take everything literally may wonder how anything can be accomplished without work, but they must bear in mind that there is work, and work. The work that is done by those who are down in the world's way is hard, wearing and tearing. It is destructive to human life and builds up one thing by tearing down another, and in the end it brings no lasting good, neither to the individual nor to the race; but the work that is done by those who have found the better way is neither hard nor wearisome. It is not done through strenuous living nor external striving, but is done by the power of the great within coming forth into expression in personal life. In this mode of work you first give your inner power right of way, then you direct it consciously and intelligently. You do not depend upon personal power and difficult personal efforts. You place yourself in the hands of higher power, and as you receive higher power you cause it to do that which you wish to have done. You have all felt power working through you, and at such times work was pleasure. You gave the commands, of course, and you knew it was your own power, your own higher power, but no hard personal effort was required. You simply opened the way somehow, then decided firmly but gently what you wished to have done; and you could feel a mighty power coming forth, seemingly from an inexhaustible source, taking full possession of thought and muscle, and doing the very thing you desired to have done. After the work was finished you discovered it was superior work, and although you had engaged in the task for many hours you actually felt stronger than when you began.

The reason why is simple. You did not depend upon personal limitations and strenuous efforts; and you did not try to make those limitations do a great deal more than they had the capacity to do. You opened your life to all the power of your life and you thus received enough power to do what you wished to have done, and more; and so long as you have power to spare you can be neither weak nor tired. When the system is thoroughly full of energy, work is a pleasure; and so long as that fullness continues weariness is impossible; and there is enough power in real life to cause your system to be full of energy, and more, at all times no matter how much you may do or how great your task may be.

When we consider the lilies of the field, how they grow, we find that they naturally permit the life that is within them to unfold; they do not try to grow; they have, as everything has, the power of growth within them and they grow because they do not hinder that interior power and growth from having their way. Likewise, when we know that divinity reigns within us we do not have to work hard nor many years to reach that state. We will grow and develop, both mentally and spiritually, when we permit the divinity within to unfold. Everything seeks self-expression. Nothing in nature, visible or invisible, will have to be forced into expression, because at the very heart of all things there is the deep, strong desire to come forth and be.

Therefore, if we wish to ascend in the scale of life, we must cease those confused and destructive states of mind that hinder expression, and become as the lilies of the field. Give the life within permission to really live in us. The life within will live our life and give us a beautiful life. The power within will do our work and do that work extremely well. The divinity within will make us God-like in all things, and never cease to give us the things of the spirit so long as we permit those things to come forth and abide in personal existence.

What we are required to do that such things may come to pass is to live, think and act in the likeness of the Infinite. God *is*, and He permits Himself to be what He *is*. Man must do likewise, and all shall be well with him. Those who do not understand may think that the individuality of man might diminish, if he were to give himself up to the life and the power within, but such a conclusion will disappear when we realize that the power from within is our own. We are simply causing ourselves to become more and more of what we already are in reality. By giving free expression to our own higher, interior powers we naturally become more powerful, and by giving free expression to our own inherent divinity we naturally become more God-like and more spiritual on every plane of being. The lilies of the field do not become inferior lilies by permitting the spirit of the beautiful to unfold from within their gentle lives. It is by this method that they become what they are, and they become so much that the glory of artificial man can never compare with theirs. It is the same with the human soul. The soul becomes great and beautiful by permitting its own greatness and loveliness to come forth unhindered and undisturbed.

Thousands of people are at present trying to develop higher powers. Many of these actually try to work hard in their efforts to gain the various gifts of mind and soul, and because they do not succeed to any great extent they frequently become discouraged and give up, wondering whether or not the real truth has been found. Others being ambitious to become great in the world try to employ spiritual laws in the furthering of their personal aims, but they find the reactions so disagreeable that the prize is not worth the labor. To fly to the top at once is the ruling passion among many and when they fail with whatever methods they may employ they conclude that what passes for truth is nothing but man-made doctrines. The fact is, however, that the truth always appears to be the untruth when misdirected. To apply the principles of real truth in the furthering of any lofty aim we may have in mind, the first essential is to establish life in perfect touch with eternal life; the second essential is to positively determine what we expect to attain and become in actual personal living; and the third essential is to proceed in the attainment of health, happiness and harmony. Without health nothing of permanent value can be accomplished. Without, happiness our talents will be as the flowers without sunshine, and without harmony most of the power we might receive would be thrown away.

To obtain health, happiness and harmony we need simply let life live. Real life already has these things, and when we let life live in us those things will be expressed through us. The next essential is to resolve that we will be fully contented simply to live. To shine in the world, to acquire fame or to do something wonderful that mankind may long remember us, that we will not think of. Many a person has worked hard for fame and died early, in obscurity. Fame in itself, however, is of no value. When you are neither happy nor well, fame cannot make your life worthwhile. If you are miserable, it will profit nothing if everybody may know your name. It is not the praise of man that we should seek, but the life of the Infinite. The praise of the world can give us nothing, but life from within can give us everything that the heart can wish for.

True fame comes to him who deserves it without his trying to get it, but those only can deserve the honor of the race who have always been their best, who have not neglected a single opportunity to be of service, and who have lived constantly for the one purpose of being an inspiration to every soul. We may look at this phase of the subject as we may, we can come to only one conclusion. He alone is great and deserving of honor who so lives that he always is all that God made him to be; and it is such a life that is lived by the lilies of the field. When man will be as true to his large world as the lilies are to their small world, mankind will become a race of gods indeed, and the Utopian dreams of the prophets will come true. This, however, the ordinary thinker may declare to be impossible, but nothing is impossible. If a flower can be true to itself in its world, man can be true to himself in his world.

Those who are accustomed to the worldly methods of thinking and working may feel that it is hardly possibly to apply these new ideas while associated with worldly minds, but we must remember that it is not where we work or at what we work, but how we work that determines what results are to be. To so work that you permit the boundless power within to work through you is the secret, and this will not only cause your work to be pleasant, but will also cause you to do better and better work every day. It is therefore the royal path to pleasantness today and greater things tomorrow. In the old way you are compelled to almost wear yourself out today in order that you might provide for tomorrow; but not so in the new. While you are providing for tomorrow you are not only enjoying life today, but you are, through the expression of greater and greater power from within, making yourself larger, stronger and greater today. In the development of talents you employ the same principle. You do not strive for greatness; you know that you are potentially great already, and by permitting this greatness to become alive in you, you will accomplish great things.

When you apply this principle in everything that you do, you will find your advancement to be steady and even rapid; you will move forward in all things, making the ideal real as you ascend in the scale. The very moment you find a new ideal you find that power within you that can make that ideal real; thus your advancement becomes continuous, your progress eternal.

To live the life beautiful we simply let life live. We know that life, itself, is beautiful and when we permit that life that is beautiful to live in us, we will live consciously and personally the most beautiful life that we can picture in the ideal without making any personal effort to do so. When we begin to live, think and act according to these principles we feel that we are carried on and on by some mysterious presence that seems to be doing everything for us while giving us the pleasure and the glory.

We soon learn, however, that this presence is ourself, our own larger, superior self-created in the image of God; therefore, able to do everything that we may wish to have done; and it is a joy, indeed, to feel everything moving so smoothly and gently, so harmoniously and pleasantly, and at the same time producing such great results.

To engage in some extraordinary work becomes one of our greatest pleasures, because nothing is hard or difficult anymore; obstacles disappear the very moment we enter their presence, and we realize inwardly that whatever we undertake to do will be accomplished. We no longer tremble when in the midst of events that require exceptional wisdom and power; we know that wisdom is ready to speak whatever may be necessary now, and that power is at hand to do whatever may be necessary to be done now. We are in touch with the greatness of the great within and may draw upon that great, inexhaustible source whatever we may need at any time. Fear takes flight, while faith becomes stronger, higher and more perfect; sorrow and despair are no more, because all things are working for the best. Even in the presence of death and loss we see more life and greater gain. We know that what passes away merely ascends that it may live more and be itself in a larger, higher measure than it ever was before. We know that whatever comes will bring the new and the more beautiful. It could not be otherwise, because having chosen to be all that we are, the all can never cease to come, and the more the all continues to come the more the all will continue to bring. We have laid aside the illusions of the world and adopted the ways of truth. We have beheld the beauties of nature and have opened our minds to the visions of the soul.

These have given us the secret, and like the lilies of the field, we have learned to be still and live.

9. COUNT IT ALL JOY.

We meet something at almost every turn that we think ought to be different. If we have high ideals, we may not feel satisfied to permit those conditions to remain as they are; we may even complain or antagonize. On the other hand, if our ideals be low, we may feel wholly indifferent, but then we find that those things go from bad to worse. What we seek, however, is our present comfort on the one hand and the betterment of everything about us on the other hand, and we wish to know how this may be brought about in the midst of the confusion, the ignorance and the ills that we find in the world. When we are indifferent to the wrong it becomes worse; therefore, even for our own good we must do something with those adverse conditions that exist in the home, in society, or in the state. We must meet all those things and meet them properly, but the problem is, how?

To antagonize, criticize or condemn never helps matters in the least; besides, such states of mind are a detriment to one's own peace and health. The critical mind wears itself out while thinking about the wrong, but the wrong in the meantime goes on becoming worse. To feel disappointed because the universe does not move according to our fancy will not change the universe, but it will produce weakness in our own mind and body. That person who lives constantly in the world of despondency will soon lose all hold upon life; he consequently does nothing in the world but bring about the end of his own personal life. The usual way of dealing with the problems of life solves nothing. The ordinary way of meeting temptation gives the tempter greater power, while the person who tries to resist is usually entrapped in adversity and trouble. But St. James has told us what to do under all such circumstances. *Count it all joy.* That is the secret. Count it all joy no matter what may come, agreeing with all adversity at once, antagonizing nothing, condemning no one, leaving criticism alone. Never be disappointed or discouraged, and have nothing whatever to do with worry. Whatever comes, count it all joy. He who meets adversity in the attitude of peace, harmony and joy will turn enemies into friends and failures into greater good.

When things do not come your way, never mind. Continue to count everything joy, and everything will change in such a manner as to give you joy. If you are seeking the best, all things will work together in such a way as to give you the best, and your heart's desire shall be realized; possibly not today, but life is long; you can wait. That which is good is always good; it is always welcome whenever it comes. In the meantime you are living in harmony and joy, and that in itself is surely a great good. That person who lives constantly in gloom drives even the sunshine out of his own mind; the clouds of gloom are so heavy that he fails to see the brightness that is all about him.

That person, however, who counts everything joy will change everything to brightness and thus receive joy from everything. When you fail to receive what you sought, never for a moment be disappointed. Count it all joy. In fact, be supremely happy; you have a reason so to be. When you fail to get what you seek it simply means that there is something still better in store for you; then why should you not count such an event great joy.

This is always the case when your whole desire is to receive the best; and when you train yourself to count everything joy, your mind develops that desire that always desires the best.

When you seek only the best, the best only will come, and you must not feel disappointed when you are taken away from a hovel in order that you may enter a palace. When you meet enemies or adversaries do not resist them or enter into warfare; look for terms of agreement. Possibly they may seem to get the best of the bargain now, but you can afford to give them the terms they ask. The Infinite is your supply. When one door closes another opens, and if you depend upon the Supreme to open that other door, it will be a door opening into far greater and far better things than what you seemingly lost; besides, by being kind to your adversary you lifted yourself up. You are now a higher and a greater being. That means that you will now draw to yourself higher and better things; consequently, it was not the enemy that got the best terms; it was you.

Whatever you are called upon to do, do it and be happy. Count it all joy that you are given the opportunity to bring sunshine into dark places and develop your own latent power by doing what seemed difficult. You are equal to the occasion, if you think so; therefore you should consider it a privilege to prove it. The world is waiting for great souls—souls that are ready to do what others failed to accomplish. You can become one of these great souls by proving to yourself that you are equal to every occasion; and you will be equal to every occasion, if you count everything joy. When you are in the midst of temptations, rejoice with your whole heart. You have found a great opportunity to turn wrong into right, and to turn wrong into right is always a mark of greatness. Millions of people have died unhonored and unsung who might have arisen to greatness and become leaders and saviors in the world, if they would have demonstrated their superiority in the midst of temptation, tribulation and wrong. Look upon all temptations and troubles as opportunities to make wrong right, and be glad that such opportunities have been presented to you. Count it all joy; besides, the result will not only produce joy to yourself, but possibly to millions. He who changes wrong into right rises in the scale, and you can think of no greater good coming to you than this. He who remains below must be counted with the small and the ordinary. He who goes up higher shall gain everything that his heart may wish for. Therefore, whatever comes, or whatever you meet, or whatever you are called upon to do, proceed with peace and joy. Be glad that you have the opportunity to prove your own power, and thus elevate yourself thereby. Be supremely happy to know that you may change many things for the better through this attitude, and thus bless the lives of multitudes.

Train yourself to look at things according to this principle, and you will find that everything can produce joy. Everything can give cause for rejoicing; that is, providing everything is met in that attitude that counts everything joy. The same principle may be employed to great advantage in overcoming difficulties. When you are asked to do what seems to be very difficult, or when you are called upon to perform duties you do not like, never refuse. Count it all joy. To excuse yourself when such occasions appear is to lose most valuable opportunities. Every person desires to make the most of himself, but to accomplish this all latent power must be awakened, and there is nothing that will bring forth our latent powers more thoroughly than the doing of what seems difficult. When you find yourself shrinking from certain tasks you have discovered a weak faculty within yourself. Refuse to let that faculty remain in such a condition. Go and do what you feared to do and let nothing hold you back. In this way the weak faculty will be made strong and your entire nature will pass through most valuable discipline and training. Nothing is really disagreeable unless we think so.

That is, we may approach the disagreeable in such a way that it ceases to be disagreeable; and the secret is, count everything joy. You may enter darkness and gloom, but if you are living in a world of brightness and cheer, that darkness will not be darkness to you, nor will gloom enter your mind for a moment. You can remain in your own happy world, no matter what may happen, no matter what may take place in your immediate environment.

When you resolve to do certain things and proceed with a conviction that you will enjoy the work thoroughly, you will find real pleasure in that work; besides, you will do the work very well. Pleasure comes from within, and when the fountain of joy within is overflowing:, it will give joy to everything that exists about us. To cause this fountain within to overflow at all times, count everything joy at all times. We should never look for weakness, but when we find it we should proceed at once to change it into strength. Whenever we meet difficulties, or whenever we are called upon to do what we dislike we have found a weakness. We may remove that weakness by doing with a will what the moment demands, and resolve to enjoy it. Never permit such occasions to pass by without being changed.

The opportunity is too valuable. Whatever your present sphere of action may require of you, that you are able to do; and the present demand upon your life and your talents must be supplied by you if you would bring out the best that is in you, and make the great eternal now full and complete.

Tasks that seem difficult and demands that seem unreasonable are after all neither difficult nor unreasonable. They are simply golden opportunities for you to become what you never were before. They are but paths to greater achievements, sweeter joys and a larger life. Therefore, when you meet such occasions, count it all joy. When you fail to gain or realize in the present what you expected, do not feel disappointed. Make up your mind to be just as happy in those conditions that are, as you expect to be in those conditions that you are looking for. The feeling of disappointment is not produced by events. It is produced by your own attitude toward events. You can meet all events in such a frame of mind that you never feel disappointed in the least, and that frame of mind is the result of counting everything joy. When you know that eternity is long and that countless joys are in store for you, you will not feel sad now because one insignificant event has been postponed. And when you have full control of your mind you will have the power to produce just as much happiness in the absence of that event as in its presence, because events themselves cannot produce happiness.

The same is true of things. We do not gain joy from things, but from the way we think about things, and we can think as we choose at any time no matter what the circumstance may be. When the present demands happiness from something different than what you were looking for in the present, grasp the opportunity to prove that you are equal to this occasion. You thus develop latent ability. When you count everything joy you know that you can always produce joy. You know that whatever happens is best, because you have the power to cause it to become the best. The best always happens to those who seek only the best; therefore, whatever comes should be received as the best, and we must give it the opportunity to prove that it is better than anything that could have happened. You are not dependent upon events for happiness. Happiness does not come from what we do or where we go. Happiness comes from what we are now or what we create out of what is present now. Whether we be alone in a garret or in a gorgeous ball room the amount of happiness we are to receive in either place will depend entirely upon our own frame of mind. The frame of mind that you desire for the present moment you may have; if it does not come of itself, you can create it; you are the master.

When things do not come the way we like, we can like them the way they are coming. This is how we agree quickly with our adversaries; we thus receive the enemy instead of fighting the enemy; and that which we receive in the true attitude of mind becomes our own. Count everything joy and every adversity will give up its power to you. That which is evil becomes good when we meet it in such a way that we draw out of it the best that it may contain, and we always attract the best from everything when we meet everything in the conviction that all things work together for good. When nothing comes to give us happiness in the external we can open the fount of everlasting joy in the great within. The heaven of the soul is ever ready to open its pearly gates, but we must look towards the soul if we would pass through those gates. We shall fail to see the fountain of joy within, however, so long as our whole attention is fixed upon those worldly pleasures that failed to come into our world; but if we count everything joy we no longer feel disappointed about what did not happen; on the other hand we enter into that joyous state of mind that will place us in direct contact with the source of limitless joy within the mind. When people speak unkindly of you, you will become offended if you thought they spoke unkindly, but if your eyes are too pure to behold iniquity you will go on your way as if nothing had been said; you count everything joy and thus you will receive joy from your own lofty position in the matter.

When you are asked to do certain things do not proceed with a feeling that you are compelled to. Go and do it because you want to; say that you want to, and count it all joy. We should never say "I have a duty to perform," but rather, "Here is an opportunity which I have the privilege to embrace. "Train yourself to want to do whatever your present sphere of life may demand. He who loves and thoroughly enjoys what he is doing today will be asked to do greater things tomorrow.

The large soul never asks if things are unpleasant or difficult; such thoughts never enter his mind. Whatever he finds to do he proceeds to do, with his mind full of will and his heart full of joy. If you dislike anybody, you have found a weakness in yourself. You have found a difficulty that must be overcome at once. Do not permit such obstacles to remain in your way. The soul that knows no weakness loves everything that God has created. The strong soul never considers those imperfections in life that man has created. Intelligence was not intended to be used in the study of nothingness, illusions or mistakes. When we hate anything we recognize the existence and the power of those things that have neither real existence nor real power; we therefore enter into a confused state of mind. What God has created we cannot help but love, but if we see something else and dislike that something else we are seeing something that God has not created. In other words, we are giving attention to illusions and mistakes, and the mind is not intended for that purpose. Remove the illusion by transforming that hate into love; this will change the point of view. You will thus see things from the upper side, the divine side, and when we look at things from the divine side we find that everything is altogether lovely.

Therefore, when you dislike anybody overcome that weakness by giving that person all the love of your heart. Love that person and *mean* it, no matter what he has said or done.

There is nothing in the world that lifts the soul so high above darkness and illusion as strong, pure, spiritual love; and it is not difficult to love a person when you know that he is God's creation, while his mistakes are simply man's creation. Mistakes must be forgiven. Our desire is to do the will of God, and to do the will of God is to love every creature in existence, and to love everything as God loves everything.

10. THE TRUE USE OF KINDNESS AND SYMPATHY.

The ordinary use of sympathy is responsible for a very large portion of the ills and the troubles we find in the world; the reason being that nearly all suffering is mental before it is physical, and that mental suffering is almost invariably produced when we enter into sympathetic touch with the ills that we meet among relations, friends or associates. The average person would suffer but little if he suffered only from the troubles that arise in his own system. It is the pain that is felt through sympathy for others that gives him most of the burdens he finds it necessary to bear. It is considered a sign of kindness, goodness and high regard, however, to sympathize with others in this manner, or rather to suffer with others, but this is not the true use of kindness.

We do not help others by entering into the same weakness that is keeping them in a world of distress. We do not help the weak by becoming weak. We do not relieve sickness by becoming sick. We do not right the wrong by entering into the wrong, or doing wrong. We do not free man from failures by permitting ourselves to become failures. We do not emancipate those who are in bondage to sin by going and committing the same sin. This is very simple; but ordinary sympathy is based upon the idea that we sympathize with a person only when we suffer with that person. We expect to relieve pain by proceeding to produce the same pain in our own systems; but we cannot remove darkness by entering into the dark. We can remove wrong only by removing the cause of that wrong, and to remove the cause of wrong we must produce the cause of right. Darkness disappears when we produce light; likewise, sickness and trouble will vanish when we produce health and harmony, but we cannot produce health and harmony by entering into disease and trouble. This, however, is what ordinary sympathy does; it has, therefore, failed to relieve the world. The ordinary use of sympathy multiplies suffering by making suffering contagious. It causes the suffering of the one to give pain to the many, and then in turn causes the pain of the many to give additional pain to each individual person whose sympathy is aroused in the same connection. We must remove everything that tends to make ills contagious, whether it is physical or mental, and it is very evident that ordinary sympathy does spread pains and ills to a very great degree. Therefore, one of the first essentials in producing emancipation or in making real the ideal is to find the true use of sympathy.

Sympathy itself must not be removed, because it is one of the highest virtues of the soul. The average person, however, misapplies this virtue continuously, and in consequence brings pains and ills both to himself and others, that could easily have been prevented. There is a better use for sympathy, and through this better use we cause all the good things in life to become contagious. Instead of entering into sympathetic touch with the weakness that may temporarily exist in the personality of man we enter into sympathetic touch with the strength that permanently exists in the soul of man. Instead of morbidly dwelling upon the ills and the wrongs which we find we proceed to gain the highest possible realization of the good, the right, the superior and the beautiful that we know has existence back of and above the superficial life of human nature. According to a metaphysical law, when we enter into mental contact with the good in man we awaken the power of that which is good in man, and the most perfect mental contact is produced by sympathy.

To sympathize with the soul is to increase the active power of the soul, because we always arouse into greater action that with which we sympathize, and when the active power of the soul is increased the weakness of the personality will become strength. To sympathize with the power of health and harmony in man will increase the power of health and harmony throughout his entire system and the elimination of sickness and trouble must inevitably follow. To sympathize with the pain a person may feel is to do nothing to relieve that person. You take the pain to yourself, but you do not take the pain away from the person with whom you sympathize. You thus double the suffering instead of removing it entirely, as you should. On the other hand, when we refuse to recognize the suffering itself and proceed to awaken in that person that something that can remove the suffering we protect ourselves from pain, while we actually do something to relieve that person from pain. We do not suffer with the person that suffers, but we do something to remove suffering absolutely from everybody concerned; instead of entering into the pain we take that person out of pain. That is sympathy that *is* sympathy. That is kindness that really results in a kind act. It does not weep, but does better. It removes both the cause and the effect of the weeping. It awakens that superior power in man that positively does produce emancipation. It does not cause suffering to be transmitted to a score of other persons who have done nothing to merit that suffering, but it stops the pain where it is and puts it out of existence absolutely.

Every form of suffering comes from the violation of some law in life. It is therefore wrong, but it cannot be righted by making a special effort to spread the results of that wrong among as many others as possible. This, however, ordinary sympathy does; it makes a special effort to make everybody feel bad because someone is not feeling as he should; but the pains of the many cannot give ease and comfort to the one, nor can many minds in bondage set one mind free. When any one is feeling bad it will not help him to have a group of morbid minds suffer with him. When any one is sorry it will not remove the cause of his grief to have others decide to be sorry also. Do something so that person will not feel bad any more. Take him out of his trouble. That is real sympathy; and while you are helping him out make him feel that your heart is as tender as tenderness itself. Do something so that the grief may be removed through the realization of that greater truth that knows that all is well.

That is kindness worthy of the name.

Those, however, who are in the habit of sympathizing in the ordinary way may think the new way cold, and devoid of feeling or love, but the fact is that it is the ordinary form of sympathy that is devoid of love. When you love a person who is in pain you will not stand around and weep pretending that you are also feeling bad. You will put on the countenance of light and cheerfulness and actually do something tangible to remove his pain. That's love; and if you have real sympathy, you will minister to him with so much depth of feeling and tender kindness that you will touch the very innermost life of his soul. All love, all tenderness, all kindness and all real feeling come from the soul.

Therefore, he whose sympathy is of the soul will receive his love and his kindness directly from the true source; in consequence, he will have more love and more kindness by far than the one whose sympathy is a form of morbid feeling.

The real purpose of true sympathy is two-fold; first, to arouse in a greater measure that finer something in life that is not only tender and sweet and beautiful, but is also immensely strong—strong with the strength of the Infinite; and second, to awaken everything in man that has quality, superiority and worth; that is, to make man feel the supreme power of his own inherent divinity. There is something in man that is greater than all weakness, all ills, all wrongs, and when this something is awakened, developed and expressed, all weakness, all ills and all wrongs must disappear. To sympathize with this greater something in everybody with whom one may come in contact will arouse this greater something, not only in others, but also in him who lives in this form of sympathy. In other words, to sympathize with the superior in man is to banish the wrong and the inferior by causing the expression of that divine something within that has the power to make all things well. Such a sympathy will tend to build a stronger life, a better life, a superior life, a more beautiful life; and to give such a sympathy to everybody is kindness indeed.

There may seem to be kindness in weeping with those who weep, but it is a far greater kindness to give those people the power to banish their sorrows completely, and he who does this is not cold; he is the very essence of the highest and most beautiful love. There is no joy in having sorrow. There is no pleasure in having pain. Therefore, what greater good can man do for man than to help him gain complete emancipation from all those things, and this is the purpose of this higher use of sympathy. True sympathy is neither cold nor purely intellectual. It is real soul-feeling, while ordinary sympathy is simply a morbid mental feeling. True sympathy is the very fire of real spiritual love, because it springs from the very soul of love and is in constant touch with the unbounded power of that love.

That such a sympathy should have extraordinary emancipating power is therefore most evident. The ordinary use of sympathy may appear to be kind. It may mean well, but it is usually misdirected kindness, and is nearly always weak. The higher use of sympathy, that is, the expression of divine sympathy, is not only kindness itself, but it has the spiritual understanding and the spiritual power to do what kindness wants to do. Ordinary kindness is usually crippled. It lacks both the power to do and the understanding to know what to do. The true sympathy, however, not only has the power to feel kindly, but has the power to act kindly. It not only gives love and makes everybody feel that they are in the presence of real love, but it also gives that something that can cause the purpose of love to come true. Real love invariably aims to produce comfort, peace and emancipation. That is its purpose, and real sympathy can fulfill that purpose. Therefore, this higher sympathy is the sympathy that *is* sympathy.

The same principle should be employed in the use of every form of emotion, because every emotion is a movement of the mind conveying mental elements and powers with certain definite objects in view. Therefore, the way the emotion acts will determine to a very great extent whether these mental powers will build for better things, or produce undesirable conditions. Those movements of the mind or emotions that express themselves in love, heart-felt joy and spiritual feeling have a beneficial effect; while that mental feeling that is usually termed emotionalism is never wholesome. True spiritual feeling is calm, but extremely beautiful and awakens orderly and harmoniously all the finer elements of human life. It is true spiritual feeling, or what may be termed emotions sublime, that gives action and expression to personal quality, mental worth and individual superiority. In other words, it is these actions of mind and soul that elevate thought, action, feeling, consciousness and desire above the planes of the ordinary. Such emotions should therefore be cultivated to the very highest and finest degree.

What is spoken of as heartfelt joy is that wholesome joy that comes directly from the heart and that has depth, reality and joyous feeling; but that joy that runs into uncontrolled ecstasy is never wholesome. Every feeling of joy that causes the mind to be carried away into excited or overwrought ecstasy is not joy, but mental intoxication. Such joy does not produce genuine happiness, and the reaction always disturbs the equilibrium of the mind. Depth of thought, clear thinking, intellectual brilliancy, good judgment, mental poise, all of these will diminish in the mind that indulges in uncontrolled ecstasy, emotionalism or pleasure that produces excitability and overwrought emotional feeling. The feeling of love, when it is love, is always wholesome and elevating, but passionate desire is weakening unless it is permeated through and through with genuine love. A deep, strong feeling of love will turn all desires, whether mental or physical, into constructive channels, but we must be certain that it is real love and not an artificial feeling temporarily produced by the misuse of the imagination. Here every mental movement that is intense, forced, overwrought or worked up to an abnormal pitch of excited enthusiasm leads to emotionalism, and emotionalism burns up energy. Nearly all kinds of nervous diseases can be traced directly or indirectly to emotionalism in one or more of its many forms; and as physical and mental weakness always follows the burning up of energy, a number of physical and mental ills can be traced to this source.

When emotionalism, fear, anger and worry are eliminated, all kinds of insanity and all kinds of nervous diseases will be things of the past; while the power, the capacity and the brilliancy of the average mind will increase to an extraordinary degree. Strong emotional feelings and intense enthusiasm will sometimes arouse a great deal of dormant, mental power. In consequence, people sometimes do exceptional things while under the emotional spell, but the entire process, as well as the final results, are very similar to that produced by alcoholic stimulants and other drugs. The system seems to be charged with a great deal of extra power for a while, but when the reaction comes the entire system becomes much weaker than it ever was before. The mind that permits itself to be aroused by intense, emotional feeling will gradually lose its power of clear thought. The understanding will become so weakened that the principles of real truth cannot be fully comprehended, while the judgment will follow more and more the illusions of an overwrought imagination. The fact that religious feeling among millions is so closely associated with this overwrought state of emotionalism proves the importance of a better understanding of the use of these finer mental elements. Emotionalism compels the mind to follow mere feeling, and mere feeling, when not properly blended with clear understanding, will be misdirected at every turn. Emotionalism also stupefies the finer perceptions by intoxicating the mind, and by burning up the finer mental energies; and since these finer perceptions are required to discern real truth we understand readily why highly emotional people cannot comprehend the principles of pure, spiritual metaphysics. Having been trained towards materialistic literalism instead of away from it, they are not to blame, however, for their present state and deserve no criticism. Nevertheless, those who wish to find real religion and real spirituality must learn to understand the psychology of emotion and must learn the true use of all the finer feelings of the mind.

There is something in man that is called religious feeling. It is present to a greater or lesser degree in everybody and cannot be removed, because it is a part of life itself. When in action, and it is never inactive very long, it expresses itself in some power of emotion. When this emotion or delicate mental movement is permitted to act without any definite purpose it becomes emotionalism; that is, mental energy running rampant, and becoming more and more intense until it destroys itself, as well as all the energy it originally contained. On the other hand, when this feeling is directed towards the highest and the most perfect conception of truth, life and being that the mind can possibly picture, all that is lofty, ideal and beautiful will be developed in the mind and soul of that individual. This is natural, because there is nothing that has greater developing power than deep, spiritual feeling; a fact that those who desire to develop remarkable ability, extraordinary talent and rare genius will do well to remember.

There is no mental faculty that is more readily affected by the emotions than the imagination, and since the imagination is such a very important faculty, no mental or physical action that in any way interferes with the constructive work of the imagination should be permitted. Emotionalism, however, invariably excites the imagination, and an excited imagination will imagine all sorts of things that are not true. The mind will thus be filled with illusions, and in consequence, false beliefs, wrong thoughts, perverted states and misdirected mental energy will follow. The result will be sickness, trouble, mistakes and failures in one or more of their many forms. It is now a well demonstrated truth that every thought has a definite power of its own, and that that power will produce its natural effect in some part of the human system. If the thought is not good the effect will naturally be undesirable, and conditions will be produced in mind or body that we do not want. But whatever we imagine, that we think; therefore, when we excite the imagination we imagine all manner of things that are untrue, unreal or abnormal; we produce false or perverted thought action in the mind; we think the wrong, and wrong thoughts invariably produce wrong conditions in mind or body, or both.

"What we imagine we reproduce in ourselves to some degree, frequently to a marked degree; but an excited imagination simply cannot imagine what is good and wholesome. In every form of development, whether in the body, the mind or the soul, the imagining faculty is employed extensively. All growth is promoted by combining and recombining the elements of life in higher and higher forms, and since it is one of the functions of the imagination to produce these higher, more complex and more perfect combinations, development cannot take place unless the imagination works orderly, constructively and progressively. An excited imagination will produce false mental combinations or may waste energy by attempting to combine mental elements that will not combine. An orderly imagination may be likened to a skilled workman who builds a beautiful mansion out of his bricks, while an excited imagination might be likened to someone who can do nothing more than pile those bricks into a heap. The fact that emotionalism always excites the imagination proves therefore how impossible it is for minds with uncontrolled emotions to develop the greatness that is latent within them.

Another fact of great importance in this connection is that emotionalism will intensify every mental tendency that may be active in mind at the time. If there is a tendency towards abnormal desires, emotionalism will intensify those desires so that it will be very difficult to resist temptation should it appear. On the other hand, pure spiritual feeling would transmute those desires, and produce instead, an ascending tendency, thus leading all the forces of mind towards higher ground.

To overcome emotionalism, intense mental feeling, anger, excitability and all overwrought or abnormal mental states, turn attention upon the spiritual heights of the soul whenever such mental feelings are felt. By training all mental feelings and emotions to move toward the deeper and the higher spiritual state of being these same feelings will become stronger, deeper, finer and more beautiful than they ever were before. We thus establish the foundation upon which we can build an ideal character, and through such a character all the qualities of mind and soul can be used beneficially in the midst of every experience, whatever the nature of that experience may be.

To cause all the emotions to follow ascending tendencies will increase remarkably the power, the fineness, the life and the rapture of every phase of feeling, not only in the soul, but in the mind and the body as well. Every trace of coldness, indifference or lack of feeling will entirely disappear, and we shall develop instead that higher form of kindness, sympathy and spiritual emotion that is created in the likeness of divine emotion. Whoever employs this method will not permit his feelings to run wild at any time, but will cause the life and the power of every feeling to accumulate in his system. He will hold them all in poise and use their energies intelligently in the building up of his whole life and in adding to the joy, the rapture and the delight of the living of a full, strong, ever-ascending state of existence. That person who controls his feelings and turns all the energies of those feelings upon the spiritual heights of the soul will actually become a living flame of love, sympathy and sublime emotion. Such a person will enjoy everything intensely, but his joy will be in such a high state of harmony that he will waste nothing in his life; instead, all the elements and powers of his life will continue to accumulate, thus giving added strength, worth and superiority to everything that he may physically, mentally or spiritually possess.

11. TALK HEALTH, HAPPINESS AND PROSPERITY.

Talk happiness. When things look dark, talk happiness. When things look bright, talk more happiness. When others are sad, insist on being glad. Talk happiness, and they will soon feel better. Talk happiness; it pays in every shape and form and manner. Give sunshine to others, and others will be more than pleased to give sunshine to you. Talk happiness, and your health will be better, your mind will be brighter and your personality far more attractive; but the qualities that happiness will give to you will also be given to those who have the pleasure to listen to you when you talk happiness.

Talk happiness, and you will always remain in a happy frame of mind. You will encourage thousands of others to do the same. You will become a fountain of joy in the midst of the garden of human life, and who can tell how many flowers of kindness and joy unfolded their rare and tender beauty because you were there. When others have lost courage, talk happiness. The future is bright for everybody. Talk happiness, and you turn on the light in their pathway, and they will see the better things that are before them. When the mind is depressed it is blinded; it sees only the darkness; but when the light of joy is admitted everything is changed. Therefore, talk happiness to all persons and on all occasions.

We cannot have too much light in the world, and the more we talk happiness the more light we produce wherever we may be. What greater pleasure could anyone desire than to realize that he has eased the way of life for thousands and sent the sunbeams and joy into the mental world of tens of thousands? You can do this by talking happiness. Thus by constantly talking happiness you produce perpetual increase in your own happiness. What we give in abundance always returns in abundance; that is, when we give in the right spirit; and he who talks happiness is always in the right spirit. When in the midst of discord, trouble or confusion, talk happiness. Harmony will soon be restored. The majority can easily change their minds for the better when someone takes the lead. You can take the lead by talking happiness.

Talk prosperity. When times are not good, man himself must make them better, and he can make them better by doing his best and having faith in that power that produces prosperity. When men have faith in prosperity they will think prosperity, live prosperity and thus do that which produces prosperity; and you can give men faith in prosperity by constantly talking prosperity. They may not listen at first, but perseverance always wins. Prosperity is extremely attractive, and the more you impress it upon the minds of others the more attractive it becomes until no one can resist it; and when we admit the idea of prosperity into our own minds we will from that moment begin to produce prosperity. Think prosperity, talk prosperity, and live prosperity; and you will rise in the scale no matter what the circumstances may be. Hold to the power that produces abundance by having unbounded faith in that power and you will overcome all adversity and reach the highest goal you have in view. The fear of failure produces more failure than all other causes combined. You can remove that fear by talking prosperity.

Talk health. It is the best medicine. When people stop talking sickness they will stop getting sick. Talk health and stay well. Talk health to the person who is sick and you will cause him to think health. He who thinks health will live health, and he who lives health will produce health. When your associates take delight in relating minutely everything they know about the ills of the community, purify the muddy waters of their conversation by talking health. Insist on talking health. Prove that there is more health than sickness, and that therefore health is the more important subject. The majority rules. Health is in the majority. Increase that majority by talking more health. Take the lead in this manner of conversation, and be positively determined to continue in the lead. Others will soon follow, and when they do, sickness will diminish more and more until it becomes practically unknown among those who have the privilege to live in your circle.

When the sins of the world are in evidence, talk virtue. When the power of virtue is in evidence, talk more virtue. Eternally emphasize the good; give it more and more power, and it will soon become sufficiently strong to produce that ideal of power that you wish to make real. Talk virtue, and people will think of virtue; they will dwell more and more upon the beauty of virtue. Ere long they will desire virtue, and that desire will become stronger and stronger until it thrills every atom in human life. To desire virtue is to become virtuous. To live for the attainment of purity is to place in action all the purifying elements in your being, and you will soon realize that perfectly clean condition that every awakened mind has learned to worship. You can purify the minds of thousands by constantly talking virtue, and these thousands will in turn convey the power of virtue to as many thousand times thousands more.

Talk virtue eternally and there is no end to the good that you may do. When the world seems bad, talk virtue. The power of good is not gone; it is just as great as it ever was, and it is here and there and everywhere. You can open the mind of man to the mighty influx of this power by eternally talking virtue. You can, through the proper use of your own words, change the tide of human thought. You can cause all mankind to desire virtue by forever talking virtue. On the surface many things may seem to be what they ought not to be, but the surface is not all there is. It is an insignificant part of the whole. There is a hidden richness in life that the many do not see, because their attention has never been turned in that direction. You can lead mankind into the gold mines of the mind and into the diamond fields of the soul, and the secret lies in the words you speak. You can guide the mind of man by the way you talk. Talking therefore should not be empty, but should ever have a sublime goal in view. Your words point the way and they who hear what you have to say will, to some degree, be influenced to go whatever way your words may point. Your power, therefore, in directing other minds towards greater and better things is hidden in every word you speak, and how important that that power be wisely employed.

We are responsible for every word we express. It will affect somebody either for good or otherwise. Talk sin, sickness and trouble, and you will cause many to go directly into more sin, sickness and trouble. Talk health, happiness and prosperity, and you will cause many to find health, happiness and prosperity in greater and greater abundance. When the world complains, do not forget to emphasize the great fact that universal good is even now at hand. The complaining mind wears colored glasses. He cannot see things as they are. You can help him to remove those glasses by calling his attention to the fact that things are not what they seem to him. Everything lies in the point of view. Look at things from the right point of view and you will be happy, cheerful and optimistic under all sorts of circumstances. But look at things from the wrong point of view, and you will see nothing clearly; everything will appear to be what it is not.

You will thus live in confusion and your mistakes will be many. Remove this confusion by placing yourself in harmony with eternal good, and you can do this by talking about the good, thinking about the good and emphasizing most positively every expression of good with which you may come in contact.

That which we think of and talk of constantly will multiply and grow in our own world.

Talk peace. You will thus not only prevent confusion, but you will remove those confused conditions that may already exist. You can still the storms of life everywhere by talking peace.

"When man thinks the most of peace he will be in peace, and he cannot fail to think of peace so long as he is faithfully talking peace. Talk success, and you will inspire everybody with the spirit of success. You will help to turn the energies of life upon the goal of success, and thus you will help all minds to move towards success. Never say that anything is impossible. Talk success, and you help to make everything possible. Everybody should succeed. It is not only the privilege of everybody to succeed, but every person, to be just to himself, must succeed.

The fear of failure, however, is the greatest obstacle. You can remove that fear by talking success. Hold the idea of success before every mind with which you come in contact; you will thus become one of the greatest philanthropists in the world.

New and greater opportunities may be found everywhere. Talk of these things and forget the missteps of the past. We can leave the lesser that is behind only by pressing on towards the greater that is before. Talk success to everybody, and everybody will press on towards the greater goal of success. Be an inspiration among all minds; and you can be by holding up the light of success, prosperity and attainment at all times. Use your words in promoting advancement, in awakening new interest in the better side, the brighter side, the sunny side, and turn the mind of man upon those things that *can* be done. He can who thinks he can, and you help every person to think that he can by talking prosperity and success. Impress the greater upon every mind, and every mind will think the greater; and he who thinks the greater is constantly building for greater things. Emphasize the sunny side in all your speech and you provide a never failing antidote for complaints; and since the complaining mind soon becomes the retrogressing mind, this antidote has extreme value. It may change for the better the destiny of anyone when brought squarely before his attention, and this your words can do.

When one door closes another opens; sometimes several.

This is the law of life. It is the expression of the law of eternal progress. The whole of nature desires to move forward eternally.

The spirit of progress animates everything. Whenever a person loses an opportunity to move forward this great law proceeds to give him another. This proves that the universe is kind, that everything is for man and nothing against him. This being the truth, the man who talks health, happiness, prosperity, power and progress is working in harmony with the universe, and is helping to promote the great purpose of the universe; and who would not occupy a position of such value and importance? Whenever you talk trouble, failure, sickness or sin you arraign your own mind against the law of life and the purpose of the universe. You will thereby be against everything, and everything will, in consequence, be against you. You must, therefore, necessarily fail in everything you undertake to do. But how different everything will be when you turn and move in the other direction. Go with the universe, and all the power of the universe will go with you, and will help you to reach whatever object you may have in view.

Harmonize yourself with the laws of life and you will steadily rise in the scale of life. Nothing can hold you down. Everything you undertake to do you will accomplish, because everything will be with you. You will reach every ideal, and at the best time and under the best circumstances cause that ideal to become real. When you cease to talk failure and begin to talk success you invariably meet the turn in the lane. You find that a new world and a better future is in store. Things will take a turn when you take a turn, and you will take a turn when you begin to talk about those things that you desire to realize. Never talk about anything else. The way you talk you go. The way you talk others will go. Therefore, talk health, happiness and prosperity, and help everybody, yourself included, to move towards health, happiness and prosperity. The power of words is immense, both in the person that speaks and in the person that is spoken to. The simplest way to use this power is to train yourself to talk the things you want; talk the things that you expect or desire to realize; talk the things you wish to attain and accomplish. You thus cause the power of words to work for you and with you in gaining the goal you have in mind. Whatever comes, talk health, happiness and prosperity. Say that you are well; say that you are happy; say that you are prosperous. Emphasize everything that is good in life, and the power of the Supreme will cause your words to come true.

12. WHAT DETERMINES THE DESTINY OF MAN.

The destiny of every individual is being hourly created by himself, and what he is to create at any particular time is determined by those ideals that he entertains at that time.

The future of a person is not preordained by some external power, nor is fate controlled by some strange, mysterious force that master-minds alone can comprehend and employ. It is ideals that control fate, and all minds have their ideals wherever in the scale of life they may be. To have ideals is not simply to have dreams or visions of that which lies beyond the attainments of the present; nor is idealism a system of ideas that the practical mind may not have the privilege to entertain. To have ideals is to have definite objects in view, be those objects very high or very low, or anywhere between those extremes.

The ideals of any mind are the real wants, the real desires or the real aims of that mind, and as every normal mind invariably lives, thinks and works for that which is wanted by his present state of existence, it is evident that every mind must necessarily, either consciously or unconsciously, follow his ideals. When those ideals are low, ordinary or inferior the individual will work for the ordinary and the inferior, and the products of his mind will correspond in quality with that for which he is working. Inferior causes will originate in his life and similar effects will follow; but when those ideals are high and superior, he will work for the superior; he will develop superiority in himself, and he will give superiority to everything that he may produce. Every action that he originates in his life will become a superior cause and will be followed by a similar effect.

The destiny of every individual is determined by what he is and by what he does; and what any individual is to be or do is determined by what he is living for, thinking for or working for. Man is not being made by some outside force. Man is making himself with the power of those forces and elements that he employs in his thought and his work; and in all his efforts, physical or mental, he invariably follows his ideals. He who lives, thinks and works for the superior becomes superior; he who works for less, becomes less. It is therefore evident that any individual may become more, achieve more, secure more and create for himself a greater and a greater destiny by simply beginning to live, think and work for a superior group of ideals. To have low ideals is to give the creative forces of the system something ordinary to work for. To have high ideals is to give those forces something extraordinary to work for, and the fate of man is the result of what his creative forces hourly produce. Every force in the human system is producing something, and that something will become a part of the individual. It is therefore evident that any individual can constantly improve the power, the quality and the worth of his being by directing the forces of his system to produce that which has quality and worth. These forces, however, are not directed or controlled by the will. It is the nature of the creative forces in man to produce what the mind desires, wants, needs or aspires to attain, and the desires and the aspirations of any mind are determined by the ideals that are entertained in that mind.

The forces of the system will begin to work for the superior when the mind begins to attain superior ideals, and since it is the product of these forces that determines both the nature and the destiny of man, a superior nature and a greater destiny may be secured by any individual who will adopt the highest and the most perfect system of idealism that he can possibly comprehend. To entertain superior ideals is to picture in mind and to hold constantly before mind the highest conception that can be formed of everything of which we may be conscious. To mentally dwell in those higher conceptions at all times is to cause the predominating ideas to become superior ideas, and it is the predominating ideas for which we live, think and work. When the ruling ideas of any mind are superior the creative force of that mind will produce the superior in every element, faculty, talent or power in that mind; greatness will thus be developed in that mind, and the great mind invariably creates a great destiny.

To entertain superior ideals is not to dream of the impossible, but to enter into mental contact with those greater possibilities that we are now able to discern; and to have the power to discern an ideal indicates that we have the power to realize that ideal. We do not become conscious of greater possibilities until we have developed sufficient capacity to work out those possibilities into practical, tangible results. Therefore, when we discern the greater we are ready to attain and achieve the greater; but before we can proceed to do what we are ready to do we must adopt superior ideals, and superior ideals only. When our ideals are superior we shall constantly think of the superior, because as our ideals are so is our thinking, and to constantly think of the superior is to steadily grow into the likeness of the superior.

When the ideals are very high all the forces of the system will move towards superior attainments; all things in the life of the individual will work together with greater and greater greatness in view, and continued advancement on a larger and larger scale must inevitably follow. To entertain superior ideals is not simply to desire some larger personal attainment or to mentally dwell in some belief that is different from the usual beliefs of the world. To entertain superior ideals is to think the very best thoughts and the very greatest thoughts about everything with which we come in contact. Superior idealism is not mere dreaming of the great and the beautiful, but is actual living in mental harmony with the very best we can find in all things, in all persons, in all circumstances and in all expressions of life. To live in mental harmony with the best we can find everywhere is to create the best in our own mentality and personality; and as we steadily grow into the likeness of that which we think of the most, we will, through ideal thinking, perpetually increase our power, capacity and worth. In consequence, we will naturally create a greater and a more worthy destiny.

The man who becomes much will achieve much, and great achievements invariably build a great destiny. To think of anything that is less than the best, or to mentally dwell with the inferior is to neutralize the effect of those superior ideals that we have begun to entertain. To secure the greatest results it is therefore absolutely necessary to entertain superior ideals only and to cease all recognition of inferiority or imperfection. The reason why the majority fail to secure any tangible results from higher ideals is because they entertain too many of the lower ideals at the same time. They may aim high; they may adore the beautiful; they may desire the perfect; they may live for the better and work for the greater, but they do not think their best thoughts about everything, and this is the reason why they do not reach the goal they have in view.

Some of their forces are building for greater things, while other forces are building for lesser things, and a house divided against itself cannot stand.

Superior idealism contains no thought that is less than the very greatest and the very best that the most lofty states of mind can possibly produce, and it entertains no desire that has not the very greatest worth, the greatest power, and the highest attainment in view. Superior idealism does not recognize the power of evil in anything or in anybody; it knows that adverse conditions exist, but it gives the matter no conscious thought whatever. It is not possible to think the greatest thought about everything while mind is giving conscious attention to adversity or imperfection. The true idealist, therefore, gives conscious recognition to the power of good only, and he lives in the conviction that all things in his life are constantly working together for good. This conviction is not mere sentiment with the idealist. He knows that all things positively will work together for good when we recognize only the good, think only the good, desire only the good and expect only the good; likewise, he knows that all things positively will work together for greater things when all the powers of life, thought and action are concentrated upon the attainment and the achievement of greater things.

To apply the principles of superior idealism in all things means advancement in all things. To follow the superior ideal is to move towards the higher, the greater and the superior, and no one can continue very long in that movement without creating for himself a new world, a better environment and a greater destiny. To create a better future begin now to select a better group of ideals. Select the best and the greatest ideals that you can possibly find, and live those ideals absolutely. You will thus cause everything in your being to work for the higher, the better and the greater, and the things that you work for now will determine what the future is to be. Work for the greatest and the best that you know in the present, and you will create the very greatest and the very best for the future.

13. TO HIM THAT HATH SHALL BE GIVEN.

The statement that much gathers more is true on every plane of life and in every sphere of existence; and the converse that every loss leads to a greater loss is equally true; though we must remember that man can stop either process at any time or place. The further down you go the more rapidly you will move towards the depths, and the higher up you go the easier it becomes to go higher still. When you begin to gain you will gain more, because "To him that hath shall be given." When you begin to lose you will lose more, because from "Him that hath not, even that which he hath shall be taken away." This is a great metaphysical law, and being metaphysical, man has the power to use it in any way that he may desire. As man is in the within, so everything will be in his external world. Therefore, whether man is to lose or gain in the without depends upon whether he is losing or gaining in the within.

The basis of all possession is found in the consciousness of man, and not in exterior circumstances, laws or conditions. If a man's consciousness is accumulative, he will positively accumulate, no matter where he may live; but whether his riches are to be physical, intellectual or spiritual will depend upon the construction of his mind. When the mind has the greatest development on the physical plane an accumulative consciousness will gather tangible possessions. When the mind has the greatest development on the intellectual or metaphysical plane, an accumulative consciousness will gather abundance of knowledge and wisdom. When the mind has the greatest development on the spiritual plane an accumulative consciousness will gather spiritual riches. However competent you may be on the physical plane, if your consciousness is not accumulative, you will not gain possession of a great deal of this world's goods. Likewise, no matter how diligently you may search for wisdom in the higher spiritual possessions, if your consciousness is not accumulative you will gain but little. In fact, you will constantly lose the knowledge of truth on the one hand while trying to gain it on the other. Therefore, to gain abundance in the world of things or tangible possessions, the secret is to become competent in our chosen vocations, and then acquire an accumulative consciousness.

To gain the riches of the mind and the soul, the secret is to develop the same accumulative consciousness and to consecrate all the powers of mind and thought to spiritual things. There are thousands in this age who have consecrated their "whole lives to the higher state of being, but there are very few who have gained the real riches of the spiritual kingdom, and the reason is they have neglected the development of the accumulative consciousness. In other words, they have overlooked the great law, "To him that hath shall be given."

Those who have nothing will receive nothing, no matter how devotedly they may pray or how beautifully they may live. But to have is not simply to possess in the external sense. Those who are conscious of nothing have nothing. Those who are conscious of much have much, regardless of external possession.

Before we can gain anything we must have something, and to have something is to be conscious of something.

We must be conscious of possession in the within before we can increase possession in any sphere of existence. All possession is based upon consciousness and is held by consciousness or lost by consciousness. All gain is the result of an accumulative consciousness. All loss is due to what may be termed the scattering consciousness; that is, that state of consciousness that lets go of everything that may come within its sphere. When you are conscious of something you are among those that hath and to you shall be given more. As soon as you gain conscious hold of things you will begin to gain possession of more and more things. As soon as you gain conscious hold upon wisdom and spiritual power, wisdom and spiritual power will be given to you in greater and greater abundance. On the other hand, when you begin to lose conscious hold of things, thoughts or powers you will begin to lose more and more of those possessions, until all are gone.

When you inwardly feel that things are slipping away from you, you are losing your conscious hold of things, and all will finally be lost if you do not change your consciousness. When you inwardly feel that you are gaining more and more, or that things are beginning to gravitate towards your sphere of existence, more and more will be given to you until you have everything that you may desire. How we feel in the within is the secret, and it is this interior feeling that determines whether we are to be among those that have or among those that have not. When you feel in the within that you are gaining more you are among those that have, and to you shall be given more. When you feel in the within that you are losing what you have, you are among those that have not, and from you shall be taken away even that which you have.

When we learn that mind is cause and that everything we gain may come from the action of mind as cause, we discover that all possession is dependent upon the attitude of mind, and since we have the power to hold the mind in any attitude desired, all the laws of gain and possession are in our own hands. When this discovery is made we begin to gain conscious possession of ourselves, and to him that hath himself all other things shall be given. To feel that you, yourself, are the power behind other powers, and that you may determine what is to come and what is to go, is to become conscious of the fact that you are something. You thus become conscious of something in yourself that is real, that is substantial and that is actually supreme in your world. To become conscious of something in yourself is to have something, and to have something is to gain more; consequently, by gaining consciousness of that something that is real in yourself you become one of those that hath, and to you shall be given.

To gain consciousness of the real in yourself is to gain consciousness of the real in life, and the more you feel the reality of life the more real life becomes. The result is that your consciousness of the reality of life becomes larger and larger; it comprehends more and takes in more. In other words, it is becoming accumulative. When this realization is attained you gain conscious hold upon life and are gradually gaining conscious hold upon everything that exists in life. This means a greater and greater mastery of life, and mastery is always followed by an increase in possession. Whatever you become conscious of in yourself, that you gain possession of in yourself. Whatever you gain possession of in yourself, that you can constructively employ in your sphere of existence, and whatever is constructively employed is productive; it produces something. Therefore, by becoming conscious of something you gain the power to produce something, and products on any plane constitute riches on that plane.

The more you become conscious of in yourself and in your life the greater your power to create and produce in your sphere of action, and the more wealth you produce the greater your possession, providing you have learned how to retain the products of your own talent. When we analyze these laws from another point of view we find the consciousness of the real in ourselves produces an ascending tendency in the mind, and whenever the mind begins to go up, the law of action and reaction will continue to press the mind up further and further indefinitely. Every upward action of mind, produces a reaction that pushes the mind upward still farther. As the mind is pushed upward a second upward action is expressed that is stronger than the first; this in turn produces a second reaction stronger than the first reaction, and the mind is pushed upward the second time much farther than it was the first time. The fact is, when the mind enters the ascending scale the law of action and reaction will perpetuate the ascension so long as the mind takes a conscious interest in the progress made; but the moment the mind loses interest in the movement the law will reverse itself and the mind enters the descending scale.

Therefore, become conscious of the law in yourself and take a conscious interest in every step in advance that you make, and you will go up in the scale of life continually and indefinitely.

When the mind is in the ascending scale it is steadily becoming larger, more powerful and more competent, and will consequently be in demand where recompense is large and the opportunities more numerous. Such a mind will naturally gain step by step in rapid succession. To such a mind will be given more and more continually, because it has placed itself in the world of those who have. The great secret of gaining more, regardless of circumstances, is to continue perpetually to go up in mind. No matter how things are going about you, continue to go up in mind. Every upward step that is taken in mind adds power to mind, and this added power will produce added results in the tangible world. When these added results are observed mind gains more faith in itself, and more faith always brings more power. On the other hand, when we permit ourselves to go down in mind, because things seem to go down, we lose power. This loss of power will prevent us from doing our work properly or from using those things and conditions about us to the best advantage. In consequence, things will actually go down more and more; and if we permit this losing of ground to make us still more discouraged, we lose still more power, to be followed by still more adversity and loss. It is therefore evident that the way we go in mind everything in our world will go also, and that if we change our minds and stay changed, everything else will change and stay changed. If we continue to go up in mind, never permitting retrogression for a moment, everything in our world will continue to go up, and there will not even be signs of reverse, much less the loss of anything which we wish to retain.

When things seem to go wrong we should stay right and continue to stay right, and things will soon decide to come and be right also. This is a law that works and never fails to work. When we permit ourselves to go wrong because things seem to go wrong, we produce what may be termed the letting go attitude of mind, and when we cease to hold on to things, things will begin to slip away. We must hold on to things ourselves, if we wish to retain them for ourselves; and the secret of holding on to things is to continue positively in that attitude of mind that is perpetually going up into the larger and the greater. The laws of life will continue perpetually to give to those who have placed themselves in the receiving attitude, and those same laws will take away from those who have placed themselves in the losing attitude. When you create a turn in yourself you will feel that things are also taking a turn to a degree; and if you continue persistently in this feeling, everything in your life will positively take the turn that you have taken. As you go everything in your world will go, providing you continue to go; the law of action and reaction explains why. In the last analysis, however, everything depends upon whether consciousness determines how every force, element, power or faculty is to act, because they are all controlled by consciousness. When your consciousness does not have the proper hold on things, the power of your being will fail to gain the proper hold on things; but when your consciousness does possess this holding power, all the powers of your being will gain the same firm grip upon everything with which they may have to deal.

To establish the accumulative consciousness, that is, that consciousness that has complete hold on things, train yourself to inwardly feel that you have full possession of everything in your own being. Feel that you possess yourself. Affirm that you possess yourself. Think constantly of yourself as possessing yourself—everything that is in yourself, and you will soon be conscious of absolute self-possession. Some have this conscious feeling naturally, and they invariably gain vast possessions, either in tangible goods or in wisdom and higher spiritual powers. But every one can develop this state of conscious possession of his whole self by remaining firm in the conviction that "All that I am is mine." When you begin to feel that you possess yourself you actually *have* something in consciousness, and according to the laws of gain and possessions you will gain more and more without end. You are in the same consciousness with those who have, and to you will be given. You have established the inner cause of possession through the conscious possession of your entire inner life, and the effect of this cause, that is, the perpetual increase of external possession, must invariably follow. In brief, you have applied the great law—To Him That Hath Himself All Other Things Shall Be Given.

14. THE LIFE THAT IS WORTH LIVING.

To the average person life means but little, because he has not discovered the greater possibilities or his real existence. He has been taught to think that to make a fortune or to make a name for himself are the only things worthwhile, and if he does not happen to have the necessary talent for these accomplishments there is nothing much else for him to do but to merely exist. However, if he has been touched with the force of ambition, or if he has had a glimpse of the ideal, mere existence does not satisfy, and the result is a life of unhappiness and dissatisfaction. But such a person must learn that there are other openings and opportunities in life besides mere existence, regardless of what the mental capacity of the individual may be. These other opportunities, when taken advantage of, will give just as much happiness, if not more, than what is secured by those who have won the admiration of the world; besides, when one learns to live for these other things real living becomes a fine art, and he begins to live a life that is really worthwhile.

There is many a person whose present position in life depends almost wholly upon his financial returns, and if these are small, with no indications of immediate increase, his life seems to be almost, if not wholly, a barren waste; not because it is a barren waste, but because he has not found the real riches of existence. The trouble with this person is the point of view; he is depending upon things instead of depending upon himself. He must learn that there is something more to live for besides his salary and what his salary can buy. The value of the individual life is not measured by the quantity of possessions, but by the quality of existence. The value of life comes not from having much, but from being much; and happiness is invariably a state of mind coming, not from what a person has, but from what he is. We must remember, however, that he who is much will finally gain much, providing the powers in his possession are practically applied; and his gains will have high quality whether they be gains in the world of things or in the world of mind, consciousness and soul.

The problem for the average person to solve is what he actually can do with himself in his present position. He may not be earning much now, and his opportunities for earning more may not be clearly in evidence, but he is nevertheless living in a great sea of opportunities, many of which may be taken advantage of at once. The first of these is the opportunity to make of himself a great personality, and in taking advantage of this opportunity he should remember that to do great things in the world is not the only thing worthwhile. To be great in the world is of equal if not greater worth, and he who is now becoming great in his own life will, without fail, do great things in years to come. The majority of those who have practical capacity are making strenuous efforts to do something great, something startling, that will arrest the attention of the world; while those who do not possess this practical capacity are not satisfied because they are not similarly favored. In the meantime neither class gains happiness, and the best forces of life are employed in the making of things, most of which are valueless, while the making of great personalities is postponed to some future time.

The capacity to make great things is not the only capacity of value in the possession of man; but all minds do not possess this capacity; all minds, however, do possess the power to remake themselves in the exact likeness of all that is great and beautiful and

198

ideal. Begin now to rebuild your own personality and proceed in the realization of the fact that you have the power to produce an edition DeLuxe out of your own present personal self. You could hardly find a purpose of greater interest and of greater possibility than this, and results will be secured from the very beginning. To find your own personality passing through a transformation process, bringing out into expression the finest and the best that you can picture in your ideals, is something that will add immensely to the joy and the worth of living. In fact, this alone would make life not only worth living, but so rich that every moment would become a source of unbounded satisfaction in itself.

The average person usually asks himself how much money he can make during the next ten years, but why should he not ask himself how much happiness he can enjoy during those same years, or how much brilliancy he can develop in his mind, or how much more beautiful he may become in body, character and soul? He would find that by living for these latter things he would not only perpetually enrich his life and live a life that is thoroughly worth living, but he would find that the earning of money would become much easier than if he simply lived for material gain alone. The ambition of the average person is to do something great in the world of things; but why is he not ambitious to do something great in the perfecting of his own being, the most wonderful world in the universe? Such ambitions are truly worth living for and working for, but our attention has not been called to their extraordinary possibilities; therefore, we have neglected the greater while wasting most of our energies on the lesser.

There are a number of ambitions outside of the usual ones that could engage our attention with the greatest of profit, because they not only have worth in themselves, but they lead to so many other things that have worth. The desire to secure as much out of life as life can possibly give will not only make living intensely interesting, but the more life a person can live the more power he will get. Live a great life and you gain great power. The increase of your power will enable you to carry out a number of other ambitions, thus adding to the richness of your life from almost every imaginable source. When a person declares that his greatest ambition is to live he is taking the most interesting, the most satisfying, the most profitable and the most complete course in life that can possibly be selected. Living, itself, when made a fine art, is one continuous feast, and the fact that all increase of power comes from the increase of life makes the ambition to live not only the greatest ambition of all, but the means through which all other ambitions may be realized.

If your present life does not hold as much as you would wish, do not think of it as an empty state of existence. Do not depend upon those few things that you are receiving from the external world; but begin to draw upon the limitless life and power that exists in the vastness of your interior world. Then you will find something to live for. Then you will begin to live a life that is thoroughly worthwhile. Then you will find the real riches of existence, and you will also find that these riches will so increase your personal power and worth that you will become able to take advantage of those opportunities that lead to things of tangible worth.

When the world of things does not seem to hold any new opportunities for you resolve to grow more and more beautiful in body, character and soul with the passing of the years. Make this your ambition, and if you do your utmost to carry out this ambition, you will gain far more satisfaction from its realization than if you had amassed an immense fortune. Live to express in body, mind and soul all that is high and beautiful and ideal in your sublime nature, and you will not only give yourself unbounded joy, but you will become a great inspiration to the entire world. The life that is not expressed through the beautiful nor surrounded by the beautiful is not worth a great deal to the mind of man; but there is practically no end to the joy and richness that man may gain through that which is actually beautiful. The beautiful not only gives happiness, but it opens the mind of man to those higher realms from which proceed all that is worthy or great or ideal. To look upon the beautiful is to gain glimpses of that vast transcendent world where supreme life is working out the marvelous destiny of man. Therefore, there can be no greater ambition than to live for the purpose of giving higher and more ideal expression to the life of that sublime world.

To give expression in personal life to the great riches of the interior world is worth far more, both to yourself and to the race, than it is to gain possession of any number of things in the external world. The man who simply gains wealth never gains happiness; besides, he is soon forgotten. But the man who will live for the purpose of giving expression to mental and spiritual wealth will gain unlimited happiness, and his life will be so illustrious that his name will never be forgotten. And remember that no matter how insignificant your position in life may be today, or how small your income, or how limited your opportunities, you can begin this moment to give expression to the vast riches of your interior life; and before you take your departure from this sphere you may become such a great light in the world of higher illumined attainment that your accomplishments in this unique sphere of action will continue to inspire the world for ages yet to come.

To live for the purpose of developing the gold mines of the mind and the diamond fields of the soul, are ambitions that might engage the attention of millions who have found no satisfaction in the world of things; and to those who will make these their leading ambitions a rich future is certainly in store; and, in addition, the present will be filled to overflowing with almost everything that can give interest and happiness to life. To develop a charming personality, to live a long life, to live a happy life, and to retain your health, your youth and your vigor as long as you live, these are ambitions that anyone can work for with the greatest interest and profit; and to him who will accomplish these things the world will give more honor than it has given to its greatest musicians, its most brilliant orators or its most illustrious statesmen.

To live for the purpose of unfolding the latent powers of your being is a work that will not only prove interesting to an exceptional degree, but will prove exceedingly rich in future possibilities. That there is practically no end to the possibilities that are latent in man is now the firm conviction of all real psychologists. Therefore, we need not weep because there are no more worlds to conquer. We are on the borderland of greater worlds than were ever dreamed of by the most illumined seers that the world has ever known. We need not feel discouraged because our position in life seems uninteresting or insignificant. We have opportunities at our very door that are so great and so numerous that it will require an eternity to take advantage of them all. Though the external world may not as yet have given us much to live for, the internal world stands ready to lavish upon us so much that is rich and marvelous that not a single moment need be otherwise than a feast fit for the gods. The doors of this internal world are open, and he who will walk in will begin to live a life that is great, indeed.

When we look into life as life really is there is so much to live for and there is so much to accomplish and attain that even eternity seems too short. The problem to solve is to know the greatest thing we can do now; and the solution may be found by resolving to live for that which is nearest at hand, whatever that may be. Accept the greatest opportunity that you can take advantage of now, and then begin to live for the working out of everything that that opportunity may contain. Do not long for opportunities that are out of reach. The majority do this and thus waste their time. Do not wait for opportunities to do great things. The opportunity to make of yourself a great soul, a marvelous mind and a higher developed personality is at hand, and by taking advantage of this opportunity you will awaken within yourself those powers that can do great things. You will thus cause your present to become all that you may wish it to be; you will build for a future that which will be nothing less than extraordinary; and you will be living a life that is thoroughly worth living in the great eternal now. You will be making the ideal real at every step of the way, but every moment will lead you into worlds that are richer and realms that are fairer than you ever dreamed of before. It is therefore evident that when we learn to live the life that is really worth living, there is no reason whatever why a single moment should be empty, dull or uninteresting in the life of any person, because there is so much to live for that has real worth, so much to enjoy that holds real enjoyment, so much to do that is thoroughly worth doing; besides, the whole of life, when actually lived, is eternally alive with interest, ever revealing the splendor of its vast transcendent domains. And he who aims to live for the purpose of gaining the realization of, and the possession of, as many spheres of this life as possible will find full expression for every ambition and every aspiration that he can possibly arouse in his mind. Life to him will be a continuous feast and existence will become an endless advancement into the highest attainments and the greater achievements that even the most illustrious mind can picture as its goal.

15. WHEN ALL THINGS BECOME POSSIBLE.

When the mind is placed in conscious contact with the limitless powers of universal life all things become possible, and faith is the secret. To have faith is to possess that interior insight through which we can discern the marvelous possibilities that are latent in the great within, and to possess the power to enter into the very life of the great within. To most minds there seems to be a veil in consciousness between the spheres of present understanding and the spheres of the higher wisdom, and though there are many who feel distinctly that there is something greater within them, yet it seems hidden, and they cannot discern it. Faith, however, has the power to perceive those greater things within that previously seemed hidden, and this is the reason why faith is the evidence of things not seen. Faith does not simply believe. It knows; it knows through higher insight, because faith is this higher insight. Faith is not blind, objective belief, but a higher development of consciousness through which the mind transcends the circumscribed and enters into the life of the boundless.

When faith is active consciousness is expanded so much that it breaks all bounds and penetrates even those realms that objective man has never heard of before. In this way new truth and discoveries are brought to light, and this is how man gains the understanding of what previously seemed to be beyond his comprehension. When we define faith as that power in mind through which consciousness can penetrate into the larger sphere of life we perceive readily why almost anything can be accomplished through faith, and we also understand why no one can afford to work without faith. When consciousness enters a larger sphere of action its capacity is naturally increased, and the greater power that can be drawn upon in performing any kind of work increases in proportion; likewise, the knowing how to work will be promoted in the same manner. To do anything successfully one must know how to do it and have the power to do what one knows should be done, and both these essentials are increased in proportion to the enlargement of consciousness. One of the principal metaphysical laws declares that whatever you become conscious of you express through your personality; therefore, according to this law more life, more power and more wisdom will come into actual possession in the personal life as we become conscious of more and more of these things in the mental life; in other words, the ideal is made real.

The art of extending consciousness into the realms of unlimited life and power and wisdom is the secret through which all great attainments and great achievements become possible; but without faith this enlargement of consciousness cannot take place, because faith is that power that perceives and enters into the greater things that are still before us. Faith looks into the beyond of every faculty, talent or power and perceives that there is much more of these same talents and powers further on. In fact, there is no visible limit to anything when viewed through the eyes of faith. Consciousness does not extend itself in any direction until it feels that there will be tangible grounds upon which to proceed. You can become conscious only of those things that seem real; therefore, to extend your consciousness in any direction you must secure evidence of the fact that there is more reality in that direction; and here we find the great mission of faith. Faith supplies this evidence. Faith looks further on into the beyond and sees real reality at every step, and proves to consciousness that things not seen are thoroughly substantial. Faith discerns that there is no danger in going on and on because there is solid ground all the way, no matter how far into the limitless we may wish to go; there is no danger of being lost in an empty void by following faith. Instead, faith gives us a positive assurance of finding more life, more power, more wisdom and a fairer state of existence than we ever knew before.

The practical value of faith is therefore to be found in its power to enlarge all the faculties and spheres of action in the mind of man, and as this enlargement can go on indefinitely, as there is no end to the visible, we conclude that anything can be accomplished by following faith. No matter how much wisdom or power we may require to reach the goal we have in view we can finally secure the required amount through the perpetual enlargement of consciousness. This is evident, and since faith is that something in mind that leads consciousness on and on into larger fields of action it becomes indispensable to all growth, to all great achievements, to all high attainments and to the realization of all true ideals. The man who has no faith in himself can neither improve himself nor his work. When nothing is added to his ability, capacity or skill there can be nothing added to the quality or the quantity of what he is doing. The effect will not improve until we have improved the cause; and man himself is the cause of everything that appears in his life.

Modern psychology, however, has discovered and conclusively demonstrated that no faculty can be improved until the conscious sphere of action of that faculty is enlarged and thoroughly developed. Therefore, to promote the efficiency of any faculty the conscious action of that faculty must become larger and imbued with more life. This is the fundamental principle in all advancement, but consciousness will not enlarge its sphere of action until it perceives that there is reality beyond its present sphere, and it is only through the interior insight of faith that the greater reality existing beyond present limitations is discovered to be real. The lack of this interior insight among the great majority is the principal obstacle that prevents them from becoming more than they are. Their minds have not the power to see the potential side of their larger nature. They are aware of the objective only and can do only as much as the limited power of the objective will permit. But they are not aware of the fact that there is limitless power within, nor do they realize that they can draw upon this great interior power and thus accomplish not only more and more, but everything that they may now have in view. Not having the power to look beyond present attainment, the little world in which they live is all that is real to them. Occasionally there is a dream or a vision of greatness, but it soon fades away, and in those rare instances when the high vision continues for some time the knowledge of how to make real the ideal is usually not at hand.

The human race is divided into three classes; first, those who live in the limited world and never see anything beyond the limited; second, those who live in the limited world but have occasional glimpses of greater things, though having neither the knowledge nor the power to make their dreams come true; and third, those who are constantly passing from the lesser to the greater, making real every ideal as soon as it comes within the world of their conscious comprehension. The last group is small, but there are millions today who are on the verge of a larger sphere of existence, and for this reason we should usher into the world at once a greater movement for the promotion of faith than has ever been known before. It is more faith that these millions need in order to enter into the beautiful life they can see before them. It is more faith they must have before they can become as much as they desire to be. It is faith, and faith alone, that can give them the power to do what this great sphere of existence may require.

To make real the ideal in any life faith must be combined with work, and no work should be undertaken unless it can be animated thoroughly with the power of faith. The reason why is found in the fact that all practical action is weak or strong, depending upon the capacity of that part of the mind which directly controls that action; and the capacity of the mind increases in proportion to the attainment of faith. To accomplish what we have in view, it is not only necessary to know how to go about our work, but it is necessary to have sufficient power, and faith is the open door to more and more power.

The very moment you obtain more faith you feel stronger; you are then certain of results and the very best results; and the reason why is found in the fact that faith always connects the mind with the larger, the greater and the inexhaustible. On the other hand, you may have an abundance of energy, but do not see clearly how to apply that energy in such a way that results will be as desired; again the remedy is more faith. Faith elevates the mind and lifts consciousness up above doubt, uncertainty and confusion. "When you go up into faith you enter the light and can see clearly how to proceed; but in this connection we must avoid a very common mistake. When we discover the remarkable power of faith there is a tendency to depend upon faith exclusively and ignore other faculties. We sometimes come to the conclusion that it matters little how we work or think or act so long as we have an abundance of faith, because faith will cause everything to come right. The fact, however, that we sometimes come to this conclusion proves that we have not found real faith, because when we have an abundance of real faith we can see clearly the great truth that all thought and action must be right to secure results, and that all faculties and powers must be employed in their highest states of efficiency if we wish to make real the ideal. Though it is absolutely necessary to have the vision, still the vision is not sufficient in itself. After the vision has been discovered in the ideal it must be made real; the principle must be applied; the new discovery must be worked out in practical action; but these things require both fine intelligence and practical skill.

Faith without works is dead, because it does nothing, uses nothing, creates nothing; it is as if it were not; and works without faith are so insignificant and ordinary that they are usually very little better than nothing. But when work and faith are combined then everything becomes possible. The power of faith is placed in action; work becomes greater and greater, and whatever our purpose may be we shall positively scale the heights. The great principle is to combine unlimited faith with skillful work. Work with all the skill that you can possibly cultivate, but inspire all your efforts with the mighty soul of a limitless faith. Become as learned, as intellectual and as highly developed in mind as possible, but animate your prodigious intellect with the supreme spirit of faith. Faith does not come to take the place of art, skill or intellect. Faith comes to give real soul to art, skill and intellect. Faith comes to fill all physical and mental action with renewed life and power. It comes to open that door through which all our efforts may pass to higher and greater things. Faith is not simply for the moral and spiritual life; it is not simply for what is sometimes called higher endeavor. It is for all endeavor, and it has the power to push all endeavor with such energy and force that we simply must succeed, no matter what our work may be. The man who has faith in his work, faith in himself, faith in the human race and faith in the Supreme—that man simply cannot fail, if he gives the full power of his faith to everything that he undertakes to do.

We must eliminate the idea that faith is something apart from every-day life, and that it is something for the future salvation of the soul only. We have held to that belief so long that real faith has actually been separated from human existence, and we find very few people today who really know what faith actually is.

The fact is that if you are not giving your faith to everything you do, be it physical, mental or spiritual, you have not as yet obtained any faith. When faith comes it never comes to give greater power to a part of your life. It comes to give supreme power to all your life, and it comes to push all your work towards higher efficiency and greater results. When you have real faith you never undertake anything without first placing your entire being in the very highest attitude of faith. Even the most trivial things you do are done invariably in the spirit of faith. This is very important, because by training yourself to be at your best in little things it soon becomes second nature for you to be your best in all things, and when you are called upon to do something of exceptional importance, something that may seem very difficult, you do not fall down; you are fully equal to the occasion. The more we exercise faith the more it develops; it is therefore profitable to use faith at all times and in everything that we do.

When we know that faith is that something that takes mind into the superior side of life and thus places in action superior powers it is not difficult to understand how to proceed when we place ourselves in faith. As we think more and more of this higher side of our nature, this better side, this wonderful side, we gradually become conscious of its remarkable possibilities and soon we can feel the power of superiority becoming stronger and stronger in everything that we do in mind or body. To develop the power of faith the first thing to do is to train the mind to hold attention constantly upon the limitless side of life; that is, to live in the upper story of being and to think as much as possible about the true idea of faith, as well as the interior essence of faith itself. When you begin to see clearly that faith is this higher development of mind, this insight that leads to higher wisdom, greater power and more abundant life, you actually find yourself entering into the realization of those greater things whenever you think of faith. By concentrating your attention upon the inner meaning of faith your mind becomes clearer, your faculties become stronger and your entire being feels the presence of more life; and that you can do much better work while in this condition is too evident to require any more elucidation. While in the attitude of faith you cannot only do your present work better, but you will steadily develop the ability and the capacity to do more difficult work— work that will prove more useful to the community and more remunerative to yourself. The world wants everything well done and is more than willing to pay for good work. We are all seeking the best and the majority aim consciously or unconsciously to give their best, but without faith it is not possible for anyone to be his best, give his best, or do his best.

Do your best and the best will come to you in return. The universe is founded upon justice, and justice will positively be done to you if you have faith in justice. Everything in life is moving towards greater worth, and since justice is universal, the greater the worth of a man the greater the value of those things that he will receive in life. The worthy soul is always rich in those things that have real worth; and when we learn to harmonize ourselves more fully with all the laws of existence we shall place ourselves in that condition where we not only can give more that has worth but will also receive everything of worth that actually is our own. Whether you are working in the commercial world, the professional world, the artistic world, the intellectual world; in brief, whatever your work may be, to have the best results you must have faith, and it is practical results in practical everyday life that determines how rapidly and how perfectly the ideal shall be made real in your own world. Whoever will do his present work as well as he possibly can, and continue to work in the highest attitude of faith will positively advance and perpetually continue to advance. He may not have accomplished much thus far; but if he takes this course, combining efficient work with supreme faith, he certainly has a splendid future before him.

If your present work is not to your liking do not plan to change at once. First proceed with your present work in this higher attitude of faith. You may thus find your present work to be the very work you want; or your present work, if it is not what is intended for you, will become the open door through which you will reach that field of action that will be to your liking, providing you animate your present work with all the faith that you can possibly realize. Make yourself the best of your kind whatever your sphere of action may be, because by so doing you are not only increasing the number of great minds in the world, but you are adding immeasurably to the world's welfare and joy; and he who combines his work with limitless faith will become the greatest and the best in his sphere. In the application of faith, however, the whole of attention must not be directed upon the improvement of your work, but more especially upon the improvement of yourself. The more you improve the better work you can do, but while you are improving yourself your improvement will be incomplete and insufficient unless you each day practically employ in your work what you have developed in yourself. Give the power of every moment to greater attainment in yourself and to greater achievement in your present occupation, and you will fulfill that dual purpose in life that invariably leads to the heights. Develop more power, more ability and more faith and combine these in everything that you do. Through the power of faith you will not only discern higher and higher ideals, but you will also give greater capacity to your practical ability. In other words, you will not only gain the power to see the ideal, but you will gain the power to practically apply what you have seen; you will make tangible in real life what the visions of the soul have revealed in the ideal life; and as you grow in faith, so great will this power become that there is no ideal you cannot make real. You will have placed yourself in touch with limitless power— the power of the Supreme, and therefore to you, all things will become possible.

16. THE ART OF GETTING WHAT IS WANTED.

We frequently hear the statement "I never received what I wanted until the time came when I did not care for it and did not need it." This statement may in most instances be based upon an unguided imagination, though this is not always the case, because there are thousands of people who actually have this very experience. They never get what they want until the desire for it, as well as the need of it, have disappeared. There may be occasional exceptions, but the rule is that what we persistently desire we shall sooner or later receive. Too often it is later, the reason being that most desires are purely personal and are not inspired by those real needs that may exist in the great eternal now. Mere personal desires are usually out of harmony with the present process of soul-growth, and therefore there is no supply in our immediate mental vicinity for what those desires naturally need. This is the reason why more time is required for the fulfilling of these desires, and frequently the time required is so long that when the desire is fulfilled we do not need it anymore. When we desire only those things that are best for us now, that is, those things that are necessary to a full and complete life in the present, we shall receive what we desire at the very time when those things are needed. What is best for us now is ready in the mental world to be expressed through us. Every demand has its own supply in the immediate vicinity, and every demand will find or attract its own supply without any delay whatever, but the demand must be natural, not artificial.

The average person is full of artificial desires—desires that have been suggested by what other people possess or require. But the question is not what we need now to compete with other people so as to make more extravagant external appearances than other people. The question is, what do we need now to make our present life as full, as complete and as perfect as it possibly can be made now. Ask yourself this question and your artificial desires will disappear. In the first place, you will try to ascertain what you are living for, and what may be required to promote that purpose of life that may seem true to your deeper thought on the subject. In the second place, you will realize that since it is the present and the present only for which you are living you will concentrate your attention upon the living of life now. This will bring the whole power of desire down upon the present moment and engage all the forces of life to work for the perfection of the present moment. The result will be the elimination of nearly everything that is foreign to your present state of existence.

To know what to desire and what to ignore in the present may seem to be a problem, but it is easily solved by depending upon the demands of the soul instead of the demands of the person.

The desires of the average person are almost constantly colored or modified by suggestions from the artificial life of the world; they are therefore not normal and are not true to real life. The desires of the soul, however, are always true and are always in harmony with the greatest good and the highest welfare of the entire being of man in his present sphere. It is the soul that lives; therefore the soul can feel truly what is necessary to fullness and completeness in present life. Real life never lives for the past or for the future. Real life lives now, and therefore knows the needs of life now. It is the soul that grows and develops; therefore the soul can feel what is required to promote present development For these reasons it is perfectly safe to follow the desires of the soul and those desires only; it will mean the best of everything for body, mind and spirit, and the right things will appear in the right places at the right time.

We live not to acquire things nor to provide for an extravagant personal appearance. We live to become more than we are. We live to live a larger and a greater life perpetually; therefore every desire must desire only those things that are conducive to growth, advancement, attainment and superior states of existence. The expression of desire, however, must not confound cause with effect, but must so place every desire that the power of cause invariably precedes the appearance of effect. To promote advancement in life we must advance in our own conscious beings before true advancement in the external world can follow. Forced advancement is artificial, and is detrimental to the permanent welfare of the soul. Do not push the person forward. Live to give greater expression to the soul and you will develop all the power that is necessary to push the person forward towards any lofty goal you may have in view. Become more than you are from the within, and external environments, demands and opportunities will ask you to come forward. Thus you promote true advancement.

There are a number of people who believe that to follow the desires of the soul is to be led into poverty, and hardships in general, but those who have this belief know practically nothing about the real nature of the soul. He who follows the desires of the soul will be led away from sickness, trouble and poverty and will enter into the possession of the best of everything, physical, mental and spiritual. This is natural, because the ruling desire of the soul is to promote the attainment of greater power, greater ability, a larger life, superior qualities and greater capacity so that things may be done that are really worthwhile.

The soul lives to unfold the limitless possibilities that are latent in the within. Therefore, to live the life of the soul and follow the desires of the soul is to become greater, more able, more competent and more worthy every day. By developing greater power in yourself you overcome sickness and trouble; and by constantly increasing your ability, your talent and your genius you pass from poverty to abundance, no matter where you may live or what your work may be.

The man who lives to perfect his entire being will naturally desire only those things that are conducive to the growth and the development that he is trying to promote, and such desires will be supplied without delay, because they are natural, and they are in harmony with real life. What life may require now that life *can* receive now. This is the law. But every artificial desire that we may hold in mind interferes with the workings of this law, and since the average person is full of artificial desires he usually fails to receive what is needed to promote the welfare of real life. Every desire that is held in mind uses up energy; therefore, if the desire is artificial, all that energy is thrown away, or it may be employed in creating something that we have no use for when it does come. It has been very wisely stated that a strong mind should weigh matters with the greatest of care before uttering a single prayer, because most of the prayers of such a mind are answered; and should he pray for something that he cares nothing for when it does come he will have a burden instead of a blessing.

The majority are entirely too reckless about their desires; they desire things because they want them at the time, but do not stop to think whether the things desired will prove satisfactory or not when they are received; and since we usually get, sooner or later, what we persistently desire, the art of knowing what to desire is an art, the development of which becomes extremely important. It is not an act of wisdom to pray for future blessings or to entertain desires that will not be fulfilled until some future time. When the future comes you may have advanced so far, or changed so much, that the needs of your life will be entirely different from what they are in the present. Let every desire be just for today, and let that desire be prompted by the ruling desire of your life; that is, the desire to become a more powerful personality, a stronger character, a more brilliant mind and a greater soul. Live perpetually in the desire that you will receive the best that life can give today, that all things will work together for good to you now, and that everything necessary to the promotion of your highest welfare will come in abundance during the great eternal now. Make this desire so strong that your heart and soul are in it with all the power of life, and let every present moment be deeply inspired by the very spirit of this desire. The result will be that the best of everything will constantly be coming into your world, and everything that may be necessary to make your life full and complete now will be added in an ever increasing abundance.

In this connection we must remember that is not best for anyone to pass through sickness, trouble and misfortune. When people have misfortune they sometimes console themselves with the belief that it is all for the best, but this is not the truth; though we can and should turn every adverse circumstance to good account. When you come into trouble you have not been living for the best. You have made mistakes or entertained artificial desires, and that is why trouble came. Had you lived in the faith that all things are working together for good, nothing but good would have come; and had you lived in the strong desire for the best and the best only, you would have received the very best that you could appreciate and enjoy now. The belief that we have to pass through trouble to reach peace and comfort is an illusion that we have inherited from the dark ages, and the belief that we are purified through the fires of adversity is another illusion coming from the same source. We are purified by passing through a perpetual refining process, and this process is the result of consciousness gaining a deeper, a higher, a truer and a more beautiful conception of that divinity in man that is created in the image and likeness of the Supreme; and it is well to remember that this refining process can live and act only where there is peace of mind, harmony of life and the joy of the spirit. Higher states of life do not come by passing through adversity but by living the soul-life so completely that you are never affected by adversity. The peace that passeth understanding does not come from the act of overcoming trouble, but is the product of that state of mind that is so high and so strong that it is never moved by trouble. The greatest victory does not come through successful warfare, but through a life that is so high and in such perfect harmony with all things that it wars against nothing, resists nothing, antagonizes nothing, pursues nothing, overcomes nothing. The life that is above things does not have to overcome things, and it is such a life that brings real peace, true joy and sublime harmony. The belief that we have to fight for our rights is another illusion; likewise, the belief that wrongs have to be overcome. The higher law declares, be right in all things and you will have your rights in all things. Be above all things and you will not have to overcome anything. Live in the spirit of the limitless supply and you will not have to demand anything from any source, because you will be in the life of abundance.

There is value in the silent demand, but it is not the highest thought. The highest thought is to desire with heart and soul whatever we may need now, and live in the absolute conviction that all natural demands are supplied now; then we shall not have to make any demands whatever, silent or audible. A mental demand usually becomes a forced mental process, and such a process, though it may succeed temporarily, as all forced actions do, will finally fail; and when it does fail the mind will not be as high in the scale as it was before. The highest state is pure realization, a state where we realize that everything is at hand for us now and will be expressed the very moment we desire its tangible possession. Here we must remember never to turn our desires into mental demands, but to make every desire an inward soul feeling united perfectly with faith.

The highest desire is always transformed into a whole-souled gratitude, even before the desire has been outwardly fulfilled, because when the desire is high in the spirit of faith it knows at once the prayer will be answered, and consequently gives thanks from the very depths of the heart.

The prayer that is uttered through the spirit of faith and through the soul of thanksgiving—the two united in one, is always answered, whether it be uttered silently or audibly. The desires that are felt in such a prayer are inspired by the divinity that dwells within and are therefore true to real life. They are soul desires. They belong to the present and will be fulfilled in the present at the very time when we want them and need them. When we fail to get what is wanted, our wants are either artificial or so full of false and perverted wants that the law of supply is prevented from doing its proper work for us. Under such conditions it is necessary to ask the great question, "What am I living for?" Then eliminate those desires that are suggested by the world, and retain only those that desire the highest state of perfection for the whole man. It is the truth that when man seeks first the kingdom of the true life, the perfect life, all other things needful to such a life will be added. He who desires more life will receive more life, and with the greater life comes the greater power—that power with which man may create his own destiny and make everything in his life as he wishes it to be. In order to get what is wanted or what is needed the usual process of desire must be reversed. Instead of desiring things, desire that greater life and that greater power that can produce things. First, desire life, power, ability, greatness, superiority, high personal worth, and exceptional spiritual attainments. Never desire definite environments, special things or certain fixed conditions. Leave those things to Higher Power, because when Higher Power begins to act you will receive the very best environments, the richest things and the most perfect conditions that you can possibly enjoy. Desire real life first, and all that is beautiful and perfect in the living of such a life in body, mind and soul, will invariably be added. Follow the desires of the soul and you will receive everything that is necessary, not only for the life of the soul but for the life of mind and body as well. Seek the Source of all good things and you will receive all good things.

17. PATHS TO HAPPINESS.

To be happy is the privilege of everybody, and everybody may be happy at all times and under all circumstances through the knowing and living of a few simple principles.

The reason why happiness is not as universal and as abundant as it might be is because the majority seek happiness for itself alone. Happiness is an effect. It comes from a definite cause.

Therefore, if we would obtain happiness we must not seek happiness for itself, but seek that something that produces happiness. He who seeks happiness directly, who desires happiness for the sake of gaining happiness or who works directly for the attainment of happiness will find but little real joy in his life. To seek happiness is to fail to find it, but to seek the cause of happiness is to find it in an ever increasing measure. Happiness, however, is not the result of any one single cause. It is the result of many ideal states of being grouped together into one harmonious whole. In brief, happiness is the result of true being perfectly lived upon all planes of consciousness.

Happiness does not come from having much, but from being much; therefore, anything that will tend to bring forth into tangible expression more and more of the real being of man will add to his joy. To promote the larger and larger expression of the real being of man; in other words, to promote the living in the real of more and more of the ideal, a number of methods may be presented; but as happiness is based upon simplicity, methods for producing the cause of happiness must also be based upon simplicity, therefore only those principles that are purely fundamental need be employed. These principles however must not be applied singly. It is necessary to combine them all in practical every-day living, and when this is done, more and more happiness will invariably follow. The principles necessary to the perpetual increase of happiness are as follows:

1. Live the simple life. The complex life is not only a burden to existence, but is invariably an obstacle to the highest attainments and welfare of man; and the majority, even among those whose tangible possessions are very insignificant, are living a complex life; but when the average person is told to remove complexity from his world and adopt simplicity he almost invariably destroys the beauty of life. The art of living a life that is both simple and beautiful is an art that few have mastered, though it is by no means difficult. Most of the life that is called simple is positively devoid of beauty and has nothing whatever that is attractive about it. In fact, it is positively a detriment both to happiness and advancement. To live the simple life is not to return to primitive conditions nor to decide to be satisfied with nothing, or next to nothing. It is possible to live the simple life in the midst of all the luxuries that wealth can buy, because simplicity does not spring from the quantity of possession but from the arrangement of possession.

The central idea in the living of a simple life is to eliminate non-essentials. The question should be, "Which of the things that are about me do I need to promote the greatest welfare of my life?" To answer this question will not be difficult, because almost anyone can determine at first thought what is needed and what is not needed to a complete life. When the decision is made, non-essentials should be removed as quickly as possible.

True, we must avoid extremes, and whatever we do we must do nothing to decrease the beauty or the harmony of life.

There are a great many things in the world of the average person that he simply thinks he needs, though he knows that those things never did anything but retard his progress. It is therefore necessary to remove non-essentials from the mind before we attempt to simplify our immediate surroundings.

The simple life is a beautiful life, with all burdens removed, and it is only the unnecessary that is burdensome. To live the simple life, surround yourself only with those things that are directly conducive to your welfare, but do not consider it necessary to limit the quantity of those things. Surround yourself with *everything* that is necessary to promote your welfare, no matter how much it may be, although do not place in your world a single thing that is not a direct power for good in your world. You thus establish the harmony of simplicity without placing any limitations whatever upon your possessions, your welfare or your highest need. You thus eliminate everything that may act as a burden; and we can readily understand that when all burdens are removed from life the happiness of life will be increased to a very great degree.

2. Live the serene life. Be calm, peaceful, quiet and undisturbed in all things and at all times. Confusion and hurry waste energy, and it is a well-known fact that depression and gloom are produced, in most instances, simply by the energy of the system running low. The serene life, if lived in poise, will keep the system brimful of energy at all times, and so long as you are filled through and through with life and energy you will be full of spirit and joy. Our saddest moments are usually the direct results of reactions from turbulent thinking and living; therefore, such moments will be eliminated completely when thinking and living are made peaceful and serene. It is not necessary to live the strenuous life in order to accomplish a great deal, although on the other hand it is not quantity but quality that we seek. Our object should not be to do many things, but to do good things. If we can do many things that are good, very well, but we must have quality first in the mind; the quantity will increase as we grow in capacity, and there is nothing that promotes the increase of mental and physical capacity more than calm, serene living. The sweetest joys that the mind can feel usually come from those deep peaceful realizations of the soul when all is quiet and serene. Therefore, to cultivate the habit of living always in this beautiful calm will invariably add happiness to happiness every day of continued existence.

3. Be in love with the world. He who loves much will be loved much in return, and there is nothing in the world that can give more joy and higher joy than an abundance of real love. The selfish love, that is only personal, and that *must* be gratified to be enjoyed, gives but a passing pleasure, the reaction of which is always pain. When we love with such a love we are always unhappy when not directly loved in return, and the purely selfish love never brings real love in return. When we love everybody with the pure love of the soul, that love that does not ask to be loved in return but loves because it *is* loved, we shall positively be loved in return; and not simply by a few here and there, but by great numbers. To feel that you are loved unselfishly, that you are loved not

because anything is expected in return, but because the love is there and *must* come—to feel this love is a source of joy which cannot be measured, and this joy everybody can receive in abundance now. The simple secret is to love the whole world at all times and under every circumstance; love everybody with heart and soul and *mean* it, and everything that happens to you will add both to the pleasure of the mind and to the more lofty joys of the soul.

4. Be useful. "Give to the world the best that you have and the best will come to you." Hold nothing back. If you have something that you can share with the world, let everybody have it today. Do all that you can for everybody, not because you expect reward, but because it is a part of your nature. Be all that you can be and do all that you can do. Never say, "I will do only as much as I am paid for." Such an attitude has kept many a person in poverty for life. Reward is an effect, not a cause. Do not place the reward first, and the service second. Increase your service and the reward will increase in proportion; you will thus not only place yourself in a position where you can secure more and more of the good things of life, but you will live in that position where you are bringing into expression more and more of the good things that exist in your own life. And we must remember that the greatest joy does not come from gaining good things from the without, but from the expression of good things from the within; and when both of these are combined harmoniously we shall secure all the joys of life—the joys that come from the outer world and the joys that come from the beauty and the splendor of the inner world. To combine these in your life, be useful; express your best; be your best; do your best. You thus bring forth riches from within and attract riches from without. Give richly of the best you have and good things in an ever increasing number will constantly flow into your life. That deep soul-satisfaction that comes to mind when we have rendered valuable service to man is entirely too good to be ignored; it is one of the deepest and highest joys that man can know. Those people who are the most valuable wherever they go are always the happiest, and we all can be of service in a thousand ways; therefore, we may add to our happiness in just as many ways, if we will always remember to be and do the best we can wherever we may go in the world.

5. Think and speak the beautiful only. Every word or thought that you express will return to you. Never say anything to make others discouraged or unhappy; it will come back to yourself. He who gives unhappiness to others is giving unhappiness to himself. He who adds to the joys of others is perpetually adding to his own joy. You can say something good about everybody. Then say it. It will give joy to everybody concerned, yourself included. Think only of the beautiful side of everybody. Everybody has a beautiful side. Find it and think of that only. You will thus live in the world of the beautiful, and he who lives in the world of the beautiful is always happy. Speak kindly and pleasantly to everybody; think kindly and pleasantly of everybody, and your days of gloom will be gone. When every word is animated with the spirit of kindness and joy, you will not only increase the power of joy in your own life, but you will be sowing the seeds of joy in the garden of the universal life; and one of these days you will reap abundantly from what you have sown. Let this sowing time be continuous and the harvest will be continuous; thus you will be reaping a harvest of boundless joy every day of your endless existence.

6. Forgive and forget everything that seems wrong. "We have spent many a weary day simply because we persisted in remembering something that was unpleasant. Forget the wrong and it will disturb you no more. Forgive others for what they have done and you will have no unpleasant memories to cloud the sky of your mental world. When people speak unkindly of you, never mind. Let them say what they like, if they must. Nothing can harm you but your own wrong thinking and living. If people do not treat you right remember they would act differently if they knew better, and you know better than to become offended. So therefore forgive it all and resolve to be happy. Forgive everybody for what is not right and forget everything that is not conducive to the right. You have no time to brood over ills and troubles that exist only in your memory. Your memory is created for a better purpose. Remember the good, the true and the beautiful; this is one of the greatest secrets of perpetual happiness. When you forgive those who have wronged you, you usually come to a place where you think more of those very persons than you ever did before, and when you come to that place you will realize a joy that is far too sweet and beautiful for pen to ever describe. It seems to be a blessing coming direct from heaven and it does not go away. This fact proves that he who learns to forgive rises in the scale of life. He who can forget and forgive the wrongs of the lowlands of undeveloped life, invariably ascends to the heights, and it is upon the heights that we find real happiness. Such is the reward of forgiveness. It will therefore not be difficult to forgive when we know that the results are so rich and so beautiful; indeed, to forgive and forget everything that seems wrong will thus become a coveted pleasure.

7. Be perfectly contented with the present. We have heard a great deal about the value of divine discontent, but discontent is never divine any more than indignation is ever righteous. Perfect contentment is one of the highest states of the soul and is one of those attainments that invariably follows ideal living. Discontent, however, in any of its shapes or forms, always indicates that we are not on the true path. So long as there is discontent there is something wrong in our living, but the moment this wrong is righted perpetual contentment will be realized. If your present lot is not what you wish it to be, discontent will not make it better. Be perfectly content with the present and create more lofty mansions for the future; thus you will not only improve your condition every year, but you will be supremely happy every day. The more perfect your present contentment the more power you will have to create for yourself a greater future, and the more mental light you will have to build wisely for days to come. The more contentment you realize in your mind the more brightness and strength there will be in your mind.

Find the good that you already possess, then enjoy it. Better things are even now on the way and through the harmony of contentment you will be prepared to receive them. You will also be in that higher state of mental discernment where you can know good things when you see them. Many people are so much disturbed by the discord of discontent that they are unable to recognize the good things already in their world; thus they add doubly to the cause of discontent. Contentment, however, does not mean to be so satisfied with present conditions that we do not care to change them.

True contentment not only appreciates the full value of the present, but also appreciates those greater powers in life that can perpetually add to the value of the present; therefore, the contented mind gains every-thing that life can give in the great eternal now, while at the same time perpetually increasing the richness, the worth and the beauty of the great eternal now. To be contented, find fault with nothing. Those things that are not quite right can be made better. Proceed to make them better, and one of the greatest joys of life comes directly from that action of life that is causing things to become better. The process of growth and advancement is invariably conducive to joy; therefore, if we cease finding fault, and use all our time in promoting improvement, we will find sources of happiness in every imperfection that we may meet in life. In other words, when we aim to improve everything that we meet, we bring out all the good that is latent in our world, and to increase the expression of the good in our world is to increase our own measure of joy.

8. Seek the ideal. Look for the ideal everywhere; live in ideal environments when possible; but if not possible in an external sense create for yourself an ideal environment in the internal sense. Live in ideal mental worlds no matter what external worlds may be. Associate as much as possible with ideal people, and if you are living an ideal life in your own mental and spiritual life, you will attract ideal people wherever you go. And one of the greatest joys of life is to associate with those who are living in lofty realms. We have no time to give to the common and the ordinary. We want the best. We deserve the best, and we can secure the best by seeking the best and the best only. Live your own ideal life. Seek the ideal both in the within and in the without, and aim to make the ideal real in every thought, word and deed; you will thus cause every moment to add to your joy.

9. Develop the whole man. To promote an orderly growth throughout your entire being is highly important, and to establish perfect harmony of action among all the various members of mind and body is indispensable to happiness. Develop everything in your nature and place all the elements in your being in perfect harmony. You will thus ascend perpetually to higher states of being and greater realms of joy. Much of the discord and unhappiness that comes into life is the direct result of one-sidedness and undevelopment, and these can be permanently removed only through the orderly development of the whole man. Body, mind and soul must be perfectly balanced in every sense of that term. The more perfectly you are balanced the greater will be your joy, because a balanced nature is conducive to harmony, and harmony is conducive to happiness.

10. Open the mind to beautiful thoughts only. The world is full of thoughts, all kinds of thoughts, but only those that are invited will come to you. There is nothing that affects life more than the thoughts we think; and the thoughts we are to think will depend almost entirely upon our mental attitude towards that which we meet in life. When we resolve to receive only beautiful thoughts from everything with which we come in contact the change for the better in life will be simply remarkable. All things will become new. "We will actually enter a new heaven and a new earth, and the joys of existence will multiply many times.

11. Be in touch with the harmony of life. The universe is full of music, and happy is the soul that can hear the symphonies of heaven; he can find no greater joy. Every soul that has been in tune with higher things is familiar with that deep pleasure that comes

to mind when the sensations of sublime harmony sweetly thrill every fibre of being; and we can all so live that we can be in tune with the music of the spheres. When you learn how to place yourself in harmony with the music of life you may for hours at a time remain within the gates of everlasting joy, and you may enter into the very life of that sublime something which eye has not seen nor ear heard. It is then that you understand why the kingdom of heaven is within and why all souls that have found that inner life are radiant with joy. Here is happiness without measure, happiness that you may enjoy anywhere and at any time. No matter what your environments may be, enter into these lofty realms and you will be the happiest soul in the world.

12. Consecrate every moment to the higher life. The mind that is ever ascending can never be sad. Perpetual ascension means perpetual joy. The happiest moments that come to you are those moments that come when you see yourself rising in the scale of sublime existence. You are then ascending to the heights. You are entering into the cosmic realms—those realms where joy is supreme; and one single moment in that lofty realm gives more happiness than we can imagine were a million heavens united in one. It is in these realms that we enter the secret places of the Most High, and to enter into that sublime state is to gain all the happiness that life can give and have that happiness while eternity shall continue to be.

18. CREATING IDEAL SURROUNDINGS.

We all believed, not so very long ago, that the circumstances in which each individual was placed were produced by inevitable fate, and that the individual himself could not change them, but would have to remain where he was until something in his favor happened from external sources. What was to cause that something to happen we did not know, nor did we give the matter much thought. We believed more or less in chance and luck, and had no definite conception of the underlying laws of things. But now many of us have changed our minds, as we have received a great deal of new light on this most important subject. The many, however, are still in the old belief; they are ignorant of the fact that man can create his own destiny, and that fate, circumstances and environments are but the products of man himself, acting alone, or in association with others. But this is the fact, and it can be scientifically demonstrated by anyone under any circumstance.

This new idea that man can change his surroundings or transport himself to more agreeable environments through the use of psychological and metaphysical laws may seem unthinkable and far-fetched to a great degree; but when we study the subject with care we find that the principles, laws and methods involved are not only natural but thoroughly substantial and can be applied in tangible every-day affairs. If the surroundings in which you live are not what you wish them to be, know that you can change them. You can make those surroundings ideal. You can make those surroundings better and better at every step in your advancement, thus making real higher and higher ideals in your life. This is a positive truth and should be impressed so deeply upon every mind that no former belief on the subject can cause us to doubt our possession of this power for a moment. The importance of thus impressing this fact upon the mind becomes very evident when we understand that no matter how much we may know, we will have no results so long as we are in doubt as to whether what we have undertaken is really possible or not.

There are thousands of people who believe, in a measure, that they can better their own conditions and they understand fully all the principles involved, but they have no satisfactory results because one moment they believe that the change is possible while at the next moment they entertain doubts. To have real results in any undertaking, especially in the changing of one's surroundings, one must believe with his whole heart that he can, and he must constantly employ all the necessary principles in that conviction. No undertaking ever succeeded that was not animated through and through with the positive faith that it could be done, and such a faith is simply indispensable if you wish to create ideal surroundings for yourself, because the process depends directly upon the way you think. You must think that you can so as to fully annihilate the belief that you cannot. Know that you can, and in that attitude continue to apply the necessary methods. Let nothing disturb your faith in the possibility of what you have undertaken to do in this respect, and you will positively succeed.

To create ideal surroundings, the first essential is to gain a clear understanding of what actually constitutes your surroundings.

The world in which you live is a state of many elements, factors, forces and activities. The physical environment with all its various phases and conditions has been considered the most important, but this is not necessarily true, because the mental environment is just as much a part of the world in which you live as the physical. The term "world" is not confined simply to visible things; it also includes states of mind, mental tendencies, thoughts, desires, motives and all the different phases of consciousness. The place in which you live physically, the place in which you live mentally, the place in which you live morally and spiritually, these places combined constitute the world in which you live. All of these states and conditions are necessary parts of your surroundings, and it is your purpose to make these necessary parts as beautiful, as perfect and as ideal as possible.

The place where you work with your hands and with your brain is a part of your world, but the same is true of the place where you work in your dreams, in your aspirations and in your ideals. The circumstances and events of your life, physically and mentally; the opportunities that are constantly passing your way; the people you meet in your work; the people you think of in your thoughts; the people you associate with and friends that are near; the various elements of nature, both visible and invisible; the many groups of things in all their various phases that you come in contact with in your daily living; all of these belong in your world. To enter into details it would be possible to mention many hundreds of different elements or factors that compose the world in which the average person lives; but to be brief we can say that your world is composed of everything that enters your life, your home, your experience, your thought and your dreams of the ideal. All of these play their part in bringing to you the good that you may desire or the ills that you may receive. Consequently, since the world in which you live is so very complex and since so much of it belongs to the mental side of life, the process of change must necessarily involve mental laws, as well as physical laws; but here the majority have made their mistake.

Many great reformers and human benefactors have tried to emancipate the race through the change of exterior laws and external conditions alone, forgetting that most of the troubles of man and nearly all of his failures have their origin in the misuse of the mind. We all know that mind is the most prominent factor in the life of man, and yet this factor has been almost entirely overlooked in our former efforts to change the conditions of the race. Everything that man does begins in his mind; therefore, every change that is to take place in the life of man must begin in his mind. This being true, we understand readily why modern metaphysics and the new psychology can provide the long looked for essentials to human emancipation and advancement. When we examine all the various things that go to make up the world in which we live we may find it difficult to discover the real source of them all. How they were produced; who produced them; why they happened to come to us, or why we went to them; these are problems that we are called upon to solve before we can begin to create ideal surroundings.

To solve these problems the first great fact to realize is that we are the creators of our own environments; but at first sight this fact may not be readily accepted, because there are so many things that seem to be the creation of others. There are two kinds of creation, however, the direct and the indirect. In direct creation you create with the forces of your own life, your own thought and your own actions, and your own creations are patterned after the ideas in your own mind; but in what is termed indirect creation someone else creates what you desire. It is your creation, however, in a certain sense, because it was your desire that called it forth. To state the fact in another manner, the world in which you live may be your own direct creation or it may be the creation of another, but you went into that other one's world to live. In the majority of cases, the world in which the individual lives is produced partly by his own efforts and partly by the efforts of others, though there is nothing in his world that he has not desired or called forth in some manner and at some time during his existence. There are a number of people who are living in worlds created almost entirely by others; in fact, the world of the average person is three-fourths the creation of the race mind; but the question is, why does a person enter into a world that is created by others; why does he not live exclusively in a world created by himself?

There are many fine minds who are living in the world of the submerged tenth, but they did not create that world.

That inferior state existed long before the birth of its present inhabitants; but why have those gone to live there who were not born there, and why have those who were born there not gone away to some better world of their own superior creation? Why do the people who live in that inferior world continue to perpetuate all its conditions? No world can continue to exist unless the people who live in that world continue to create those conditions that make up that world. Then why do not those people who live in the world of the submerged tenth cease the creating of that inferior world and begin the creation of the superior world when we know they have the power to do so? These are great questions, but they all have very simple answers. To answer these questions the first great fact to be realized is that the mind of man is the most important factor in everything that he does, and since no person can change his environments until he changes his actions we realize that the first step to be taken is the change of mind. Learn to change your mind for the better, and you will soon learn how to change your surroundings for the better. Before you proceed, however, there is another important condition to be considered; it is the fact that a portion of what is found in our world is created by ourselves, while the rest is the product of those minds with which we work or live. In the home each individual contributes to the qualities of the world which all the members of that home have in common, but each individual lives in a mental world distinctly his own, unless he is so negative that he has not a single individual purpose or thought. When the mental world of each individual is developed to a high degree it will become so strong that the fate of that individual will not be affected by the adverse conditions that may exist in the home.

The same is true of the environments that we meet in our places of work. No man need be affected very long by adverse surroundings or obstacles that he may meet in his work. He will finally become so strong that he can overcome every adversity that may exist in his physical world and thus gain entrance to better surroundings. However, we can readily see how a great deal of discord can be produced in a home or in our place of work where the different members are not in harmony with each other, and we can also understand how the events, circumstances and conditions of all those members, as well as each individual member, will be affected more or less by that inharmony; providing however, that each individual is not developing that power of his mental world that can finally overcome all adversity. We can also understand how harmony and co-operation in a home or in a place of work would become a powerful force for good in the life of each individual concerned. Where a few are gathered in the right attitude there immense power will be developed; in fact, sufficient power to do almost anything that those few may wish to have done.

This has been fully demonstrated a number of times; therefore, where many minds are associated in the creation of a world in which all will live, more or less, these higher mental laws should be fully understood and most thoroughly applied.

To enter a world that does not correspond with yourself and to go in and live where you do not naturally belong is to go astray, and such an action will not only cause all the forces and elements of your life to be misdirected, but you will place yourself in that position where nothing that is your own can come to you. There are vast multitudes, however, who have gone astray in this manner, and that is the reason why we find so many people who are misplaced, who do not realize their ideals, and who have not the privilege to enjoy their own. But we may ask, why do people go astray in this manner; why do we associate with people that do not belong in our world; why do we enter environments that do not correspond to our nature; why do we enter vocations for which we are not adapted, and why do we pursue plans, ideas and ambitions that lead us directly away from the very thing that our state of development requires? These are questions that we must answer, because no one can get the greatest good out of life or make the most of himself unless he lives in a world where he truly belongs. It is only when you live in a world created by yourself or in a world that others have created in harmony with you that you can be your real self, and since one must be truly himself to be wholly free and to promote his own advancement naturally and completely the subject is of great importance.

There are two reasons why we stray from our own true world and enter worlds where we do not belong; first, because we frequently permit the inferior side of our nature to predominate; and second, because we permit the senses to guide us in almost everything that we do. No person who has qualifications for the living of life in a superior world will ever enter an inferior world if he does not permit inferior desires to lead him into destructive paths; and no person, no matter what his work may be, will go down the scale so long as he follows the highest mental and spiritual light that he can possibly see during his most lofty moments. Follow the highest and the best that is in you, and you will constantly ascend into higher and better worlds; all your creative forces will thus build for you better and better surroundings, because so long as you are rising in the scale everything in your life in the external as well as in the internal must necessarily improve continuously. There is no need whatever of any person ever entering an inferior world.

No one need pass into environments and surroundings that are less desirable than the ones in which he is living now. In fact, a person may take the opposite course. Endeavor constantly to attain superiority and you will steadily work yourself up into superiority, and as you become superior you will find an entrance into those worlds, those environments and those surroundings that are superior. There is a higher light, a better understanding within yourself that will guide you correctly in all your associations with people and environments. Do not follow physical desires or physical senses; let these be servants in the hands of higher wisdom. Follow this higher wisdom and you will make few mistakes, if any. You will constantly pass into better and better surroundings, because you will constantly pass into a higher, a better and a superior life. To follow the highest and the best that is within you under all circumstances does not constitute supernaturalism. It is simply good sense enlarged, and those who take this course will continue to make real the ideal in everything that may exist in the world in which they live. In consequence, both the mental world and the physical world in which we live will perpetually change for the better; and all our surroundings will improve accordingly, becoming more and more ideal until everything that exists about us is as beautiful as the visions of the soul.

19. CHANGING YOUR OWN FATE.

When you discover that you are living in a world that you did not create and that does not correspond with your ideals, there is a tendency to break loose from external conditions at the earliest possible moment; but this tendency must be checked. Nothing is gained through an attempt to change from one world of effect to another world of effect without first changing the cause. The majority believe that when things are wrong in the outer world the only remedy is to change external conditions; but the fact is that external conditions are simply effects from internal causes, and so long as those internal causes remain the same, no attempt to change external conditions will prove of permanent value. So long as there are adverse causes in your inner life there will be adverse effects in your outer life, no matter how many times you may change from one condition to another or from one place to another.

When you begin to seek emancipation from the false world in which you are living now; in other words, when you begin to take positive measures to change your own fate, the first thing to do is to resolve not to make any forceful effort to change external conditions without first changing the inner cause of those conditions. Let outer things be as they are for the time being and continue to remain where you are until you can open a door to better things; but while you are waiting for this door to open do not be idle in any manner whatever. Although you are letting things be as they are in the external sense, and although you are not forcing yourself into different places or circumstances, still your purpose must be to entirely remake yourself. You came into this false state of life because you were misled by your own judgment, and if you should break loose, this same judgment will mislead you again; you will thus pass from one world that is not your own into some other world that is not your own, and there will be no improvement in the change. If you have not improved yourself in any manner whatever, your judgment will be just as inferior and unreliable as it was before, and no attempt to follow this judgment into different conditions will help matters in the least. Your object is not to set yourself free from the false world in which you are living now and then enter some other world that is not your own. You are not ready to move, neither physically nor mentally, until you have created a world of your own just as you would have it in your present state of development. Therefore, all thought of change will but divert your attention from the real purpose in view. So long as you are constantly thinking about external changes your mind cannot concentrate upon internal changes. So long as you are trying to change external conditions you cannot change yourself, and as you, yourself, are the cause of the new world which you are trying to create, you must recreate yourself before you can create the external world as desired.

To change your fate begin with yourself. If the environments in which you live are beneath your ideal, nothing can be gained by leaving those environments until the way is opened naturally to better things. If you simply get up and leave, you will gravitate into something elsewhere that will be just as uncongenial as those conditions you left behind. First, find the reason why you are living in your present adverse environments, then proceed to remove that cause. There may be many reasons, but in most cases the principal reason is a lack of ability or the lack of power to apply the ability you possess.

In such a case you must remove inability by becoming more proficient, and as soon as you are competent to render better service you will readily find a better place. This means larger remuneration, and you will thus be able to secure more desirable surroundings. The many, however, will think that to promote sufficient improvement so as to command greater recompense, and do so in a short time, is practically impossible under the average conditions; but all difficulties that may be met in this connection may be readily removed through the principles of modern metaphysics.

Continuous improvement in everything pertaining to the life, the power, the capacity or the mentality of the individual can be readily promoted by anyone and decided results secured in a very short time. Therefore, no person need remain in adverse or limited conditions. He can, through the awakening and the expression of the best that is in himself, become competent to take advantage of greater opportunities and thus change his fate, his future and his destiny. If you wish to improve your physical environments, remain content where you are while you develop the power to earn and create better environments. Contentment with things as they are and harmony with everything about you are indispensable essentials if you wish to increase your ability, your capacity and your worth. To continue to kick against the pricks is to remain where pricks are abundant; but when we cease this mode of action and begin to polish off all the rough corners of our nature and improve ourselves in ever manner possible, things will take a turn. We will leave the world of pricks and enter a smoother path. The polished man is admitted to the polished world where there are no rough places and where adverse conditions are few, if existing at all.

"When circumstances are against you, do not contend with circumstances. So long as we contend with things, things will contend with us. Do not resist present conditions; you prolong their existence by so doing. Whatever comes, meet all things in the attitude of perfect harmony and you will find that all things, even the most adverse, can be readily handled and turned to good account. We all know the marvelous power of the man who can harmonize contending factions, be they in his own life or in his circumstances. He not only gains good from everything that he meets, but he becomes a most highly respected personage, and is sought wherever opportunities are great and where great things are to be accomplished. Learn to harmonize the contending factions in your own life and experience, and you will find yourself entering new worlds where circumstances are more congenial and opportunities far greater. You will thus meet more desirable events, more desirable people, and superior advantages of every description will appear in your pathway. If your present friends are not to your liking admire them nevertheless for every good quality that they may possess. Emphasize their good qualities and ignore everything in their nature that seems inferior. This will help you to develop superior qualities in yourself; and this is extremely important, because as you develop superiority you prepare yourself for places higher up in the scale.

Make yourself over, so to speak, in your own friendship; increase your personal worth; polish your own character; refine your mind, and make real more and more of the ideal; double and treble your love and your kindness and constantly increase your admiration for everything that has real quality and high worth. Continue thus until you have results, whether those results begin to come at once or not; they will positively come here long, and the things that you develop in yourself you will meet in your external world. Change yourself for the better in every shape and manner, and you change your fate for the better, but the change that you produce in yourself must not simply be negative in its action. It is the positive character, the positive mind, the positive personality that meets in the external world what has been developed in the internal world.

The fact that a change in yourself can produce a similar change in your fate, your environments, your circumstances, in brief, everything in your outer world, may not seem clear at first; but it is easily demonstrated to be the truth when we analyze the relationship that exists between man and the world in which he lives. Everything that exists in your outer world has a correspondent in your inner world. This inner correspondent is the cause that has either created or attracted its external counterpart, and the process is easily understood.

To state it briefly, environment corresponds with ability. Circumstances are the aggregation of events brought about by your own actions and associations and friends, which follow the law of like attracting like. That environment is the direct effect of ability may not seem true when we observe that there are many people living in luxury that have practically no ability, but we must first demonstrate that these people have no ability. We shall find that those who have actually accumulated their own wealth have ability, in fact, exceptional ability, though they may not always have employed it according to the exact principles of justice. On the other hand, when we understand the process of creation we shall find that ability employed according to principle will produce far greater results than when it is employed unjustly. Therefore, the law underlying the power of ability to create its own environment acts wholly in the favor of him who lives according to the highest ideals of life.

This fact becomes more evident when we discern that success is not measured simply by the accumulation of things, but also by the accumulation of those elements in life that pertain to quality and worth in man's interior nature. It is wealth in the mental and the spiritual worlds that has the greatest value or the greatest power in promoting the welfare and the happiness of man, and this higher wealth can be accumulated only by those who are living according to their ideals. However, the accumulation of mental and spiritual wealth will have a direct tendency to increase the power and the capacity of practical ability, and practical ability when scientifically applied will tend to increase tangible wealth; that is, to improve the value and the worth of external environments. When we consider this subject from the universal view-point we shall find a perfect correspondent existing between the size of a man's possessions, physical, mental and spiritual, and the size of his brains, taking the term "brains" to signify ability, capacity and worth in the largest sense; but the size of brains can be increased perpetually. We therefore conclude that possessions in the larger sense can be increased perpetually, and he who is perpetually increasing his possessions on all the planes of his life is constantly changing his fate for the better. We shall also find that when a person increases the power of his own life he will bring about, through his own actions, new events, and these new events will produce new circumstances.

To change circumstances is to change fate; and whatever the change may be in fate, circumstances or events it will be a change for the better, if the increase of power is applied according to the principles of ideals. Again, when a person develops quality and superiority in himself he will, through the law of attraction, meet friends and associations that are after his own heart. In other words, he will enter a world where his ideals, both as to persons and as to things, are constantly being made real in every sphere of his present state of existence. He is thus creating for himself a better fate in every sense of the term and opening doors and pathways to a larger and a more beautiful future than he has ever realized before; but the beginning is in himself; in fact, every change for the better must begin within the life of man himself, and whoever will begin to change for the better in the within will positively realize greater and greater changes for the better in the without.

20. BUILDING YOUR OWN IDEAL WORLD.

To build your own ideal world, the first essential is to begin to build in the real everything that you can discern in the ideal; and the second essential is to continue to rebuild your ideal world according to higher and higher ideals. However congenial or desirable or perfect our world may be, we should continue to improve upon it constantly. When we cease to promote progression we return to the ways of retrogression. One of the principal causes of undesirable environments or unexpected reverses among the more capable is found in the tendency to "stop, rest and enjoy" what we have gained whenever conditions are fairly satisfactory. It is the mind; that is ever creating the new and ever recreating everything according to higher ideals that is always free and that is always enjoying the best. No one can be in bondage to the lesser who is constantly rising out of the lesser, and he who is ever growing into the best is constantly enjoying the best. In the last analysis, retrogression is the only cause of bondage, while constant progression is the only cause of perfect freedom; and constant progression is promoted by the continuous recreation of everything in your world according to higher and higher ideals.

To begin, your entire mentality must be changed and constantly changed so as to correspond perfectly with your newest thoughts on every subject and your highest ideals of everything that you can discern in your life. The mind is the cause and is the source of every force that can act as a cause of whatever may be developed, expressed or worked out through yourself into your external world. Therefore, begin with the mind and with all the elements of the mind. All desires, motives and ambitions must be concentrated upon the larger and the perfect in their various spheres of action. All the mental states must be in harmony with each other, and with the outer as well as the inner conditions of life. All mental qualities must be expanded and enlarged constantly, and consciousness must be trained to act perpetually upon the verge of the limitless. The entire world of thought must be perpetually renewed, enlarged and perfected, and every step taken in the mental world must be practically expressed and applied in the outer world. In order to bring all the creative forces of mind into harmony with the goal in view the ideal wished to be realized must be thoroughly established in consciousness, and the goal in view must be constantly held before the mental vision.

In the rebuilding of your own world one of the principal causes of failure will be found in a tendency to change in your plans, motives or desires; therefore, do not permit yourself to entertain one group of desires today and a different group tomorrow, and do not permit your faith to fall into periodical states of doubt. Decide upon what you wish to do, accomplish, promote and attain, and proceed to live, think and work for those things, regardless of what may happen. The powers within you follow the predominating states of mind, and when these states are constantly changing, the creative forces will be employed simply in taking initial steps, but never in completing anything. On the other hand, when your mental states, desires, motives, plans, etc., continue to concentrate upon the one supreme goal in view your creative forces will perpetually build towards that goal, and you will be daily rebuilding your entire world according to the higher, the better and the greater that you have in view. There are thousands of fine minds that are down in the scale today and cannot get up, because they are constantly changing their plans, motives and desires. To create a new world you must fix in your mind what you wish to create, and then continue to build until the complete structure is finished. Recreate your present world, then constantly make it better, larger and more beautiful. All the elements of your mind, both conscious and subconscious, must be constantly inspired with your highest thought of the larger, the better and the more beautiful. Not a single thought should enter your mind that is inferior or in the least beneath your ideal of life, and not a single moment of discouragement or doubt should ever be permitted. Fix your mind on the soul's vision and hold it there through all sorts of circumstances or conditions. Do not waver for a moment. Keep the eye single upon the heights and all the powers of your being will build that great world that you can see in your mental vision as you concentrate attention upon the heights.

The mind must be clean, strong and high. It is the mind that does things. It is the mind that originates things. Therefore, if you wish to build for yourself an ideal world, the mind must be ideal in every sense of the term, and every element of the mind must always be its best and act at its best. To promote the right use of mind the imagination must be guided with the greatest of care. The imagination is one of the most important powers in the mind. The imagination when misdirected can produce more ills than any other faculty, and when properly directed can produce greater good than any other faculty. In fact, the imagination when scientifically applied becomes a marvelous power in the great creative process of the vast mental domain.

Train the imagination to picture, not only the goal you have in view but all the highest ideals that you can possibly imagine as might exist within the realms of that goal. Train the imaging faculty to impress upon the mind only those superior qualities that you wish to incorporate in your new world, and whatever you impress upon the mind will be created in your mental world. To create superior qualities in the mental world means that you will create, as well as attract, the superior in your outer world, and you thus promote the building of an ideal world.

To build your own ideal world, the more opportunities that you can take advantage of the better, but opportunities come only to those who have demonstrated their worth. Prove to the world that you have worth, and you can have your choice of almost any opportunity that the world can offer. There is nothing that is in greater demand than great men and women— minds of ability and power, people who can do things. The great mind is constantly in the presence of opportunities to change his environment and his field of action; therefore, he may enter into a new world almost any time. Those opportunities, however, do not come of themselves; they come because he has made himself equal to those opportunities. Make yourself equal to the best and you will meet the best. This is a law that is universal and is never known to fail. Make yourself a great power in your present sphere of action. Learn to do things better than they have ever been done before. Produce something for the world that the world wants and the gates to new and greater opportunities will open for you. Henceforth, you may secure almost anything that you may wish, and all the elements that may be necessary for you to employ in order to build the ideal world you have in mind may be readily obtained because you have placed yourself in touch with the limitless supply of the best that life can give.

Those who are in search for new and greater opportunities should eliminate the belief that the best things have been said, that all great things have been done and that all remarkable discoveries have been made. The fact is we are just in the A B C of literature, invention, art, music, industrial achievements and extraordinary human attainments. The human race is now on the verge of hundreds of undeveloped fields that have just been discovered, and they have more possibilities in store than we have ever dreamed. Many of these possibilities when developed will supply the world with the very things that the present development of the race is demanding in every expression of thought and desire. It is therefore easier to attain greatness, and do something of exceptional value at the present time than it ever was before. The opportunities of this age are very numerous, and some of them hold possibilities that are actually marvelous. Those who will prepare themselves to meet the requirements of this age will therefore find a number of rich fields already at hand, and all minds can prepare themselves as required. Every person of moderate intelligence can, in a short time, place himself in the path of some of these new opportunities, and all minds can find better opportunities in their present spheres if they will proceed to become more than they are.

Train all the elements of your being to work towards a higher goal and you will bring forth into expression those greater powers that will make for you a mentality that the world will demand for its highest places of action and achievement. When you proceed to build in yourself an ideal mental world—a mental world of power, ability, capacity and high worth you will find it necessary to adapt this mental world to the external world in such a way as to promote harmony of action. The added power of your new mental world must work in harmony with your external world if practical results are to be secured. Circumstances come from personal actions; therefore, to change circumstances, personal actions must be changed, and to change personal actions your ideal mental life must be expressed in your personal life, and to this end the development of a high degree of harmony becomes necessary. Harmony, however, will not only promote the united action of the inner world with the outer world, but will also tend to eliminate mistakes from personal actions, and when we eliminate mistakes from personal actions we will cease to produce adverse circumstances. When you are in perfect harmony with yourself and everything you eliminate mental confusion. You thus place your mind in that position where you can think clearly, reason logically and judge wisely. The result is, you will do the right thing at the right time. The elements of your life will be properly blended, and this is necessary in order to create an ideal world.

Another essential in the practical application of your ideals to real life is the development of what may be termed interior insight. This faculty will guide you perfectly in your expression of the finer things of life through the tangible things of life; in other words, you will see clearly how to combine the ideal with those actions that are promoted for the purpose of rebuilding the real. To combine the ideal with the real and make the two one, we must come into the closest possible relationship with the finer things in life and learn to use that phase of mind that is always in a cleared-up condition. The lower story of the mind is often darkened with false conclusions about things, and is frequently more or less filled with ideas that have been impressed through the senses; but in the upper story we can see things as they are; we can think clearly, and invariably come to the right conclusions. The power to think in the upper story of the mind, the cleared-up side of consciousness where the sun is always shining and where there are no clouds, is called interior insight. This interior insight not only discerns the ideal, but can discern the practical possibilities that every ideal may contain, and we make the ideal real when we proceed to develop and apply in actual life those practical possibilities that our ideals may contain. Interior insight will also elevate all our mental faculties and cause those faculties to function with far greater efficiency. In fact, the entire mind will be lifted up into a state of greater power, greater brilliancy and greater ability for high and efficient mental expression.

To develop interior insight aim to use consciousness in the discernment of what may be termed the spirit of all things. Do not simply think of things as they appear on the surface, but try to think of things as they are in the spirit of their interior existence. The mere effort to do this will develop the power to look through things or to look into things; and the growth of this power promotes interior insight. You may thus discern clearly the real worth and the real possibilities that exist in the lofty goal that you have in view, and by keeping the eye single upon that lofty goal, never wavering for a moment, all the powers of your being will work together and build for those greater things that you can see upon the heights of that goal. Thus your entire world in the within as well as in the without will constantly be recreated and rebuilt according to the likeness of your supreme ideals; in consequence, you will not only build for yourself an ideal world, but you will be building for yourself a world that is ever becoming more and more ideal, and to live in such a world is ideal living indeed. The world that is ever becoming more and more ideal is *the* world in which to live, and the power to create such a world is now at hand in every human mind.

THE END

BOOK THREE

MASTERY OF FATE

ATTAINING THE SUPREME SELF THROUGH SUPERIOR THOUGHT

ABOUT THIS BOOK

"What Man is, and what man does, determines in what conditions, circumstances and environments he shall be placed. And since man can change both himself and his actions, he can determine what his fate is to be."

With this phrase, Larson starts this amazing book, full of the spirit of motivation and success. You can create any fate by creating the spirit of success. It is all in your mind, and, as "he can who think he can", if you develop your internal insight and a firm belief in yourself and your forces, you will think you can, and do it!

"To change himself, man must change his thought, because man is as he thinks; and to change his actions, he must change the purpose of his life, because every action is consciously or unconsciously inspired by the purpose held in view."

1. MASTERY OF FATE

What Man is, and what man does, determines in what conditions, circumstances and environments he shall be placed. And since man can change both himself and his actions, he can determine what his fate is to be.

To change himself, man must change his thought, because man is as he thinks; and to change his actions, he must change the purpose of his life, because every action is consciously or unconsciously inspired by the purpose held in view.

To change his thought, man must be able to determine what impressions are to form in his mind, because every thought is created in the likeness of a mental impression.

To choose his own mental impressions, man must learn to govern the objective senses, and must acquire the art of original thought.

Everything that enters the mind through the physical senses will produce impressions upon the mind, unless prevented by original thought. These impressions will be direct reflections of the environment from whence they came; and since thoughts will be created in the exact likeness of these impressions, so long as man permits environment to impress the mind, his thoughts will be exactly like his environment: and since man becomes like the thoughts he thinks, he will also become like his environment.

But man, in this way, not only grows into the likeness of his environment, but is, in addition, controlled by his environment, because his thoughts, desires, motives and actions are suggested to him by the impressions that he willingly accepts from environment.

Therefore, one of the first essentials in the mastery of fate is to learn to govern the physical senses so thoroughly, that no impression can enter mind from without, unless it is consciously desired.

This is accomplished by holding the mind in a strong, firm, positive attitude at all times, but especially while surrounded by conditions that are inferior.

This attitude will bring the senses under the supremacy of the subconscious will, and will finally produce a state of mind that never responds to impressions from without unless directed to do so.

To overcome the tendency of the physical senses to accept, indiscriminately, all sorts of impressions from without, mind should, at frequent intervals, employ the physical senses in trying to detect the superior possibilities that may be latent in the various surrounding conditions. And gradually, the senses themselves will become selective, and will instantaneously inform the mind whenever an undesirable impression demands admission.

While the senses are being employed in the search of superior possibilities, the impressions thus received should be analyzed, and recombined in the constructive states of consciousness, and according to the mind's own original conception. This will promote original thinking, which will, in turn, counteract the tendency of the objective side of mind to receive suggestions from without.

Every original thought that mind may create, will to a degree, change man and re-make him according to what he inwardly desires to be; because every original thought is patterned after man's conception of himself when he is at his best.

Thoughts inspired by environment are inferior or superior, according to what the environment may be; but an original thought is always superior, because it is inspired by man himself while the superior elements of his being are predominant.

When every thought that mind creates is an original thought, man will constantly grow in greatness, superiority and worth; and when all these original thoughts are created with the same purpose in view, man will become exactly what is indicated by that purpose.

Therefore, since man can base thinking upon any purpose that he may desire, he can, through original thinking, become whatever he may choose to become.

Fate is the result of man's being and doing; a direct effect of the life and the works of the individual; a natural creation of man; and the creation is always the image and in likeness of the creator.

Therefore, when man, through original thinking, acquires the power to become what he chooses to become, his fate will of itself change as man changes; and through this law he can create for himself any fate desired.

That man will consciously and naturally create his own fate when he gains the power to recreate himself as he desires to be, is evident for various reasons. And the power to re-create himself is simply the power of original thought. Because man becomes like the thoughts he thinks, and original thoughts are created in the likeness of man's ideal impressions of his superior self.

That the fate of each individual person is the direct or indirect result of what that person is and does, can be demonstrated by the following self-evident facts:

1. The mental world in which a person lives is the exact reflection of what that person is, feels and thinks; therefore, when a superior life and worthier thoughts are attained, the mental world will also change accordingly.

2. The circumstances and conditions of man's physical world are the direct or indirect effects of the active elements in his mental world; a fact we shall thoroughly demonstrate in the following pages.

3. Like attracts like; therefore, the associations of man are after his own kind; and as he changes for the better he will attract, and be attracted into better associations.

4. The events that transpire in the life of man are the consequences of his own efforts to express himself in his individual world of action. Therefore, what happens to any person is the reaction of what that person has previously said or done.

This being true, man has the power to cause any event to transpire that he may decide upon; though to accomplish this it is necessary to understand the law of action and reaction as applied both to the physical and metaphysical worlds.

When man begins to re-create himself, he will rise superior to his present position; and since new and better opportunities always appear when man proves himself superior to his present position, he can, by changing himself as he desires, call forth any opportunity that he may desire.

To have the privilege to take advantage of better opportunities, is the direct path to better conditions, better circumstances and better environments; and since man can create this privilege at will, he can create his own fate, his own future, his own destiny.

However, the secret of creating this privilege at will lies in man's power to form only such impressions upon his mind as will originate constructive thought. Because when all the thought he thinks is constructive, every mental process will be a building process, and will constantly increase the ability, the capacity and the personal worth of man himself. This in turn makes man competent to accept the larger places that are waiting everywhere for minds with sufficient capability to fill them.

Every thought has creative power; and this power will express itself according to the desire that was in mind when the thought was created. Therefore, if every thought is to express its creative power in the building up of man, mind must constantly be filled with the spirit of that purpose.

When the desire for growth and superior attainment does not predominate in mind, the greater part of the creative energy of thought will misdirect, and artificial mental conditions will form, only to act as obstacles to man's welfare and advancement.

The creative power of thought is the only power employed in the construction and reconstruction of man; and for this reason man is as he thinks.

Consequently, when man thinks what he desires to think, he will become what he desires to become. But to think what he desires to think, he must consciously govern the process through which impressions are formed upon mind.

To govern this process is to have the power to exclude any impression from without that is not desired, and to completely impress upon mind every original thought that may be formed; thus giving mind the power to think only what it consciously chooses to think.

Before man can govern this process, he must understand the difference between the two leading attitudes of mind – the attitude of self-submission, and the attitude of self-supremacy; and must learn how to completely eliminate the former, and how to establish all life, all thought, and all action absolutely upon the latter.

When this is done, no impression can form upon mind without man's conscious permission; and complete control of the creative power of thought is permanently secured.

To master the creative power of thought is to master the personal self; and to master the personal self is to master fate.

2. THE STATE OF SELF-SUPREMACY

MAN IS inherently master over everything in his own life, because the principle of his being contains the possibility of complete mastership; and the realization of this principle produces the attitude of self-supremacy.

While mind is in this attitude, only those impressions are formed that are consciously selected; consequently, only those thoughts are created that conform to the purpose that may predominate in mind at the time.

To remain constantly in the attitude of self-supremacy, is therefore the secret of original thinking; and since the mastery of fate comes directly from original thinking, everything that interferes with the attitude of self-supremacy must be eliminated completely.

The most serious obstacle to this attitude is the belief that man is, for the greater part, the product of his environment; and that man cannot change to any extent until a change is first produced in his environment.

The result of this belief is the attitude of self-submission; and the more deeply this belief is felt, the more completely does man submit himself to the influence of his surroundings.

While mind is in this attitude, it has only a partial control over the process of thinking; it accepts willingly every impression that may enter through the senses, and permits the creation of thought in the likeness of those impressions without the slightest discrimination.

To remove the attitude of self-submission, man must cease to believe that he is controlled by environment, and must establish all his thinking upon the conviction that he is inherently master over his entire domain.

This, however, may appear to be not only impossible, but absurd, when considered in the presence of the fact that man is controlled by environment. To tell a man to cease to believe as true that which he knows to be true, may not, at first sight seem to contain any reason; but at second sight it proves itself to mean the same as to tell a man to leave the darkness and enter the light.

When man ceases to believe that he is controlled by environment, he departs from a belief that is detrimental; and when he begins to realize that he has the power to completely control himself, he enters a conviction that is favorable to the highest degree.

While he is in the attitude of self-submission, he is controlled by environment, and the belief that he is thus controlled, is true to him. But when he enters the attitude of self-supremacy, he is not controlled by environment; therefore, the belief that he is controlled by environment is no longer true to him. While we are in the dark, we can truthfully say that we are in darkness; but when we enter the light, we cannot say, truthfully, that we are in darkness.

There is such a thing as being influenced by conditions that exist in our surroundings; but when we transcend that influence we are in it no more; therefore, to say that we are in it when we are out of it, is to contradict ourselves. And we equally contradict ourselves when we state that we are controlled by environment after we are convinced that we are inherently masters of everything in the personal life. What is not true to us now, we should not admit now, even though it had been true to us for all previous time.

To state that you are controlled by environment, and to permit that belief to possess your mind, is to submit yourself almost completely to the control of environment.

To recognize the principle of your being, and to realize that within that principle the power of complete supremacy does exist; to establish yourself absolutely upon that principle, and to state that you are not controlled by environment, is to depart from the control of environment.

While you are conscious of the principle of self-supremacy, you are unconscious of the influence of environment; therefore, to speak the truth, you must declare that you are complete master in your own domain.

When you know that the possibility of self-supremacy is within you, you cannot state truthfully that it is not there; and to state, in the presence of your knowledge of self-supremacy, that you are controlled by environment, is the same as to state that there is no self-supremacy.

The very moment that you admit the possibility of self-supremacy, the control of environment is no longer a real fact to you; because in the state of self-supremacy, it is not possible for the control of environment to exist.

When man discovers the state of self-supremacy, he can no longer believe in the control of environment as a principle; and is therefore compelled to declare that the control of environment is no longer true to him. And, as he is permitted to speak only for himself, and judge only his own life, he must refuse absolutely to believe in the control of environment under any condition whatever.

To believe that others are controlled by environment, is to judge where he has no authority, and also to place himself once again in the belief that environment controls man. To place himself in that belief is to enter the attitude of self-submission, and submit himself to the influence of everything that enters his sphere of existence.

It is therefore evident that the principal reason why those who know of self-supremacy do not master fate, is because they are not true to their own convictions. They believe that the principle of self-supremacy exists, but they also believe that the control of environment exists. They try to believe both to be true at the same time, which is impossible.

If the one exists as a living power in the life of a person, the other does not exist in the life of that person. It would be just as reasonable to believe that light and darkness could exist in the same place at the same time.

To try to believe in the idea of self-supremacy and the control of environment at the same time, is to live in confusion; and he who lives in confusion controls practically nothing. He is therefore more or less controlled by everything,

When man is convinced that he is, in himself, master over his life, he can no longer believe that his life is controlled by environment. He must absolutely reject the latter belief; both cannot be true to any one mind; therefore, every mind must decide which one of these beliefs to accept as absolutely true, and which one to reject as absolutely untrue.

The mind that does not wholly reject one of the two, is trying to serve two masters, which is impossible. He who tries to serve two masters will serve the one only, and that one will be the false one; because whoever tries to serve two masters is false to himself, and will consequently serve that which is false. In this connection it may be questioned how we know that the principle of self-supremacy does exist; and how we know that complete mastership is inherent in man.

But we do know; because man does exercise complete mastership over certain parts of his being at certain times; and the fact that he does this proves the existence of the principle.

If the principle of self-supremacy did not exist, man could not exercise complete control over anything at any time; but every mind demonstrates supremacy many times every hour.

The mastership exercised over mind and body in various ways may be confined to limited spheres of action; but within those spheres of action the mastership is complete. And those spheres will expand constantly as the principle of self-supremacy is applied on a larger and a larger scale.

Since the principle of complete control exists in man, there is a way to apply that principle in everything, and at all times. But to accomplish this, the attitude of self-supremacy must prevail at all times, and under all conditions.

While man is in the attitude of self-supremacy, he exercises complete control over certain things in his life; but when he enters the belief that he is controlled or influenced by other things, he leaves the attitude of self-supremacy, and ceases to exercise his complete control.

In the present state of human development, the average mind is so constituted that it oscillates from one state to another, remaining the greater part of the time in the attitude of self-submission; due principally to the fact that we are seldom absolutely true to the higher conviction, and also because we try to think that both beliefs are true at the same time.

Consequently, the great essential for man in his present state is to accept the high conviction as an absolute truth, and be true to that truth every moment of existence.

To be true to that truth he must refuse absolutely to believe that he can be controlled or influenced by anything or anybody. He must depart completely from the belief in the control of other powers, and must recognize in himself the only power to control -the power to control completely, everything in his own domain.

Nor is this a contradiction, because when man enters the consciousness of self-supremacy, he cannot submit his self to any outside influence; therefore, there are no outside influences in action in his life. And when this is the case he cannot believe in the existence of outside influences, as far as he is concerned. When nothing is trying to control him, he cannot truthfully say that he is being controlled, nor even that he is liable to be controlled.

When man is in a state of self-supremacy, he is in a state where no, influence from without exists; he is in a world where the power of self-mastery is the only controlling power; therefore, he cannot truthfully recognize any other.

While in the attitude of self-submission, your mind is open to all kinds of impressions from without; and consequently, your thinking will be suggested to you by your environment. The result is that you will become like your environment, and will think, act and live as your environment may suggest.

If your environment be inferior, you will think inferior thoughts, live an inferior life, and commit deeds that are low or perverse, so long as you are in the attitude of self-submission. But if you should submit yourself to a better environment, your life, thoughts, and deeds would naturally become better. In each case you would be the representation of the impressions that enter through the senses.

However, the very moment you pass from a superior environment to one that is inferior, you will begin to change for the worse, unless you have in the meantime attained a degree of self-supremacy.

To enter a superior environment will not of itself develop self-supremacy, nor the art of original thinking; because so long as you permit yourself to be influenced by environment, you prevent your mind from gaining consciousness of the principle of self-supremacy.

A change of environment, therefore, will not give man the power to master his fate. This power comes only through a change of thought.

While in the attitude of self-supremacy your mind is not open to impressions from any source; but you can place your mind, at will, in the responsive attitude, so that it may receive impressions from any source that you may select.

By proper selection, consciousness can, in this way, be trained to express itself only through those mental channels that reach the superior side of things, and thereby come in contact with the unlimited possibilities of things.

From impressions received through this contact with unlimited possibilities, mind will be able to form original thoughts that embody superior powers and attainments; and as man becomes like his thoughts, he will, through this process, become superior.

Instead of being controlled by the impressions received from environment, he will control those impressions, and use them as material in the construction of his own larger life, and the greater destiny that must follow.

While mind is in the attitude of self-supremacy, man's contact with the world will not affect him contrary to the way he desires to be affected; because he controls the impressions that come from without, and can completely change their natures before they are accepted in consciousness. Or, he may refuse to accept them entirely.

In the midst of adversity he does not permit the adverseness of the circumstances to impress his mind, but opens his mind to be impressed by the great power that is back of the adversity. His mind is not impressed by the misdirection of power, but by the power itself.

Therefore, instead of being disturbed, he is made stronger.

There is something of value to be gained from every disagreeable condition, because within every condition there is power, and there are always greater possibilities latent than the surface indicates.

Through original thinking these greater possibilities are discerned; and when mind is in the attitude of self-supremacy, it may choose to be impressed by the greater possibilities only, thus providing more material for the reconstruction of man, and his destiny, on a larger and superior scale.

It is therefore evident that self-supremacy is indispensable; and it is attained by placing all life, all thought and all action upon the principle that man is inherently master over everything in his life; and by refusing absolutely to believe that we can be controlled by environment under any condition whatever.

3. SUPERIOR THOUGHTS

THE STATEMENT that the conditions and circumstances of man's physical world are the direct, or indirect effects of the active elements in his mental world, is fully demonstrated by comparing the external and internal phases of life in any person. The correspondence between the two is exact.

Every misfortune in the life of any individual, barring accidents produced by nature, can be traced to incompetence in some way, or to the misapplication of ability. And even those adverse conditions that come from nature's seeming irregularities can be wholly avoided through the development of superior insight.

The largest number of misfortunes comes from doing the wrong thing at the wrong time; and this is caused by confusion in the mental world, or by an obtuse judgment.

The mind that is constantly in a state of poise and harmony, judges well, and will never misdirect any thought, force or action. Therefore, by cultivating those states, anyone can gain the power to do the right thing at the right time.

A great many conditions that surround the average individual are not produced by himself and for this reason he does not hold himself responsible; but when a person enters circumstances that have been created by others, he simply enters something that corresponds with his own mental world.

No person with normal mind will voluntarily enter conditions that are inferior, or that do not correspond in any way to himself. The fact that he accepts, or borrows the environments produced by others, proves that he either belongs there, or that he does not know where he belongs.

When we enter blindly into disagreeable circumstances, our own blindness is at fault; therefore, the external circumstance is the indirect effect of a certain action in our own minds.

A person with great ability, who can practically apply his ability, will never be found at work where recompense is inadequate. Though a person with great ability who does not possess the practical element, may remain in a position that is inferior. In this case ability is misdirected, and the person's own mentality is the indirect cause of the undesirable circumstance.

The mind that is gentle, orderly and beautiful in character will inspire admiration in many places where associations are exactly to his liking. He is wanted among the best of his kind, and has the privilege to select the characters of his social world. Others may call him fortunate, but he has attracted ideal associations because he himself can give ideal companionship. Having developed a worthy mind, he belongs where minds of worth congregate; and through such associations gains inspiration for the development of still greater worth. This not only promotes his advancement in his field of action, but enables him to attract, meet and enjoy still better associations in the future.

When a beautiful character is found among inferior associations, the cause is usually a lack of positive quality. A number of beautiful characters are purely negative, and are therefore hiding the greater part of their true worth. They are far better than they appear to be, and they possess more than they use; but as it is only what we use that counts, such characters will be found in associations that measure exactly, not with what they are, but with what they use and express.

A genius may have no opportunity to employ his great ability; and if so, there is a reason. If he is really competent, there are a hundred excellent places open to him; but if he has only genius and little or no talent, he is not competent. If he has only the capacity, but not the art of turning his power to practical use, he can do nothing of value; and it is results that merit the good places in life.

His misfortune is therefore not due to any exterior adversity, but is caused directly by a state of his own mind.

His misfortune, however, will vanish, and great and good things come instead, when he transforms his genius into talent, and learns to do something that the world wants done.

There is many a skilled workman who keeps himself down because he is constantly out of harmony with his associations. By resisting everything and antagonizing everybody, he keeps his own inferior side always in view. His skill is submerged beneath his personal inferiority, and he is judged, not by what he hides, but by the imperfections that he willingly presents to the world.

A man who persists in revealing nothing but his inferior side, cannot expect promotion; to promote such a man would be a loss to the institution; and those in authority usually feel this fact instinctively. Every enterprise is continued for results; therefore, everything that interferes with results should be eliminated. To give a conspicuous place to someone who breeds discord, hatred and confusion, will positively interfere with results; therefore, such a person does not justly deserve promotion, no matter how perfect his individual product may be.

The man who is against the world will array the world against himself, and must take the consequences. His fate will not be pleasant, but he alone is to blame.

To do good work is necessary; but it is also necessary to make good as a man, if the best places are to be secured. Therefore, hide your inferior side until you have destroyed it entirely. Surround your skillful labor with a personal atmosphere that breeds harmony, wholesomeness and character, and the best position in your field of action will be opened to you.

There are thousands of people who claim they have not secured a fair chance; but if that be true, the mental worlds of those very persons are the causes. There is something in their mental make-up that places their ability and skill in a false light before the world.

The same is true of the man who is constantly misunderstood. He is not revealing himself as he really is; his real nature is misdirected during the process of expression, and everybody is deceived. That something that produces the deception exists in the person's own mind, and so long as that something remains, he will misplace himself, and will not meet the friends nor the opportunities that really are his own.

The misplacing of oneself is due to a lack of judgment, or to a bad arrangement of one's personal powers and characteristics.

But judgment can be remarkably improved in anyone through the development of original thinking and interior insight; and the various powers of the person can be placed in perfect order and harmony with each other through the practice of bringing out the greater possibilities in every phase of being.

The habit of permitting everything we come in contact with to impress our minds, and suggest this course or that method is responsible for a great deal of misdirected effort; therefore, the attitude of self-supremacy becomes indispensable.

A large number of people have been induced to enter circumstances where they do not belong, through the exercise of an abnormal sympathy. Such a sympathy, called forth by a few selfish friends, has also kept many a great mind working in a narrow field, while scores of large, and even extraordinary opportunities were constantly waiting.

To correct this condition, train yourself to sympathize only with the superior side of people and the greater possibilities of things.

When you sympathize naturally and constantly with the superior side of people, all the desires of mind will gradually fix their attention upon the superior; and when all the desires of mind desire the superior you will be irresistibly drawn into superior association. And nothing, not even old abnormal sympathies can keep you away from your own.

When you sympathize with the greater possibilities in things, your attention will be constantly turned upon the greater; your mind will be more and more impressed with the greater, until every thought becomes a power for greatness; and with this power you will move into greatness, regardless of any obstacle that may appear in the way.

The power of sympathy is one of the greatest powers of attraction in existence; therefore, when we sympathize only with the superior, we will be drawn into superiority, and this will steadily change our environments for the better. Thus, by producing a change in the mental world, we can revolutionize the external world.

When life is viewed comprehensively, it becomes very evident that the actions of the person determine what the external conditions and circumstances of that person are to be; but every personal action is caused by a mental action; therefore, the change of environment must be preceded by a change of mind.

To master thought is to master fate; but thought cannot be mastered until mind acts exclusively upon the principle that man is inherently complete master over his entire domain.

The strongest evidence that can be produced in favor of the statement that man's circumstances are caused by the active elements of his mental world, is that of creative ability, because it is being demonstrated every day that the man with a strong creative mind has destiny at his feet.

Creative ability can absolutely change all circumstances; but it is not an external power; it is simply an active element in mind.

4. CREATING THE SPIRIT OF SUCCESS

THE MASTERY of fate implies the constant improvement of everything in one's world – physical or mental; and since the improvement of one's exterior environment requires financial increase, the problem of recompense and reward must be solved.

There are vast numbers who claim they are not being remunerated according to their worth, and this claim is keeping the industrial world in constant turmoil.

The result is detrimental to everybody, whether they are directly connected with industrial activity or not.

Therefore, to find a solution for the problem would be one of the greatest discoveries that could possibly be made.

That a great deal of injustice exists in the world, is true; and that many who are strong are taking advantage of multitudes that are weak, is also true; but there is a peaceful way for every individual to secure his own. And it remains wholly with the individual.

There is no remedy in sight that the whole world can adopt, through which industrial justice can be established by law; but each individual can so relate himself to the world that his recompense will correspond exactly with his worth. To do this he must neither under-value nor overvalue his work; and he must not compare his legitimate efforts with the efforts of those who employ questionable means. There are a great many who think they are worth more than they really are, because they compare themselves with the unscrupulous.

When a certain person gains great wealth through illegitimate means, many imagine that they ought to gain as much; they are just as good and just as able as he, and work equally as hard.

But in the mastery of fate all kinds of unjust methods must be eliminated completely, because in the creation of one's future there must be no flaws, or the entire structure may have to be discarded.

There is no wisdom in making any comparison between oneself and the man who is gaining wealth by undermining his own future welfare. We do not care for the destiny of such a personage, and there is only loss in store for those who imitate his ways.

Whether we are gaining as much as this one or that one is not the question at all; the question is, are we receiving what we are actually worth? If we are not, we must find the cause, and the way to remove that cause.

If you are receiving all that you deserve, make yourself more deserving, and you will receive more; but if you are not receiving your share, learn the reason why. If you are to blame, change yourself; if your present work is to blame, use your present work as a stepping-stone to something better.

The average person, who thinks he is underpaid, will find himself to be the real cause; therefore, the change of himself is the remedy. And he is usually to blame in this respect, that he overvalues his work and undervalues himself.

No one can advance in life unless he values himself correctly. The man who lives a "common" life, and continues in "ordinary" attitudes of mind will stay "down," no matter how hard he works or how well he performs his particular labor. For this there are several reasons.

It is not simply the visible product of brains or skill that the world pays for; the world also pays for what man contributes to life.

If your personal life is inferior, you give your vocation the stamp of inferiority; and a "common" atmosphere, so detrimental to the progress of any enterprise, goes with you, wherever you may be employed.

If you carry an atmosphere of worth, advancement is in store without fail, because the world does recognize worth, and pays well to secure it.

It is not only the work, but the life that surrounds that work that counts. It is not only the idea, but the words through which it is expressed that carry conviction. And it is not only the ability of the man, but the way he presents that ability that commands attention from the world.

When you present your ability in a crude, common attitude, and present yourself in an atmosphere of inferiority, you are hiding the larger part of your worth, your ability and your skill. And you will be paid only for that which the world can see.

The rays of a skilled mind or a brilliant intellect cannot be seen at first sight, through the dense atmosphere of personal recklessness and crudeness; and the world does not possess the second sight.

But no man can surround himself with a clear atmosphere -an atmosphere that reveals the best there is in him – unless he values himself, and aims to express his real worth in every thought and action.

If a man has superior ability, let him demonstrate by his own presence that he is neither common, inferior nor ordinary. The world demands demonstration; and anyone can detect a real man, no matter what clothes he may wear.

The world is constantly in search of competent men, and when you prove yourself to be competent, you will have more rare opportunities than you can fill.

When the average man begins to live, and takes just as much pride in living a real life as he does in producing a good machine, the industrial world will be revolutionized for the better, and every man will receive all that he knows he is worth.

To value yourself correctly, understand the unbounded possibilities that are latent within you, and live in the realization of the greater things that you know you have the power to do. This will produce in mind the consciousness of superiority, and through this consciousness, superior impressions will be formed in mind. From these impressions will come superior thoughts; which in turn will develop superiority in you; because a man is as he thinks.

The principal reason why a man who is down, remains there, and continues to appear as ordinary as his environment, is because he permits his mind to be impressed with everything that his environment may suggest. His thoughts are therefore the reflections of his surroundings, and he is like his thoughts.

Therefore, the man who would become different from his environment must learn the art of original thinking, and must enter the attitude of self-supremacy.

The principal reason why a man is underpaid is because he does not value himself, and therefore hides behind personal inferiority the greater part of his ability.

Another reason is because he works only for the wages that are coming to himself. He refuses to do more than is absolutely necessary, lest someone might be benefited. This attitude produces the cramped condition, which in turn reacts upon the purse.

The man who is afraid to do too much, usually fails to do enough; at any rate, he produces that impression, and his recompense is lowered accordingly.

On the other hand, the man who does his best at all times, regardless of the scale of wages, not only produces an excellent impression everywhere, but makes those in authority feel that he wants the enterprise to succeed. He is therefore better paid, because such men are valuable. They are wanted everywhere, not because they do more than they are paid for, but because they are a living power for success wherever they are called upon to act.

The spirit of success breeds success; and the man who takes a living interest in the enterprise for which he works, even doing more than he is expected to do when the occasion demands, is creating the spirit of success, and will soon share in the greater success that follows.

Among the underpaid, by far the largest number is composed of those who submit absolutely to their present conditions, and therefore remain not only in bondage to unscrupulous taskmasters, but also to their own environments and mental limitations. They are the many weak, of whom some of the strong take advantage; and it is in behalf of these that reformers demand a change in the order of things. But it is not a change in the order of things that the world requires; it is a change of mind. And when the change of mind is produced, all other necessary changes will inevitably follow.

If you are underpaid because you have submitted to the power of the unscrupulous, cease to live in the attitude of mental submission. Do not antagonize the powers to which you have submitted, and do not resist your present condition. In your external life, continue as usual for a period; but change absolutely your internal life.

What we resist we fear; and we always continue in bondage to that which we fear.

What we antagonize, we meet on the inferior side, and thus enter into contact with the very things we desire to avoid. We shall never get rid of the inferior so long as we resist the inferior; and whatever stays with us will impress our minds. Therefore, by resisting the inferior, we produce inferiority in ourselves.

Begin your emancipation by removing your attitude of self-submission; cease to believe that you must remain down where you are. Change your mind; know that inherently you are master over everything in your own domain, and resolve to exercise your supremacy. Refuse to be impressed by your environment; and learn to impress your own mind with superior impressions only. Re-create your own mind according to a higher standard of power, ability and character; thus you will re-create both yourself and your surroundings; because by making yourself stronger and more competent, you will be wanted where surroundings are better, and recompense greater.

The reason why those who are mentally weak remain in submission to inferior environments, is because they either do not attempt to become strong, or because they use up their mental powers resisting adversity.

Every person, no matter how submerged he may be, who will arouse his own interior strength, exercise his own supremacy over his thoughts, thus thinking his own superior thought, will gradually rise out of his condition; and before long he will find both emancipation and the reward of a better place in life. This is the only orderly method to freedom; and will produce permanent freedom. And it is the only natural method to greater gain and better conditions.

However, attention must not be centered too much upon mere financial gain. The principle is abundance of everything that is necessary to produce a complete life on all conscious planes; and the perpetual increase of all these things as life eternally advances.

But these things man himself must create; and creative power increases through the development of character, ability and self-supremacy.

5. WE CAN CREATE ANY FATE

TO MASTER fate it is necessary to approach all the elements of fate in the proper mental attitudes; because since everything in the external world responds to the active forces in one's mental world, these forces should so act as to call forth only the response desired.

The idea of mastery will arouse in the average mind a tendency to control objective things with the will; but we must remember that fate is not controlled; fate is created.

When we can create any fate that we may desire, we have mastered fate; but not until then.

The mastery of fate does not call for the controlling actions of the will, but for the constructive actions of the creative energies; and since the domineering use of the will scatters creative energy, such an attitude of mind must never be permitted.

All desire to control or influence persons or things must be eliminated completely, because such a course will only defeat our purpose.

We do not master fate by compelling things to come our way; or by persuading persons to promote our objects in view. Things will come of themselves when we demonstrate our ability to use things; and persons will cooperate with us in every way possible when we prove the superiority of both ourselves and our work.

The weakest mind of all is the domineering mind, and since such a mind has but little creative energy, the man who domineers cannot fulfill, legitimately, a single desire.

And what he does control through force, will later on react to his own downfall.

It is the meek that inherit the earth, because such minds have the greatest creative power. What we create, we inherit; no more, no less. Therefore, when we gain the power to create much, we shall inherit much.

To meet everything in the attitude of harmony is of the highest importance, because whatever we enter into harmony with, while in a state of aspiration, that we meet on the superior side.

The qualities that we enter into mental contact with, we absorb; therefore, it is a great advantage to mentally meet the superior only.

When we constantly aspire, and live in harmony with everything, we enter into true relationship with the better qualities that are latent in every person or condition with which we come in contact; and consequently permit the superior things in life to impress our minds at every turn.

And the value of having only superior impressions in mind is so great that it cannot be calculated.

Superior impressions originate superior thoughts; and as man is as he thinks, superior thoughts will develop superiority in him. And the superior man creates a superior fate, a better future and a more wonderful destiny.

By entering into harmony with all things, and by constantly dwelling in the aspiring attitude, you absorb the good qualities from your enemies and your adversaries. And since evil is only the good perverted, when you take the good out of anything, there is nothing left to be perverted; consequently there can exist no more enmity nor adversity in that place.

Absorb the good power that is back of adversity, and adversity ceases to be. In this way, we can truthfully say, "We have met the enemy, and they are ours," because the very life of that which was against us has been appropriated by ourselves and engaged to work for our interest and promotion.

This principle, if carried out in every detail of life, would completely revolutionize physical and mental existence; and would reduce trouble, discord, adversity and enmity to practically nothing.

The most disagreeable circumstances will change and become models of perfection simply through our attitude in calling forth the superior side; and when we enter into harmony with any circumstance while we are in the aspiring state of mind, we call forth the superior qualities of that circumstance, and the greater possibilities that are always latent everywhere.

When we meet circumstances of any description, we should never resist the undesirable elements, if there be any; nor find fault with the deficiency; but should search immediately for the possibilities. The questions are, what that circumstance can give; and how we may secure everything of worth that it can give.

Every circumstance you meet contains something for you; because it is made to enrich your life, to serve you, and to promote your welfare in every way possible.

By meeting a circumstance in the harmony of aspiration you call forth its real possibilities, and especially if you look directly for those possibilities. When you take an active interest and a friendly interest in the constructive powers of a circumstance, those powers will place themselves in your hands, and every disagreeable element will disappear.

By taking the best out of every circumstance, and by transmuting all the forces you meet so that they become your forces, you add so much to your present life that you rise readily to a higher position, where superior circumstances and still greater possibilities will be met.

Any circumstance can be changed, if constantly approached in this way; or you will change so much that far better circumstances will be ready to receive you.

Directly connected with the attitude of harmony is the attitude of love; and the way we love, as well as what we love, is of the highest importance in the mastery of fate.

The law is that we steadily grow into the likeness of that which we love; and the reason is that what we love is so deeply impressed upon mind that it never fails to reproduce itself in thought.

Anything that enters mind while mind is in the state of deep feeling, is deeply impressed; and it is the deepest impressions that serve as patterns for the creative energies.

Love only that which has high worth, and never permit the common, the ordinary or the inferior to enter the world of feeling.

Love the true side of life; love the soul side of persons; and love the greater possibilities that are latent in circumstances, conditions and things. And love these things with a passion that thrills every atom in your being. The result will be simply remarkable.

Where the heart is, there we concentrate; and where we concentrate we give our life, our thought, our ability and our power. Therefore, if we wish to build up the superior, we must deeply love the high, the true and the worthy, wherever these may be found.

When difficulties are met, they should be met in the attitude of joy; and we should look upon the experience as a privilege through which greater power may be brought into evidence.

To count everything joy is not a mere sentiment, but the application of a great scientific principle. The mind that meets everything in joy, conquers every time, because the attitude of joy is an ascending attitude; it transcends, and goes above that with which it comes in contact.

Therefore, whatever we meet in the attitude of joy, we rise above; and whatever we rise above, that we overcome in every instance.

The feeling of joy is also expansive, enlarging and constructive, and is a developing power of extreme value.

To count everything joy may at first seem difficult; but when we realize that the attitude of real joy rises above everything, and overcomes everything by taking life to a higher level, we shall soon find it easier and more natural to meet everything in joy than otherwise.

6. He Can Who Thinks He Can

A GREAT many new ideas of extreme value have recently appeared in current thought, but one of the most valuable is the idea that "he can who thinks he can;" and in the mastery of fate it will not only be necessary to keep this idea constantly in mind, but also to make the fullest possible use of the law upon which this idea is based.

To accomplish anything, ability is required; and it has been demonstrated that when man thinks he can do a certain thing, he increases the power and the capacity of that faculty which is required in doing what he thinks he can do.

To illustrate: When you think that you can succeed in business, you cause your business ability to develop, because by thinking that you can succeed in business you draw all the creative energies of the system into the business faculties, and consequently those faculties will be developed; and as those faculties are being developed, you gain that ability which positively can produce success in business.

You develop the power to do certain things by constantly thinking that you can do those things, because the law is that wherever in mind we concentrate attention, there development will take place; and we naturally concentrate upon that faculty that is required in the doing of that which we think we can do.

If you think that you can compose music, and continue to think that you can, you will develop that musical faculty that can compose music. Even though you may not have the slightest talent in that direction now, by thinking constantly that you can compose music you will develop that talent.

Results may begin to appear in a few months, or it may require a few years; nevertheless, if you continue to think that you can compose music, you will, in a few years be able to do so. Later on, you can develop into a rare musical genius.

Persistence, however, is required and all thought must be concentrated daily upon that one accomplishment. But this will not be difficult, because before long the entire mind will form a tendency to accumulate all its power and creative energy in the region of that one faculty; and constant development will take place both consciously and unconsciously.

Whatever a man desires to do, if he thinks that he can, he will develop the necessary power, and when the necessary power and ability are gained, the tangible results inevitably follow.

The secret is persistence. After you have decided what you want to do, begin to think that you can, and continue without ceasing to think that you can. Pay no attention to temporary failures; know that you can, and continue to think that you can.

To continue in the consciousness of the law that underlies this idea will bring greater results and more rapid results, because in that case you will consciously direct the developing process, and you will know that to think you can is to develop the power that can.

To keep constantly before mind the idea that "he can who thinks he can," will steadily increase the qualities of faith, self-confidence, perseverance and persistence; and whoever develops these qualities to a greater and greater degree will move forward without fail.

Therefore, to live in the conviction that "he can who thinks he can," will not only increase ability along the desired lines, but will also produce the power to push that ability into a living, tangible action.

In addition to thinking that you can do, try to do; put into practice at once what power and ability you possess, and by continuing to think that you can do more, you will develop the power to do more. To keep before mind the idea that "he can who thinks he can" will also hold attention upon the high ideals we have in view, and this is extremely important.

The fact is if we do not give ideal models to the creative energies of mind, those energies will employ whatever passes before them, as the senses admit all sorts of impressions from without.

The creative energies of mind are constantly producing thought, and these thoughts will be produced in the likeness of the deepest, the clearest and the most predominant mental impressions. Therefore, it is absolutely necessary that the predominant impressions be those into the likeness of which we desire to grow, because, as the impressions are, so are the thoughts; and as the thoughts are, so is man.

When man thinks that he will succeed, the predominant impression is the idea of success. All his thoughts will therefore contain the elements of success, and the forces that can produce success; and he himself, will become thoroughly saturated with the very life of success.

Nothing succeeds like success; therefore, the, man that is filled with the spirit of success can never fail; and what is more, the forces that contain the elements of success will give that man the very qualifications that are essential to success, because like produces like.

And again, the faculty required to produce the success desired, will be the one upon which all these success-energies will be concentrated.

When a man has the ability to do certain things, those things will be done; that is a foregone conclusion; and the ability to do what we want to do, comes when we constantly and persistently think that we can do what we want to do.

In the mastery of fate, the law upon which this idea is based will be found indispensable; because, since fate is created, and not controlled, all the elements of fate will have to be constantly re-created.

But no one can do this unless he thinks he can. To change many of the circumstances and conditions that now may surround us, requires more ability and power than we now possess; and to secure this greater power we must proceed to change and improve everything in our world by working in the conviction that we can.

By constantly thinking that we can change all our conditions, we gain a power to produce that change, and will consequently reach our goal.

The man who faces his environment with the belief that he is helpless before so many insurmountable obstacles, will remain where he is; but the man who thinks he can, will proceed to surmount everything, overcome everything, change everything and improve everything; and by constantly thinking he can, he will gain the power to do what he thinks he can do.

7. EXPRESS YOUR INDIVIDUALITY

THE PURPOSE of life is continuous advancement, and this necessitates the constant appropriation of the new, and the constant elimination of the old. To promote the first essential, a practical system of ideals is required; and to promote the second, we must master the art of letting go.

If we desire the new to be created, the creative process of mind must be supplied with new and better impressions.

Should we fail to do this, the creative energies will employ the old ideas, or impressions that are suggested from without.

In the mastery of fate, one of the greatest essentials is to prevent environment from impressing the mind; and to prevent this, your mind should be filled with your own ideal impressions. But this is not possible to any satisfactory degree unless a definite system of idealism is adopted, because no impression will become strong and predominant unless it is given constant attention.

In this connection, the true use of the imagination becomes extremely important. Everything that we imagine we impress upon mind; therefore, through the imagination we can work ourselves into almost any condition or state of being. In meeting circumstances and events imagination can be made to serve a most valuable service, and thus become directly instrumental in changing environment and fate.

When adversity comes we usually try to find the silver lining; but when we fail to find this, discouragement follows, which in turn but intensifies the darkness and the trouble.

However, we can create a silver lining with the imagination that will serve the same purpose; because when we picture the better side of things, and keep mind steadily upon that picture, the better will impress itself upon the mind. The result is that our thoughts change for the better, and we improve with our thoughts; and the improvement of man means the improvement of his environment.

Anyone who is in trouble can work himself out by creating in his imagination the silver lining of emancipation, and keeping the eye single upon that ideal picture.

Anyone who wishes to change his fate can do so by imaging upon mind a different fate, and by keeping that image so constantly before mind that every thought becomes the likeness of the new fate.

The law is that the external world of man changes when his mental world changes; and through the constructive use of the imagination the mental world can be changed in any way that we may desire.

When failure seems near, we should image success, refusing absolutely to think of the dark side. By imaging success, we impress upon mind the idea of success; thoughts will be created containing the elements of success, and from these thoughts we shall receive the power that can produce success. Any threatening failure can be overcome and entirely averted by this simple process, providing we live and work as we think.

By training the imagination to serve the system of ideals that we may have adopted, we shah soon gain full control of the process that forms impressions upon mind; and when this is accomplished every high ideal, every great purpose and every superior quality that we have in mind will be so well impressed upon the mental creative process that perpetual growth into every desirable condition must positively take place.

But to promote this advancement, we must learn to let go completely of everything that has served its purpose, or that in any way interferes with the steady progress of the whole man.

To acquire the art of letting go is an accomplishment with few equals, and is easily attained by learning to act upon the subjective side of everything in our own systems. It is the subjective side that holds; therefore, the subjective side alone can let go. The subjective contains the root of every thought, every desire, every tendency, every physical condition and every mental state that exists in the human system; it is the foundation of everything in the personal man, and originates the cause of everything that takes place in the life of man.

Whatever we place in the hands of the subjective, the subjective will continue to hold until it is called upon to let go. Every cause that gains a foothold in the subjective will continue to produce its effects, until the subjective is directed to have it removed; and every impression that is formed upon the subjective will continue to act as a pattern for the creation of thought until a different impression is formed in its place. To know how to deal with the subjective is therefore one of the greatest essentials; and the reason why so few have the power to master their fate is because the conscious direction of the subjective is almost unknown.

Mind has two sides, the outer and the inner; or the objective and the subjective. The objective is the conscious mind; the subjective is the subconscious mind. The objective acts; the subjective reacts. The objective mind gives orders; the subjective carries them out. The objective selects the seed and places that seed in the subjective; and the subjective causes that seed to grow and bear fruit after its kind. Whatever the objective desires to have done, the subjective has the power to do, and will do, if properly directed; though it must be properly and consciously directed.

In the average mind the subjective is directed ignorantly and irregularly; sometimes for good, more frequently otherwise. Therefore, the results are as they are; uncertain, unsatisfactory and limited. However, when we learn to direct the subjective consciously and with method, we shall be able to produce any result desired, at any time desired.

To direct the subjective, the will must be employed, as it must be in all forms of direction; and in the use of the will is where the real secret is found. The will must not act upon the external phase of any idea, desire or condition, but must intentionally act upon the internal side only.

When you move a muscle, the will acts upon the subjective side of that muscle. If the will should act upon the objective side, the muscle would become stiff, unable to move at all. Likewise, when the will acts upon the objective side of any idea, desire, tendency, habit, mental state or physical condition, no change whatever will take place. But the very moment that the will acts upon the subjective side of those things, they will begin to change according to the desire predominant in mind at the time.

Therefore whatever we wish to remove from the subjective, we should direct the will intentionally upon the subjective side of that which we desire to remove, and desire deeply to have that something removed.

It may require some training to master this process, but when the process is mastered, we can drop anything from mind instantaneously. Any idea, any habit, any desire, any state of discord or confusion, any diseased condition – all can be eliminated completely from the system, when we acquire the art of letting go.

To train the objective mind to act directly upon the subjective, consciousness should be more thoroughly developed in the realms of the finer feelings and the finer elements of life. Efforts should be made to come in touch with the higher vibrations in the system, because whenever we act in the higher vibrations, we act upon the subjective.

Whatever we desire the subjective to do while we act in the finer feeling of the higher vibrations that the subjective will proceed to do.

To act consciously and directly upon the subjective will also deepen the realization of life, which is extremely important; because the deepest life gives the strongest power, and in the creation of a greater destiny we need all the power we can secure.

When this deepening of life is continued in the serene attitude, mind is kept constantly in touch with the source of unbounded power, and thus receives as much power each day as may be required.

This brings us to one of the greatest essentials in the mastery of fate living; because there is nothing that contributes so much to the supremacy of man as a real, full life.

To bring out the best that is within him, man must not merely exist; he must live. When man actually lives he is what he is, and is all that he is. He does not try to be something else, or someone else. He does not imitate, but continues to be himself. And this is one of the secrets in the creation of a greater destiny.

The average person does not try to be himself, but tries constantly to imitate. He does not try to bring out his own individuality, but tries to fashion his personality and personal life according to some exterior model that is supposed to be the standard in the world's eye. The result is, he misplaces himself; because a person is always misplaced and misdirected when he tries to imitate the life of another; and no misplaced person can master his own fate.

Such a mind goes willingly and unconsciously into all sorts of foreign conditions, and then wonders what he has done to bring about such a mixed and undesirable fate.

When the individual tries to be himself, he will begin to act wholly in his own world, the only world where he can be his very best. And by trying to be himself, he begins to draw upon the unbounded possibilities that exist within himself, thus making himself a larger and a greater being constantly.

The individual that tries to imitate persons or environments does not express himself; therefore, his own hidden powers continue to lie dormant.

To express one's own individuality, and to be oneself, the greatest essential is to live real life; the life that is felt in the depth of inner consciousness.

To be yourself, be all that you are where you are, and greater spheres of action will constantly open before you.

Be satisfied to be what you are, but do not be satisfied to be less than all that you are.

When one begins to live – in the depth of real life, and begins to draw upon his own inexhaustible self, he will find that he is so much that there is no end to the possibilities that exist in his own life and his own world.

8. THE FOUR PARTS OF FATE

EVERY PERSON finds himself in a certain environment, in a certain physical condition, in certain mental states, with certain abilities and opportunities, and with certain obstacles and limitations.

In a world with others, he finds himself in a world of his own; and he calls this world his fate. But what is the cause of it all?

He knows that he is responsible for some of it, but he is quite sure he is not responsible for all of it. But who is? He wishes to know, in order that he may eliminate the undesirable, and constantly improve upon that which he wishes to retain.

When we analyze fate we find that it has four distinct parts, each of which comes from its own individual cause.

The first is the creations of nature that man has voluntarily entered into; the second is the creations of the race that man as an individual has accepted as his own; the third is the creations of certain individuals to which man has closely related himself; and the fourth is the creations of the individual himself.

That man voluntarily entered into the first three, is a fact easily demonstrated; though he might not have been wide awake when he did so. Those parts of your fate that you have not created, you have selected; though too often you made your selection in the dark.

In the mastery of fate it is therefore not only necessary to produce the very highest creations through your own creative efforts, but it is also necessary to obtain that wisdom, or interior insight through which the proper selections may be made from those other sources that do invariably contribute to your fate.

Those creations of nature that we may find in our own environment, are filled with unlimited possibilities, whether they appear favorable or not. What they are to do to us depends upon what we decide to do with them.

We may take the elements of nature and convert them into high and constructive uses, or we may permit ourselves to remain in bondage to those elements. The bondage, however, is not produced by nature, but the way we relate ourselves to nature.

To master that part of fate that we receive from nature, the secret is to be in harmony with nature at all times, and under all conditions, and to try constantly to employ constructively every element in nature with which we may come in contact.

That part of fate that has been received from the race is called heredity, and is usually looked upon as a permanent factor in life; but there is no heredity that cannot be changed.

Acquire the art of letting those things go that you do not want, and proceed to improve upon those that you do want.

Use undeveloped hereditary conditions as channels through which to reach the greater things you have in view. Back of every condition there is a power; that power can be developed, and when it is, the old, inferior condition disappears.

What is called the "world," with all its perversions and obstacles, is simply raw material, out of which the strong mind can build almost anything that he may desire.

But the "world" must not be met in the belief that things as they are, are permanent and insurmountable; but as the builder meets his material.

Work in the idea that "he can who thinks he can;" develop interior insight so that you may know how to select the material you desire; and develop your mind into a strong mind by entering the attitude of self-supremacy.

We have the same mental power over circumstances and conditions as we have physical power over iron, lumber and coal. Every event that transpires in daily life contains an opportunity; but we must have the insight to see it, and the power to employ it.

The creation of those individuals with whom we come in personal contact, constitute frequently a predominating factor in our destiny, because since we are more or less wedded to our associations, our minds accept impressions from such sources to a very great degree; but this interferes with original thinking, and consequently, with our own mastery of fate.

Therefore, that part of fate that we receive from friends, relatives and personal associations, must be carefully selected through insight and through the principle that "when we become better, we meet better people." Instead of being indiscriminately influenced by our friends, we should accept their mental gifts as we accept their hospitable repast -to be masticated, digested and assimilated by ourselves.

What to do with close relations that refuse to co-operate with us, is a great problem that becomes extremely simple when we decide to live our own life in such a way that no person's liberty or idea of liberty is disturbed.

Be a model character that does things; and everybody will soon go with you to the superior life you have in view.

Give your best to everybody and the best will certainly come to you if you give the law the time required, and do not force changes by impatience and lack of faith. Change yourself, and all other desirable changes must positively follow.

9. MAKING THE IDEAL REAL

EVERY FACTOR in the fate of man responds to the life of man; and every element in the life of man is governed, directed, changed or modified by the thought of man. Therefore, as thought goes, so will the creative causes of fate go also. For this reason, if fate is to be improved, thought must move upward and onward; and since thought follows ideals, to him who would master his fate, ideals become indispensable.

But it is not only necessary to have ideals; it is also necessary to make real our ideals. This, however, seems difficult for the average person to do, because between the real and the ideal there appears to be a gulf that he does not know how to bridge.

Even many of the greatest philosophers in the world have failed to realize in a practical way what their finer perceptions had discovered; though this is not strange, because it is the prophetic faculty that sees the ideal, and the scientific faculty that makes the ideal real; and these two faculties are not always found in the same man.

The complete man, however, has both; and he who would master his fate must be complete.

By the prophetic faculty we do not me the power to discern the future, because with the future we are not concerned; we are living in the eternal now and in the eternal now we shall always continue to live.

The prophetic faculty is the power to look back of things, within things and above things; thus discerning basic laws, fundamental principles and the unbounded possibilities that exist everywhere. It is seeing the ideal; and the ideal is not a mere mental picture, but the discovery of something higher, something better and something greater than what is actually realized now. The prophetic faculty discovers what can be done now if we choose to do it.

This faculty is developed through the constructive use of the imagination, the constant use of interior insight, and the practice of looking for the greater possibilities in everything with which we come in contact.

The mere discovery of the great is not sufficient; the ideal must be made real. It is not the dreaming of things, but the doing of things that produces a better fate and a larger destiny. But we must perceive the greater things before we can do the greater things; and to perceive the greater things is to have ideals. To make real the ideal, the scientific faculty is required; and this faculty develops through scientific thinking and through the practical application of every principle and law discovered.

To make real the ideal, the first essential is to remove from consciousness the gulf that seems to exist between present attainment and the greater possibilities. Refuse to think of this gulf, because to think of it is to impress the mind with the idea that the greater is beyond us. This impression will prevent mind from reaching the greater, and will also produce frequent states of despair. Such states not only weaken mind, but cause man to give himself up to the influence of environment.

A discouraged mind, submitting itself to environment, is impressed with failure, weakness, inferiority, and the tendency to go down grade; while the mind that is to master fate must go the other way.

To remove the seeming gulf from mind, turn attention not only upon the ideal you desire to reach, but try to see the ideal of yourself as well. By so doing you impress the ideal of yourself upon your mind; thoughts like the ideal self will be created, and your personal self becomes like the thoughts you think. Consequently, by a simple process, the personal self is made to improve constantly, daily becoming more and more like the ideal.

To realize constant personal advancement is to prevent all thoughts of discouragement, and also to enter the power of that law through which gain promotes gain, and much gathers more.

The law is that you begin to realize the ideal in your personal life when the personal self begins to grow into the likeness of the ideal. Therefore, to yearn for ideals while nothing is being done to make yourself more ideal, is to continue to keep yourself away from your ideal.

It is like that attracts like, and only those who are alike will be drawn into the same world; consequently, to live in the same world with your ideal, you must become like your ideal.

The ideal cannot come down to you; ideals never move that way; but you can go up to your ideal, and that is the true way for you to move.

To make any part of the personal self-ideal, place before the creative powers of mind the corresponding ideal of your true self; and it must be remembered that your true self is not something distinct from your ideal self, because the two are one.

The ideal of yourself is you; you are the ideal side of yourself; the actual or external side of yourself is only a partial expression of the ideal or true self. The ideal side of man is the complete side; and the complete side is you. You are not the incomplete side, because if you were there would be no source for anything in your being; not even the incomplete or external side would have a source, and consequently could not exist.

Incompleteness cannot come from incompleteness, because an incompleteness is a partial effect of a complete cause. Incompleteness can come only from completeness; therefore, the fact that the personal self is incomplete proves that it comes from a self that is complete; and since you, yourself, cannot be complete and incomplete at the same time, you, yourself, must be the complete self, while the personal self is but a partial expression of the completeness that exists in you.

When you see this clearly, you will know that you are already ideal; that is, complete, and in possession of unlimited possibilities; and when you know that you are ideal, you will think of yourself as ideal. You will impress the ideal, and the greater possibilities upon mind, and your thoughts will not only be ideal, but will contain the power of the greater possibilities. This power will be expressed in the personal self, because the power of every thought is expressed in the personal self; consequently, the personal self will become larger, greater and more perfect, constantly making real the ideal.

To realize your ideal it is not necessary to change your present environment, or to adopt some radical mode of living; nor is it necessary to be transported to some other sphere.

The ideals that you see are in your own path, directly before you, and will positively be reached through a forward movement. We cannot see the ideals of another mind; therefore, the ideals that you see are in your own path, and can be reached by you. The secret is to move forward in your own life. Be yourself, and bring out all that exists in yourself, and you will gain both the power and the ability to reach what you have in view.

There will be no waiting time; and it is not necessary to become absolutely perfect to make real the ideal. The very moment you begin to develop the personal self into the likeness of the ideal self, the ideal life will begin to become real in the personal life; and the mind that impresses itself only with its own selected and superior impressions, will develop the personal self with the greatest rapidity.

To make real the ideal, the principle is to make everything in your life more and more like the ideal. Ideal friendship brings ideal friends; refinement in action, thought and speech brings refined people; greater ability brings greater results in the world of achievement; and better environments come when we develop the power to create the better. A beautiful mental life produces a beautiful physical existence; and by giving the best to the world, the best will surely return.

10. DIRECTING CREATIVE FORCES

FATE IS created by the powers in man; therefore, in order to master fate, man must acquire control over the creative forces in his being. And this is accomplished, not by trying to control these forces, but by changing their courses.

Every force in the system moves through the field of consciousness, and by training the will to act upon consciousness so as to open or close the channels of consciousness in any place, the different forces in the system can be directed wherever desired.

No force can be driven. We cannot drive the force of electricity; but by providing suitable conductors, electricity will go wherever it is wanted, because we have the power to move the conductors about as we like.

The channels of consciousness, more correctly designated the tendencies of mind, are the conductors of the creative forces of the system; therefore, by regulating the tendencies of mind we may cause all, or any desired part of our creative power to accumulate at any time in any place of mind or body.

To regulate the tendencies of mind, the will must act upon the finer or inner side of consciousness; and whatever the will wills to have done while acting upon the finer side, the same will be done.

To reach this finer side, mind must enter a perpetual refining process, and must establish this process in every part of the system. Create a strong desire to transform, refine and improve everything with which you come in contact, and the finer consciousness will develop steadily. This is the first essential.

The second essential is to properly meet the forces that come into your life, because every force that comes, comes to act; and how it is met will determine whether its action upon you will be favorable or not.

When you meet a force, you must do something with it, or it will do something with you; you must direct it, or it will pass through your system aimlessly and be lost. Or, if it is an undeveloped force, as most forces are, you will permit the formation of adverse conditions by permitting such a force to pass through your world unguided.

It is the nature of all forces to do things; they cannot be idle; therefore, if you do not give them something definite to build, they will build aimlessly, or destroy ruthlessly.

We are constantly in the midst of powerful forces, and they are all at our command when we know how to command them; but they do not pass under our dominion until they enter our systems.

It is the forces that pass through our own systems that we can direct; and when these are properly, directed, anything we desire to have done can be done; because an enormous amount of energy is generated in the average person, and hourly passes through the person.

When we learn to direct and constructively employ all those forces, it matters not whether we have highly developed parents or not; whether we have a good ancestry or not; whether we were born under favorable conditions or not; whether we have any talents and opportunities or not; we can make ourselves over absolutely; we can change and improve everything in ourselves and in our environments, and proceed in the creation and realization of a great and superior destiny.

When we place ourselves in a favorable attitude towards all the forces that enter the system, and learn how to direct those forces into favorable channels of construction, every force that passes through the system will become favorable to us, no matter where it comes from, nor how unfavorable it may be before it enters our favorable world.

The secret is to make your own system a transforming, refining and transmuting power. Establish in your system two predominating tendencies and desires – to refine everything and to construct superiority out of everything. And every force that enters your system will become a superior constructive power for you; and will build up your talents, promote your purpose, and change your fate as you wish it to be.

The whole world of power is ready to build for the man that is thoroughly permeated with the desire to become more and accomplish more; therefore, the man who lives constantly in the spirit of transformation will reach the highest goal he has in view.

Make no effort to control or influence any force within yourself, or outside of yourself. Simply control yourself to remain constantly in constructive touch with the finer vibrations of the world of force.

It is necessary to meet every force in the serene attitude, and to feel an interior oneness with the real life of all power. When you feel this deeper unity, every force will unite with you, work for you, and promote your purpose.

When the presence of a force is felt in the system, we should enter into mental touch with the inner, finer side of that force, and hold strongly in mind what we desire to accomplish. This will produce the tendency required, and the force will follow the new channel, to do what we desire to have done.

To develop this finer and interior feeling, enter into constant sympathy with the inner life of everything, and be always in poise.

Employ the finer senses of perception, discernment and deep feeling as frequently as possible, and try every day to feel through your entire system.

Concentrate several times daily upon the higher vibrations that are back of, within and above every atom in your being; and whenever you use the will, turn attention upon the soul or real substance of things.

11. HOW TO DEVELOP INTERNAL INSIGHT

THE CREATIVE forces that are generated in man, and the cosmic forces that work through man are fundamental causes of fate; therefore, if man would master his fate, he must consciously direct these so that the creations may be what he desires. When he fails to do this, the creative forces will be directed or influenced by suggestions from external conditions and environments; and this is what takes place in the life of the average person; therefore, his fate is so uncertain, so mixed and so unlike his secret ideal.

The methods presented in the previous chapter will enable anyone to get into that state of consciousness where the forces of the system can be turned in any direction; but after a power is under our control, we want to use it wisely, and to the very best advantage.

Good judgment, reason, understanding, and a brilliant intellect will serve this purpose to a degree; but to make the very best use of every power, under every circumstance, another faculty is required. The necessary faculty is interior insight; or the power to discern the causes, principles and laws that lie beneath the surface. It is that sense that all possess to a degree, that feels and knows how things are going, and how they ought to go; and may therefore be called the inside secret of all success, of all great attainments and achievements.

It is through this faculty that man does the right thing at the right time, with or without the aid of external evidence.

The great minds who have taken advantage of exceptional opportunities at the psychological moment, have been prompted to do so by this very faculty; and what is usually termed extraordinary good fortune is but the result of actions that interior insight was instrumental in producing.

No one has ever reached the pinnacle of attainment and achievement without this faculty, and no one ever will. In the absence of interior insight, the greater part of the best ability would be misdirected, and most of the powers of the system would be lost.

Interior insight is not a faculty that has to be acquired; everybody has it to a considerable degree; it is only necessary that it be further developed and consciously employed. And as it deals directly with the finer forces of life, discerning the nature, the present movements and the latent possibilities of those forces, it is in connection with the world of those forces that the faculty must be exercised for greater efficiency.

To bring this faculty into full expression so it may be employed with accuracy in any field desired, the first essential is to exercise interior insight at every possible opportunity. Not that its verdict should be invariably accepted; but its verdict should always be sought. It will be profitable to do this even in minute and unimportant daily affairs, because it is by discerning the law of action in small things, that we gain the power to discern the same law in greater things.

When this faculty is developed, we shall no longer judge according to appearances, and be misled; but we shall judge according to the real facts that are at the foundation of things; and since it is the underlying causes that must be dealt with in the mastery of fate, interior insight becomes indispensable.

Whenever you are in the midst of changes, or have anything to decide, expect to discern the proper course, and decide correctly through the action of interior insight. And have perfect faith in the power of this faculty at all times. This will not only strengthen the faculty, but will in most instances produce the decision desired.

When conflicting ideas come at such times, enter into a deep, serene state of mind, forgetting the various ideas received, and desiring with the whole of life to discern what you wish to know. Remain in this attitude for days if necessary, or until you receive only one leading decision on the subject. You will get it, and the strong, prolonged effort will have developed your interior insight to a remarkable degree.

To determine the reliability of an idea received through insight, test it with reason, from every point of view; and if it continues to remain a predominant conviction, it is the truth of which you are in search. While expecting information through this faculty, mind should be kept as quiet and as elevated in thought as possible. All sentimental or emotional feelings should be avoided, and the imagination must be perfectly still.

The upward look of mind, devoid of restless yearning, but fully serene and responsive, is the true attitude.

Expect to receive the desired information from the superior wisdom of your higher mentality, and know that there positively is such a wisdom.

While expecting this superior wisdom to unfold what you desire to know, be positive to your environment and to everything in the without. Do not permit the senses to suggest anything on the subject. But be responsive to your interior life; that is, feel in the within that your mind is open to the -real wisdom from the within.

Never doubt the existence of the superior wisdom within. This will close the mind to that wisdom. You know that there is such a wisdom; you have evidence to prove it every day; and the more faith you have in its reality, the more perfectly will your mind respond to its unfoldment.

Another essential to the full expression of interior insight is to refine the physical brain so that the finer mental actions may produce perceptible impressions. This is accomplished by awakening the finer forces of the system, and directing those forces through a deep, serene concentration, upon every part of the brain. This exercise should be taken for a few minutes, several times a day; and the more highly refined you feel throughout the system at the time, the greater the results.

In the use of interior insight, reason and objective understanding should not be ignored, because the best results are secured when the exterior and interior aspects of judgment are developed simultaneously and used together at all times. In this way the mind acquires the power to discern the internal causes on the one hand, and on the other, understands how to adapt the present movements of those causes to present exterior conditions. This brings the ideal and the practical into united action at every turn, which is absolutely necessary.

While exercising the faculty of interior insight, the predominant effort should be to see through things; because the predominant desire, if continued, is always realized.

12. CHARACTER, ABILITY AND FAITH

THE PLACE that each individual is to occupy in the world is determined principally by character and ability; there are other factors, all of which have been mentioned, but these two predominate.

When character is absent, the powers of mind or body will be turned into wrong channels, because nothing in the being of man can go right unless it passes through the life of character.

When ability is absent, man becomes a negative personality, incapable of creating a single course of individual action, and is consequently influenced and controlled by everything with which he comes in contact.

The reason why so many beautiful characters are found in undesirable environments is because they lack positive creative ability.

It is ability that supplies the power to do things; and it is character that directs the power so that the things done will be worthy and true.

By character, however, we do not mean simply a state of being good in the ordinary sense of that term; nor is it a mere attitude of mind that holds preference for the right.

Character is an established quality of being, based upon the principle of absolute right. It is a living power with divine consciousness as its source; it is a life that is right, and that thrills every atom in being with the force of justice, righteousness and truth.

Character is a permanent attainment; it cannot be shaken; it cannot, under any consideration, be influenced from without; but it can at all times be unfolded from within.

That character should be necessary in the mastery of fate, is evident when we realize that all the creative powers of man must express themselves through the principle of the absolutely right, if they are to create a better and a greater destiny; because it is through character alone that the right expression of any force or any talent can take place.

Develop ability, and develop character, and you have the foundation for any fate you may desire to create. You have that something that wins every time, regardless of seeming exceptions.

With character and ability combined, no one can fail; and with a high development of these two, anyone can attain, not only great things, but the very greatest of all things.

To promote the highest development and the most thorough use of character and ability, faith becomes indispensable.

Faith awakens everything within us that is superior, and brings out the best that is within. Faith unites man with the Infinite; and no one can accomplish the great things in life unless he works constantly in oneness with the Infinite. No mind can do much without the Supreme; and no one can do his best in any sphere of action unless he lives so near to the Supreme that the divine presence is consciously felt at all times.

We are helped by a higher power, and we can receive far greater assistance and far superior assistance from this same source when our faith is high and strong.

A highly developed mind may accomplish much without faith, but with faith that same mind can accomplish a great deal more; and the same is true of every mind in every stage of development. Faith increases the power, the capacity and the efficiency of everything and everybody.

One of the greatest essentials in the mastery of fate is to have a high goal, a definite goal, and to keep the eye single upon this goal. And there is nothing that causes the mind to aim as high as faith. Faith goes out upon the boundlessness of all things; it passes by the borderland and proves there is no borderland. It demonstrates conclusively that all things are possible, and that there is no end to the path of attainment; and what is more, it demonstrates that this path to greater and greater attainment is substantial and sound all the way.

There is no seeming void; all is solid rock; therefore, it is perfectly safe to go out anywhere into the universal. In the eyes of faith, there is no gulf between the small and the great; from the smaller to the greater there is a path of smooth and solid rock, and any one may safely reach the greater by simply pressing on.

To master fate, the mind must be determined to reach the highest goal in view, and should realize that the goal can be reached -that it is being reached. And there is nothing that makes the mind more determined to reach the heights than a strong, living faith.

Faith sees the heights; faith knows they are there, and can be reached. Therefore, to a mind that would create a grander fate, nothing is more valuable than faith.

To attain faith we must understand that it is not blind belief; it is not belief at all. Faith is a live conviction, illumined knowledge received at first hand through the awakening of that power within that sees, knows and understands the spirit of things.

Consequently, faith not only awakens higher and mightier powers, and illumines the mind with light, wisdom and truth of incalculable value, but it also brings mind into perfect touch with those laws and principles that lie at the very foundation of all life, all attainment, all achievement, and all change; and it is these laws that mind must employ if fate is to be mastered, and a greater destiny created.

To attain faith, have faith; have faith in the Supreme; have faith in man; have faith in yourself; have faith in everything in the universe; and above all, have faith in faith.

Last, but not least, the man who would master his fate must do things in love. A tangible fate is the result of tangible deeds; but no tangible deed can contribute to a better fate unless is it the product of love.

Desire to do things with a desire that sets every fibre in being aflame; love everything, is being done, with a love that is the living power of the soul itself; and give yourself, your largest self, your whole self to your life and your work. And what you give that will be your fate.

The End.

BOOK FOUR

HOW THE MIND WORKS

Using The Greatest Human Power

ABOUT THIS BOOK

Man is as he thinks; therefore he can change himself, his life, and even his circumstances, by changing his thought. But before he can change his thought he must understand those laws and processes through which thought is produced; that is, he must know how the mind works.

This book analyzes the most important of the mental and metaphysical laws known to date are considered from every possible viewpoint, the principal object being to ascertain their real nature as well as their power and use. In addition, a number of psychological ideas are presented that will throw light both on the inner and the outer workings of the mind.

No effort, however, has been made to delve into the mysteries of the mind; this will be done in another work, the object here being to present the practical side of mental action, and present it in such a way that anyone may learn to use the powers of the mind properly. And at the present stage of psychological study, this is the most important.

We want to know how the mind does work so that we may, in all mental work, use the mind in the best, the fullest and the most effective manner.

FOREWORD

EVERYTHING THAT is in action must necessarily work through definite laws. And as the mind is in constant action, alternating its actions at almost every turn of thought or feeling, it is evident that a vast number of laws are employed by the mental process. To know how the mind works, therefore, we must know something about these laws.

In the following pages the most important of the mental and metaphysical laws known to date are considered from every possible viewpoint, the principal object being to ascertain their real nature as well as their power and use. In addition, a number of psychological ideas are presented that will throw light both on the inner and the outer workings of the mind.

No effort, however, has been made to delve into the mysteries of the mind; this will be done in another work, the object here being to present the practical side of mental action, and present it in such a way that anyone may learn to use the powers of the mind properly. And at the present stage of psychological study, this is the most important. We want to know how the mind does work so that we may, in all mental work, use the mind in the best, the fullest and the most effective manner.

The fact that we have, in the past, known practically nothing about the real workings of the mind, and also that there are only a few minds, even in the present, that have gained the power to direct and control mental action according to system, design and law, should make the study of this book both interesting and profitable. In fact, we are convinced that all who understand the purpose and the message of this book will become highly enthused over its practical value; and will accordingly gain more from its perusal than tongue can ever tell.

That this number may be very large in the present, and constantly become larger in the future, is our dearest wish in this connection; for when you know that a certain thing is so very true and so very important, you want everybody else, if possible, to gain all that you have gained from the understanding and use of that particular thing.

And this is natural; we all want to share the truth with others; we all want everybody to gain that power through which the richest and the best that life has in store may be realized; and this fact proves that there is far more of the noble in human nature than we have previously believed. However, it is only as we learn to use the mind in harmony with the natural and orderly workings of mental law, that everything that is noble in human nature will find expression.

1. THE GREATEST POWER IN MAN

IT IS now a demonstrated fact that the powers and the possibilities that are inherent in the mind of man are practically unbounded. And this conclusion is based upon the discovery that no limit can be found to anything in human nature, and that everything in human nature contains a latent capacity for perpetual development. This discovery, and no discovery of greater importance has appeared in any age, gives man a new conception of himself, a conception which when applied will necessarily revolutionize the entire sphere of human thought and action.

To be able to discern the real significance of this new conception will naturally constitute the greatest power in man, and should therefore be given the first thought in all efforts that have advancement, attainment or achievement in view. The purpose of each individual should be not simply to cultivate and apply those possibilities that are now in evidence, but also to develop power to discern and fathom what really exists within him. This power is the greatest power because it prepares the way for the attainment and expression of all other powers. It is the power that unlocks the door to everything that is great and wonderful in man, and must therefore be understood and applied before anything of real value can be accomplished through human thought or action.

The principal reason why the average person remains weak and incompetent is found in the fact that he makes no effort to fathom and understand the depths of his real being. He tries to use what is in action on the surface, but is unconscious of the fact that enormous powers are in existence in the greater depth of his life. These powers are dormant simply because they have not been called into action, and they will continue to lie dormant until man develops his greatest power; that is, the power to discern what really exists within him.

The fundamental cause of failure is found in the belief that what exists on the surface is all there is of man. And the reason why greatness is the rare exception instead of the universal rule can be traced to the same cause. When the mind discovers that its powers are inexhaustible and that its faculties and talents can be developed to the very highest degree imaginable, and to any degree beyond that, the fear of failure will entirely disappear. In its stead will come the conviction that man may attain anything or achieve anything, provided, of course, he works within the natural sphere of universal law. Whatever circumstances may be today such a mind will know that all can be changed; that this condition can be made to pass away, and that the vacancy may be filled with the heart's most cherished desire.

That mind that can discern what exists in the depths of the real life of man does not simply change its views as to what man may attain or achieve, but actually begins to draw upon the inexhaustible power within, and begins at once to develop and apply the greater possibilities that this deeper discernment has revealed. When man can see, feel and understand what exists beneath the surface of his life, the expression of this deeper life begins, because whatever we become conscious of that we invariably bring forth into tangible expression.

And since the deeper life contains innumerable possibilities as well as unbounded power, it is evident that when the deeper life is clearly discerned, anything within the human sphere may be attained or achieved.

The idea that there is more and more of man than what appears on the surface should be so constantly and so deeply impressed upon the mind that it becomes a positive conviction, and no thought should be placed in action unless it is based upon this conviction. To live, think and act in the realization of the fact that there is "more of me" should be the constant purpose of every individual. When this is done the more will constantly develop, coming forth in greater and greater measure, giving added power, capacity and life to everything that is in action in the human system.

When the average person fails he either blames circumstances or comes to the conclusion that he was not equal to the occasion. He is therefore tempted to give up, and tries to be content with the lesser. But if he knew that there was more in him than what he had applied in this undertaking he would not give up. He would know that by developing this "more" he positively would succeed where he had previously failed. It is therefore evident that when man gives attention to his greatest power, that is, the power to discern the more that is in him, he will never give up until he does succeed; and in consequence he invariably will succeed.

That individual who knows his power does not judge according to appearances. He never permits himself to believe that this or that cannot be done. He knows that those things can be done because he has discovered the more which really exists within him. He works in the conviction that he must and will succeed because he has the power. And this is the truth. He does have the power. We all have the power.

To live, think and work in the attitude that there is more of you within the great depths of your being, and to know that there is more of you within the great depths of your being, and to know that this "more" is so immense that no limit to its power can be found, will cause the mind to come in closer and closer touch with this greater power. And you will in consequence gain more and more of this power. The mind that lives in this attitude opens the door of consciousness, so to speak, to everything in human life that has real quality and worth. It places itself in that position where it can respond to the best that exists within itself. And modern psychology has discovered that this "best" is extraordinary in quality, limitless in power, and contains possibilities that cannot be numbered.

It is the truth that man is a marvelous being, and the greatest power in man is the power to discern this marvelousness that really does exist within him. It is the law that we steadily develop and bring forth whatever we think of the most. We shall therefore find it highly profitable to think constantly of our deeper nature and to try in every manner and form imaginable to fathom the limitlessness and the inexhaustibleness of these great and marvelous depths.

In practical life this mode of thinking will have the same effect upon the personal mind as that which is secured when placing an ordinary wire in contact with a wire that is charged. The great within is a live wire. When the mind touches the great within it becomes charged with the same immense power.

And the mind is more or less in touch with the great within when it lives, thinks, and works in the firm conviction that there is "more of me," so much more that it cannot be measured.

We can receive from the deeper life only that which we recognize, because consciousness is the power between the outer life and the great within; and we open the door only to those things of which we become conscious. The principal reason, therefore, why the average person does not possess greater powers and talents is because he is not conscious of more. And he is not conscious of more because he has not recognized the depths of his real life, and has not tried to fathom the possibilities that are latent within him.

The average person lives on the surface. He thinks that the surface is all there is of him, and therefore does not place himself in touch with the live wire of his great and inexhaustible nature within. He does not exercise his greatest power the power to discern what his whole nature may contain, and therefore does not unlock the door to any of his other powers. This being true, we can readily understand why mortals are weak. They are weak simply because they have chosen weakness. But when they choose power and greatness they shall positively become what they have chosen to become. And we all can choose power and greatness, because it is in us.

We all admit that there is more in man than what is expressed in the average person. We may differ as to how much more, but the more should be developed, expressed and applied. It is unjust both to the individual and to the race to remain in the lesser when it is possible to attain the higher, the richer and the greater. It is right that we all should ascend to the higher and the greater now. And the greatest power in man reveals the fact that we all can.

2. THE BEST USE OF THE MIND

WE HAVE at the present time a number of metaphysical systems, and though they differ considerably in many respects they all produce practically the same results. We find that no one system is more successful than the others, and yet they are all so remarkably successful that modern metaphysics is rapidly becoming one of the most popular studies of today. The real secret of all these systems is found in their power to draw consciousness more deeply into the realization of the absolute.

The absolute is unconditioned; therefore the more deeply consciousness enters the absolute the less conscious will the mind become of conditions. That is, the mind will be emancipated more and more from conditions as it grows into the realization of that which is unconditioned, or rather above conditions.

Any method that will tend to develop in the mind the consciousness of the absolute will produce emancipation from physical or mental ills, the reason being that there are no ills in the absolute, and it is not possible for the mind to be conscious of ills when it is in the consciousness of that which is absolutely free from ills. In other words, the mind cannot be in darkness, weakness or disease when it is in light, power and health.

Although it is not exact science to state that all is mind, because it can easily be proven that all is not mind; nevertheless, the statement that all is mind has a tendency to resolve consciousness into the allness of infinite mind, that is, the mind of the absolute. This will eliminate from the personal mind the consciousness of personal limitations and thus produce the realization of the absolute, that state of being that is free from conditions. It will also cause the personal mind to function in the consciousness of its unity with the impersonal mind which again is the infinite mind.

In like manner it is not scientific to deny the existence of matter, because matter does exist. Nevertheless the persistent denial of the existence of matter has a tendency to eliminate from mind the consciousness of shape and form, also the limitations and the conditions of shape and form. The result will be a certain degree of emancipation from conditions, and accordingly the ills that may have existed in those conditions will disappear.

The purpose of metaphysical methods is to prevent superficial mental action by deepening thought into the understanding of real action; that is, to prevent bondage to the limitations of form by awakening the consciousness of that limitless Life that animates all form, and also to prevent the creation of imperfect conditions by producing in the mind the realization of absolutely perfect states. Any method that will tend to promote these objects in view will prove healthful to a degree in producing personal emancipation from sickness, adversity or want; but if the method is not strictly scientific its value will be very limited, and will prove to be nothing more than a temporary aid in the lesser aspects of life.

In this connection we must remember that no metaphysical method can fully promote the purpose in view unless it recognizes the reality of the whole universe and aims to produce advancement in every individual expression of universal life. However, every method is at first incomplete, therefore not strictly scientific. But to be scientific we must give everything due credit for what it is doing, no matter how limited it may be in its personal power.

To awaken the consciousness of the real, the unconditioned and the absolute, it is not necessary to declare that all is mind, nor is it necessary to deny the existence of matter. On the contrary, such methods should be avoided, because they will prove detrimental to the highest development of the individual if employed for any length of time. And we realize that our purpose is not simply to emancipate man from the ordinary ills of personal life, but also to develop man to the very highest heights of real greatness.

There is a world of absolute reality that exists within and about all things. It permeates all things and surrounds all things. It is an infinite sea in which all things live and move and have their being. It is the source of everything, and being limitless can give limitless life and power to anything. All science recognizes this world of absolute reality, and it is the purpose of metaphysics, that is, the best use of the mind, to gain that understanding that will enable any individual to place himself in perfect conscious touch with that world. This absolute reality is the perfect state of being upon which all individual being is based. Therefore the more perfectly conscious the individual becomes of the absolute, the less imperfection there will be in the life of the individual. And when individual consciousness is completely resolved in absolute consciousness, the cosmic state is realized a state with such marvelous beauty and such indescribable joy that it is worth a thousand ages of pain to come within its gates for just one single moment.

To develop the consciousness of the absolute and to grow steadily into the realization of the reality of perfect being the fundamental essential is to live habitually in the metaphysical attitude. This is a distinct attitude, by far the most desirable attitude of the mind, and comes as a natural result of the mind's discernment of the existence, the reality and the absoluteness of the universal sea of unconditioned life. This attitude is emancipating because it removes the imperfect by resolving the mind into the consciousness of the perfect. It produces the realization of the real and thus floods human life with the light of the real, that light that invariably dispels all darkness, whether it be ignorance, adversity, want, weakness, illusion or evil in any form or condition.

The secret of all metaphysical methods of cure is found in the peculiar power of the metaphysical attitude. To enter this attitude is to resolve mind in the consciousness of the absolute, and since there is no sickness in the absolute it is not possible for any mind to feel sickness while in the consciousness of the absolute. For this reason any method that will cause the mind to enter the metaphysical attitude will give that mind the power to heal physical or mental ailments. However, it is not the method that heals. It is that peculiar power or consciousness that conies when the mind is in the metaphysical attitude. And this power simply implies the elimination of imperfect conditions by resolving consciousness into the perfection of absolute states.

The actions of the mind are back of all personal conditions, therefore when the mind begins to act in the consciousness of absolute states it will express the perfection, the health, the wholeness and the power of those states. And when the qualities of such states are expressed, imperfect conditions must necessarily disappear. Light and darkness cannot exist in the same place at the same time; neither can health and disease. When the former comes the latter is no more. When the mind is placed in the metaphysical attitude the conscious realization of the more powerful forces of life is gained. This means possession and mastery of those forces, at least in a measure, and the result will be a decided increase in the power, the capacity and the ability of every active faculty of the mind.

It is therefore evident that every person who desires to become much and achieve much should live habitually in the metaphysical attitude, for it is in this attitude that the best use of the mind is secured. The metaphysical attitude is distinct from the psychical attitude, and it is highly important for every person to clearly understand this distinction. Both attitudes will place the mind in touch with the more powerful forces of life, but the metaphysical is based upon the conviction that all power is in itself good, and that the mind naturally controls all power; but the psychical attitude has no definite conviction or purpose regarding the real nature of power. The metaphysical attitude takes hold of those finer powers and applies them constructively, while in the psychical attitude those powers are more or less in a chaotic state. For this reason the psychical attitude is nearly always detrimental, while the metaphysical is never otherwise than highly beneficial.

To approach the universal life of unbounded wisdom and limitless power is usually termed occultism. We find therefore that metaphysics and occultism have the same general purpose, and deal largely with the same elements and powers, but they do not make the same use of those elements and powers, nor are the results identical in any sense whatever. The psychical attitude opens the mind to more power but takes no definite steps in directing that power into constructive channels. If the mind is wholesome and constructive while in the psychical attitude the greater powers thus gained will be beneficial because it will in such a mind be directed properly. But to enter the psychical while there are adverse tendencies, false ideas or perverted desires in mind, is decidedly detrimental because this greater power will at such times be misdirected. And the greater the power the worse will be the consequence when misdirection takes place.

To state it briefly, no mind can safely enter the psychical attitude unless it has a spotless character, a masterful mind, and knows the truth about everything in this present state of existence. But as this requirement is practically beyond everybody, we must conclude that no one can safely enter the psychical state. To enter the psychical attitude is to fill the personality with new forces, some of which will be very strong, and if the mind is not constructive through and through, at the time, some or all of those forces will become destructive.

However, it is not possible to make the mind constructive through and through without entering the metaphysical attitude; that is, the mind is not fit to enter the psychical attitude until it has entered the metaphysical attitude. But as the same powers are secured in the metaphysical attitude, the psychical attitude becomes superfluous. Therefore, to give a single moment of thought or attention to occultism is a waste of time.

When a mind enters the metaphysical attitude it becomes constructive at once, because the metaphysical attitude is naturally a constructive attitude, being based upon the conviction that all things are in themselves good and working together for greater good. All power is good and all power is constructive. All power is beneficial when applied according to its true purpose, but no mind can apply power according to its true purpose until it becomes thoroughly constructive, and no mind can become thoroughly constructive until it enters the metaphysical attitude.

In this attitude all thought and attention is given to that which makes for better things and greater things. The mind is placed in such perfect harmony with the absolute that it naturally follows the law of the absolute, and to follow this law is to be all that you can be. It is therefore the very soul of advancement, attainment and achievement, having nothing but construction in view.

The fact that the practice of occultism produces extraordinary phenomena, either upon the physical plane or in the world of mental imagery gives it an atmosphere of the marvelous, and therefore it becomes extremely fascinating to the senses. Metaphysics, however, does not aim to appeal directly to the senses nor does it produce mere phenomena. On the contrary, metaphysics appeals directly to the superior understanding, and its purpose is to develop worth, greatness and superiority in man.

Those persons who live habitually in the metaphysical attitude have a wholesome, healthful appearance. They are bright, happy, contented, and they look clean. They are thoroughly alive, but in their expression of life there is a deep calmness that indicates extraordinary power and the high attainment of real harmony. We realize, therefore, why it is only in the metaphysical attitude that we can secure the best use of the mind.

The metaphysical attitude is rich in thoughts and ideas of worth. Such ideas are always constructive, and when applied will invariably promote practical and tangible advancement. To entertain pure metaphysical thought is to grow in the power to create higher thought and also to grow in the conscious realization of the real, thereby eliminating imperfect conditions of mind, thought or personality by resolving the mind in the consciousness of the unconditioned.

Metaphysics deals fundamentally with the understanding of the principle of absolute reality, that is, that complete something that underlies all things, permeates all things and surrounds all things. It deals with the all that there is in the world of fact and reality, and we can readily understand that the mind must aim to deal with the all if its use is to be the best. In other words the best use of the mind naturally implies that use of the mind that gives the highest, the largest and the most comprehensive application of everything there is in the mind. And this the metaphysical attitude invariably tends to do.

The understanding of the principle of absolute reality, that is the soul, so to speak, of all that is real, also reveals the great truth that all individual expressions of life have their source in the perfect state of being, and that the growth of the individual mind in the consciousness of this perfect state of being will cause that same perfection of being to be expressed more and more in the personal man. The term "perfection," however, in this sense implies that state of being that is all that it can be now, and that is so much that nothing in the present state of being can be added.

We all seek perfection, that is, that state where the mind realizes in itself those ideals that are discerned as possibilities within itself; and this form of perfection the metaphysical attitude has the power to produce in any mind at any time. In fact to enter the metaphysical attitude is to give higher and higher degrees of this perfection to every power, every faculty, every function and every talent in human life.

There are various methods for producing the metaphysical attitude, but the better way is to give the first attention to the development of a metaphysical sense; that is, to train the mind to think more and more of that state of consciousness wherein the perfection of the real is the one predominating factor. When this sense is awakened each mind will find its own best methods. The majority, however, have this sense and need only to place it in action. To give full action to the metaphysical sense we should aim to discern the absolutely real that is within everything of which the mind can be conscious. We should try to carry out this aim in connection with every process of thought, especially those processes that involve the exercise of the imagination.

3. WHAT DETERMINES MENTAL ACTION

EVERY FORCE and faculty in the mind has a tendency to act in a certain way, to move in a certain direction and to produce certain results. It is evident, therefore, that when we control the tendencies of the mind we may determine the actions of the mind and also what results those actions will naturally produce. In addition we may determine whether we are to go forward or backward, towards inferiority or superiority. To control mental tendencies we must control that from which tendencies arise, and all tendencies are born of desires. But desires can be made to order or eliminated, as we may decide.

We are all familiar with the fact that it is not an easy matter to stop "when we get a-going" in any particular direction. For this reason we should direct our movements in the right direction before we begin. And to learn in what direction we are moving we shall only have to examine the tendencies of the mind. When any tendency is established the mind will act unconsciously in that direction and will carry out the desires involved.

In this connection it is highly important to understand that the creative forces in the mind invariably obey and follow tendencies, and always go with those tendencies that have the greatest intensities and the most perfect concentration. When you think that you should like to have this or that you establish a mental tendency to create a desire for that particular thing. And that desire may become uncontrollable, so that, although the tendency comes from a desire that you could control, it may create a desire that you cannot control. Every tendency that is formed in the mind has a tendency to multiply and reproduce itself because an impression is energy centralized, and creative desire always appears with such centralizations. When the tendency of an impression to produce itself is permitted that tiny impression may become a powerful mental state and may become so strong that all other states in mind will have to obey. Under such circumstances the man himself will become more and more like that particular state of mind, which fact explains a great many mysteries in human character that have heretofore seemed beyond comprehension.

Some people are exact externalizations of a single predominating mental state while others form their personalities from a group of mental states. But since every mental state originated in some tiny impression, we understand what may become of us when we permit every impression to follow its natural tendency. Every large object, physical or metaphysical, has a tendency to draw all smaller objects into its own path, and also to make all things in its atmosphere like unto itself. This, however, is partly prevented by counteracting tendencies, though the law is an important one and should be thoroughly understood.

In the metaphysical world the understanding of this law is especially important in the building of character and in the development of talents. If you have good character it means that the strongest tendencies of mind are wholesome, elevating and righteous in their nature, while if your character is weak there is not one elevating tendency that is strong enough to predominate in the world of conduct. A perverted character is always the result of descending tendencies with the ascending tendencies too insignificant to exercise and influence.

The fact that weak characters as well as perverted characters sometimes perform noble acts, and that the finest characters sometimes degrade themselves, is readily explained by the law of mental tendencies. In the first case the better tendencies are permitted occasionally to act without interference, while in the second case we find degrading tendencies arising temporarily, possibly through the influence of suggestion. These adverse tendencies, however, could not have exercised any power over conduct had the strong, ascending tendencies been active. But the strongest tendencies may at times be inactive, and it is at these times that a good man may fall, and the other kind show acts of goodness.

When you think more of the external things of life than that which is within, you create in consciousness a tendency to dwell on the surface. The result is you become superficial in proportion and finally become much inferior to what you were. On the other hand, when you think much of those things that are lofty and profound you create in consciousness a tendency to penetrate the deeper things in life. And the result is you become conscious of a larger world of thought, thereby increasing your mental capacity as well as placing yourself in a position where you may make valuable discoveries or formulate ideas of worth.

When you place questionable pictures before minds that are not established in purity, you create in those minds a tendency to immoral desire, and if those tendencies are continued such desires may become too strong to be controlled, and the victims will seek gratification even at the risk of life. This illustrates how powerful a mental tendency may become and how easily a wrong tendency may be produced when we do not exercise full control over those impressions that may enter the mind.

That man who thinks a great deal about spotless virtue and keeps the idea of virtue constantly before attention will soon create such a strong tendency to virtue that all desires and feelings will actually become virtuous. In consequence it will be simplicity itself for such a person to be virtuous, for when you are virtuous you do not have to try to be. You do not have to resist or fight desires which you do not want because all your desires have become tendencies towards clean and wholesome living. Your energies do not create grosser feelings anymore, but have been trained to create vitality, energy, force and power instead.

Here we should remember that when the predominating tendencies of mind are towards virtue all creative energies will become constructive, and will build up body and mind instead of being dissipated through some desire that is not even normal.

Another illustration of mental tendency and how mental tendency determines mental action is found in the man who is ambitious. Through the efforts of that ambition he is daily training all the tendencies of the mind to act upon the faculties needed to carry out his plans, and he is in consequence building up those faculties with the added force and nourishment thus accumulated. This proves that whenever you resolve to accomplish certain things you will certainly succeed in proportion to your ability. But by resolve we do not mean mere mental spurts. A resolve to be genuine must be constant, and must never waver in the strength of its force and determination. The reason why such a resolve must eventually win is found in the study of mental tendencies; that is, in the realization of the fact that we go as our tendencies go, where we directed them in their first stages.

When we think a great deal about the refined side of life we create tendencies that will cause all the forces within us to recreate everything in our systems according to a more refined pattern. Therefore, to be refined will ere long become second nature, provided we keep constantly before our minds the highest idea of refinement that we can mentally picture. This illustrates how the control of mental tendency may absolutely change an individual from the most ordinary state of grossness to the highest state of refinement.

A striking illustration of the power of mental tendency is found in connection with the belief of the average mind that the body decays and grows old. For this reason we find in practically all human personalities a tendency to produce decay and age in the body. And this tendency is actually bringing about decay and old age where there would be no such conditions whatever were the tendency absent. Nature renews your body every few months and there is no natural process of decay in your system. If your system decays, you yourself have created the process of decay, either through mental or physical violation of natural laws, and by permitting those violations to become permanent tendencies.

If there is a process in your system that makes you look older every year, that process is a false one. It is not placed there by nature. You yourself have produced it by perpetuating the tendency to get older, a tendency that invariably arises from the belief that we must get older. The tendency to become weaker in body and mind as the years go by is also a creation of your own. It is not natural to become weaker with the passing of years. On the contrary, it is natural to become stronger the longer you live, and it is just as easy for you to create a tendency to become stronger the longer you live as it is to create the reverse. In like manner you can also create the tendency to become more attractive in personality, more powerful in mind, stronger in character and more beautiful in soul the longer you live.

However, we must eliminate all detrimental tendencies of the mind, and to do so we must find their origin. In many instances we are born with these adverse tendencies although many of them are acquired later in life. Those tendencies with which we are born generally become stronger and stronger through our own tendency to follow the groove in which we are placed. We find, therefore, that it is always a mistake to live in a groove or to continue year after year to do a certain thing in the same usual way. Our object should be to break bounds constantly and to improve upon everything. Nothing is more important than change, provided every change is a constructive change.

Every impression that we form in the mind is a seed which may grow a tendency. Therefore we should not only eliminate all such impressions as we refuse to cultivate, but we should also prevent inferior and perverse impressions from entering the mind in the first place. To do this, however, we must be constantly on watch so that nothing can enter the mind through our senses which we do not wish to possess and perpetuate.

When we see people growing old, or rather becoming old through the operation of certain false tendencies, the impression of an aging process will stamp itself upon our minds if we permit it. Such impressions contain the tendency to produce the same aging process in us and it usually receives our permission to have its way. Thus we cause the aging process to become stronger and stronger in us the more we see it in others until we soon discover that we are actually creating for ourselves older bodies every year. The new bodies that nature gives us every year are thus made to look older than the new bodies of the year before, which is a direct violation of natural law. Then we also sing with much feeling about the death and decay that is everywhere about us, and entertain thoughts of a similar nature by the wholesale. But all these indications of death and decay in our environments were not produced by nature. They were produced by false mental tendencies which arose through false belief about life and human nature.

The same is true regarding all other adverse tendencies that may exist in us or in those with whom we associate. When we see the action of those tendencies in others we receive impressions upon our own minds that have it in them to produce the same tendencies in us, which will later bring about the same adverse consequences in us. Therefore we must not permit our minds to be impressed with anything in our environment that is contrary to what is true in the perfect nature of man. In other words, we must never permit any mental impression that comes from the weak, the adverse or the wrong conditions about us, but we should permit all things that are good and constructive to impress our minds more and more deeply every day.

We have been in the habit of thinking that various things were natural and inevitable because we see them everywhere about us, but when we discover that we have made a great many of these things ourselves and that they are all wrong, and that it is just as easy to make them different, we conclude that it is time to begin all over again. But to begin, we must transform all the tendencies of the mind so that all of them will move in the way we wish to go.

We may wish to enter health, but if there are tendencies to disease in our systems, and especially in the subconscious, our physical bodies will evolve more or less disease every year. Therefore this tendency must be changed to one of health before we can have what we desire in this respect. In other words, every action in the human system must be a health producing action and such will be the case when all the tendencies of the system have perfect health as their goal. The same is true regarding all other desires, tendencies or objects we may have in view.

The first question, therefore, to ask is this:

Where am I going? or rather, Where are the tendencies of my mind going? Are those tendencies moving towards sin, sickness, decay, weakness and failure, or are they moving towards the reverse? We must look at ourselves closely and learn whether those tendencies are moving where we wish to go, or moving towards conditions that we know to be wrong or detrimental. And when we find where these tendencies are moving we must proceed to change them if they are wrong, and this we can do by producing right mental tendencies in their stead.

When we look at the tendencies of our mind we can largely determine what our own future is to be, provided we do not change those tendencies later on. Then when we know that our present physical conditions, our present strength, our present ability, our present character, our present attainments and our present achievements are all the consequences of the way our mental tendencies have been moving, and also that we have lived, thought and acted according to those tendencies when we know these things, we shall have found knowledge of priceless value, and by applying that knowledge we can make our own future as we wish it to be.

The question is, whether are we drifting, not physically but mentally, because it is the way we drift mentally that determines both the actions of the mind and the actions of the body. And our mental tendencies answer this question. As they go, so do we. What we are creating, what we are building, what we are developing these things depend upon how the tendencies of the mind are directed. Therefore the proper course to pursue is to determine where we wish to go, in what direction and when. Then establish in mind what we wish to accomplish and how soon.

Know what you want and what you want to be. Then examine all the tendencies of your mind. All those which are not going the way you want to go must be changed, while all those that are already going your way should be given more and more power. Then do not waver in your purpose. Never look back, let nothing disturb your plans, and keep your highest aspirations too sacred to be mentioned.

You will find that if you will pursue this course you will go where you wish to go, you will achieve what you have planned, and your destiny will be as you desire.

4. THE LEADING METAPHYSICAL LAW

WHATEVER ENTERS the consciousness of man will express itself in the personality of man. This is one of the most important of all the laws of life, and when its immense scope is fully comprehended thousands of perplexing questions will be answered. We shall then know why we are as we are and why all things about us are as they are; and we shall also know how all this can be changed. When we examine the principle upon which this law is based we find that our environments are the results of our actions and our actions are the results of our thoughts. Our physical and mental conditions are the results of our states of mind and our states of mind are the results of our ideas. Our thoughts are mental creations patterned after the impressions that exist in consciousness and our ideas are the mental conceptions that come from our conscious understanding of life. Thus we realize that everything existing both in the mental field and in the personality, as well as in surrounding conditions, have their origin in that which becomes active in human consciousness.

We may define consciousness by stating that it is an attribute of the Ego through which the individual knows what is and what is taking place. Consciousness may usually be divided into three phases, the objective, the subjective and the absolute. Through absolute consciousness the Ego discerns its relationship with the universal that phase of consciousness that is beyond the average mind and need not necessarily be considered in connection with this law. Through subjective consciousness the Ego knows what is taking place within itself, that is, within the vast field of individuality. And through objective consciousness the Ego knows what is taking place in its immediate external world. Objective consciousness employs the five external senses, while subjective consciousness employs all those finer perceptions which, when grouped together are sometimes spoken of as the sixth sense.

In our study of this law we shall deal principally with subjective consciousness because it is this consciousness that rules over real interior action. The subjective plane is the plane of change and growth so that there can be no change in any part of life until the cause of the desired change has been found or produced in the subjective. What enters objective consciousness will not produce any effect upon the personality unless it also enters subjective consciousness, because it is only what becomes subjective that reproduces itself in the human entity.

In our present state of existence the center of conscious action is largely in the subconscious mind, that is, the interior or finer mental field, and in consequence all the actions of consciousness are directly connected with the subjective. In this connection it is well to state that the terms subjective and subconscious mean practically the same. Whatever enters consciousness and is deeply felt will impress itself upon the subjective so therefore in order to control the results of this law we must avoid giving deep feelings to such impressions, thoughts, ideas or desires as we do not wish to have reproduced in ourselves. There are many impressions and experiences that enter objective consciousness to a degree, but never become subjective since they are not accompanied with depth of feeling. We may be conscious of such experiences or impressions, but we are not affected by them. For this reason we need not give them our attention, which is well because the majority of the impressions that enter the conscious mind pass off, so to speak, without affecting life in any way.

Whatever actually enters consciousness is always felt by the finer sensibilities of mind, and whatever enters into the finer state of mind is taken up by the creative energies; and impressions are accordingly produced. From these impressions will come similar expressions, and it is such expressions that determine thought, character, conduct and life. To state this law in a slightly different manner we may state that whatever enters subjective consciousness will produce an impression just like itself, and every subjective impression becomes a pattern for thought creation while it lasts. Therefore whenever an impression is formed in the mind, thoughts will be created just like that impression. And so long as that impression remains in subjective consciousness thought will continue to be formed after its likeness. Then we must remember that every thought created in the mind goes out into the personality, producing vital and chemical effects according to its nature.

Thus we understand the process of the law.

First, the impression is formed upon subjective consciousness. Second, the creative energies of the mind will produce thoughts and mental states just like those impressions, and all such thoughts and mental states will express themselves in the personality, producing conditions in the personality similar to their own nature. To illustrate this process from everyday life we may mention several experiences with which we are all familiar.

When you view a very peaceful scene and become wholly absorbed in it your entire being will become perfectly serene almost at once, and this is the reason: The scene was peaceful and produced a peaceful impression upon your mind. This impression entered your subjective consciousness because you became deeply absorbed in the scene. If you had simply viewed the scene in a superficial way you would have felt no change because then the impression would not have entered your subjective mind; but you responded to the impressions that entered the mind through the organ of sight and thus admitted those impressions into the deeper or subjective state. In other words, the scene actually entered into your consciousness, the serenity of it all was impressed upon the subjective; and as explained in the process above, the creative energies of your mind at once began to create thoughts and mental states containing the same serene and peaceful life. These thoughts entered into your entire personality, as all thoughts do after being created, thus conveying the life of peace to every atom in your being.

When you view an exciting scene and are carried away by it you lose your poise and may even become uncontrollable. The reason is you admit confusion into your mind, and according to the law, confusion will be produced in yourself; that is, discord has entered your consciousness and has become the model for the creative processes of the mind. The mental energies will enter such states and create thoughts and mental states that are just AS confused as the confusion you saw in the without. And when these confused states go out into the personality, as they do almost at once, your entire nervous system will be upset, disturbed and in a state of inharmony. Thus you have produced the same confusion in your own mind and body that you saw in your environments. However, if you had prevented the confused scenes from entering your mind, you would have been perfectly calm in the midst of it all; but by permitting the excitement to enter your consciousness it was reproduced in yourself, and the discord that entered your consciousness from the without was thereby expressed in your own personality.

There may be indications of threatening failure in your work and you may begin to fear that such failure will come, but so long as you do not feel the inner dread of failure the impression of failure will not enter your consciousness; and accordingly conditions of failure will not be produced in your own mind. But if the fear continues until you actually feel fearful deep down in your heart, the idea of failure has entered your consciousness, and if not prevented will be deeply impressed in the subjective.

When failure is impressed upon your subjective mind, a condition of mental failure will permeate all your faculties, and in consequence they will fail to do their best. And we all know very well that the very moment our faculties begin to go back on us, doing less work and less effective work, we are on the down grade to failure and loss. Failure means going down to the lesser, and if you have admitted thoughts of failure into your mind you have given your creative energies bad models. These energies will create thoughts and mental states just like those models, no matter what those models may be. If those models are based upon the idea of failure all the thoughts created will contain the failing attitude, or the losing ground attitude. When such thoughts express themselves in the system they will produce weakening conditions and disturbances everywhere in mind and personality. Your faculties will not be able to do their best; they will begin to fail in their work because they are being permeated with a losing ground tendency, and you will make many mistakes on account of the increasing confusion. The result will be inevitable failure unless you are able to check this tendency or retrace your steps upward before it is too late. We have all noticed that the man on the down grade makes more mistakes than anyone else, and also that his genius or his talents become weaker the further down he goes. The above explains the reason why. We are all familiar with the folly of judging from appearances and permitting temporary conditions to impress and govern our thinking, the reason being that our object is not to follow the whims of circumstances or the uncertainties of fate, but to carry out our purpose in life regardless of what happens. On the other hand when we do not judge according to external indications, but proceed to impress the subconscious mind with the determination to succeed, we are placing in consciousness an idea that stands for growth, advancement and increase. Immediately the creative energies of mind will proceed to create thoughts and states that have advancing, upbuilding and constructive tendencies. Such thoughts will give push, power, life and added talent to your faculties, and you will very soon begin to do better work; the superior forces will build up your mind, make your mind more brilliant, and add constantly to your capacity. Thus you will become a success within yourself; that is, your own forces and faculties will begin to work successfully which is the first essential to the gaining of success in the external world. You will be moving forward in your own being and you will be gaining in worth in every respect. The results will be better work, better impressions upon the world, and fewer mistakes. And when the world discovers that there is success in you they will want your service with recompense according to your full worth. When we understand this process of the mind we realize how we can bring upon ourselves almost anything simply through permitting the corresponding impressions to enter consciousness. Therefore we should learn to prevent all such things from entering consciousness as we do not wish to see reproduced in ourselves and expressed through our personality. Then we should learn to impress permanently in consciousness the image and likeness of all those things that we do wish to develop and express.

The workings of this law are very well illustrated in conditions of heath and disease, because when we are constantly thinking about disease and fearing disease we permit the idea of disease to impress itself upon consciousness. In other words, we become more and more conscious of disease, and cause the image of sickness to get a firm foothold in the subjective. The result is that the creative forces of mind will create thoughts, mental states and conditions just like the image of disease, and that which is just like the image of disease actually is a disease. Therefore since every mental state conveys conditions similar to itself to every part of the body, such thoughts will constantly carry diseased conditions into the body, tending thereby to produce the very ailment that we feared, thought of, or impressed upon consciousness in the first place. Nature may resist these adverse conditions for a while if the body is full of vitality, but when the vital forces run low these sickly mental conditions will have full sway, and the result will be a siege of illness which may be prolonged, and even result in death, which happens thousands of times under just such conditions.

The law, however, works both ways. We can just as easily impress the idea of perfect health upon subjective consciousness and thus give the creative forces a better image as a model for their creative processes. At such times all thoughts and mental states will be wholesome and health producing, and will constantly carry better health, more harmony and greater strength to the body. This is how the law works, and as anyone can understand the process, further details are not required. Briefly stated, the law is this: That everything entering subjective consciousness will impress itself there and become a pattern for the creative energies of the mind. These energies will proceed to create thoughts and conditions just like the impression formed, which will carry their own conditions to every part of the human system.

In this way conditions are produced and expressed in the personality just like the original idea, thought or impression that entered subjective consciousness. Everything that enters the mind through the various senses may also enter subjective consciousness, that is, if deeply felt, and thus produce a permanent impression. In like manner, all our own concepts of things will become impressions, that is, if they are inner convictions. For this reason we must not only watch all those things that enter the mind through the senses, but we must also govern our own thinking so that every mental conception formed will be one of quality, worth, wholeness, health, growth and advancement.

To employ this law properly nothing must be permitted to enter the subjective unless we wish to have it reproduced in ourselves. We should refuse therefore to take into consciousness that which we do not wish to see expressed through mind or body. We should train consciousness to respond only to those external impressions that are desirable; and we should v train our own imaging faculties to impress deeply and permanently in consciousness every good thing or desirable quality that we wish to see reproduced in ourselves and expressed through our personality.

5. HOW THE MIND MAKES THE MAN

MAN GRADUALLY grows into the likeness of that which he thinks of the most. This is another important metaphysical law, and is so closely related to the law presented in the preceding chapter that the analysis given for one will naturally explain the process of the other. However, this second law is distinct from the first one in many of its phases, and it is so full of possibility that the understanding of its application opens up a vast world of change and attainment along a number of lines.

Man is the reflection of all his thought; that is, his body, his character, his mind, his spiritual nature all are fashioned according to his thought; even the elements that compose the flesh of his body are gross or fine just as his thought happens to be. Whenever we think a great deal of the material, most of our thoughts will become material in their nature and will carry material conditions to every part of the system. This explains why gross thoughts stamp grossness upon every fiber of the body, while refined thought refines every fiber, improving the quality and perfecting the structure.

The mind that thinks a great deal of the perfection of the Supreme will think a great deal of divine qualities and spiritual attainments. In brief, nearly all the thought created in such a mind will be of a superior nature and will carry superiority to every part of the system. When we think more of the spiritual than we do of other things the entire system will constantly pass through a refining and spiritualizing process, the possibility of which if carried on to the ultimate would be nothing less than marvelous. When we think a great deal of power, ability and attainment we are actually creating a great deal of ability in us. We are increasing our power and we are moving forward into far greater attainments.

The mind that thinks constantly of perfect health refusing to entertain for a moment the thought of disease is steadily growing into a state of health that will ere long be absolutely perfect. Such a person may be suffering from a score of maladies now, but all of them must pass away before the constant influx of health, wholeness and life. All darkness must finally vanish from a place that is constantly being filled with more and more light. In like manner any condition that may exist in the person of man will have to change and improve if the person is constantly being filled with a superior condition.

We become like the thoughts we think because the creative power of thought is the only creative power that we have within us. And the energies of mind are constantly creating; and what they create now is just like the thoughts we think now. Since every physical condition, every mental state, and every phase of character since all these things are fashioned after our predominating thoughts, and since the capacity of every faculty and the quality of every talent are determined by the thoughts we think, we must naturally conclude that there can be no greater art than the art of correct thinking.

In fact, to think is to occupy a position involving far greater responsibility than that of a thousand absolute monarchs. And when we realize this, we will not permit a single thought to take shape and form in our minds without first determining upon the value of that thought.

Why we grow into the likeness of that of which we think the most has been fully explained in the preceding chapter, and it is found in the fact that every impression formed in the mind will reproduce its kind and express its creations throughout the entire system. And though these impressions usually come from without in the first place, still they do not become real impressions until we accept them into our consciousness, or in thought, or in conviction. That is, many minds will think only what is suggested to them by environment, or what they are told to think by those in authority; still it is their own thought that shapes their lives.

Wherever the suggestion may come from, it is your thought about that suggestion that produces the effect.

The analysis of thought presented in the preceding chapter explains how the person is affected by thought, and how thought is always created in the likeness of those ideas, states or impressions that have established themselves in consciousness. But to carry this analysis to its final goal we must discover why man becomes like his thought and also how he can think thought of a superior nature. And this we discover through the workings of the law now under consideration. In the first place man becomes like his thought because there is no other pattern in his being besides his own thought. The creative forces of his mind and personality always create according to the image and likeness of the strongest and deepest impressions in consciousness, and all such impressions are produced by the process of thinking.

When we use the term "thought," however, we may refer either to the mental model, which is the result of mental conception, or we may refer to that thought which is the result of mental creation. The mental creation is patterned after the mental conception, and the mental conception is the result of our efforts to understand what we are thinking about. Mental conception is conscious and is therefore under our control, while mental creation is subconscious and is therefore beyond our control; but we do not have to control mental creation. Those creations will be just like our mental conceptions; therefore when we form only such mental conceptions as we like we shall have only such mental creations as we like. In consequence when we see mentally that which is superior and can form a true conception of what we see, we give to the creative energies a model that is higher than any we have given them before. Accordingly the mental creations will be superior.

And here we should remember that these creations are not wholly abstract, but are in most instances as concrete or tangible as the body itself. The creative energies of the human system act both in the mind and in the body, though their central field of action is always in the subjective or inner side of things. In the body these energies constitute the vital forces and the nerve forces of the system, while in the mind they constitute all those energies or powers employed in thought, feeling or mental action of whatever nature.

When we examine these energies we find that they do not simply create conditions after the likeness of the predominating thought, but that they themselves also become just like the predominating thought, which fact illustrates the power exercised by such thoughts as hold the ruling position in our minds. From this fact we conclude that these forces states of the mind. So, that if there is anything wrong in the subjective states of the mind these forces will convey those wrong conditions to the body, the reason being that these forces come from the subjective and cannot be different from the ruling conditions of their source.

The fibers and cells of the body are built up by these energies. Therefore the quality as well as the structures of the cells must correspond with the nature of the creative energies at the time. These energies build cells just like the patterns before them, and the patterns are formed by the subjective conceptions. When that part of the subjective mind that governs cell structures in the body becomes imbued with a more perfect idea of construction the creative energies will build more perfect cells. And when that part of the subjective mind that governs physical shape and form receives a better conception of shape and form, these creative energies will naturally build a body that is more perfect as to shape and form. Every function in the body is governed by a certain part of the subjective mind and the creative energies act through that particular function according to the present state of the subjective mind.

Therefore when more perfect patterns are placed in .those parts of the subjective that govern the body, the creative energies will build a more perfect body. And when we know that these creative energies are building us a new body every year, according to the predominating pattern of the subjective, we can see how easily the new body we receive every year can be made more perfect if we will improve the subjective pattern. The creative energies construct brain cells in the same way, the quality being governed by the state of mind. And that part of the brain that is to receive the largest group of cells is determined by the tendencies of the mind.

In the world of talents and faculties the creative energies construct concepts so that every talent is actually composed of all the conceptions that the mind has formed while trying to understand the nature and possibility of that talent. In the formation of character the creative energies do their work in constructing desires, motives, purposes and the like. And in every instance they form these characteristics according to the predominating thought on the subject. In the construction of the spiritual attitudes and higher attainments the process is very similar though in these instances the pattern is gained through faith instead of subjective mentation.

Why man grows into the likeness of that which he thinks of the most becomes perfectly clear when we understand how the creative energies work; that is, that they always create after the likeness of the subjective pattern. And when we learn that the subjective pattern can be changed in any part of mind by thinking a great deal of a higher conception of that particular phase, we have the whole secret. When we think a great deal along any line with a higher conception before us we finally establish that higher conception in the place of the old one. When we hold an idea in mind a long time that idea will become a predominating idea; it will become larger and stronger than the other ideas and will consequently be selected as a model by the creative energies.

The next question before us is how to think only of those things that we desire to grow into the likeness of. And this question is answered through the following metaphysical law: Man thinks the most both consciously and unconsciously of that which he loves the best. The simplest way to govern thought is to do so through love. When we love the lofty and the noble we naturally think a great deal of those qualities without trying to do so, and in consequence we become more noble in thought, character and motives. If we wish to develop the greater and the higher within us we must love everything that contains greatness, and our love must be with the whole heart: that is, every fiber of our being must actually thrill with a passion for that higher something which we desire to develop.

Here we must remember that all intellectual or metaphysical methods for the development of talents or character, or anything of a superior nature within us, will fail unless we passionately love superior attainments. The man who loves honesty, justice and virtue will become honest, just and virtuous; though if he does not naturally love those things no amount of moral training can change his character. Millions of people are praying to become better, more noble and more spiritual, but too many fail to receive answers to such prayers. And the reason why is found in the fact that they do not love as deeply as they should those superior attainments for which they are praying. They may desire those things in a superficial way, but that is not sufficient. Real love alone will avail because such love goes to the very depth of life and touches the very essence of being itself.

When we, as a race, will begin to love the superior and the divine with the same depth that we love gold or material pleasures, we shall become a superior race. When we love divine qualities with the whole heart we shall think a great deal of such qualities and the more we will try to understand the inner nature of those qualities. The higher this understanding becomes the higher will our conception of the divine and the spiritual become. And the higher those conceptions are the higher will be our thoughts. And since the outer man is fashioned after the ruling thoughts of his mind, we shall in this way steadily rise in the scale of life until we become in mind and personality like those higher thoughts we have learned to think. In other words, we shall manifest in the without more and more of the divinity that is within. And that such a process would in time transform humanity into a superior race anyone can readily understand.

Love, however, is not mere sentiment, nor is it ordinary emotionalism. Love also has quality. There is ordinary love and there are the higher forms of quality. Therefore, the love with which we love must be developed into greater worth if we are to penetrate the realms of worth through our love. The reason why we naturally think the most about what we like the best is found in the fact that there can be no division in love. When you actually love something that something will receive your undivided attention. And as all your thought goes where your attention is directed you will in this manner give all your thought both consciously and unconsciously to that which you love. This we all know from our own personal experience, and we shall find that everybody has had the same experience, thus proving universally the absoluteness of this law.

We have all seen people become beautiful in countenance and character after they had begun to love some high and noble purpose. And we can find thousands who have become more and more common because they have continued to love the ordinary. By living the ordinary they naturally became like the ordinary thus their mental actions became inferior, and both mind and personality became inferior in proportion. The elements of the body may be in a low state of action and express grossness, or they may be in a high state of action and express refinement; and the state of the mind determines what those actions are to be, whether they are to be crude or refined. The low, common mind invariably gives sluggish or crude actions to the system, and in such a person the physical form looks very much like ordinary clay. But a lofty mind, a mind that is living in the ideal and the beautiful, and in the realization of the marvelous possibilities of mind, gives highly refined actions to the body; and such a body will naturally be superior in fineness, quality and substance. It is therefore true that there are people who are made of a finer clay; not because they have come from so-called noble ancestors, but because their thoughts have become beautiful, lofty and high.

The attitude of love towards all that is superior should be cultivated with the greatest enthusiasm, and the love itself should also be made superior as we advance in the realization of true worth. It is in this way that we shall find the true path and the simple path to high thinking, noble thinking and right thinking. And man grows into the likeness, steadily and surely, of that which he thinks of the most.

Since we think the most of what we love the best we should love passionately all that is beautiful and sublime; we should love all that is lofty and ideal; we should love the true side, the superior side and the genuine side in all persons and in all things.

But we should never think of the inferior at any time. We should love the perfect, the divine and the spiritual in every soul in existence, and give the whole heart to the love of the sublime qualities of the Supreme. Thus we shall find that body, mind and soul will respond to the perfect thought that we thus form while living on the mental heights. Gradually we shall find all the elements of our nature changing for the better, becoming more and more like those sublime states of mind of which we are so vividly conscious while on the heights.

6. HOW MENTAL PICTURES BECOME REALITIES

EVERY THOUGHT is patterned after the mental image that predominates at the time the thought is created. This is another great metaphysical law and its importance is found in the fact that thoughts are things, that every thought produces an effect on mind and body, and that the effect is always similar to the cause. According to these facts we can therefore produce any effect desired upon mind or body by producing the necessary thought or mental state, so that when we have learned to control our thinking we can control practically everything else in life, because in the last analysis it is thinking that constitutes the one great cause in the life of the individual.

To control thinking, however, we must understand the process of thought creation. To think is to create thought, and to control thinking is to create any thought we like at any time and under any circumstance. When we analyze the process of thinking we find three factors involved; that is, the pattern, the mental substance and the creative energy. The pattern is always the deepest impression, the clearest image, or the predominating idea.

The quality of the mental substance improves with the quality of the mind; and the quantity increases with the expansion of consciousness, while the creative energies grow stronger the less energy we lose and the more we awaken the greater powers from within.

When an idea or image is impressed upon the mind the mental energies will proceed to create thought just like that image; and will continue while that image occupies a permanent position in consciousness. When the mind is very active a great deal of thought is created every second, though the amount varies with the activity of the mind. It is therefore more detrimental for an active mind to think wrong thought than for a mind that is dull or stupid; proving the fact that responsibility always increases as we rise in the scale. It is the function of the creative energies of the mind to create thought that is just like every image impressed upon mind and to continue to create thought in the likeness of that image while it lasts. The creative energies do this of their own accord and we cannot stop them. But we can make them weak or strong, or give them better patterns.

Mind is an art gallery of many pictures, but only the most prominent are selected for models in thought creation. Only those pictures that are sufficiently distinct to be seen by consciousness without special effort are brought before the creative energies as patterns. We thus find that the art of controlling one's thinking and the power to determine what kind of thought is to be created is acquired largely through the training of the mind to impress deeply only such mental pictures as are desired as models for thinking. The law, however, is very simple because as the picture in the mind happens to be at this moment so will also be the thoughts created at this moment, and the mental pictures are in each case the ideas and impressions that we permit in mind.

Whatever enters the mind through the senses can impress the mind, and the result will be a picture or mental image which will become a pattern for the creative energies. What takes shape and form in your mind through your own interior thinking will also impress the mind and become an image or pattern. It is therefore possible through this law to determine what kind of thoughts you are to create by impressing your mind with your own ideas regardless of what environment may suggest to you through your senses. And it is by exercising this power that you place the destiny of body, mind and soul absolutely in your own hands.

As we proceed with this process we find another vital law which may be stated as follows: What we constantly picture upon the mind we shall eventually realize in actual life. This law may be spoken of as a twin sister to the one stated above as they are found to work together in almost every process of thought creation and thought expression. The one declares that all thought is patterned after the predominating mental pictures while the other declares that the entire external life of man is being daily recreated in the likeness of those mental pictures. The fact is, as the mental tendencies are, so is thought; as thought is, so is character; and it is the combined action of character, ability and purpose that determines what we are to attain or accomplish, or what is to happen to us.

Through the law of attraction we naturally meet in the external world what corresponds to our own internal world, that is, to what we are in ourselves. The self constitutes the magnet, and like attracts like. This self which constitutes the magnet is composed of all the active forces, desires, tendencies, motives, states and thoughts that are at work in mind or personality. When we look at everything that is alive throughout our whole being and put all those things together we have what may be termed our present active self. And this self invariably attracts in the external world such conditions as correspond to its own nature. This self and all its parts in the person corresponds to the thoughts that we have been creating in mind. In fact the nature of the self is actually composed of thought, mental states and mental activities. We realize, therefore, that when we change our thought, the nature of the self will change, and this change will be good or otherwise depending upon the change of thought.

Your external life is the exact counterpart of this active self. This self is the exact likeness of your thought, and your thoughts are patterned after the pictures that are impressed upon your mind. Therefore we understand that whatever is pictured in the mind will be realized in external life. And the reason why is not only simply explained but can be proven along strictly scientific lines. However, to determine through the law of mind picturing what our external life is to be, every process of mind picturing which we desire to carry out must be continued for a sufficient length of time to give the creative processes the opportunity to make over the whole self.

When a certain picture is formed in the mind thought will be created in the likeness of that picture. This thought goes out and permeates the entire self and changes the self to a degree. But as a rule it takes some time to change the entire self; therefore we must continue to hold the desired picture in mind until the whole self has been entirely made over and has become just like the ideal picture. And you can easily discern when the self has been wholly changed because as soon as the self is changed everything in your life changes. Then a new self will attract new people, new conditions, new environments, new opportunities and new states of being. It is evident therefore that so long as there is no change in the outer life we may know that the self has not been changed. However, the changing process may be going on, but the new has not as yet become stronger than the old, and for the time being things continue as they were.

When the self has been changed to such an extent that the new becomes positive and the old negative we will begin to attract new things. We may therefore begin to attract new and better things for some time before the entire self has been completely changed. When we are changing only a part of the self that part will begin to attract the new while those parts of the self that have not been changed will continue to attract the old as usual. This explains why some people continue to attract trouble and adversity for a while after they have begun to live a larger and a better life.

In promoting the art of mind picturing we must not change ideas or plans at too frequent intervals for such changes will neutralize what has been gained thus far and here is the place where a great many people fail. The average person who wishes to change his life for the better does not hold on to his ideals long enough; that is, he does not give them a fair chance to work themselves out and bring the expected results. When he does not receive results as soon as he expects he changes his plans and produces new pictures upon the mind. Thus he begins all over again, losing what he had built up through previous plans; but ere long becomes discouraged once more, so tries still other ideas or methods. When our ideals are the highest we know we do not have to change them. They cannot be improved upon until we have so entirely recreated ourselves that we can live in a superior state of consciousness. It is therefore highly important to determine positively upon the ideals that we wish to realize, and to hold on to those ideals until they are realized regardless of what may happen in the meantime.

However, we must not infer that we can realize in the external the correspondence of every picture that we hold in mind, because the majority of the mental pictures that we form are so constituted that they can be worked out in practical action.

We must therefore distinguish between such ideals as can be made practical now and those that are simply temporary dreams, having no connection with real life here and now.

To be realized a mental picture must be constant, but only such pictures can be constant as are sufficiently elaborate to involve a complete transformation in yourself, and that are so high that they can act as an inspiration until all your present ideals are realized. When we form such pictures in the mind and continue to hold on to them until they are externally realized we shall certainly obtain the desired realization. At such times we can proceed with the perfect faith that what we have pictured will become true in actual life in days to come, and those days will not be far away. But to use this law the mind must never waver; it must hitch its wagon to a star and never cut the traces.

In scientific mind picturing it is not necessary to go into minor details, though we must not be too general. The idea is to picture all the essentials, that is, all those parts that are distinct or individualized. But we need not include such things as are naturally attracted by the essentials. In other words, apply the law, and that which will naturally come through the application of that law, will be realized.

If you wish to realize a more perfect body it is not necessary to picture the exact physical appearance of that body. You may not know at present what a perfect body should look like. Therefore picture only the quality of perfection in every part of the physical form and those qualities will develop and express themselves more and more throughout your personality. And if you wish to enter a different environment do not give your thought to some special locality, nor to persons and things that would necessarily be included in such an environment. Persons come and go and things are generally the way we wish them to be.

To proceed realize what constitutes an ideal environment and hold that picture in your mind. In analyzing an ideal environment we would find it to contain harmony, beauty, love, peace, joy, desirable opportunities, advantages, ideal friends, wholesome conditions and an abundance of the best of everything that the welfare of human life may require. Therefore we should picture those things and continue to hold them in mind with the faith that we will soon find an environment containing all those things in the highest degree of perfection. Gradually we shall find more and more of them coming into our life until we shall find an environment that comes up in every respect to our ideal.

The law of mind picturing will also be found effective in changing physical conditions. Any physical malady must eventually disappear if we continue to hold in mind a perfect picture of health and wholeness. Many have eliminated chronic ailments in a few weeks and even in a few days by this method, and all would succeed if they never pictured disease but perfect health only. In the field of achievement we will find the same facts to hold good. Whenever we fear that we shall not succeed we bring forth the wrong picture thus the wrong thoughts are created and wrong conditions are produced; in consequence the very thing we feared comes upon us. When we are positively determined to succeed, however, we picture the idea of success and attainment upon the mind, and according to the law, success will be realized in external life.

Mental and spiritual attainments respond remarkably to mind picturing, principally because all true mind picturing draws consciousness up into the world of superiority. The same is true in the field of talent. If there is any talent that you wish to develop draw mental pictures of yourself in full possession of that talent and you will comply with the requirements of the steady growth of that talent. This method alone will accomplish much, but when it is associated with our processes of development the results desired will surely be remarkable.

In the building of character, mind picturing is of exceptional importance. If you continue to associate only with impure minds and continue to think only of deeds of darkness you will picture only the wrong upon your mind. Thus your thoughts will become wrong and wrong thoughts lead to wrong actions. The contrary, however, is also true. So therefore if we wish to perfect our conduct we must impress upon the mind only such ideas as will inspire us with desires and aims for greater and higher things.

We all admit that character can be influenced most decidedly by mind pictures, but everybody may not be ready to accept the idea that ability, attainment, achievement, environment and destiny can be affected in the same way. However, it is only a full analysis of the law of mind picturing that is necessary to prove this also to be an exact scientific fact. It is the way we think that determines the quality of the mind, and it is the quality of the mind that determines what our ability, mental capacity and mental force is to be. And we can readily understand that the improvement of ability will naturally be followed by increase in attainment and achievement as well as a greater control over fate and destiny.

Man is constantly increasing his ability, is making his own future and is making that future brighter and greater every day. Therefore, if mind pictures can affect mental quality, mental power and mental ability they can also affect environment and achievement, and in brief, the entire external life of man. In looking for evidence for the fact that mental pictures can affect ability, simply compare results from efforts that are inspired by high ideals and efforts that are inspired by low ideals, and you have all the evidence you need.

When your mind is filled with pictures of superiority you will think superior thoughts – thoughts that have more quality, power and worth – and such thoughts cannot fail to give power, quality and worth to your talents and faculties. We also find that tendencies, desires and motives originate largely from mental pictures, and we also know that these factors exercise an enormous power in life. The active self of man is so dominated by desires and tendencies that it is absolutely impossible to change the self until tendencies and desires are changed. But tendencies and desires as well as motives cannot be changed without changing the mental pictures a fact of extreme importance.

Through scientific mind picturing you can create or eliminate any kind of desire; you can produce or remove any tendency that you like. All that is necessary is to impress upon the mind the perfect picture of a desire or tendency that you wish and then continue to hold that picture in the mind until you have results. A mental picture, however, is not necessarily something that you can see in the same way as you see external, tangible things. It is an impression or idea or concept and is seen only by the understanding. In order to hold a mental picture constantly in mind keep all the essentials of that picture before your attention; that is, try to be conscious of the real nature of those powers and possibilities that are represented by the picture. In other words, enter into the very nature of those qualities which that picture represents.

The mind is very large. It is therefore possible to form mental pictures of as many ideals as we like, but at first it is best to choose only a few.

Begin by picturing a perfect body, an able mind a strong character and a beautiful soul; after that an ideal interior life and an ideal external environment. Thus you have the foundation of a great life, a rich life and a wonderful life. Keep these pictures constantly before your mind in fact, train yourself to actually live for those pictures. And you will find all things in your life changing daily to become more and more like those pictures. In the course of time you will realize in actual life the exact likeness of those pictures; that is, what you have constantly pictured upon your mind you will realize in actual life. Then you can form new and more beautiful pictures to be realized in like manner as you build for a still greater future.

7. THE INCREASE OF MENTAL POWER

ALL MENTAL actions that consciously move towards the within tend to increase the capacity, the power and the quality of mind. The majority of mental actions in the average mind, however, move towards the surface, and this is one reason why advancing years bring mental inferiority as the converse of this law is also true. That is, that all mental actions that move towards the surface will decrease the power of mind.

According to the law of growth the more we use a faculty the larger and stronger and more perfect it should become, provided it is used properly.

Therefore continuous use in itself should invariably bring increase.

However, the use of anything may follow the lines of destruction as well as construction. For this reason we must train all mental actions along constructive lines. And we find all constructive action tends to deepen mental action; in other words, tends to move towards the within.

The value of the increase of mental power is clearly evident along all lines. Everything must increase in the life of him who is perpetually increasing his own personal power. We know that a large mind creates more extensively than a small one. The creations of a highly developed mind are more worthy than the creations of an inferior mind, and the achievements of any one are in proportion to that one's capacity and power. Therefore when we begin to increase the value of life everything pertaining to life as well as everything coming into life will increase also. Perpetual development in ourselves means perpetual increase of everything of worth required in our sphere of existence. This is the law; but so long as mental actions move towards the surface, mentality is diminished; therefore the opposite process must be established.

By training all mental actions to move constantly towards the within we increase perpetually the capacity, the power and the quality of mind and the reason why is very simple. When mental actions move towards the surface consciousness will be centered upon the surface of things and will therefore picture in mind the lesser and inferior side of things. Those mental energies that serve as patterns for the creative energies will in consequence be formed in the likeness of the smaller. And the result is that the mind will be created according to the lesser and more inferior conception of itself.

On the other hand, when all the actions of mind move toward the great within, the eye of the mind will concentrate upon the world of greater possibilities. The conception of things will in such a mental state constantly increase because attention at such times is concerned only with that which is larger and superior. Thus the mental energies will be directed towards the idea of superiority, and the creative energies will naturally rebuild the mind gradually and steadily upon a larger and more perfect scale. This is all very simple and anyone who will examine the workings of his own mind will find it to be absolutely true. We understand therefore how each individual has in his own hands the power to create for himself a greater mind, a more perfect personality, a richer life and a more desirable destiny.

In all methods for mental development this law must be wisely considered for no matter how perfect the method may be, if the mental actions move towards the surface, no results will be gained. While on the other hand, if the mental actions move towards the within results will positively be gained even though the methods be inferior. Nearly all minds in the past that continued to develop through life did so without system, but gained increase through aspiration, or rather concentration upon the greater possibilities of life, which in turn caused mental actions to move towards the within.

When your attention is turned upon the inner and the larger phases of life your mind will begin to turn its actions upon the great within. Accordingly all mental tendencies will begin to move toward superiority, and all the building forces in your life will have superiority as their goal. That you should constantly rise in the scale when thinking and acting in this manner is therefore evident. Remarkable results have been gained and can be gained simply through aspiration, but if a complete system of the best methods are employed in conjunction with the fundamental law, these results will naturally increase to a very great degree. For this reason all things that are conducive to the growth of the mind should be employed in harmony so that the increase of mental power may be gained in the largest possible measure.

To train the mental actions to move towards the within we should concentrate attention upon the greater possibilities of life, and think as deeply and as much as we can upon those possibilities. In fact we should train the mind to look towards the within at all times and view with great expectations those superior states that ere long will be attained. In addition all tendencies of life should be trained to move towards the higher and the larger and every thought should have an ascending spirit.

When you feel that you are becoming too much concerned with the superficial, turn attention at once upon the depths of existence. And when you feel that you have fallen down temporarily into the world of inferiority use every effort at your command to rise again towards the heights. The leading purpose should be to train all the forces, desires, tendencies and actions in life to move upward and onward at all times. This will cause the greater powers and possibilities within to be awakened, which will be followed by the perpetual increase of the capacity, the power and the quality of the mind. And with this increase conies also the increase of everything else in life that is required for our highest welfare.

When this increase of power begins it will naturally be felt in various parts of mind, and in order to know how to make the best possible use of this increase, as well as of the power we already possess, we should remember the great law, that whatever you feel that you can do, that you have the power to do. There are many methods through which we can determine what the mind really can do and what work we may be able to carry out successfully, but this particular law is the best guide of all, provided it is properly understood. And it is extremely important to discover what we are able to do because the majority are not in their true spheres of action.

To be in your true sphere of action means better work, greater results and more abundant good both to yourself and to others with whom you are associated. It also means that you can be at your best at all times and he who is at his best at all times is on the way to perpetual growth and perpetual increase.

To do your best work and your true work you must employ the largest and the strongest faculty that you possess. But to learn what this faculty actually is, this is the problem. This problem can be solved, however, if we live in compliance with the law just mentioned. The power that we possess is always felt, therefore when you feel that you can do a certain thing it means that there is sufficient power in that particular faculty that is required. But a faculty must be large before it can contain enough power to be consciously felt. Consequently the fact that you feel power in a certain faculty proves conclusively that that faculty is large, and is possessed of considerable ability.

From this point on, the question to decide is, where you feel the greatest amount of power because where you feel the most power there you will find the greatest ability. This is conclusive, but here another question arises, that is, if the feeling of the average person is always reliable. The answer is that it is not. But it can be made so with a little training.

All psychologists have come to the conclusion that there is but one sense, the sense of feeling and that all other senses, both in the external and the internal are but modifications of this one sense.

It is also admitted that the sense of feeling can be cultivated along scores of lines where it is now wholly inactive, and that there is no perceptible limit to its development along any line. This being true we shall go to the very foundation of all the senses, and all the modes of discerning things, when we take the sense of feeling for our guide in the selection of that work for which we have the greatest talent and power.

To train the sense of feeling in detecting the exact place in mind where the greatest power resides, the first step is to make this sense normal, which is highly important because the average person has so many artificial desires, and permits the mind to be stimulated by every successful venture that is heard of.

There are a great many people who become aroused with ambition to enter the literary world whenever they learn of remarkable success attained in that world. Thus their energies are temporarily turned upon the literary faculties and they feel considerable power in that part of the mind. This they think is sufficient evidence that they have literary talent and make attempts to get results in such work; but they soon find that the inspiration in that direction did not last and they are compelled to try something else.

Then these people may learn of remarkable success in the business world. They become enthused over the possibilities of commercial ventures and turn their energies in that direction. But they soon find that their commercial faculties are not large enough to carry out their ambitions along this line. In consequence they turn their attention to the next venture that looks promising. There are thousands of minds who are constantly affected in this way, drifting from one thing to another. They imagine that because someone is succeeding in a certain work they may also succeed in that work, provided they have inclinations along that line. They also imagine that they are the very ones to enter every particular field where the demand for great service and great ability is required. The reason is their minds are controlled by appearances and what they feel as the result of the switching of energy here and there from one faculty to another. Such people therefore cannot rely upon the sense of feeling in any line of action because it is seldom normal.

To produce a normal sense of feeling for the purpose in question we should never pay any attention to what others have done or are doing because the success of others proves nothing as far as we are concerned. We must not look at the power of another man's brain, but try to find what there is in our own brains. We should never permit the enthusiasm of others to intoxicate our own minds. We should let others be enthused in their way and we should let them concentrate upon what work they like. But we should not imitate others either in thought, enthusiasm or feeling.

The course to pursue is to watch yourself closely for some weeks or months and try to discover in what faculty you feel the most power. If you feel the greatest power in a certain faculty and in that one only, you may choose that faculty without further examination and give it all your force, energy, ambition and desire, realizing that the application of that faculty will bring the greatest results that you could attain in your life. But if there are several other faculties that seem to be equally strong, wait and watch more closely until you finally discover the seat of the greatest power. When two or more seem to be equally strong, and continue thus under the most rigid self-examination, choose the one that you can use to the best advantage now, and turn all your power for attainment and achievement in that direction.

When there is prolonged uncertainty as to where the greatest amount of power is expressed try to increase the power of every part of your mind by directing the subconscious to express more power from within. The value of this is found in the fact that the greatest amount of power always goes to the largest faculty so that an increase of power will in every case reveal the existence of the leading talent or faculty in your possession.

After you have made the sense of feeling normal so that you can feel the state of your mind as it really is, you can always depend upon the law that whatever you feel that you can do you have the power to do. And you may proceed to act along that line knowing that you will succeed, no matter how difficult the undertaking may seem to be. It is the presence of great power in a certain faculty that makes you feel that you can do things by using that faculty. Therefore when you can feel what faculty is the largest and strongest you know positively what you can do, what you can accomplish and what you should undertake. True, a great deal of training of that strongest faculty may be required, but since the talent, the ability, and the power are there the results must follow when the practical application is made.

8. THE WITHIN AND THE WITHOUT

IT HAS been stated that the average person is nine-tenths environment; that is, nine-tenths of his thoughts, ideas, desires and motives are suggested by environment, or created in the likeness of what he has come in contact with in the outer life; and this is largely true. He is therefore almost wholly patterned after the things that make up his surroundings, and instead of being himself is a reflection of his circumstances. That such a person can master himself and control his destiny is out of the question because we cannot control external things so long as we are almost entirely in the control of those things.

When we analyze this phase of human life we find that the multitudes float with the stream like dead logs; therefore can never go where they wish nor accomplish what they wish. However, no life is complete until we can have things the way we like; that is, until we can consciously change ourselves and our environments according to those higher views of life that we are constantly receiving as we promote our progress. For this reason we must find some way that will lead us out from the control of environment if we wish to live a complete life and a life really worth living.

To proceed we find the law to be that anything in the without that is permitted to impress its likeness upon the mind will influence character, conduct, thought, action and living. And when you give such impressions full right of way they will actually control your life, the reason for which has been explained in preceding chapters. To avoid this influence from environment therefore, we must refuse to receive impressions from without that we do not desire. But since the greater part of these impressions come unconsciously the question will be how to avoid them. This question, however, is answered through the understanding of the law of receptivity.

It is natural for the mind to receive impressions from the without. It is also necessary. That is what the senses are for. But it is not natural to absorb through the senses all sorts of impressions from everything with which we may come in contact. When such impressions are absorbed without discrimination and without our cognizance of the fact we have a mental state called unconscious receptivity, and this state is produced by a weak character.

But here we must remember that a weak character is not necessarily a bad character; because when you are very weak you may not even be able to do mischief. To be really bad you must be strong because a bad character is a strong mind misdirected, while a weak character is a negative sort of goodness, a goodness that means well but is wholly incompetent. What is called character is that quality of mind that discriminates, selects, chooses and holds in possession what has been selected. Character therefore has two functions. The one selects the right and the other holds the mind in the right. When character is absent or so completely negative that it is almost wholly inactive it is not possible for the mind to select the right or to hold the right. Such a mind will absorb nearly everything that environment may suggest and will therefore be a reflection of the present sphere of existence.

Most minds have some character and therefore have a few ideas and motives of their own; they accordingly eliminate some of the undesirable impressions that may try to gain entrance to the mind. But we are all aware of the fact that the average person is entirely too much under the influence of those things that surround him. The majority are affected to a large extent by surroundings, climatic conditions and atmospheres in general, though it is a sign of weakness to be influenced in this manner. The coming and going of events and the opinions of others also play a very large part in molding the thought of most minds. But no mind should be modified by such influences unless he accepts those modifications by personal choice.

Every mind should be able to be himself, no matter what happens or fails to happen, and every mind should be able to think his own thought regardless of anyone's opinion on the subject. This, however, requires a strong character; that is, the ability to make your own selections and the power to stand by that which you have selected.

The attitude of receptivity has frequently been looked upon as a weakness, but it is the lack of character in this connection that constitutes the weakness. Receptivity in itself is indispensable. There are any number of illustrations to prove this fact. The mind that is not receptive to the finer things of life, such as music, art, love, the beauties of nature and so on, has not begun to live. Without the attitude of receptivity, however, no one can respond to anything.

But here we must remember that in becoming receptive we should train ourselves to respond only to such things as we consciously select. The most receptive mind has the greatest opportunities for enjoyment as well as for the increase of wisdom. But this receptivity must be guided, and character alone can do this. Receptivity must be employed consciously only, and unconscious receptivity must be entirely avoided.

The mind must be able to use consciously that to which it wishes to respond, and must also be able to respond perfectly when the choice is made. When such an attainment is secured you will always be yourself, you will never be influenced by anything but your own thought and you will get many times as much enjoyment out of those things of life that you are able to appreciate. And the path to such an attainment is a strong, highly developed character.

Continuing this study of man, and man's relations to his surroundings, we meet a metaphysical law of extreme importance, and it may be stated as follows: Man's welfare depends upon what he does in the within and how he relates himself to the without. The inner realm is the cause realm; therefore this inner realm must be acted upon consciously and properly when certain special effects are desired. But when these effects do appear the personal qualities through which they appear must be related correctly to their sphere of action.

There are many good effects that are spoiled because of discord in those personalities through which they appear, and there are many most excellent and most harmonious states of mind that remain unproductive because they are not supplied with the effect required. This proves that the within should act to the fullest degree possible and To promote the welfare of man all thought should be constructive and all outer relations should be harmonious. We should aim to agree with all adversaries. We should refuse to be out of harmony with anything or anybody. We should meet all things in their own world and meet them with the attitude of harmony towards their better side. And this we can do because it is possible to be harmoniously related to everything in life; and what is more it is absolutely necessary. When true harmony is absent full expression is prevented, and since it is the bringing forth of the best alone that can give us the best, we find that the full expression of what is in us becomes indispensable to our highest welfare.

What we do in the within makes us what we are. And how we are related to the without determines what we are to receive from the world. When we do much in the within we become much, and the more we can accomplish and attain, or create, in our sphere of action. When we are properly related to the world we receive the very best from the world, that is, the best that we can appropriate, appreciate and use now. We can all understand therefore why man's welfare depends upon what he does in the within and how he relates himself to the without. However, to promote constructive action in the within we must learn to apply the law of growth in every part of the human mind, and we find that all growth and development is preceded by the expansion of consciousness. To expand consciousness therefore becomes one of the great essentials in everything that may pertain to perfect advancement and higher welfare.

Mental growth involves three stages unfoldment, development and cultivation; and in each stage new fields of action are appropriated. Whenever anything in the life of an individual is enlarged a new field of activity has been entered. Unfoldment is the bringing out into a larger sphere that which previously occupied a smaller sphere. Development is the multiplying of modes of action. And cultivation is the perfecting of those channels or vehicles through which the various modes of action may find expression. The term development is usually employed to cover the entire process because it merges with unfoldment on the subjective side and with cultivation on the objective side. Therefore when used by itself the entire process of growth is implied.

Since development in any sphere cannot take place until consciousness has been expanded in that sphere no process or system of development is complete until provided with practical methods for promoting such expansion. This being true we see how inadequate modern systems of training must be; and accordingly it is not difficult to find numerous reasons why the race is not more highly developed. However, any process of development will expand consciousness in a measure, provided the desire for expansion is held in mind when such a process is employed. But this desire must be present and must be very strong.

To try to feel the life of all life, or rather to place mind in conscious contact with all existence, will also promote the same purpose to a degree because in this attitude the mind actually transcends present limitations. In fact all limitations are eliminated in this way and the mind is set free to enter new regions whenever it may desire. This method, however, must be employed with wisdom and perfect self-control. There are many minds that have recently set themselves free from all limitations of consciousness through the exercise of universal sympathy; but not all have gained anything thereby. A few have been afraid to venture beyond what they already felt to be substantial, while others have roamed here and there and everywhere on the borderland of the unknown, wasting their energies in search of pastures green. They have had no definite aim except to find the new, and therefore have accomplished nothing. For the fact is that to find the new is not all that is necessary. When we find the new we must stop there awhile and get out of it what it may contain.

As a rule the imagination runs wild after limitations of consciousness have been removed, and only fragmentary impressions are gained whenever a slight pause for observation may be taken when in the midst of these new fields. The result is, ideas arid conclusions that have no foundation whatever, or opinions that seemed plausible to the one that produced them, but wholly devoid of truth, in fact mere freaks of aimless creative power. And it is a well-known fact that such creations are entirely too numerous in the mental world at the present time. Imagination is a splendid servant, but as a master it will invariably lead you into chaos. And in the expansion of consciousness imagination is liable to take the lead unless controlled, because at such times it becomes intensely active.

To control the imagination at such times we should not permit it to do anything but construct the more perfect mental images according to such principles of life as have proven themselves to be scientifically true. The imagination should never be permitted to roam aimlessly. Whenever employed it should be put to work on something definite that you are resolved to perfect or work out.

Do not accept every new mental image as an exact truth, for a truth is usually represented by a large group of mental images. But such images cannot properly group themselves until the mind gets down to sound, rational and analytical thinking.

It can therefore be stated as a fact that no mind really understands new ideas until its thinking concerning those ideas has been reduced to system.

In order to expand consciousness in any sphere, after the limitations of that sphere have been eliminated, the imagination must be controlled and the feeling of real life intensified. A highly active imagination, however, must be avoided because new ideas created by an act of the imagination does not necessarily indicate the expansion of consciousness because an active imagination is not always deep. It usually skims the surface or acts on the borderland of new fields and generally acts in the most haphazard manner. It is the quiet orderly imagination combined with deep feeling that indicates expansion of consciousness, and that actually creates new ideas that are really true as well as of actual worth.

When we proceed to expand consciousness we find that consciousness will not enter the new field until the faculty of interior insight has established the reality of that field. In other words, we must discern that the larger mental world is real before consciousness will proceed to work itself out into that larger world. For this reason we realize that all great minds must of necessity have interior insight, or that something within them that reveals the fact that the larger field is also solid ground.

The man who attempts great undertakings usually does so because he feels within him that success will crown his efforts. Something has told him that he can move out upon the beyond of present thought and action without any fear whatever. To the senses the new realms may look empty, and to venture on may appear to be nothing more than a wild leap into the fathomless abyss of utter destruction; but interior insight takes a different view.

This superior sight can see further and knows that the seeming void of the larger conscious field is actually solid rock. It also knows that this seeming void is rich with possibilities, many of which can be worked out in practical life now.

Interior insight may be defined as faith taking shape and form for practical action. Faith itself is a mental state that dwells constantly on the borderland of the unknown, while interior insight is a mental faculty the function of which is to examine things at a long range. Far sightedness among practical men of affairs is the same thing, and is one of the chief secrets of success in all important undertakings. Interior insight may be called the telescope of the human mind, and the more perfectly it is developed the better you understand the greater possibilities as well as the difficulties that lie before you.

It is therefore evident that when you have this insight you will know not only how to proceed, but also how to deal with those things that you know you will meet in your advancement toward greater achievements. When equipped with a well-developed faculty of this kind you will know what to do to make all personal actions work together for the speedy realization of the greater things in store.

In other words, you can plan ahead to advantage and you can turn all effort, thought and attention in the right direction. Many a time we fail to see the great opportunities that are almost within reach and instead of working up to them as we should if we saw them, we turn our efforts into channels that have practically nothing for us. Millions of mistakes of this kind have been made, but all of them could have been avoided through the use of interior insight.

According to the fact under consideration this insight must establish the reality of a new field before consciousness will naturally expand in that direction; that is, it must prove to the mind that the new field is substantial and full of possibilities. The development of interior insight is therefore absolutely necessary to the promotion of all other kinds of development and without it neither great attainments nor great achievements are possible. But with it there is no mental field, however large or marvelous, that the mind may not finally enter, explore, acquire and possess.

9. FINDING YOUR PLACE IN LIFE

ACCORDING TO the natural workings of things, man gravitates towards those environments that are the exact counterparts of his own active nature.

This is invariably the law. However, those who are living in undesirable environments may not take pleasure in accepting the idea presented in this law. It is more agreeable to place the blame elsewhere. But the fact that your surroundings are ordinary does not necessarily prove that you are an inferior person, although it does prove that you have not brought forth into full action the superior qualities that you may possess.

Here we should remember that it is the active nature that determines the surroundings in which we are to be placed, and the active nature in most persons is a mixture of conflicting forces, many of which are constantly neutralizing each other, or disturbing each other, thus preventing the more desirable of those forces to produce such results as they have the power to produce.

In addition, we must remember the fact that a disturbed nature always attracts inferiority or is drawn into disagreeable conditions. When the active forces in your nature conflict and neutralize each other your nature becomes like a leaf in the whirlwind, and you may become a victim of all the unpleasant conditions you meet.

There are a number of people with high and strong powers who never meet anything but the dark side of things and the reason is that their active forces are in conflict. One desire goes this way and another that way. Some intentions are constructive while others move at random. Their objects in life are constantly being changed and what they build up one day is taken down the next. Thus we understand why such people fail to build for themselves such environments or surroundings as they have the power to build, and also why they are found in situations that are inferior to the best that may exist in their own nature.

If the average mind should look closely at his own nature and ask himself if all the forces of his being are moving constructively and harmoniously towards his one great goal, he would find that they are not. He would discover far more conflict in his own mind and consciousness than he expected, and he would have to admit that his surroundings are the exact counterpart of those things that are active in his own self.

There is one exception, however, to this rule, an exception that must be considered before we proceed further, and this exception is found in misdirected sympathy. We frequently find excellent people in environments where we know they do not belong. At first we may fail to discover the reason, and in failing to do this we may conclude that there is nothing in the idea that people attract their own environments, or are drawn into environments similar to themselves. But a close examination of these cases will reverse this conclusion. There are many people who remain where they are, and frequently in most undesirable environments, not because they belong there, but because their sympathy keeps them there. They do not wish to break away for fear others may suffer. We all know of many such cases, and when we look into this subject closely we find that misdirected sympathy is one of the greatest obstacles to the proper adjustment of persons with their true surroundings.

If it were not for misdirected sympathy several million people would today be living in far better environments – environments that would be directly suited to their present natures and needs. But to break loose from old associations and accept new opportunities may at times seem unkind. However, we must remember that we are living for the whole race, and not only for a few friends. And also that we can render the best service to the race, including our present friends, by being perfectly true to ourselves; that is, by living and working where we actually belong.

Sentimentalism and abnormal feelings have kept down thousands of fine minds, and compelled many a human flower to wither among weeds; but this is always wrong. The entire race is kept back in a measure whenever a single worthy person is held down. Therefore we must seek to avoid such a circumstance whenever we can. Each individual must be permitted to be true to himself; and it is wrong for us to shed tears when a friend finds it necessary to go elsewhere to promote his progress.

You may be living today in uncongenial or unpleasant environments, or your work may call you where you know you do not belong; and there are several causes. You may be held where you are on account of misdirected sympathy. If so, give reason a chance to prove to you that you are wronging everybody by staying where you are. You cannot do the right thing for yourself nor for anyone else unless you are at your best, and to do your best you must be where you belong.

Then you may be held where you are because you have no definite purpose in life, and if so, decide upon a purpose, proceeding at once to train all the forces of your being to work for that purpose and that alone. Gradually you will work away from your present surroundings and doors will open through which you may pass to better things. There is nothing that will take you into better environments more quickly than to have a fixed and high purpose, and to marshal all the powers of mind and soul to work together for the promotion of that purpose. And since this is something that all can do, there is no reason whatever why a single person should live in surroundings that are inferior to himself.

Then there is another reason, possibly the most important of all. You may be held where you are because your good qualities are negative and have neither working capacity nor practical application. If the better side of you is negative and if such adverse tendencies as you may have inherited are positive and active, you are making for yourself a world that is anything but ideal. In this case it is not the best that is in you, but the worst that is in you that determines what kind of surroundings you are to receive, build up or attract. However, when your better side becomes strong and positive; when your good intentions are filled with living power, and when you turn all the forces of your being into the promotion of larger and higher aims, there is going to be a great change. You will soon begin to build for the better, you will begin to gravitate towards better environments and you will meet everywhere more congenial conditions.

But in this connection one of the great essentials is that all the forces of your better nature be in harmony and trained to work together for those better environments that you have in view. It is not what you are negatively, inherently or potentially that determines your present conditions in life. It is what you use and how that something is used.

There are people with small minds and insignificant abilities that are now living in most desirable environments simply because the active forces of their nature work together for a definite object constantly in view. Then there are others with splendid minds and remarkable talents that are living in the midst of failure and distress simply because they did not make constructive use of the powers they possessed; in other words, the better elements in their nature were not in harmony and therefore could not produce results.

It is strict adherence to the quiet, steady, orderly and constant forward movement that will bring you to the goal in view, and even when your forces are so weak that you have to move slowly. But when you are endowed with extraordinary capabilities you will through this process rise rapidly, and finally attain everything you have had in view. A man may not be strictly honest or moral, nevertheless, if he has ability and employs his faculties constructively and harmoniously, he will build for himself a superior environment. And through his power to achieve the greater things he will be attracted towards opportunities that will promote still further the improvement of his environment. But it must be remembered that if this man were honest, moral and true his power would be still greater, and he would enjoy far better the richness and beauties of his delightful surroundings.

There is a belief among many that honest people ought to have the best that life can give, but the mere state of being honest is not sufficient. The best man in the world will be a failure if he does not employ his ability constructively, because it is doing things that counts. And to do things the powers we possess must work in harmony and work with a definite object in view.

In this connection we must not forget that the mind that is pure, honest and just can accomplish far more with a given ability than one who does not have these virtues. Virtues do not create but they do have the power to give proper direction to the process of creation. It is constructive ability that does things. Character simply guides the doing so that the product may be of the highest order and the greatest worth. That the person, therefore, who has character only and no constructive ability will accomplish very little in the world and will have to submit to the inconsistencies of fate.

The course to pursue is to combine ability with character, and to turn all powers and talents towards the attainment of some definite goal. When we take this course we are going to rise out of our present conditions and enter steadily and surely into the better and the superior. It is your active nature that counts. You may have a score of good qualities, but if those qualities are not active they will contribute nothing to the building up of your environment or your destiny. Therefore the more development, the more power and superiority that you can express through your active nature, the greater will be the results in the external world.

But all the qualities of your active nature must have worth and must work together. Superior qualities working at variance with each other will take you down into inferior environments, while inferior qualities if constructive and united in action will take you into better environments than you may be living in now. The whole problem therefore is to express your best in action, and to train the active powers and qualities in your being to work in perfect harmony; that is, to work together for the same purpose and in the same attitude.

Conflicting tendencies of mind have given poverty, distress and misfortune to many of great ability and superior goodness, while properly united tendencies have given success to many a man who was neither able nor true. However, nature is just. We receive according to what we have accomplished; not according to what we have tried to do, but what we actually have done; or in other words, not according to what there is in us, but according to how much of what is in us we applied in a thorough and practical manner.

We will receive material success and delightful exterior surroundings if we have worked properly for those things. But if we have neglected to work for the finer things of life we will receive nothing that has permanent value in human existence, and we will not have the capacity to enjoy our ideal surroundings. For this reason the wise man works for all that is beautiful and true, both in the material sense and in a higher sense. Accordingly he will receive riches both in the without and in the within; thereby gaining the privilege to live the full life, the complete life and the life that is really worth living. You may conclude therefore that if things are not right in your world you are to blame. Accept the blame and resolve to take things into your own hands and make them right. This you can positively do because your environment will be exactly what your active nature is, and you can change your active nature as you may desire.

10. WHEN ALL THINGS WORK FOR GOOD

IN ANALYZING the workings of the mind there is no subject of more importance than that of the relation of good and evil. Concerning evil there are many doctrines, some of which declare that it is a real and permanent power battling with the good, while others declare that it is nothing, or simply the absence of good. Then between these two extreme beliefs almost any number of other beliefs may be found. To prove that evil is an actual principle personified in some form is not only difficult, but impossible. On the other hand, to prove to the world that evil is nothing is by no means simplicity itself. Nevertheless, this doctrine comes very nearly being the truth.

However, it is not our purpose to analyze the nature of evil in this connection. That is a subject so large that separate attention would be required. Our object here is to make clear what we wish to bring out in connection with a most important law, viz., that when we give conscious recognition to the existence of an evil we tend to increase its power and multiply its effects. And in dealing with this law it will be necessary to define briefly what evil actually is, or rather what the new psychology has found it to be.

To say that evil is the absence of the good is not sufficiently explicit; while to say that evil is undeveloped good is simply to play upon words. The process of development is continuous; therefore the fully developed of today is undeveloped in comparison with the possibilities of tomorrow. So that according to that idea the good of today would be evil in the light of tomorrow which is by no means a scientific idea. The truth in this connection is that when we employ the undeveloped just as if it were developed we produce what we call evil, and it is this fact that has given rise to the belief that evil is undeveloped good.

When we look closely at those things that are called evil we find that in every case force has been employed contrary to the natural laws involved. It will therefore be correct to say that evil is misdirected good, or that it is the improper use of a power that is in itself good. In fact, all powers, forces and elements are good in themselves because all that is real is good. Everything is created for a good purpose and is actually good, but it is possible to employ it for a purpose that is not in accord with those laws under which we live at the present moment. And here is where evil may arise.

Every act is good, proper and useful when performed in its own sphere of action, but when performed outside of its own sphere it is not good. It produces conditions that we call evil. This being true the fact that every act has its own sphere of action is one of the greatest facts in the universe. We can do only such things at such times that harmonize with the laws that obtain at the time and under the circumstance. And it is absolutely necessary to the persistence of the universe that such laws be absolute, because if they were not the universe would be chaos.

To simplify the subject we may state that evil is a condition produced by an act that is performed outside of its natural sphere, and that the power and effects of that condition depend upon how much life the mind throws into that particular act. It is a well-known fact that the mind gives its life to those actions and conditions upon which consciousness is directed, and consciousness is always directed where reality is supposed to exist. Therefore when we give conscious recognition to the existence of an evil we give more life and power to those conditions that we call evil, and in consequence make them much worse than they were. This is very simple because the more attention you give to anything the more life and power you add to that particular thing, be it good or evil. Accordingly it is unwise to give attention or recognition to evil under any circumstance.

However, the question is how we can prevent giving conscious attention to the evil and the wrong. When evil seems so very real how can we avoid giving conscious recognition to its existence? The answer is that we must get a better understanding of the real nature of evil and the real nature of good, because when this understanding is gained we can train the mind to act correctly in this connection. When we know that evil is not a thing, not a principle, not a reality, but simply a certain temporary and mistaken use of reality; and when we know that the use of that reality has its origin in our own minds, our attention will at once be transferred from the unpleasant condition surrounding the evil, and be directed instead upon our own inner mental domain. Thus consciousness will be withdrawn from the condition called evil and will become concerned with the change of mental action. Accordingly the power of the evil will at once be diminished.

Actual experience in life has demonstrated the fact a number of times that pain or even a severe disease will disappear instantaneously when consciousness is fully and completely taken into another sphere or thought or action. This proves that an evil condition can live only so long as we give it life, and we give it life only so long as we consciously admit or recognize its existence. When an evil condition is felt, attention should at once be directed upon the opposite good that exists in the inner world of perfection. This action of the mind will take consciousness away from the unpleasant condition and will cause all the faculties of the mind to work in realizing the absolutely good.

When we proceed to trace all perverted action to its inner mental source consciousness will follow, leaving evil behind, and coming to give its life to the change of the said source which proves itself simply to be a misunderstanding of things. Then if the desire of the heart is to change the source of that action, or in other words, to gain a correct understanding of things, the new and the ideal image of the good will appear in the mind, and according to laws previously presented a change for the better will follow at once.

To illustrate, we will take a depressed condition of mind or body and proceed to remove it by this method. First, we will picture clearly upon the mind the perfect image of harmony so that we can almost see harmony with the mind. Second, we will prove to ourselves through reason that this depressed condition is not a thing, but the temporary result of valuable power misdirected. And since this power is misdirected by our own mind, our own mind must contain the origin of that misdirection. Then we will turn attention upon our own inner mentality with a view of removing the source of perversion, establishing a state of harmony; and while thus directing attention upon the inner mentality we will hold the mind in such an attitude that it is moving directly upon the image of perfect harmony.

The result will be that consciousness will become so absorbed in creating the new state of harmony that it will withdraw completely from the outer evil condition. This outer condition will in consequence disappear as it is deprived of life, while the new state of harmony will be firmly established by receiving all the attention and all the life. In other words, when consciousness leaves the condition of evil, evil has nothing further to live on, and will disappear; and as consciousness enters the condition of harmony and good in the within those conditions will receive all the life that consciousness has to give, and will accordingly grow and develop until they become sufficiently strong to take possession of the entire human system.

This is a simple process that works perfectly and that can be employed successfully in removing any undesirable condition from mind or body. However, before we begin we must picture clearly upon the mind the image of the perfect state that we seek to realize and develop, and proceed as above in the elimination of the wrong through the creation of the right. A perfect understanding of the law under consideration will aid remarkably in turning our attention as required because there is nothing that can change the mind so readily as the reasoning process involved in a clear understanding of the subject at hand.

To realize fully that life and power always go wherever consciousness goes, is extremely important and also that consciousness can be directed anywhere by becoming thoroughly interested wherever we wish it to go. In applying these methods people who feel deeply always have the best results because deep feeling tends to produce deep interest in those conditions into which we wish to direct attention.

Closely connected with this process we find a most important metaphysical law which may be stated as follows: All things work together for good to him who desires only the good. And as it is possible for anyone to desire the good and the good only we realize that it is possible for anyone to cause all things to work together for good in his life. This law proves that the way to better things is not nearly as difficult as we have supposed it to be, and also that the straight and narrow path is by no means a path that the few alone can enter.

The doctrine of the straight and narrow path has been misinterpreted as it does not refer to something that is so extremely difficult to pass through, nor is it a path that leads directly away from everything that is pleasant in life. Neither is it so narrow that we can pass through it only when we have given up everything else in life. The belief that everything in life must be left out if we wish to take this path is not only absurd, but is the very opposite to the real truth. The path that leads into life, the full life, the complete life, the beautiful life is straight because it is established upon law. When you take this path you begin to use all the laws of life properly and will therefore gain all the good things that life has the power to give.

Here we must remember that a law is not a cruel something, the function of which is simply to punish. A law is a path that leads to greater and better things. Therefore to follow a law is to move directly towards the better and the greater. When we live according to a law we are constantly receiving the greater riches that lie in that path, and when we live according to all the laws of life we receive everything good that life can give. However, when we violate law we go outside of the path, where there is nothing to be gained and nothing to live for. In fact, we step out of everything that pertains to life and thus enter chaos, the result of which is pain, loss and retrogression. It is not the law that gives us punishment when we go astray. When we go astray we deprive ourselves of the good things of life by going away from that path where those good things are to be found. And when we are deprived of the good, the good is absent; and the absence of the good means evil, the entering into of which means punishment.

The path that leads into life is narrow because it gives room only for your own individuality, and only for the true self. You cannot be a double self, one part good and the other not, when you enter this path. There is only room for the true self. Neither can you lean on someone else. There is no room for anyone upon which to lean, as the path is for yourself alone. On this path you must live your own life and give all others freedom to live their own life.

Life is given us to be lived, and to live life we must live to ourselves according to our own light and our own individual needs. The path to life is the path to better things; in other words, it is the advancing path and is therefore not a dismal, disagreeable or difficult path. On the contrary, it is the very opposite and is found by seeking the good and the good only. So long as we have only the good in mind we will be on this path. We will live according to the laws of life and will receive only good things because the laws of life can give only good things. But when we begin to desire what is not good we are at once drawn out of the path. Thus we will be deprived of the essentials of life, and instead we will enter into emptiness, weakness, perversion, confusion and all kinds of disaster.

When all our desires are directed upon the attainment of the highest good our creative powers will proceed to create and rebuild everything within us and about us, thus causing all things to become better. Everything in life will improve. We will be in more perfect harmony with our surroundings and will attract more agreeable persons, circumstances and events. We will become creators of the good. Everything that we do will produce good and everything that we attempt will result in good. We will meet all persons and environments on the better side, and will in consequence receive the best things that such persons and environments have the power to give. Every change that we make will be an open door to greater good because we are moving towards the good and the good only as every change is being made.

Here it is very important to remember that when we desire only the good we are always moving towards greater good, and must without fail realize the greater good in the near future. If we pass through a few unpleasant experiences while we are waiting we must not pay attention to such seeming inconsistencies. The fact that all will be well when we reach the goal in view should so fully occupy our minds that we will not be disturbed by any defect that may be found in the way over which we must for the present pass.

To desire the good, however, does not mean to desire mere self-satisfaction. It is the universal good that must be held in mind, the greatest good for everybody. And this must not only be held in mind but deeply desired with the whole heart and soul. The proper course is to desire only the highest good and then turn all the life and power we possess into that desire. In fact we should make that desire far stronger than all other desires and we should live in it constantly.

As you proceed in this manner all the laws of the mind will work with you in promoting the realization of the good that you have in view and will gradually eliminate the results of past mistakes. Should the personal self tend to make new mistakes or take missteps, thereby leading your plans out of the true path, something will occur to prevent you from doing this before it is too late. The laws of your being will cause something to come in your way and thus turn your life in another direction, that is, in a new direction where the highest good you have in view may be finally realized.

When you have set your heart and soul upon the attainment of the good and the good only, the predominating powers in your being will work only for good, and all lesser powers will, one after the other, be taken into the same positive current so that ere long all things in your life will work together for good. We may not understand at first how these powers operate, but we shall soon find that the results we had in view are being realized more and more. And as this realization is gained we shall come positively to the conclusion that all things do work together for good when we desire the good and the good alone.

11. WITH WHAT MEASURE YE METE

HE WHO gives much receives much. This we all know, but the question is what it means to give. When we speak of giving we usually think of charity and poverty; and believing that the latter is inevitable we conclude that the former must be an exalted virtue; but poverty is not inevitable. It is not a part of life's plan. It is simply a mistake. Therefore charity cannot be otherwise than a temporal remedy. Such remedies, however, though good and necessary, do not always constitute virtues because virtue is permanent and is a part of a continuous advancement in man.

He who gives in charity does not receive anything in return unless he also gives himself. It is therefore not the giving of things that brings reward, but the giving of life. But to give much life one must possess much life, and to possess much life one must live a large measure of life. According to the law, life is measured out to us with the same measure that we employ in the measuring of our own existence. In other words, we will receive only as much life as our own measure can hold; but it is not only life that is measured out to us in this way. Everything that pertains to life is measured in a similar way.

We conclude, therefore, that he who sets out a large measure to be filled will receive a large measure full, and that he who gives himself simply offers his own life for further enrichment. He who gives much of himself will be abundantly enriched because he places in life a large measure of himself to be filled. He who gives things may lose all that is given. But he who gives himself, the best that is in himself, loses nothing. Instead he gains a larger and a richer self. He who gives himself to the race gives life and life can supply all needs.

To have an abundance of life is to have the power to help yourself and to recreate your own world according to your highest desires. The gift of life is therefore the highest gift. It is also the largest gift because it includes all gifts. He who gives life does not give to relieve poverty, but to build strong souls, and when strong souls appear poverty disappears of itself. To give one's life is to express in thought, word or action everything of worth that one may possess in mind or soul; that is, everything that one may live for. And how much we live for depends upon how largely the life is measured in our understanding. When we measure life largely, life will give us a large measure of itself.

When we blend consciousness with the universal we will receive universal consciousness in return.

When we think only of the boundless, our thought will be limited no more. When we take a larger measure of our talents the wisdom that fills the universe will also fill that larger measure. When we take a large measure of man and have faith in the superior side of every mind, every mind will give to us as much as our measure of that mind can hold. Realizing these great facts we should dwell constantly in the world of greater possibilities.

We should expect much, work for much, live for much, have faith in much, and we shall find that as much will come to us as we have thought, lived and worked for. We should never limit anything nor anyone. The measure of all things should be as large as our conscious comprehension and we should refuse to be contented with anything except that which is constantly enlarging its measure. Accordingly we should live for great things and press on. Thus the greater and the greater will surely be measured out in return. This is the law and it cannot fail.

Very few, however, apply this law and that is the reason why the majority accomplish so little. They undertake so little and they never reach the high places because they nearly always aim at the low ones. Many minds that aim high for a while lose their lofty aspirations later on because they fail to reach the mountain top the first week or the first year. Others again aspire to the high things though at the same time think of themselves as limited, insignificant and even worse. But if we would become great we must blend all though with greatness and measure ourselves with that measure that is large enough to contain all the greatness we can possibly conceive of.

He who expands consciousness so as to measure things largely gains capacity, while he who takes a small view of everything remains incompetent. We do not get power, growth or ability by trying to cram a small mind, but by trying to expand the mind.

And to expand the mind we must take the largest possible view of all things. We must live with the limitless and blend all thought with infinite thought. When the senses declare you cannot do this, reply by saying, It is in me to do it; therefore I can.

While the person is working with the limitations of the present, the mind should transcend those limitations and constantly take larger measures of both life and attainment. And as soon as this larger measure is taken the larger will begin to appear until even the person is called upon to enter a larger work with increased remuneration. Make yourself worthy and greater worth will come to you. Take a larger measure of your own capacity, your own ability, your own worth. Expect more of yourself. Have more faith in yourself and that something that supplies everybody will completely nil your measure.

It is the law that no matter how large your measure will be it will be filled. And your measure of things is as large as your conscious realization of those things. Therefore to take a larger and a larger measure of anything is to expand consciousness beyond the present understanding of that particular thing. Therefore all that we are conscious of is but a partial expression of something that is in itself limitless because everything in existence is limitless. Therefore by gaining a larger consciousness of those partial expressions we will become conscious of a larger expression. And a larger expression of those things will appear through us, which means that our own life has been enlarged and enriched. This is all perfectly simple and proves conclusively why the boundless measures out to each individual only as much as the measure of that individual can hold.

But since there is nothing to hold consciousness in bounds except our own limited view, and since we can take a larger view of anything whenever we choose, it is in our power to increase the measure of anything in our own life or in our own sphere of existence. Perpetual increase and perpetual expansion of consciousness go hand in hand in the life of man. The former is produced by the latter and the latter is produced by man himself. We conclude, therefore, that anyone can make his life as large as he wishes it to be, and can bring into his life as much of everything as he may desire.

In considering this great subject we must give due attention to the process of growth. And in this connection we must remember that the desire for growth and the effort to promote growth must be constant. This law, however, is frequently neglected as it is the tendency of nearly every person to lean back, fold arms and suspend all desire and every effort whenever a victory has been won, or an onward step taken. But we can never afford to stop or to suspend action at any time and what is more it is impossible to suspend action.

We cannot stop living, therefore we cannot stop thinking, and so long as we think, some part of our being will act. And that part should act with some definite goal in view. When you leave the field of action to rest, so to speak, you permit that part of your being that does act to act aimlessly, and aimless actions always produce perversions, false states and detrimental conditions. It is the conviction of every thorough student of life that aimless action is the fundamental cause of all the ills that appear in life. And aimless action is caused by the attempt to stop all action when we try to rest. However, the fact that action will go on perpetually in some part of our system proves that the individual Ego should be constantly at hand to guide that action.

The Ego does not need any rest, nor need it ever suspend activity, because rest simply means recuperation, and it is those organs that receive and use up energy that require recuperation. The Ego does not create and does not employ energy, but simply governs the distribution and use of energy. So that the real you should always be active in some sense, and should always desire the promotion of growth as well as carry out the promotion of growth, regardless of how many special parts of your system have suspended action for the time being.

When we understand the real purpose of rest we perceive clearly why the governing conscious Ego requires no rest whatever, and also why it does require ceaseless conscious action. To prevent aimless action the Ego should guide action on the mental or spiritual plane whenever rest demands suspension of activity on the physical plane. It has been demonstrated conclusively that the body rests most perfectly when some constructive action takes place in mind or soul, and it is for this reason that the first day of the week has been consecrated to the spiritual life. By giving this day entirely to higher thought, and the contemplation of the finer things of life, the body and the mind will recuperate so perfectly that you can do more work and far better work during the coming week than ever before; although not simply because you have properly rested mind and body, but also because you have through your higher devotions awakened new life, more life and a number of higher, stronger powers.

The principle that the body rests most perfectly when consciousness is actively at work on some higher plane is a principle that should receive the most thorough attention, and every person should adopt some system of living by which this principle could be carried out completely in every detail. Such a system of living would prolong the life of the body, increase the power of the mind and remarkably unfold the soul.

The metaphysical law under consideration is based upon this principle. Therefore to live according to this principle, this law must be constantly employed; that is, the desire for growth and effort to promote growth must be constant. In addition, the desire for growth must be constructive because no action is constructive unless it is prompted by the desire for growth. And every effort to promote growth must be constant, because efforts that do not aim at growth are destructive, while suspended efforts cause aimless action. To carry out this law transfer your desire for growth from one faculty to another, and from one plane to another, as conditions may demand, or as your work may require, but never suspend that desire.

When you feel that a certain faculty, through which you have been acting, needs recuperation withdraw action from that faculty and begin to act through another faculty, expressing through this other faculty all the desire for growth that you can possibly create. Or, when you feel that the physical plane needs recuperation act upon the mental. When both mental and physical planes require recuperation enter the spiritual and express there your desire for soul unfoldment. Then whenever you express your desire for growth do something to promote that growth use what methods you possess and gradually you will evolve better and more effective methods.

As you apply all these ideas, consciousness will constantly expand, development will be constantly taking place in some part of your being, and you will be improving in some way every minute. In addition, you will prevent all aimless action and all retarded growth. Every part of the system will receive proper rest and recuperation whenever required, and this will mean complete emancipation because all ills come from aimless action, retarded growth and their consequences. It will also mean greater achievements and higher attainments because all the faculties will improve steadily and surely, and the entire system will be at its best under every circumstance.

12. FINDING MATERIAL FOR MIND BUILDING

TO LIVE is to move forward but there can be no forward movement without new experience. Therefore in all advancement, in all progress, in all attainment, in all achievement, and in the living of life itself experience is indispensable. Experience being necessary to the promotion of advancement as well as to the increase of the value and the welfare of life, it becomes necessarily a permanent and continuous cause in the world of every individual, and as like causes produce like effects, both in quality and in quantity, experience should be sought and selected with the greatest possible care.

It is also highly important that we seek an abundance of experience because so long as the cause has quality it cannot be too extensive in quantity. Experience is the material from which character and mentality are constructed. Therefore the richer and more abundant our experience, the stronger and more perfect will our character and mentality become. Everything has its purpose and the real purpose of experience is to awaken new forces, new states, new phases of consciousness, and to originate new actions in the various parts of being.

To unfold and bring forth what is latent in the being of man is the principal object of experience. And it is well to remember that without experience no latent quality or power can ever be aroused and expressed. The power of experience to bring forth what is latent and to originate the new gives cause to enjoyment and happiness, as well as progress, and since experience is the only cause of enjoyment, it follows that what the enjoyment is to be in the life of any individual will depend directly upon what experience that individual will select.

The average mind makes no effort to select experience wisely, therefore fails to promote the real purpose of experience; and failing in this he also fails to awaken and develop those things in himself that can produce the most desirable of all experience, that is, the consciousness of a perpetual increase of all that has real worth in life.

The more experience the better, provided it is rich, constructive and wholesome, though no person should seek experience for the mere sake of passing through experience. The belief that experience itself builds life is not true, nor is there any truth in the doctrine that all kinds of experience, good and otherwise, are necessary to the full development of life. It is only a certain kind of experience that can add to the welfare of life and promote the purpose of life. Therefore to understand the psychology of experience and how experience is connected with the workings of mind is a matter of exceptional importance.

The daily purpose of each individual should be to seek the richest experience possible in order that the best material possible may be provided in the building of himself. To this end he should place himself in daily contact with the best that is moving in the world, and the more of this the better. Such a practice will develop the mind, perfect the character, refine and re-polish the personality, and increase perpetually the health and the wholeness of the body. It will also tend directly towards the promotion of a long and happy life.

The mind should be wide awake to everything in its sphere of existence that can give expression to superior action, and seek to gain the richest possible experience by coming in contact with that action.

To place one's self in mental contact with the best that is in action in the world is to originate similar actions within one's own mentality. These will arouse the superior forces that are latent in the deeper mentality and ere long a superior mental life will have been evolved.

The more experience that the mind can gain by coming in contact with the best things that are alive in the world the larger, the broader and the more perfect will the mind become. It is therefore evident that the recluse must necessarily have a small mind whether he lives in the world or apart from the world. To live a life of seclusion is to eliminate experience to the smallest degree possible and thereby cause the mind to become so small that only a mere fraction of its power and intellect can be in conscious action. In consequence such a person can never be his best in anything, not even in a single isolated talent, nor can his ideas as a whole have any practical value, being based wholly upon one sided opinions.

In this connection it is most important to understand that the philosophy of the hermit is useless in practical life. And the same is true of moral or physical views as formulated by those who live in seclusion. Such ideas may look well in theory and they may be accepted by millions of people, but nothing outside of mere intellectual satisfaction will be gained. Intellectual satisfaction, however, when not directly associated with physical, mental and moral progress is detrimental; the reason being that it produces a phase of mental contentment which culminates in mental inactivity.

The only intellectual satisfaction that is normal and that can be beneficial, is that satisfaction which comes from the consciousness of continuous advancement. Any other satisfaction means mental inaction, and mental inaction leads to death invariably, not only in the intellectual but also in body, mind and character.

Those who live in the world and who are daily required to meet the problems of the world should seek guidance and instruction when necessary only from those superior minds that have had experience in the world. Those who live apart from the world do not appreciate the conditions that exist in the world. They have not been awakened to the real nature of those conditions. Therefore the solution that they may offer for the problem which may arise from such conditions can be of no practical value. He alone really knows who has had experience, though experience is not the whole of knowledge.

It is only a small part, but that part is indispensable.

Minds that live only for themselves or for a selected few only, will also become narrow in mentality and dwarfed in character. Such living invariably results in retrogression because too many of the elements of life, both physical and metaphysical, are compelled through the lack of experience to remain inactive. The entire mentality and the entire personality should be active, and to promote such activity the entire individual life should be entirely filled with rich, wholesome and intellectual experience.

In brief we should live while we live and not simply exist. The lives of young people in particular should be well provided with an abundance of wholesome amusements and of every imaginable variety, though this practice should not cease with the coming of the thirties. We should all enjoy this life to the fullest extent so long as we remain in this life, though not simply because it is the privilege of us all to enjoy every moment to the fullest extent, but also because there are few things that are more conducive to wholesome experience than that of wholesome enjoyment. We gradually grow into the likeness of that which we enjoy. An abundance of wholesome amusement therefore will invariably produce a wholesome nature. And by enjoying the greatest possible number of the best things we shall naturally and steadily develop the best that is latent within us.

Every experience that we pass through awakens something within us that was not active before, and this something will in turn impress upon the subconscious the nature of the thought that was created during the experience. In fact the nature of the experience will determine what is to be awakened in the conscious mind and what is to be impressed upon the subconscious. And since subconscious impressions determine the character, the mentality and the personal nature of man, it is of the highest importance that only such experiences be selected as are rich, constructive and wholesome.

What is awakened in the mind of man is awakened by experience alone. For this reason no change in the mind can take place, unless preceded by some experience whether that experience be tangible or imaginary. And what is awakened in the mind of man determines first what he is to think, and second what he is to do and to be. These facts prove conclusively that experience is the material from which character and mentality are constructed. And therefore experience should receive the most thorough consideration during every period of life, and especially during the first twenty-four years of personal existence.

The experience that a person passes through during this early period will determine to a very great extent what is to be accomplished in later years; the reason being that the early tendencies are the strongest as a rule, be they good or otherwise. We are not inferring, however, that man cannot change his nature, his character, his mentality, his habits, his desires or his tendencies at any time, because he can. But time and energy can be put to better use in later life than to that of overcoming the results of mistakes that could have been avoided if the proper mental tendencies had been produced early in life.

We should take advantage of favorable periods when we have them, and we should create such periods when we do not have them. This we can do, but when they come of themselves, as they do in the early years of personal existence, everything possible should be done to make these periods become a permanent power in our favor.

To permit the young mind or any mind to pass through experiences that are unwholesome or adverse is to cause tendencies to be produced that will work against him all his life, that is, if those tendencies are not removed later on, and they usually are not. But to limit the supply of experience at this period or at any period is equally detrimental. That person who enters the twenties in the consciousness of an abundance of rich experience is prepared for his career, and if he has a fair degree of ability he will succeed from the very beginning. He is ripe, so to speak, for his work. His mind has found normal action in nearly all of its phases and he will make but few mistakes of any consequence.

It is totally different, however, with that person who has entered the twenties in what may be called the green state. Even though his mind may be highly active he will accomplish but little, because being as yet unconscious of his real nature, his real capacity and his true state of normal action, he will misdirect most of his energies and they will be used up before his success can begin.

The mind that lacks experience does not know its own power, its own possibilities, its own desires nor its own natural sphere of action. It has not found its bearings, and even though it may have remarkable ability it will invariably misplace that ability, and will in consequence fail utterly where lesser minds, with an abundance of wholesome experience to begin with, have nearly everything their own way.

It is therefore evident that the practice still prevalent in thousands of homes of compelling young people to be ignorant of what is going on in the world is most detrimental to the future welfare of those people. Such a practice has caused many a young mind to be a complete failure until he was thirty-five or more, though if he had received an abundance of wholesome experience early in life he could easily have entered into real success more than ten years before. An abundance of rich experience secured early in life will awaken the best that is in the person. He will thus become acquainted with himself and will know what to do with himself.

He will also know what to do with others and how to apply himself in the outer world.

However, we must remember in this connection that it is not necessary for anyone to do wrong or to mix with the wrongs of the world in order to gain experience. The fact is that such experience is not experience simply a misuse of mind, thought and action. The proper kind of experience is just as necessary to the young mind as the proper kind of education, and parents should in no way eliminate the opportunities of their children to gain experience of value and worth. But they should not let their children loose, so to speak, without paying any attention to the kind of experience that children seek to enjoy. To pass through experience that is neither rich nor wholesome is to cause tendencies, desires, habits and traits to be formed that are adverse to everything worthwhile that the person may try to do. The results of such experience will have to be removed before real living and real achievement can begin.

All young minds should be given the freedom to enjoy every imaginable form of enjoyment that can be found, provided such enjoyments are wholesome. And here we should remember that those young people who stay at home ignorant of the world are not any better in character than those who go out to enjoy the best that is living and moving in the world. And as to mental power they are much weaker than those who have come in contact with the movements of life and thought in all its phases. Moral purity does not come from keeping the mind in a state of inaction, nor does goodness come from the absence of desire. The best way to make the mind pure and the character strong is to give the person so much rich and wholesome experience that he will not care for that which is inferior or perverted. No normal mind will care for the lesser after he has gained possession of the greater. And those minds that are not normal do not need ethics, they need a physician.

An abundance of wholesome and most interesting enjoyment may be found anywhere, and the supply will increase with the demand. It is possible for any person to go out and come in contact with the world without going wrong, and the experience is invaluable, not only in a practical way but also in a way that touches the very cause of everything that has worth in the being of man. The more constructive experience that a person passes through the larger will the mind become and the more substantial will everything become that is active in his nature. An abundance of rich experience will invariably be followed by a larger subconscious life and this will add remarkably to the power and capacity of every talent and faculty. Such experience will also tend to give every force in the system the proper direction and thus prevent the waste of energy.

The more experience we seek the better, provided that experience is sought for the purpose of awakening the larger and the better that is latent within us. And since experience in some form is absolutely necessary to the promotion of this awakening, the art of securing experience becomes a fine art, in fact one of the finest and most important in the world.

Every experience produces a subjective impression and when a number of such impressions of the highest order are secured there is not only a feeling of completeness and satisfaction that is beyond price, but the entire individuality gains a marked degree of superiority and worth. An abundance of rich experience will also give a substantial foundation to the mind, a foundation that no circumstance, however trying, will be able to disturb. And so long as the foundation of the mind is secure the various elements and forces of the system will be able to perform their functions well, no matter what temporary conditions may be.

One of the greatest secrets of success in any undertaking, or in any vocation in life, is found in the possession of a mental foundation so strong and so substantial that it is never disturbed under any circumstance. And as the right kind of experience will tend to build such a mental foundation, we realize the extreme value of the subject under consideration.

To feel that you have received your share of the good things that have come your way is one of the rare joys of life. And this feeling comes invariably from the subjective memory of rich and abundant experience. This feeling produces the consciousness of mental wealth and without it life is not complete; but with it any person can pass through physical poverty and not feel poor in the least. While the mind that has had little or no experience is poverty stricken, no matter how extensive external possessions may be. Such a mind is practically empty, it finds no satisfaction in life and is incapable of turning its energies into constructive action. In brief, it flows with the stream and is almost completely in the hands of fate.

Experience, however, in the true sense is not synonymous with hardship. And to pass through trials and tribulations does not necessarily mean to gain experience. Occasionally it does, but as a rule it does not, and real experience awakens new life.

It gives new points of view and enlarges the mental world. Instead of crushing individuality as hardships sometimes do it strengthens individuality, and makes the man more powerful both in mind and character than ever before.

To enjoy real experience, therefore, is not simply to pass through certain mental or physical conditions, but it is to gain something of permanent value while passing through those conditions. Experience of this kind may sometimes be gained through mistakes; that is, when the mistake causes the mind to seek the other way; otherwise the mistake does not produce experience of value, and nothing is gained. However, it is not necessary to make mistakes or to go wrong in order to gain valuable experience. Neither is hardship, pain nor adversity necessary to growth, progress and advancement.

The most valuable experience comes, not through mistakes, but through the mind's sympathetic contact with the best that is alive in the world. Such experiences, however, may not be had for nothing. But to employ a small percentage of one's earnings in procuring such experiences is to make a most excellent investment. The bank of rich and wholesome experience pays a very large interest. It will be profitable, therefore, for everybody to deposit as much as can be spared every week in this great bank. To keep in constant touch with the best that is living and moving in the world will give new ideas, new mental life, greater ambition, greater mental power, increased ability and capacity, and will in consequence increase the earning capacity of the individual. It will also increase the joy of living and make every individual life more thoroughly worthwhile.

The good things in the world, however, should not be sought for mere pastime. They should invariably be sought for the purpose of gaining conscious possession of the richness which they may contain. This will increase immeasurably the enjoyment of the experience, and will cause the experience to add directly to the power, the quality, the worth and the value of life. It will make living more and more worthwhile, and nothing is worth more.

13. BUILDING THE SUPERIOR MIND

ACCORDING TO the conclusions of experimental psychology the possibilities that are latent in the soul of man are both limitless and numberless. It is evident therefore that when we learn to draw on the abundance of the great within we can readily build within ourselves all the elements of a superior mind. In applying this idea, however, the first essential is to recognize the fact that every effort to build for greater things must act directly upon the soul, because the soul is the only source of that which is expressed or that which may be expressed in the human personality.

In trying to build the superior in mind, life and character two methods have been employed. The first has been based upon the belief that man is naturally imperfect in every part of his being and that advancement may be promoted only by improving upon his imperfect qualities. The other method, which is the new method, is based upon the principle that man contains within himself all the qualities of superiority in a perfect state and that advancement is promoted, not by trying to improve upon his imperfections, but by trying to bring forth into personal expression more and more of the many perfect qualities that already exist within him.

The first method is necessarily a failure. And the reason why the race has improved so slowly is because this method has been used almost exclusively. A few, however, have in all ages, consciously or unconsciously used the second method, and it is through the efforts of these, that the advancement that we have made has been brought about. That the first method must be a failure is clearly understood when we realize that nothing can be evolved unless it is involved, and that it is impossible for man to bring forth the more perfect unless the more perfect already exists in a potential state within him.

This principle is well illustrated by the fact that we cannot produce light by acting upon darkness, nor produce perfection by trying to improve upon such things as do not have the possibilities of perfection. We cannot develop quality, worth or superiority in ourselves unless those elements which go to make up qualities of worth and superiority already exist within us. Development means the bringing out of that which is already within. But if there is nothing in the within no development will take place, no matter how faithfully we may apply ourselves. Thus we realize that before development along any line can be promoted, we must recognize the fact that we already possess within us all those elements that may be needed for the promotion of that development even to the highest possible degree. In other words, we must recognize the fact that all the possibilities of perfection already exist within us, and that we are therefore in reality perfect through and through as far as our real or interior nature is concerned.

Those who employ the first method do not recognize the greater possibilities within and therefore they do not try to bring forth what is already within them. They simply try to improve the imperfect in their personal nature by acting upon the imperfect. But we cannot fill an empty space by simply acting upon emptiness. We must bring something into that empty state if we wish fullness to take place. The imperfect lacks something; that is the reason why it is imperfect. And that something must be supplied from some other source before improvement or change for the better can be brought about. That something, however, that is lacking may be found in the great within because the great within contains everything that man may require to produce perfection in any part of his mind, character or personality.

The possibilities of the within are limitless and numberless. Of this fact we have any amount of evidence. Therefore by adopting the second method for building the superior in the human mind it is evident that any individual may steadily rise in the scale until he finally reaches the high goal of attainment that he may have in view.

To proceed, realize that the source of perfection and the source of all the elements of quality and worth exist already within you. Then by becoming more deeply conscious of these superior qualities that you possess within yourself those qualities will be expressed more and more, because the law is, that whatever we become conscious of within ourselves that we shall naturally express through mind and personality.

If you wish to improve any faculty or talent realize that the interior foundation of that faculty is perfect as well as limitless, and that you can make that faculty as remarkable as you wish by unfolding the perfection and the limitless power that is back of, beneath, or within that faculty. There is nothing to be gained by trying to patch up, so to speak, the imperfections of the exterior side of mind or personality through the application of some superficial or artificial method, though this is practically all that modern systems of mind building have attempted to do.

When we examine the results of those systems we realize how futile such methods necessarily are in this connection. However, when we proceed to enlarge the actual capacity of a faculty by drawing upon the interior and limitless source of that faculty we secure something with which to work. And by employing a scientific system of objective training in addition to the perpetual enlargement of a faculty from within, we build up not only a powerful faculty, but we learn to apply all of its power and talent in practical use.

The same methods will hold in the building of any part of the mind or the whole of the mind. And it is such methods through which we may secure not only satisfactory results in the present, but a perpetual increase of results for an indefinite period. Before we can employ these methods, however, we must recognize the fact that the real man within is already perfect and limitless and that the subconscious root of every talent or faculty is also perfect and limitless.

Therefore our object must not be to perfect our external selves by trying to improve upon our external selves regardless of what we may possess within us, but our object must be to bring forth into expression an ever increasing abundance of the power, the quality and the worth that is already latent within us. We must live, think and act with this great purpose uppermost in mind regardless of circumstances. In fact, everything we do must be done with the desire to bring forth more of the wonderful that is within us. And it is in this way that we may build the superior mind.

Those who have gone beneath the surface of mere existence and have familiarized themselves with real life know that the personal man is as he thinks. Therefore to perfect the personal man thought must be more perfect. But here we must remember that thought is created in the likeness of our own conception of ourselves. Therefore, so long as we think that we are imperfect in every part of body, mind and soul it is

327

natural that our thought will be imperfect, and the personal man will accordingly in body, mind and character continue to be imperfect.

The law is that thought is the cause of every state or condition that appears in mind, character or personality. Thus we realize that so long as we think of ourselves as imperfect we will create imperfect thoughts; and imperfect thought will produce nothing else but imperfect conditions and states in every part of our being.

However, when man discovers that he himself in the real and in the soul state of his existence is absolutely perfect, he will think of himself as perfect, that is, he will not consider himself as an imperfect personality, but constantly think of himself as an individuality possessed of all the elements, powers and qualities of the highest state of perfection. Accordingly his thought will be perfect as far as he has developed this higher conception of himself. And since the personal man is in his nature the result of thought, more and more perfection will accordingly be expressed in every part of the personal man.

As man grows in the understanding of his own interior perfection his thought of himself will be higher and higher, better and better, more and more perfect. His mind, body and character will in consequence improve in proportion. And since there is no limit to the latent possibilities of perfection any individual can by attaining a larger and deeper conscious realization of the perfect qualities within develop himself perpetually, because whatever we become conscious of within ourselves that we naturally express through the life of the personality.

The art of building the superior in the human mind as well as in personality and character is therefore based upon the discovery that the real interior man is not only perfect in all his latent elements and qualities, but is actually a marvelous being; in fact is within himself limitless in power, having superior qualities that are actually numberless.

To unfold these possibilities and gradually bring out into expression more and more of the marvelous man within, we must become more and more conscious of this power and worth and perfection that exists within us. And this consciousness may be attained by thinking constantly with deep feeling of this interior perfection; and also by actually living for the one purpose of unfolding more and more of this interior perfection.

In brief, the principle is this: The superior already exists within us. When we become conscious of the superior we will, according to a leading metaphysical law, express the superior; and what we express in mind or personality becomes a permanent part of the personal man. Mind building, therefore, is based upon the bringing out of the greatness that is within, and in learning to apply in practical life that power which naturally comes forth, through mind and personality, as this interior greatness is unfolded.

14. THE SECRET OF THE MASTER MIND

THE MIND that masters himself creates his own ideas, thoughts and desires through the original use of his own imaging faculty, while the mind that does not master himself forms his thoughts and desires after the likeness of impressions received through the senses; and is therefore controlled by the conditions from which those impressions come, because as we think so we act and live. Accordingly the master mind is a mind that thinks what he wants to think regardless of what circumstances, environments or associations may suggest.

The average mind desires what the world desires without any definite thought as to its own highest welfare or greatest need, the reason being that a strong tendency to do likewise or to imitate is always produced in the mind when desires are formed in the likeness of impressions that are suggested by external conditions. It is therefore evident that a person who permits himself to be affected by suggestion will invariably form artificial desires. And to follow such desires is to be misled in every instance. The master mind, however, desires only that which is conducive to real life here and now and in the selection of those desires is never influenced in the least by the desires of the world.

The power of desire is one of the greatest of all powers in the human system. It is therefore highly important that every desire be normal and created for the welfare of the individual himself. But no desire is normal that is formed through the direct influence of suggestions. Such desires are always abnormal and cause the individual to be misplaced.

This explains why a very large number of people are misplaced. They do not occupy those places wherein they may be their best and accomplish the most. They are working at a disadvantage and are living a life that is far inferior to what they are intended to live, and because of abnormal desires. They have imitated the desires of others without consulting their own present need. They have formed the desire to do what others are doing, permitting their minds to be influenced by suggestions and impressions from the world, forgetting what their present state makes them capable of doing now. Thus, by living the lives, the habits, the actions and the desires of others they are led into a life not their own; in other words, they are misplaced.

The master mind is never misplaced because he does not live to do what others are doing, but what he himself wants to do now, and he wants to do only that which is conducive to real life, a life worthwhile, a life that steadily works up to the very highest goal in view.

The average mind requires a change of environment before he can change his thought. He has to go somewhere or bring into his presence something that will suggest a new line of thinking and feeling. The master mind, however, can change his thought whenever he may so desire. A change of scene is not necessary because the master mind is not controlled by external conditions or circumstances. A change of scene will not produce a change of thought in his mind unless he so elects for the master mind changes his thoughts, ideas, or desires by imaging upon the mind the exact likeness of those new ideas, new thoughts, or new desires that have been selected.

The secret of the master mind is found wholly in the intelligent use of the imaging faculty, for man is as he thinks, and his thoughts are patterned after the predominating mental images, whether those images are impressions suggested from without or impressions formed by the mind through original thinking. When any individual permits his thoughts or desires to be formed in the likeness of impressions received from without he will be more or less controlled by environment. He will be largely in the hands of circumstances and fate, but when he proceeds to transform into an original idea every impression received from without and incorporates that idea into a new mental image he will use environment as a servant, thereby placing fate in his own hands.

Every object that is seen will produce an impression upon the mind according to the degree of mental susceptibility. This impression will contain the nature of the object of which it is a representation. Thus, the nature of that object will be reproduced in the mind, and what has thus entered the mind will be expressed more or less throughout the entire human system. Therefore, the individual who is susceptible to suggestions and external impressions will reproduce in his own mind and system conditions that are similar in nature to almost everything that he may see, hear or feel. He will, in consequence, be a reflection of the world in which he lives. He will think, speak and act as his surroundings may suggest. He will flow with the stream of his circumstances and he will be more or less of an automaton instead of a well individualized character.

However, every person who permits himself to be largely and continually affected by suggestions is more or less of an automaton, and accordingly is more or less in the hands of fate. So, therefore, in order to reverse matters and place fate in his own hands he must proceed to make intelligent use of suggestions instead of blindly following such desires and thoughts as his surroundings may suggest.

We are all surrounded constantly by suggestions of every description, because everything has the power to suggest something to us, provided we are susceptible. But there is a vast difference between permitting ourselves to be susceptible to all sorts of suggestions and by training ourselves to use intelligently all those impressions that suggestions may convey c The average student of suggestion not only ignores this difference, but encourages susceptibility to suggestion by constantly emphasizing the belief that it is suggestion that controls the world.

But if it is really true that suggestion does control the world, we want to learn how to so use suggestion that its indiscriminate control of the human mind may decrease steadily. For the human mind must not be controlled by anything, and this we can accomplish, not by teaching people how to use suggestion for the purpose of affecting their minds, but in using every impression conveyed by suggestion in the reconstruction of our own minds.

Suggestion is a part of life because everything has the power to suggest and all minds are open to impressions. Suggestion, therefore, is a necessary factor, and a permanent factor in our midst. But the problem is to train ourselves to make intelligent use of the impressions received, instead of blindly following the desires produced by such impressions, as the majority do.

To carry out this idea never permit the objects discerned by the senses to reproduce themselves in your mind against your will. Form your own ideas about what you see, hear or feel and try to make those ideas superior to what was suggested by the objects discerned. When you see evil do not form ideas or mental impressions that are similar to that evil. And do not think of the evil as bad, but try to understand the forces that are back of all evil, forces that are good in themselves though misdirected in their present state.

By trying to understand the nature that is back of evil or adversity you will not form bad ideas, and therefore will feel no bad effects from experiences that may seem undesirable. At the same time you will think your own thought about the experience, thereby developing the power of the master mind.

Surround yourself as far as possible with those things that suggest the superior, but do not permit such suggestions to determine your thought about the superior. The superior impressions that are suggested by superior environments should be used by yourself in forming still more superior thought. For if you wish to be a master mind your thought must always be higher than the thought your environment may suggest, no matter how ideal that environment may be.

Every impression that enters the mind through the senses should be worked out and should be made to serve the mind in its fullest capacity. In this way the original impression will not reproduce itself in the mind, but will become instrumental in giving the mind a number of new and superior ideas. To work out an impression try to see through its own nature; that is, look at it from every conceivable point of view while trying to discern its causes, tendencies, possibilities and probable effects.

Use your imaging faculty in determining what you want to think or do, what you are to desire and what your tendencies are to be. Know what you want, then image those things upon the mind at all times. This will develop the power to think what you want to think. And he who can think what he wants to think can be what he wants to be. In this connection it is most important to realize that the principal reason why the average person has not realized his ideals is because he has not learned to think what he wants to think. He is too much affected by the suggestions that are all about him. He imitates his environment too much, following desires and tendencies that are not his own, and therefore he is misled and misplaced.

Whenever you permit yourself to think what persons, things, conditions or circumstances may suggest, you are not thinking what you yourself want to think. You are following borrowed desires instead of your own desire. Therefore you will drift into strange thinking, thinking that is entirely different from what you have planned and that maybe directly opposed to your present purpose, need or ambition.

To obey the call of every suggestion and permit your mind to be carried away by this, that or the other, is to develop the tendency to drift; your mind will wander, the power of concentration will weaken and you will become wholly incapable of really thinking what you want to think. In fact one line of constructive thinking will have scarcely begun when another line will be suggested, and you will leave the unfinished task to begin something else, which will in turn be left incomplete. Nothing, therefore, will be accomplished.

To become a master mind you must think what you want to think, no matter what your surroundings may suggest. And you must continue to think what you want to think until each particular purpose is carried out and every desired idea realized. Make it a point to desire what you want to desire and impress that desire so deeply upon consciousness that it cannot possibly be disturbed by such foreign desires as environment may suggest.

Then continue to express that desire in all thought and action until you get what you want.

When you know that you have the right desire do not permit anything to influence your mind to change. Take such influences and suggestions and convert them into the desire that you have already decided upon, thereby giving that desire additional life and power. However, you should never close your mind to impressions from without. Try to gain valuable impressions from every source, but do not follow those impressions. Use them in building up your own system of original thought. Then think what you want to think under every circumstance and so use every impression you receive that you will gain still greater power to think what you want to think. Thus you will readily and surely develop the master mind.

15. THE POWER OF MIND OVER BODY

IT IS through the law of vibration that the mind exercises its power over the body. And through this law every action of the mind produces a chemical effect in the body, that is, an effect that actually takes place in the substance of the physical form. The process of this law is readily understood when we find that every mental action is a vibration, and passes through every atom in the body, modifying both the general conditions and the chemical conditions of every group of cells.

A chemical change in the body is produced by a change in the vibrations of the different elements of the body because every element is what it is by virtue of the rate of vibrations of its atoms. Everything in the universe is what it is because of its rate of vibration; therefore, anything may be changed in nature and quality by changing the rate of its vibrations.

When we change the vibrations of ice it becomes water. When we change the vibrations of water it becomes steam. When we change the vibrations of ordinary earth in one or more ways it becomes green grass, roses, trees or waving fields of grain, depending upon the changes that are made. Nature is constantly changing the vibrations of her elements thus producing all sorts of forms, colors and appearances. In fact, the vast panorama of nature, both that which is visible to the senses and that which is not all is produced by constant changes in the vibrations of the elements and forces of nature.

Man, however, is doing the same in his kingdom, that is, in mind and personality. We all are changing the vibrations of different parts of our system every second, though all such changes are, of course, produced within the bounds of natural law. We know that by exercising the power of thought in any form or manner we can produce the vibrations both of our states of mind and our physical conditions. And when we exercise this power to the fullest degree possible we can change the vibrations of everything in our system and thus produce practically any condition that may be desired. This gives us a power that is extraordinary to say the least. But it is not a power that we have to secure. We have it already and we employ it every minute, because to think is to exercise this power. This being true the problem is to use this power intelligently and thus not only secure desirable results, or results as desired, but also to secure superior results to anything we have secured before.

When we analyze this law of vibration we find that every unpleasant condition that man has felt in his body has come from a false change in the vibrations of some of the elements in his body. And we also find that every agreeable condition has come from a true change in those vibrations, that is, a change towards the better. Here we should remember that every change in the vibrations of the human system that takes us down, so to speak into the lesser grade is a false change and will produce unnatural or detrimental effects, while every change that is an ascending change in the scale is beneficial.

To apply this law intelligently it is necessary to know what chemical changes each particular mental action has the power to produce, and also how we may so regulate mental actions that all changes in the vibrations of our system may be changes along the line of the ascending scale. This, however, leads us into a vast and most fascinating subject; but on account of its vastness we can only mention it here, which is all that is necessary in this connection, as our object for the present is simply to give the reason why every mental action produces a chemical change in the body.

Since every element in the body is what it is because it vibrates at a certain rate; since every mental action is a vibration; since every vibration that comes from an inner plane can modify vibrations that act upon an outer plane; and since all vibrations are within the physical plane of action, we understand perfectly why every mental action will tend to produce a chemical change in the body. Although it is also true that two different grades of vibration on the same plane, or in the same sphere of action, may modify each other, still they do so only when the one is much stronger than the other.

All mental vibrations act more deeply in chemical life than the physical vibrations; therefore the former can entirely change the latter, no matter how strong the latter may seem to be. And this is how the mind exercises power over the body. Some mental vibrations, however, are almost as near to the surface as the physical ones and for that reason produce but slight changes, changes that are some times imperceptible. Knowing this we understand why the power of mind over body becomes greater in proportion to the depth of consciousness and feeling that we enter into during any process of thought.

Therefore when we promote such changes in the body as we may desire or decide upon we must cultivate deeper consciousness, or what may be called subjective consciousness. This is extremely important because we can eliminate practically any physical disease or undesired physical condition by producing the necessary chemical change in those physical elements where that particular condition resides at the time. This is how medicine aims to cure and it does cure whenever it produces the necessary chemical change. But it fails so frequently in this respect that it cannot be depended upon under all circumstances.

Mental vibrations, however, when deep or subjective can in every case produce the necessary chemical change in the elements concerned. And the desired vibrations are invariably produced by positive, constructive and wholesome mental actions, provided those actions are deeply felt. Thus we realize that the power of mind acting through the law of vibration can, by changing or modifying the vibrations of the different elements in the body, produce almost any change desired in the physical conditions of the body.

What we wish to emphasize in this connection are the facts that every mental action is a vibration; that it permeates every atom of the body; that it comes up from the deeper chemical life, thereby working beneath the elements and forces of the physical body; and that according to a chemical law can modify and change the vibrations of those elements and forces to almost any extent within the sphere of natural law.

To modify the vibrations of the physical elements is to produce a chemical change in the body. But whether this change will be desirable or undesirable depends upon the nature of the mental action that produces the change. Therefore by entertaining and perpetuating only such mental actions as tend to produce desirable changes, or the changes we want in the body, we can secure practically any physical change desired;

and we may thereby exercise the power of mind over body to an extent that will have practically no limitation within the natural workings of the human domain.

16. THE POWER OF MIND OVER DESTINY

THE DESTINY of every individual is being created hourly by himself, and that something that determines what he is to create at any particular period in time is the sum total of his ideals. The future of the person is not preordained by some external power, nor is fate controlled by some strange and mysterious force that master minds can alone comprehend and apply. It is our ideals that control and determine our fate. And we all have our ideals, whether we be aware of the fact or not.

To have ideals is not simply to have dreams or visions of that which lies beyond the attainment of the person, nor is idealism a system of ideas that the practical mind would not have the privilege to entertain. To have ideals is to have definite objects in view, be those objects very high, very low or anywhere between those extremes. The ideals of any mind are simply the wants, the desires and the aims of that mind, and as every normal mind will invariably live, think and work for that which is wanted by his present state of existence, it is evident that every mind must necessarily follow his ideals both consciously and unconsciously.

However, when those ideals are low or inferior the individual will naturally work for the ordinary and the inferior, and the products of his mind will correspond in quality to that for which he is working. Thus inferior causes will spring up everywhere in his life and inferior effects will inevitably follow. But when those ideals are high and superior he will work for the superior; he will develop superiority in himself and he will give superiority to everything that he may produce. Accordingly every action that he originates in his life will become a superior cause and will be followed by a superior effect.

The destiny of every individual is determined by what he is and by what he is doing. And what any individual is to be or do is determined by what he is living for, thinking for, or working for, be those objects great or small, superior or inferior. Man is not being made by some outside force, nor is the fate of man the result of causes outside of himself. Man is making himself as well as his future with what he is working for and in all his efforts he invariably follows his ideals.

It is therefore evident that he who lives, thinks and works for the superior becomes superior while he who works for less becomes less. And also that any individual may become more, achieve more, secure more and create for himself a better future and a greater destiny by beginning to think, live and work for a superior group of ideals.

To have low ideals is to give the creative forces of the system something ordinary to work for. To have high ideals is to give those forces something extraordinary to work for. And the fate of man is the result of what those forces are constantly producing. Every force in the human system is producing something and that something will become a part both of the individual and his external circumstances.

It is therefore evident that any individual can improve the power, the quality and the worth of his being by directing the forces of his system to produce something that has quality and worth. Those forces, however, are not directed or controlled entirely by the will, because it is their nature to produce what the mind desires, wants or needs. And the desires of any mind are determined directly by the leading ideals entertained in that mind.

The forces of the system will begin to work for the superior when the mind begins to entertain superior ideals. And since it is the product of those creative forces that determine both the nature and the destiny of man it is evident that a superior nature and a greater destiny may be secured by any individual who will adopt, and live up to, the highest and the most perfect system of idealism that he can possibly comprehend.

To entertain superior ideals is to picture in the mind, and to hold constantly before the mind, the highest conceptions that can be formed of everything of which we may be conscious. To dwell mentally in those higher conceptions at all times is to cause the predominating ideals to become superior ideals. And it is the ruling ideals for which we live, think and work.

When the ruling ideals of any mind are superior the creative forces of that mind will produce the superior in every element, faculty, talent or power in that mind. Thus the greater will be developed in that mind, and the great mind invariably creates a better future and a greater destiny.

To entertain superior ideals is not to dream of the impossible, but to enter into mental contact with those greater possibilities that we are not able to discern. And to have the power to discern an ideal indicates that we have the power to realize that ideal. For the fact is we do not become conscious of greater possibilities until we have developed sufficient capacity to work out those possibilities into practical tangible results.

Therefore, when we discern the greater we are ready to attain and achieve the greater, but before we can proceed to do what we are ready to do we must adopt superior ideals, and live up to those ideals according to our full capacity and power. When our ideals are superior we shall think constantly of the superior because as our ideals are, so is our thinking. And to thing constantly of the superior is to grow steadily into the likeness of the superior. Thus all the forces of the mind will move toward the superior. All things in the life of the individual will work together with greater and greater goals in view, and continuous advancement on a larger and broader scale must inevitably follow.

To entertain superior ideals is not simply to desire some larger personal attainment, nor is it to dwell mentally in some belief that is different from the usual beliefs of the world. To entertain superior ideals is simply to think the best thought about everything and to try to improve upon that thought every day. Superior idealism therefore is not mere dreaming of the great and beautiful. It is also the actual living in mental harmony with the very best we know in all things, in all persons, in all circumstances and in all expressions of life. To live in mental harmony with the best we can find anywhere is to create the best in our own mentalities and personalities.

And as we grow steadily into the likeness of that which we think of the most we will in this manner increase our power, capacity and worth, and in consequence be able to create a better future and a more worthy destiny. For it is the law under every circumstance that the man who becomes much will achieve much, and great attainments are invariably followed by a greater future.

To think of anything that is less than the best or to dwell mentally with the inferior is to neutralize the effect of those superior ideals that we have begun to entertain. It is therefore absolutely necessary to entertain superior ideals only, and to cease all recognition of inferiority or imperfection if we want to secure the best results along these lines.

In this connection we find the reason why the majority fail to secure any tangible results from higher ideals, for the fact is they entertain too many lower ideals at the same time. They may aim high, they may adore the beautiful, they may desire the perfect, they may live for the better and they may work for the greater, but they do not think their best thoughts about everything; therefore the house in their case is divided against itself and cannot stand.

Superior idealism, however, contains no thought that is less than the best, and it entertains no desire that has not greater worth in view. Such idealism does not recognize the power of evil in anything or in anybody. It may know that adverse conditions do exist, but it gives the matter no conscious thought whatever. And to pursue this course is absolutely necessary if we would create a better future. For it is not possible to think the best thought about everything while the mind gives conscious attention to adversity and imperfection.

The true idealist therefore gives conscious recognition only to the power of good. And he lives in the conviction that all things in his life are working together for good. But this conviction is not mere sentiment with him because he knows that all things will work together for good when we recognize only the good, think only the good, desire only the good, expect only the good and live only for the good.

To apply the principle of superior idealism in all things, that is, to live, think and work only for the highest ideals that we can comprehend means advancement in all things. To follow the superior ideal is to move towards the higher, the greater and the superior. And no one can continue very long in that mode of living, thinking and acting without creating for himself a new world, a better environment and a fairer destiny.

We understand therefore that in order to create a better future we must begin now to select a better group of ideals, for it is our ideals that constitute the cause of the future we expect to create. And as the cause is so will also be the effect.

17. THE X-RAY POWER OF THE MIND

THERE ARE many things that the human mind can do and all of them are remarkable when viewed from the highest pinnacle of consciousness; but one of the greatest and most wonderful is the power of mind to see through things; that is, to cause the rays of its insight and discernment to pass through the problems of life just as the X-ray passes through opaque and tangible substances. This power is latent in every mind and is active to a considerable degree in many minds; and on account of the extreme value of this power its development should be promoted in every possible manner.

When this power is highly developed practically all mistakes can be avoided. The right thing can be done at the right time, and every opportunity can be taken advantage of when the psychological moment is at hand; and in addition that finer perception of life will be gained through which consciousness may expand into larger and larger fields until the mind goes beyond all limitations and lives in the spirit of the universal.

We are all surrounded by possibilities that can never be measured, possibilities which, if employed even in a limited degree, would make life many times as rich and beautiful as it is now. The average person, however, does not see these many larger and greater ways of adding to the value and worth of existence. In other words, he cannot see through the circumstances of his life and thus take possession of the more substantial elements of growth, attainment and realization. Therefore life with him continues to remain a very ordinary matter.

He may know that there are better things in store and that there is something just beyond his present conception of life that could change his life completely if he could only lay hold upon it; still here is where he fails. He is in the dark. He cannot see how to proceed in gaining those greater and better things that life must contain. There is something in the way of his vision, a cloud, a veil, or an obstacle of some kind that hides the path to better things. And he cannot see through the obstacle. For this reason he remains where he is, wondering why he has not the power to reach what he is absolutely certain could be reached.

Millions of minds complain "if we could only have things cleared up." This is the problem everywhere. Therefore, if they could all see their way clear what might they not accomplish both for themselves and others. But as a rule they do not see their way clear. Occasional glimpses of light appear when the real path to all good things seems to reveal itself, but before they are ready to take this path another cloud comes in the way and they have no idea what to do next. This is the experience of the average person along these lines.

And there seems to be no hope for the average person of ever passing from the lesser to the greater. The reason seems to be that when everything looks bright and the way is clear for greater results, desirable changes, more happiness and a larger life, something invariably happens to confuse things again, and the way to pastures green has for the time being been closed up once more. However, there is a way out of all sorts of conditions and everybody can find this way. Though it is a fact well to remember that every individual must always see this way for himself.

To proceed, everybody must develop the power to see through things. In fact, see through all things, or in other words, learn to use the X-ray of what may be termed superior degrees of intelligence. Every mind has this X-ray, this higher power to penetrate and see through the difficult and the confused. And there is no condition, no circumstance, no obstacle, no mystery through which this ray cannot penetrate. Therefore, when we employ this X-ray of the mind we clear up everything, we see exactly where we are going, where we ought to go and where we should not go. So that to live constantly in the light of these finer grades of intelligence is to live in the cleared up atmosphere perpetually, no matter where our sphere of activity may be.

That those minds that live in the lower atmosphere of thought cannot see clearly where they are going is quite natural. Because in the first place these lower atmospheres of life are usually dense, being surcharged with the confused thought of the world; and in the second place, those who live in these lower grades do not employ the higher and finer rays of mental light.

We all know that the lower vibrations of physical light cannot pass through objects that are opaque. And we have also learned that the lower rays of mental light cannot pass through conditions and circumstances that are confused with discord and materiality. But it has been demonstrated that the higher rays of physical light can pass through almost any physical object. In like manner the higher rays of intelligence or mental light can see through almost anything in the mental world. And, therefore, the one who employs these higher rays of his mind will have the power to see through all things in his life.

However, when we speak of higher grades of intelligence as being the power that can see through things we must not infer that such intelligence is too high to be gained by the average individual. For the fact is that we all have this higher intelligence or finer rays of mental light active within us at all times. The secret is simply to learn how to apply these finer rays of mental light; thus we shall all be able to exercise the power to see through things.

The difference between the lower and the higher rays of light is found almost wholly in the attitude of the mind. That is, it is materiality on the one hand and spirituality on the other hand. By materiality we mean the attitude of mind that looks down; an attitude that is absorbed wholly in things; that dwells on the surface, and that lives exclusively for the body, not being consciously interested in anything but the body.

By spirituality we mean that attitude of the mind that gives an upward look to every thought, every desire, every motive, every feeling and every action of the entire being of man. But this upward look is not an attitude that looks for the invisible, nor an attitude that dreams of the glories of another sphere of existence. It is an attitude that simply looks for the greater possibilities that exist everywhere now, and for the beauty and the truth that crowns the whole world.

The mind that is material or that lives exclusively in the world of things is more or less in the clouds of confusion, therefore employs the lesser rays of intelligence, those rays that do not have the power to see through things. Such a mind, therefore, can never be in a cleared-up mental atmosphere. At times those minds that have been conscious of higher grades of mentality and that have seen the superiority and the brilliancy of

340

this higher intelligence within them, may fall down temporarily into materiality, and for the time being they may lose sight completely of the higher consciousness of truth which they previously gained. Thus they frequently forget every principle in higher experience that once was so vivid, and while in this state of depression they generally conclude that all is sin, sorrow and human weakness after all; that is, it seems so to such a mind, because at such a time it is only the discord of the world and the results of mistakes that are discerned.

While in this submerged state the mind cannot see the splendors that are immediately beyond, and he cannot feel the supreme joy that higher realms have in store. Accordingly he comes to the conclusion that all is trouble and pain; he feels nothing else, knows nothing else and has temporarily forgotten the light and the joy that he knew while in higher realms of consciousness. The wise man who wrote the proverbs was in this lower mentality when he declared that all is vanity and vexation of spirit. And he spoke the truth about that lower world, that is, that material state that is composed wholly of the mistakes of man.

That material state, however, is not the only world that there is. There are other and finer worlds in the mind of man worlds where vanity does not exist and where nothing vexes the spirit. It is these higher and finer worlds of the mind that we must train ourselves to love, if we wish to see through things and thus learn to understand things as they really are. Then we shall find that the wrong is insignificant compared with the immensity of the right and the good.

When we look at things from a worldly or materialistic point of view, things do not appear very well, nor are things always very well in that particular state. They are frequently wrong and misdirected. But when we learn to see through things and see all things as they are we change our minds. Then we discover other worlds and other and higher stories to the mansion in which we live. The cellar is usually dark and damp, but how much better we find it further up. And yet when the average person is in the cellar of his mind he imagines that it is the only place there is and that there is neither light, comfort nor joy in the world. But why should we ever enter the cellar of the mind, and why should we permit a dark damp cellar to exist in our minds at all? There is no need of it in human life, for it is simply the sum total of our mistakes, and does not represent the real mansion of existence in any sense of the term.

The whole of the being of man should be illumined and every atom should be filled with harmony, comfort, joy and life. When the mind that had fallen down comes up again it realizes how absurd it was to forget all the truth and all the joy of real existence simply because there were a few clouds for a little time. However, after a few such experiences the mind learns to interpret the experience of the cellar and does not consider it real anymore, but on the contrary makes haste to prevent that experience as well as all other descending attitudes in the future.

The mind that has never experienced the higher phases of consciousness does not know how to proceed to prevent the more adverse experiences of ordinary existence, and therefore will remain among the dense fogs of confusion more or less until taught how to rise into the finer grades of mental light. To proceed in rising above these undesirable conditions the first step to take is to make harmony, happiness and brightness of spirit the great objects in view. Even when we simply think of these states we elevate the mind in a measure, and whenever the mind is elevated to some extent we find that finer light comes into our world of intelligence; that is, the higher rays of mentality begin to express themselves and many things begin to clear up.

In this connection it is well to remember that our brightest ideas come while we are on the mountain top of intellectual activity, and also that we can find the correct answer to almost any problem that may appear in personal life if we only go up in mind as high as we possibly can reach at the time. While the mind is up in those finer grades of intellect the most abstract principles are comprehended with almost no mental effort, and the path to greater things becomes as clear as the midday sun.

It is therefore a great and valuable accomplishment to be able to go up in the mind as high as one may wish. For to bring superior intelligence into constant use is to live in the world of absolute light itself, the reason being that this intelligence actually does possess X-ray power of penetration in the mental world. There is nothing that this ray cannot see through, and there nothing is hidden that it cannot reveal to light.

Again we must remember, however, that it is not necessary to attain an enormous amount of wisdom and knowledge in order to gain the power to see through things in this way, because every stage of development that exists has the power to see through everything that may appear in that particular stage. Every individual in his present state has the power to see through everything in that state, that is, a finer grade of a mental light that belongs to that particular state and it has the X-ray power of penetration in its own sphere. Accordingly he can learn to see through everything where he is without becoming a mental giant, or without acquiring wisdom which belongs exclusively to higher states of mental attainment.

The idea is to live in the upper story of your mental world whatever that world may be now, because by entering the upper story of your mental world you enter that state of your present intelligence that can see through everything that pertains to your present world. In order to enter the upper story of the mind the whole of life should be concentrated so to speak, upon the most superior states of existence that we can conceive of. This will cause the mind to become ascending in its attitude and the power of the ascending mind is immense. Such a mind will steadily grow upward and onward towards higher and finer grades of intellect, wisdom and mental light, and gradually this power to see through things will be gained. In addition everything will be turned to greater use and better use, and thus be made more conducive to a life of beauty, richness and joy.

However, when we proceed to consecrate a life to the superior in this manner we do not leave the world of things. We simply turn the life and the power of all things towards the higher, the larger and the better. We thereby cause the world of things to move steadily towards superior states of life and action. As we enter more and more into this upper realm of thought, light and understanding we should employ this penetrating power of finer intelligence in connection with every move we make. For it is the constant use and the true use of a power that develops that power. Therefore, we should do nothing without first turning on the X-ray of the mind. In other words, we should view every circumstance from the standpoint of a clearer perception before any decision is made, and we should seek to secure the very highest viewpoint under every circumstance. This will not only give the mind a better understanding of how to proceed, but the faculty of finer discernment will be developed constantly, and our growth in wisdom and intellectual brilliancy will in time become remarkable. In this connection we should remember that nearly all the missteps that are taken in the average life are the results of the mind's failure to penetrate the surface of things and conditions so as to see the real nature of the factors at work. But the lower mental rays, that is, that phase of intelligence that we use while in the lower story of the mind, do not possess this penetrating power. Therefore, if we learn to live, think and act correctly under all sorts of circumstances we must learn to employ the X-ray of the mind; that is, that light of the mind that we are conscious of when living in the upper story of the mind; and it is when we are in that light that we can see through all things.

18. WHEN MIND IS BROAD AND DEEP

IT HAS become a virtue to be broad minded, but there are times when certain virtues become so extreme in their actions that they cease to contain any virtue. In like manner it is possible for the mind to become so broad that it contains practically nothing of value being too superficial in its effort to cover the whole field to possess a single idea of merit.

To be progressive in thought is another admirable trait in the eyes of the modern world, but there are not a few of our advanced thinkers who advance so rapidly, according to their own conception of advancement, that their own minds are literally left behind; that is, they become so absorbed in the act of moving forward that no attention is given to that power that alone can produce advancement. In consequence their remarkable progress is in the imagination only.

Here it is well to remember that all is not thought that comes from the mind or that is produced in the mind. For the mere fact that we are thinking does not prove that we are creating thought. A large percentage of the products of the average mind is but heaps of intellectual debris accumulated in one place today and moved to another place in the mind tomorrow. In brief, too much of our modern thinking is simply a moving of useless mental material from one side of consciousness to another. However, in promoting the right use of the mind this practice is something that must be avoided absolutely for the mind cannot work to advantage under such conditions.

Thought that really is thought is the product of design and purpose, and is invariably the result of systematic efforts to work out principles. Accordingly such thought contains the power to serve certain definite objects in view. We should therefore realize that no product of the mind constitutes real thought unless it is the result of designed thinking and is created for a certain special purpose. A pile of brick is not a house, but a house may be built from those bricks if they are arranged according to special design and put together for a definite purpose.

The broad mind should endeavor to embrace much, but should not attempt to hold more than can be applied practically and thoroughly and according to the purpose which it is desired to fulfill. In other words, the object is not to see how much we can hold in the mind, but how much we can actually possess or use; not how much ground we can cover, but how much we can take care of in the best manner, and cultivate scientifically.

In this connection it is most important to understand that the mind that becomes broad enough to accept everything will also accept the illusions, the vagaries and the foundationless theories that are so numerous everywhere. There are a number of people today who do this very thing and call themselves liberal, advanced, charitable and broadly progressive. But the fact is that their minds constitute a hopeless mixture of truths, half-truths and illusions. Accordingly they accomplish very little, and what is more serious they confuse the beginners in genuine advanced thought and thus tend to place the real truth of our progressive movements in a false light.

However, there is a progress that is progressive. There is an advancement that actually does advance and we have much of it today. But there are many movements and many people claiming to be broad who are broad only in the sense of keeping the mental doors wide open to everything that may desire to come in. But such broad mindedness must be avoided at every turn because it tends to make the mind shallow, superficial and inefficient, thereby rendering the mentality incapable of actually taking possession of a single genuine idea or mental power.

The mind that is broad in the true sense of the term does not try to embrace everything, but tries to penetrate everything. Its object is not to simply take in and hold, but to enter into and understand and thereby gain real control and possession of facts, talents and powers. The truth is that to be broad minded is not to be ready to believe everything, but to be ready to examine everything, and to accept everything that proves itself true regardless of how it may conflict with objects, views or opinions.

A broad mind never takes things on authority, but is eternally in search of the one authority truth that is back of and within all things. In brief, to be able to see the true side of every belief, every system, every idea and every experience this is genuine broad mindedness.

In considering this subject we must remember that what we accept becomes a part of ourselves. Therefore it is a most serious mistake to take into the mind everything that may come along. The fact is we cannot possibly exercise too much care in selecting our ideas, although we must not go to the other extreme and become so particular that we remain dissatisfied with everything. There is a happy medium in this connection that everyone can establish by training the mind to penetrate everything for the purpose of understanding the principles that underlie everything.

It has been well stated that we gradually grow into the likeness of that which we admire the most and think of the most. And it is true that we nearly always have special admiration for that which we constantly defend, whether we have fully accepted the same as true or not. The mind that is willing to accept almost anything for the sake of being broad will also be ready to defend almost anything to justify that position. Therefore to defend all theories the past has advanced, is to reproduce our minds more or less in the likeness of all those theories. But since those theories contradict each other at almost every turn, many of them being illusions, we can readily imagine the result. In fact, the mind will, under such circumstances, be divided against itself and will be incapable of doing its work according to principle and law.

A confused mind is the greatest obstacle to real progress and the attempt to take in every new idea as true because it is new will invariably confuse the mind, and what is more such a practice will so derange judgment that after a while the mind will not be able to discriminate intelligently between the right and the wrong in any sphere of life.

In this connection we must remember that among the new ideas that are springing up in the world the larger number are either half-truths or illusions. And the reason why so many of these ideas are accepted as true is because real broad mindedness, that is, that attitude of mind that does not embrace everything but attempts to penetrate everything, is an art yet to be acquired by the majority. The average mind is ready to take in and hold almost any belief or idea if it happens to produce an impression that is favorable to his present condition of life, but there are few who are training their minds to penetrate everything for the purpose of understanding everything. For this reason a mass of ideas are accepted that contain neither virtue, truth nor power.

The attitude of tolerance is closely connected with broad mindedness and is usually considered an exceptional virtue. But again we are liable to be misled because there are two kinds of tolerance; the one holds a passive charity for everything without trying to find out the truth about anything; while the other enters into friendly relation with all things in order that the good and true that may exist in those things can be found.

The attitude of tolerance, however, is always valuable, in so far as it eliminates the spirit of criticism, because the spirit of criticism can never find the truth. But the spirit of friendly research always does find the truth. For this reason the penetrating mind must be kind, gentle and sympathetic. If it is not, the very elements that are to be examined will be scattered and misplaced. Besides it is the substance of things that contains the truth, and to enter into this substance the mind must be in sympathetic touch with the life and the soul of that which it seeks to understand.

That attitude of tolerance that is passive, is either indifferent, or will soon become indifferent; and mental indifference leads to stagnation, which in turn makes the mind so inactive that it is completely controlled by every condition or environment with which it may come in contact. Such a tolerance, therefore, must be avoided and avoided absolutely.

True tolerance refrains from criticism at all times but that is only one side of its nature. The other side enters into the closest mental contact with all things and penetrates to the very depths of the principles upon which these things are based. In this way the mind readily discovers those ideas and beliefs that constitute the true expressions of principles, and also discovers those which are mere perversions. However, the tolerant mind does not condemn the perversions. It forgets them entirely by giving added life and attention to the true expressions , and thereby proceeds to give lull and positive action to all those ideas and powers of which it has gained possession by being broad as well as deep.

19. THE GREATEST MIND OF ALL

IN ORDER that we may rise in the scale of life the mind must fix attention upon the ideal. And the ideal may be defined as that possible something that is above and beyond present realization. To become more and accomplish more we must transcend the lesser and enter the greater. But there can be no transcending action unless there is a higher goal toward which all the elements within us are moving; and there can be no higher goal unless there is a clear discernment of the ideal.

The more distinctly the mind discerns the ideal, and the more frequently the ideal is brought directly before the actions of attention the more will the mind think of the ideal; and the mind invariably moves towards that which we think of the most.

The man with no ideals will think constantly f that which is beneath the ideal, or rather that which is the opposite of the ideal; that is, he will think the most of that which is low, inferior and unworthy.

In consequence he will drift more and more into the life of nothingness, emptiness, inferiority and want. Tie will steadily go down into the lesser until he wants for everything, both on the mental and physical planes.

The man, however, who has high ideals will think the most of the greater things in life, and accordingly will advance perpetually into the possession of everything that has greatness, superiority and high worth. The wise men of the past declared that the nation with no visions would perish. And the cause of this fact is simple. When we are not going up we are going down. To live is to be in action and there is no standstill in action. To continue to go down is to finally perish. Therefore to prevent such an end we must continue to go up. But we cannot continue to go up towards the higher unless we have constant visions of the higher. We cannot move mentally or physically towards that which we do not see.

Nor can we desire that of which we have never been conscious.

In like manner the individual who has no ideals and no visions of greater things will continue to go down until his life becomes mere emptiness. Thus everything in his nature that has worth will perish, and finally he will have nothing to live for. When he discovers himself he will find that there are but two courses to pursue: To continue to live in the valley of tears he has made for himself; or to ascend towards the heights of emancipation, those heights which can be reached only by following the lofty vision.

It is the visions of greater things that arouse the mind to greater action. It is higher ideals that inspire man to create more nobly in the real, and it is the touch of things sublime that awakens in human nature that beautiful something that makes life truly worth living. Without ideals no person will ever attain greatness, neither will there be any improvement in the world. But every person who has ideals, and who lives to realize his ideals, will positively attain greatness, and will positively improve everything, both in his life and in his environment.

It must be clearly evident to all minds who understand the true functions of the ideal that the life of man will be worthless unless inspired by the ideal, and also that everything that is worthwhile in human existence comes directly from man's effort to rise towards the ideal. Such men, therefore, who are constantly placing high ideals before the world in a manner that will attract the attention of the world it is such men who invariably have the greatest mind of all.

The majority have not the power to discern the ideal clearly without having their attention aroused by the vivid description of some lucid mind that already does see the ideal. But when their attention is aroused and the ideal is made clear to their minds, they will begin at once to rise in the scale. That individual, therefore, who is constantly placing ideals before the minds of the many is causing the many to rise towards the more worthy and the more beautiful in life. In consequence he is not only doing great things himself, but he is causing thousands of others to do great things. He is not only awakening the superior powers in his own nature, but he is also awakening those powers in the natures of vast multitudes. His mind, therefore, is doing work that is great indeed.

However, to place ideals before the minds of others, it is not necessary to make that particular purpose a profession, nor is it sufficient to reveal idealism in the mere form of written or spoken words. Actions speak louder than words and the man who does things exercises a far greater power for good than the man who simply says things. The ideal can be made a vital and a ruling element in every vocation. And all men and women can reveal the ideal through their work without giving voice to a single word concerning any particular system of idealism.

But it is not necessary to be silent concerning those sublime visions that daily appear before the mind, although it is well to remember that we always secure the best results when we do a great deal more than we say. The man who makes his work an inspiration to greater things will invariably do greater and greater work and he will also cause thousands of others to do greater work. He will make his own ideals practical and tangible, and will thereby make the ideal intelligible to the majority. For though it is true that great words inspire the few, it requires great deeds to inspire the many.

The man who makes his own life worthwhile will cause thousands of others to make their lives worthwhile. In consequence the value and happiness that he will add to the sum total of human existence cannot possibly be measured. He is placing great and living ideals before the world and must therefore be counted among those who possess the greatest mind in the world.

The man who performs a great work has achieved greatness, but his work is the work of one man only. That man, however, who places high ideals before the minds of the many, thereby awakening the greatness that is latent within the many, causes a greater work to be performed by each one of the many; thus he gives origin to a thousand great deeds, where the former gives origin to a few only. That he is greater in exact proportion is therefore a fact that cannot be disputed. For this reason we must conclude that the greatest mind of all is invariably that mind that can inspire the greatest number to live, think and work for the vision.

To awaken the greatness that is latent in man is to awaken the cause of everything that has real worth in the world. Such work, therefore, is the greatest of all great work and it is a work that lies within the power of everybody. For we all can awaken the greatness that is latent in other minds by placing high ideals before those minds.

The great soul lives in the world of superior visions and aims to make those visions real by training all the powers of mind and personality to move towards those visions. And here it is highly important to realize that when the powers of mind and personality steadily move towards the ideal they will create the ideal more and more in the present, thereby making the ideal real in the present.

To live where there is neither improvement nor advancement is to live a life that is utterly worthless. But improvement and advancement are not possible without ideals. We must have visions of the better before we can make things better. And before we can make things better we must discern the greater before we can rise out of the lesser. To advance is to move towards something that is beyond the present; but there can be no advancement until that something is discerned. And as everything that is beyond the present is ideal, the mind must necessarily have idealism before any advancement can possibly take place.

Everything that is added to the value of life has been produced because someone had ideals; because someone revealed those ideals; and because someone tried to make those ideals real. It is therefore evident that when lofty ideals are constantly placed before the mind of the whole world we may add immeasurably to the value of life, and in every manner conceivable.

The same law through which we may increase that which is desired in life we may apply for the elimination of that which is not desired. And to remove what is not desired the secret is to press on towards the ideal. The ideal contains what is desired, and to enter that which is desired is to rise out of that which is not desired. Through the application of this law we eliminate the usual method of resistance, which is highly important, because when we antagonize the wrong or that which is not desired we give life to the wrong, thereby adding to its power. For the fact is we always give power to that which we resist or antagonize. In consequence we will, through such a method, either perpetuate the wrong or remove one wrong by placing another in its stead.

However, no wrong was ever righted in the world until the race ignored that wrong and began to rise into the corresponding right. And to enter into this rising attitude is to become an idealist. It is not the iconoclast, but the idealist who reforms the world. And the greatest reformer is invariably that man whose conception of the ideal is so clear that his entire mind is illumined by a brilliant light of superior worlds. His thought, his life, his word, his action in brief, everything connected with his existence, gives the same vivid description of the ideal made real. And every person with whom he may come in contact will be inspired to live on those same superior heights of sublime existence.

When we try to force any ill away from any part of the system, be the system that of an individual, a community, or a race, we invariably cause a similar or modified ill to appear in some other part of that system. For the fact is that no ill can be eliminated until it is replaced by wholeness. And wholeness will not enter the system until the system enters wholeness. We must enter the light before we can receive or possess the light. And to enter wholeness is to enter the ideal and perfect existence.

To enter the ideal, however, it is necessary to understand the ideal. Every form of emancipation, as well as, as every process of advancement will depend directly upon the mind's understanding of the ideal, and its aspiration towards the ideal. A strong ascending desire to realize the ideal will in the life of any individual cause the entire system of that individual to outgrow everything that is inferior or undesirable. In consequence complete emancipation and greater and greater attainments must invariably follow.

When we understand this subject thoroughly we realize that if all the strong minds in the world would constantly face the idea!, giving all their power to the attainment of the ideal and living completely in the reality of the ideal, a live current permeating the whole race would begin to move towards the ideal. And so strong would this current become that its power would be irresistible. The natural result would be that the ideal would be realized more and more in every individual life of the race. This possibility demonstrates the extreme value of the ideal and the importance of living absolutely for the ideal. It also demonstrates the fact that all such men and women who are constantly placing the ideal before the minds of the world possess the greatest minds in the world. For it is only such minds that can inspire the masses of minds to discern the ideal, to desire the ideal and to live for the realization of the ideal.

20. WHEN MIND IS ON THE HEIGHTS

WHEN THE great soul transcends the world of things it invariably begins to dream of that which is greater, finer, more perfect, more beautiful and more sublime than what the life of present experience has been able to produce. But those dreams are not mere dreams; they are actually glimpses of what is possible or what may be near at hand; that is, prophetic visions of what is to be. The dreams of the small soul are usually temporary creations of an unguided imagination. But the dreams of the great soul are flashes of light emanating from the realms of supreme light, revealing secrets that man shall some day be able to make his own.

What the great soul discerns in his visions and dreams is nothing less than that greater life and those greater things into the possession of which he is being prepared to enter. But if we would gain those greater things which are in store we must proceed to claim our own, and not simply continue to dream. The prophetic vision of the great soul does not reveal what will come to pass of its own accord, but what such a soul is now competent to bring to pass, provided he will use the powers that are in his possession now. In brief, a prophetic vision does not reveal something that is coming to you, but reveals something that you now have the power to bring to yourself if you will.

The soul that can transcend the world of passing things and dream of the world of better things is now in possession of the necessary power to make his dreams come true. For the fact is, we cannot discern the ideal until we have the power to make it real, nor can the mind arise into worlds sublime until it has gained the power to make its own life sublime. Therefore the soul that can look into the mystic future and discern a more beautiful life is prepared for such a life, has found the secret path to such a life, has the power to create such a life, though not merely in ages to come, but now. For what we see in our visions today we have the power to bring to pass in the present. This is indeed a great truth, and than this, nothing could possibly bring greater joy to the soul of man.

If we can see better days while our minds are on the heights we can rest assured that we have the power to create better days. But we must proceed to use that power if we would enter into the pastures green that are before us. The law is that what we see in the ideal we must work for in the actual, for it is in this way alone that our dreams can come true without fail.

The dreams of the great soul always appear when the mind is on the heights. And it is such dreams alone that can contain the prophetic vision. What we dream of while on the low lands of life has no value. The fact is that if we would know the next step; if we would know what today can bring forth; if we would know what is best now; if we would know what we are able to attain and achieve now; if we would know those greater things that are now in store for us, we must rise to the mountain top of the soul's transcendent existence. It is there, and there alone, that these things are made known. And every mind can at times ascend to those sublime heights. The great soul can readily rise to these mountain tops; in brief, such a soul has no other visions than those that appear on the mountain tops. Therefore the dreams of the great soul are not mere dreams;

they are positive indications of what can be done, of what will be done; they are glimpses of the splendors of a greater day.

The soul that can rise to the mountain tops and see the splendor of greater things can indeed rejoice with great joy for such a soul is not destined for an ordinary life. Greater things are at hand and a wonderful future will positively be realized. But such a future, with its richer possibilities and its more worthy attainments, will not come back to us where we now stand. We must move forward and work for what we have seen in the vision. That which is greater does not come back to that which is lesser. We must press on into the life of the greater if we would realize such a life. And if we dreamed the dreams of the great soul those dreams will indicate that we can. What we have seen on the heights reveals what we can do if we will. We have gained the power; the gates are ajar, and in the beautiful somewhere our own is waiting.

End.

BOOK FIVE

THINKING FOR RESULTS

ABOUT THIS BOOK

THIS IS THE PRINCIPLE.—You are constantly thinking. To think is to place energy in action. All active energy tends to produce certain results. Then the question is what those results are to be. Are they to be favorable or detrimental, superior or inferior, for you or against you? This you can determine by thinking according to design— by thinking for a definite purpose—by placing in action energies that will act for your advantage—by training all the powers of your mind to work for your purpose.

This book was among the first ones ever written by Larson, and contains a very nice summary of his philosophy on the power of thought, and the importance of keeping always good thoughts, as the way to have a happy, fulfilling life, full of "results".

"Man is as he thinks he is, and what he does is the result of the sum total of his thought" says the author. "The average person, however, thinks at random and therefore lives at random and does not know from day to day whether good or evil lies in his path. What he finds in his path is invariably the result of his own thinking, but as he does not know what results different kinds of thought produce he creates both good and evil daily not knowing that he necessarily does either of these. When he knows what each mental state will produce, however, and has gained the power to think as he likes under all sorts of circumstances, then he will have fate, destiny, environment, physical conditions, mental conditions, attainments, achievements and in fact everything in his own hands."

This book is about teaching the reader, precisely that: what each mental state will produce, and how to control them.

1

THAT man can change himself, improve himself, recreate himself, control his environment and master his own destiny is the conclusion of every mind who is wide-awake to the power of right thought in constructive action. In fact, it is the conviction of all such minds that man can do practically anything within the possibilities of the human domain when he knows how to think, and that he can secure almost any result desired when he learns how to think for results.

Man is as he thinks he is, and what he does is the result of the sum total of his thought. The average person, however, thinks at random and therefore lives at random and does not know from day to day whether good or evil lies in his path. What he finds in his path is invariably the result of his own thinking, but as he does not know what results different kinds of thought produce he creates both good and evil daily not knowing that he necessarily does either of these. When he knows what each mental state will produce, however, and has gained the power to think as he likes under all sorts of circumstances, then he will have fate, destiny, environment, physical conditions, mental conditions, attainments, achievements and in fact everything in his own hands.

It is a well-known fact that we can produce any effect desired when we understand causes, and can master those causes. And as the process of thinking is the one underlying cause in the life of man we naturally become master over all life when we can understand and master the process of thinking. Each process of thinking produces its own results in mind and body and acts indirectly upon all the actions and efforts of mind and body. Therefore, through adverse thinking almost any undesirable condition may be produced while almost any condition of worth and value can be produced through wholesome thinking. Certain processes of thought will lead to sickness, others to poverty, while processes of thought that are entirely different from these will lead to health, power and prosperity. Through chaotic thinking one can bring about years of trouble and misfortune, while through a properly arranged system of thinking one can determine his own future for years and years in advance.

Everything that happens to a man is the result of something that he has done or fails to do. But since both actions and inactions come from corresponding states of mind he can make almost anything happen that he likes when he learns to regulate his thinking. This may seem to be a very strong statement, but the more perfectly we understand the relation of mental action to physical and personal action the more convinced we become that this statement is absolutely true.

When we study the laws of nature we find that certain results invariably follow certain uses of those laws; and that other results follow the misuse of those laws. We find that a misused law can finally carry you to the lowest depths, and that a law that is perfectly understood and properly applied can carry you to the greatest heights. In the use of natural law, however, we are at liberty to change our mind at any time; that is, when we find ourselves going down we can turn about and go the other way; though the fact remains that if we continue the down grade we will finally reach the lowest depths. The same is true when we find ourselves advancing; we may become negligent and fall back, but the law in question can carry us on higher and higher without end if we choose to go. The laws that govern thinking are just as absolute as the well-known laws of nature and will serve man just as faithfully after he has begun to apply them with understanding.

When we understand the laws of thought and think accordingly, we have begun what may properly be termed scientific thinking; that is, we have begun designed thinking; thinking with a purpose in view; thinking in accordance with exact scientific system; and thinking for results. When we think in this manner we think according to those laws of thought that are required in order to produce the results we have in view; therefore all the forces of mind will be directed to produce those very results. In this connection we should remember that every mental process produces its own results in the human system; therefore we can secure any result desired when we place in action the necessary mental process.

You never think scientifically unless you think for a purpose; it is therefore purposeless thinking that you must avoid. And all purposeless thinking is wrong. Every process of thought that works at random is wrong because it leads to waste, destruction and retarded growth. For this reason all thoughts that we may create at any time that have no special purpose in view are wrong thoughts and are detrimental to the welfare of the individual. But here we must remember that wrong thought is not simply thought that has base motives; it is also thought that has no motives. A right thought always has a definite motive with some higher goal in view. In fact, to be right a thought must have a motive, and that motive must be constructive; that is, it must aim to build, and to build for something worthwhile. Wrong thought, however, is scattering and destructive and retards growth. This is the real difference between thought that is wrong and thought that is right. The same is true with other things. Everything in life that retards growth is wrong. Everything that promotes growth is right. If we are in doubt as to whether any particular thing is right or wrong we can readily discover where it belongs if we apply this principle; that is, if it promotes growth it is right, while if it retards growth it is wrong. We shall find that all true systems of ethics or morals will be found to harmonize perfectly with this idea.

The purpose of life is continuous advancement and all the laws of life are created for the promotion of advancement in all things and at all times. Therefore, to retard growth is to violate the laws of life while to promote growth is to properly employ those laws of life. When we go with the laws of life we move forward, but when we go against those laws we begin a life of retrogression. According to this principle nothing is wrong unless it retards growth and nothing can be right unless it promotes growth, because nothing can be wrong unless it is against the laws of life and nothing can be right unless it is in harmony with the laws of life. And the laws of life demand continuous advancement.

Since our object is advancement and progress in every way, and since thinking is the key to all results, it is evident that all thinking must be established upon the principle of continuous advancement. For this reason all thinking that in any way retards growth in any part of the human system must be discontinued, and all thinking must be so arranged or rearranged that it will tend to promote growth and advancement in every phase of human life. In other words, all thinking must be designed, and designed according to the laws that underlie the purpose we have in view. To apply this principle we should never think unless we have a purpose that we wish to promote through that thinking. Before we begin any process of thought we should determine clearly what we wish to promote at the time, and we should then employ that process of thinking through which the purpose in view may be promoted to the best advantage. In this manner every action of mind will become constructive and will build up something that we wish to have constructed. Neither time nor mental energy will be thrown away by aimlessness, and no chaotic states of mind will exist for a moment. All our mental processes will be arranged according to such a system of action as can promote progress, and all the various forces of mind will work together in the creation of that which we wish to realize and possess.

To think according to the laws of growth and to think for a definite purpose—this is the foundation of scientific thinking. This is the principle upon which to act when thinking for results, and whoever resolves to think in this manner only will soon find remarkable changes for the better taking place in every department of his life.

In training the mind to think according to the exact science of right thought, to think according to system, to think for a definite purpose and to think for results, there are four essentials that will be required and we shall proceed to give these essentials our best attention in their proper order. The first essential is to provide what may be termed the mental attitude of normal states of consciousness for all our thinking; that is, to promote only right states of mind whatever the process of thought may be, because such states are always wholesome and are invariably conducive to mental development. In addition, such states tend to hold the various energies of the mind in a working attitude which is highly important when our purpose is to work for results.

To train the mind to think only in the right states of mind we must learn to distinguish between right and wrong mental states, though this is a matter that becomes very simple when we understand that the difference between right and wrong states of mind is found in this, that the former tends to relate the mind properly to the laws, the principles and the powers of life, while the latter tends to prevent that relationship. When we are at variance with our sphere of existence or out of harmony with the world in which we think and live we can accomplish nothing, but when we are in harmony with that world we place ourselves in a position where we can accomplish practically anything if we learn the full use of all the powers we possess. Therefore, if we wish to accomplish what we have in view we must work with those laws and principles of life that govern the sphere in which our work is to be done. But wrong mental states will prevent us from working with the laws of life while right mental states have a tendency to bring us more perfectly into harmony with those laws. Wrong mental states are wrong simply because they prevent this necessary relationship, and they are wrong for no other reason. The first problem before us therefore is to distinguish between the two states of mind, to eliminate the wrong and to cultivate the right. But to distinguish between the two is not difficult when we know that right states o£ mind always produce harmony between ourselves and those powers in life that we must use in order to realize our purpose in life, and that wrong states of mind always take us away from everything that has quality, superiority and worth, or that can serve us in realizing the greater and the better. However, that we may all understand what mental states to cultivate in order to make our thinking more scientific, more exact, more effective and more conducive to the production of the results we desire, we shall proceed to give a brief description of the most important of these states, or what may be termed the normal and the true state of consciousness.

2

AMONG the right states of mind the attitude of peace naturally comes first because at the foundation of all true action we find a state of deep calm. No growth is possible in confusion nor can we enjoy the steps already taken while strife and disturbance prevail. But if we find that we are not in a perfectly peaceful attitude the matter cannot be remedied through a strenuous effort to secure peace. Peace of mind comes most quickly when we do not try to be peaceful, but simply permit ourselves to be normal. To relax mind and body at frequent intervals will also aid remarkably, but the most important of all is the attainment of the consciousness of peace.

There is a state within us where all is still, and as nearly all of us have been conscious of this state at different times we know that it actually exists. To cultivate the consciousness of this state is the real secret of attaining a permanent mental state of peace. When we become conscious of that state we enter what may be termed the permanent condition of peace and thereby realize the peace that passeth understanding; and when we are in that state of peace we know why it does pass understanding.

A further proof of this idea is found in the fact that the center of all action is absolutely still, and that from this center all action proceeds. In like manner there is an absolutely still center in your own mind, and you can become conscious of that center by turning your attention gently and frequently upon the serene within. This should be done several times a day and no matter how peaceful we may feel we should daily seek a still finer realization of this consciousness of peace. The result will be more power because peace conserves energy. The mind will be kept in the necessary attitude for growth and you will avoid all such ills and failures as originate in mental confusion. According to the law that we always become in the without as we feel in the within you will naturally become more and more conscious of peacefulness in your personality as you become more conscious of the calm that is within you. In other words, the same stillness that you feel within yourself when in the consciousness of peace, will unfold itself through your entire system and you will become peaceful in every part of mind and body.

Closely related to the attitude of peace we have that of poise, and this is an attitude that is simply indispensable. The attainment of peace tends to conserve and accumulate energy while the attainment of poise tends to hold that energy in such a way that not a particle is lost. Peace is a restful attitude while poise is a working attitude. In peace you feel absolutely still. In poise you feel and hold the mighty power within you ready for action.

The well poised mind is not only charged with enormous energies, but can also retain those energies in any part of the system and can direct them towards any effort desired. The poised mind combines calmness with power. Through the attitude of calmness it retains its touch with the depths within and is thus constantly supplied with added life and power. Through the attitude of strength it relates itself to the world of action and thus becomes able to go forth and do things. The attitude of poise, however, is not well developed in the average person as the art of. being peaceful and powerful at the same time is an art that has received but little attention; but it is something that is extremely important and no one who desires to learn to think and act for results can afford to neglect this high art for a moment.

To proceed with the development of poise we should work, act, think and live in the consciousness of peace and in the consciousness of power; that is, we should aim to combine peace and power in everything that we feel or do. Here we should remember two great truths; that is, that unlimited power is latent within us and that at the depth of our being everything is perfectly still. When you realize these great truths you will feel more and more that enormous energies are alive in your being, but you will find that they never force themselves into any particular line of action, and that they never run over on the surface. On the other hand, you will find that you can hold those energies in perfect repose or turn them into your work just as you wish. When you have poise therefore all those energies will also have poise. They will be as you are because they are your creations.

The effect of poise upon thinking is very great because the attitude of poise is the one essential attitude through which constructive work of mind or thought can be promoted. The object of exact scientific thinking is to bring about the results we have in view, but results follow only the true application of power, and power cannot be applied constructively unless it acts through the state of peace. We therefore understand why poise, the action of power in peace, is indispensable to every mode of thinking that aims to produce results.

Another mental state of extreme value is that of harmony; and as there is only a step from peace and poise to harmony we may readily acquire the latter when we have acquired the former. In the attitude of peace the mind finds its true self and its own supreme power. Through the attitude of poise this power is brought forth into action and is held in its true spheres of action, but it is only through harmony that this power can act properly upon things or in connection with things. Nothing comes from the application of power unless it acts directly upon something, but it cannot act upon anything with the assurance of results unless there is harmony between the power that acts and the thing acted upon. No action should be attempted therefore until harmony is secured between the two factors involved. In this connection we find that thousands of well-meant actions lead to confusion, sickness and failure because no attention was given to the attainment of harmony. But the importance of attaining harmony before undertaking anything is realized when we learn that the real purpose of harmony is to bring the two factors concerned into that perfect relationship where they can work together for the promotion of the object in view.

To secure harmony it may be necessary for both factors to change their present positions. They may have to meet each other half way, but there can be no objection to this. Our object in life is not to stand where we are, but to do something; and if we can do something of value by changing our present position, that is the very thing we should do. In fact, we can even return with advantage to positions that we imagine have been outgrown if something of value can be accomplished by such a move. The one thing to consider, however, is the result. Any movement that leads to results is a movement in the right direction.

Harmony is not cultivated by isolation nor exclusiveness. There are many minds who think they are in perfect harmony when they are alone, but they are not. They are simply at rest and the sensation is somewhat similar to certain states of harmony. We are in harmony only when we are properly related to someone else or something else. There must be at least two factors before there can be harmony and those two factors must be properly related.

The best way to cultivate the mental state of harmony is to adapt yourself consciously to everything and everybody that you meet. Never resist or antagonize anything nor hold yourself aloof from anybody. Wherever you are aim to look for the agreeable side of things and try to act with everything while in that attitude. After a while you will find it an easy matter to meet all things and all persons in their world, and when you can do this you can unite with them in securing results that neither side could have secured alone.

To secure results two or more factors must work together, but they cannot work together constructively unless they are in harmony; that is, unless they are perfectly related to each other. To be in harmony, however, does not mean simply to be on good terms. You may be on good terms with everybody and not be in harmony with anybody. We are in harmony with persons and things when the two factors or sides concerned can actually work together for the promotion of some actual purpose. In the mental world this law is very easily discerned and its operations found to be exact. You may have a fine mind, but if the different parts of your mind do not harmonize and work together you will accomplish but little, and there are thousands of brilliant minds in this very condition. Then we find minds with simply a fair amount of ability who accomplish a great deal, and the reason is that the different parts of such minds are in harmony working together according to the laws of constructive action. And here we should remember that wherever two or more factors actually work together desirable results will positively follow. To agree with your adversary has the same significance. There is a certain side of every form of adversity to which you can adapt yourself. Look for that side and try to relate yourself harmoniously and constructively to the power of that side. You will avoid much trouble thereby and bring to pass scores of good things that otherwise would not have been realized.

To harmonize with the adverse does not mean that you are to follow or imitate the adverse. At all times we should be ourselves. We should change nothing in our own individuality, but should aim primarily to adapt the actions of our individuality, whether physical or mental, to those things with which we may be associated. Under all adverse circumstances we should remember that vice is virtue gone wrong and that the power in the one is the same as the power in the other; the good misdirected, that is all. But you are not to harmonize with the misdirection. You are to harmonize with the power that is back of the action and try to use that power for some valued purpose. Here we find a subject upon which volumes could be written, but the real secret that underlies it all is simple. Adapt yourself to everything and everybody with a view of securing united action for greater good. You will thus continue in perfect harmony, and you will cause every action that may result from your efforts to work directly for the production of the results you have in view.

3

THE three states of mind mentioned in the previous chapter will naturally lead us to a place where results can be secured, but how great these results are to be will depend upon the loftiness of our aim. Therefore a mental state will be required that will constantly center attention upon the high places of attainment, and such a state we find in aspiration. But here we must know the difference between aspiration and ambition especially when they act separately. When ambition acts aside from aspiration the aim of the mind will be to promote the personal self by calling into action only those powers that are now active in the personal self. Such an action, however, tends to separate the personality from the greater powers within which will finally produce a condition of personal inferiority. We have seen this fact illustrated so frequently that it has become proverbial to say that personal ambition when in full control of the mind invariably leads to personal downfall.

It is a well-known fact that no mind that is simply ambitious can ever become great, and the reason is that personal ambition prevents mind and consciousness from ascending into those superior states of thought and power which alone can make greatness possible. This ascension of mind and consciousness, however, invariably takes place through the attitude of aspiration, and therefore the force of ambition should always be inspired by the spirit of aspiration. Both are necessary and they must combine perfectly in every case if results worthwhile are to be realized.

The attitude of aspiration causes the mind to think of the marvels that lie beyond present attainment and thereby inspires the creation of great thoughts which is vastly important. There must be great thoughts before the mind can become great, and the mind must become great before great results can be secured.

Aspiration concentrates attention upon superiority always and therefore elevates all the qualities of the mind into that state. This being true every effort in life should be directed towards those possibilities that lie beyond the present attainment if we wish to cultivate and strengthen the attitude of aspiration. When we are simply ambitious we proceed as we are and seek to make a mark for ourselves with what power we already possess; but when we are alive with the spirit of aspiration we seek to make ourselves larger, more powerful and far superior to what we are now, knowing that a great light cannot be hid, and that anyone with great power must invariably reach the goal he has in view. The ambitious mind seeks to make a small light shine far beyond its capacity, and through this effort finally wears itself out. The aspiring mind, however, seeks to make the light larger and larger, knowing that the larger the light becomes the further it will shine, and that no strenuous efforts will be required to push its powerful rays into effectiveness. But when the attitude of aspiration looks beyond the personal self it does not necessarily look outside of the self. The purpose of aspiration is to enter into the possession of the marvels of the great within because what is found in the within will be expressed in the without. Therefore, when we constantly rise above the personal self we perpetually enlarge the personal self, thus gaining the capacity to accomplish more and more until we finally accomplish practically everything we have in view. The attitude of aspiration therefore should never leave the mind for a moment; but we should on the contrary keep the mental eye single upon the boundless possibilities that are within us and deeply desire with heart and soul a greater and a greater realization of those possibilities in practical life.

The attitude of contentment may truthfully be said to be the twin sister of aspiration and its important function is to prevent aspiration from losing sight of what has already been gained. When contentment is absent the present seems more or less barren, and when aspiration is absent the present seems sufficient. But the present is never barren nor is it ever sufficient. The present is rich with many things of extreme value if we only train ourselves to see them. These things. however, are not sufficient to the advancing soul. Greater things are at hand and it is our privilege to press on through the realization of those greater things. We must therefore conclude that the true attitude of mind in this connection is to be content with things as they now are, and at the same time reach out constantly for greater things.

When contentment is absent the present is not fully utilized and we cannot attain the greater things until we have fully employed what has already been received. When aspiration is absent the present is used over and over again like the air in a closed room, and the result must be mental stagnation to be followed by failure and final extinction. When, we look at this subject from another point of view we find that the mind that is not contented cannot be developed; nor can such a mind make the best use of the powers it may now possess. Every moment therefore should be filled with contentment and perfect satisfaction, but every moment should also be filled with a strong desire for still greater attainments and achievements. In such a state where contentment and aspiration are combined we shall find life to be a continual feast, each course being more delicious than the one preceding. We shall also find such a life to be the path to perpetual growth and continuous joy.

To cultivate the state of contentment we should live in the conviction that all things are working together for good, and that what is best for us now is coming to us now. The truth is that if we are trying to make all things work together for good, and live in the faith that we can, we actually will so order things in our life that all things will work together for good. And what comes to us every day will be the very best for us that day. When we live, think and act in this manner we shall soon find that the best is daily coming to us, and that the best of each day is better than that of the day preceding. The result will be perfect contentment, and the placing of life in that position where it can receive in the great eternal now all that the great eternal now has to give. In brief, when we so live that we permit the present moment to be filled with all the richness that it can hold, then we shall have the contented mind and the ever-growing mind, the mind that is proverbially described as a continuous feast.

The attitude of gratitude is closely related to that of contentment and is one of the greatest of all mental states; and the reason why is found in the fact that no mind can be, right nor think constructively unless it is filled with the spirit of gratitude. The fact is that new life is coming to us every day and with it new opportunities. Every moment therefore is richer than the one before; but if this coming of new life and new opportunities does not add to the richness and value of our own personal life there is a lack of gratitude. And the explanation is that where gratitude is lacking the mind is more or less closed to the many good things that are coming our way. The grateful mind, however, is always an open mind, open to the newer, the higher and the better, and therefore invariably coming into possession of more and more of those things.

The entire race is moving forward with the stream of continuous advancement; better things therefore are daily coming into the life of each individual. If he does not receive them the reason is that his mind is more or less closed on account of the lack of gratitude. For let us remember in this connection that the mind simply must be grateful for everything in order to be open to the reception of new things and better things. We simply cannot receive better things unless we are truly grateful for that which we already possess. This is the law in this matter, and it is a law that will bear the most rigid analysis. To give thanks therefore with the whole heart for everything that comes into life, and to express constant and whole souled gratitude to all the world for everything that is good in the world—this is the secret through which we may open the mind to the great cosmic influx; that influx that is bringing into the life of every individual the richness and the power that complete life has in store for every individual.

But in order to be grateful in the best and most perfect manner we must have appreciation. We must be able to see the real worth of that which comes into life before we can express the fullness and the spirit of the grateful heart. The attitude of appreciation is also valuable in another direction. When we appreciate worth we always gain a higher consciousness of worth and thereby make our own minds more worthy.

To cultivate the mental state of appreciation we should eliminate all tendency to fault finding, criticism and the like, and we should make a special effort to see the worthy qualities in everything and everybody with which we come in contact. The result of such a practice will not only be a better appreciation, with a deeper insight into the superior qualities of life, but also the building of a more wholesome mind. Realizing the value of appreciation we should, whenever we discover a lack of appreciation in ourselves, proceed at once to remove the cause. We shall not hesitate in doing this when we find that a lack of appreciation also tends to give the mind a false view of things thereby preventing the acquisition of the best that life has in store.

The appreciative mind has a natural tendency to look upon the better side of things, but this tendency becomes complete only when the optimistic attitude is added. To be optimistic, however, does not mean to think that black is white or that everything everywhere is all right. The true optimist can also see the flaws and the imperfections in life, but he gives direct attention to the good side, the better side and the strong side. And having this larger view he always knows that the strong side is much larger and far superior to the weak side. He never becomes discouraged therefore because he knows that failure and wrong are only temporary, and that the right finally wins every time. In addition, he knows that he can aid the right to such an extent that the victory can be gained now.

The pessimist lives in the false and does not see things as they are. His conclusions are therefore worthless. For this reason we should never pay any attention to the words of the pessimist as we shall be misled in every instance if we do. Instead we should listen to the prophecy of the optimist, and then put all our ability and all our faith into the possibilities of that prophecy thereby making it come true, proceeding of course in the conviction that we can. The value of the optimistic attitude in scientific thinking

363

therefore is very great; because to think correctly on any subject the mind must have the mountain top view, and we must think correctly if we wish to think for results.

Though the optimist may live on the sunny side, still the full value of life's sunshine cannot be gained until we add the attitude of constant cheerfulness. To be cheerful, bright, happy and joyous is absolutely necessary if we wish to think scientifically, think constructively and think for results. When we proceed to think for results we think for a purpose. We employ correctly the constructive mental processes so that we may work ourselves up to the goal in view. Growth and development therefore must take place all along the line of action, but no mental growth can take place without mental sunshine. Accordingly, we should resolve to be happy no matter what may transpire. We cannot afford to be otherwise. Sunshine will melt the most massive iceberg if the rays are direct and the clouds are kept away; and it is the same in daily life. No matter how cold, disagreeable and uncongenial your present environment may be, plenty of mental sunshine can change it all.

It pays to be happy. Cheerfulness is a most profitable investment and there are no riches that are greater than constant joy. This attitude is not for the few or for occasional moments because all the sunny states of mind can be made permanent in a short time by a very simple process. Make it a practice to go to sleep every night with cheerfulness on your mind and with a feeling of joy in every atom of your being. Through this practice you will carry the cheerful idea into the subconscious, and gradually the joyous state will become an established state in the subconscious mind. The result will be that the subconscious will express cheerfulness and wholesomeness at all times, and it will become second nature for you to have a sweet disposition, a sunny frame of mind and an attitude of perpetual joy. This method may seem to be too simple to be of value, but the simplest methods are usually the best. And anyone can prove through a few weeks of trial that this method will produce the desired results, and will through more continuous practice actually transform mind and disposition to such an extent that the mind will henceforth live in constant mental sunshine. And there are few things that are more important than this if we wish to train the mind to act and work in those attitudes that are necessary in order that we may proceed successfully in thinking for results.

4

THE attitude of kindness is one of the greatest among the right states of mind. Therefore to be kind to everybody and to feel kindly towards the whole of creation, this must be the attitude if the right use of mind and thought is to prevail. Kindness enlarges the inner consciousness thus promoting the enlargement and the expression of life. And it also creates the tendency to give one's best and there is nothing that brings forth the greater life and power within us so quickly and so completely as the giving of one's best in all things and at all times.

Both the soul and the mind, with all their powers and possibilities, tend to unfold themselves through the actions of the strong whole souled attitude of kindness. In fact, no one Can begin to unfold his larger life and receive the greater richness from within until he begins to give, through the attitude of kindness, all that which he already has in his personality. And the more one gives of the richness of one's own life, ability and power, the more he will receive from the limitless realms of the within. This is a law that no one, not even the most materialistic, can afford to ignore. But giving is not giving unless it comes from the heart, and it must invariably be an act of expression for some great purpose. Your expressions, either of thought or action, will not open the way for inner unfoldment unless you give richly through a fuller and larger expression, and in all such expressions you must feel kindly. The attitude of kindness is therefore indispensable to growth, mental unfoldment and constructive thinking.

The attitude of sympathy always acts in close connection with kindness, and though it is a most important state of mind it is also a much abused state. There are few people who sympathize correctly and there is possibly nothing that interferes with correct thinking as does misdirected sympathy. When we sympathize with anyone we enter into a certain unity of that one's mind and we almost invariably imitate to a degree the mind that we unite with in this way. Two minds with but a single thought will imitate each other in nearly everything and will actually grow to look alike. It is therefore very important to know with what we should sympathize. When you sympathize with a person in distress you will think the thought of distress at the time, and will reproduce in a measure the same state in your own mind, and possibly in your own life and personality. Many a person has failed in life because he has sympathized too much with the weak side and inferior side of those who have had misfortune. When you sympathize with a person that is sick your mind will create within itself a similar condition of disease, and this expression will express itself in your own body, a fact to which thousands can testify. We realize again therefore that it will not do to sympathize with anything and everything that may arouse our sympathy.

Why does it hurt to see a friend punished? Why do we usually feel bad when those of whom we think a great deal feel bad? Why is there a tendency of most minds to think and feel like the prevailing thought in their community? Why does a mob lose its head, so to speak, and proceed to think, feel and act precisely like the leader? Why do scores of incidents of a similar nature take place in our midst constantly? Sympathetic imitation explains such phenomena. And the law that underlies this phenomena is a law that we must understand thoroughly if we wish to master our own thinking and our actions wherever those actions may be expressed. When you sympathize with weakness you are liable to become weak. When you sympathize with disease you are liable to get the same symptoms and frequently the very disease itself. When you sympathize with the wrong you are liable to think that same wrong and possibly act it out in your own life. These are facts with which we are all familiar. It is therefore a subject of extreme importance. The law that governs sympathy is this, that you enter into mental unity in a measure with everything with which you sympathize, and that whatever you enter into mental unity with you tend to imitate and produce in yourself to a degree. Understanding this law we realize that we cannot afford to sympathize with everything, but on the contrary find it absolutely necessary to make a careful selection of those things with which we may sympathize.

When you sympathize with a person who is in trouble do not think of the trouble or the pain or the weakness, but think of that something within him that is superior to all pain and that can annihilate all the trouble in existence. Then remember the great statement that "he that is within you is greater than he that is in the world." Make it a practice never to sympathize with the inferior side, but only with the superior side. But this will not make you cold and indifferent as many suppose, for it is impossible for you to become mentally cold while being in touch with the very life of the soul itself which must be the very essence of tenderness, kindness and love. In applying this principle we find that the more perfectly you sympathize with the higher, the finer and the stronger side of man the more love you feel, the more tenderness you express and the more helpful you become in all of your efforts. Nothing is lost, therefore, but much is gained by training the mind to sympathize only with the true side of human life.

The man who is sick and in trouble does not want more tears. He has had enough of them. What he wants and what he needs is that sympathy that can banish all tears and that can reveal the way to emancipation, power and joy. This being true we must try to banish completely every form of morbid sympathy. It hurts everybody. It perpetuates weakness and keeps the mind in bondage to inferior imitations. In applying this higher form of sympathy do not tell the unfortunate that you are sorry. Tell them how to get rid of their sorrow. Then do something substantial to speed them on the way. This is sympathy that is worthy of the name.

Right thinking cannot be promoted so long as we sympathize in the. old fashioned way. We cannot think constructively so long as we permit the mind to imitate the wrong, the weak, the inferior and the destructive. Here, however, we find a problem that we must solve because it is natural for the mind to imitate to a certain degree. We should therefore give the mind something to imitate that has quality and superiority. In brief, we should train the mind to imitate the strong, the worthy, the superior and the ideal, and thus cause all mental actions to produce the strong, the worthy, the superior and the ideal in ourselves. For the mind invariably tends to create that which we think of the most. The true attitude of sympathy will be promoted to a very great extent if we train ourselves to live in the upper story or rather the idealistic state of mind. There are two planes upon which the mind can dwell and they are usually called the idealistic and the materialistic. The ideal plane is the upper plane while the materialistic is the lower. In the idealistic all the tendencies of the mind move towards the qualities of superiority and worth; all the desires are for the higher and the better; all thoughts are created after the likeness of our higher conceptions of the perfect, the true and the superior. To live in such an attitude is to be an idealist and this is the meaning of idealism. An idealistic mind therefore is a mind that is constantly ascending, and thus taking a larger view and a more beautiful view every day of the richness and splendor of real existence.

In the materialistic attitude all the tendencies of mind move toward the superficial, the inferior and the imperfect. In this attitude we usually think according to those false conceptions of things that have been handed down by the race, and all our desires are concerned principally with satisfying the needs of the body. The materialistic mind is the descending mind, the mind that is losing ground gradually, and that is daily being overcome more and more by its own perverted and materialistic thought habits. But to live in the upper story is to keep the mind concentrated upon the great possibilities that are latent within us and to desire with the whole heart the daily realization of more and more of the wonders that are in store for those who are steadily pressing on towards greater things. In the upper story we live with greatness. In the lower story we live with mistakes and inferiority. In the upper story we see that man is daily unfolding the greatness of the super-man. In the lower story we see only the depravity or weakness of error and sin. In the lower story we are in partial or complete darkness. In the upper story we are in the full light. It is therefore easily understood why the mind must dwell in the upper story before right thinking can begin.

After beginning to live in the upper story the consciousness of superiority and supremacy will naturally appear, and these two states should be thoroughly developed. We should all train ourselves to feel that we are superior beings; not superior to others because we are all superior, but superior to everything that pertains to personal existence; superior to ills, pains, weaknesses, mistakes and failures; and superior to everything that is imperfect or undeveloped. Here we should remember that the consciousness of superiority does not produce vanity or egotism. When a person has really become conscious of the superiority of his true being he is above all small and questionable states of mind.

When you are superior you do not have to make any display of the matter to prove it. It will show in your life and in your work, and actions speak more eloquently than words. The principal reason why the attitude of superiority is so important is because it unites the mind with everything in your life and your thought that has quality, and thereby gives everything in your mind and personality the stamp of greater worth. And it is a well-known fact that whenever we enrich our thought, or any expression of thought, we tend to enrich everything in our life and those things that we produce through our work.

The attitude of supremacy should refer to your own being only. To rule supremely in your own domain and not interfere with the domain of anyone else —this is the true purpose of self-supremacy. And the value of self-supremacy is realized not only in its power to give the individual self-mastery, but also in the fact that when the mind feels that it is superior it can more easily think its own thoughts and thereby prevent the practice of imitating false actions or ideas. It must therefore be quite evident that this state is absolutely necessary to scientific thinking and to the art of thinking for results.

The mind that recognizes its own supremacy is a strong mind and will therefore seek to extend its power wherever the enlargement of life can be promoted, but to accomplish this the mind must be positive; that is, every action of the mind should be filled, so to speak, with a thought current that tends to press on and on to the goal in view. The positive mind, however, does not force its way, but wins because it is strong, and every mind becomes strong when constantly filled with thoughts that are positive and determined. To the attitude of positiveness we should add those of push and perseverance because these two attitudes tend to promote the increase of the results that are already being gained; and there is nothing that succeeds like that which is constantly pressing on to greater success.

When we proceed to think for results we are invariably imbued with the spirit of advancement. Therefore to increase the power of this spirit the mind should cultivate the persevering attitude and should feel a strong desire to push forward into the ever enlarging realms of perpetual growth. But in this connection we must not forget courage and patience, nor the progressive attitude. It has been well said that we all could accomplish far more if we would only attempt more, but in the majority courage generally fails when in the presence of great undertakings. This, however, we cannot afford to permit. To the attitude of courage we should add the mental states of self-reliance and self-confidence and still greater gain will be realized. In fact, these two states are of such value that their importance cannot be described in words. They are not sufficiently developed in the average person, however, because he depends too much upon environments, opportunities and associates, and not enough upon himself. The great soul depends upon nothing exterior to himself. Such a soul makes opportunities to order and changes environments to comply with requirements. Such a soul turns adversity into a willing servant and makes every obstacle a new path to greater achievement. But no soul can become a great soul until faith in its own power has become unbounded.

The strong, positive mind may at times go beyond its own domain and may sometimes act in realms where it has no legal right, but this can be prevented through the attitude of non-resistance, another most important attitude in the art of constructive thinking. The attitude of resistance is always destructive and therefore interferes with the real purpose of right thinking. But it is not necessary to resist anything. That which is inferior will disappear when we produce the superior and not until then. It is therefore a waste of time and energy to try to remove wrong through resistance. The proper course to pursue is to build up the right and the wrong will disappear of itself. In this connection, however, it may seem to be difficult to continue in a non-resisting attitude when we are constantly in the presence of adverse conditions. But here we should remember that the mind that is constantly creating the larger and the better will hardly be aware of the imperfect in his life because the imperfect is constantly passing away with the ceaseless coming and upbuilding of the more perfect. Our purpose should be never to resist evil; though we should not on the other hand fold our arms and let things be as they are. While we are turning away from lesser things we should concentrate our whole attention upon the building up of the greater. This is a method that will give perfect freedom and continuous advancement to us all. ◆

To the practice of non-resistance we should add forgiveness. Forgive everybody, even yourself. To condemn anything or anybody is a misuse of the mind. So long as we condemn the wrong the mind is forcefully directed towards the wrong. The mental picture of wrong becomes more deeply stamped upon the subconscious, and more thoughts and mental states will be created in the likeness of those impressions or pictures. These impressions will reproduce themselves in us and this is how we tend to create in ourselves what we condemn in others. The reverse of this principle is also true; that is, that we tend to create and build up in ourselves the good that we commend and appreciate in others.

To promote the cultivation of forgiveness we should become conscious of real purity, and the reason for this is readily understood when we remember the statement about the eye that is too pure to behold iniquity. Why the pure eye does not see evil is a subject too large to be discussed here. But we shall find that the more perfectly we develop the consciousness of purity the smaller and more insignificant evil becomes to us, and the easier it becomes to forgive everybody for everything. In the attitude of mental purity we look upon the mistakes of the world in the same way as we look upon the false notes that the child makes while learning to play. We want those false notes corrected, but we do not call them bad. We know that the child will learn to play perfectly later on, not by being punished or scolded, but by being taught thoroughly and persistently. It is the same with the mistakes of the human race, and those mistakes should be dealt with in the same manner.

One of the very important states of the mind is that of justice, or the consciousness of justice, and it is most necessary that we cultivate the habit of being just even in minute details. The just mind can readily direct its processes of thought and creation into those channels of action that are in harmony with the laws of life, while the mind that is not just will misdirect many of those processes and thereby produce all kinds of detrimental conditions of mind and body. In a state of justice everybody has his own. Therefore to be just is to so act that you never deprive anyone of his own nor fail to render to anyone that which is his own. To know what really belongs to you and what really belongs to others, however, may at first sight seem to be a difficult problem, but we cannot solve it by looking at external possessions. We become just by developing the consciousness of justice and not by measuring this to one and that to the other. To execute justice in the world, or in connection with any of our own actions, we must realize justice in our own soul because effects do not precede causes. And if all moral teachers in the world would cease their criticisms of powers and systems and give their entire attention to the development of the consciousness of justice in the mind of the race, we should soon have an order of things which would be absolutely just to all. In our own thinking, however, the attainment of this consciousness of justice is so absolutely necessary that it should be given a most prominent place in all our efforts, because it is only through the consciousness of justice that all misdirection of thought and energy can be prevented.

There are three additional States of mind required to make this study complete, and these are refinement, receptivity and faith. But we need not take the time to give them special attention as we all understand their nature and importance. Faith and receptivity have special functions to perform in all kinds of mental actions and development, and the advancing process of the mind must of necessity be a refining process; otherwise growth would be an impossibility. The purpose of scientific thinking therefore cannot be promoted unless the entire system is permeated with the consciousness of refinement. And to attain this consciousness we should picture before us the most refined state of the ideal that we can possibly conceive, and keep this picture before us constantly with the deep desire to make it real.

The above is a brief analysis of the most important of the right mental states —those states that are needed to place the mind in that state of action that is absolutely necessary if we wish to think for results. We are now ready therefore to proceed with the real process of thinking.

5

EVERY normal person has a definite goal that he expects to reach; some purpose for which he is living, thinking and working; one or more objects that he is trying to gain possession of. But how to realize this ambition is the problem, and though he hopes to find the solution in some way, that way is not always as clear as he should wish it to be. A study of natural laws, however, both physical and metaphysical will readily reveal the secret.

When we study natural laws we find that aimless living is wasteful, deteriorating and detrimental both to the individual and to the race, and the same study reveals the fact that all the laws of nature are constructed for the promotion of progress and growth. Therefore to be natural we must move forward, and to move forward we must have a definite purpose. From this we conclude that the life with a definite purpose is the only natural life.

And as it is natural, nature must be able to provide a way by which such a life can be perfected fully and completely. In other words, there must be a solution for every problem, and this being true, he who seeks the solution will certainly find it.

Nature is dual, physical and metaphysical. What we fail to find in the one, therefore, we shall certainly find in the other; and the study of the larger metaphysics gives us the solution for the problem under consideration. This solution is based upon the discovery that thought is the one power that determines the life, the position, the circumstances and the destiny of man, and that to use that power we must learn to think for results.

Whether the individual is to move forward or not depends upon what he thinks. His actions, his intentions, his motives, his plans, his tendencies, his efforts—all of these play their part, but they are all the products of thinking, and therefore are invariably like the process of thinking from which they sprang. Every thought is a power in the life where it is created and will either promote or retard the purpose of that life. Every thought you think is either for you or against you. It will either push you forward or hold you down. When your own thought is against you all your actions, efforts, tendencies, plans, intentions, and everything that is produced by thought or directed by thought will also be against you; and conversely everything that you do with muscle or brain will be for you when your thought is for you. This is a fact the importance of which is certainly great. And since it has been fully demonstrated to be a fact we cannot afford to give it less than our most profound attention.

Since it is natural to have definite aims in life, in fact absolutely necessary in order to be in harmony with the purpose of life, and since it is natural to move forward, it must be natural to have only such thoughts as are for you; thoughts that can push you forward and that will be instrumental in promoting the purpose you have in view. In other words, to comply with the laws of nature, physical and metaphysical, it is necessary to think in such a way that all mental action tends to produce growth, advancement and progress. In this connection we find that nature's laws do not conflict. One law declares that the individual must move forward constantly if he would be in accord with nature, and another law declares that our thoughts will either promote or retard the forward movement. Therefore when our thinking retards our progress we violate natural law and will consequently produce conditions that are detrimental.

To discriminate between right and wrong thinking, between scientific and chaotic thinking, and all thinking is chaotic that is not scientific, becomes very simple when we define the former as being in accord with natural laws, and the latter as being at variance with natural laws. Or to be more explicit, scientific thinking is the formation of all such mental actions, mental states and mental forces as have the power to produce in our efforts what nature has given all things in the human system the power to produce. It is the intention of nature that all things shall work for perpetual advancement of all things. Therefore a thought to be in accord with nature must have the inherent impulse as well as the power to promote advancement in its sphere of action.

To be scientific is to be in accord with nature; to work physically and mentally with nature, and to carry out the fundamental intentions of nature. And since all the actions of man are produced and directed by his thinking, he cannot work with nature unless his thinking is in accord with nature, and is designed and applied with definite results in view. In brief, thinking is scientific and designed when its purpose is to produce advancement, and when it has at the same time both the power and the knowledge to carry out that purpose.

Every intelligent person tries to live in accord with natural laws, but as a rule complies only with those laws that deal with the physical side of life. He therefore cannot be in perfect accord with nature because to obey one group of laws and ignore another group will produce nothing but confusion and ultimate failure. And what is important, it is not possible to comply perfectly with physical laws unless we understand metaphysical laws. Physical actions are both produced and directed by mental action. Not a muscle can move unless the mind moves. Therefore, if the mental action is not fully in accord with natural laws it will not be possible for the consequent physical actions to be in full accord with nature. It is not difficult to understand therefore why the majority of those who have tried to live in accord with nature, and tried to apply fully the powers and possibilities of nature, have not succeeded in as large a measure as their ambitions might desire. They have tried to bring physical actions into harmony with nature while their mental actions have been more or less at variance with nature. They have tried to make their actions scientific while their thinking remained unscientific. And here we have the cause of practically all the trouble, confusion and failure in the world.

The statement that nature's fundamental intention is the perpetual advancement of all things, may be questioned when we take note of the many processes of nature that appear to be destructive, and find that those processes invariably work in harmony with natural law. But when we look beneath the surface we find that the consuming process is necessary to the refining process, and that the decomposing process is indispensable to growth. That which destroys does not tend directly to build up, but the inferior must be removed before the superior can be constructed. The force of destruction, however, can be used in many ways. It can be turned into the gross actions of the sledge that tears down the present structure. Or it can be employed through the channel of transmutation which removes the present structure, not by tearing it down, but by changing it into something better. In the grosser forms of action destruction is usually separated from construction, and may or may not be followed by the latter, but in the higher forms of action destruction and construction are one. The inferior is destroyed by being immediately transmuted into the superior. And here we should remember that everything in nature regardless of its present condition can be transformed into something higher, finer and better because every process in nature can promote advancement, being created for that purpose. Therefore to be in accord with nature man must have the same purpose. He must live, think and work for perpetual advancement, constant growth and eternal progress.

In preceding pages it has been stated that the foundation of scientific thinking consists of thinking only in the attitude of right mental states, and the principal right mental states were enumerated and defined; and in this connection it may be added that the reason why such states of mind constitute the foundation of scientific thinking is based upon the fact that wrong mental states tend to pervert and misdirect the original intention of every process of thinking, while right mental states tend to hold in position, so to speak, or properly direct the original intention of every mental process. To think scientifically and to think for results is to think with a definite object in view; that is, to so think that every thought will aid in the realization of that object. Therefore it cannot be scientific to originate a mental process with a certain object in view and then permit that process to be misdirected, but this is what we continue to do so long as wrong mental states are permitted to act in the mind. A misdirected mental process always creates thoughts and mental actions that are foreign or adverse to the original intention of that process and are in consequence detrimental. Such thinking therefore does not only waste time and effort, but places serious obstacles in the way of our constructive and properly directed efforts. In the average mind we find mental states that are right as well as mental states that are wrong. The one group assists the forward movement of mind while the other not only retards or misdirects, but usually acts as an obstacle as well. This, however, we cannot afford to permit. The proper course to take therefore in the very beginning is to eliminate absolutely all mental states that are wrong and to shun them completely in the future. Should we be in doubt as to what states are wrong, we need only remember that every mental state is wrong that has no tendency to build, and that every state is right that does have a direct upbuilding tendency. And in eliminating the wrong states of mind the simplest method is to give so much attention to the creation and the strengthening of right mental states that not a single mental action is ever permitted to create or perpetuate wrong states. In other words, there will be no power with which to produce the wrong when all the power of the mind is used in building up the right.

We may proceed, therefore, upon the principle that right mental states constitute the foundation of scientific thinking, and that the very first thing to do in learning how to think for results is to train the mind to create, entertain, and perpetuate only right mental states. When we have established this foundation we may proceed with the first story of the superstructure. To this structure there are several stories, but the first one is to give every thought you think the tendency and the power to promote your own individual purpose in life; that is, every mental action, every mental creative process and every form of thinking should be so constituted that everything that transpires in the mind will work both fully and directly for your welfare and advancement. In other words, train your mind to think only thoughts that will push your work, and every thought you think can push your work if properly constructed. But the opposite is also true. Every thought you think can interfere with your work if not properly constructed. We realize therefore the importance of discriminating between the right and the wrong even in the most insignificant of our mental attitudes, because we want everything that takes place in our system to act to our advantage.

Before you can apply scientific thinking in your own life it is necessary to make a definite decision as to what purpose you wish to live, think and work for. And in most minds this purpose will assume a threefold aspect. The first will be to succeed in your vocation; the second will be a continuous development of the leading mental qualities; and the third will be the attainment of higher and higher states of ideal existence. To these three many may wish to add the development of one or more special talents, or the attainment of certain special objects, and these different things can easily be added without interfering with the full promotion of the general purpose. The idea is that you must clearly fix in mind what you wish to think and work for in the great eternal now. In the future, some or all of your plans may be changed, but you may do that when the future comes. While the present remains there must be something definite to work for now, and that something should receive your undivided attention. By doing justice to the present we shall be far better equipped for the opportunities of the future. In fact the very best way to prepare for the future is to be your very best in the present, and if you are your best in the present your future will certainly be better.

Whether you have a few object or many that you wish to realize, place them properly in your mind giving each a special position before your mental vision, and then hold these objects constantly before you as the great goal for which you desire to live, think and work. Center all attention upon that goal, mentally moving in that direction every moment, and turning on the full current. No force of thought or action must go to the left or to the right. Every force you place in action in your system must aim upon that goal, and must proceed with the definite purpose of helping you reach that goal. In brief, you must actually live in every sense of the word for the purpose you have in view. That does not mean, however, that you must ignore the interest of others or become oblivious to the many phases of life that exist about you. The mind is complex and consciousness is capable of many grades of action; therefore you can in general be interested in everything that has worth. But all these other interests must be made a channel through which your fundamental purpose can be promoted, or rather an aid to the great plan for which you live, think and work. If you are a business man you need not

Ignore music, art or literature. The more you have of these the better for your business provided you employ them as forces of inspiration. Though it is necessary for you to concentrate your life upon your business, still you must constantly enlarge your mind, character and soul in order to insure increased success in your business. Your capacity for work and your power to improve the quality of your work must develop. And everything in life that has worth can be made to promote your own individual growth. In other words, be interested in everything that has quality and worth anywhere in life and use everything you gain through this interest for the making of your own life larger, richer and more successful.

It is not the narrow mind that succeeds. The mind that invariably realizes the greatest success is the mind that is broad, and at the same time has the power to focus the whole of its larger capacity upon the one thing that is being done now. When you constantly focus your mind upon that which you are living for and working for you are giving all your creative powers to those faculties and talents that are required in the realization of your objects in view. It is therefore evident that the larger your mind is, both in its capacity and power the greater will be the results. It requires ability and power to do things. Therefore the more ability and the more power you can apply in any line of action the more you will accomplish and the more rapidly you will advance in that direction. For this reason we do not wish to throw away ability and power upon those things that cannot promote our present progress. We do not wish to give thought and attention to plans that are of no use to us now. We may need those plans some day, but the plans that we can use now are the only ones that have a right to our present attention.

The idea is to think that you can, to think for results and to give your life in the present to that which can use your life in the present. This is not done, however, when we permit aimless thinking. And the amount of life and ability that is thrown away in this manner is enormous. Aimless thinking has the same effect upon your capacity and ability as punching holes in the boiler has upon the capacity of the engine. But the giving of attention to foreign or temporary plans is just as wasteful. When you decide upon a plan see it through. Give your whole life to it. Turn the full force of your whole mind upon it and keep at it until you are ready for some greater plan. You will thus build yourself up and prepare yourself for a greater plan, and when such a plan arrives, which it positively will, drop everything else and give this new plan the full force of your undivided attention.

Too many minds are constantly wishing they were in some other kind of work, thus diverting their attention every few moments from the work in which they are engaged now. The result is not only poor work, but they place themselves in a position where they can never find opportunity for advancement. If you want something better to do, do your present work so well that it becomes a stepping stone to something better. It is the man who thoroughly fills his present place that is asked to come up and fill a larger place, but no man can fill his present place to full capacity unless all the life and all the power that is in him is applied directly in producing results in that place.

Since thought is a definite power, with great constructive possibilities, the more thought we give to our work the more successful we shall be in that work provided our thought is scientific, designed and constructive. This is simple. On the other hand whenever we encourage aimless thinking or wishing for something else to do we are taking power away from our work thereby decreasing results. One of the first principles in thinking for results therefore is to give your whole attention to your present work; to give all your creative power to the building up of the purpose at hand; and to cause every mental action to act in such a way that it will act with the plans and for the plans you are now seeking to push through.

6

THE next question that will naturally arise is that of knowing what to think about our work and the objects we have in view. Every mental state becomes the mother of ideas; every idea can produce a tendency of mind, and every tendency tends to draw mental actions in its own direction. A false conception will produce false ideas, false ideas will originate false tendencies and false tendencies will lead the mind into mistakes. To promote any purpose, however, mistakes must be avoided as far as possible. Everything must be done correctly, and whatever is done should be done better and better every time. The way we think therefore of what we are to do or the objects we have in view will directly determine the results that are to be attained.

When you think about your work as being difficult you form a wrong mental conception; for the fact is that no work IS more difficult than we make it, and we can relate ourselves to our work in* such a way that we shall always be equal to the occasion. When you think about your work as difficult you will usually approach it in the attitude of doubt and fear, and no mind can do its best while in such states. Nor can you relate yourself to your work under such conditions because the false mental tendencies that follow such false conceptions will mislead many or all of your faculties. To think of your work as being completely under your personal control is correct because the possibilities within us are unlimited and we can make ourselves equal to any occasion. From this we are not to infer, however, that we can do now whatever our personal opinions may conclude that we can do now; for such opinions are not always based upon the whole truth in the matter. But the idea is that you can succeed in that work which your best judgment has decided upon, and that you can increase your success in that line more and more for an indefinite period.

To think of your work as trivial, mean or burdensome is wrong because such an attitude of mind will tend to make you inferior, and there is no success for you while you are on the downgrade towards inferiority. To think of your work as ordinary or trivial is to think ordinary thoughts, and as such thoughts will decrease the power of your mind they will naturally interfere with your work and therefore be directly against you in their actions. To think of your work as drudgery, or as something disagreeable that is to be gone through with is in like manner a mistake; the reason being that such thinking prevents the mind from being its best and giving expression to its best. You cannot give your heart and soul to that which you despise, and you cannot do your best in any kind of work unless you give it your whole heart and soul.

If you want to think and work for results you must love your work, and you can, though such love is not to be sentimental, but rather the feeling of intense admiration for those lines of action that you know will lead to greater things. Think therefore of your work as a channel through which you are to reach the higher places of life because that is what your work really is if you approach it in the right way and apply its possibilities on the largest scale. To find fault with what you have accomplished is wrong as it tends to turn attention upon defects and inferiority. Every mind should constantly expect to do better and should with every effort try to improve upon what was done before, but no actual or chronic fault finding must be permitted. To find fault with what you have done is to belittle yourself; in brief, to place a wet blanket, so to speak, over your hopes and aspirations. Instead, you should think of your work as very good considering your present development, but you should set your whole heart and soul upon the attainment of something far superior. Think constantly of your work as being susceptible to perpetual improvement. Then proceed to make that thought come true, and you will positively succeed.

Every mental process that you turn into your work must be constructive. Your object is progress towards the goal you have in view. Therefore, every process that you place in action whether in mind or personality must be a building process. But your desire to make those processes constructive will not alone make them so. The idea of constant enlargement must be the very soul of every thought, and the whole of your mentality must live and act in a state of expanding consciousness. In the growing mind there is an interior ever-increasing feeling of the consciousness of enlargement and expansion which we should cultivate extensively, and in this feeling every process of thinking should move. The thought that you put into your work will increase or decrease your capacity, and will consequently either promote or retard your progress. And here we should remember that the thought you put into your work is the thought you think while you work. While you work you are actually giving a part of yourself to that which you are doing, but if you are giving your life and power correctly you will receive more than you give; that is, the reaction will be greater than the action. In order to give correctly of your life and power in this manner, or rather to think correctly while at work, every mental action in expression at the time should be permeated with the spirit of expansion, improvement and advancement. In brief, you should feel that the effort you put into your work is actually developing yourself. And this is precisely what is taking place in every mind that thinks scientifically, constructively and according to a definite purpose while at work. Your thought about the progress of your work is very important and such thought should always be that of success. If you are determined to succeed your work is already a success, and it is strictly scientific to think of it as such. When the seed is good and has been placed in good soil we can truthfully say that a good harvest will be forthcoming. In like manner, you can truthfully say that you are a success when all the elements needed to produce success have been placed in action in your own mind and personality. Too many minds, however, do not recognize success until they see the physical results and for this very reason the physical results are frequently limited or of inferior worth; the reason being that the real spirit of success was absent during the actions of that process through which the physical results were being produced. But the cause of success has the same right to recognition as the effect of success, and if the cause is recognized in the beginning the effects will become much larger because the process will contain a much larger measure of the spirit of success. When we give conscious recognition to a cause we increase its power. When you have selected a work and have resolved to put your whole life into it you are already a success in that work, and it is perfectly right for you to think of yourself as a success. The cause of that success has been created; therefore that success already does exist. And by giving it faith, encouragement and mental power it will continue to grow, and will finally produce all kinds of rich harvests or tangible results in the external world.

When a powerful cause has been created the effect is inevitable, provided it is not destroyed during its process of expression. Wrong thought, however, has a tendency to destroy every constructive cause that may have been placed in action in the mind. Therefore we must think correctly, harmoniously and constructively of every process of thought or action all along the line; that is, we should give every good cause definite recognition as an individual power and give it full right of way in our world. To create a good cause and then ignore it is to deprive it of life during its infancy, but this is the very thing we do when we proceed in the belief that we may succeed some day. Say instead, and say it with all the power of mind and soul, I AM SUCCESS NOW. Every true effort is successful because it not only has the power to produce success, but is actually working out successful results; and if it is encouraged, pushed and promoted it will positively express the success desired in real life. To push or promote a true effort we should think of it as being already an individual power for success, because that is what it is, and by dealing with it as such we turn our creative powers into its sphere of action which means that the desired results will invariably follow.

The progress of anything will necessarily depend upon the methods employed. Therefore, the way we plan for greater achievements and the methods we employ in promoting our advancement, are matters of extreme importance. Every plan should be directly related to the purpose which it is intended to promote, and every method we employ should be based upon the laws required to carry it out. It is also important to increase the capacity of every new plan as much as possible. In formulating the best plans and methods, however, the laws of life should be thoroughly understood especially those laws that act in the metaphysical field because all physical action to be effective must be preceded by effective mental actions. But in addition to having the right methods, the right plans and the knowledge of constructive action, physical and mental, we must also have a powerful faith if we wish to work and think for results. When we plan for greater things and have faith in greater things we shall certainly see those greater things realized. In fact, the power of faith in the promotion of any plan or purpose is so great that no one can afford to give it otherwise than the most thorough attention. Though faith in one of its phases is what may be termed a mental attitude, an attitude with an upward look, still it is in its most important phase a positive mental force. The mental force or action of faith is always elevating, expanding and constructive. Therefore, to have faith in yourself and in your work is to cause all the powers of your mind to become elevating, expanding and constructive in all their actions. Faith always tends to build and it builds the loftier, the perfect and the more worthy. Doubt, however, retards and retreats; it is a depressing mental state that we cannot afford to entertain for a moment. But such a state can be removed at once by cultivating faith; and as we proceed to get faith we should by all means get an abundance of faith for in all efforts that aim for great results we cannot have too much faith.

It has been said that faith and science can never harmonize, because according to some they are antagonistic, and according to others they act in domains that are wholly dissimilar. But no matter what the views of the past may be on the subject the fact is that there is nothing more scientific than faith, and also that there is nothing that will aid the mind more in becoming scientific and constructive than a thorough realization, as well as expression, of the spirit of faith. The more familiar we become with real faith the more convinced we become that faith is indispensable in every effort we make, physical or mental, if the best results are to be secured. In fact, faith must be made the very soul of every thought, and the living spirit of every mental action. For this reason we realize that no greater step forward can be taken than to give faith the first place in life if our purpose in life is to think and work for results.

7

MAN is as he thinks and his thoughts are invariably created in the likeness of his mental conceptions of those things of which he thinks about habitually. Therefore as man improves his mental conceptions of all things he will improve himself in the same measure. To improve these mental conceptions attention should always be concentrated upon the ideal of everything of which we think. That is, all thinking should move toward the greater, the larger and the superior. Whatever we think about we should always think about its ideal side, its larger side and its superior side. Everything has two sides, the limited or objective side and the unlimited or subjective side. When we consider only the limited objective side of those things we think about our mental conceptions will be small, superficial and materialistic. But when we consider the unlimited subjective side of those things our mental conceptions will be larger, finer and of far superior worth.

The capacity, the power and the brilliancy of the mind depends entirely upon its mental conceptions. If the mental conceptions are formed in the likeness of the external, common or the ordinary, the mind will be inferior in every respect, and vice versa. It is therefore of the highest importance that every mental conception be as high, as perfect and as ideal as it is possible to make it. And to bring this about it is necessary to train the mind to concentrate attention upon the ideal side of everything and to think with the larger, the greater and the superior always in view.

When thinking about persons no mental conceptions should be formed of the mere external or personal side. The superior man alone should receive direct attention. To look through the person, so to speak, and view the inner possibilities, and all the worthy qualities that we know to exist back of the imperfect manifestation—this is the correct and the scientific way to think about the people we meet. When we analyze the inferior things we see about a person and permit those things to affect our minds we form inferior and detrimental conceptions in our own minds. When we think a great deal about the smallness we imagine we see in others we tend to breed smallness in ourselves. But when we think only of the larger and the better side of others we cause our minds to rise in the scale and thus gain power and understanding we never had before. In this connection the law is that when we look with deep interest for everything that is superior in others we actually develop the superior in ourselves.

When we think of the body we should not think of it as common flesh as the majority do, because the physical form will tend to express the crude and the common when we think of it in that way. When your mental actions are low, crude and coarse your body will have an ordinary earth-earthy appearance, but when those actions are highly refined your body will express a more refined appearance to correspond. All such actions constitute, or are produced by, the thoughts we think. Therefore all our mental actions are as crude or as fine as our thoughts themselves. To be scientific in this, however, we should think of the body as a great temple with millions of apartments, each one furnished most gorgeously with nature's own wealth and beauty, and this is what the body really is. Every cell of the body when viewed under a microscope is like a crystal palace, and the body is composed of millions of such. We should always think of the body as a divinely formed structure, as an ideal creation, and we should mentally view its perfect elements, its forces and laws in this manner as they perform their daily miracles. We should think of the body as it is in its true inner self, as it is in its fine and delicate structures and we should not think of those imperfections in its appearance which our own crude mental actions have produced; for when we form in mind the highest conception possible of the ideal physical form we will not only cause the body to grow more beautiful every year, but we will also enrich the mind with thoughts of high and superior worth.

When we think of the mind we should not think of its flaws or undeveloped states, but try to realize how great and wonderful the mind really is, and then hold attention upon our highest conception of true greatness. When all our mental activities move towards this lofty idea of a brilliant and prodigious mind we shall steadily develop our own mind up to that superior state; for according to a well-known metaphysical law we mentally move towards the ideals we persistently hold in mind. Therefore by directing our attention upon the greater side of the mind we shall actually arise into mental greatness thus tending directly to develop superiority in our own minds. This is the path to mental greatness, but it is so simple that few have found it.

When we think about life we should always view the sunny side of personal existence and the real life of interior existence. Instead of viewing life as a burden or as a misery to be endured now, that glory may come in the future, we should think of the unbounded possibilities that real life has in store here and now. Our mind should be concerned with the real life itself and should seek to form the very highest conceptions possible of such a life. There is no greater subject for thought than life when we look at life as an eternity of rich and marvelous possibilities. And to view life in this way will not only elevate and enlarge the mind, but will also give us the conscious realization of a continuous increase in life. And as life increases everything in mind and personality will increase to correspond. A great life produces a great mind and a high soul, but to attain the greater life we must enlarge our view of life. And this we do by turning all attention upon real life itself, and the marvelous possibilities of real life. Realizing these facts we should never think of that which is small when we have the capacity to think of that which is great. And we all can think of the great. There is a beautiful and a wonderful side to all life, and the possibilities of all life are unbounded. We therefore understand the value of training ourselves to take the correct view of life, for to think of the larger and the more beautiful side of all life is to enlarge and beautify the life that is in us. The same principle should be observed in all our thought about nature, and to learn how to enter into that perfect communion with nature where we can see her real beauty and her wonderful power, is to apply a faculty that deserves the highest state of cultivation in every mind. Those mental conceptions that are formed while we are in perfect touch with the true in nature are of exceptional worth and will add largely to the power and superiority of mind. Therefore when we think of nature all attention should be concentrated upon the ideal, the beautiful and true side. When we see what may seem to be flaws it is wisdom to pass them by and never permit them to impress our minds. Even a weed should be thought of with respect because it is also a product of natural law, and it is our privilege to transform the weed into something that has real beauty and worth. But here it is highly important to remember that our power to perfect anything in nature can only increase as we think less of its flaws and more of its hidden splendors.

When we come to the subject of our own personal life and experiences we cannot apply too well the principle of scientific thinking, because what we think of the experiences of to-day will largely determine what experiences we are to have to-morrow. What we receive from life passes through the channel of experience and every channel tends to modify that which passes through. The subject therefore is vitally important. As frequently stated before, scientific thinking is thinking that produces the larger, the better, the greater and the superior; thinking that promotes progress ; thinking that produces results. And such thinking is scientific because it is in harmony with the purpose of life which is to advance constantly in the producing of greater and greater results; consequently to think scientifically about experience every mental conception formed by experience should be formed in the likeness of those facts that will be found back of the experience. Every experience can teach us something we do not know; therefore instead of deploring the experience we should receive it with joy and proceed at once to look for the truth it has come to convey. No experience will be unpleasant if we meet it with the one desire to know what it has to teach; and what is better still when we think of experience as a messenger of truth we will form only lofty mental conceptions of all experience. We will thus not only gain much new truth, but we will enrich the mind with these many superior conceptions. In the usual way we meet unpleasant experiences with a heavy heart, and we meet the pleasant ones with the thought of personal gratification. Those mental conceptions that we form while thinking of our experiences in the usual way will therefore be ordinary and frequently detrimental. In the meantime, the new truth that those experiences could have conveyed will remain unlearned and undiscovered.

The reverses and misfortunes of life are usually looked upon with regret, and are deplored as so many obstacles in our way, but such thought is not conducive to good results. Reverses come because we have failed to comply with the laws of life, therefore instead of regretting the experience we should use it as a means of finding wherein we have failed. And having done this we may proceed once more with the positive assurance of gaining increased success. Misfortunes may also be employed as builders of character because there is nothing that strengthens the mind and the soul so much as to pass through reverses without being mentally or morally disturbed. The spiritual giant can pass through anything and gain good from anything. To him misfortunes are not disagreeable; they are simply opportunities to bring out greater life and power, to learn more laws, to gain a better understanding of things, and thus achieve still greater things when the next attempt is made. But though we may not have attained such a lofty state we can at least pass through reverses with our minds fixed constantly upon the high goal in view. The result will be greater moral stability, greater mental power and the turning of fate in the direction we ourselves desire to move.

That knowledge and power is gained through pain is a well-known belief and it is one of those beliefs that contains much truth; and it is also true that when we have learned the lesson the pain came to teach the pain disappears. When the pain is felt attention should at once be directed upon that finer and larger life that lies back of the personal man. We feel pain because the outer forces are not in harmony with the more perfect life within; therefore to remove the pain this harmony must be restored. To restore this harmony we should proceed to gain consciousness of the finer forces of the inner life because when we become conscious of the inner life, which is always in harmony, the disorder of the outer life will disappear. The more we think of the pain the more conscious we become of the discord in the outer life and the more difficult it becomes to gain consciousness of the harmony of the inner life. Therefore to think scientifically about pain is to take the mind beyond pain into the inner realms of life where perfect harmony reigns. The result will be freedom from pain and the discovery of a new interior world.

When, we take this higher view of pain, reverses, misfortune, troubles and the like we gradually work ourselves out of the lower and the confused, and will be no long before we get out of them entirely. It is therefore evident that when we think scientifically about the ills of life we proceed directly to rise above them and will therefore meet them no more. This is perfectly natural because when your thoughts are high you will rise in the scale; you will leave behind the inferior and the wrong and you will enter into the possession of the superior and the right.

When we think about ourselves we should always think about the unlimited possibilities of the within. Attention should be directed upon the larger self, and every thought should be formed in the likeness of the highest mental conceptions that we can form of the superior. We may, however, recognize the existence of flaws in our nature; in fact, it is necessary to know where the weak places are in order to remove them; but the mind should never hold its attention upon those weak places.

The mental eye should never look upon the imperfect, but should go through it and direct its vision towards the ideal. And here we find the reason why the average person does not improve as he should. The fact is he thinks of himself as he appears to be in the limited personal self. He patterns his thought after the small life that he can see in the outer self. And as man is as he thinks he will therefore not rise above the quality or the nature of his own thought. No one can rise any higher than his thoughts. Therefore, so long as your thoughts are like your present limited personal life you will never become any more than you are now. The mind, however, that transcends its present states, talents and qualities and tries to gain mental conceptions of the larger and the superior will steadily rise and become as large as those new conceptions that have been formed, and may later rise still higher thus reaching greater heights of consciousness, ability, and power than was dreamed of before.

In the world of feeling the thorough application of the law of scientific thought is extremely important, the reason being that we generally live upon those planes where our feelings are the strongest. All our feelings therefore should be transformed to the highest planes of thought and living that we can possibly think of. But since feelings deal principally with forces, whether in mind or personality, it is in the world of force that we shall have to direct our attention if a change of feeling is to be made. And this is done very simply by training the mind to always try to feel the finer and the more powerful forces that are back of every state, condition or action. Whenever anything takes place in your system try to feel the finer forces in that part of the system where the action is taking place. This experience may not give you any new sensation at first, but you will gradually become conscious of a whole universe of finer life and action within yourself. Then your mind will be living in a much larger world and in a much richer world. These finer life forces that you feel within yourself are the powerful creative energies of the subconscious, and it is these energies that are so valuable in the development of the mind and the reconstruction of the body. Therefore, whenever you exercise the sense of feeling try to feel the higher and the finer that is in you. You will soon succeed and the results will not only add enjoyments, both to mind and personality, but will also give you the mastery of new and powerful forces.

An expanding and ascending desire should be back of every action of the mind, and all efforts to gain the conscious realization of the new should aim at the very largest mental scope and realization possible. Every desire should desire the largest, the purest, the most refined and the most perfect expression that present mental capacity can be conscious of. This will add remarkably to the joy of living and will have a refining effect upon the entire system. The most refined expressions of desire give the greatest pleasure, whether the channel of expression be physical, mental or spiritual. But no desire should be destroyed. The proper course is to refine it and turn it into channels through which the forces back of that desire can be wisely employed now. When we refine our desires those desires will never lead us into wrongs or temptations because the fact is that a refined desire never desires to do wrong. On the contrary, every desire that desires higher and higher expressions will, through such a desire, tend to enter into the right, the more perfect and the superior. In this connection, we should remember that all ascending actions are right actions, that all descending actions are wrong actions, and that this is the only difference between right and wrong.

Every mental aim should have the greater in view, and every plan that is formed should embody the largest possibilities conceivable. Too many minds fail because their plans are so small and their aims too low; but the larger and the higher is invariably the purpose of scientific thought—thought that thinks for results. Every mental force, therefore, should be an aspiring force and should have the power to spur us on to greater efforts and higher goals. This is extremely important as we shall know when we learn that all forces are creative. When all the forces of your system are trained to aspire, everything that is being created in your system will be created more perfectly and you will steadily advance. In like manner, when every mental action is constructive, everything that may be placed in action in your mind will tend to build you up and will tend to work for the purpose you have in view. Mental actions that have no particular aim are usually destructive, but every action of the mind can be made constructive if we make it a point to always think for results. The first step in this connection, and the only really important step, is to have a strong desire for mental construction constantly held in mind, and to give this desire increased attention when our mental actions are especially strong. In all our efforts our object should be greater things, and to realize this object no building power in mind or personality must be idle or misdirected. On the contrary, everything within us should be trained to work for all those definite results that we have in view, and all actions of mind and body should be so perfectly directed upon the production of those results that everything we do under any circumstance will tend to work constantly and directly for those results. It is when we proceed in this manner that our thinking is right, designed and scientific, and it is such thinking alone that we can employ when we aim to think for results.

8.

TO make the right use of thought we must make it a practice to think that which is inherently true. Therefore whatever we think about we must formulate our thoughts according to the truth which we know to exist within that of which we think. When we think about life we must think of life as it is in itself and not as it appears to be in the personal existence of someone who does not know how to use life. There are people who make life a burden, but life in itself is anything but a burden. On the contrary it is a rare privilege. Therefore, to think of life as a burden is to take the wrong view of life. It is to think the untruth about life. It is to view life from the standpoint of one who has misapplied life. Accordingly what we judge is not life, but a mistaken opinion about life. Our thought in the matter will thus be foreign to life and will naturally mislead us when we try to apply it in connection with real living. When we think about life we must think about real life and not about some illusion that we might have of life. The average person's thought about life, however, is simply an opinion about his misunderstanding about life and therefore his thinking is never designed, constructive nor scientific. Life itself is a joy, a rich blessing and it means so much that an eternity of mental growth will be required to comprehend it entire meaning. Life is not something that comes and goes; it is something that always is. Neither is life something that can be produced or destroyed. Life is inexhaustible and indestructible and contains within itself a definite and eternal purpose. We should therefore view life according to this idea. And when we gain this right idea of life we can become more deeply conscious of real life and thus gain possession of more life. This is extremely important because it is only as we gain added life that we can gain added ability and power. When we gain a correct conception of life we also enter into harmony with the purpose of life which means to enter the path of continuous advancement along all lines, the result of which will be perpetually increased in all things.

When you think about yourself view yourself as you are at your best and not as you appear when in the midst of failure. You never fail when you are at your best and you are true to yourself only when you are at your best. Therefore if you wish to think the truth about yourself think about yourself as you are when you are true to yourself and not as you appear to be when you are false to yourself. Scientific thinking does not recognize weakness of mind or body because you yourself are not weak, and you would never feel weak if you were always true to yourself. Thoughts should never be formed in the likeness of a weak condition because such thinking will perpetuate the condition of weakness. When weakness is felt think the truth about yourself; that is, that you are inherently strong and the weakness will disappear. Form your thought in the likeness of yourself as you are in your real and larger self; that is, as you are when you are true to your whole self—full of life, strength and vigor. And your thought will become the thought of strength conveying strength to every part of your system.

In the right use of thought we never permit ourselves to say that we cannot. On the contrary we continue to believe and say, "I can do whatever I undertake to do and I am equal to every occasion." This is our firm conviction when we have come to that place where we really know what is in us, and it is a conviction that is based upon actual scientific fact. Unlimited possibilities are latent in every mind; therefore man is

386

inherently equal to every occasion and he should claim his whole power at all times. If he does not make himself equal to every occasion the cause is that he fails to express all that is in him. But the greater capacity that is within anyone cannot fully express itself so long as thought is created in the likeness of weakness, doubt and limitations. Therefore the right and scientific use of thought becomes the direct channel through which the greatness that is within man may come forth and act in real life.

Man is not naturally in the hands of fate for the truth is that fate is in the hands of man. Man may appear to be controlled by a destiny that seems distinct from himself, but the real truth is that he himself has created the very life and the very tendency of that destiny. The destiny of every man in his own creation, be it good or otherwise, but so long as he thinks he is in the hands of this destiny he will fail to intelligently employ his own creations, and will accordingly originate adverse circumstances. Many have speculated as to the real cause of adverse circumstances, bad luck and the like, but the cause is simply this, that when man finds himself in adversity he has neglected to direct, consciously and intelligently, the forces which he himself has placed in action; and this neglect can invariably be traced to the belief that we are all controlled more or less by what we call fate. For this reason the sooner we eliminate that belief absolutely the better.

No man will attempt to control the forces of life so long as he thinks he is unavoidably controlled by those forces; but if those forces are not intelligently controlled, their action will be aimless and we shall have that confusion which is otherwise termed adversity. Every word, every thought and every action gives expression to certain life forces, and what those forces will do depends first upon their original nature and second upon how they are directed in their courses. The sum total of all the words, thoughts and actions expressed by man will constitute the forces of his destiny, and the result of those forces will constitute his fate. What those forces are in the beginning depends upon what man created them to be, and what those forces will unitedly produce will depend upon whether they are directed by man himself or left to act aimlessly. But man can make his words, thoughts and actions what he wishes them to be. He can direct them intelligently into channels of constructive and perpetual growth. It is therefore simply understood how man is unconsciously the cause of his fate, and how he can consciously and intelligently create his own fate. To create his own fate, however, he must make the right use of thought; that is, he must think for results.

To think scientifically about the people we meet it is necessary to apply the same principle which we apply to our true thought about life. We must think of people as they are in themselves and not as they appear to be while out of harmony with existence. When we are judging man we should judge the real man and not his mistakes. The mistakes of the man do not constitute the man any more than the absence of light constitutes light. The usual way, however, of judging man is to look at his weak points and then after comparing these with his strong points call the result the man himself. But this is as unscientific as to combine black with white and speak of the result as pure white. The weaknesses that we find in man may disappear in a day. They frequently do, while his virtues and superior qualities may double in power at any time. Then we have another man, and we say he has changed, which is not strictly true. The real man has not changed. The real man is already unbounded in life and power and does not have to change. The change that we see is simply this, that more of the true worth of his real being has been expressed.

Our thoughts about other people are more or less deeply impressed upon our own minds; therefore we cannot afford to think anything wrong about anybody. The better we understand life the more convinced we become that the average person is doing the best he knows how. For this reason we shall be training our minds to think the whole truth about the human race when we take this view, and what is highly important, such a view will tend to keep our own minds wholesome and clean. Then when we add to this the larger view of man himself, in his true glory and power, our thought about man will become as we wish it to be, strictly scientific.

In thinking for results all circumstances should be viewed as opportunities because that is what they are in reality. And to think correctly we must think of things according to what there really is in them. No circumstance is actually against us though we may go against a circumstance and thus produce a clash. A circumstance is usually similar to an electrical force. It may destroy or it may serve depending upon how it is approached. The power, however, is there and we are the ones to determine what that power is to do. Our relation to anything in the external depends upon how we view the circumstances involved. When we think of circumstances as adverse we become antagonistic to those circumstances and in consequence produce discord, trouble and misfortune. But when we think of circumstances as opportunities to take advantage of and control, we relate ourselves harmoniously to the power that is contained in those circumstances. Thus by entering into harmony with that power we will perpetuate more and more of it until we have made it our own altogether.

When disappointments appear it is not scientific to feel depressed nor to view the experience as a misfortune. To the advancing mind a disappointment is always an open door to something better. When you fail to get what you want there is something better at hand for you; that is, if you are moving forward. Therefore to every advancing mind so called disappointments may be viewed as prophecies of better things. If you are not moving forward a disappointment indicates that you have not made yourself equal to your ideal. But the fact that you have felt disappointment proves that you have seen the ideal, and to see an ideal indicates that that ideal is within your reach ready for you to possess if you will press forward steadily and surely until the goal is reached. Therefore no matter what your condition may be in life a disappointment indicates that there is something better at hand for you if you will go and work for it. For this reason, instead of feeling depressed you should rejoice, and then press on with more faith and enthusiasm than ever that you may meet your own at the earliest possible moment.

These thoughts are not presented simply to give encouragement or cheer. The fact is they are thoroughly scientific and based upon two well established laws in metaphysics. The first law is that no person can feel disappointed unless he has had a perception of something better. And the second law is that whoever is far enough advanced to perceive the better has the capacity to acquire that something better, though he must make full use of the power at hand. Too many minds that see the ideal simply dream about it and feel depressed because the ideal has not been reached, while in the meantime they do nothing to work themselves up to that ideal. Instead such minds should take a scientific view of the entire subject and then press on towards the goal before them. They positively will succeed.

When we look upon a disappointment as a misfortune the depressed thought that follows will take us down and away from the open door of the better things, and will in consequence prevent us from realizing the greater good which was in store. We shall then have to give much time and effort to the bringing of ourselves back again to the gates of the ideal we had in view But such tactics we cannot afford to employ if our object is to work and think for results. We conclude therefore that whatever comes or does not come the best way is always to smile and press on.

It is scientific to recognize only the sunny side of everything and to expect only the best results from every effort, because the sunny side is the real side and the substantial side, and our thinking should be concerned only with the substantial, or with that which has real or possible worth. Failure is an empty place, so to speak, or a condition involving a group of misdirected actions. To think of failure therefore is to produce a mental tendency towards misdirected or abortive actions, and at the same time create thoughts that waste energy. To dwell mentally on the sunny side, however, is to turn all the actions of the mind towards the construction of greater worth in the mind; and accordingly the habit of dwelling upon the sunny side will invariably tend to develop brilliancy of mind, clearness of thought and greater intellectual capacity. The principal reason for this is found in the fact that such a mind deals almost entirely with the larger, the greater and the limitless of the potential. Mind therefore naturally expands and develops and steadily gains in power, comprehension and lucidity along all lines. To act in harmony with this principle we should expect the best results from every effort because the best results do exist potentially in every effort; and to be scientific we must think of things as they really are in themselves and not as they appear while in the hands of the incompetent. It is not our purpose to dwell mentally upon the absence of results, but to give all our thought and attention to the right use of those powers within us that actually can produce results.

To think scientifically about the health and the wholeness of mind and body is one of the most important essentials of all because health is indispensable to the highest attainments and the greatest achievements. The principle, however, is that the real man is well, and that you yourself are the real man. When you are thinking about yourself as you really are and since you, the real YOU, the individuality, are always well, your thought of yourself is not right and constructive unless you think of yourself as absolutely and permanently well. Every condition in the personal man is the result of habits of thought. Therefore when you think of yourself as being absolutely and permanently well you will through that mode of thinking give absolute and permanent health to the entire system. This is a law that is as strong as life itself. And we are not making extravagant statements when we declare that if this law were universally employed disease would be practically banished from off the face of the earth. This law is the absolute truth and every student of modern metaphysics knows that it is the truth. That its power is invincible no one can deny. Therefore the wise course to pursue is to apply this law thoroughly under all sorts of circumstances and never lose faith in its effectiveness for a moment.

In training ourselves to think for results we must constantly bear in mind the great fact that man invariably grows into the likeness of that which he thinks of the most. Therefore, think constantly of what you want to become and your life will daily grow in that direction. Think constantly of health, power, ability, capacity, worth and superiority and the powers of your being will gradually and steadily produce all those qualities in your own system. But all such thinking must be deep, persistent and of the heart. It is that thinking which is in touch with the under currents of life that shapes human destiny; therefore all such thinking should always be as we wish to become. No thoughts should ever enter the mind that do not contain in the ideal the very things that we wish to attain or accomplish in the real. But to train ourselves in this mode of thinking is not difficult. It is only a matter of deciding what we want in life; then to think the most of those things and make such thinking deep, persistent, positive and strong.

9.

TO train the mind to think for results there are four essentials that must be provided. The first is to carry on all thinking in the attitude of right mental states. The second is to think only such thoughts as will push your work and that will constantly promote your present purpose in life. The third is to employ only such creative processes in the mind as will tend directly to produce the larger, the better and the superior. And the fourth is to think only the real truth about all things; that is, to fashion all thought according to the most perfect mental conception that can be formed of the real in everything of which we may think. The first three essentials have been fully considered in the preceding pages. We shall therefore conclude by giving our attention to the fourth. And in doing so we must prepare ourselves for thought that is somewhat deeper than the usual.

To begin we must realize that there is a vast difference between what seems to be true and what really is true, and that all thinking to be right, wholesome, constructive and scientific must deal directly with that which really is true. To illustrate we will consider the being of man. Viewed externally man seems to have many imperfections, to be limited in all things and to be more or less in the hands of fate. But when we consider, not the present conditions of the personal man, but the possibilities of his marvelous interior nature, we find that imperfections are simply greater things in the process of development. We find that there is no limit to his power and inherent capacity, and we find that he is strong enough, if he applies all his strength, to overcome any fate, to change any circumstance and to positively determine his own destiny.

When we examine other things we find the same to be true; that is, that there is more in everything than what appears on the surface. And therefore what appears to be true of things when viewed externally is not the whole truth; in fact, it may frequently be the very opposite of the real truth. The right use of thought, however, must concern itself with the real truth, or the inside facts in the case; therefore, in thinking for results we must fashion our thoughts according to what really is in those thoughts of which we may be thinking.

In dealing with the inside facts of any case, condition or object the question always is: "What are the possibilities; what can be done with what is in the thing; and what results can be gained from the full use of everything that this circumstance or that object may contain?" And it is highly important to answer this question as fully and as correctly as possible because we are as we think and our thoughts are always like the things we think about. Besides we must be conscious of the real interior possibility of those things with which we deal in order to secure the greatest results. If we think only of the imperfections and the limitations that appear on the surface our thinking will be inferior, and we will become ordinary both in mind and personality. But if we think of what is really true of the greater possibilities of all things we will think far greater thoughts, and we will think inspiring thoughts—thoughts that will stir the mind to greater ambition and greater achievement, and the mind will accordingly enter more and more into a larger, greater and richer world. In consequence our mental powers along all lines will steadily increase.

To think what is really true about all things is therefore to think of the greater powers and possibilities that are in all things; and to think the truth in the broadest sense is to direct the mind upon the whole of life, with all its possibilities, and to deal mentally with all the richness, all the power and all the marvelous-ness that can be discerned in everything pertaining to life. Or to state it briefly, you have begun to think what is really true when your mind has begun to move constantly towards the vastness of the greater things that lie before us. And here we must remember that there is no end to that vastness; no limit to the greatness that is inherent in life. Therefore, we may go on and on indefinitely thinking more and more truth about everything; and as we do we shall continue to enrich and enlarge both the talents and the powers of the mind.

It is therefore evident that when we think the truth about all things, that is, think of what is really possible in all things, we will cause the mind to enlarge and expand constantly, because as we think of the larger we invariably enlarge the mind. And the real truth about all things grows larger and larger the further we advance in the pursuit of truth. And the importance of such a mode of thinking becomes more and more evident as we realize that an ever enlarging mind is an absolute necessity if our aim is to think for results.

When we proceed to think the truth about things we naturally think of the true state of affairs within those things. We think of the power itself and not of its past use. Therefore, such thinking will invariably keep the mind in a wholesome and harmonious condition. That which is true of the real nature of things must be good and wholesome, and therefore to think of that which is true must necessarily produce wholesome conditions in the mind. And here it is well to emphasize the fact that the mind that is wholesome and harmonious is far more powerful than the mind that is not. Such a mind therefore may secure far greater results, no matter what its work or purpose may be.

To think what is really true about everything will for the same reason prevent the formation of detrimental and perverted states of mind, and will also prevent the misdirection of mental energy. This is a fact of great importance to those who aim for results, because in the average mind the majority of the energies placed in action are either misdirected or applied in such a way as to be of no permanent value. Another fact that needs emphasis in this connection is that the thinking of truth will tend to bring out all that is in us. And the reason is that when we think of what there really is in everything the mind becomes more penetrating as well as more comprehensive in its scope of action. The result therefore will naturally be that our own mental actions will penetrate more and more every element and power that is in us, and thus arouse more and more of everything that is in us. In other words, the mind will proceed to act positively upon everything that exists in the vast domain of our own mental world, conscious and subconscious, and will actually think into activity every power and faculty we possess.

When we think the real truth about everything in life, including our own self, we invariably focus attention upon the best, the largest and the richest that exists in everything. And this we must do if our purpose is to secure greater and better results the further we go in our progress toward attainment and achievement. Your mind, your thought, your ability, your power, in brief, everything of worth in your system, cannot be fully and effectively applied unless your attention is constantly concentrated upon the greater; unless you are mentally moving towards the greater; unless you are giving your whole life and power to the greater; and to this end your attention must constantly be focused upon the best and the greatest that you can possibly picture in your mind.

When you think the truth you think of what can be done. You do not think of weakness, obstacles or possible failure; nor do you consider what may be dark, adverse or detrimental in your present circumstances. Instead you think of the tremendous power that is within you, and you try to turn on the full current of that power so that what you want to accomplish positively will be accomplished. But in turning on that full current you make a special effort to make every action in your system constructive, whether it be physical or mental, because in working for results you want all that is in you to work thoroughly, continuously and directly for those self same results. We realize therefore the importance of training the mind to think the truth according to this larger view of the truth in order that the best use, the fullest use and the most effective use of every power of mind and thought may be applied; and we shall find as we proceed that the art of thinking the truth in this manner can be readily mastered by anyone whose desire is to make his life as large, as rich and as perfect as life can be made.

To restate the principles and ideas upon which the right use of the mind is based, we need simply return to the four essentials mentioned in the beginning of this chapter. We proceed by placing the mind in certain mental states called right mental states because the mind has more power while acting in such states, and can act more effectively while acting through the wholesome constructive attitudes of those states. We continue by thinking only such thoughts as will tend to work with us, and give their full force to the promotion of our purpose. We avoid thoughts and mental states that are against us and permit only those that are positively and absolutely for us. We place in action only such mental processes as tend to create the larger, the better and the superior in ourselves because our object is not simply to secure results now, but to secure greater and greater results ; and to promote this object we must constantly develop the larger, the better and the superior in ourselves. Lastly we make it a special point to think the real truth about all things; that is, we form our mental conceptions, our ideas and our thoughts in the exact likeness of the great, the marvelous and the limitless that is inherent in all life.

We aim to fashion our thoughts according to everything that is great, lofty and of superior worth so that we may think great thoughts because we are as we think. When our thoughts are small we will become small, weak and inefficient; but when our thoughts are great we will become great, powerful and efficient. This is the law, and as we apply this law as fully and as effectively as we possibly can, we shall positively become much and achieve much, and the object we have in view—the securing of greater and greater results—will be realized. Therefore in all our thinking we focus all the actions of mind upon the unbounded possibilities that are inherent in ourselves, that are inherent in all things, that are inherent in the vastness of the cosmos. We turn all our thoughts upon the rich, the limitless and the sublime so that we may live constantly in a larger and superior mental world—a world that we are determined to make larger and larger every day. And as we live, think and work in that ever-growing mental world we insist that everything we do shall, with a certainty, build for that greater future we now have in view; and that every action of mind and body shall be a positive force moving steadily, surely and perpetually towards those sublime heights of attainment and achievement that we have longed for so much while inspired by the spirit of ambition's lofty dream.

THE END.

BOOK SIX

BRAINS, AND HOW TO GET THEM

ABOUT THIS BOOK

"When we consider the human brain, together with mental brilliancy, mental power and mental capacity, we find three factors in particular that stand out distinctly; and we also find that the more we have of these three factors, the more brains we possess.

The first factor is the physical cells of the brain; the second factor is the quality of the mind acting through the brain; and the third factor is the actions of the mind itself."

From this premise, Larson takes us in a Journey of discovery of the brain, and how we can actually develop our capacity, and become smarter and more capable people. Through his secrets and practical methods of brain building, the reader will be able to develop its mental power, and make every brain cell alive!

INTRODUCTION. NEW DISCOVERIES IN BRAIN BUILDING

When we consider the human brain, together with mental brilliancy, mental power and mental capacity, we find three factors in particular that stand out distinctly; and we also find that the more we have of these three factors, the more brains we possess.

The first factor is the physical cells of the brain; the second factor is the quality of the mind acting through the brain; and the third factor is the actions of the mind itself.

The actions of the mind we may also speak of as mental force; that is, that power in the mind that is distinct both from mental quality and the physical side of the brain; and we always find that the possession of an exceptional degree of this mental force or power, always means mental brilliancy as well as high mental activity.

The fact that these three factors, when highly developed, invariably produce a greater quantity and a higher degree of brains, leads us to inquire how the further development of these factors may be promoted; and we now know that these factors can be developed.

In the past we lived largely in the belief that the increase of talent or ability was something that we might not expect—something that was hardly possible in any case; and therefore we felt it necessary to be content with what ability we might happen to be born with. This however, we do not believe anymore, because any number of intensely interesting experiments conducted along these lines have proven conclusively that brains can be developed.

This same fact is being proven every day by a great number of individuals who are constantly building up the mind and its power, through the best methods that they have been able to find in modern psychology. We have all noted how certain people have improved during certain periods of time when they gave attention to the newest principles of mind development; and in many cases such improvement has been remarkable. We may therefore proceed in the conviction that brains can be developed, and that an individual can develop his own brains, not only to a certain degree, but to any degree desired.

Considering the first factor—the cells of the brain—we come face to face with a very interesting fact that has been evolved in recent years through certain laboratory experiments, and this fact is, that the cells of the brain can be increased in number and improved in quality through the mere act of increasing life and power in the various groups of the brain cells. To illustrate, we will suppose that you divide your brain into five or six divisions, and take, say, one-half hour, twice every day, for the purpose of concentrating attention upon those various divisions, for the express purpose of increasing life and energy throughout the brain; you will find, in the course of a few weeks' time, that every part of your brain will be more active than it was before; and you will note a remarkable increase in the power and capacity of the mind as a whole. We all are familiar with the fact that whenever we concentrate attention upon any group of cells, cither in the body, or in the brain, we invariably increase life, energy, and nourishment among those cells; and the result must be development. These experiments in concentration prove that the circulation can be increased anywhere in the human system, at the point of concentration; and we know full well that whenever we increase the circulation, we supply added nourishment as well as added life force. We understand therefore, that by providing the different divisions of the brain with added nourishment and life force, through this process of concentration, we provide those very essentials that nature requires in order to build more cells, as well as develop further the cells already existing in that particular group.

This same mode of concentration tends to increase brain activity, and wherever brain activity is increased, there we always find a corresponding improvement in quality, together with finer mental action, deeper mental action, and a more refined mode of mental functioning, which invariably leads to superior thinking.

The development of the brain through this method does not necessarily mean an enlargement of the brain on the whole, for the fact is that the higher development of the brain tends to produce more cells and smaller cells, so that where one crude cell might have existed before, we may produce a dozen or more finer cells; and the law is, that the finer the cells of the brain, the more perfect the brain becomes as an instrument through which ability, talent and genius may be expressed. However, if this process of brain development is continued for a number of years, the entire cranium will have increased in size to some extent. We find in great men and great women who have used their brains and minds extensively all through life, that the measurement of the cranium has increased slightly every ten years; and in some instances we find that the circumference of the cranium has increased one entire inch after the age of sixty. This fact proves conclusively that brain development may be continued far beyond the half century mark; and that ability may be increased remarkably even after the three score and ten has been passed; in fact, the new psychology is proving conclusively that we can increase ability, talent, brain capacity and mental power every year as long as we live, so that any man may become far more brilliant at the age of one hundred than he might have been at any previous time in his life.

When we consider this process of brain development, and the possibility of increasing the number of cells in the brain, we meet a very interesting fact. We will suppose that a certain group of cells in your brain is composed of just one hundred cells. This means that there would be one hundred points of action through which the mind could act in that particular part of the brain; but if you could double that number of cells you would have two hundred points of action through which the mind could be expressed along that line; and in consequence mental capacity and power would exactly double along that particular line of expression. Then suppose that you would promote your development further, and build twelve small, highly refined cells for every one brain cell you previously had; the capacity of the mind would become just exactly twelve times as great as it was before. You would have twelve times as many channels for the expression of talent and genius as you had previously; and the creative power of your mind would be twelve times as large as it was in the past.

It may not be possible for every brain to increase the number of cells to this extent; but every brain can double and treble its number of cells; and a large number, especially those who are faithful, will find it possible to increase the number of brain cells to eight, ten, and twelve times during the course of several years of steady brain development.

This fact brings us face to face with marvelous possibilities; it proves conclusively that there is no need of any one, at any time, being discouraged on account of a lack of ability or lack of opportunity, because even a few months of development of the brain will bring the individual to a place where he will be able to handle and master problems and propositions that he never could have managed before. Besides, this increase of development of the brain will give added ability and power in proportion and we all know very well that however discouraging the present may be, we shall find it possible to take advantage of new and exceptional opportunities the very moment we can add to our ability and power.

In this connection, we must remember that every cell in the brain serves as a channel for mental action. Therefore, the more cells we have in the brain, the more mental actions there will be; and the increase of mental actions means increase of mental capacity, mental power, and also mental creative force.

Mental action, however, does not depend on size, so that a brain cell does not have to be large in order to serve as a perfect channel for mental action. The fact is that the smaller the brain cell is, the more perfect it becomes as a channel for mental action. Therefore, we see the advantage of securing smaller brain cells and more brain cells; and this we may accomplish through the process of brain development, which we shall here outline.

We find that all such development tends to rebuild all the cells of the brain; and in re-building those cells, the brain texture is made finer, and the cells themselves smaller and more numerous. The psychology of all of this is very simple, as we shall find the more deeply we study this important subject.

The study of brain development also proves conclusively that the brain or the mind does not wear out. We had that opinion in the past, but it has been discarded as absolutely untrue. The use of the brain does not, in itself, tend to wear upon the brain, for the fact is, that use should constitute, and does constitute exercise; and the more we exercise any faculty or factor, the greater will be the development of that faculty or factor.

The same is true of experience. We have been in the habit of believing that experience will wear on the human system; but the contrary is the truth. Every experience should increase the power of the mind, and the reason why is simple. Every new experience you pass through, should, and naturally does, lead the mind into a new field. It adds a new dominion to the field of consciousness; and our capacity to apply consciousness must increase accordingly. When consciousness acts in a limited field it is limited; but when that field is enlarged consciousness is enlarged in proportion; and the larger the field of consciousness, the larger, the greater and the more brilliant becomes the mind.

Every new experience, every new line of growth, and every new line of mental activity, will naturally add to the powers and the domains of the mind. Thus we secure a larger mental field, and this is one of our principal objects in view. We should always look upon experience in this way; and if we take this view of experience, we tend to encourage the mind to go farther and farther in the expansion of consciousness, whenever a new experience is entertained or enjoyed. The result will be that every experience will have a tendency to enlarge the mind and add to the field of consciousness.

In building up the cells of the brain, we may consider a few simple methods that have proven themselves most effective through actual experience. This study, however, is very recent, and there are only a few who have undertaken to demonstrate the effectiveness of the principles involved ; but we have secured enough facts to substantiate absolutely the science of this new brain development. We may therefore proceed with the full conviction that the results desired will be secured.

The first principle to consider is that of concentration, and the power of concentration to increase life, energy and circulation in any part of the human system where we may choose to concentrate. You can prove this power through various experiments. Concentrate your attention upon your hand, and in a few minutes your hand will become warm. Very soon you will note the veins on the back of the hand beginning to swell, proving conclusively that the circulation there has been increased to a very large extent. Concentrate your attention upon your feet, with a desire to increase the circulation all the way down through your body, and you will soon feel a glowing warmth all over the surface of the skin, and the feet themselves will become quite warm. This method has been found very effective in preventing a cold, in case we should feel such a condition coming on; because it is a well-known fact that the increase of the circulation all over the body will tend to open the pores of the skin, and thus enable nature to eliminate those very conditions that are brewing in the system when a cold is threatened.

There are many ailments in the human system that can be prevented or overcome in the same way, because we know very well that the increase of the circulation, with life and energy is all that is necessary to cure a disease, or prevent any ailment, whatever the circumstances may be. We understand therefore that we can, through the process of concentration, increase life, energy and circulation anywhere in the system, and therefore in any group of cells in the brain.

Begin by concentrating attention upon the different parts of the brain; and during the process of concentration try to feel deeply; that is, try to enter into the spirit of this concentration; and express, through your concentration, a very deep desire for the increase of life, energy and action in that group of cells upon which your concentration is directed. It is a positive fact that this method alone will, during a year's time, if practiced every day, increase brain capacity from fifty to three hundred per cent in almost any brain that we might mention.

The mere development of the brain, however, and the cells of the brain, is not all that will follow through this method; for the fact is, that most of us have talents and powers within us that are constantly clamoring for expression, but that cannot find expression, because the brain is not sufficiently developed to act as a proper channel. There are many people in this condition. They feel genius within them, but that genius cannot find expression. They are restless and ambitious, but they do not know what to do with themselves, because the power within them is pent up, so to speak, and is unable to do anything along any definite line. In the minds of these people the brain cells are not attuned to the powers and genius within them, and therefore they accomplish nothing. But if these people would take up this method of concentration upon the brain, they would soon develop the brain sufficiently, and refine the brain sufficiently, to give at least a part of this genius and power within them an opportunity for this expression; and gradually as they continued this development, more and more of the genius within them would find expression, until they would pass from what appeared to be ordinary mental capacity to exceptional genius.

The fact is that there are thousands of people in the world who have exceptional genius within them, but their brains are not fine enough to give this genius an opportunity to come forth and act. All of these people therefore would become highly talented and possessed of genius in actual action, if they would develop their brains; and this simple method of concentration will do far more than we ever dreamed along this particular line.

There are many instances in history where people have been practically of no value mentally, until after forty, fifty or sixty; then suddenly exceptional ability came forth; and this fact can be explained when we know that remarkable genius, if active in the within, will continue to try to express itself and refine the brain, until finally the brain becomes sufficiently developed to give that genius expression; but if we do not assist this genius within, it may take a half a century or more before the brain will, in this indirect way, become fine enough through which genius may act. But we need not wait for this slow and indirect process ; in fact, we must not wait; we must proceed at once to build up our brains so that we may give what genius we have full opportunity to work itself out and become a power in life.

In applying this mode of concentration, give a few moments, two or three times every day, to every part of the brain, dividing the brain into eight or ten divisions; and always concentrate with deep feeling, and in a calm, gentle attitude; but be tremendously in earnest. Try to feel the finer life and the finer forces of life as you concentrate and try to enter into the very spirit of the process. The result will be increased brain and mental activity in every instance; and as this process of development is continued, brain development will continue until we may succeed in building up the brain with ten or twelve times as many cells as the brain had before; and also in building up cells that are highly refined, highly cultivated, thereby becoming perfect instruments, through which the highest degree of genius and talent may find expression.

.—Another exceptional advantage to be gained, through this mode of concentration is this, that the entire brain will come more perfectly under our control so that whenever we want to change mental action, we can bring about that change almost immediately. We are all familiar with the fact that the average brain responds very slowly to any changed line of thought. It moves and lives in a groove; and where the individual may desire to act along another line for a time, it is almost impossible to do so, because the brain does not respond to the new field of mental action selected. In other words, such brains find it necessary to work at about the same thing every day, and they continue this all through life, a state of affairs which is by no means desirable, as it means a narrow world of nothing beyond mere existence.

However, if we make it a practice to concentrate upon the brain every day, we train the will to gain more and more perfect control of the brain; and we also make the brain itself more responsive to all our desires and intentions. Therefore, whenever we wish to act along another line, or take up some other work, the brain will adapt itself almost immediately to the new demand; and we can proceed with the new line of work with practically no loss of time. This, we realize is of an immense advantage, for we all come to places, every few days, when we are called upon to consider subjects and problems with which we are not dealing constantly; and if we can direct the brain to respond immediately to this new line of mental action, we can take up those problems at once, and deal with them as if we had been working along that line for years.

In this process of brain development, the principal thing to consider is that of making the entire brain active. We know that in the average brain, only about one cell out of every ten is active; and even among very fine brains, fully one-half of the cells are almost totally inactive. Therefore, if we would wake up, so to speak, the whole brain, and make every cell active, we might in that way alone, increase mental activity and brain capacity fully 100 per cent; and in some instances, to a far greater degree.

Here we find the principal reason why most minds are so limited in capacity and endurance. We know that the average mind becomes exhausted very soon and the reason is that the average mind uses only about one-tenth of the cells of the brain. If the mind could use all the cells of the brain instead of only one-tenth, we should have ten times as much brain capacity and endurance as we had before. We realize therefore the tremendous value of this simple method of brain concentration; but in all this work, we must remember that the brain is a very delicate instrument, and responds only to those actions that are deeply calm and tremendously in earnest. We must train ourselves therefore, to feel the deeper, finer mental forces of body, personality and mind; and we must try to get into constant touch with those finer elements that are at work in the deeper subconscious field. Most minds feel this energy to a considerable extent, and most people who are ambitious have moments when these finer energies are felt to the very depth of the soul; and it is at such moments that ambitious minds feel as if they could accomplish anything, and it is certainly true that we can accomplish anything if we learn to apply all the talent and genius and power that we possess. But we must awaken the deeper, finer and more penetrating forces of mind and soul, because these forces are both limitless and invincible.

For practical purposes, it might be suggested that each individual take five or ten minutes every morning for brain concentration; then five or ten minutes more in the middle of the day; and possibly ten or fifteen minutes in the early part of the evening; but whenever we have three or four minutes at any time of the day, it is a splendid practice to become quiet and turn attention upon various parts of the brain, with a desire to promote the increase of life, energy and power. We should go about this process, however, in a very gradual manner, and always be calm and serene, but tremendously in earnest. We should look for results from the very beginning, although we must never permit ourselves to become discouraged, should results fail to appear at once. This system will do the work. It will develop the brain; and all we need do is to persevere to secure the results we desire.

An important fact to remember is, that this mode of brain concentration is not to be used for a short time only. It should be used constantly all through life, because it will not only promote continuous development, but will prevent brain cells from becoming dormant; that is, it will continue to make the whole brain alive; and as long as the whole brain is alive the brain will be young, vigorous, virile and wide awake.

The reason why people lose their memory and their mental brilliancy after they have lived thirty, forty or fifty years, is because they permit so many brain cells to become dormant; but this can be prevented by the simple practice of concentrating upon the entire brain for a few moments every day; and as we proceed with this concentration, we should turn on the full current, and try to increase steadily the natural amount of energy that is generated by the brain and the mind. And one thing is certain, that after we have continued this mode of development for a time, until the brain begins to respond to the will, we shall find a decided increase of power, talent, ability and capacity along every line. We may not notice much increase until the brain begins to respond to the will, and to this process of concentration, but this response will come in a few days or a few weeks to most minds; and after that time most excellent results may be expected in a greater and greater measure.

The second factor is that of quality; and quality consists of any number of elements, the principal ones being mental refinement, high mental activity and complexity of mental activity. To improve the quality, therefore, of the brain and of the mind, the first essential is to refine all our thinking; and the most direct course to pursue in mental refinement is to try to form correct and finer mental conceptions of everything of which we may be thinking. In other words, we should train ourselves to think towards the ideal side of every circumstance, every condition, every factor and every living entity that we may observe or meet in life; in this manner our thinking will become more and more refined, and the quality of mind and brain will improve accordingly.

Another essential in the improvement of quality is to cause the mind to pass from the simple to the complex in all its mental conceptions. To illustrate: If you are thinking of a certain object and have only one general idea of that object, your thinking at that time is very simple. But if you try to consider that object from every imaginable point of view, you will find, that instead of forming one idea of the object, you will form a score or more. Your mental conception therefore of that object will become very large, very extensive and very complex. That object will give you ten, twenty, fifty or possibly one hundred different ideas, instead of one idea which would be the case if you thought of that object in a general way only, and only along a certain line. It is a most excellent practice to make it a point to try to think of every object or subject from as many viewpoints as possible. This will not only give the mind many new ideas, but it will train the mind to act along many new lines, and in addition will improve the quality of the mind in every form and manner.

An important gain in this connection is that of enjoyment. We all have the privilege to enjoy life in as many ways as possible, provided the enjoyment is wholesome and beneficial; and we shall find that the more complex the mind becomes, that is, the more channels there are in the mind, through which we can think and act, the greater will be our enjoyment of everything that we may entertain in life. We will be able to appreciate an immense universe instead of merely a few elements, as before; and we will begin to live in a world that will contain hundreds and even thousands of times as many interesting states or fields of consciousness as we found in the world in which we lived in the past. In brief, our state of existence will become a harp of a thousand strings instead of merely a harp of a few strings, as is the case with the average person.

Our object should always be to enlarge life, to enlarge consciousness, to enlarge the field of the mind, and to multiply the number of channels through which the mind can find action, because the more lines of expression there are, the more talent and genius we can apply in practical life; and we shall find that the practice of making all thinking more complex, that is, learning to see everything from every imaginable viewpoint, will tend directly to produce this enlargement of the mental field; and results will be numerous as well as highly desirable, in every form and manner.

The study of mental quality is one that is very large and very deep; and it is a subject that will be considered more thoroughly as we proceed in this study; but for practical purposes the above will be sufficient; and we will therefore proceed to the third factor— the increase of the actions of the mind itself.

Every faculty must have a certain amount of energy and life; and to increase the energy and life of each particular faculty, we must learn, first, that it is what we realize in that faculty that actually finds expression.

We might define the actions of the mind as the inner power of thought, or what might also be called, the thinking of the faculty or the talent that is being employed. To illustrate, take the faculty of music. We shall find that it is large, active and brilliant in proportion to how well the musician can really think music; and to think music, we enter into the spirit of music itself. The mind acts in the world of music, or in the real soul of music instead of simply viewing the element of music from a distance. We shall find it to be a fact, that if we wish to increase mental activity through any talent or faculty, we must think that talent, and think that talent more and more: and we think a talent whenever mind or soul expresses itself through the soul of that talent, forming at the time distinct and definite ideas of the talent itself. Whenever we employ a faculty, we find that a certain force is being expressed through that faculty, and that force consists of thinking what is absolutely in that faculty itself.

To illustrate: When you think music, you do not think of music, but you really think music; and there is a vast difference. You must understand the difference, if you wish to attain genius. When you think invention, you do not think of invention, but you think invention itself. When you think business you do not think of business, but you think business itself; that is, you think through the life and spirit of the business faculty in your possession; and when you think business, your business faculty is acting, not round about the business element, but is acting through the business element; and is consequently producing definite and valuable business ideas. You will find that when you think business according to this definition, /our mind will naturally create better business ideas, better business plans and methods than it has ever done in the past, because you are acting in the business faculty itself, in the very spirit, soul and essence of it, and in that part of the mind that has the power to apply itself in the commercial world.

It will be very evident to the student that it is difficult to define in words, what it is to "think" your talent, or to think a faculty. It is something that we must realize through our own experience; but when we attain this realization we shall find that when we make a special effort to enter into a faculty and talent whenever we think of that talent, and at the same time try to think what the talent already is and can do, we are getting down to rock bottom in this immense field.

We should proceed therefore to try to think the ability or talent we possess, or the ability and talent we wish to develop, whatever that ability may be; and by so doing, we will increase the real vital activity of that ability or talent in itself, and thus enter into that indefinable something in the mind that we speak of as native talent or as native genius. It is indefinable; it is real; it is natural; it is inherent; it is second nature. It is an inseparable part of the mind.

We should also make it a point to think of every talent as a growing talent. Think of your faculties and talents as evolving, developing and creating more power. Picture in your mind every talent as being in a process of building. Think of your consciousness as delving deeper and deeper into this vast interior mental process, where talent and genius are created. Think of your whole mind as becoming more and more alive. We know there is something alive in the mind that we call talent. There is a mental power that comes from the depth of the soul; and when the brain begins to respond to that power from within, that power will work itself out through all the cells of the brain, and the result will be that all those cells will become direct channels for a larger, a greater and a stronger expression of all the ability, talent, power or genius that we may arouse within. It is then that the mind becomes a live wire, so to speak; and when the mind becomes a live wire, we shall have no more dormant brain cells and no more inactive forces in our mental world. Every power, faculty and talent v/e possess will begin to work, and will work constructively as well as effectively along the lines that we have decided upon. The result will be that capacity, power, ability, talent and genius will increase along all lines; and this increase may be continued steadily and uninterruptedly as long as we live.

We must proceed in the conviction that we not only have the power to arouse all the latent capacity and talent within us, but we also have the power to build up and develop that capacity and talent to any degree desired, and for an indefinite period; and here we should remember that the mind has the faculty of rebuilding itself, again and again, on a larger and a larger scale for any length of time. The mind that you have today can double its own power and talent during the present year; and next year this mind that has been doubled, can repeat the process and double once more this larger life and capacity that has been gained. Later, this process can be repeated again and continued indefinitely.

It matters not therefore how small a mind you may have today, you can double the power of that mind again and again as long as you live, until it becomes a prodigious mind, and you become a mental giant. Remarkable possibilities therefore lie before us in this wonderful study; and those who will persevere in the correct application of these principles, will succeed in making real the ideal of these possibilities, steadily and surely in every direction; so therefore no matter how high our ideals may be, or how difficult the undertakings we have in view, those undertakings can be carried out successfully, and every ideal realized. The power to do those things does exist within us; and whenever we want more power than we have now, we need only remember that every human mind has the faculty of rebuilding itself on a larger scale, again and again, for any length of time.

1. BUILDING THE BRAIN

Function of the Brain —The brain is to the mind what the piano is to the pianist, or what any instrument of expression is to that which is being expressed. To develop the brain, therefore, to the very highest degree is necessary if the mind is to make full application and tangible use of every power that' may be latent in the great within of the subconscious. The brain as a whole, as well as every cell in the brain, must become perfectly responsive to every action the mind may make, and must possess the capacity to give that action the full volume of power required. The brain must possess the capacity of much work, and must also possess that fineness of quality that is necessary to the highest order of work. In brief, to supply the demands of genius, the brain as well as the mind must be able to furnish both quantity and quality.

Modern Methods —The methods employed in modern education tend in a measure to develop the brain. The practical use of the mind will develop the brain in parts, but such development is both indirect and inadequate. The average mind is much greater than the brain it is trying to use; therefore, it does not accomplish what It has the power to accomplish. To develop the brain even to a slight degree, would in many instances give the mind almost twice as much active capacity and ability as is possessed now, while if such development were promoted thoroughly and in conjunction with further mental development, there would be a decided increase in ability; and in many instances actual genius would appear. In the average brain there are millions of cells that are practically dormant. They are never called into action, and in consequence serve only as obstacles to the efforts of the mind. In fact, in many brains more than half of the cells are not in use. They are constantly being enriched or reconstructed, but they do not serve the mind in any way; and such brain cells as do not permit the expression of the mind will invariably prevent that expression.

Active Brain Cells —The more active brain cells we possess the more mental power we can express. The mental power and ability that is back of the physical brain is limitless, but the cells of the physical brain arc only channels through which talent and genius are coming forth. To increase the number of active brain cells, therefore, is one of the chief essentials in the development of genius. When all the cells that now exist in the brain are made active, the mind, if correspondingly developed, will become exceptional in brilliancy and power. But if the mind should so develop that the present number of cells would not be adequate, the number could be increased without changing the regular size of the brain to any extent, although the brain as a whole always becomes a little larger when high development of both brain and mind is taking place. In the crude brain the cells are large and sluggish. In the developed brain the cells are small, refined and very active. In fact, the smaller the brain cell the better it becomes as an instrument of the mind, the reason being that the more closely the cell approaches a point of action, the more perfect the concentration of mental action; and the more perfect the concentration of any action, the greater the power and efficiency of that action. When the brain is well developed all the large sluggish cells will be removed, and the space will be filled with an extra number of small active cells; in consequence a well-developed brain has several times as many cells as an undeveloped brain, although the size of the two brains may be the same. And since the cells of the well-developed brain will all be alive ready to respond to the mind, we can readily see the advantage of thorough brain development.

The Three Essentials —The brain of the genius is always very fine in the quality of its substance; and this is the first essential. The second essential is an increase in the number of active brain cells. In fact, where we feel real genius we find every brain cell thoroughly alive and in a high state of vibration. The third essential is the awakening of the subconscious life of every brain cell. The brain of the genius is very strong on the subconscious side; and this is one reason why such a brain sometimes gives expression to what seems to be superhuman attainments. Every cell contains a subjective or subconscious life; that is, an inner life that is far greater in power, capacity and efficiency than any phase of life that may exist merely on the surface; and when this subconscious life is fully alive in all the brain cells, we will naturally have a brain that is inexhaustible in capacity and power.

Necessary Elements —There are a number of elements that go to make up genius. One of these is unlimited capacity for work; and this is secured when the subconscious life and power of every cell in the brain becomes alive. Such a brain will not be used up no matter how complex, how intricate or how extensive the actions of the mind may be. It is equal to every occasion that the mind may meet, no matter how difficult, and it can easily hold out until the task is finished. The average brain is used up after a few hours of full mental action; and the reason is found in the fact that its capacity is limited. In such a brain the deep, inexhaustible subconscious life is not awakened, therefore it has but little to draw upon. In the brain of the genius, however, there is any amount of life and power upon which to draw. Every cell is literally alive with unlimited subconscious life, and therefore no matter how great the demands of the mind may be, the brain is fully equal to all of those demands. Increased Capacity —When the mind is inspired by great ambitions, the desire to do great things in the world becomes stronger and stronger. In consequence, the mind will attempt to obey these desires; in fact, it will have no peace until it does. But if the brain does not have the power and the capacity to work as much and as long as the mind may require in order to carry out these ambitions, failure will inevitably follow. And here we have one reason why so many important undertakings with every opportunity for remarkable success have failed almost from the beginning. The men behind those undertakings had the ambition and the courage to proceed, but they did not have the brain capacity to hold out, the reason being that their brain cells were not alive with the limitless powder of the great within. This inexhaustible brain capacity, however, can be developed by anyone, because the subconscious life of every cell is very easily awakened, and the more we draw upon this larger interior life, the easier it becomes to secure more The problem is to take the first step; that is, to enter into conscious touch with the subconscious side of things; and when this is done, we have the key that will unlock all the greater powers that are latent within us.

How to Proceed —To give more life and action to every part of the brain is necessary before real brain development can begin; but to promote this, the three great divisions of the brain must receive special and distinct attention. Each part must be dealt with according to its special function, and every effort to increase the life and action of that part must be animated with the desire to promote the power and efficiency of that function. The function of the fore brain embraces principally the power of intellect, memory and imagination. The mind acts directly upon this part of the brain when it reasons and knows, and also when it creates ideas, forms plans, evolves methods, analyzes laws and principles, understands, comprehends, discriminates, or exercises the elements of insight, perception or discernment. The function of the back brain embraces working capacity, force, determination, push, power, reserve force and kindred elements. The mind draws upon the back brain whenever force is required in the actual doing of things, and acts upon this part of the brain when trying to control, direct and master anything in the physical personality. The function of the top brain embraces aspiration, ambition, consciousness of quality and worth, attainments of superiority, perception of ideals and the realization of higher mental states of conscious existence. The mind acts through the top brain whenever it soars to greater heights, or whenever it builds for greater things anywhere in the physical or mental domain. When the top brain is large and active the finer things of life are readily discerned, but when this part of the brain is small or sluggish nothing is appreciated but that which can be weighed or measured.

Full Development —The combined use of all the different parts of the brain is necessary to secure results along any line. Every effort requires intelligence and imagination as well as power and working capacity. And no effort is worthwhile unless it is prompted by the desire to press on towards the greater, the superior and the ideal. Every part of the brain, therefore, should be well developed. Every part helps every other part, and the best results are secured along any line when all parts of the brain are equally developed. Abnormal development in some parts may give expression to exceptional genius, but such genius is one-sided. It is not properly balanced, and for that reason can never be at its best. When genius is queer, eccentric, peculiar, or addicted to what is called **"the artistic temperament" it is not the best developed form of genius; it is not real genius, but the expression of extraordinary powers that are only under partial control; that is, they may be controlled to do great things through a certain faculty, but they are not controlled to act in harmony with all the faculties; and it is only when all the faculties act in harmony that the highest attainments and the greatest achievements become possible.

Real Genius —Where we find real genius we find exceptional capacity for work and remarkable talent for high efficiency. But we do not find such genius to be eccentric, very sensitive or difficult to get along with. The real genius is broad minded and can get along with anybody. He is a master mind and can therefore adapt himself to all kinds of conditions, and can use all kinds of conditions through which to reach the greater goal in view. The real genius is well balanced, and therefore has not simply the power to do great things, but also the power to live a great life. The reason why so many among those who possess certain grades of genius are eccentric or oversensitive, is found in the fact that certain parts of their brains are not sufficiently developed to act in harmony with those better developed parts through which the genius in question is expressed. But when these neglected parts become well developed, those people will not only become well balanced characters and charming personalities, but they will also gain the power to do greater things than ever before. Building Brain Cells —To develop any part of the brain more energy and more nourishment will be required in that part, and these two essentials may be provided through subjective concentration. When we concentrate subjectively upon any part of the human system we produce more mental action in that part. This increase of mental action will cause more life and energy to be generated in that part. It will also attract surplus energy from other parts of the system because much gathers more; and in brief, will increase the circulation in that part, thus supplying the added nourishment required. When we concentrate upon any part of the brain we promote the building of brain cells. Wherever an increase of energy and nourishment is provided the cell building process will be promoted. And if that concentration is inspired with a strong desire to attain the greater and the superior, the new brain cells will have superior qualities. Accordingly they will become fit instruments for the expression of real genius. The concentration of attention upon every part of the brain will also cause all the inactive cells to become alive, though in order to secure the best results in this respect the mind should try to feel the finer forces of the brain, and the finer activities of those forces while concentration is taking place. So long as concentration is mechanical there are no results, but when the process of concentration works through the finer life forces it becomes a living process, and the desired results will invariably follow.

Special Methods —To build brain cells in any part of the brain, and to cause all of the cells in that part to become alive, concentration should aim to promote the natural functions of that part; that is, when we concentrate upon any part of the brain we should express a strong, deep and persistent desire to do that which that particular part has the natural power to do. When concentrating upon the back brain, be determined. Mentally act in the positive, determined attitude; desire power, and aim to push forward every purpose you have in view. Feel the increase of capacity and try to realize that the energies of the back brain are constantly accumulating, becoming stronger and stronger, until you feel as if you had sufficient power to see anything through. This process of concentration will accomplish three things. The inactive cells of the back brain will become alive. And the more living cells there are in any part of the human system the more power and capacity there will be in that particular part. Secondly, new brain cells will be formed; and as all of these new cells will be alive, there will be further increase in the power and the working capacity of the back brain. And third, the natural function of the back brain will be promoted. You will have more force and more push. You will become more positive and more determined, and your power to see things through to a finish will increase in proportion. In addition, there will be a steady increase of creative energy, and this is very important, because to possess an enormous amount of creative energy is one of the principal secrets of genius. When concentrating upon the fore brain use the imagination extensively. Create mental pictures of every mental state of being that you can imagine. Form plans of all kinds, and try to promote practical methods for every imaginable undertaking in the world. Use the power of analysis thoroughly upon every idea, law or principle that you may encounter in your thinking, and try to form your own original conclusion as to the nature of it all. Try to feel intelligence, and picture mental brilliancy in every cell throughout that part of the brain. But do not permit your thinking to become heavy or laborious. Keep attention in touch with the finer forces of the brain, and have expansion of mind constantly in view.

This concentration will do for the fore brain what it was stated the previous exercise would do for the back brain, and in addition it will develop the power to create ideas of merit; and there is no mental power that is more important than this. Everything that man has formed in the visible world was first an idea. And as the best ideas produce the best results in practical life, we realize therefore, that those who develop the power to create better and better ideas will steadily rise in the scale, occupying more important places every year in the world's work. When concentrating upon the top brain aspire to the highest you know. Give full expression to all the powers of your ambition. Desire superiority, and try to feel consciously all the elements of worth that you know to have existence. Live in the ideal. Transcend the world of things and let your mind soar to empyrean heights. Think of everything that is high, noble and great, and desire with all the power of your soul to realize it all. Then know that you can. Have full confidence in yourself. Have faith in all your desires and ambitions. Think that you can. Feel that you can, and inspire that feeling with the loftiest thoughts that you can possibly form in your mind. Concentrate in this manner every day, or several times every day when convenient. A few minutes at a time is sufficient, and if done properly, a year's time will produce improvements that no one at first could believe.

Additional Methods —Another most excellent exercise is to concentrate upon every group of cells in the brain, giving a few seconds to each group, and then picture genius in every cell during the process. What we mentally picture, we create; therefore by daily picturing genius in every brain cell, we will tend to create genius in every brain cell. We thus develop the brain of the genius, and whatever we may wish to attain or accomplish we will then have a brain that can positively do what we wish to have done. To awaken and increase the subconscious life in the brain cells, the following method should be employed : Turn attention upon the back brain and think with deep feeling of the subconscious life that you know permeates every fibre. Continue for a few moments, and try to enter into this finer mental life. Do not be anxious for results, but be calm and well poised, and deeply determined to secure results. In a few moments move attention to the right of the brain and repeat the process. Then move attention to the left of the brain, repeating the process in each case. In each part try to enter into the finer subconscious life, and desire the awakening of this life with the deepest and strongest desire possible. The entire exercise may continue for ten or fifteen minutes, and may be taken once or twice a day.

Important —Pay no attention to the way you feel after the exercise. You may feel drowsy or you may feel mentally exhilarated. In either case keep calm, retain your poise and know that every brain cell in your possession has increased its volume of life and power. Immediately after the exercise relax mind and body. Let your thought pass down through the body so as to distribute equally among all the nerve centers the added life which you have gained. Then proceed to think of something else. The art of concentration, when fairly well mastered, may be exercised at any time. To use spare moments for this work is a most excellent practice, because it will not interfere with the regular duties, and besides it will make those moments very interesting as well as highly valuable We may promote brain building at any time when engaged in work that is purely mechanical or that does not require direct attention; and in fact, we should try to train ourselves to build the brain at all times, no matter what our work may be. We

411

should train the forces of the mind to pass through certain parts of the brain, so to speak, while doing their work, and we should expect those forces to promote development wherever they are directed to act. The energy employed in thinking should build brain cells and develop mental faculties during the process of thought, no matter what that thought might be. The same should be expected of energy employed in study or in any form of mental work, and all mental energy in action will promote brain and mind development when trained to do so.

FIG I.

1. Power. 2. Intellect 3. Aspiration

2. MAKING EVERY BRAIN CELL ALIVE

The greater the number of active brain cells, the greater the supply of mental energy; and the more mental energy, the greater the power, the ability and the working capacity of the mind. Every active brain cell generates mental energy. To keep all the cells in action is to accumulate energy; and as much accumulates more, the practice of making alive all the brain cells every day will ere long give the mind far greater capacity and power. In the average brain only one half of the cells are active, and of those that are active only a fraction are thoroughly alive. That ability could be doubled and even trebled in the average mind through a practical system of brain development is therefore evident.

When a majority of the brain cells are dormant the mind is dull, stupid, and even lazy. When the cells in the back brain or in the lower part of the brain are dormant or partly so, a tendency to physical inactivity follows almost invariably. To remove this condition therefore, we must arouse the dormant cells in those parts that are affected. The fact that a person is indolent or stupid does not indicate that there is nothing in him. In fact, he may have remarkable ability along certain lines, but not enough mental energy to put that ability into action. And a lack of mental energy is always due to inaction among the majority of the brain cells. Any person who is inclined to be sluggish in his activity can never do his best. He will accomplish only a fraction of what he has the latent power to accomplish, and will gain very little as far as comfort, happiness and attainment are concerned. An inactive person is never healthy, because there are too many dead cells in his system, and he cannot possibly enjoy life to any degree of satisfaction because his mind is partly in a stupor. His contentment, if he has any, will be the contentment of partial insensibility and not that which comes from having entered into harmony with the life that is alive. There is no real comfort in being sluggish or indolent. The man who takes it easy does not get one-third as much satisfaction from his life and his work as does the one who turns all his energy into his work, and who makes himself the very personification of industry, enterprise and achievement. The happiest man is the one who works with all his power and lives with all his life, but who works and lives in poise. He is also the healthiest man because a live personality is always wholesome and full of vitality.

When the entire personality is not thoroughly alive, waste matter will accumulate in various parts, clogging the blood vessels, obstructing the nerve forces and interfering in general with the normal functions of the system. This waste matter will also cause the tissues to ossify, to harden, to wrinkle up and look old. This is one reason why the man who retires from business and tries to do nothing becomes old very fast. A man, however, does not have to remain in the business world all his life in order to live a long and interesting life, but he must keep his entire system alive and active. And to do this, the first essential is to exercise daily the cells of the brain and the cells of the various nerve centers. The belief that no one can afford to give time or attention to any other part of the mind than that which is employed directly in his vocation, is a mistake, because when the whole of the mind is kept alive and every brain cell is continued in action, the amount of mental energy upon which any faculty may draw will increase to a very great extent. True, those faculties that we use directly in our leading occupations should be developed to a greater degree than the rest of the mind, but the whole of the mind and the whole of the brain should be put to work generating energy. The more energy any faculty may have at its command the greater its capacity for work, and the more thoroughly will its work be done. Every cell in the brain, therefore, should be employed in generating energy, so that the faculties we do employ may have unlimited power upon which to draw. The fact that an increase of mental energy will increase the ability and the working capacity of the mind, and the fact that strong minds, competent minds and able minds are in great demand everywhere makes this subject extremely important.

Another fact that must not be overlooked is that the brain is the instrument of the mind, and must, therefore, be placed in the best possible working condition before the mind can do justice to itself. If every other string in a piano were out of tune, no musician, not even the very best, could produce music through that instrument. But it is just as impossible for the mind to carry on real thinking with a brain wherein a large percentage of the cells are dormant. The fact that so few minds are able to think clearly or produce original thought on any desired subject is due almost entirely to the presence of so many inactive brain cells. Every dormant brain cell is an obstacle to mental action. The energies of thought cannot act upon or act through such cells. We therefore understand that the presence of such cells will interfere decidedly with the natural action of thinking, and that clear, consecutive, constructive thinking becomes almost impossible where dormant cells are numerous. The fact that the mind may be very active does not prove that all the brain cells are alive, because that activity may be confined almost entirely to certain limited portions of the brain; and the fact that most active brains tire easily proves that the majority of the cells are not doing anything. When all the brain cells are alive and generating energy, there will be so much energy in the brain that the mind will never feel tired, provided of course it works in poise; and the entire brain will naturally become transparent so that the mind can see through every thought, so to speak, and thus think clearly upon every subject. To emphasize this fact, we may add that every dormant cell is like a daub of paint upon a window pane, so therefore, we can realize how the presence of such cells will interfere with clear thought.

The belief that every part of brain and mind will be kept in action through an attempt to exercise all the mental faculties at frequent intervals, is not true. First, because no one has the time. To give five minutes of thought in the field of every faculty would require from six to eight hours, something that only a few could do every day. And those few who might have so much time on their hands would naturally have neither the ambition nor the ability to carry out such an extensive regime. Second, to exercise thought in the field of a certain faculty does not necessarily bring into action all the brain cells in that particular part of the brain where the said faculty functions. Ordinary thinking, about faculties, talents, qualities, attributes or definite subjects seldom bring into play other cells than those already in action. Nor does the direct use of the faculty arouse all the cells in the field of action in that faculty. The ordinary use of any part of the mind simply draws upon the energy that is already being generated without doing anything directly to arouse those cells that arc dormant. To stir up the dormant brain cells, it will therefore be necessary to employ a different process; in fact, a special process, a process, that will act upon every cell, and that will have the power to arouse that cell into the fullest possible action.

The process that we shall outline for this work need not require more than ten minutes of time each day, although it would be well to give the matter two or three times as much attention, and even that would be possible for anyone, no matter how busy he might be. It has been demonstrated conclusively that you can arouse to action any cells in the system by concentrating attention upon that cell, provided your mind is acting in a state of deep, but highly refined feeling at the time. To awaken a cell, however, it is not necessary to concentrate attention upon that one cell individually. Just as good results may be secured by concentrating upon a large group of cells; and this is especially true when attention aims to move in what may be termed the expansive attitude. To proceed, divide the brain into eight or ten parts, viewing each part as a special group of cells. Then concentrate subjectively for one, two or three minutes upon each group. Take this exercise every day and give it all the interest and enthusiasm that you can possibly arouse in your mind. In a few weeks every cell in your brain will be at work generating energy, and you will discover that the power and the working capacity of your mind will have almost doubled; but this will be only the beginning. If you continue this exercise, and try to make constructive use of all the added power you gain, you will soon come to the conclusion that your ability along any special line can be increased and developed to a remarkable degree. When concentrating in this manner upon each group of brain cells, try to picture mentally all the cells of that group that you can imagine as existing there. This will cause attention to penetrate the entire group through and through, and thus act upon each cell with the full force of thought. The fact that there are millions of cells in the brain need not disturb the imagination in its effort to mentally see them all. The imaging faculty is fully equal to the task. If not at first, it will become so after a little cultivation.

When concentrating upon the brain cells, there should be a strong, deeply felt desire to arouse every cell, but this desire should invariably act in perfect poise, and should never permit the slightest trace of forced action. To establish a full life, a wholesome life, a strong life, a wholly active life and a smooth, calm, harmonious life in every brain cell should be the purpose, and during the process of concentration the mind should be thoroughly determined to carry out this purpose. In many minds certain parts of the brain are very active, while other parts are not. Such minds, therefore, should give most of their attention and concentration to the inactive parts for a while, or until a balanced, thoroughly alive mental action is established in every part of the brain.

The process of concentration should begin at the lower part of the back brain, and should move forward gradually, ending at the upper part of the fore brain. During this concentration all the finer creative energies of the system should be drawn gently, with deep feeling and strong desire, towards the brain. And after the exercise is over, both mind and body should relax completely for a few moments, as this will produce perfect equilibrium. The result of this exercise, if taken daily, will be to eliminate all sluggishness, all stupidity, all dullness and all tendency to indolence or inactivity in any part of the mind, the brain or the nervous system. The mental power will increase remarkably, thinking will become clear and the brain will become such a perfect instrument that the mind can always do justice to itself no matter how highly it may be developed or how great its ambitions may be.

3. PRINCIPLES IN BRAIN BUILDING

The Leading Principle —To increase the size, to improve the quality and to multiply the energies of every faculty, talent or power that exists in the human mind, and to promote in general or in particular the development of ability, talent and genius, the leading principle is to combine the brain, the mind and the soul in every effort made to this end. This, however, is a new idea. No attempt has ever been made in the past to combine these three factors in an orderly and scientific manner for the promotion of any form of development; but we shall find as we proceed that it is this principle that constitutes the real secret of this important work. Many scientists have devoted themselves to the study of the brain. Many meta-physicians have searched for the mysteries of the mind. And others have spent a lifetime trying to fathom the depths of the soul, but no definite effort has been made to combine these three factors for practical results. But this we must do if we are to promote this system of development. And as we carry out this principle we shall find that there is no reason why-anyone may not become as much and achieve as much as his loftiest ambitions hold in view. As this principle is applied the weakest mind can be made strong, the dullest mind can be made to improve constantly in activity and brilliancy, and such minds as are already brilliant can be improved to an extent that will in many instances approach the extraordinary.

The Process Simple —We shall understand 'presently how these exceptional possibilities can be realized. And we shall also find that the process involved is very simple. This, however, is natural, because the greatest things are always the simplest. This is one reason why we fail to find them at once, because there is a tendency in the human mind to look constantly for the complex, laboring under the delusion that the complex alone is great. But now we realize that man can improve himself only as he learns to get down to rock bottom and apply the laws of mental growth in their original simplicity. The obstacle that most of us have met is this, that instead of applying the laws of nature, we have tried instead to apply somebody's interpretation of those laws; but interpretations are usually complex, confusing and misleading, while the laws themselves are sufficiently simple for a child to comprehend and apply.

Important Questions —Proceeding directly to the consideration of this great subject, we will naturally find ourselves asking the following questions: What makes a mind great? Why does one person have ability and another not? What is talent and what does it come from? What is the secret of genius? What is the reason that some minds become so much and achieve so much while others accomplish practically nothing? These are important questions and there must be definite answers to them all; in fact, there must be an inner secret that makes the difference in each case. When we look at a person with a great mind we cannot at first find the secret, and as few are able to look beyond the exterior person, we have remained comparatively in ignorance on this great subject, admittedly one of the greatest of the ages. In most minds the secret of greatness, ability and genius is looked upon as a hidden something that can possibly not be found. But when we analyze man as he really is, and find that he is not simply personal, but mental and spiritual as well, this secret is no longer hidden. We find it to be composed of a few natural laws in orderly application. And we also find that both the understanding and the application of these laws are very simple.

Essentials Required —When we speak of ability in any particular mind, we usually consider only one or two faculties in that mind, as there are but few minds that are really great in more than two things. For this reason, to answer the questions presented above, we must analyze those individual faculties and try to discover why they are so remarkable. When we study such faculties, we find that there are three reasons why they are different from ordinary faculties; and these reasons are, that in all superior faculties we find size, quality and power exceptionally developed and properly combined. So this, therefore, is the simple secret of ability, talent and genius; and being so simple, we can readily understand why it has been overlooked. However, as we proceed in harmony with its natural simplicity, and try to apply it, we find that any one of these three essentials can be developed to almost any degree. And as the combined and harmonious application of the three essentials is a matter that anybody can master, we realize again that there is no reason why we all should not become much and achieve much. In fact, there need be no end to what we can develop and accomplish along any line. The talents we now possess can be developed far beyond anything we have ever imagined or dreamed of. And those greater powers that are still latent in the potential may be brought forth so that man will still accomplish what the race has never imagined possible.

Essentials Explained —Before we proceed further, it will be necessary to know what is really understood by the term size, quality, and power as applied to the faculties and talents of man; and also how those essentials were produced in such minds, as we have made no effort to develop and build through any method whatever. When we meet an exceptional mind we usually come to the conclusion that that mind secured remarkable ability and power without knowing anything about systems of development, and also that ability and genius are for this reason born in those who have them. To the average mind, this conclusion may seem to prove that only those can be able who are born able, and that therefore there can be no use for the ordinary mind in trying to develop added ability. But here we should remember that as it is possible to improve the trees and the flowers as well as all kinds of animals, there necessarily must be some way to improve man both physically, mentally and spiritually, as man needs improvement more than anything else, having greater responsibility, and being at the highest point, so to speak, of the creative powers of nature. We all must admit the logic of such ideas, but we need not depend upon logic. We also have the facts. We have the evidence in the case, and there is nothing more evident than evidence. The human mind as well as all the faculties and powers in man can be developed, and there is nothing to indicate that there is any end to the possibility of such development. We have found the secret, and that it works, is being demonstrated every day. The wise course to pursue, therefore, is to give our whole attention to the application of the laws and the methods involved, so that the best in view may be realized. The size of the faculty is determined by that part of the brain through which the faculty functions. The quality of the faculty comes from the state of the mind, and the power that enables the faculty to do its work comes from the within, and increases as the within is awakened and developed. To give a faculty size, therefore, we must deal with the brain. To give a faculty quality we must deal with the mind, and especially the states of the mind. And to give a faculty power we must deal with the soul, or rather the entire interior realms of life and consciousness. Thus we understand why the brain, the mind and the soul must be combined if we wish to provide the three essentials—size, quality, and power—required in the increase of ability or genius along any line.

Further Explanation —The reason why these three essentials are required can be simply illustrated. The engine must have steam or it will not have the power to do what it is built to do. It may be very large and have enormous capacity, but if there is little or no steam it can do practically nothing. Then the engine may have any amount of steam to draw upon, but if it is very small it cannot use all of this power, and will accordingly accomplish but little. Then again the engine may be large and the steam abundant, but if it is poorly constructed it will not work. In other words, if the engine is to perform its purpose, it must have size, quality and power, and the more it has of these three, the more it can do. It is exactly the same with the human mind, and when we realize this we understand why so many large brains accomplish nothing, why so many fine minds accomplish nothing, and why so many strong minds accomplish nothing. The large brain must have mental quality back of it, and abundance of creative energy from the subconscious. The fine mind must have plenty of power back of it, and a large brain through which to act. The strong soul must have mental quality so as to give its power superior ideas with which to work, and a large brain through which these superior ideas can find full expression.

Increase of Size —It is therefore evident that those who wish to become much and accomplish something of worth must give their attention to the three essentials mentioned, and to give special attention to that essential that is most deficient in development. If you have a large well developed brain, but low mental quality with but little power, give your attention principally to the development of mind and soul. But if you have plenty of energy and ambition with good mental quality, but a poorly developed brain, give your attention to the brain, and have its size increased especially in those parts through which the talent you desire naturally functions. And here we must remember that each faculty functions through a special part of the brain—a fact that is not only important, but that is in perfect harmony with the laws of nature. The function of sight employs the eye while that of hearing employs the ear. The other senses have their own particular channels, and the same is true of the various faculties of the mind. Each individu.il faculty finds expression through its own part of the brain, and therefore it is necessary that that particular part be well developed if the faculty in question is to function with exceptional ability and power. The increase of size, therefore, in any part of the brain becomes a matter that will require the very best attention we can possibly provide, though the process through which this increase may be brought about is very simply applied. It is a well-known fact that any part of the system will grow and develop in size if more nourishment and vitality is supplied; and increased nourishment and vitality can readily be supplied by increasing the circulation in that particular part. This is a fact that has been thoroughly demonstrated, so that we may proceed with the full conviction that as we apply the principle involved we shall positively secure the desired result.

Interesting Experiments —The following experiments will illustrate how nourishment and vitality can be increased in any part of the physical form: Place a dog's paw in a vacuum at stated intervals for some period of time, and that paw will become twice as large as the other one. And the explanation is that the vacuum draws more blood into the paw thus providing additional nourishment and vitality. The same experiment can be applied along a number of other lines, proving the same idea; but here we may enquire how increased circulation can be produced in any part of the brain. We cannot employ mechanical means for such a purpose; therefore, must find another plan. It is admitted that added development will naturally take place wherever there is an increase of nourishment and vitality; and this increase is supplied by an increase of the circulation in that part; but the problem is, how to increase the circulation in any part of the brain. The solution, however, is simple, as the following experiments will illustrate: Place a man upon an oscillating platform, and have him so placed that the body is perfectly balanced, the feet and the head being at equal distance from the floor; then tell him to work out a difficult problem, or tell him to think of something that requires very deep thought. In a few seconds the circulation will increase in the brain sufficiently to cause the head to go down considerable, and even to the floor, as the feet or the other end of the body rises accordingly. Here is an illustration of how the circulation can be increased in the brain simply by carrying out a certain line of thought. Then tell this same man to imagine that he is running a foot race, and in a few seconds the circulation will increase in the feet to such an extent that the feet will become heavier than the head, and go down as the head goes up. This is an experiment that most anyone can try with most interesting results, and it gives tangible evidence to prove that the mind can control the circulation. While the mind was thinking about the deep problem, extra energy and circulation was drawn to the brain; but when that same mind was imagining the running of a foot race, this extra energy and circulation went towards the feet because attention was concentrated upon the feet at the time. Another interesting experiment is to imagine yourself taking a hot foot bath. You will soon find your feet becoming very warm, the veins beginning to swell, indicating that increased circulation has been produced in that part of the body. Here we have the same principle; that is, the power of mind to increase the circulation in any part of the body by concentrating with deep interest upon that particular part. A number of similar experiments can be carried out, proving the same law; and as the law is so simply applied, we find that there is no reason whatever why the increase of the size of any part of the brain may not be produced as we may desire.

Power of Concentration —To apply this law we must understand how to concentrate. If we concentrate simply in an objective sense, we have no effect upon the forces of the system, and the above law will not act. But when we concentrate subjectively, that is, with deep interest and feeling, we find that the forces of the system invariably accumulate at the point of concentration; and where the forces of their system accumulate, an increase in circulation will invariably follow. To explain this matter more fully, we might state that real concentration upon any part of the body causes mind and consciousness to increase activity in that part. Wherever there is an increase of mental activity, the finer life currents will become more active; and where those currents become more active the circulation will increase. This is how the law operates, and it is based entirely upon how deeply the mind feels at the time of concentration, and how deeply interested the attention is in the project we wish to carry out. In other words, it is the concentration that is felt that controls the circulation, because such concentration acts through the finer forces of the system; and the circulation is controlled by those finer forces.

Deep Feeling Necessary —The above may seem to lead us into difficulties, and take away the ease and simplicity that was previously indicated; but we need not be disturbed. This inner consciousness of finer feeling is simply secured, and what is better still, we all have it already. What we wish to make perfectly clear is the fact that you cannot draw additional vitality and nourishment to any part of the brain unless you concentrate your attention upon that part while your mind feels the action of the finer life current. You do not govern functions or activities anywhere in your system until you act through subjective mentality because all physical functions, including the circulation, are controlled by the subconscious mind. Whenever you feel deeply, however, you act directly upon the subconscious, and may, therefore, originate and direct any new subconscious act desired. The principle is to feel deeply whenever you concentrate. Nothing else need be attempted. If you know that you feel deeply whenever you turn your attention to any part of the brain, you will know that there will be an increase of nourishment and vitality in that part, and that the brain cells of that part will be developed and built up accordingly.

Unconscious Development —In answering the question why a great many minds have been developed without the understanding of this law, we need simply state that it is possible to use some of the most important laws of mind and body without really understanding the nature of those laws. In fact, we are doing this all the time. When you wish to succeed in any undertaking, and you concentrate all your efforts upon that purpose, you develop to a certain extent the faculty employed in that undertaking. And the reason is that the concentration that was unconsciously practiced caused the added nourishment and vitality to be supplied to that part of the brain through which the faculty in question was expressed. In other words, you employ unconsciously the same law that we are trying to use consciously and according to exact science. But here we must remember that although the unconscious use of a certain law may produce results, the conscious and intelligent use of that same law will naturally produce far greater results. Therefore, we wish to understand the inside secret of this entire theme, so that we can make the best use of all the principles involved.

The Power of Ambition —In this same connection we learn that ambition is also a channel through which unconscious development is constantly taking place. When you have a strong ambition to realize a certain goal, the force of that ambition naturally tends to build up those faculties that you need in order to reach your goal. And we find that the force of ambition also involves the force of concentration, because we always concentrate upon those things that we are deeply ambitious to realize. We find, therefore, that both the mind and the brain may be built up through the exercise of a strong, determined ambition. But here as elsewhere, we should not be satisfied simply with the unconscious use of the principle involved. If we would, instead of simply being ambitious, proceed to direct the force of ambition upon that part of the brain through which the desired talent naturally functions, we would find that that talent would develop with far greater rapidity than through the old general method of simply being ambitious; in other words, we would have another illustration of the power of concentration and intelligent action. Illustration —To illustrate this idea further, we will suppose that you are ambitious to become a great musician, but instead of being simply ambitious, you concentrate you mind upon that part of the brain through which the faculty of music functions. The result will be that the power of your ambition will express itself directly in building up your musical faculty, because the additional mental energy that you will provide for that faculty will not only build up the mind in that part, but will also tend to supply additional nourishment and vitality for the corresponding part of the brain. Here we find a new use for that great mental force usually called ambition, especially since it can be employed in the building up of any faculty whatever. We realize that those who will make the right use of this force in building up any faculty, the increased development of which is desired, will naturally secure decided results from the very beginning; and if the process is continued with perseverance, will secure results that will be nothing less than remarkable. In this part of our study we have given special attention to size as previously defined, and have illustrated how size could be secured by building up any part of the brain. Later on, we shall consider quality and power. But we should all remember in pursuing this study that size is of exceptional importance, the fact being that there are very few brains that are sufficiently developed to give the proper expression to the ability and the genius that most of us already possess.

4. PRACTICAL METHODS IN BRAIN BUILDING

Important Faculty —The power of the mind is limitless; that is, the power that is already active in the mind can, as it is directed, reproduce itself in larger and larger quantities. This faculty is latent in every mind, and is employed to some degree by every mind. The more mental power we generate, the greater becomes the mental capacity to generate more. But only as much of the power of the mind can be expressed as the development of the brain will permit. Therefore, the cultivation of the mind and the increase of mental power will not produce an increase in ability, talent and genius unless the brain is developed just as thoroughly as the mind.

The Highly Organized Brain —To develop the brain there are three essentials that must be constantly promoted. First, every brain cell must be made more active; second, the number of brain cells must be increased; and third, the brain as a whole must be more highly organized. Dormant brain cells obstruct the expression of ability and power, while active brain cells tend to promote that expression. An active brain cell not only permits the expression of mental power, but actually calls forth more and more of that power. The more brain cells you have, the more channels for mental expression you will have, and the greater the number of these channels, the greater your mental capacity. The highly organized brain is superior in quality, and, therefore, can respond readily to the highest forms of genius. The brain that is gross, crude or dense cannot act as an instrument for any form of genius, not even for the simplest forms of practical ability; and the fact that most brains are crude and undeveloped, either as a whole or in parts, explains why extraordinary ability is the exception rather than the rule.

Ability Trebled —Extraordinary ability need not remain the exception, however; there are thousands of minds with ordinary ability that would double and treble their ability by simply taking a thorough course of brain development. They already have the mental power, but their brains are not sufficiently developed to give full expression to that power. And there are other thousands who are not conscious of any talents whatever that would become talented if their brains were sufficiently developed to give full expression to all that is in them. A thorough development of the brain will also reveal what a person is best adapted for, for when every faculty can fully express itself, it is an easy matter to discover which one is the strongest; and if that one is given further development, extraordinary ability will be the result.

More Brain Cells —To know how much you can do through any faculty, is not possible until every cell in the brain is fully alive, and when you do discover what you can do through any special faculty, you can double your ability in that faculty by doubling the subconscious power back of that faculty, and by doubling the number of cells in that part of the brain through which that faculty functions. To double the number of cells in the brain, or in any part of the brain, is possible without increasing the usual size of the cranium, because the cells invariably decrease in size as the structure of the brain is improved in quality. The smaller the cells of the brain the better; and the more active and the more highly organized the brain, the more nearly the brain cell approaches the form of a mere point of expression. And for the same reason, the smaller the cells of the brain, the more easily and the more thoroughly can the mind concentrate upon any special subject.

The Vital Secret —To make every cell alive, the secret is to concentrate attention upon every part of the brain, thinking of the finer substance of the brain at the time, and proceeding with the desire to promote increase in life, energy and power. Turn attention first upon the center (a point midway between the opening of the ears) and think i of the finer life and substance that permeates the region of that center. Then, while in that deeper state of thought and feeling, move attention through any part of the brain you like, and toward the surface. This movement should be gradual, and you should try to deeply feel and gently arouse the finer life that permeates the brain cells through which your thought is passing. When your concentration comes to the surface of the brain, move it back again gradually, passing through the same region until you come to the brain center. Take about two minutes for the process of passing concentration from the brain center to any part of the surface of the brain and back again to the center. This exercise may last from ten to twenty minutes and should be taken once a day, but should never be taken immediately after a meal.

Subjective Concentration —When you concentrate upon any part of the brain, do not think of the physical brain, or the physical brain cells, but think of that finer or metaphysical substance that permeates the physical cells. This will hold concentration in the subjective state; and all concentration must be subjective to be effective. All actions of concentration should move smoothly, easily, deeply, and harmoniously; the process should be animated with a deep, calm, self-possessed enthusiasm; be positively, but calmly determined to secure results, and constantly expect results. Think of the brain as a perfect instrument of genius, and hold such a mental picture of the brain in your thought at all times.

The Real Principle —The number of cells in any part of the brain may be increased by concentrating subjectively upon that part. Whenever you concentrate attention upon any group of cells, you cause creative energy to accumulate in that group. Wherever creative energy accumulates, the circulation will increase, and in consequence there will not only be an increase of the power that builds, but also added nourishment with which to build. This is the principle: Concentrate upon any part of the brain, and you bring more energy and more nourishment to that part; and when more energy and more nourishment meet in any place, there will be more cells in that place. Concentration will cause these two essentials to meet wherever you may desire. But the concentration must be subjective; that is, do not concentrate upon the physical part of the brain, but upon that finer life and substance that permeates the physical. If you do not realize the existence of those finer life forces that permeate the physical cells, imagine the existence of finer cells as being within the physical cells, and concentrate upon those finer cells. You will soon begin to realize-the finer substance and the finer life that fills or permeates the physical cells, and in the meantime you will have results; you will build the brain; you will develop those parts of the brain wherein you concentrate subjectively and with regularity.

Where to Concentrate —To impress ability in any faculty, concentrate regularly upon any part of the brain through which the faculty in question functions. Every leading faculty employs its own part, or parts, of the brain. Some faculties express themselves through one part only, while other faculties employ several parts. When you know what part of the brain is employed by some special faculty, build up that part; that is, concentrate daily upon that part and aim, not only to increase the number of cells, but also to refine and develop those cells. You will thus give your special faculty a more perfect instrument with which to work, and that faculty will steadily become stronger, more able and more efficient.

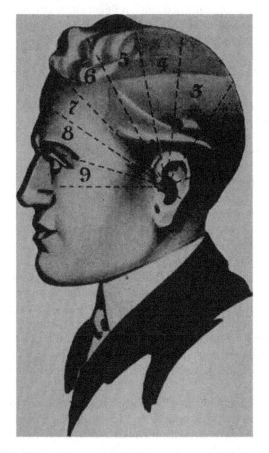

FIG. III

1. Creative Energy
2. Love
3. Individuality
4. Interior Understanding
5. Emotion
6. Intuition
7. Intelligence
8. Application

Improved Quality —The predominating thought of the mind during any period of concentration will determine the quality of the new cells that are conceived during that period. Therefore, to improve the quality of the brain cells and make the brain structure more highly organized, the quality of thought that is formed in mind during any exercise in concentration should be the highest that can possibly be imagined. When you concentrate upon any part of the brain, think of quality, refinement, worth, superiority, power, ability, talent, genius. Think of all these things in their highest forms and draw upon your imagination for higher and higher forms. Enrich your thinking to the very highest degree possible; this richer, higher, superior thought will permeate the very life and essence of every cell in your brain, and thus you will constantly improve this quality of your entire brain. When you concentrate upon any special part of your brain, use the same method, and in addition, picture in mind the superior genius of that faculty that functions through this special part. Try to impress this picture of superior genius upon every cell in that part of the brain, and try to feel that the spirit of superior genius is alive in every cell. You thus develop both the faculty and that part of the brain through which the faculty functions.

All Around Development —The balanced brain should be the first object in view. No matter what your vocation may be, every part of your brain should be well developed. The balanced brain has always the greatest capacity and the greatest endurance, because those parts that are not employed directly furnish added power to those parts that are employed directly. The balanced brain is also the most practical, having the power both to create ideas and the power to make actual use of those ideas. Compare the shape of your own brain with that of Figure II and you will see at once where the greatest amount of development is required in your own case. But do not give your whole attention to those parts that seem to be small; proceed to develop your whole brain so as to make every cell alive, and aim to improve the quality of your entire brain; give most of your time, however, to those parts that lack in size and activity. If your brain seems to be fairly well balanced, give most of your time to those parts that you employ directly in your daily work and the remainder of your time to the entire brain in general.

Where to Begin —Begin your development of the brain by taking from ten to twenty minutes every day and concentrate for a minute or two on the nine fundamental divisions outlined in Fig. III. Always begin with the region of "creative energy," and close with the region of expression. To increase creative energy is always the first essential in every undertaking; and expression is the final outcome, the climax, the goal in view. When you concentrate upon the region of creative energy, think deeply of accumulation, and try to feel the possession of limitless power. Be in perfect poise and harmony, and realize that your back brain is actually becoming charged with tremendous energy. Be as quiet as possible, try to hold it all in your system, and feel deeply so that the process of concentration will be subjective. When concentration ceases to be subjective, you lose your hold upon energies, and development will be interrupted; but so long as your concentration continues to be subjective, you will hold your energy in your system, you will also awaken more, and every desire for development will promote development.

Individuality —The largest conception of love that you can possibly realize should be deeply felt when you concentrate upon the region of "love." Think of everything that is tender, lovable and sweet; in fact, enter into the very world of immeasurable love; try to feel that you are absolutely at one with everything that is, and that you love with all your heart everything that is. The region of "individuality" is the principal channel of expression for the will; therefore when you concentrate upon the brain cells in this region, proceed to will with all the power of will. This region is also the principal seat of stability, firmness, self-confidence and faith. Accordingly, your desire to express these qualities should be combined with your own concentration. When you concentrate for the development of individuality enter into the spirit of faith; have faith in yourself; have faith in everybody and everything; have faith in your mission in life; have faith in the Supreme and have faith in faith. Be strong- and firm; feel through and through that you are yourself—your superior self, and that you can master everything that is in yourself.

Discerning the Within —The inner world of things, as well as the higher side of things, is discerned through "interior understanding." It is also the channel through which the mind acts when we try to discern the ideal, the superior and those elements of true worth that exist within all things, and in the higher life of all things. When you concentrate upon this part of the brain think of the ideal, the higher, the greater, the superior, and try to mentally enter into the soul of your every thought. As you develop interior understanding you will gain the power to understand the metaphysical nature as well as the physical nature of all life, and no one can fully understand life, properly use life, or master life, until he can look at all things both from the metaphysical and the physical points of view.

Feeling the Real —When concentrating upon the region of "emotion" every effort should be made to enter into the most tender feelings of the soul; but all tendencies towards the sentimental should be avoided. Try to feel sympathetic; try to sympathize most keenly with everything and everybody, and try to realize the sublime state of oneness with the higher side of all that is. When trying to develop sympathy do not think of that which is wrong, pitiful or distressing; this will simply develop morbidity, a condition that is frequently mistaken for real sympathy. The true function of sympathy is to place the mind in touch with the real, the true, the sublime and the beautiful; in brief, to feel the touch of life; not false life, imperfect life, or misdirected life, but the life that is life, the life that makes all life truly worthwhile. The more perfectly we develop the finer emotions, the more keenly we can enjoy that something that may well be termed the music of sublime existence, and the more readily can we rise to those lofty heights in consciousness where we can see all things from all points of view. Therefore when we concentrate upon the region of emotion, we should try to enter into the music of sublime existence; we should try to rise to the mountain tops of consciousness; we should try to feel the tender touch of everything that is real, beautiful and true, and we should try to realize that something within us that binds the soul of man to every breathing, living thing in all the vastness of the cosmos.

Function of Intuition —Interior insight, discernment, judgment, decisions and all the finer perceptions of the mind function through that part of the brain termed "intuition." Intuition is indispensable, no matter what our vocation may be, because we are constantly called upon to decide as to what step to take further, or to judge as to the best course to pursue, or to look through this matter or that. It is a faculty, however, that has never been developed, and that is the principal reason why practical minds make so many mistakes, adopt the wrong plans almost at every turn, and so frequently walk right into failure when they could just as easily walk directly into success. The most successful men in the world possess natural intuition to a very great degree, and that is why they usually do the right thing at the right time. They know real opportunities when they see them, and they know when and how to take advantage of those opportunities. But they do not know these things through external evidence; they usually go contrary to external evidence and what is called safe and sane business sense. They follow a "finer business sense." They may not call their superior business judgment intuition, but it is the same thing, and it may be developed to a remarkable degree by anyone. Proceed first to make alive and build up that part of the brain through which this faculty functions. Concentrate for a few minutes upon this region several times a day, and especially just before you are to decide upon some important matter. While concentrating, think of interior insight, try to see through every thought or idea that enters the mind at the time, and desire deeply to see the real truth in everything of which you are conscious. Learn to depend upon your interior insight at all times, whenever you are called upon to judge, select, look through or decide ; and the constant use of this faculty in practical life, combined with daily concentration upon this part of the brain, will develop this faculty to almost any degree desired.

Building Intellect —Mental brilliancy and rare mental activity may be developed by concentrating upon the region of "intelligence." Think of pure intellect and picture in mind the highest form of mental brilliancy imaginable when concentrating upon this part of the brain. Also, enter the feeling of mental expansion and limitless intellectual capacity, and try to picture calmness and lucidity in every thought you think. You thus, not only develop and enlarge that part of the brain through which pure intellect functions, but you also become more brilliant; and at the same time your power to think, understand, comprehend and realize is steadily increased. This method, if practiced for a few minutes several times a day, will, in the course of a few years, produce a prodigious intellect. There is no reason, therefore, why anyone should remain in a state of mental inferiority. Rare mental brilliancy and remarkable intellectual capacity are possible to all, but the high places are for those only who will go to work and make their possibilities come true.

Producing Results —Practical application is the art of combining the world of ideas with the world of things; or, rather, the turning of ideas into actual use. The faculty of "intelligence" produces the idea; the faculty of application puts that idea to work. To develop the faculty of application, concentrate upon that part of the brain marked "8" in Fig. II, and think of system, method and scientific application at the time. Impress upon every cell in that part of the brain a deep, positive desire to do things, and you will develop the "knack" of being practical, as well as increase the actual power of application.

The Real Purpose —The great climax of all life, all thought, all effort, is expression. The real purpose of man is to bring forth all that is in him—the whole of himself, and although every force and element in his system is employed, directly or indirectly, in promoting expression, the entire process is governed by the mind acting through a certain part of the brain. This part is the region marked 'V in Fig. II, and therefore as this region is more fully developed, the power to promote expression will increase in proportion. Some faculties employ this part of the brain directly, while all the other faculties employ it indirectly. The singer, the orator, the actor, the artist, the writer and the man who sells things, employ the faculty of expression directly; therefore, all such people should develop this part of the brain to the highest possible degree. But all others should give the faculty of expression thorough attention, because we all must express ourselves if we would be much and do much. When concentrating upon this part of the brain, think of the perfect expression of that which you desire to express more fully. If you are an artist, mentally see the expression of the ideal and the beautiful. If you are a singer, mentally feel the expression of tone. If you are an orator, mentally feel the power of eloquence. If you are a writer, mentally realize the expression, in language, of the ideas that you wish to express in literature. If you talk much, or write much, in a business way, with a view of promoting the sale of your product, mentally see yourself expressing yourself in the most forceful, the most persuasive and the most effective manner imaginable. Imagine yourself expressing yourself as you wish to express yourself, whenever you concentrate upon this part of the brain; and do not fail to draw upon your imagination for the most perfect expression possible. Impress upon your brain cells the greatest thoughts that you can imagine, and you thus train your brain to become a perfect instrument for the expression of those thoughts. In the general development of expression, desire deeply to express the best that is in yourself whenever you concentrate, and try to feel the all that is in yourself coming forth in an ever increasing measure.

Special Rides —It is important to remember that all concentration for brain development should begin at the brain center. First, turn attention upon the brain center; gently draw, with your thought, all the finer forces of the mind towards this center; then move the action of concentration toward the surface of the brain, thus passing through that region that you wish to develop. Move the action of concentration to and fro from the center of the brain to the surface, but give more attention to those groups of cells that lie near the surface of the brain, as it is these through which the mind functions to the greatest degree.

What to Expect —The time required to secure results through these methods will depend upon present development and how faithfully this process of development is applied. Results will usually begin to appear in a few days, and very marked results within a few weeks. An increase of mental life, mental power and mental capacity will be noted almost from the very beginning, and a decided improvement in practical efficiency will shortly follow. After a few weeks or a few months, you will discover that your general ability is growing, and at times, you will feel the power of genius finding expression through one or more of your faculties. You will then begin to realize that it is only a matter of perseverance in the daily application of these methods, when ability, talent and genius of the highest order will be attained.

When to Exercise —Apply these methods at any time or anywhere whenever you have a few moments to spare. Take twenty minutes once or twice a day, for regular practice if you can; and it is an excellent practice to use spare moments, as they come, for this purpose. Make it a point to concentrate for development upon some part of your brain whenever you have a minute or two. And, if you concentrate properly, you will not only reinvigorate the brain, but you will rest the mind from its regular work. Proper concentration is always subjective; that is, in the field of deeper, finer feeling. Never begin to concentrate until you feel deeply serene, and feel that your mind is acting calmly in those finer elements and forces that permeate the physical cells. To enter this subjective or finer state of thought and feeling, become very quiet for a few moments; breathe deeply but gently, and do not move a muscle; when you inhale, imagine that you are drawing the force of your personality into that finer subconscious life that permeates your personality; and when you exhale, imagine that all the forces of your system are moving down through your personality toward your feet. What you imagine you do during this exercise, you very soon will do; then you can master your forces in any way desired by simply thinking of your forces as doing what you wish them to do. During these breathing exercises, turn your attention upon the inner life of your system; try to feel this life, and try to enter mentally into the vast interior world of this life. You will soon realize that there is another world of force within the physical world of force. You are then in the subjective state; you are then in touch with the real power within you— the power that lies beneath every cell, and that can therefore change, reproduce or develop every cell. You may then proceed with your concentration; and this deeper power with which you are in touch will proceed to do whatever your predominant thought may desire at the time.

5. VITAL SECRETS IN BRAIN BUILDING

Remarkable Possibility —The brain is the instrument of the mind or the channel through which the unbounded possibilities of the mind are to find expression. It is therefore of the highest importance that the brain receive the most thorough and the most perfect development possible. The reason for this is readily understood when we learn that the average mind could do two or three times as much if the brain was properly developed, and that the quality of the work done could be improved not less than tenfold in many instances. It is a well-known fact that the better the instrument, the better the results, other things being equal, and that no performer can do justice to himself unless his instrument is perfect. But this fact has not been considered in connection with the mind and its instrument. In consequence thereof not one person in ten thousand is giving his mind a fair chance.

Special Exercises Required —That the brain needs development, is admitted by everybody, but there is a current belief that the brain naturally develops as the mind develops, and that to exercise the brain in the mere act of thinking is sufficient to promote this development. This conclusion is based upon the idea that the mind is the unconscious builder of the brain, and that therefore the brain will be at each stage of mental development exactly what the mind requires it to be. But it would be difficult to find a more serious mistake than this. That the mind is the builder of the brain is true in a sense; that is, every change in the brain will be determined by the actions of the mind, and it is the mind that governs the chemical and creative processes that carry on construction and reconstruction. But that function of the mind that governs construction is a distinct function, and is not directly connected with the process of thinking. Thinking in itself does not necessarily develop the brain, nor does ordinary work always develop the muscles of the body. If thinking developed brains and working developed muscle, we should all be marvels of mental capacity and physical power. But the fact that the average person remains undeveloped both in mind and body, no matter how much he thinks or works, proves that special exercises are required for every form of development.

Two Distinctive Processes —To bring a crude, sluggish and perverse brain up to the highest state of action by mere thinking, is just as impossible as it is to bring a discordant piano into perfect tune by mere playing. To play the piano is one thing. To tune a piano or build a more perfect piano is quite another thing. In like manner, the regular creation or thinking of thought and the reconstruction of a more perfect physical brain are two distinct processes, and accordingly require different applications of the mind. It is man who builds the musical instrument, and it is man who employs that instrument to produce music. According to the same analogy, it is the mind that determines what its physical instruments are to be, and it is the mind that acts upon those instruments when thought or expression are to be produced. It is the mind, therefore, that must develop the brain. But the application of the mind in brain development is far different than that of usual thinking.

How Exercise Develops —To apply the mind in brain development, we must eliminate the belief that the use of anything in mind or body necessarily promotes the development of the thing used. It is not use or exercise in itself that develops. It is the extra supply of nourishment and energy that is drawn to the place through use or exercise that alone can promote development. The process of construction in body or brain is not possible without nourishment and creative energy. Therefore, when we increase the supply of these two in any part of the system we cause that part to develop more rapidly. The exercise of the muscle or faculty, however, does not always draw more nourishment and energy to those places where the exercise occurs. If it did, we should have physical giants and mental giants by the millions. And what is important, it is not the exercise itself that draws the circulation or the increased energy to those parts that are being exercised; it is the attitude of the mind that we sometimes enter while body or brain is in action. This is a discovery of exceptional value because when once understood all systems of mental or physical culture will be revolutionized. Instead of systems that produce occasional and accidental results, we shall then have systems that produce definite and positive results in every case. In brief, the idea is that physical or mental exercise does not draw increased circulation and increased energy to the part exercised unless the mind is in a certain attitude at the time; and it is absolutely necessary that increased circulation and increased energy be supplied at the point of exercise if development is to take place.

Subjective Concentration —That attitude of mind that invariably draws nourishment and energy to the part that is exercised is called subjective concentration, and the fact that it is subjective concentration and not exercise, in itself that develops, is a fact that all should understand more perfectly who have greater development for mind or body in view. Whenever any muscle is used, the act attracts attention and the mind will naturally concentrate upon that muscle to a degree. If the concentration is subjective, more nourishment and energy will be drawn to that muscle with development as the result. But if the concentration is not subjective, no added supply of nourishment or energy will be provided. The result will be that the muscle that is being exercised or used will use up the nourishment and energy already there and finally become tired or exhausted. No development, therefore, of that muscle can under the circumstances take place.

Accidental Development —In this connection we may well ask how people have succeeded in developing muscles and faculties before subjective concentration was understood. We know that a large number who have been ignorant of this mode of concentration have improved themselves through various systems. Then how did they do it? The secret is this; whenever you concentrate attention in the attitude of whole-hearted interest, you enter the subjective to a degree and thus concentrate subjectively without being aware of the fact. No matter what system of culture you employ, if you are not interested in the exercise you gain absolutely nothing; but on the other hand, the most perfect system will help you if you are thoroughly interested in the exercise. And the reason is that when you are interested you concentrate subjectively to a degree, and it is through that subjective concentration that you get your results. This idea is well illustrated by the fact that we are always helped the most by those methods that arouse our deepest interest and our most wide-awake attention. By being interested in our work, our studies and our exercises, we have accidentally, so to speak, entered to a degree into subjective moods of concentration, and through such concentration have drawn much nourishment and energy to the parts exercised, thus promoting development in a measure. To depend upon accidental or occasional results, however, will not and should not satisfy those who have greater things in view. We have scientific, exact and unfailing methods for reaching every goal and brain development is no exception. Therefore, we should find the best methods and apply them thoroughly so that every effort we make towards improvements will positively produce results.

Deep Interest —Since more nourishment and more energy are required where development is to take place, and since these two essentials will be provided wherever we concentrate in the subjective attitude, we understand why subjective concentration is the real secret to brain development as well as all other forms of development. For this reason we should enter the subjective attitude directly before we begin to concentrate, and not depend upon indirect means to produce this necessary attitude. By entering directly into the subjective attitude before we begin our concentration we shall have positive results in every instance, and thus avoid unnecessary delays. But if you feel that you do not clearly understand the idea of the subjective, use the term "deep interest" instead. The two terms mean the same. That is, become deeply interested in that upon which you proceed to concentrate, and train yourself to think, study and work in an attitude of deep feeling. Thus you will concentrate subjectively in the most natural and the most perfect manner, and invariably accomplish what you have in view. Living Brain Cells —The discovery that the development of brain and body can be promoted thoroughly and rapidly through subjective concentration will prove valuable beyond belief because every brain almost is in such great need of special development. That a fine mind can work properly through a brain that is crude or sluggish is impossible, and yet the majority of brains are very crude in places and so sluggish in parts that hardly any activity is evident. It is a matter of fact that many parts of the average brain are almost entirely dormant—a condition that no one should permit to continue for a moment, because the full capacity of mind can find expression only when every cell in the brain is thoroughly alive. To bring life and full action into every cell, and to cause every cell to continue to be a living cell, attention should be concentrated subjectively upon every part of the brain several times each day. Ten minutes three times a day will produce great improvements within a few months. Then let no one say that he has not the time. The truth is we have not the time to neglect this matter. The possibilities that are within us are marvelous to say the least, but those possibilities cannot express themselves through a brain that is crude, sluggish or undeveloped.

Finer States of Action —To refine the substance of the brain is highly important, because it is only through a refined brain that superior mental qualities can find expression. For this reason a refining process should permeate the entire brain several times every day, or it may be applied in conjunction with regular concentration for development. While concentrating upon the brain, try to perceive or feel the finer elements of the brain that permeate the physical elements. This will draw the entire developing process into a finer state of action, which will tend to refine more and more every cell in the entire brain structure. To comprehend the finer elements of life and to gain conscious power of that something that is within things, beneath things, and above things, is absolutely necessary if we desire to become as much as nature has given us the power to become. But to respond to the life of that finer something, the brain must be so highly developed or refined in its substance and essence that every trace of crudeness and materiality has been removed. A clear understanding of all the finer processes of life and action will aid remarkably in giving this refinement and responsiveness to the brain, because every ascending tendency of the mind will, if applied to the brain, give higher and finer states of action to all the elements and forces of the brain.

Additional Results —When subjective concentration is perfectly understood and thoroughly applied, we shall find that in addition to continuous development of the brain, all undesirable conditions will be removed from the mind. No forms of mental exhaustion, lack of mental energy or mental depression of any kind will ever occur so long as the brain is properly supplied with nourishment and energy; and since subjective concentration if applied daily will provide the brain perfectly with these two essentials, all mental troubles can be brought to an end through the art of this concentration. This is certainly a fact that will mean much, and great will be the gain to those who apply it thoroughly. In addition to subjective concentration upon the brain, a similar concentration should be directed every day upon the body. This will keep the entire system balanced and strong, and will constantly create new avenues for the upbuilding of the entire personality. Every cell in the human person contains the possibility of a new group of cells of a higher order which when formed will supply the requisite channels through which a higher expression of mind and soul may be promoted. The art of cell building in the brain or body is therefore an art we should all cultivate to the very highest degree. When we concentrate daily upon all parts of the brain, every form of mental sluggishness will disappear, and activity will be steadily increased in every cell. But in the increase of life and action in the brain, we must never lose sight of the idea of perfect poise. When we give high, strong, well poised activity to every part of the brain, the mind will secure an instrument through which the greater things we have in view will positively be accomplished.

What Is Needed —In this connection it is well to repeat and emphasize the fact that in the development of ability along any line, there are three principles involved. First, the number of brain cells must be increased in that part of the brain through which the faculty in question functions. Second, the quality of the mind and the faculty must be improved. And third, the power back of the mind must be made much stronger. In other words, we must have size, quality and power, and these must be properly combined if we are to have the best results. Size, however, does not mean quantity alone, because when any part of the brain is made larger, we should also aim to make the substance of that part much finer. The more cells you can build in a given cubic inch of brain matter and the more delicate you can make the structure of those cells, the greater becomes the capacity of that part of the brain. The smaller the cells of the brain, the finer the brain. Common brain matter has large cells, and the structure of such cells is nearly always crude. The higher order of brain matter always has small cells with a fine delicate structure, and their number to each given amount of space is very large. In consequence when we proceed to develop the brain, the brain itself should be made somewhat larger. The cells should be smaller and more numerous, and the brain matter itself should be more delicate as to substance and texture. Very fine brain matter approaches the ethereal in essence and reminds you of the petals of flowers instead of crude clay. In the development of ability, the brain must receive special attention, because it is the vehicle or the instrument or the tool that the mind employs. Not that the tool is more important than the workman, but the tool in most cases has been neglected. We have tried to improve our minds and have succeeded to some extent; but we have given practically no attention to the scientific development of the brain. We have left the brain as it is and have expected the mind to do its best under such circumstances. That only a few in every age have really acquired greatness is therefore a matter that is easily explained.

All Faculties Localized —It has been thoroughly demonstrated that every talent employs one or more distinct parts of the brain, and that the development of these parts of the brain will increase the capacity and the efficiency of the talent. Consequently, when we know what part of the brain each special talent employs, the development of any talent becomes a matter of simplicity, and is placed within easy reach of everyone. As we proceed to take a general view of this idea of localization, we find that the lower half of the forehead is employed by the scientific and the practical functions of mind, and that the development of this part of the brain will increase one's ability to apply in practice what has been learned. The same development will give method, system and the happy application in the world of details. The man whose mind and brain are well developed in this region has the power to do things. He may not always have the best plans or the best methods, but he always produces results. To develop this part of the brain, concentrate attention first upon the brain center, which is a point just midway between the ears; then gradually move attention towards the lower half of the forehead until you concentrate subjectively upon all the brain matter that lies between the brain center and the lower half of the forehead. All the cells that are found in this region are concerned in the function of application. Therefore, when you concentrate, do not simply give your attention to the surface of the brain, but to the whole of that part of the brain that lies between the surface in question and the brain center.

Thought of Expansion —Another very important idea to remember is that all such concentration must contain the thought of expansion, and must be very gentle, though deep and strong. The necessity of finer consciousness while concentration is taking place must never be overlooked. For this reason we should enter into this finer consciousness before we begin. Such concentration upon any part of the brain for promoting development may last ten or fifteen minutes, and may be repeated several times a day. In your work it is a very good plan to concentrate mildly, but constantly upon that part of the brain that you use in your work; thus development will go on steadily while you are engaged in other efforts. Pure Intellect —The upper half of the forehead is employed by the function of pure intellect. Therefore, if we wish to increase intelligence, the power of reason, understanding and intellectual capabilities in general, that part of the brain should be developed. And again we must bear in mind that it is not simply the surface that should be developed, but all the convolutions that lie between the surface and the brain center. The function of pure intellect occupies all that part of the brain that is found between the brain center and the upper half of the forehead; concentration, therefore, for the development of intellect must be directed upon all the cells found in this region. To help give quality to the intelligence you seek to perfect, try to enter into the real meaning of intelligence while you are concentrating upon this part of the brain. Try to realize as deeply as possible the true significance of intellect, and what it means to reason and understand. You will thus find that results

435

will increase decidedly. At first, you may not gain any considerable insight into the depths of intellect, but by trying to form the most perfect conceptions of intelligence while concentrating in this manner, the brain will actually become more lucid. Your comprehension will enlarge its scope and the intellect will become more brilliant. If you have some deep subject under consideration, and you do not quite succeed in penetrating its depths, you will find the solution coming almost of itself, if you concentrate in this manner upon the upper half of the forehead while that subject is being analyzed. Perplexing problems can be solved in the same way, although the method will have to be carried out properly; that is, all the essentials involved must be given due attention. We find that we can, therefore, in this way make our intellects more brilliant than usual when occasions so demand. And we can, by daily practice, so improve intellect that we may ere long be able to understand perfectly almost any subject that is brought before our attention. To Develop Individuality —One of the greatest faculties possessed by man is that of individuality, because it gives not only stability to what he is doing, but also causes the individual to be himself, which is highly important. No one can do his best and become all that he is capable of unless he is himself under all circumstances; and this desired trait is invariably brought out through individuality. To develop individuality, you must increase the size and the quality of that part of the brain through which it functions. And this part is illustrated in Fig. II. Individuality includes self-confidence, firmness, stability, faith and the faculty of keeping on. Thousands of fine minds fail because they do not continue right on regardless of what happens. In most instances, however, they cannot help it, because they lack individuality. We all can develop individuality, however, and we must if we wish to succeed in every undertaking for which we are fitted. To develop this faculty, concentrate upon that part of the brain indicated, and animate your concentration with a firm, self-possessed attitude of mind. In brief, as you concentrate, try to feel that you are a strong, masterful individuality, absolute monarch of your own domain. Feel that you have the power to be and do what you want to be and do, and realize that you as an individuality constitute the power that is back of and above everything that transpires in your own life. In addition to this, add faith; that is, have unbounded faith in your own individuality, and believe thoroughly that the purpose you have in view can positively be realized.

Energy and Push —The lower half of the back brain is the seat of energy, and when this is well developed we have what may be called push; that is, we will not give up our efforts because there is too much power back of those efforts. When individuality is well developed, we continue because we know that we can; and when a great deal of power is added to individuality and self-confidence, nothing can induce us to give up what we feel can be successfully pushed through. A great many people feel conditions of weakness at times, and even pain in the back brain whenever they try to push through something of importance, and the cause is lack of energy. It is therefore well to give this part of the brain attention, before we undertake any kind of work that requires a great deal of energy and perseverance. And when we feel exhaustion in the back brain, we can produce perfect relief almost at once by gently concentrating upon that part while trying at the same time to feel the presence of the finer creative energies. The development of the back brain is promoted in the same way as that of other parts with this exception:

436

During subjective concentration upon the back of the brain, the attitude of mind must contain the thought of greater power, and you must try to feel that creative energies are accumulating more and more where your attention is directed.

Insight and Judgment —A faculty of remarkable value is that of insight or real judgment, and its place of expression is found in that part of the forehead where the cranium begins to recede. To develop this part of the brain, that is, all the brain cells that lie between the brain center and the surface of the region indicated, the process is as usual, and the mental attitude should be that of interior insight. In other words, try to exercise the power of interior insight in connection with everything that you may be thinking of while concentrating for the development of this faculty. We all come to places at times where we have to make some important decision, but frequently we are uncertain as to what course to pursue. Thousands have under such circumstances taken the wrong path, and thousands in the midst of many opportunities have selected the least because they have no power of knowing which was the best. Mistakes have been made without number because we did not possess the judgment to know what was right at the time, and a number of similar conditions could be mentioned all arising from the same deficiency. The development, therefore, of judgment, discernment and insight is of more than usual importance. When two opportunities present themselves there ought to be something that could inform us as to the nature of each one. There ought to be a way to know when to do things, when to act, which course to pursue, and what plan to adopt. There ought to be such a way and there is. We have the faculty of judging these things properly. And when this faculty is well developed, our decisions and selections will always be the best. To proceed with the development of this faculty, the following method may be adopted: When you have something to decide, something of great importance, but do not know what decision to make, do not think of the matter for the time being, but proceed instead to give special attention to this faculty of insight. Concentrate subjectively at frequent intervals upon the brain cells involved. Try to increase their number; refine the substance of which they are composed, and try to give the faculty of judgment and decision the most perfect vehicle of expression possible. Continue this for a few hours or a few days if you can put off the decision that long. Then take up the problem and try to see the best way. If the faculty in question is sufficiently awakened, you will know almost at once what course to pursue, and you will lose all desire for other plans. But should you fail to receive a decided answer, let the problem go for a while longer, and proceed to awaken this faculty still further. You will soon bring this faculty up to the desired state of lucidity, and the decision will be made. In addition to this method, carry on regular development every day as you do with all your other faculties.

Improvement of Quality —We gain size in any faculty through the use of subjective concentration, but quality and power are developed in other ways. The first essential in the production of quality consists of forming the highest mental conceptions possible of the faculties themselves as well as every thought or idea that may enter the mind. The term "mental conception" simply means the idea that you form of anything of which you may be thinking. Every idea you form in mind is a mental concept and it serves as a vital factor in the upbuilding of the talent you have under consideration. Metaphysically speaking, every idea is composed of the ideas which you have formed

437

concerning that talent, and every faculty is as large and as perfect as your conscious or interior understanding of the function of that faculty. Therefore, the more perfectly you understand the inner life, the soul, the essence, the true nature, the scope and the possibilities of a talent, the higher will be your mental conceptions of that talent. And the higher these conceptions are the higher will be the quality of the talent itself. To state this matter more simply, we might say that the first law in the improvement of quality among the faculties of the mind, is to have as great and as lofty thoughts as possible at all times. To carry out this idea, we should hold our minds in the loftiest attitude possible whenever we concentrate for the development of any part of the brain. Thus we will develop mental quality at the same time as we develop brain capacity. When we concentrate attention upon the upper half of the forehead, we should hold in mind at the time the highest, the broadest and the deepest conceptions of pure intellect that we can form. The result of this dual process will be increased quality in our intelligence and a more perfect brain through which this improved intellect may be expressed. In promoting development along other lines, the same idea should be applied, and we may thus secure results along several lines through every individual process.

Increase of Power —The first step in the increase of power is to preserve the energies we already possess. There is an enormous amount of energy generated in the average personality, but the larger part of this is usually wasted. Therefore, if we simply prevented this waste, we should, in many instances, have more energy than we could use, no matter along how many lines we wish to promote development. To prevent this waste of energy, all discord must be avoided and perfect poise attained; there must be no anger, no worry, no despondency and no fear; the mind must be composed, the nervous system in harmony and the entire personality in tune with the serenity of the soul. When this has been accomplished, we shall feel a great deal stronger both in mind and body.

Important Fact —We shall realize a decided increase in the force and energy throughout every part of our systems. The personality will feel as if it were charged, so to speak, with energies we never felt before, and we realize that we have come into possession of new and stronger forces than we have ever supposed in the past. When this accumulation of energy is felt, however, we should not become too enthusiastic nor too determined, as such a course may tend to destroy our poise, and thus produce the waste we have tried to avoid. Instead these great moments should be employed in gently directing attention towards those parts of the brain and the mind that we wish to develop. In this way we will give added power to the building up of any particular talent towards which we may be giving our attention ; but when our minds become so large that we require more energy than what is being generated in our systems now, we shall find it necessary to secure an additional supply; and this is done by awakening the great within; that is by directing the subconscious to give expression to more and more energy as we may require.

Transmutation —In the increase and use of creative energy, the process of transmutation becomes absolutely necessary; and to transmute any force in the system means to change that force from a lower to a higher state of action; or to change any creative power from its present purpose to some other purpose than we may have in mind. To change any force to a higher or finer state of action, we should enter into the conscious feeling of the finer forces of the system. And this is not difficult as anyone will find after making a few attempts along this line. Through the process of transmutation, all the forces of the system at any time can be changed to different forces, and can be gathered for special work in that part of the system where special development is to take place. The value of transmutation, therefore, is very great, and should receive thorough and constant attention.

Added Lines of Expression —Whenever the creative forces accumulate, the predominating thought held in mind at the time becomes the pattern, and what the creative forces produce will always be similar to the nature of this predominating thought. Therefore, when we concentrate upon any part of the brain for the purpose of development, the thought of development, expansion and growth should receive our first attention. This practice will aid remarkably in the increase of brain cells, and as each brain cell is a channel of expression for the conscious action of that talent that functions through the part in question, we realize its great value. The more brain cells there are in a given place, the more channels of expression will be secured for that talent; and the more channels of expression we provide for a talent, the greater the capacity and power of that talent. To help increase the number of cells in any part of the brain, all the essentials of the talent that function through that part should be held in consciousness during such concentration. And the essentials of a talent are all those different parts of the talent that one can become conscious of by trying to examine that talent from every possible point of view. The more essentials or actions of the talent we are conscious of while we concentrate upon any part of the brain, the more lines of expression we will produce in that part. And since each line of expression tends to create its own cell, provided there is sufficient nourishment and energy in that particular place, the number of brain cells will necessarily increase in proportion to the number of essentials we hold in mind during the process of concentration.

Multiplication of Ideas —In the beginning all that is necessary is to have a clear idea of the nature of the talent you wish to develop, and then hold that clear idea in mind during concentration. As you proceed, this idea will subdivide again and again until it becomes a score of ideas, and each of these ideas will become an essential, that is, a distinct part of the talent and an individual line of action for that talent. You realize, therefore, that to see all the essentials of a talent with the mind's eye, is to dissect that talent and see all its parts as parts, and how they are united to form the one talent. The value of this process is found in the fact that the more parts of the talent you are conscious of while concentrating, the more cells you will create in that part of the brain upon which you concentrate, provided, you hold in mind very clearly the principal ideas of the talent that functions through that particular part. Another gain from the same process is found in the fact that it tends to increase the channels of expression for the talent itself. And the more channels of expression we provide for a talent, the greater that talent becomes.

The Brain Center —When concentrating upon any part of the brain, we should always begin at the brain center; that is, where all the lines meet as indicated in Figure II. We should begin by drawing all the forces of the mind towards this center, and when we feel that consciousness is concentrated, so to speak, at this point, we should turn attention upon that part of the brain we wish to develop. Then we should concentrate upon the entire region from the brain center to the surface of the cranium as it is all the cells within that space that we wish to multiply, refine and develop.

The Metaphysical Side —That part of the brain marked "interior understanding" is employed by the metaphysical side of the mind. Through this region the mind discerns the interior and higher aspects of life, and is therefore of great importance. When this part of the brain lacks in development the mind sees only the surface of things, and the deeper things of life are therefore beyond his understanding. But since the attainment of real worth depends upon our ability to understand the inner and real side of things, this part of the brain must never be neglected. When we concentrate upon this region we should open the mind fully to thought from the depths of consciousness. We should begin by turning all attention away from things and external ideas, and think only of the most perfect ideas that we can form of everything of which we are conscious. It is not necessary to attempt any profound analysis of the abstract, but simply to hold attention upon that perfect something that permeates everything. We should not at this time think of flaws, defects, mistakes or imperfections, but should hold the idea of absolute perfection uppermost in mind. The possibility of absolute perfection is a matter we need not discuss with ourselves because we know that there is such a thing. It is upon our most perfect idea of the perfect that we should turn attention. In the development of this faculty we should remember that there is such a thing as metaphysical consciousness, a consciousness that is distinct from intellectual understanding, and the distinction is this, that the intellectual understanding understands how things are related to each other, while this inner metaphysical understanding understands the things themselves. The intellectual understands phenomena. The interior understands that which produces the phenomena. It is this metaphysical consciousness or understanding that we should seek to realize when we concentrate for the development of this region of the brain. Therefore, all thought must be directed upon the perfect; that is, that something that we discern when metaphysical consciousness begins. The real value of this consciousness will be more fully realized when we come to study special talents, as we shall then find that every talent has a metaphysical foundation, and that to perfect the quality and true worth of that talent we must express more fully the metaphysical nature of that talent. But since we cannot increase the expression of anything until we become conscious of it, we realize that metaphysical consciousness becomes indispensable to those who wish to grow in genuine quality and true worth.

The Use of Emotion —That region of the brain marked "emotion" is the channel of sympathy and every tender feeling of mind or soul. It is through the functions that employ this region that the mind finds unity and at-one-ment with everything that exists; and as the realization of unity and harmony with all things is absolutely necessary to the highest development of mind, this faculty should be well developed. In a great many people the emotional side is more or less perverted, and takes the form of

440

sentimentalism. But this does not come from an over-development of this faculty. On the contrary, it is due to a false conception of the finer things in life, and is therefore caused principally by the lack of intelligence. In concentrating upon this part of the brain, the purpose should be the development of a larger channel for the expression of true sympathy. Everything should occupy the foremost place in mind at the time. But when we think of sympathy, we should think of it as being the essence of the highest unity conceivable, and not as a mere mode of sympathizing with people. When the average person sympathizes, he usually comes down and feels like those with whom he sympathizes; he does not try to realize that finer and higher unity that exists among all things. Therefore he is not in sympathy. He simply imitates the emotions of the other person, and this is a violation of all the laws of man. To feel that deep and high unity that makes all creation one is the purpose of sympathy, and when we feel this sublime unity, we become conscious of the most beautiful and the most tender emotions that the soul can possibly know. Accordingly, the value of such development becomes two-fold; first, the most beautiful qualities of life are brought into expression; and second the mind learns to view all things from that higher state of consciousness where the unity and the harmony of all is discerned. And here we find the secret of knowing the truth, because to know the truth is to see all things from the viewpoint of unity; it is to stand at that place from which all things proceed and to see clearly what they are, where they are going, and what their purpose in life or action happens to be. True sympathy, or the realization of the finer emotion, will tend to bring the mind to this place, because all these high emotions will draw irresistibly upon the mind, thereby leading consciousness up to that place where perfect unity is absolutely real. We all know that the finest emotions of the soul constantly lead us towards higher places. And we also know that the higher we go in consciousness the more perfect becomes our understanding of all things. The value of sympathy, therefore, in its true sense is very great indeed.

The Power of Intuition —The most successful men in the world have had the faculty of intuition developed to a high degree and have thus been able to take advantage of the best opportunities at the proper time. History is full of incidents where men and women have arisen to high places by following the indications of this great faculty. It gives the mind the power to see through things as they are and therefore reveals, not only the facts in the case, but also indicates how to deal with those facts. Intuition may work consciously or unconsciously, but whenever it is well developed it works, and works well. As previously stated, we may develop this faculty by concentrating subjectively at frequent intervals every day upon that part of the brain indicated in Figure II, and we should, during the process of concentration give our attention to the idea of interior insight; that is, we should try to see through things and try to know directly or at first hand without resorting to reason or analysis. In this connection a strong desire for deeper discernment is of the highest value if such desire is expressed persistently whenever we concentrate for development. The development of this faculty can be promoted decidedly by making it a point to have more and more faith in its judgment, and also by depending upon it for judgment in every case that comes up. Like all other things, it develops through use if that use is thorough and continuous. It is a splendid practice to make it a point never to decide upon anything without first getting the highest possible light of intuition on the subject, and also to have perfect faith in your ability to get the real truth in this way. Through this practice you will give more and more energy and life to this faculty. And accordingly it will develop steadily and surely until it becomes sufficiently developed to express its function even to a remarkable degree. The Most Important Faculty —All the faculties of the mind are important and necessary to each other, but the most important of all is unquestionably that of intellect. This faculty, therefore, should receive our first attention unless it is already well developed. Through the proper concentration upon that part of the brain that is employed by the intellect, remarkable intelligence can possibly be developed, and results will appear at the very beginning. The very first time you concentrate upon that part of the brain with the thought of brilliancy in mind you realize that your mentality becomes clearer and more lucid; you can think better; fine thoughts come more readily, and you can understand things with a clearness that is sometimes remarkable. You do not simply think that the improvement has been realized, however, because in dealing with difficult problems you actually demonstrate that the lucidity of your mind has been decidedly improved. To promote this development we should concentrate attention upon the upper half of the forehead whenever we think or study, as we shall increase the capacity of intelligence at the very time when we are making direct use of it; and we shall accordingly have better results both in our thinking, or study, and in our development. But all such concentration should be easy, and should be associated with the consciousness of the finer creative energies. When you feel the action of these finer forces, you do not have to compel them to work. They work easily, smoothly and harmoniously of their own accord when placed in action. In fact, they act and work as if directed by some superior power; and this is really true because when you awaken the higher powers within you, you are actually bringing into action powers that are superior, powers that have no limitations whatever.

Application and Expression —That region of the brain that is marked "application" is employed by the mind in the doing of things; that is, those faculties that express themselves through this region have the power to use what we understand, and therefore unites intellect with the world of things. When we develop this faculty we shall find that it is just as easy to practice as to theorize, and that every idea of value can be turned to practical use in the tangible world. When trying to develop this faculty, we should hold in mind thoughts of system, method and scientific application. And we should try to feel that we are consciously related to all things in the outer world. Then, to this attitude we should add a strong desire to do things and achieve much, and we shall find ourselves laying the foundation for a power of application that will be a practical power indeed. Through this same region we find the action of the faculty of expression, and though this faculty is employed largely in connection with musical, artistic and literary talents, it is by no means confined to those talents. The power of expression, generally speaking, is used by all faculties and is absolutely necessary to everybody in bringing forth what there is in them. When we develop the power of expression we tend to bring forth our own individuality and make the personality far more powerful than it has been before. And in addition all the talents we employ will express themselves with more thoroughness, efficiency and power. For general purposes we should concentrate upon this part of the brain in the attitude of a strong desire for full expression of mind, soul and personality. And we should try to feel at the time that every power or faculty in our possession is being expressed more and more through its own channel. Perseverance and Enthusiasm —In all concentration for development we should give the most time to those faculties that we need in our work, and especially to those that are weak and inferior. Our object should be to secure a well-developed brain in all respects, and to give special development to those faculties that we use in our vocation. When concentrating upon a certain part of the brain we should think only of that talent or faculty that functions through that part, and we should try to realize as fully as possible the interior or potential nature of that talent. To think of the unlimited possibilities that exist within the talent is of the highest value during concentration, because in this way the richest thought that we are capable of creating will be introduced into the process of development. In all these efforts perseverance and enthusiasm are indispensable. Principles must be applied and to all such application we should give our whole life and soul. The first essential is to understand the principles of mind development. And the second is to persevere in every application, giving so much enthusiasm to all our efforts that every element and force within us is called to action. It is in this way, and in this way alone, that results will be secured, and when we persevere in this manner results will positively be secured. The amount of time that will be required to secure decided results will depend upon our own efforts. To develop ability or genius up to a high state will require years, but in the meantime, we shall be gaining ground steadily. And so long as we are steadily improving we know that we shall finally reach the goal in view, no matter how high or how wonderful that goal may be. Anyone, however, who will faithfully apply the above principles as well as the other principles presented in this study, will realize a decided improvement from the very beginning, and may secure even remarkable results in a few months' time. In fact, the majority of those who take up this study should at least double their mental power and ability every year, and a large percentage will positively do far better than this.

6. SPECIAL BRAIN DEVELOPMENT

The Eight Principal Divisions —That every faculty of the mind functions through one or more distinct parts of the brain is no longer mere theory; it is a fact that leading scientists of the world are demonstrating to be true. And that any part of the brain can be developed through the art of subjective concentration, is also a fact that is being conclusively demonstrated at the present time. It is therefore evident that when we know exactly through what part of the brain each faculty functions, we can increase the power and the efficiency of that faculty to any degree desired, provided we develop the mental faculty itself as well as that part of the brain through which it functions. It is with the development of the brain that we are now concerned, however, because this phase has been entirely neglected by all previous systems of mental training. In Fig. IV we present the eight principal divisions of the brain, although these divisions do not represent the same number of individual faculties. On the contrary, a group of faculties function through each division, but in each case the individual faculties of any one group are so closely related that they can be developed together. Thus time is saved, and a more thorough development is secured.

The Practical Brain —That part of the brain that is marked No. 1 in Fig. IV may be very appropriately termed the practical brain, as it is through this part that the mind functions when direct practical action is being expressed. Whenever you try to be practical your mind begins at once to act upon the practical brain, and when the practical brain is well developed you are naturally of a practical turn of mind. The practical brain should be developed by everybody, and especially by those who are engaged in vocations where system, method and the mastery of details are required. Concentrate subjectively upon this part of the brain for a few minutes several times a day, and whenever you are engaged in the actual doing of things, think of the practical brain; that is, aim to focus the power of thought, attention and application upon this part of the brain, and aim to act through the practical brain whenever you apply yourself practically.

The Mechanical Brain —Every building process and all the faculties of construction function through the mechanical brain (See No. 2, Fig. IV). Engineers, mechanics and builders of every description should develop this part of the brain; and these are the two methods that may be employed. First, use subjective concentration whenever you have a few moments to spare; and second, train your mind to work through the mechanical brain while you are engaged in your special line of constructive work. When you are laying bricks, do not think at random; think of improving your skill; and as you think, try to turn the full power of your thought into the mechanical brain. The power of your mind, instead of being aimlessly scattered, will thus accumulate in the mechanical brain, and will daily strengthen, develop and build up that part of the brain. In the course of time you will become a mechanical genius, and scores of valuable opportunities will be opened for you. If you are building a bridge, digging a tunnel, running an engine or working on some invention, apply the same principle. Train your mind to act directly upon the mechanical brain while you are at work, and deeply desire the active powers of your mind to steadily build up that part of the brain. You will soon become an expert in your line of work, and later on a genius.

444

The Financial Brain —We all need a very good development of the financial brain (See No. 3, Fig. IV), because the full value of life cannot be gained so long as there is the slightest trace of poverty. When the financial brain is so well developed as to balance properly with all the other leading faculties, the use of those other faculties will result in financial gain; but where the financial brain is weak and small, financial gains will be meager, even though there may be extraordinary ability along other lines. No matter how remarkable your talents may be along any special line, you will not make much money through the use of those talents unless your financial brain is well developed; but if this part of the brain is exceptionally developed, everything you touch will be turned to money. The making of money, however, is not the sole purpose of life; the making of money will not, in itself, produce happiness, nor make living worthwhile, but it is a necessary part of the real purpose of life; therefore everybody should develop the financial brain to a good degree. If you are not directly connected with the financial world, give your financial brain a few moments attention, through subjective concentration, every day; that will prove sufficient. And as you concentrate, think of accumulation, desire accumulation, and try to feel that you are in the process of accumulation. But if you are engaged directly in the financial world, whether in banking, brokerage, financial management, financial promotion or in any form of actual financial work whatever, give your financial brain thorough development. Aim to work through this brain, and use subjective concentration for a few minutes every hour if possible.

The Executive Brain —That part of the brain marked "'4" in Fig. IV is employed by the mind in all forms of management. Those who govern, rule, manage, superintend or occupy positions at the head of enterprises, should give special attention to the development of the executive brain. When this part of the brain is large, strong and well developed, we possess what is termed "backbone"; and we have real, substantial "backing" for every purpose, plan or idea that we may wish to carry through. We have force and determination, and have the power as well as the "knack" of guiding the ship of any enterprise through the storms of every obstacle, adversity or difficulty, to a safe landing, at the haven of great success. The true executive governs perfectly without giving anyone the impression that he is trying to rule; he governs, not by personal force, but by superior leadership; he has the power that can rule, therefore does not have to try to rule. The strong man never domineers; it is only weak men who would like to rule that ever domineer; but it is time and energy wasted. Never try to domineer over anything or try to forcefully rule anybody if you would attain superior executive power. To develop the executive brain, try to realize the position and power of true leadership whenever you apply subjective concentration in that part, or apply executive power in daily life. Aim to make the executive brain as large and strong as possible, and whenever you use the executive faculty, try to feel that it is the executive brain that gives the necessary power.

The Volitional Brain —The development of the fifth division of the brain produces will power, personal force, determination, push, perseverance, persistence, self-confidence, firmness and self-control. When the volitional brain is well developed you are no longer a part of the mass; you stand out as a distinct individuality, and you are a special power in the world in which you work and live. The volitional brain, therefore, should be thoroughly developed by every mind that aims to become something more than a mere cog in the industrial machine. The best way to proceed with this development is to concentrate subjectively upon the volitional brain for ten or fifteen minutes every morning. This will give you the power to control more fully your thought, your actions and your circumstances during the day. When you concentrate hold yourself in the attitude of self-control, and deeply will with all the power of will that you possess. Whenever you are called upon to use exceptional will-power or "stand your ground" against temptations or adverse circumstances, turn your attention upon the volitional brain; that is, think of the volitional brain when you use your will, your determination or your self-control, and you will feel yourself becoming stronger and stronger in personal power and will-power until nothing in the world can cause you to budge in the least from the true position you have taken.

The Aspiring Brain —When the mind aspires toward the ideal, the beautiful, the sublime, the actions of the mind function through that part of the brain designated in the sixth division in Fig. IV. When you "hitch your wagon to a star" you act through the aspiring brain; you do the same when you feel ambitious, or express real desire for higher attainments and greater achievements. It is the aspiring brain that prompts you to advance, to improve yourself, to push to the front, to do great things in the world, to live a life worthwhile; and it is the same brain that keeps you in touch with the greater possibilities that exist in every conceivable field of action. Develop the aspiring brain and you will become ambitions; you will gain a strong desire to rise out of the common; all the tendencies of your mind will begin to move toward greater things; you will discern the ideal; you will begin to have visions of extraordinary attainments and achievements, and you will be inspired with an "upward and onward force" that will give you no peace until you begin to work in earnest to make your lofty dreams come true. So long as the aspiring brain is small and weak, you will have neither the power nor the desire to get above mere, common existence; but when this part of the brain becomes large, strong and thoroughly developed, you will have the power and the desire to reach the top; and to the top you will positively go. To develop this part of the brain two things are necessary. Concentrate subjectively upon the aspiring brain whenever you have a few moments to spare, and during every moment of such concentration, "Hitch your wagon to a star."

The Imaging Brain —This part of the brain (See No. 7, Fig. IV) may be properly termed the "idea factory." It is the imaging brain that creates ideas, that forms plans, that formulates methods and that combines, adjusts and readjusts the various elements that are embraced in whatever the mind may create. To accomplish greater things we must have greater ideas, more extensive plans and more perfect methods. The imaging faculty can furnish all three precisely as we may desire, provided the imaging brain is developed to higher and higher degrees. To proceed, turn your attention upon the imaging brain whenever you use your imagination or whenever you picture anything in your mind. When you are in search of new ideas, look into the imaging brain, and use subjective concentration in arousing this part of the brain to higher and finer activity. Think with the imaging brain whenever you are engaged in forming new plans or formulating new methods, and always aim to express the expansive attitude through that part of the brain. In other words, when you use the imaging or concentrate

446

subjectively upon that part of the brain, think of the imaging faculty as expanding into larger and greater fields of thought. Your mental creative power will thus become greater and greater; you will grasp a much larger world of thought, action and possibility, and the superior ideas and plans desired will soon be secured.

The Intellectual Brain —The eighth division of the brain, as illustrated in Figure IV, is the seat of pure intelligence, reason, judgment, analysis, conception and understanding. Every cell in the brain is animated with intelligence, because intelligence is an attribute of every faculty of the mind, but it is through the intellectual brain that the mind functions when it thinks with that form of intelligence that not only knows, but knows that it knows. Whenever you attempt to understand any particular subject or object, turn your attention upon the intellectual brain, and try to think directly with that part of the brain. Do the same when you reason about anything, when you proceed to analyze anything, or try to find the solution of any problem. Concentrate subjectively upon the intellectual brain for a few minutes several times a day; and while you concentrate, try to see through every thought that comes into your mind at the time. This will increase remarkably your power to know, and will, at the same time, increase the general power of your mental ability. All ability depends, to some degree, upon the power of your intellect; therefore, whatever your work, give special and daily attention to the development of the intellectual brain. As the faculty of pure intellect, reason and understanding is increased in efficiency and power, every other active faculty in the mind will also increase in efficiency and power. It is the intellectual brain that guides the whole brain; and, therefore, intellectual advancement means general advancement; but this general advancement in every part of the brain and the mind will not be satisfactory unless the whole of the brain is developed in proportion. Develop the intellectual brain continuously, no matter what your work; give special and continuous development to that part of the brain that is employed directly in your work; and give general development to your whole brain; this is the perfect rule to follow in order to secure the proper results.

7. THE INNER SECRET

In order to develop any part of the physical system, two essentials are required. The first is more nourishment in that particular part, and the second is an increase in creative energy. The circulation conveys nourishment to all parts of the system, and the nerves transmit the creative energies; therefore, wherever we increase the circulation, additional nourishment will be supplied, and wherever the activity of the nerves is increased or intensified, there creative energy will accumulate. Accordingly, the question will be how to increase the circulation wherever we like, and how to intensify the activity of any desired nerve center. Experiments, however, have demonstrated that this problem is not as difficult as it may seem, because wherever mental attention is concentrated, an increase both in the circulation and in the nerve activity takes place. But this concentration must be in the right mental attitude, and here we come to the inner secret.

It has been discovered that all functions of the personality are under the direct control of what is termed the finer subjective forces, and in order to master any physical function or mental faculty, these finer forces must be employed. Wherever these subjective forces display the greatest activity, there the circulation is the strongest, and there the creative energies naturally accumulate; and these subjective forces will display the greatest activity wherever attention is concentrated during subjective consciousness. The secret, therefore, is to enter subjective consciousness before we begin to concentrate for any desired development; and by subjective consciousness we mean that mental state wherein the finer forces of the system can be felt. But this is not something new or something difficult to attain. We all are more or less on the verge of this consciousness all the time, and most of us enter into it frequently.

When you are thrilled by music that stirs the very soul of your being you are in subjective consciousness, and it is the finer forces or interior vibrations that produce the delightful sensation you feel at the time. When you are inwardly touched by the beauties of nature, you are in this same consciousness; and it is these finer forces that create the lofty thoughts you think during such moments. There are any number of experiences that could be mentioned to illustrate what is meant by subjective consciousness, but the two just mentioned will give anyone the key. And here we must remember that it is this state that we must enter whenever we concentrate for development, either for mind, brain or body; the reason being, that while the mind is in this finer subjective state, the actions of mind will directly control the subjective forces. When the mind is in subjective consciousness, the subjective forces will follow concentration, thus drawing more creative energy and a stronger circulation to that place upon which attention is directed. This is the law, and it is just as unfailing as any law in nature. But how to take the mind into subjective consciousness at any time is of course the problem, although the solution is by no means difficult to find.

When we know what subjective consciousness really is, and remember the sensation we have felt while in such a state at previous times, we can readily transfer the mind to the field of the finer forces by simply desiring to do so, but we must not make a strenuous effort in that direction. To keep the mind upon the ideal and the more refined for a few moments is usually sufficient to awaken subjective consciousness in most

448

instances; and to think of anything that is lofty and sublime, or that touches the soul will invariably produce the same result. In brief, anything that will cause your mind to pass from the mere surface of thought into the finer depths of life may be employed in the beginning to induce this finer state. Possibly few external helps would be better than that of listening for a few moments to sweet, tender, soulful music, and the reading of poetry that really is poetry will usually serve the same purpose. It must be remembered, however, that when we employ external aids in this connection we must make a deep, but gentle effort to enter into sympathetic touch with the soul of that which we employ at the time.

When we gain the mastery of our own consciousness we can enter the subjective state or withdraw from that state at any time as we like. In fact, we can do this just as easily as we can open or close our eyes. This mastery, therefore, should be our great object in view when we are depending upon temporary or external helps. Another method for assisting the mind in producing subjective consciousness is the study of the different planes of vibration with a view of gaining a perfect understanding of the true nature of each individual plane. This is an immense and a most interesting study, and will prove extremely valuable in mental development, for the reason that the mind can consciously enter and consciously act upon any plane that it understands. Therefore, when the mind understands the nature of subjective consciousness, it can enter that state at any time by simply deciding to do so. To gain a better understanding of the various planes of consciousness and the ascending scales of vibrations, the latest discoveries both in physical science and in psychology should be noted with the greatest of care. The X-rays and the N-rays demonstrate conclusively the existence of finer forces and higher vibrations in nature; and the fact that every plane in nature has a corresponding plane in man has been known for a long time. It is also a well-known fact that man has a higher sense or consciousness to correspond with every higher force or plane in nature. Therefore the fact that there are higher forces in nature proves that there are higher states of consciousness in man; and it is our privilege to have all of these developed whenever we may so desire.

Many minds look upon the visible physical body as all there is of the body, but chemistry has demonstrated conclusively that within the purely physical body there exists a finer grade of elements, and within this finer grade a still finer grade and so on for a number of grades, the exact number of which has not been determined. The physical body therefore is, strictly speaking, composed of a number of forms, the outermost form being in the lowest grade of vibration, while the innermost forms being in such a high grade of vibration that they approach what scientists call ethereal elements. Just at this point the subconscious begins and we have a vast interior world, the immensity of which will possibly never be fully demonstrated. It is this interior world that we call "the great within," and it is the source of the boundless possibilities that are latent in man. Whenever we are more or less in touch with this inner or finer realm we are in subjective consciousness, and it is only necessary to touch the subconscious to gain control of the finer forces.

Subjective consciousness deals with a boundless realm and therefore we may expand the mind into this vast realm perpetually, gaining mastery over greater and greater powers as we advance. In usual brain development the mere feeling of these finer forces of the subjective field is all that is necessary to secure results. And those who employ the helps already presented will find no difficulty whatever in reaching this deeper or finer state of feeling. When you are in subjective consciousness during concentration, you can readily feel those finer forces in that part of the brain that you are trying to develop, and you can also feel an increase in the circulation in the same place. The finer creative energies are not always as distinctly felt, but they are always present in abundance where the finer activities are at work. When we begin to gain control of the subjective forces so that we can draw all the creative energies of the system into any part of the brain or body where we desire development, we find we are beginning to master another great process, without doubt one of the greatest processes in the being of man; in other words, what may be truthfully called the inner secret of all human development; and as we advance in the application of the principle of this secret, we shall advance in development in proportion. But as there is no end to the possibilities of this secret, there is necessarily no end to what man may develop in his own mind and soul as he advances in the scientific use of the principle involved.

8. THE FINER FORCES

The consciousness of and the proper direction of the finer forces in mind and personality, is absolutely necessary in all development of brain or mind, and therefore we must learn to know those forces whenever their actions are felt in the system. One of the first signs of the presence of these finer forces is indicated by peculiar warmth in the deeper life of the body, especially when the forces are strong; though it is not necessary that they should produce this warmth nor that they should produce any pronounced physical sensation whatever. It is very important, however, that we learn to distinguish between the finer forces and the other forces in the system because when the finer forces are discerned they may be directed anywhere to promote development. And here we must remember that unless these finer forces are placed in action, no development can possibly take place.

The inner forces are the interior creative energies of the human personality. They are the invisible builders of every force in the body and every state, quality and faculty in the mind.

Therefore to promote growth anywhere in the human system, the action of the finer forces in that part must be increased.

When the finer forces are felt or discerned they will readily accumulate wherever attention may be directed; and wherever they accumulate there life, nourishment, vitality, and everything necessary to growth and construction, will accumulate also. To discern the finer forces it is necessary for the mind to enter into the consciousness of those elements that permeate the physical elements; that is, conscious action must act not upon the physical person, but upon the real life that thrills every atom in the person. During this conscious action no thought whatever must be given to physical matter nor must the mind dwell upon shape or form. When the mind thinks of shape, form, or physical matter during the process of concentration, attention will be directed upon physical matter instead of upon that life that gives animation to matter. The desired results therefore will not be forthcoming. To arouse the finer forces, attention must be concentrated upon those forces; the mind must think of those forces, and consciousness must seek to enter into the very life of those forces. This, however, is not possible while one is thinking of the body or giving attention to its shape and form. To develop any part of the brain, the cells in that part should be made more refined and more numerous. To accomplish this, more energy, more life and more nourishment will be needed in the part to be developed; and all of these will accumulate where desired if the finer forces are active in the system, and attention is concentrated upon the exact place where development is to take place. During this concentration, however, no thought must be given to the physical brain cells. Attention must be devoted exclusively to the finer elements, the finer forces, the finer life that permeates the finer forces, and the finer life that permeates the physical cells.

Concentrate attention upon the finer forces in any part of the system, and those forces from any part of the system will accumulate at the point of concentration; and whatever you desire to develop at the time, those forces will proceed to develop. When this accumulation of the finer forces or energies is taking place, their presence can sometimes be felt, and they produce a very delicate vibratory sensation. Sometimes

451

these vibrations produce electric thrills, a sensation that is most delightful, and sometimes they cause the personality to feel, as it were, a living magnet, which is true. When the finer forces are highly active, the personality actually becomes a living magnet and gains at the time the creative power of rare genius.

The actions and the vibrations of the finer forces never feel as if they were on the surface, nor even in an external state of physical sub-stance. On the contrary, they always feel as if they were deeply permeating physical substance, giving external power, so to speak, to external shape and form. To try to feel the finer forces, however, is not desirable. Our purpose is to arouse them into high and full action, and whenever they are in action, we shall feel them without trying to do so. When we try to feel those forces, the mind will give its attention to sensation, and sensation is simply effect; but to produce the action of those forces as well as the feeling of their presence in the system, we must act upon those forces themselves; that is, we must act upon the cause, and whenever we produce the desired cause, the desired effect will invariably follow.

9. SUBJECTIVE CONCENTRATION

To concentrate upon the finer essence, the finer life of the finer forces in any part of the brain, or in any part of the personality, is termed subjective concentration, and there is no other form of concentration that has any value for any purpose whatever. To accomplish anything in any field of action, concentration is indispensable, but that concentration must be subjective to produce results. And to concentrate subjectively is to act mentally in the conscious feeling of that finer life, essence or force that permeates the objective or physical life.

There are two sides to the human system, the objective and the subjective. The objective is the external, the tangible or the physical side. The subjective is the interior, the finer, or the metaphysical side. The subjective permeates the objective. The metaphysical or the subjective is the cause, or constitutes the realm of cause, and therefore controls the physical, and determines every effect that will be produced in the physical. For this reason, the mind must concentrate upon the metaphysical and produce the desired cause in the metaphysical in order to secure any desired effect or result in the physical. It is the finer metaphysical forces that control the vital forces and the chemical forces in the body, and it is these same forces that are usually termed creative energies. It is these that create and develop, and therefore to promote development, these finer forces must be awakened, directed and properly applied.

To awaken the finer forces of the system, the mind must concentrate attention upon the finer essence or substance that permeates the physical substance of the personality, and this is accomplished by trying to feel the finer forces while the mind is thinking deeply of the subjective or finer life of the system. The principle is this, that the substance of which the body is composed is actually permeated with a much finer substance, just as water permeates a sponge, and that this finer substance or essence is filled with forces that arc much finer and far more rapid than the ordinary physical forces. To concentrate subjectively is to direct attention upon this finer essence and these finer forces, and when the mind actually succeeds in acting upon this finer essence the finer forces of the system will be placed in action.

Wherever these forces begin to act, there development will take place. Therefore, to promote development in any part of the brain or in any part of the personality all that is necessary is to concentrate subjectively on that part, and have clearly fixed in mind at the time the degree of development that is desired. To concentrate upon the finer essence of the brain center is to think about the finer substance that permeates the physical brain center, and then turn attention upon that finer substance. In this way the finer forces of the brain will be acted upon, and when these forces are acted upon they will do whatever the mind may desire to have done at the time.

What to think while concentrating subjectively depends upon what one desires to develop, attain or accomplish through such concentration. And this can be determined by applying the principle of scientific thinking. The most important principle in scientific thinking is to think only of that now that you are trying to accomplish now, and turn all the power of thought, life, consciousness and attention upon that one subject. And here we must realize that without scientific thinking concentration is of no value; in fact, it ceases to be concentration; because to try to concentrate upon one subject while thinking of something else is a mere scattering of force. When concentrating upon a certain faculty one should think about the more perfect state of that faculty and also what one desires to accomplish through the use of that faculty. In this connection the constructive use of the imagination will prove highly profitable, because what is imagined in the mind during any process of subjective concentration will be created and developed in the mind. What is imaged in the mind when concentration is not subjective, will not be developed in the mind, because the creative forces, those forces that develop, are not brought into action unless concentration is subjective. To awaken these forces attention must act in the subjective field of consciousness ; and this field is simply a field of finer life and action permeating every part of the human system.

To enter mentally into this finer field is not difficult. In fact, when anyone feels deeply, the mind is more or less in the subjective. The same is true when attention enters an attitude of deep, whole-souled interest, a fact that can easily be demonstrated because concentration is always perfect when the interest is absolute; and a finer, stronger life is always felt at such times. Whenever a person concentrates with a deep, living interest, he concentrates subjectively, and if he would analyze the experience he would find that he was not interested in the outer phase of the subject, but actually entered into the real interior life of the subject itself. The simple principle is that when we enter into a subject we concentrate subjectively upon that subject. And when we enter into the finer essence or life of an object, we concentrate subjectively upon that object. The process of subjective concentration, therefore, is easily understood and applied. It is not something special that we have to learn because we are concentrating subjectively more or less all the time, that is, whenever we direct attention upon anything with a deep, living interest. It is a process, however, that should be developed thoroughly and completely mastered as it constitutes the principal secret to all attainment and achievement.

10. PRINCIPLE OF CONCENTRATION

To do one thing at a time and to give one's whole thought and attention to what is being done now is the principle upon which concentration is based, and nothing worthwhile can be accomplished without concentration. This principle, however, is not confined to definite lines of action, nor does it necessarily mean that the well concentrated mind moves in a groove. On the contrary, the more perfect the power of concentration, the more easily can the mind turn its attention with full force to any subject or object that may be considered. To be able to concentrate well does not simply mean to be able to give one's whole attention to present action; it also means the power to turn one's complete attention upon any new subject or object at will.

In the first place, concentration is a function of the conscious mind only. It is not necessary to concentrate upon that which the subconscious is doing; and all the automatic actions of mind or body are directed by the subconscious; that is, after the subconscious has been given the proper directions, no further concentration along: those lines will be necessary. It is only such actions as have not been given definite tendencies and such modes of thought or effort as require special attention, that need concentration. What is termed mechanical work, therefore, that is, work that can be done without special thought or direction, can be carried on perfectly by the automatic action of the subconscious while the conscious mind may be thinking about something else. But it is not well to carry this practice too far.

To place certain kinds of simple work in the hands of the subconscious while the conscious mind is otherwise engaged may have a tendency to separate the actions of the conscious and the subconscious phases of mind; but this separation must be avoided as it is perfect unity of action between the conscious and the subconscious that we seek to attain, because when this unity becomes perfect, the subconscious will always respond to the directions of the conscious mind. We have discovered that the subconscious can do and will do whatever it is properly impressed or directed to do, but the conscious mind cannot direct the subconscious properly unless there is perfect unity of action between the two.

To think of something else while you are doing mechanical work is permissible to a degree, but it must not be made a general practice. The wisest course is to give your whole attention to what you are doing now whatever that work may be; and if you give soul to that work it will cease to be mechanical. Besides, such a work can be made a channel for a fuller and a larger expression of self. All kinds of work may become channels of expression for the superior powers of mind and soul, and the secret is to give soul to everything that is being done. To give soul to your work is to work in the conscious interest of what you are doing; in brief, to feel that your work is an expression of more and more life, and that expression will steadily increase the power of your entire mind and personality. In other words, you give soul to your work when your whole heart is in your work; when you are thoroughly interested in the work itself and the final result; when you deeply love it and thoroughly enjoy it; and when you give it your very best thoughts, ability and power. In this connection it is important to remember that what you give to your work you give to yourself. The more ability and power you give to your work the more ability and power you develop in yourself. And the more interest you take in your present work the better will your concentration become. To take only a halfhearted interest in what we may be doing now is to weaken the power of concentration; in fact, the power of concentration will almost disappear if such a practice is continued. No one, therefore, can afford to be otherwise than thoroughly interested in the work of the present moment, no matter what the work may be. Occasionally, however, simple tasks may be left to automatic mental action; that is, when we have done those things so many times that their doing has become second nature, so to speak; and we may thus give our conscious attention at the time to other matters. But such a practice should be the exception, never the rule.

A fact of exceptional importance that we shall all discover as we apply the principle of concentration, is that no task can be disagreeable when approached in the attitude of real concentration. The reason why is found in the fact that when we concentrate properly we approach a subject or object from the most interesting point of view; and nothing can be really disagreeable when approached from the most interesting point of view. The value of this fact will increase as we realize the importance of avoiding every attitude of mind that is in any way antagonistic to our work. And as real concentration will perfect all such attitudes, we find what a gain we shall make in every respect when we learn to concentrate in the right way. We concentrate naturally upon that in which we are interested. For this reason the natural method for the development of concentration is always to look for the most interesting points of view; and we should apply this method, no matter what we may be thinking about or what our work may be. Everything has an interesting side, and when we look for it we shall invariably find it. In fact, to look for the interesting side will in itself create interest; and to create interest is to develop concentration. In this connection it is well to remember that no work can possibly be drudgery when entered into in the right frame of mind. And also that all work that is performed in the right frame of mind will open the way to something better. This is a law that never fails, and the right frame of mind in each case consists of the right use of concentration; that is, producing concentration by becoming deeply interested in what we may be thinking of or doing. In other words, to look for the most interesting points of view regardless of what conditions or circumstances may be.

IMPORTANT RULES.

1.—In all efforts to develop the brain through subjective concentration always concentrate upon the brain center first, and from that point gradually move attention to the outer surface.

2.—During concentration the mind should be in a well-poised, serene attitude, and strongly determined to secure results. 3.—Fifteen or twenty minutes is long enough to practice at a time, and two or three times a day for regular exercise, although it is well to practice for a few minutes every hour if opportunities present themselves.

4.—Never concentrate for brain or mind development immediately after a meal. The digestive functions for about an hour after each meal require a full circulation and all available surplus energy. Therefore, neither the circulation nor additional energy should be drawn elsewhere at that time.

5.—The mind should continue in the attitude of perfect faith during the process of concentration. The more faith you have in the methods you employ the greater your results, because faith invariably awakens higher and more powerful forces.

6.—Affirmations, suggestions and strong positive statements may be combined with the process of concentration. To illustrate; while you are concentrating upon the faculty of intelligence, you may affirm, "My mind is clear, lucid and brilliant," "My mind is alive with exceptional intelligence," "My mind is constantly growing in the capacity to think, understand and create ideas,*' and statements of a similar nature. Statements to correspond with what you desire each faculty to become may be formulated by yourself, and affirmed as you concentrate for the development of that faculty.

7.—When concentrating, have superiority and worth constantly in mind, and train all the mental tendencies to move towards the higher and the greater.

8.—Never begin concentration until you have permeated the entire system with a refining process, and drawn all the forces of your system into finer states of life and action.

9.—While you are at your work, train your attention to act directly upon and through the faculty that you are using in your work. This will increase the power and the activity of that faculty, thereby developing the faculty at the time, as well as producing better work.

10. Never be over anxious about results, because you know that results must inevitably follow; then let results come when they are ready. If you proceed in this attitude you will begin to secure results from the very beginning.

11.—It is not always well to try to develop a number of leading talents at the same time. Select one or two that you expect to develop for your life work; then give these fully three-fourths of your attention, and divide the remainder of your time among all other faculties so as to produce a balanced mentality.

12.—It is not necessary to form any mental picture of the brain or the brain cells while you concentrate. In fact, it is best not to do this, as such a practice will tend to draw consciousness away from the subjective into the objective. Do not think of the physical brain itself or of the physical cells, but simply keep in mind those higher and greater qualities that you desire to develop. And hold your attention upon the interior subjective process that is promoting the development. Concentrate your attention upon that part of the brain that you desire to develop, but think only of the finer or metaphysical counterpart of your brain at the time. In other words, give your attention to the finer mental elements that permeate the physical brain. Thus you will awaken those energies and elements that alone have the power to produce the increase in talent and power you desire.

11. DEVELOPMENT OF BUSINESS ABILITY

To become successful in the commercial world, that entire region marked "business ability*' in Fig. V. should be developed. Concentrate subjectively upon this region for ten or fifteen minutes every morning before going to work, and repeat the concentration for a few minutes several times during the day. When you concentrate upon this region animate your concentration with a deep, strong desire to make this part of the brain larger, more powerful and more efficient. Be alive and enthusiastic during the concentration, but be fully poised and self-possessed, and positively expect results.

It will be noticed that that part of the brain marked "business ability" in Fig. V. includes the first four divisions as indicated in Fig. IV. Therefore in concentrating upon the region of "business ability" it will be well to take these four divisions separately at various times of the day. Take ten or fifteen minutes every day for the development of this region as a whole without any thought as to its divisions. Sometime during the day give a few minutes to the practical brain; at another time during the same day give a few minutes to the mechanical brain and the executive brain. Give most of your attention, however, to that division that seems to be smaller or less efficient than the others.

The practical brain and the financial brain should receive the most thorough development when the individual is engaged in the general business field. But the mechanical brain should always be a close second, as the power to construct, build up, enlarge and develop is absolutely necessary in the working out of a successful business enterprise. When the management of an enterprise demands the greatest amount of attention, the executive brain should receive the most thorough development, while the practical brain should receive the first thought when the working out of details constitutes the principal line of action.

Speaking in general, the manager of an enterprise should constantly develop the executive brain; the general office force should constantly develop the practical brain, so that the ideas of the manager would be actually and efficiently carried out; the financial heads of the concern should constantly develop the financial brain, while everyone connected with the enterprise should give daily attention to the entire region of "business ability." In addition to the development of general business ability, the man who would become a great power in the commercial world, should also develop "originality," the secret of greatness, and "intuition," or finer insight, the power to sec through every circumstance and condition, and thus take advantage of the right opportunity at the right time.

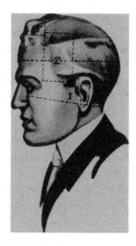

FIG. V.

1. Business Ability

2. Construction and Imagination

Men and women who occupy stenographic or clerical positions should develop the practical brain in particular, and the entire region of "business ability" in general. Those who are employed in any form of constructive work should give special attention to the mechanical brain and the practical brain. If your clerical position is principally in connection with money, develop the practical brain and the financial brain. Foremen, superintendents and managers in factories should develop the executive brain and the mechanical brain; while those who manage financial institutions, or who superintend the selling of products, should develop the executive brain and the financial brain. The executive brain and the practical brain should be developed by those who manage the detail work of any business concern; and it must be remembered that those who manage or superintend, in any manner whatever, must also develop the volitional brain. Whenever you concentrate subjectively upon any division of the brain, try to increase the active power of the faculty that functions through that part; and also try to improve the quality of that faculty. This is readily done by combining the proper desires and mental attitudes with the action of concentration. When you concentrate upon the practical brain, desire the power of practical application; think deeply of what it actually means to be practical, and try to evolve perfect system out of every group of thoughts, ideas or plans that may appear in your mind at the time.

When concentrating upon the mechanical brain, deeply desire to construct, invent and build up; try to put together the different parts of your business in every imaginable combination, and try to work out a combination that will be far superior to the present arrangement. You thus develop the constructive brain and the mental faculty of construction at the same time; besides, you may, at any time, invent a combination in your business affairs that will double your success.

459

When you concentrate upon the financial brain, desire wealth; desire a vast amount of legitimate wealth, and make up your mind to secure it; think deeply of that power in human action that accumulates, that gathers together, that produces increase, and try to feel that the power is becoming stronger and stronger in you. When concentrating upon the executive brain, think constantly of the practical art of management; examine the governing power from every point of view, and analyze as perfectly as possible that faculty in the human mind that is naturally adapted to manage, govern and rule. Deeply desire this faculty, this power, and inspire your desire to govern with the positive conviction that you can. In this manner you not only develop and enlarge the executive brain, but you also bring forth into practical action all the mental qualities that go to make up executive power. In consequence you will constantly gain greater and greater executive power; and if you continue in your development you will, in the course of a reasonable time, be able to manage successfully the most extensive enterprise in the world.

12. ACCUMULATION AND INCREASE

The upper half of the brain is devoted to the abstract, to the world of ideas. The lower half of the brain is devoted to the concrete, to the world of things. And since the commercial world deals directly with the concrete, the lower half of the brain must necessarily be well developed if the increase of business ability is desired.

It is usually not difficult to formulate plausible theories concerning what ought to be done, but to apply such theories is quite a different matter; and application invariably demands the ability to apply in the world of things what has been worked out in the world of ideas. Most theories may be good, but not one in a hundred is ever applied, the reason being that there is a decided lack in the power of application among most minds. In the business world it is the man who can do things and who can put ideas into practice that is in the greatest demand. It is such a man who secures the best positions and a princely recompense; and on account of his exceptional worth he deserves all that he receives.

The man who can evolve system in his work, who can formulate methods for the more thorough application of his work, and who can practically apply for actual results all those methods, is never going to fail in his undertakings. And this proves that the power of application has such extreme value that even the man who has no other accomplishment can achieve great things in life if this particular power is highly developed. Though the power of application is of unusual value in every line of work, it has its greatest value in the business world, because in that world results cannot be secured unless the practical element is present in a large measure. The business man should therefore give a great deal of attention to the development of that part of the brain through which the faculty of application naturally functions.

When concentrating upon the faculty of application try to evolve system out of everything that you may be thinking of at the time. And this is very important as there must be system in all action before actual results can be secured. During such concentration, it is best to think principally of the work in which we are now engaged and try to perfect system in that work. In this manner you will apply your efforts in brain building more directly, and accordingly will develop your business ability to a much greater degree and in much less time.

The power of construction is absolutely necessary in the business world; therefore while concentrating for the development of constructive power, think deeply about your work and try to bring the different parts of your work into just such combinations as you desire. In brief, try to think out combinations that you feel will prove superior to every combination along constructive lines that you have worked out before. Thus you develop not only the brain in that particular region, but you also build up the corresponding faculty in the mind—that mental faculty that is applied in all constructive efforts.

You may not adopt all the new combinations that you will evolve in this manner, but you will develop the power of construction in your mind the more you try to evolve superior combinations ; and through this practice you will finally evolve some exceptional combination from which the greater results you desire will be secured. It is a well-known fact that success in the commercial world depends largely upon the way the business is constructed. Therefore, better and better results will inevitably follow as you increase your power to combine the various parts of your business in such a way as to give the entire enterprise, in which you are interested, the most perfect working system available.

In the world of things we find both the scattering process and the process of accumulation, and when we examine the subject closely we find that each individual has both of these processes in his own hands. He can control things to such an extent that he may positively determine how much is to be scattered in one place and how much is to be accumulated in some other place. In brief, he controls absolutely the disposal of all things and all possessions in his own world. In the majority, however, this faculty has not been developed, and for this reason we find only a small majority who are in possession of abundance, or who have the power to recuperate instantaneously should losses be incurred. But nature is able to give us abundance, and we all can secure abundance if we apply ourselves fully and in harmony with natural law. One of the most important essentials in this connection is the mental power of accumulation, for we must remember that we must be able to accumulate in the mind before we can accumulate in the external world. And as previously stated, this power can be increased more and more for an indefinite period through the proper development of the mind, and through the full development of that part of the brain through which this faculty functions. To proceed, concentrate for the development of accumulation as outlined elsewhere in this study; and hold in your mind as clearly as possible the idea of accumulation at the time. Realize that you are an individual center, and that you can cause all the rich things in life to gravitate toward yourself as this center. Establish in your mind a deep feeling of what you imagine the process of accumulation to be, and try to feel that the various forces and elements in your system are actually accumulating within you. Hold yourself in a strong attitude of poise, and realize that through this attitude you are holding all things together in your system. Practice these things while concentrating until you realize your own supremacy over things, and feel distinctly the process of accumulation constantly at work in your entire system. The result will be a rapid and steady development of the power of accumulation, not only in your own mind, but in all those faculties whose function it is to gather abundance in the world of things.

It is a fact well known among all minds who have studied these deeper laws, that whenever you establish a certain process in your own system you can establish the same process in your environment. In other words, should you apply this law to the idea of accumulation we would find that you would have gained the power to accumulate possessions in your external world, when you have gained the power to accumulate the richer elements of your own mind. And experience proves that this law is absolutely true. Accordingly, we should seek to attain the consciousness of accumulation and create the accumulating process in our own mental world; that is, we should hold the mind in this consciousness while concentrating for the development of those faculties of the mind that are directly concerned with accumulation; and we will thereby, not only develop the brain in the region of those faculties, but will also develop the mental power to acquire and hold possessions both in the mental world and in the world of things.

13. INDIVIDUAL ADVANCEMENT

Progress and Success —The true meaning of success may be expressed in the one word "progress." You are successful only when you are moving forward, when you are constantly gaining ground in the most comprehensive sense of that term. Therefore, the first essential to those who have success as their goal, is to make individual progress their first and leading aim. And to this aim should be added the constant desire to find better and better methods through which individual progress may be gained.

The Right Vocation —To begin, select the right vocation. In making your selection follow your strongest ambition; that is, if you can do something in that particular field now. Though if this is not always possible, there is another way that may be entered upon temporarily. Accept the best opportunity that you can find under present conditions, and resolve to make good. Then, in the meantime, proceed to improve your whole mind. This will not only enable you to do better work where you are, but it will also make you more familiar with what ability and power you really possess. A great many young men are very ambitious along certain lines, and therefore imagine that their greatest success lies in those lines. But after their entire mentalities become fully alive, they discover that their strongest powers lie in an entirely different direction. Accordingly, their ambitions change; they find their first ambitions to be simply the result of surface action in the mind, while their new ambitions are the result of their real, inherent ability, now awakened to action.

Arouse the Whole Mind —The first ambitions of most young men are "false alarms," due to shallow mental actions produced by some external suggestions. The small boy who wants to be a street car motorman, because that particular work fascinates his boyish notion of responsibility and position, is an illustration. And though those young ideas usually pass away on short notice, still they are frequently followed by other ideas and ambitions equally false and superficial. The necessity, therefore, of waking up the whole mind in order to develop the true ambition and get the proper clue to the correct vocation in each case is most evident. When you accept the best opportunity you can now find, and proceed to develop your whole mind while working in that particular position, you will soon re-adjust your ambitions, if those ambitions happen to be "false alarms." But if your ambitions actually are genuine, proceeding directly and naturally from your greatest natural ability, the waking up of your whole mind will only tend to make those ambitions stronger and more persistent than ever before.

Your True Ambition —When you find a certain ambition becoming stronger and stronger the more you improve your mind, you may rest assured that that is your true ambition. And if you follow that ambition, you will enter your true vocation. But if you find your ambitions changing as you proceed to build up every part of your mind, you will find it advisable not to follow any special ambition, or select any special vocation until your whole mind is thoroughly aroused, and the strongest faculties determined with a certainty. Wherever you begin in your chosen vocation, you will find it absolutely necessary to promote your own individual progress if you wish to succeed. And by individual progress we mean the constant improvement of your whole self— your mind, your faculties, your powers, your character, your mode of thinking, your conduct, your disposition, your personal life, your personality, your power of application, your habits, your views of life, your personal worth, your ideals—in brief, everything that pertains to your own individual Life, thought and action.

Individual Progress —If you are already in the right vocation, individual progress will enable you to meet the ever growing demands of that vocation. And here we must remember that the man who does not improve himself in this age is the man who will be left behind, and later placed "on the shelf." The man who is constantly improving himself will be wanted in the world of action as long as he lives, regardless of his age or the color of his hair. But self-improvement is no hardship; it is a pleasure; in fact, there are few things that help more to make life worthwhile. If you are not in the right vocation, individual progress will soon bring out the best that is in you, so that you will not only know where you belong, but will be competent to go to work where you belong. Then, if you continue this progress and self-improvement, you will constantly advance externally by noting a steady improvement in your conditions. Improve yourself, and your conditions will also improve. This is the law; and it cannot fail when systematically applied. Realize that individual progress must precede individual success, and that individual progress must continue if success is to be permanent. Work unceasingly for the progress and improvement of yourself. Make it a point to build your- self up; and never bring this building process to a standstill. If you are in an uncongenial position, do not try to get out at once; do not force yourself out; but proceed where you are to build yourself up, and improve yourself to such an extent that you become indispensable where you are. You will soon secure a better position, and you will become much stronger and more valuable, on account of the discipline gained by "holding out" under adversity.

Secret of Advancement —Make difficulties and obstacles serve the greater purpose you have in view, and they will, if you enter every position with a view of using the demands of that position for making your whole mind alive. But in this connection do not make the mistake that thousands have who have entered temporary positions. After entering those positions they have failed to improve themselves; instead, they have permitted their minds to retrograde, and therefore have either continued for life in those "temporary" positions, or have been pushed lower still. This accounts for the fact that so many capable and well educated men are now holding inferior positions. They took the best they could find in the beginning, but ignored the necessity of individual progress, and therefore had to continue where they began year after year until they finally gave up hope of ever getting anything better. The mistake of these men must be rigorously avoided at every turn, and every tendency to fall into a "rut" must be stamped out completely. Work for individual progress every minute, and no matter where or how you begin, you will steadily advance in the scale. New and better opportunities will come to you all along the line as you are prepared to accept them. You will prove the fact that better opportunities are always waiting for the better man, and that the better man is invariably the man who makes individual progress his first and greatest aim.

14. THE GENIUS OF INVENTION

There are few worlds that hold richer possibilities than the world of invention, and there are few things that are more easily developed than inventive genius. Everything can be improved. Even the most perfect products of the industrial world have defects, and the man whose genius can remove those defects will be most richly rewarded. In the world of new and original inventions there are no limitations whatever. The field is simply inexhaustible because there is no end to the realm of ideas, and invention is simply a new combination of ideas that can be turned to practical use. Another reason why the world of invention is so immense is because inventive genius is not confined to a single field of action. It is, on the contrary, employed in nearly every field of action. A certain grade of inventive genius is absolutely necessary to the writer; another grade is indispensable to the musical composer; still other grades are required by the artist, the mechanic and the skilled worker; while no business man will succeed to any extent unless he has the power of invention developed to a high degree.

The secret of inventive genius is the power to create new ideas, and to produce new combinations of ideas using both old ideas and new ideas as the case may require. The power to combine ideas for practical use is the most important phase in the development of inventive genius at the present time. There are innumerable ideas afloat in the world today that have not been turned to any account; even a few of these if properly combined, and practically applied would revolutionize the industrial world. It is, therefore, not necessary to search for new ideas at the present time while the world is waiting for a genius to tell us how to use the best ideas we already possess.

To proceed with the improvement of any invention a definite plan should be employed, but new inventions, new and original combinations frequently come of themselves while inventive genius is being developed; or they may come when the inventive genius, one may already possess, is aroused to an extraordinary degree by some powerful suggestion or experience that bears directly upon the necessary phases of mind. The first essential in the improvement of the invention is to gain a clear understanding of the principle upon which that invention is based, and the purpose which it is intended to fulfill. If the old invention does not fulfill that purpose with satisfaction, find the reason why. If your objective mind cannot give you your real reason, consult the subconscious. The subconscious can work out the most difficult problems in mathematics while you sleep; then why should it not be able to discover the real cause of imperfections in the invention you desire to improve, and also discover the key to the necessary improvements. The fact is that the subconscious can find out almost anything provided it is properly impressed and directed. And since we all can learn to direct the subconscious in any way desired, we should never permit ourselves to ever use the term impossible. When you have found the cause of the imperfections of any invention, the proper combinations required to remove those imperfections can be easily made by applying the faculties of imagination and construction, though in this as well as in all other efforts, the subconscious should be brought into the fullest use possible. In its last analysis every improvement is the result of a better mental conception of the workings of the thing to be improved. Therefore, before undertaking to make the proposed improvement, the object under consideration should be analyzed

465

from every possible point of view. In this connection it is highly important to know that there is nothing that will produce so many new combinations of ideas as the practice of looking at every object from every imaginable point of view; and this is especially true when we look at things with an interest that is deeply felt and thoroughly alive. The average person looks at things from a single point of view only; therefore his mental conceptions are one sided. His ideas are incomplete, and such ideas as are required to produce the new combinations or inventions desired are not forthcoming. Those necessary ideas, however, may be gained by taking new points of view, one after the other, until the object under consideration has been viewed and examined in every conceivable manner.

When you have examined something from every viewpoint, you have gained all the ideas of that something that your present mental capacity can comprehend. By combining those ideas, you will have a combination that must necessarily be an improvement upon that which you originally examined, and by turning this new combination to practical use you will have an actual improvement. The simple practice of looking at all things from every imaginable viewpoint will alone develop the power of invention to a remarkable degree, and when this practice is combined with a practical system of development in the art of invention, the attainment of real inventive genius is absolutely certain.

The principal faculties to develop in order to gain inventive genius are imagination, construction and intuition. The latter may also be termed insight, discernment, or the power of discovery. To begin, concentrate upon those faculties twice every day, giving about ten minutes to each faculty, and while concentrating upon a certain faculty exercise that faculty in the work which it is being developed to perform. To determine where to concentrate for the development of the brain in this connection see Figure VI. To illustrate, when you concentrate upon that part of the brain through which the imaging faculty is expressed, use the imagination to the fullest extent and use it in picturing the various parts of the invention you desire to perfect. This invention may be a book, a musical composition, a machine, an architectural structure or a group of plans and methods for the promotion of some commercial enterprise. In other words, while you are concentrating upon that part of the brain which is used by the faculty in question, put that faculty to work. You will thereby develop both the brain and the mind at the same time, which is highly important.

FIG. VI.

1. Imagination 2. Construction. 3. Interior Sight

To develop the mental faculty alone is not sufficient. You might just as well expect a great musician to do justice to himself on some crude, primitive instrument as to expect a highly developed faculty to express talent or genius through a crude sluggish brain. For the same reason it is not sufficient to develop the brain alone. The brain is the instrument of the mental faculty; therefore when the faculty itself is not developed, there will be nothing in the mind to make full use of the highly developed brain that may have been secured. For this reason the faculty should be exercised whenever attention is concentrated upon that part of the brain through which the faculty naturally functions.

When exercising the imaging faculty during concentration the imagination should be used with some definite purpose in view. We should never permit the imagination to work at random, but should give it something special to work out into a complete mental picture. And here we should remember that the imagination is one of the greatest mental faculties in the mind. In fact, it is so important that no matter how practical or matter of fact your work may be, you will find it absolutely necessary to develop your imagination to the very highest degree if you wish to secure the best results obtainable through that particular work.

It is imagination that plans the greater "enterprise and that supplies the necessary methods for successfully promoting that enterprise. Nothing great was ever done that was not first worked out in the imagination, and no improvement was ever made that was not first conceived and pictured in the imaging faculty. It is the power of imagination that lifts the products of mind above the crude and the ordinary, and that gives real worth to that which has worth. Everything that man has made was born of the imagination. And man has made some things that are truly marvelous, regardless of the fact that imagination has never been systematically cultivated. We can therefore imagine what we may expect when this remarkable faculty is thoroughly cultivated and highly developed.

When concentrating upon the faculty of construction, use that faculty in carrying on a definite building process in your mind, directing attention principally upon those ideas that you wish to combine with a view of procuring a new invention or a new system for practical application in your work. During concentration on this faculty, all the ideas, plans and systems imaginable, in connection with the subject under consideration, should be arranged and rearranged in every conceivable manner until the best arrangement or construction has been secured. This exercise, if practiced during the proper concentration upon the brain, will develop rapidly and thoroughly that faculty that produces new combinations of ideas, and that turns those combinations to practical use; that is, that faculty which can invent, or that IS usually defined, when in its highest state of expression, as inventive genius.

When concentrating upon that part of the brain through which the faculty of intuition functions, we should exercise the faculty of insight and discovery, by trying to see through everything that has been brought before our attention. In brief, we should turn our attention upon the hidden parts of those phases of life and work in which we are directly interested, and try to discern the real nature of those parts. We may not discover anything of value at the time, and still we may; but the exercise will positively develop the faculty of insight; and if we continue this development, that faculty will finally discover something, something that may prove of exceptional value. In addition, we should give as much attention as possible to the development of that faculty that is defined as interior understanding, and especially if we desire to employ the power of invention in the fields of art, music or literature. Or, if we wish to devote our genius to mechanics or architecture, we should develop the mechanical brain in addition. While if we wish to apply ourselves principally in the commercial world, we should develop business ability in addition to the other faculties mentioned.

Another essential in the development of inventive genius is the fullest preservation and the proper direction of creative energy. Invention Is naturally a creative process in all its phases, and therefore requires more creative energy than almost any other use of the mind. For this reason it is highly important that the faculties of invention be well supplied with such energy. To this end, the development of poise is indispensable, so that all waste of energy may be prevented. And at least fifty hours of sleep should be taken every week so that the subconscious may keep the system well charged with its various creative forces. Try to average from seven to eight hours of sleep in every twenty-four, but if this allowance should be cut short one night on account of important engagements, retire earlier the next night and make it up. This is a rule that should be kept as rigidly as possible, as it will not only aid decidedly in supplying the system with the necessary amount of creative energy, but it will also aid remarkably in preserving good health for mind and body. Lastly, learn to transmute all those energies in the system that are not required for the normal functions, and turn all of that extra energy into the faculties of invention. The more of this energy you can give to those faculties, the greater will be the creative power of your inventive genius, and the greater will be the inventions that will spring from your brain.

IMPORTANT FACTS.

When thought and attention are concentrated subjectively upon any group of cells in the brain, those cells will multiply in number, and there will be a decided increase in their efficiency and energy-producing capacity. Accordingly, that mental faculty that functions through those cells, will express greater power and a higher degree of ability. Any part of the brain can be developed to an exceptional degree by this method, but the concentration must be subjective; that is, it must be deep and alive, and must actually feel the real or inner power of its own action.

Every division of the brain is in two corresponding parts, one part appearing upon the right side of the brain and the other on the left; every group of brain cells on the right side has a corresponding group on the left side; therefore, in concentrating for brain development, give attention to both sides, first changing from one to the other, and later, as you become more proficient in the art of subjective concentration, give your attention to both sides at the same time. Always begin all concentration at the brain center, and move the action of your concentrated thought toward the surface of the brain, giving special attention to the cells on the surface, as these are the most important. Whenever your ambition is aroused, concentrate the force of your ambition upon that part of the brain through which you must work to realize your ambition. That is, if you are ambitious to become a great financier, turn your attention upon the financial brain, or if you are ambitious to become a great inventor, turn your attention upon the mechanical brain and the imaging brain whenever you feel the power of ambition arising within you; or whatever you are ambitious to become, turn the force of your ambition directly upon that part of the brain that must be developed before your ambition can be made true. You thus develop the necessary faculty, and gain the power to do the very thing you desire to do.

To push the development of any one faculty, concentrate subjectively for ten minutes every hour on that part of the brain through which that particular faculty functions. But before you begin, always place your thought in the conscious feeling of the finer forces of your mind. When concentrating upon any part of the brain, picture in your imagination the faculty that functions through that part, and draw a mental picture of that faculty in the largest, highest and most perfect state of development that you can imagine. You thus impress superior mental development upon every brain cell, and gradually every cell will grow into the exact likeness of that superior development.

During subjective concentration the mind should be well poised, deeply calm, but strongly determined to secure results. Act in the feeling of unbounded faith, believe thoroughly and deeply in the process, and you will arouse those finer and greater forces in your system that can make the process a remarkable success. Ten to fifteen minutes is usually long enough for an exercise in brain development; but you may continue for twenty minutes if you feel that you are having exceptional results. Exercises may be taken every hour or two, but never directly after a meal, as a perfect digestion demands that your mind be perfectly quiet for at least an hour after partaking of food.

When you concentrate upon any part of the brain, use such good suggestions and affirmations as tend to work in harmony with the development you desire to promote. When you concentrate upon the region of intellect repeat mentally with enthusiastic conviction, "My mind is clear and lucid," "My mind is becoming more and more brilliant," "My mind is growing steadily and surely in the power of genuine understanding," "My intellectual capacity is constantly on the increase," "I am gaining the power to know, to discern, to comprehend and to realize every fact and every truth that I may desire." Formulate similar suggestions and affirmations as your needs may require, and try to feel that you are moving into those greater things that your affirmations tend to suggest. When you concentrate upon the volitional brain, use suggestions that suggest greater will-power, greater personal force and greater self-control. When you concentrate upon the practical brain use suggestions that suggest the increase of the power of application, the power that does things. In brief, whenever you concentrate use suggestions that will prompt your thought to work with the process of development. You thus cause all your forces to work together in promoting your purpose, and great results will invariably follow.

15. THE MUSICAL PRODIGY

The Power of Music —In the promotion of human culture, refinement and a higher order of life, consciousness and thought, there is no power greater than that of music. It is therefore an art that should be cultivated universally and cultivated to the very highest possible degree. Though all music tends to elevate the mind, it is the music of quality that exercises the greatest power and the most permanent effect. But such music is not as abundant as we would like, the reason being that really great musicians are rare. The number of people who are studying music is very large and is constantly on the increase, but the majority of these are simply learning to apply what talent they already possess. They are not trying to develop talent of music itself. This, however, must be done if real musical genius is to be gained, although it is evident that in order to accomplish this we must have new and superior methods.

Use Plus Development —To learn how to use the talent you possess is one thing, but to develop that talent itself is quite another. The educational systems of today are concerned almost wholly with the former. But the coming systems must concern themselves also with the latter or the many opportunities for superior attainment now at hand will be lost. There are thousands of excellent minds that could develop rare genius if permitted. But most of the systems in vogue do not develop, their object being simply to train. To give these thousands an opportunity to get away from the routine of mere training, and to give expression to the genius that is within them is one of the aims of this study. Not that training is to be neglected, for thorough training is indispensable, but there must also be something more. We must not rest content with simply the training of our talents. We must also do something definite and effective to enlarge and constantly develop those talents.

Possibilities —To state that anyone who already has considerable musical talent could, through the proper system of development, become a musical prodigy may seem to be far beyond the realm of actual fact. Nevertheless, it is scientifically true. And it is also true that those who have no musical talent whatever, can, if they have a strong desire for musical development, become talented to a considerable degree. And here we must remember that the possibilities of the mind are both limitless and extraordinary, so that if these possibilities are given a fair chance to express themselves there is no reason whatever why genius should not positively appear.

The Three Factors —To develop the musical faculty, the three great factors in all development, the brain, the mind and the soul must receive thorough and scientific attention. The soul, however, should be given the first place, because in music, soul expression is indispensable to high quality. The best music becomes mechanical and, actually ceases to be real music, when the soul is neglected in its expression; and the soul is neglected in too many instances. We find that the lighter forms of music, that music that in itself appeals only to the superficial sentiments, actually becomes superior in its tenderness and sweetness when expressed through someone who has soul; and it is a well-known fact that the sweetest music always comes from the sweetest souls, the reason for which will be readily understood.

Brain Development —It has been stated before, and deserves emphasis as well as repetition, that the brain must be thoroughly developed whatever the faculty may be that is to be expressed, because the brain is the instrument of the mind. To neglect the development of the brain is to remain in the ranks of inferiority, no matter how powerful or talented the mind may be; but as the development of the brain has been almost wholly neglected, we must proceed to give this matter most thorough and most enthusiastic attention. That part of the brain through which the musical faculty proper functions is indicated in Figure VII, and it is this region that needs development where musical genius is the object in view. To develop this part of the brain we should concentrate as before upon the brain center, so as to accumulate as much creative energy as possible at that important point; and while concentrating in this manner gently draw the finer forces from all parts of the system towards the brain center. In a few moments energy will flow to this point through all the nerves, because all the nerves meet at the brain center. All the brain convolutions also meet at the same point, and it is therefore the point of accumulation of energy as well as the point from which energy must be directed to that part of the brain that is to be developed.

Abundant Energy — The accumulation of energy at the brain center by this process will not deprive any part of the body of its necessary power, because far more energy is generated throughout the system than is ever used, and most of it is lost on account of never being taken up and applied in any way. There are various ways to prevent this waste or loss, but none of these methods will be of value unless the energy thus preserved is taken control of and practically applied in some part of mind or body. Since fully three-fourths of the energy generated in the average system is lost, we shall, by preventing this loss, secure more than enough for the most extensive system of development that we wish to apply, without depriving any part of the body of its necessary supply. We may proceed, therefore, according to the method indicated, and after a few moments of concentration upon the brain center cause abundant energy to accumulate at that point. This energy should be directed towards that part of the brain through which the musical faculty functions. The first step should be to direct this energy to the right side of the cranium; the second step to cause concentration to be returned to the brain center; the third step to direct this energy to the left side of the cranium; and the fourth step to concentrate upon the brain center again as before. These four steps may occupy one or two minutes each, and when taken, the same process may be repeated several times, and the whole exercise taken two or three times every day.

Exercises in Concentration —All exercises in concentration for brain development should be deeply serene and well poised, but should also be very strong. Force and intensity, however, must not be permitted, because such actions are disturbing, and disturbed actions always prevent growth. But so long as the mind is well poised, the concentration may be very strong and persistent without producing any discord whatever. In all these exercises, we should remember that the object is to produce more cells, smaller cells and finer cells in that part of the brain through which the faculty of music functions; and this is accomplished when the concentration is full, strong, well poised, harmonious and subjective, so that the finer creative energies are supplied in abundance. When taking lessons in music, the pupil should, during practice, concentrate attention as much as possible upon both sides of the forehead as indicated in the Figure. This will not only develop the faculty of music itself, but will also increase the activity of that faculty at the time, which will mean that better results will be secured in the study of music, and each lesson mastered in less time.

Undivided Attention —When the mind is concentrated upon these regions of the brain while you are taking lessons in music, or performing in music, the quality of the music you produce will be far better, though it may be argued that such concentration will divide attention, and take the mind of from the music in a measure. But this is not the case. When you concentrate upon the music you are producing, you should aim to cause your mind to pass through that part of the brain, so to speak, that is employed by the musical faculty. This can be accomplished with a little practice; and in a very short time the one mode of concentration will keep your attention upon the music as well as causing the activity of your mind at the time to act directly upon the proper brain regions as you perform.

Continuous Improvement —The great value of this method is that it not only increases and improves results in the person, but also develops the musical talent itself, so that far greater results may positively be secured in the future. This will insure continuous improvement, and since the possibilities of every talent are unlimited, there is no end to what can be gained through that talent, provided the methods necessary to continuous development and improvement are constantly and faithfully applied.

Feeling in Music —To secure more feeling in your music give special attention to the development of the region of emotion as indicated in Figure III. And this is most important because the more real feeling you can give to your music, the deeper will be the impression produced by your music upon all minds that have the privilege to be present when you perform. For this reason every good musician must be highly developed in the realms of emotion, although in this connection it is necessary to cultivate a well-balanced and well poised mind, so that those emotions are always under control, and always full and harmoniously expressed.

Appreciation of the Classical —When the faculty of interior understanding as indicated in Figure III is well developed, you will be able to appreciate classical music. Classical music is, strictly speaking, metaphysical music, and therefore appeals only to those minds that have become conscious of the deeper and the higher realms of thought. This does not mean, however, that those who appreciate classical music will necessarily appreciate the philosophy of metaphysics, as metaphysics is very large, and gives room for a thousand phases, and ten times as many more combinations; but the fact is that classical music comes directly from the realms of superiority and worth, and is therefore appreciated only by those minds that are conscious in a measure of superiority and worth. Such music also awakens in the minds of those who respond a still finer consciousness of the real quality of all things. During a classical performance you invariably withdraw from the superficial side of existence, and dwell more or less in the great depths of mind and soul. And the more highly you are developed in the broader metaphysical consciousness, the more real enjoyment you will secure from classical music. It is therefore well for everybody to enlarge the faculty of interior understanding, and it is absolutely necessary for those who wish to produce classical music. In this connection we must emphasize the fact that no one can become a genius in music without developing most thoroughly the faculty of interior understanding. And for this reason all such methods as have been given in previous lessons for the development of this faculty should be studied and applied with the greatest of care. When we examine classical music, we find that much of it is incomplete, due to the fact that interior consciousness or consciousness of high worth was not in full activity in the mind of the composer during every moment while the production was penned. When the great musicians of today, however, begin to give attention to this matter, and secure a higher state of interior understanding, we shall have classical compositions that will be far superior to anything that the masters of the past have produced.

Consciousness of Harmony —One of the first essentials to higher musical development in the musical world is the consciousness of harmony. The musician should not only live in perfect harmony, but should constantly seek to attain a deeper and a deeper realization of the very principles of harmony. And this being true, we realize that every musician who permits a single feeling of discord in mind or body, places thereby an obstacle in his way both with regard to the expression of music and the further development of the musical faculty. All real music contains the life of harmony to a greater or lesser extent; but how much of this harmony it contains will depend both upon the composition and upon the performer. A performer, however, who has found the world of harmony will express that lofty state even though the music may be lacking in a measure in this respect. To become a great musician, the mind must master the very life of music. To do this, the consciousness of this life must be secured, and it may be secured through the realization of higher and higher states of harmony. We conclude therefore that it is absolutely necessary to be in harmony with one's self, with everything and with everybody if high musical development is to be attained.

Principle of Music —Closely connected with the attitude of harmony is the understanding of the inner principle of music itself, and this is a great essential. But as it is a very deep study, the average mind will necessarily be slow in grasping its full meaning and import. In this connection daily efforts in trying to consciously comprehend music itself will prove of great value. And as such meditations can be enjoyed during spare moments, the results desired can be realized without loss of time. Another essential along this same line is to try to key the mind to finer vibrations of thought, feeling and consciousness. To accomplish this, the study of the law of vibration will be necessary, because it is only when we know the scale of vibrations that we develop the consciousness of grade and qualities. It is an immense field, however, and interesting and fascinating beyond the expectations of the most imaginative. But to those who cannot give the subject thorough attention at present, very good results will be secured by trying to concentrate the actions of the mind upon the highest and the finest grades of thought and feeling that can possibly be imagined. Subjective consciousness will help greatly and the practice of transmuting the finer energies will help still more, so that by combining all these various methods, even though to a slight degree, the mind will soon be keyed to much higher grades of quality and action than before.

To Secure Quality —To dwell constantly in the attitude of superiority and worth is extremely important, because to become a genius quality must be considered; and to secure quality the mind must create only such thoughts as are patterned after that which has quality. It is therefore necessary to hold attention upon the superior side of life, and to live in such close touch with the world of real worth that you can actually feel the superior taking possession of your system. In furthering these efforts, no superficial, common or ordinary states of mind must be permitted. The mind must never dwell on the empty side or on the surface of things, but must be trained to move constantly towards the depths and the heights of the superior within. In addition, it will be necessary to do everything possible to develop a beautiful character and a complete mind of the highest order.

The Soul of Music —As stated before, it is the soul that should receive the first attention in musical development; and by the soul we not only mean the real you, the individuality, but also everything within you that pertains to the lofty, the beautiful and the sublime. All those things that emanate from the ideal side, the finer side, the transcendental side in your life belong to the soul, and these things will give soul to everything you do, provided they are permitted to be expressed. To come into perfect touch with this finer side or those loftier things that we feel at times but cannot define or describe, is the purpose we have in view. It is these things, when expressed, that give soul to music, and it is such music that carries the mind away upon the wings of sublime ecstasy. When we hear such music existence is transformed, life becomes a dream of eternal bliss, and we find ourselves in a higher, more perfect and more beautiful world than we have ever known before. When we soar to those heights we ask for nothing more than simply to live. And the reason why is simple. We have found real life, and whenever we find real life it is sufficient simply to live. When we return to this world again we sometimes wonder if our experience was a mere vision, but we soon conclude that it was real. It must have been real, because we have been changed. We have been immersed, so to speak, in the crystal wonders of real life, and we are decidedly different. Something has been added to our minds, to our feelings and to our thought; and that something keeps watch so that we can never again go down completely to where we were before. There are many ways through which the mind can be awakened to the beauty and the real worth of life, and music that has soul is one of the highest and one of the best of these ways. It is the one way that can touch the greatest number. Therefore, to be able to give soul to your music will not only enable you to become greater in your chosen vocation, but also enable you to become a greater power for good, the equal of which may not be found anywhere.

The Soul In All Things —There are reasons why the soul should be given first place in musical development, and those who will bear this in mind will find their future study of music to be far more successful than it has been in the past. But in order that we may bring ourselves into more perfect touch with this finer something that we speak of as the soul of music, it is necessary to recognize and understand the soul in all things. There is nothing that will aid us more in the beginning along this line than to live in perfect tune with nature, and to try to listen constantly to the music of the spheres. Those who try to learn the spirit of nature's physical forms are usually looked upon by the practical as mere visionaries of no real value to the world, but history proves the fact that the creations of such minds are immortal. It is from such minds that the world has received everything that is worthwhile. We may, therefore, listen to the music of the spheres as much as we like. We may try to live more closely, and ever more closely, to the great spirit of nature, for nothing but good can come from such efforts; and when we employ wisely the inspiration thus received we shall give to the world real life. We shall create something that will never die. We shall write our own names upon the eternal rock of time, and beneath those names nature shall write genius, the highest title she can give to man.

Inspired Music —All real music is in a sense inspired, as it comes into mind when we are on the verge of the cosmic or in touch with the great soul of things. In brief, it is when we hear the symphonies of the vastness of the cosmos that we produce real music. When we hear real music we know where it came from, and we know that it came from the soul that was on the heights. We all long for such music principally because too much of the music we hear is simply "put together." It may pass away time pleasantly, but it does not open the heavens before us, nor awaken the spirit of man. If you would compose real music, therefore, live constantly on the verge of the cosmic. Thus you may do consciously and perfectly what the great souls of the past have done only in part. And here we should remember that there is such a thing as being touched by the spirit. The experience is real. It indicates that your mind is open to revelations, to higher and finer worlds; and this is something that should be encouraged whenever possible, because it is the great secret, or the open way, so to speak, through which man receives everything that is lofty, marvelous, wonderful or sublime. We have not considered these things in the past; but we must consider them now if we would give soul to all our music, and develop our musical faculties to the very highest states of real genius. For here be it remembered that no music is true music unless it has soul.

Soul Expression —Another essential is soul expression, or rather the living of the life of music; that is, the giving of full expression to that finer, higher something that may be described as the music of human existence. The importance of this will be realized when we learn that the more soul we express in our living, the more soul we can give to whatever may be expressed through us either in our thought or in our work. To apply this idea the musician should aim to give soul to every note, and the more soul that is given to every note, the more rapidly will the superior musical faculty develop. The inner meaning of every tone should also be felt, and that feeling should be expressed through every vibration of the personality. Begin by attaining as high and as perfect a consciousness of soul as you possibly can, and aim to express that soul whenever you perform or practice. You will soon discover the real meaning of it all; and when you do, you will know how to express consciously and perfectly the soul of every tone. From that time on your music will begin to attain a quality it never had before. Your progress will be rapid both in your power to perform and in the development of your musical talent. You will not simply produce a succession of concordant sounds, .but will begin to produce real music; and it is such music that the world wants. Therefore, whoever can produce such music may look forward to a most brilliant future.

FIG. VII.

1. Expression 3. Imagination

2. Tone 4. Intellect

5. Memory

The Subconscious —To employ the best methods known for the training of the subconscious, will be found extremely valuable in musical development as well as in every other form of development. To awaken the great within, and to train the subconscious to respond perfectly to the directions of the conscious—this is one of the greatest secrets in the development of genius along any line. But before the increase of talent from within can be of real value, the brain and the mind must be made perfect channels of transmission and expression; and the soul must be called upon to give quality, superiority and high worth. Leading Essentials —It is therefore necessary to give justice to all the factors involved, and to give special attention to those things that we may lack the most. The methods given for brain development are of special value; and as no practical system for brain development has been presented before, thorough attention must be given to this matter at once. To place the mind in a perfect and harmonious condition is an absolute necessity, because discord cannot produce harmony; and in music especially, harmony is the great principle. The soul must receive special attention, though in the development of that quality called "soul" we shall find it necessary to depend largely upon individual soul consciousness. Since the soul is beyond tangible rules no regular system of rules and methods can be given in this respect. But those who aim to realize higher and higher states of soul consciousness will soon secure the results desired. In addition, we should employ all the helps that we can find from every source, and to employ all these things as thoroughly and as perfectly as we can, for it is in this way that we shall reach the high goal we have in view.

The Spirit of Genius —The most important of all is to train both mind and personality to give full right of way to the spirit of genius, and especially when using the musical faculty in actual performance. Do not try to play or sing. Instead let the spirit of genius play; and let this same spirit sing. How it feels to be touched by the spirit of genius no one can describe, nor is it necessary. Those who will apply this system of development will soon feel this spirit themselves. Then they will know at first hand. They will also know how to give way to the spirit of genius, and give expression more and more to the musical prodigy of the great within. Then remember that there is something wonderful slumbering within you. That something can make you great. That something can make you a prodigy. That something, when fully awakened and fully trained for tangible action, can make you even a greater genius than the world has ever known.

16. TALENT AND GENIUS IN ART

In every vocation possibilities are both great and numerous when genius and talent are employed, and since we all can improve ourselves indefinitely, the greater possibilities of life may be realized more and more by everybody. For this reason no one should think that he must remain in a small insignificant world all his life simply because he is living in such a world now. In every field of action opportunities in an ever increasing number are at hand always waiting and watching to be accepted.

The idea that opportunities come but once is an idea without any foundation whatever, because the fact is that the opportunities that come into your life never take their departure. They continue to remain in a sense until they are accepted when they become a part of the life that receives them. Another fact of equal value is this, that the more opportunities we take advantage of, the more new opportunities we shall meet. It is therefore detrimental to our own interest to keep a single opportunity waiting. And there are many most excellent opportunities waiting for us all this moment, no matter what or where we may be. We shall find this to be absolutely true, because the more familiar we become with the subject the more convinced we become that the opportunities in one field are neither greater nor more numerous than in any other field. Therefore there is, strictly speaking, opportunity for all everywhere.

At present there are few worlds that hold so many opportunities for genius and talent as the world of art. And the reason is that the present age is nearer to the ideal than any other age in history. Thousands of people have recently entered that finer state of consciousness where they can appreciate real art, so therefore the time is ripe for the real artist. When we speak of the real artist, however, we do not mean someone who can simply paint well. Thousands can do that who have not the slightest genius for art. Something more is required besides the ability to place pictures on canvas for the work of the real artist is alive. It has character and soul and is not only a living thing now, but is immortal.

Too much of the good art with which we are familiar has very little character. It may be correct from an artistic standpoint and it may be beautiful. It may also be true to life; that is, true to the life that it pictures, but it does not always inspire that finer, higher something that makes man feel that he is more than a mortal creature. This, however, real art can do and should do. But the artist himself must inwardly feel those higher qualities before he can express them in his pictures. In this connection we find that laxness whether in mind or character always appears in the product of the individual. When his genius lacks character his work also lacks character. His admirers may rave over his remarkable creations, but something is absent that ought to be there, and on account of that absence the creation fails in its real mission. This is also true in every other vocation. The mind that has both character and ability produces far greater and far more lasting results than the mind that has simply ability alone. It is therefore to everybody's advantage to develop character, no matter what their work may be, and this is especially true of the artist.

The work of the artist appeals to the finer elements in man, and when there is character combined with idealism in his work, the effect of his work will always be increased accordingly. Idealism without character has a tendency to produce idle

479

dreaming, aimless imagination and various forms of sentimentalism that frequently react into morbid moods of depression. But when idealism and character combine, a constructive process begins in the mind, a process with a sound substantial foundation, and a goal as high as perfection itself. For this reason it is highly important to awaken in the mind those elements that tend to combine idealism and character. And there is no one that can awaken those elements to a higher degree than the real artist. And therefore the artist has it in his power to render exceptional service to the human race.

To become a real artist there are a number of faculties and qualities that should be developed, though the three greatest essentials are soul, character and the proper development of the brain. The artistic talents employ several parts of the brain, the first of which is form, or that part of the brain that extends from the brain center to the region between the eyes. The second is construction, occupying the region between the temples. When form and construction are well developed, the faculty of drawing will appear, but if there are no other artistic faculties in evidence this power to draw well will be simply mechanical, and will be of service to those who are employed in mechanics or architecture. The third brain faculty is the perception of color, and is found in or about that region that occupies the outer half of the eyebrow. The fourth is the imaging faculty located directly above construction. And the fifth is the perception of the ideal, the sublime and the beautiful, located directly back of the imaging faculty. To determine the exact location of these faculties see Figure VIII.

To concentrate subjectively upon these various parts of the brain, for three minutes several times every day will, in a few months, begin to show decided results in the development of artistic talent, although these results will be greater when the process of concentration is carried on in the proper mental attitudes. To illustrate, we should aim to analyze and measure shape and form with the mental vision whenever we concentrate upon the region of form; that is, we should take the three dimensions, length, breadth and height and mentally combine them in every shape and form imaginable. This will develop the mental shape of form as well as that part of the brain through which the faculty of form functions. When concentrating upon the region of construction, a similar mental process should be employed though with this difference, that more attention should be given to the size, the form and the shape of the structure in building; that is, instead of simply combining dimensions in the mind, we should try to build up or actually construct according to our highest ideal of form and construction. The faculty of form conceives the exact form and shape of every individual part, while the faculty of construction tries to take all these various parts and build them up into some definite and ideal structure.

FIG. VIII.

1. Expression of Form 4. Imagination

2. Perception of Color 5. Perception of The Beautiful

When concentrating upon the faculty of color we should analyze with the mind all the colors that we know, and try to blend them mentally in every way imaginable. The mental experience that is enjoyed in connection with this practice is beautiful beyond description. During the practice color scenes and panoramas of color will frequently appear before the mental vision. And in many instances they will outrival in gorgeousness everything that the imagination has ever been able to picture. When concentrating upon the imaging faculty try to paint pictures in the mind. Proceed to paint imaginary pictures upon imaginary canvas, and try to make these pictures, not only original, but extraordinary. Do not copy in your imagination something that you have seen, but try to picture something that physical sight has never seen. This will not only develop the imaging faculty, but will also develop originality, which is the secret of greatness. When concentrating upon that faculty through which the beautiful is received, turn attention directly upon the ideal. Try to see and perceive the ideal of everything in your physical world as well as in your mental world. Think about the high, the lofty and the sublime, and try to actually enter into the world of sublimity and grandeur. Also awaken the life and power of aspiration, and try to gain the largest consciousness possible of everything that has real worth and high superiority.

In addition to the above faculties, we should also cultivate the faculties of love and emotion, because this will give sympathy, a quality that is absolutely necessary in all art. The real artist must be in sympathy with nature in general and with human nature in particular, though this sympathy should always seek the finer touch of the more beautiful side of everything. We should never sympathize with the undeveloped conditions of nature nor with the weakness of man; that is, we should not enter into mental contact with those things nor imitate mentally those conditions. Such a sympathy is always unhealthful; and unhealthful states of mind are not conducive to genius. It is not the shortcomings of nature nor the crude side of man that you are to love and admire, but it is the unbounded possibilities that we have the power to unfold and develop that we should select as our ideals, not only in art, but in living.

481

To understand the laws of harmony and gradation is indispensable to the artist. In addition to what is already being taught on these subjects in art schools, the development of mental harmony should be sought most earnestly. The real artist must convey the spirit of real harmony, and to give this quality to his art he must be conscious of the deeper harmonics of the soul. To this end, therefore, he should seek higher consciousness; that is, that consciousness which reveals the beauty, the serenity and the soul of all things. When a work of art has soul it will forever remain an inspiration, and that which inspires has the power to elevate man to higher states of living. In this connection we should remember that everything we see has a tendency to impress the mind. As these impressions are so are our thoughts, and as our thinking is so are we. Therefore, if we wish to become more than we are, and rise to the subconscious states of a better and a more beautiful life, we should surround ourselves as much as possible with those things that have the power to inspire; and there is nothing that will serve this purpose to a greater degree than works of art that have soul.

Whatever we may be doing, if we feel the soul at the time, we give soul to that which we do; and our work will therefore be classed with that which is superior. In the development of genius, however, many conclude that genius alone is sufficient to produce great ability and promote great achievements. But we have already discovered that this mysterious something that we call soul is just as necessary as genius itself, and in fact must be present before genius becomes real genius. Genius not only does its best work through the avenues of virtue, truth, lofty mindedness and high spiritual qualities, but what is more, genius cannot do itself justice unless those qualities are present to a very high degree. In other words, genius is not genius unless it has soul and character; for without soul and character, genius is but a cheap imitation of its great and wonderful self.

Another essential in the development of ability and genius in art, as well as in the development of all other forms of ability, is to educate the subconscious along proper lines. The subconscious can do anything if properly impressed. This is the law. Therefore the subconscious has the power to bring forth everything that is required for the faculties of art. From this statement we are not to conclude, however, that the direction of the subconscious is all that is necessary. To awaken the subconscious is one essential and an essential that is indispensable, but to train the objective and develop the brain so that the greater subconscious powers can find orderly expression are other essentials equally important. To impress the subconscious along artistic lines, realize clearly in mind what constitutes artistic talent; gain a perfect consciousness of art itself, and try to understand the artistic spirit. In other words, form definite ideas of art and of the art of which you wish to become a master. Then impress those ideas upon your subconscious mind many times every day, being convinced at the time that what you impress upon the subconscious the subconscious will later on express in your mind and faculties. What we give to the subconscious will be returned to us in thirty, sixty or an hundred fold. Therefore, we must impress upon the subconscious the real ideas of art; and when we do we shall receive that power and genius in return that will give us great and even extraordinary talents in the wonderful world of real art.

17. TALENT AND GENIUS IN LITERATURE

The faculties required for literary work depend largely upon the field selected although there are a few faculties that all writers need in common. These are expression, construction and a highly active imaginative intellect. Where there is a desire to write on metaphysical or psychological subjects, interior understanding should be developed in addition to the ones mentioned. And to write well on scientific and practical subjects a thorough development of application is required because this gives one ability to connect principles and laws with the practical world. It also gives system, method and the faculty of turning the abstract into actual use. To become a good writer of fiction, develop the faculties of expression, intellect, intuition, emotion and originality. To these should be added what might be called universal consciousness, or the power to sympathize and enter into harmony with all phases of life.

In this connection it is important to mention that there are several new fields—fields that hold excellent possibilities for those who will prepare themselves for such a work. Ordinary fiction pictures life as it is lived by human nature in its weakness. It is true to life as it is lived by those who really do not know how to live. Therefore, it is largely a picture of flaws, perversions and mistakes. People read such fiction usually for no other reason than to pass time or to be entertained, although a great deal of fiction is read through a morbid desire to devour what is hardly wholesome. It is therefore evident that very little good can come from the reading of ordinary fiction, and to be just to ourselves we cannot afford to do what does not bring good in some way. In addition to the usual fiction we have fiction that is out of the ordinary; that is, that constitutes superior and real literature. Such fiction is highly valuable for the richness of its language, and no one can read such fiction without being decidedly benefited along the lines of higher literature; but such fiction does not as a rule contain anything of direct value concerning the secret of life. Many will contend that it is not the purpose of fiction to teach anything. But the fact is that there is no class of literature that could teach the secrets of life in a more thorough and more convincing manner than fiction. Therefore, fiction that does not aim to be constructive as well as entertaining ignores its greatest opportunity.

To define the new fiction is hardly possible in a brief paragraph, but its object is to picture life as it might be lived by people who have mastered or are trying to master the secrets of life. In other words, it would not deal with ordinary people and their modes of living, but it would deal with the life and the conduct of such people as have taken it upon themselves to attain and achieve the greatest and the highest things that are possible in life. That such fiction could be made more interesting and more fascinating than anything that has ever appeared in print is evident, and if produced by a master mind would constitute a higher form of literature than has ever appeared in the world. The time is now ripe for such fiction, and to those who can produce it, fame and fortune in a large measure are surely in store.

To develop literary genius, the first essential is to develop those faculties of the brain and the mind that are required for such work. These faculties are indicated in Figure IX and full instruction as to their development has been presented in previous chapters. The second essential is to educate the subconscious along literary lines. This is extremely important, because there are few talents that respond as readily to subconscious training as the literary talent. Besides, it is in the subconscious alone that we can find real genius along any line. In the subconscious we find the limitless state of every faculty, talent or power; and we can steadily bring Into expression more and more of this capacity, as no limit has been found to its power or possibilities. The real secret of becoming a genius is to awaken and properly train the subconscious mind, though we must not forget that the objective mind and the physical brain must be cultivated in such a way that subconscious genius can find full expression. To bring out the literary genius that may be latent in the subconscious is a process that cannot be perfected in a few weeks, but those who have considerable literary talent may, in a few weeks, realize a remarkable improvement from the application of right methods; and if they will continue indefinitely in the application of these methods, continuous advancement will positively be the result.

Those who may not be talented along literary lines, but who desire to develop such talents, can make their desires true to a very great extent if they will persevere for a year or more in the application of the two essentials mentioned. In this connection it must be remembered that the subconscious contains all the talents in a potential state, and it is our privilege to choose which one we desire to express, develop and apply. If that talent is already expressing itself in a measure it will take less time to increase its subconscious power, but if time, perseverance and the right efforts are combined, any talent desired can be developed to a remarkable degree, whether we have much ability along that line or not at the present time.

The first step is to gain a clear mental conception of what you desire to develop; and this desire should be full and strong at all times, as the subconscious will never respond to half-hearted desires nor divided attentions. When the desired purpose has been clearly pictured in mind, the next essential is to impress this with deep feeling upon every thought. Every thought which has deep feeling enters the subconscious and carries into the subconscious the desire with which it was impressed. As previously stated, the subconscious must be expressed in the present tense; therefore, do not simply desire to become a genius, but desire to bring forth the genius that already exists in the depths of your mind. Never impress the subconscious with the idea that you hope to become this or that. On the contrary, live in the strong, deep conviction that you have those things now, and this is true. A genius is asleep in the subconscious of every mind, and the subconscious is a part of you. It belongs to you. Therefore, you possess now all that is in the subconscious. For this reason it is strictly scientific and absolutely correct to affirm positively that you now have, and that you now are, what you wish to possess or become.

Live in the conviction that you already are a literary genius. Know that it is true, and stamp that conviction upon every thought you think. If necessary use affirmations to establish that conviction. It is always well to use affirmations provided we feel the real truth that is contained in all such statements. These affirmations may be made at any time, but they should without fail be impressed upon the subconscious every night before going to sleep. Take fifteen or twenty minutes every night after you have retired, and impress deep, positive statements upon the subconscious, affirming such ideas as you wish the subconscious to perpetrate and develop. Then go to sleep with the conviction that you now are a literary genius. Statements like these may be employed: "I am a literary genius;" "I am a brilliant writer;" "I have strong, clear, lucid mind." "My literary ability is unbounded, and of the highest order;" "T am complete master of the richness of language;" "I have at my command innumerable ideas;" "I am original in thought and in expression;" "Well constructed expressions are always ready to flow through my mind;" "I am alive with my subject and can give it the fullest, the freest and the most perfect expression." Many other statements of a similar nature can be formulated and employed, though it is not well to use too many. The object is to carry into the depths of the subconscious the idea that there is genius within you, and that this genius is now ready to express itself in rare literary ability. While affirming these statements your attention should be concentrated upon the subconscious side of those parts of the brain that are employed in literary work. Then expect results now; and persevere until results do come, never permitting yourself to become discouraged in the least even though you have to work for months before you secure the desired subconscious response. Through perseverance and the right methods, results positively will come; and when they do come, you will be on the way to a development that will certainly mean much for the future.

CONCLUSION: VITAL ESSENTIALS IN BRAIN BUILDING

Moments of Tranquility —In all growth the passive is just as necessary as the active. Moments of action must invariably be followed by moments of repose, and the mode of repose should be selected with the same scientific care as the mode of action. To know how to properly apply a faculty is highly important when certain results are held in view, but it is equally important to know how to rest, relax and amuse that faculty in order to secure those same results. The reposeful attitudes accumulate; the active attitudes take up the new mental material thus secured, and proceed to build more largely. But the amount accumulated during any moment of repose is always larger when the mind expects accumulation during that moment.

When to he Still — Immediately following any form of positive action, physical or mental, the mind should be perfectly still for a few moments. Whether the action be actual work or simply exercise, the same rule should be observed. And also certain periods of tranquility should be taken at frequent intervals, varying from a few moments to a few days, depending upon the circumstances involved. The general purpose of such periods would be rest, recuperation and accumulation; and these are just as necessary to progress, growth or advancement as the periods of exercise, work and action. It is the moments of repose that give the moments of action the necessary material with which to work. This is a law that must receive constant and judicious attention wherever scientific attempts are made in the development of ability, talent and genius.

Relaxation —Any action of the mind tends to produce what may be termed the "keyed up" attitude, and this attitude is necessary to the highest state of efficiency. When you are "keyed up," all your faculties are at their best; they are fully aroused, thoroughly alive and are worked up to the most perfect point of practical ability. But when you are through with your work, the "keyed up" attitude should be discontinued for the time being. The majority, however, fail to do this; they sometimes continue in the "keyed up" attitude for hours after they have ceased to work; they even go to sleep in the same attitude, and then wonder why they do not sleep well, why they tire so easily or why their systems are almost constantly on the verge of breakdown. The attitude for work is for work only; when the work is done enter the attitude that is not for work; that is, relax, and give the system the needed opportunity to place itself in proper condition for the next day's work. To relax the system, breathe deeply, easily and quietly, and think of your thought as going towards the feet every time you exhale.

Restful Harmony —The attitude of restful harmony should be entered at frequent intervals every day. A moment or two in this attitude is often the means of doubling the working capacity of the mind for the next hour. The restful attitude accumulates energy, while the harmonious attitude tends to place this new energy in the proper position for efficient action. Harmony always tends to set things right; therefore, the value of combining the feeling of harmony with the attitude of rest, repose or relaxation is readily appreciated. A few moments of restful harmony are especially important immediately after some exercise in brain building or mental development.

Recreation —What kind of recreation to select depends entirely upon your work. The two should always be opposites in nature, tendency and effect. If you are engaged in heavy mental work, choose recreation and amusement that is light, bright and sprightly. But if your work requires but little mental energy, choose recreation that tends to arouse mental energy. A stirring drama would prove highly beneficial to a mind that had been practically a blank during the day; in fact, such recreation might in time arouse enough mental energy to take, him into some position where he could apply the full capacity of his mind. To a mind, however, that had been dealing all day with profound problems, a different form of amusement would be required. If you are stirred up continually by your work, do not select forms of recreation that have the same effect. Hundreds do this; they are in the midst of excitement all day in business; at night they choose some form of amusement that has the same exciting effect. In consequence, life is cut short a half a century or more too soon. Whether in amusement, entertainment, outdoor sports or reading for recreation, aim to select something that produces an effect directly opposite to that produced by your work. Through this practice you will do far better work, and you may add a quarter of a century or more to your life.

Diversion in Concentration —The actions of concentration will be thoroughly effective only when alternated with passive diversions. Concentrate regularly upon your leading purpose, and when you do concentrate, give the subject at hand your undivided attention; but have several interesting diversions to which you can give your passive attention at frequent intervals. To live exclusively for one thing is not to succeed in the largest sense of that term; nor can any mode of concentration produce the results desired unless it is placed at rest occasionally, and the actions of the mind turned, for the time being, in other directions. To cease action in a given line, it is necessary to promote action in a different line; therefore, diversions are necessary. And every action must cease at intervals in order to give that which is acted upon the opportunity to adjust itself to the results of that action.

Imagination in Repose —During moments of repose and relaxation the imagination should be directed to give its attention to that which is quiet and serene. When you are resting the mind, picture scenes of tranquility, and try to enter into that restfulness that such scenes will naturally suggest. The imaging faculty is never completely inactive. So long as you live you will think, and so long as you think you will imagine. Therefore, during serene moments, imagine the serene, and you will give perfect repose to your entire system. The power of the imagination is used extensively in the development of talent and ability; in fact, no development can possibly take place unless imagination is properly incorporated in the process. It is therefore evident that those moments of complete relaxation that should always follow every exercise for development must, to actually produce relaxation, direct the imagination to picture that which is in perfect repose. To relax mind and body is not possible so long as the imagination is picturing something that is not in repose.

Soul Serenity —This is that deeper feeling of calmness and peace that tends to tranquilize the finer forces and the undercurrents of the system. And this is very important, as it is this deep, interior state of poise that makes man a power. Soul serenity should be entered into several times every day; and the result will be that those mental forces that have been aroused through positive exercise in development will become more deeply established in the subconsciousness of the mind. That is, the result of every exercise will take root; it will find deep soil, and will live and grow as a permanent factor in the continual upbuilding of the mind.

Sleep —The mind should be deeply impressed, before going to sleep, with that degree of development that is desired; but before sleep is actually entered, every faculty should be placed in a state of perfect calm. To go to sleep properly is just as important in any form of mental development as any exercise we may take when awake for the promotion of that development. But all that is necessary in securing these results is to think deeply with a strong desire for the development we have in view, and calm the entire mind as we go to sleep. To accomplish this, simply relax, using the method for producing relaxation as stated above.

Recuperative Thinking —During moments of rest and repose, do not think of doing things, but think of enjoying things. The man who is always thinking of doing things may produce the quantity for a time, but the time will be short, and the quality will be absent entirely. The best results are always secured when thoughts of doing things are frequently alternated with thoughts of enjoying things. The simplest, the easiest and the quickest way to recuperate the mind is to think of enjoying things. A few moments of such thoughts are usually sufficient to restore full mental vigor; but those moments must be given over completely to thoughts of enjoyment; the doing of things must be wholly forgotten for the time being, and the mind must give its all to the pleasing picture it has elected to entertain.

Meditation —The practice of tranquil meditation is absolutely necessary in every form of mental development. It is a practice, however, that is rare, and this accounts for the fact that deep, profound, substantial minds are also rare. The many have not discovered the real riches of their own mental domains, and the reason is they have neglected meditation. The purpose of meditation is to "turn over" in the mind every idea that we know we possess. We thus gain new viewpoints, and, in turn, new ideas. Through meditation we become acquainted with the wonderful that is within us. We discover what we are, what we possess, and what we may attempt. When we meditate we take a peaceful tour of investigation through the many realms of our own mind; we are thus brought face to face with many things that are new, and the tour will prove both a recreation and an education. It is always a diversion, and it will never fail to entertain. Meditation will also properly place every new impression that has been received; thus it becomes a building process in the mind, and a factor of absolute necessity. To practice meditation regularly is to become more and more resourceful, because meditation invariably gives depth, to every phase of the mind. The mind that meditates frequently does not live simply on the surface anymore; such a mind is daily becoming enriched with the gold mines of the great within, and is gaining possession of larger and larger interior domains. In consequence it finds more and more upon which to draw, and it will never be at a loss, no matter what the needs or the circumstances may be.

Rest —To give any part of the system rest, we must withdraw attention from that part, and to withdraw attention from any special part we must give the whole of attention to some other part. When the mind needs rest, exercise the body. When the body needs rest, read something of real interest, or listen to soothing music, or think of something that takes attention away from physical existence. Give proper rest to the body, and you will never lose your vitality, your virility or your vigor. Give proper rest to the brain and the mind, and you will never lose your brilliancy no matter how long you may live. But real rest for any special part is not secured by simply trying to cease action. You cease action in one part by becoming vitally interested in some other part. People wear out simply because they do not know how to rest. They are partly active in every part of the system continually. By becoming wholly active in a certain part, you become wholly inactive in all the other parts; and the inactive parts are perfectly rested. Then change about, regularly, giving each part of the system perfect rest for some moments several times every day. This is the art of resting; and he who rests well will work well and live well; he will also live long and do much that is truly worthwhile.

THE END.

BOOK SEVEN

CONCENTRATION

1. THE ART OF CONCENTRATION

THE art of concentration is one of the simplest to learn, and one of the greatest when mastered; and these pages are written especially for those who wish to learn how to master this fine art in all of its aspects; who wish to develop the power to concentrate well at any time and for any purpose; who wish to make real concentration a permanent acquisition of the mind.

Whatever your work or your purpose may be, a good concentration is indispensable. It is necessary to apply, upon the object or subject at hand, the full power of thought and talent if you are to secure, with a certainty, the results you desire, or win the one thing you have in view. But the art of concentration is not only a leading factor in the fields of achievement and realization; it is also a leading factor in another field — a field of untold possibility.

The exceptional value of concentration is recognized universally; and still there are comparatively few that really know how to concentrate. Some of these have a natural aptitude for concentrated thought and action, while others have improved themselves remarkably in this direction, due to increased knowledge on the subject; but as yet the psychology of concentration is not understood generally; and that is why the majority have not developed this great art, although they are deeply desirous of doing so.

When we do not know how to proceed, we either hesitate or proceed in a bungling fashion; or, we may proceed under the guidance of a number of misleading beliefs. And in connection with concentration there are several ideas and beliefs that have interfered greatly with the development of this art. In fact, methods have been given out, and published broadcast, that are supposed to develop concentration, but that produce the very opposite effect. These things, however, clear up when we learn the psychology of the subject.

Among these misleading beliefs we find one of the most prevalent to be that we must, in order to concentrate well, become oblivious to everything but the one thing before attention now; but the fact is that when we become oblivious to our surroundings we do not concentrate at all; we have simply buried ourselves in abstraction, which is the reverse of concentration. The mind is highly active and thoroughly alive when we concentrate perfectly; and sufficiently alive and keen to be aware of everything in the mind and all about the mind, although giving first thought and attention to the work in hand.

Another belief is this, that we must use great force in the mind in order to concentrate well; that is, we must literally compel the mind to fix attention upon the object or subject before it; but here we must note that forced action, although seemingly effective for a while, is detrimental in the long run. This is true of the body as well as of the mind, so that we must find a better method. However, when we learn the real secret of concentration we find that no special effort is required; there is neither mental strain nor hard work connected with the process; the mind becomes well poised and serene; and, in that attitude, full power and capacity is applied where attention is directed. The mind that concentrates well does not work in the commonplace sense of that term; wear and tear have been eliminated; there is no strenuous action; there is no desire to force or drive things through; and no tendency whatever towards the high strung or keyed up condition. On the contrary, all action is smooth, orderly, easy and harmonious; and work has become a keen pleasure. This we can fully appreciate when we learn that, in real concentration, the mind has gained that peculiar faculty through which it can at will open all the avenues of energy in such a way that all those energies flow into one stream; and that stream flows into the one place where work is going on now. Therefore, it is not a matter of main force, but a matter of knowledge; knowing how and where to open the gates of energy in the mental world. When we study the psychology of concentration, we find that most of our previous beliefs on the subject will have to be discarded. They have only acted as obstacles; and as those obstacles have prevented the development of real concentration, another obstacle has arisen in nearly every mind — that of adverse suggestion — the most detrimental of all. Briefly, the majority, feeling the lack of concentration, continue to think and speak of this factor as weak. They continue to suggest to themselves, ignorantly and unintentionally, that they are very poor in concentration; and therefore they hold this factor down in a perpetual state of weakness. No mental faculty or power can develop to any extent so long as we think or speak of that faculty as weak or inferior. Adverse suggestion acts as a blight, and must not be permitted under any circumstance. We should think as little as possible about our weak points. When we know that we have a certain weakness, we need not speak of it further. To dwell mentally upon weakness is to live mentally in weakness; and they who live mentally in weakness cannot develop strength. Therefore, we will not think or say,* again and again, that we are unable to concentrate, or that we are weak or inferior in any respect whatever. We will eliminate all manner of adverse suggestion. We will think and say that we can. We will not complain that we concentrate poorly, but we will proceed to train ourselves to concentrate wonderfully.

2. PRINCIPLES OF CONCENTRATION

CONCENTRATION in general may be defined as an active state of mind wherein the whole of attention, with all available energy and talent, is being applied upon the one thing that we are doing now. We concentrate in the full meaning of the term when we give ourselves completely to the thought or the action of the present moment; and this is true whether we work with muscle, brain or mind, or express ourselves through thoughts, 1 words or emotion.

The principle of concentration is to do one thing at a time, and to do that one thing with all the talent and power we possess. We literally turn on the full current of mental and personal energy — not only the full current of what we may feel on the surface of thought — but all that we can arouse in deeper consciousness, and bring forth from the greater self within. It is a leading purpose in concentration to lay hold upon deeper and greater possibility; for we are not giving our whole best self to the work in hand unless we apply all the life, energy and talent that we can through super-effort awaken and develop now.

How this may be accomplished we will understand clearly as we proceed with our analysis of the many phases of the subject; and we will discover that the power to concentrate well means vastly more and involves vastly more than most minds ever imagined. Although the general purpose of this art is to give undivided attention to the work in hand, the development of that purpose will presently lead us beyond this point, and we will enter a new field; we will discover in concentration a new power and a marvelous possibility.

There are many things that we may expect to accomplish through concentration; and in order that we may become familiar with this art from every aspect — which is necessary to its highest development— we will consider briefly the most important of these accomplishments. First of all we gain the power to hold attention upon any object or subject for a sufficient length of time to complete the work in hand, and the power to do this at any time and under any circumstances. This is vitally important as we all meet distractions at every turn, and must learn to give our work undivided attention whatever our surroundings may be.

When we concentrate well we may, at will, cause all the available energies of mind and personality to work together, with full capacity, upon the work in hand. This will increase remarkably the working capacity and the dependable endurance of both mind and body, and will mean a high degree of mental mastery. To be able to master the elements and energies of the mind sufficiently to bring them all together to work together anywhere any time— this is an advantage for which we would pay almost any price; but it comes as a natural emolument with the development of concentration.

We all appreciate the value of speed, and especially among the thinking processes of the mind. The mind that moves slowly is never brilliant; while the mind that can think and act with lightning rapidity is on the verge of attaining genius; and may reach the goal of genius in this way if depth and range are combined with the element of speed. It is not possible, however, to produce mental speed through forced action; it comes naturally through concentration; and it will mean more work and better work; more perfect plans and more brilliant ideas — a combination that will go very far towards the high goal we have in view.

You are equal to any occasion when the whole of your mind is called into action; and this very thing concentration has the power to do. More than that, the whole of the mind will be called to higher ground, thereby working itself out of mediocrity and restricted channels, and gradually developing itself into that wonder state where everything seems possible. Real concentration can lead the way; the whole mind will follow; and concentration invariably leads into worlds of greater results. When we concentrate well we exercise a peculiar influence over the whole mind; we create, in every part of the mind, an irresistible desire to go to work; and we inspire every element of the mind with a definite ambition to excel.

The act of concentration tends not only to apply effectively all available energy of mind and personality; but tends also to draw forth latent energies. The fact is that real concentration becomes in the mind a remarkable force of attraction — attracting to itself unused and latent energies from all sources in the mental world. That is one reason why the mind that concentrates well becomes so powerful, and why such a mind will invariably forge ahead, regardless of what the obstacles or difficulties may be. It is now a known fact that the subconscious supply of latent energy is enormous; and as concentration tends to attract latent energy from all sources, we perceive here possibilities that assume tremendous proportions. Concentrated action will grow into greater action, and upon the principle that "much gathers more"; "nothing succeeds like success "; "make expert use of what you have and Nature will bountifully increase your supply." All things in life flow into the main stream — because the main stream is going somewhere — concentrating its movements upon a definite goal.

Concentrate the mind upon any problem, and if you concentrate wonderfully well, you will find the solution. The solution of any problem is locked up in that problem; and concentration is the key. The psychology of this involves a most fascinating study; but sufficient in this stage of our study to know that these things can be done. The same is true of any subject, situation or circumstance. You can, through concentration, find the main points or the inside facts of any subject or situation that you may consider. Real concentration has the power to break through the shell; to get beneath the surface; to get in behind the scenes; to enter into the very life of the thing, and thus get hold of bed-rock information.

These things we may accomplish through concentration; and there is good reason therefore why it has always been looked upon as the master art; but there is one thing more, the greatest of them all. Mental action, when perfectly concentrated, tends to go farther and farther into the life, substance or principle that is acted upon at the time. Concentration develops a penetrating tendency — a tendency to lead the mind out of the usual and on into the unknown. Concentration forges ahead. It goes straight on. It does not tarry with known facts. It goes farther. It sets out upon a journey; and such a journey will invariably prove a journey of discovery. The mind will find and enter new fields of thought. New laws and principles will be discovered. A new region of possibility will open before the mind, and long sought secrets may come to light. Positively, we can, through a highly developed concentration, cause Nature to give up her secrets, and cause the mysteries of Life to be revealed.

3. DEVELOPING INTEREST

WHEN we realize what may be accomplished through concentration, we shall make every conceivable effort to develop this master art; and our persistence, determination and enthusiasm will know neither pause nor measure; we will purpose positively to learn how to concentrate, and therefore will want to know how to proceed — what principles to adopt and what methods to apply.

When we examine the psychology of concentration, we find that it is based upon mental actions that are deeply interested in a certain subject or object; that is, we concentrate naturally and without effort whenever or wherever we are vitally interested. This then is the first principle. Be really interested in that to which you are to address yourself, and you will give it your undivided attention.

The problem, however, is how to become really interested in subjects or objects that do not, on their own account, attract our attention; or that do not, on the surface, appeal to us in the least. This is the first and possibly the greatest obstacle we have to meet in the development of concentration; but the solution is very simple; and we proceed upon the fact that everything is interesting from a certain point of view — that everything can attract our attention if permitted to reveal its chief attraction.

To the superficial mind many things may seem useless or uninteresting; but not so to the mind that has learned to think. It is only on the surface, or from a commonplace viewpoint, that most things may seem unworthy of passing notice; and it is only when looked upon through the eyes of prejudice or ignorance that our associations may repel or produce indifference, or that life and its work may offer slight appeal. The situation changes entirely when we see things as they are; and especially when we seek for the deeper cause of every condition, and discover the greater possibilities that are awaiting back of the scenes everywhere.

The most commonplace object in existence, such as a simple rock or a turf, becomes a wonder-world when examined scientifically; and the ordinary duties of life, if examined from all points of view, will reveal opportunities and possibilities that will positively startle the mind. It is certainly true that everything is interesting from a certain point of view, and we may multiply illustrations indefinitely. The universe in all of its realities; life in all of its manifestations; and existence in all of its actions and changes — these things, when looked into, with eyes that see, will prove interesting to a wonderful degree, and frequently fascinating to an amazing degree.

Understanding this aspect of the subject, which is the all important aspect, we may make the following proposition: We concentrate naturally and perfectly when we are vitally interested. Everything is, in its chief attraction, extremely interesting. Therefore, we may, by seeking the chief attraction in everything, concentrate naturally and perfectly anywhere any time. This is simple and conclusive, provided we find the chief attraction; but here we meet another problem. We may grant that everything is interesting from a certain point of view, but is it possible to find that interesting viewpoint anywhere and on short notice?

It is true that we can, in due time, find elements of real interest anywhere — of sufficient interest to attract our undivided attention; but we may not always do so at the moment; therefore we have another problem to solve; and again, the solution is simple — within easy reach of anyone who will try. It is only necessary at first to proceed upon the conviction that everything is interesting from certain points of view; and to drill that fact into the mind with positive action and depth of thought. A situation will arise that can solve this other problem absolutely.

When you convince the mind that everything is interesting from a certain point of view, you establish, in the subconscious, a natural tendency to be on the alert for this interesting viewpoint. Your mind will, unconsciously and unfailingly, look for the interesting element in everything you meet in life, or that you may take up for consideration. And when the mind is on the alert, and keenly looking for the interesting element, the mind is really interested in that subject or object. Vital interest in the situation has sprung up subconsciously, without your making the least effort to become interested. So there you have the first and most vital essential for concentration.

The importance of this principle is so great, and the methods connected with it are so effective, that we should emphasize and reemphasize these things in our minds in every way conceivable. We should think on these things repeatedly; dwell upon this situation with the utmost of faith and confidence; and give special time and thought to the facts involved. There is a tendency in nearly every mind to take natural interest in a few things only; to work and act largely in grooves, and to think of things in the most general and superficial fashion. But real concentration is out of the question in such a state of mind; that is why special attention should be given to the facts under consideration, so that the tendency of indifference may be supplanted by one of whole-hearted interest.

In practical life this is how the plan will work. You are called upon to give attention to something you do not understand, or something that does not appeal to you in the least. You are not interested, and therefore you cannot, at the moment, concentrate properly, or give the matter undivided attention. But you remember the great fact noted in this study, that everything is interesting from a certain point of view. Instantly you become curious to know what the interesting element in the matter in hand might be. You have made your own mind curious; and a curious mind is on the verge of becoming an interested mind.

If this be your first attempt in the application of this method, nothing more than a mild interest may arise; and even that might aid you decidedly at the time; but suppose you make use of this method many times every day for weeks and months. Suppose you make it a part of your daily work to impress upon your mind, again and again, the fact that everything is interesting from a certain point of view. The subconscious will soon receive these impressions and make that fact its very own. Then suppose you are called upon to consider a subject towards which you have been wholly indifferent. But the subconscious has been advised that there are elements of interest everywhere, and the subconscious never forgets what it has once really learned. Accordingly, the mind will be prompted, by powerful impulses from within, to seek the interesting elements in the subject before you; and, before you are hardly aware of the fact, this subject has become interesting and attractive. Suddenly, a keen desire has come over you to look into this subject thoroughly. You want to know. You are vitally interested. You are giving the matter undivided attention. You are concentrating perfectly in that direction.

When it becomes a part of your mind to know and feel that there are interesting elements in everything, and that everything, when looked upon with eyes that see, becomes a wonder-world, you develop a permanent faculty for looking into the vital elements in all things. You are interested, deeply and permanently, in the workings and possibilities of all aspects of life; you are wonderfully attracted to the real and the true everywhere; and therefore you will instantly, and without effort, give your whole attention to anything that you may meet, or that you are called upon to consider. Wherever you think and act, you do so with your whole mind; you concentrate perfectly, not because you are trying to do so, but because you have developed that something in yourself that produces perfect concentration.

4. METTING EVERYTHING WITH CURIOSITY

TO develop this idea farther, and secure all possible results, we should make it one of the permanent rules of life to meet everything with the desire to discover its real worth and chief points of interest; and whether the element of interest be found or not, the act of looking for that element will create interest in the mind, thereby producing a certain degree of concentration. Whether we meet the commonplace or the exceptional, this rule should be rigidly observed; and whenever we have moments to spare we should apply the rule definitely to any subject or object at hand, so that the mind may develop a permanent and a powerful tendency in that direction. To illustrate, we may take an ordinary looking rock and ask ourselves what there is about this rock in which we may become interested. We would ask what this rock is composed of, how many elements it may contain, how they combine, how they are attracted to each other and how they happen to hold together. We might proceed asking questions, and we would find that we could ask anywhere from fifty to one hundred very interesting and most scientific questions about this very ordinary looking rock; and every one of those questions would arouse the deepest interest in the mind because they would be questions that would involve some of the greatest principles in science.

The same method may be applied in connection with any object or any subject we may wish to consider; and in every instance we shall be surprised to find how many points of interest will come forth to attract and even amaze the mind. The truth is, that if we are wide awake to the meaning and purpose of everything in existence, we shall not find anything to be commonplace or uninteresting. What appears to be uninteresting appears so simply because we have not taken the time to make an intelligent examination. The moment, however, that we really examine the thing itself, and look into its elements, its nature, its qualities, its powers, its possibilities and its very soul, we shall find so much that is interesting that we might occupy the mind for days, weeks and months in a deeper and further examination.

We shall find nothing to be of greater value as a daily practice than to take up objects or subjects, in which we are not actually interested, and direct the mind to look for interesting viewpoints, elements or factors in connection with those objects or subjects. We shall be richly rewarded, because we will not only find much that is interesting, but we will, through this practice, train the mind to look naturally for that which is of interest everywhere; and we know that there is nothing that adds so much to our fund of knowledge as the happy faculty of being able to look for facts, or for the truth everywhere; and the same faculty tends to develop, not only intellect, but all the finer mental faculties as well.

This practice will produce a permanent tendency in the mind to look for the interesting in connection with everything that we may see, or hear, or think about; and this tendency will expand and develop the mind, and place us in a position to secure direct or first-hand information from every experience and from every object or subject that we meet on the way. More than this, the same tendency will develop in the mind the faculty of searching for the chief essentials, or the real thing, that invariably exists in the actual life or soul of that with which we come in contact; and it is hardly possible to over-estimate the value of such a faculty, knowing as we do that the average mind skims over the surface continually, and seldom, if ever, discovers the real, vital principle involved anywhere. When we develop the faculty of finding the real thing, the real truth, the real principle, the real power, the real factors that exist in everything we meet in life, we have gained immensely. Whenever we meet what does not seem interesting, we should proceed at once to examine that particular thing with a view of finding something of interest; and we will find it. And when we have work that does not seem interesting — work upon which we must concentrate in order to do it well — we should take up such work in the same attitude; that is, we should inquire deeply and scientifically as to what there is about such work that is in reality interesting. This question coming up, will cause the mind to become interested; and at once concentration will begin. And as we continue this practice, the tendency to look for the interesting everywhere will become second nature; that is, concentration will have become a permanent power in the mind, and will act thoroughly and effectively of itself, wherever the mind may proceed to act. The rule is simple: Look for the interesting, and the mind becomes interested; and wherever the mind is interested, there you concentrate naturally and effectively; provided, of course, that you subconsciously feel that there are ; interesting elements in everything; and, provided further, that your mind is keenly alive with the desire to know, to achieve, to excel.

5. CONTROLING THE ACTIONS OF THE MIND

A MOST important essential in the development of concentration is to learn to control the actions of the mind — all the leading actions, both objective and subjective; and although this may seem to be a difficult undertaking, it is really quite simple, for in fact we exercise this power almost hourly to some degree. We all have experienced moments when the forces of the mind seemed to be under perfect control — when it seemed as if we could know those forces, in any mode or manner desired, just as we move our hands or feet. And when we analyze our states of mind during such moments, we find that we are in deeper or closer touch with the finer forces of mind and personality — that is the secret. To acquire the art of entering into this closer touch therefore must be our purpose; and to begin, it is deeper feeling that prepares the way for that desired state of mind.

Whenever we proceed to concentrate, we should try and deepen the feeling of all thought and all mental action; in fact, we should try and feel so deeply about everything that we think or do that the mind actually enters into the very spirit of the process; that is, into the undercurrents of mental life, those finer currents that determine results in everything that is being done. We may, when concentrating in a superficial manner, secure some slight results temporarily, but it is those deeper, finer, more penetrating currents that produce real results, and that alone have the capacity to produce extraordinary results. Besides, it is the consciousness of those finer currents that gives the mind the power to exercise complete control over all the actions and forces of the mental / world — an attainment that is most important in the development of concentration.

You may find it a problem at times to enter into this state of deeper feeling; but you can, by giving special attention to the principle, master this situation absolutely; and the secret will be found in comparing the two ways of listening to music. When you listen to music and remain in a superficial state, you are simply aware of pleasing sound, but nothing more. However, if you are in a deeper state of mind at the time, wherein you can appreciate the very soul of music, you will not simply hear pleasing sound, but infinitely more. Every tone of that music will actually thrill the atoms of your being, and arouse feelings in mind and soul that are so deep, so lofty and so beautiful that you could not possibly describe them. Briefly stated, your entire being would be alive with the deepest and finest and most sacred emotions, and the experience would be such that its effect would remain with you for weeks, months and possibly years.

This illustrates what happens when we meet experiences, or anything in life, in the attitude of deeper and finer states of mind. At such times we do not simply discern the surface of things, or come in mental contact merely with the outer meaning; we actually discern the very life of things, and come in mental contact with the very kingdom of the soul. We find that we invariably enter into this deeper feeling when we try to live every act, thought or experience that may appear in our world; and the reason why is found in the fact that whenever we try to live anything, we enter into the very life of that particular thing. To develop the tendency to enter the deeper states of the mind, we should work in harmony with a leading law in the mental world; that is, the peculiar proneness of the mind to produce within itself any state, condition or tendency that we continue to desire with persistence and sincerity, fit is the truth that your mind will do anything for you if you really want it done.

When we make it our purpose to enter into deeper states of feeling in connection with every thought and action, the mind will soon develop a tendency that will invariably take all mental action into deeper states of feeling. To encourage the mind in this connection, we shall find it a most excellent practice, whenever we hear good music, to look for the soul of music, to try and feel the finer touch of the real life of music, and to try to appreciate the most delicate harmonies that exist in the very spirit of music itself.

We shall find it an excellent practice to apply the same principle in connection with anything that is beautiful, or anything that may appeal to the mind as being worthy of our deepest and highest attention; and in fact, whatever we may be thinking about, we should try and enter into the very soul of the thought or the theme. In this manner, we will develop a natural desire to seek for the real, to enter into the depths of life, thought and feeling; and gradually consciousness will deepen all of its activities until we find we can feel more deeply in every thought or experience; and we shall also find that the conscious domain has been increased remarkably.

We shall find it profitable to apply the same principle to every aspect of physical sensation, and to every experience of the sense life. If we make it our aim, not to be satisfied with the grosser side of physical sensation, but try to discern and feel the finer elements that are invariably expressed through all forms of sensation, we shall not only find every sensation more delightful than before, but also that it has been lifted to a higher plane — that grossness and crudeness have disappeared, and that the physical body, as a whole, has become more refined in every form and manner. These exercises and experiences will tend directly to prepare the way for the development of those states of mind that we must possess in order to enter into this closer and finer touch with the higher and finer forces of the mind — a most important essential in the art of controlling all the actions of the mind; for we know that when we have gained perfect control over all the actions of the mind, then we shall be able to concentrate all the energy we possess upon any object or subject we may have in view.

The purpose must be to live beneath the surface; to make the great within our chief realm of life and concern. We may act upon and with the external aspects of life; but we must make the deeper fields of thought our real place of business. For surely if we would master the deeper forces of life, we must live and think where those forces arise and develop. This, therefore, is a matter of imperative importance.

6. WILL POWER

AN indispensable element is that of a good strong will; and the use of the will in connection with concentration may be illustrated variously; but we will first examine the effect of will power, correctly applied, in the process of thought creation. To illustrate, we will suppose that you have several facts concerning a proposed invention, but have not as yet succeeded in bringing those facts together in the combination required for the perfecting of that invention. If you understand the use of the will, you will apply will power upon that group of facts, knowing that you thereby increase mental activity in that particular part of the mind; and wherever mental activity is increased, there the creative process is intensified and expressed to a higher and more perfect degree. The fact is this, that whenever an idea may seem indistinct, although you know you have all the elements required, the reason is that the mind is not sufficiently active in connection with the creative process that is working to perfect that idea. The use of the will, however, will not only increase activity throughout this creative process, but will also make concentration more perfect, because the power of will, when applied in connection with concentration, increases invariably both the power and the capacity of the force of concentration.

You will find it possible to perfect almost any idea you have in mind, if you can bring to bear upon that idea all the available energy existing in your mind; and this may be accomplished through concentration, provided concentration is deeply expressed, and in a positive manner — results we may secure through the full action of the will. For when we fully apply the will, we increase power and activity. We intensify the process involved; and there is nothing that tends more directly to increase the power of concentration than the act of increasing the rapidity of action wherever con- \ centration may be taking place.

We all appreciate the value of brilliant ideas; and most minds are in a position to create brilliant ideas at frequent intervals, but as a rule they merely come up to the point of creating a brilliant idea; they do not quite reach the point itself. The reason is that they have not the power to bring together all the elements required for this new idea; and this power is lacking because the will is weak and concentration undeveloped. The same is true regarding the perfecting of plans or methods. We may have the essentials, or all the factors required, but we may not always have the power to bring them together to a focus, where the required combination can be brought about so as to evolve the idea or plan we desire. The use of the will, however, in this connection will produce remarkable results. The will always intensifies any mental process, and thereby tends to bring to a climax any creative process that may be going on in the mind. The creation of rich and valuable thought may be furthered in the same manner, because such thought is almost invariably the result of the bringing together, in the proper combination, of the best impressions that may have come into the mind through our own study or experience.

Regarding the psychological use of the power of thought, we shall find the same principle of exceptional value, because whenever we use the power of thought, whether for the overcoming of physical ailments, for the elimination of adverse mental states, or for the building up of character or mental faculties — wherever we may apply the power of thought — a perfect concentration is indispensable; and the use of the will in connection with concentration invariably tends to increase both the force and the capacity of the process. In fact, we never can concentrate with all that we are unless we express through concentration, the full power of the will. To express the full power of the will, however, every action of the will must be positive, and the will must act subjectively; that is, it must act through the undercurrents, or through the attitude of finer feeling—the importance of which we have previously considered. We understand therefore that if we would learn to concentrate well we must also acquire a thorough knowledge of the will, and develop the will to the highest possible degree.

7. PERSISTENT DESIRE

THE power of persistent desire is invaluable wherever increased results are wanted; and therefore the full force of desire must invariably combine with concentration. When we desire persistently the object in view, we become deeply interested in that object and we cause the whole mind to work for its realization. Besides, the element of desire will instill a something into concentration that is really alive. It will eliminate the tendency to make mental or personal actions mechanical or forced, and will give to every action that vital spark that means so much. The force of desire will also deepen and expand every mental process involved — a situation that may, at times, become the opening way to remarkable results.

To concentrate successfully we must direct and focalize all the creative energies of the mind upon the object of concentration; but these energies must first be aroused; and here is where real desire becomes invaluable. Wherever we turn on the full current of persistent desire, every energy and force in the mind becomes alive, and may be enlisted for good work in any place where the power of concentration has been directed. We find therefore that the force of desire becomes a direct and powerful aid to concentration in two distinct particulars; first, by creating wide-awake interest all through the mind — by causing the mind to become vitally interested in the goal in view; and second, by arousing, or making alive, the latent or dormant energies of the mind, thereby providing the process of concentration with a vast amount of additional power.

All of this we understand perfectly; and the more we investigate the psychology of the process, the more reasons we find why we always get what we want when we want it "real bad." The secret then is to want what you\ want with all the life and power there is in you. We can reach any goal, or realize any ideal when we concentrate perfectly, and with the full force of a perfect concentration; and persistent desire proceeds to give concentration more and more of the two chief essentials; that is, deeper mental interest and greater mental power.

In this connection inquiry may arise as to the best methods for creating this deeper and more persistent desire, especially where we may not be personally interested in the final results; but here we should remember that we always gain personally from anything that is done right. If we develop greater Oriental power through the use of any psychological law, we gain to that extent, even though the greater portion of the tangible results may, in this instance, go elsewhere. The future is long; every form of gain will come to each one of us in due time — in a very short time if we take advantage of every opportunity to increase our own capacity and power. We should therefore be interested, personally, in the best and most thorough use of every psychological law we may have the privilege to employ.

Realizing this fact, we will want to desire success, the greatest possible success, for every enterprise with which we may be connected. Such a desire will improve remarkably, not only our own concentration, but also all other powers and talents we may possess. Our own gain therefore will be strictly personal, and most direct; and although tangible gain may not come at once, it positively will come in the near future. The future is both larger and richer for those who improve themselves in the present; and greater opportunities are waiting everywhere for greater minds; but improvements must be genuine, not merely superficial.

To increase the power of desire we should deepen and intensify all such desire in every form and manner, realizing the fact that the more the mind acts in a certain direction the greater becomes its power to act still more in the same direction. The force of desire therefore may through this simple rule become immense. And the more we increase the force of desire the more we increase results in every field of thought or action. Furthermore, we may cause the forces of concentration and desire to act and react upon each other to great advantage; that is, the more we concentrate for the increase of desire — worthwhile desire — the more powerful and persistent will such desire become; and the more deeply we desire the power to concentrate well — wonderfully well — the more life, energy and action we express in the building of real concentration.

8. IMAGINATION

THE greatest faculty of all is that of imagination; but it is the least understood, due principally to the fact that most minds have remained in grooves of thought, and therefore have not given extensive attention to their own creative possibilities, the richest and most numerous of which exist in the fields of imagination. In the development of any power or talent, however, these creative possibilities must receive direct and scientific attention; and this is especially true with regard to the power of concentration. Besides, some of the functions of concentration are so closely related to those of imagination as to seem almost identical. When you employ the faculty of imagination, one of your chief objects is to bring together ideas or mental images with a view of creating some new or greater idea; and in concentration this bringing together " tendency — this uniting the many in one, is the leading object in view. It is clearly evident therefore that a better training of imagination will largely increase the power of concentration.

When you employ the faculty of imagination, you also tend to bring together the many creative energies of the mind, combining those energies in the one process to which you are giving attention at the time. A highly developed faculty of imagination therefore naturally becomes an invaluable aid to the power of concentration; and when we understand how concentration can, by working with imagination, bring together, into one powerful line of mental action, all the best ideas of the mind and all available creative energy, we know why we usually find an excellent imagination wherever we find a remarkable concentration.

Analyzing the subject farther, we find that a vivid, well-trained imagination tends to " light up " the entire mental world; or, in other words, to make everything in the mind more clear. The result is, that the idea or object upon which we concentrate becomes more distinct; and accordingly, we not only concentrate better, but the entire mind becomes interested in this idea on account of its vividness and distinctiveness. Thus we call into action the many aspects of mental attention, an action that increases directly and instantaneously the power of concentration. We all know through experience how much better we can think when the ideas with which we are dealing are vivid, or stand out clearly in the mind; and also how much better we can concentrate when we have a distinct mental picture of the object in view. And imagination, if well trained and scientifically applied, will invariably turn the light upon any idea that we may call up for examination or further development.

When imagination is vivid, every mental process will be literally filled and surrounded with light; and we all can appreciate what an immense advantage this will be in the practical application of concentration. To illustrate, we will call imagination into action wherever we wish to concentrate, and immediately that place or process in the mind will become so vivid, and stand out so clearly, that all our faculties will become interested. The entire mind will turn its attention towards the point of concentration; and in a moment the entire mind will concentrate. And when we have the whole mind working for the object in view, the results desired will positively be realized.

As a practical suggestion we should, whenever we begin to concentrate, proceed to imagine all the forces of the mind coming to a focus at the point of concentration. This simple rule will not only produce some startling results in the process of concentration itself, but will also train imagination for definite and practical work. Herewith, let us note that imagination does have the power to take the lead in the mental world; and therefore whenever we imagine that a certain thing is being done in the mind, we lead a majority of the energies of the mind to go and do that very thing; provided of course that imagination be vivid and highly positive in its actions. Here then we have within easy reach a most remarkable possibility.

9. CONCENTRATE WITH THE WHOLE MIND

TO concentrate well is not sufficient; we must also concentrate with the greatest possible capacity; and therefore, we should train ourselves to concentrate with the whole mind; or to express more and more of life and power in every thought and action. But the average mind makes actual use of only a small fraction of what is possible in ability and power; and that is one reason why the concentrated efforts of such a mind are so weak or utterly futile.

Where concentration is weak and imperfect, we always find most of the mind in a dormant state; and vice versa, where concentration is exceptional, we find marked activity all through the mental world. The problem then is to awaken more of the mind, and express more of the power of the mind in everything we do — a problem that would largely solve itself if we would abandon completely all half-hearted modes) of thought and action.

We should make it a practice to express the whole self in everything we do, think or say; and the increase in mental capacity would be remarkable. We should eliminate indifference absolutely. Whether we turn to the left or to the right, we should turn with all we have in feeling, purpose and will. Wherever we act, we should be a power, and aim to make all action constructive — conducive to greater capacity for action tomorrow. There is no gain in saving up power for another day. If we use it all now, we will have still more when the other day arrives. The power that is generated in the system to-day should be used to-day — not scattered — but used — used in constructive expression. And the law is, that the more power we use to-day, the more we shall have tomorrow.

When we think, we should not simply think with the brain, but think with every force and element in the entire personality. There is nothing that will increase mental capacity so quickly and so effectively as the training of the mind to use the whole personality in every thought and expression. And when the mind can, in concentration, draw upon the entire personality for power, conscious and subconscious, we can imagine what the force of such concentration will be. Our principal object, therefore, should be in this connection to awaken the vast regions of dormant energy all through the mental world, and express more and more of this new energy in everything we do. Thus we provide concentration with an ever-increasing measure of power.

A most excellent practice, in order to express more of the mind in every thought and action, is to lay hold upon all the energy of the mind with deep feeling and will, and actually take up that energy as we would take up a book with the hand, and place it where we want it now. This can readily be done; and with practice we will find that we can control our mental energies just as effectively as we control the movements of hands or feet. When this control is gained we shall be able, at any time, to increase the expression of the power of mind, thereby increasing directly the power of concentration; and when we realize that even exceptional minds use less than five per cent of their latent energies, we gain some idea of the vast-ness of our own possibilities.

To further this increase in mental capacity, we should give definite and frequent directions to the subconscious for this particular purpose. In fact, there is nothing that will avail so much for such a purpose, which fact we can readily appreciate when we note what the subconscious is, and what it can do. We should make it a daily practice therefore to direct the subconscious to awaken the whole mind, and to express, in constructive action, the full power and capacity of the mind. Remarkable increase will be realized, as the weeks pass, both in working capacity and in thinking power.

Then we should proceed farther and direct the subconscious to develop and perfect concentration itself; and we shall be amazed at what can be done in this regard. We know that the subconscious can do anything within the range of human possibility, if properly directed; therefore the creative power of the great within can build for us all the most effective and the most perfect concentration conceivable. This marvelous power is latent in every mind — waiting to be used with intelligence, super-effort and real faith.

IN the science and art of concentration, it is the deeper forces and the finer energies of mind and personality with which we deal directly; and therefore we increase the power of concentration as we acquire the ability to take up or control those forces at will, and according to our purpose or desire. To accomplish this, we must gain interior hold of those forces, because they do not respond to any action of mind or will that is merely superficial. And here we find another reason why it is only the few who really can concentrate; it is only the few who think deeply and who cause the actions of the mind to work among the powerful undercurrents of life, thought and mentality; but anyone can acquire this power; and the first step towards that end is to gain this interior hold of the finer energies of the mind.

When we can take hold of the forces of the mental world, and direct or sway those forces in any way desired, just as we sway or extend the arm in any mode or direction desired — when we can do this, then we are beginning to acquire the power of real concentration. This inner mastery of the forces and energies of the mind, is a purely subjective process, and is developed only as we learn to act consciously and positively in what we call the inner field of thought, consciousness and mind action. And although there are many who can and do act, to some extent, in this inner field, the majority can acquire this power only through extensive practice.

The value of this power, even aside from that of concentration, is very-great, especially in connection with the creation of effective and brilliant ideas; for the fact is, that it is only in this inner field of mind and thought that brilliant ideas are created; and besides, every mental creative process of genuine worth depends directly upon the action of these finer energies. If we would develop the real power of concentration, therefore, and also master the art of creating brilliant ideas, we must think and act in the consciousness of the " inner field " of mentality, and gain, more and more, this interior hold upon the forces of mind and personality.

To advance in this direction, we should endeavor frequently to take up and apply the deeper forces of the mental system; that is, to take positive hold of those forces with mind and will, directing them first upon one sphere in the mental world, then upon some other sphere; to move those forces to and fro as we may desire; to cause them to move in circles one moment and in straight lines, either towards the depths or the heights of the mental world, the next moment; to gather them in large groups or in small groups according to desire; to focalize them all upon any subject or idea we have in mind, and to see how long we can continue such focalization without losing interest in the subject or becoming oblivious to our surroundings. And here we should remember that the moment we lose interest in the subject before us, that moment we cease to concentrate; and also, that the moment we become oblivious to our surroundings, that moment we cease to concentrate. Concentration involves, on the one hand, undivided attention to the subject or object before us; and, on the other hand, complete wide-awakeness to everything going on among our surroundings. The moment we become oblivious to our surroundings, the real power of concentration is lost for the time being; it is very important therefore that we continue to be wide-awake, both to the objective and to the subjective; in fact, in as wide and deep and large a sphere as possible.

To gain this interior hold upon the deeper forces of the mind, it is continuous practice that will give the power desired; and every imaginable method should be employed, because the more ways through which we can handle, sway or manipulate those forces, the greater will become our conscious hold upon those forces; and when this conscious hold becomes remarkable, then we can apply those forces anywhere at any time, and with full capacity and power. In other words, we shall be able to concentrate perfectly, and turn on the full current of all the talent, energy and power we possess.

An excellent practice is to turn attention frequently upon the great within, concentrating the deeper forces of the mind upon the vast and marvelous possibilities that exist in the fathomless depths of the mental world. This practice will not only aid the mind remarkably in gaining this interior hold upon the finer energies, but will also awaken latent forces and new talents; and will invariably arouse increased capacity and power in every faculty and talent we may be using now.

When we find that the faculties and talents we employ do not possess sufficient force and capacity to make that work a success, it is most important that we take up the above practice and do so with determination and enthusiasm. We will soon experience most marked improvement; the mental engine will have more " steam," and we shall be able to speed on with twice and thrice the usual cargo of plans, propositions and achievements. Furthermore, this practice will enlarge immensely the field for concentration; and here it is important to remember that the greater the scope and range of the mental world, of which we are actively conscious, the greater becomes the power of concentration. Every faculty or power in the mind gains exceptional advantages when given more and more to work with; and the practice of concentrating frequently upon the great within will give every faculty more to work with, besides giving the mind, as a whole, an ever-increasing world for attainment and achievement.

10. CLEARING THE WAY FOR ACHIEVEMENT

THE possibilities of concentration are many; but there is one possibility in particular that we all should seek to understand most thoroughly, and develop to the highest degree conceivable. The results will be amazing; and every step in advance will open new worlds to conquer.

The principle is this, that we can through concentration clear the way for almost any achievement, attainment or discovery within the range of human life and power; and this range is a thousand times greater than we have supposed; in fact, no limits or restrictions can be found.

This principle can be applied to almost anything that we may wish to find or accomplish; and for practical illustration we will consider first the problems we meet in daily life. It is the usual custom, when we have difficult problems to solve, to waste a vast amount of time and energy worrying about how we are to find the solution; and as we know this is an easy way to failure and defeat.

The new way is to concentrate; to concentrate upon the problem with all the energy and intellect we possess; and this is what will happen: The full light of the mind will be focused upon that problem; that problem will be placed under the penetrating gaze of a powerful mental search light; and, accordingly, the mind will be able to look into and look through the entire situation. Thus the solution will be found; for the fact is, that situations or problems seem difficult or perplexing only when viewed in the dark or in subdued light. When we can look through the thing, then we know what to do.

Turn on sufficient light and all mystery disappears. Problems cease to be problems when viewed in the clear light; and we can, through a highly developed concentration, turn the full light of the mind upon any subject, circumstance or situation. Therefore, we should concentrate upon those things; concentrate with all the energy and intellect we possess; concentrate for days or weeks, if necessary, and with unflinching faith and determination. We will soon penetrate the mystery and find what is wanted. We will see through it all, and see clearly what to do.

The same principle will apply if you are working on some invention. Do not give up at any stage; concentrate upon the thing you wish to develop or perfect; and concentrate with more and more persistence until the thing is done. Nothing is impossible. Nature will give up her secrets to those who really want them, or to those who will come into her greater realms and get them; and concentration has the penetrating power to go on in anywhere.

It is a well-known fact that most inventions have come through persistent concentration; or through mental processes that involved lightning speed creative power; and such processes are always due to previous moments of exceptional concentration. Furthermore, the possibilities of the mind become simply marvelous when the full light and the full creative power of the mind are concentrated upon the goal in view. We realize therefore that greater inventions than the world has ever dreamed of may be expected when a much larger number learn to master the wonder working art of concentration.

Inventive genius involves, among other things, the power to create new ideas; and we can realize that the more intellect and energy we apply in any creative process the greater and more brilliant will that idea become. We also realize that when we apply all our faculties and forces upon the creation of an idea or the perfecting of an invention, the results will be far greater than if we applied only a fraction of those faculties and forces. And it is the function of concentration to apply, upon the work in hand, the full power of the mind and the highest and most effective actions of that power.

Rich things grow where producing power is abundant; and the producing power of the mind at any point will be abundant in profusion when we concentrate the best that we have and the best that we are upon that point. And to emphasize this fact, let us note again that the power of concentration when persistent and highly developed, will not only cause all the talents and forces of the mind to work together at the point of action, but will also awaken latent energies in mind and personality — sometimes an enormous amount of new energy — until you feel as if you were a living dynamo.

When you are in need of a new plan in your business, or in your field of endeavor, do not consult all the people you know, the majority of whom may not be really interested. That is the old way, and it leads to confusion. The new way is to concentrate upon the plan you want, and with the highest and greatest actions of the mind. Thus you cause the highest and greatest in your mind to go to work and evolve the plan you desire. They can do it; and if you concentrate exceptionally well, you will cause those actions to make a super-effort — the result of which will go far beyond your every expectation. Here you should note well the fact that your own mind has the power, active or latent, to work out any plan you may require for your best welfare and continued progress. Nothing is more true than this, that your own mind is fully able to take the very best care of you. This is a statement that should be shouted from the house tops, and drilled so thoroughly into every human brain that it becomes a positive and ever conscious realization. Your own mind can solve your problems and work out the plans that you need for advancement in your life and your work. And your own mind will do these things if you concentrate persistently upon that which you want, and concentrate wonderfully well.

A large and valued field for the application of the same principle, is the field of ideals. And in this connection we should consider well the great fact that whenever the mind gains the insight to perceive an ideal it also gains the power to make that ideal real. But it is only through a well-developed concentration that this power can be applied effectively. The majority, however, among those who entertain high ideals, do not give sufficient thought to concentration. They dream and dream, hoping the dream will come true; or, when they do try to concentrate, they journey off into abstractions and transcendental speculations — a process that does not call into action the power that is able to make those dreams come true.

The same is true of young minds who are ambitious. Most of them merely hope and hope that their ambitions will be realized somehow; but they do not concentrate persistently and continually upon the great goal they have in view. They do not call into concerted and organized action the sum-total of their forces and faculties; and, in consequence, their ambitions never materialize. The fact is that where one ambitious mind scales the heights of achievement, fifty give up their early ambitions after a few years and decide to resume an average existence; and the chief reason is, that these fifty do not concentrate; or, if they do concentrate, it is only for a time and in a weak, uncertain fashion. The successful one, however, turns on the full current of concentration, and persists, with undaunted faith and determination, until the goal in view is realized.

This should be the rule: Whatever you want, concentrate; concentrate upon the purpose you have in mind; concentrate upon those greater forces and possibilities within you that can get you what you want — that can see you through successfully. For it is positively true that your own mind can get you anything within reason; provided of course that your whole mind is working for you; and your whole mind will work for you — will work for you with the highest degree of effectiveness — if you concentrate wonderfully well. The possibilities of concentration are not confined, however, to the usual fields of achievement, or to those mental domains with which most of us are familiar. There are other and greater worlds that we may discover and take possession of through the use of this master art. To illustrate, if we wish to evolve or develop something that is entirely new, or decidedly different, the principle is to concentrate in that direction. Thus we shall make a super-effort in that direction; that is, if we concentrate with full capacity and marvelous skill; and we will, with absolute certainty, develop something that is beyond all previous effort — something that is distinctive, that stands out in a class by itself, that reveals clearly the master touch of genius. The elements of genius are latent in every mind; and any mind may, through the super-efforts of a marvelous concentration, call those elements together into positive, creative action. Thus something new or startling may be developed. It may be a new and most brilliant idea; or, a new and superior plan for the realization of certain highly desired changes in life; or, an entirely new way of doing things — ways and methods, which when applied, might revolutionize everything in that sphere of human thought or endeavor.

The most wonderful possibility of all is this, that concentration can lead the mind on and on, out of present restrictions and beyond present states of knowledge and consciousness, into new realms, richer kingdoms and greater worlds. We know that concentration does have the tendency to go farther; and that it has real penetrating power, so that it may delve into anything in the vast domains of Life, Mind or Nature. It is possible therefore to cause the power of concentration to go so far into any state of reality that new and marvelous domains will open before the mind. Thus we might find long sought secrets in the natural world, or make discoveries in any field or region that would prove amazing to the mind and invaluable to human progress.

It is the positive truth that a highly developed concentration can carry the mind farther and deeper in any direction. This is something that the great minds of every age have demonstrated repeatedly. And if we go deeper or farther into Life, into Mind, into Nature, we are going to make discoveries. We are going to find secrets that no mind has known before. We are going to meet forces, laws and principles, the knowledge of which may reduce to simplicity a thousand so-called impossibilities. We are going to discern the inner workings of things in many fields and regions, and thus secure information that wise men have sought all through the ages.

These things are not exaggerations nor the mere picturing of a highly stimulated imagination; for when we accept the fact that concentration can lead the mind farther and deeper in any direction — which fact we all accept absolutely — we realize that we may, through this use of concentration, discover or accomplish almost anything; that is, if we carry on the process far enough. It is a matter therefore of deciding to concentrate until we find or secure what we want. The outcome will be as expected; for in due time we shall meet the great and the wonderful; we shall learn how this remarkable power can open to the mind regions beyond regions of untold possibility.

Here then is food for thought whatever our work may be, or whatever our fields of study may be. Here we have promises rich and rare for those who aspire to excel; for those who are looking for new worlds to conquer; for those who are in search of the deeper secrets of life everywhere. And as we give thoughtful attention to these things, we perceive most keenly that we are ever on the brink of wonders and marvels — with the power to go on into those fabulous regions and take possession.

To the practical mind it is clearly evident that if we train the mind thoroughly along all essential lines, and learn to concentrate wonderfully well, we are going to move forward steadily and surely, gaining capacity, power and speed as we proceed. And if we continue in this manner, we will not only accomplish what we have in view, but we may at any time strike a new trail leading directly and quickly to the highest pinnacle of achievement.

To the mind of ideals, and to all who have faith in greater possibilities, it is equally evident that a well-trained mind can, through a highly developed concentration, take a charmed journey into Nature's wonder world — with the positive assurance that something of untold value will be found. For when we realize that the mind holds marvels and possibilities far beyond what we ever dreamed; and when we know that these mental marvels can be gathered and trained for super-effort—for creative work on any scale — or for going out upon expeditions of discovery, even entering into the secrets of life and the heart of things — when we note these things we stand amazed at what might be done. But the mind of faith and courage will stand amazed only for a moment. Such a mind will resolve to master this wonder art at once — for in it there is a power that never knew failure nor defeat — a power that is fully able to cast the mountains of impossibility into the sea of oblivion.

THE END.